Promises of
Freedom

Books by David Grinstead

The Earth Movers
Promises of Freedom

Promises of Freedom

by
David Grinstead

Crown Publishers, Inc., New York

Author's Note: This work is fiction and the characters (except public figures such as Lyndon Johnson who were witnessed to have behaved as recounted) are fictional.

Published by Crown Publishers, Inc., 201 East 50th Street, New York, New York 10022. Member of the Crown Publishing Group.

CROWN is a trademark of Crown Publishers, Inc.
Manufactured in the United States of America

Library of Congress Cataloging-in-Publication Data

Grinstead, David.
Promises of freedom / by David Grinstead.—1st ed.
p. cm.
1. Vietnamese Conflict, 1961-1975—Fiction. I. Title.
PS3557.R533P7 1990
813'.54—dc20 90-36615

ISBN 0-517-57659-7
10 9 8 7 6 5 4 3 2 1
First Edition

For Nicholas and Eve

Acknowledgments

M any people helped me on background. The talented and perceptive Esther S. Yntema gave me the first push and clarified the New England spirit for me. Specific information was provided by Dr. John Constable, Professor Ithiel de Sola Pool, Professor Walter J. Slote, Mrs. Walsh McDermott (Marian MacPhail) and other *Life* staffers, Barbara Orcutt, Lt. Col. Nguyen Van Giang, Mr. Nguyen Luan, the historical divisions and public information offices of the United States Marine Corps and the United States Army, and veterans, peace activists, and *attentismistes* who told me what they saw.

Vietnamese tales are from *Land of the Seagull and Fox, Vietnamese Folk Tales*, R. Q. Sun, ed. Tokyo: Charles Tuttle, 1966.

Promises of
Freedom

VIP
Shot

He walked fast along First Avenue, swerving around people in front of restaurants and shop windows bright with things to buy for Christmas. He turned into the quiet dark street of trees and fine townhouses.

In a few steps he sensed something wrong, an extra shadow among the bare trees.

A small dark kid stepped out.

"Hey." Wide dark eyes. "Yeah, you, man. Stop."

Someone else sitting in a car at the curb. American car. Man at the wheel. His hand moved. Some kind of signal.

He kept walking, away from the kid, letting his clothes show he should be unassailable—the camel-hair coat, silk scarf, black English shoes.

"Hey, man, you stop. Stop now!"

The kid didn't sound authoritative or angry. He sounded scared, unpredictable.

Then he saw the gray shine of the large automatic. His gut lurched. *Don't panic.* He stopped and faced the kid, made a reassuring smile. "Okay. I've stopped."

The kid smiled too. He was mocha-colored, with a flat nose, pustular mouth, and straight hair under his leather cap.

"Well, I know what you want."

"Yeah, ha-ha-ha-ha-ha, you know what I want. Yeah. Gimme the watch."

Shit. His gold Cartier. He held it out, black lizard straps dangling. The kid did not glance at it but put it in his pocket. Vacuous face. But not poorly dressed. His jacket was dark glove leather. The fat dark man in the car said, *"Bale! Bale!"*

"Money, man, I don' got all night. Move! Come on!"

He removed his wallet. The kid opened it, looked beyond him to the fat man, and nodded. The wallet had four or five hundred and itself was worth over a hundred dollars. He wondered if the little shit knew that.

"What else you got, man?"

"Nothing."

"Come on! Come on, what else you got? Come on, lessee your pockets, man."

He didn't like the kid's tone. He got eye contact with the little shit and stared at him. He couldn't help it. That ugly mouth. "What do you mean?" he said, his voice hard.

"Yo! Open pockets!" the fat man said behind him. *"Los todos!"*

" 'Side out, man," the kid said.

He reached into his pockets and pulled them out. A money clip with a few singles, fives, and twenties fell to the street. Keys. Coins.

"Pick 'em up, sir," the fat man said. "Don't do that no more."

"Pick 'em up fast!" the kid said. "Move!"

He bent over and handed them to the kid, glaring. The kid avoided his eyes. Without that pistol a coward. He let contempt seethe into his voice. "Have you got what you want? I'd like to go now."

The kid said, "I don't like you, man."

At his hand, a white flash—what? Hard punch in the ribs. He stepped back, became aware he was falling backward, ears ringing from a bang he couldn't remember hearing: *My God, I'm shot!*

"Hey, no," the fat man said.

He fell. The pavement hit his butt. The iron tree grate hit his thigh. Hurt, but didn't hurt, strangely. A dull, distant feeling. His gut burned. He breathed and couldn't get air. He tried to turn away. Another shot. He was punched sideways, his shoulder numb.

"No! *Garde!*" the fat man said. *"Vámanos!"* Car door opened. Kid didn't say anything.

Okay. They'd leave, he could crawl to First, hail a cab, go to New York Hospital or Lenox Hill. On his hands and knees, palms felt the hard, gritty, cold concrete. Didn't hurt. He could handle it. He saw the fat man above him through the open door of the car. The fat man gestured at him, pointing.

Whack! White flashing blow to his head, gray yellow glow, receding, dimness, he was falling, speeding, he knew it, over, over, racing toward something blinding and dark and solid and nothing.

Phoebe Bishop got to the Brick Church after the service started. She was one of the best-known reporters on television and the CBS crew swung on her as she climbed the wide steps, a good-looking brunette with good hair, good invisible surgery under her chin and around her lovely eyes. She made a pretty face dodging the reporters.

She wasn't covering this. When she had heard about the killing two days earlier, she said, "Fuck him." The dead man had destroyed her lover and been a part of the great upheavals two decades earlier. But she wanted to confirm the kill, as they said in war, and she wanted to pace a rival journalist, Ashleigh Loakes, who had had one of his infuriating smug think pieces in the *Times* Op Ed about each of us having fifteen minutes of fame and what this man had done in the sixties and What It Meant.

She saw Loakes's fat head far down the filled rows. The sanctuary was plain wood and the pews were filled with, she supposed, other Yale men and their ilk. The handsome silver-haired minister who spoke in cultivated tones about "tragedy" may have been a Yale man, too: ". . . This daunting problem of our cities," he said. "Violence unleashed, alas, here at home." His words had that moral tone so elevated it sounded fatuous if you didn't buy the style.

Stuffed shirt, she thought on the way out. Pain in the ass. She was a Vassar graduate from a very good family and liked to talk tough off-camera. No one else there she wanted to see.

She rode in a network sedan to the West Side. Many of her friends had raised hell in the course of normal life, as killers, anarchists, and leaders in a time of War Peace Love Death Sex Drugs and Rock&Roll. They took it from the top, too, and chose what they'd do. The ones who came along a half-dozen years later found the war already running, the demonstrations chanting, the music playing.

The studios and newsrooms were in a big building, like a garage, and when you walked down the carpeted corridors you were aware that the picture-hung walls were moveable and the low ceiling just a

skin under a high space where noises echo, where things happen that
you can't see and your surroundings can change shape overnight.
That's not symbolism, it's television.

"They've confirmed they have the killer!" Tom Hurley said,
throwing himself into a soft chair in Phoebe's office. He was in his
twenties, tall and slender, hair touching his ears. He wore an expensive Italian windowpane shirt and a green silk knit tie. He was Phoebe's writer/researcher. He was new. She wondered if they'd have an
affair. She'd had lousy luck in love and, like Lady Lazarus, she ate
men like air.

Pat Mulkin, the associate producer, came in shielding her chest
with her clipboard. Thirties, dark-haired, brisk. She hated Tom.
"The killer's at Central Booking. We've got a follow-up on the six
o'clock but Barry Pendleton's wondering about a segment for 'Spotlight.' "

Barry was one of the news vice presidents.

"The idea is this kid was on the bottom and killed someone who
had a name," Pat said. "Profile the mugger. Look at his family. Ask
why."

Phoebe said, "Does he have a family? Who is he?"

"His name's Angel Acevedo," Pat said. "Nineteen. Grew up on
Avenue B."

"Very trendy," Tom said, and looked at Phoebe with hot, mad
eyes. They laughed. He was the kind of sensitive bitchy male she'd
come to like. The other kind had nearly killed her.

Pat showed strips of yellow paper from the B wire, bulletin
updates marked xxx building a story by accretion.

Dateline Manhattan December 12: Police on anti-mugging surveillance had a shoot-out at York and Seventy-seventh. Follow-up:
Killed one suspect and arrested Acevedo. Follow-up: Acevedo had a
9-millimeter pistol that could be linked to the VIP slaying last week
on Seventy-second. Ballistics tests slated. More follow-ups gave names
and addresses.

"We still have an open segment next show," Pat said.

"Need to get the killer and his family," Phoebe said. "Pictures of
the victims. I know there's file stuff on our hero who's just been sent
to heaven. The next 'Spotlight'? That's the nineteenth. How happy
will *that* holiday story be?"

"There's the street-life angle," Tom said. "This has been a *fero-*

cious season." Street robbers were busiest between Thanksgiving and Christmas.

"What else do we have?"

Pat looked at her clipboard and read off features culled from the newspapers. Nothing appealed to Phoebe. She said, "I want to see this killer."

Central Booking was down by Chinatown. Painted steel doors clanged, electric releases buzzed. The cop who let Phoebe through looked like he'd been inside too long himself. His skin was pale and his light-and-dark-blue uniform was grimy. He took her to a semiprivate conference room and stayed at one end.

A door opened and another cop led in Angel Acevedo, who was about Phoebe's height, five seven, and thin. Coffee-colored skin, purple zits ringing his mouth, bad teeth, eyes never settled—sweeping across her face, around the room to the cops, checking out her breasts, swinging to the door. He wore leather pants and a long-collar cream-colored silk shirt—dirty collar. He was looking at the door when he said, "Yeah, wha'd you wan', man?"

Phoebe said she wanted to do a story about him. In truth, she wasn't sure she wanted to go ahead but wanted to gauge how he'd look on camera. And she wanted to see for herself the one who'd killed the man who'd caused her lover's death.

"No, no, don' fuck with me, man," Angel said, looking at her breasts and then up. "You TV, you got plenty money. I wan' *two thousand* dollars talk to you, man."

"No. We don't do that."

"I want a better lawyer, then."

"We can't get involved that way."

"Yeah," he said. "Yeah," glancing at her. "Yeah, what do you wan'? *Diga me* wha'd you wan'!" He looked as if he wanted something but didn't know what. In the end he said yes. She arranged to interview him and his family and gang friends.

The few questions she'd asked him in the dingy room established one thing: He had no idea whom he'd killed. But she had a feeling about Acevedo, this mindless thug. So many like him had hatched in the chaos of the sixties. The man Angel had killed, the man she hated, had helped unleash the chaos, that time of killing, hope, and big talk when the country was crazy with war, love, and promises of freedom.

She had met the Yale men in those last calm months before the crazy times. Kennedy was President. It was just after the Bay of Pigs, before the missile crisis. Her last spring at Vassar. She'd had mono one year, studied two, had her first serious affair, with a lacrosse player named Krafter from Deerfield, RPI, and a good family upstate like hers. He was a brutish defenseman with a thick neck and meaty shoulders. He could lift her with one finger. Once he slapped her; she screamed loud enough to embarrass the bejesus out of him and walked out of his life.

She and Carole Tiddens spent their last year hitting every party they could. Carole had a car in Poughkeepsie. In those days that was against the rules. They drove over black leaf-stickered roads to Amherst, Wesleyan, Princeton, and sometimes Yale. Men all around knew them as "Phoebe and Carole—a couple of hot tickets!" Many saw them in polo coats and shirtwaists, holding drinks and making noise, this good-looking brunette, Phoebe, with her high forehead and Eastern WASP voice, and Carole, the flushed, exuberant big blonde from Oklahoma oil money.

Carole said, "You can always tell you've had a good date when you throw your panties at the ceiling and they stick." The idea was to be charming, cool, go far enough but not give it away, and snag a husband, the M.R.S. degree, but Phoebe had no plans for that. She wanted to go to Paris as an intern with *The Paris Review*. She was a good photographer and sometimes wrote for *Miscellany News*. This is how she met Ashleigh Loakes, who was big at the *Yale Daily News*. He asked her to come to New Haven for a weekend in May. She thought Ash was pompous and bad news but agreed because it was, after all, a Yale weekend cha-cha-cha. It was part of her being an undergraduate cynic. She'd never been in love.

She rode up on the train from Manhattan that Friday; she'd been doing research for a paper and visiting her Aunt Amanda, who had an apartment on Park Avenue and said it was "swell" for Phoebe to have "a bid from New Haven." Amanda had gone up there in the F. Scott Fitzgerald years, when evenings were luminous and all the world's young were charming. When Phoebe reached New Haven she knew she was in trouble.

The town was not inviting, let alone luminous: From the train she saw empty factories; broken windows; littered streets; sullen men idling on sidewalks; dented, rusty autos with out-of-date fins and colors like turquoise and pink; tarpaper houses. No, New Haven was not luminous so far. But as the train shambled into the station, the old

Yale scene rolled past her window like a stage traveler: Yale men dressed up to meet girls and off-campus gays. Weekend Date Time! Theater posters for *The Fantasticks* and *Camelot*. Earnest faces. Men in seersucker, cords, madras. There was Ash Loakes. Glasses on his large moon face. Yellow ascot. Blazer over his large, soft body.

"Pheebs!" he yelled, as much to attract attention to himself as to call to her. "Come on! We've got *lots* to see!"

He was going to show off this good-looking date.

"Here's my freshman dorm!" He pulled her along over the stone-and-brick campus. "Let's go to the *Yalie Daily!*" Into the smoky office on Fraternity Row, unshaven boys gazing dumbly at her. "Let's get a bevo at Zeta!" At Mory's she ate dinner in a wooden booth carved with jammed-together initials. She shrank under overhanging oars, crowded team photos, and his spate of words.

Escape! How? Carole, her ride back, was with this boy *she'd* just met, Peabody, but she wasn't sure where.

"Let's go to the hoot at Beta!"

When they walked back up the Row she saw the man she fell in love with and went crazy over. The first one, that is.

He stood on the Fence Club terrace at the end of the alley. Light from the windows fell dazzling on his clothes—a frayed white shirt, wash pants, a white cast on his arm. His skin pink and his hair reddish gold. Muscular, but not a brute like Krafter. A jock? He *looked* like a jock, so scrubbed, his grin cockeyed and jocky. As they approached she saw tiny freckles across his short nose. He grinned at her and looked her down and up. "Hi."

"Hey, Howze," Ash said, pulling her past. "That's Houston Bridles!" He pronounced it Howston. "Fantastic athlete. Letters in football, hockey, and lacrosse! A star! He just broke his arm playing lacrosse against Cornell! I saw it happen!"

Beta was crowded. She drank beer. They sang "Tom Dooley," "Take This Hammer," "Rock Island Line" (Kingston Trio, Odetta, Pete Seeger); they sang fervently about poor and black people who couldn't go to college as they could.

She had to pee. Girls stood in line. One coming out said, "Drip dry, no paper," so she walked next door, used the john at Zeta, and heard Calypso coming from Fence. She walked in through a foyer of painted wainscoting and turned into a big crowded room where four blacks in Jamaican shirts sang under a Queen Anne chandelier.

Houston C. G. Bridles III, the shining hero, held a beer can in his cast hand and watched them, his mouth half open in that appealing crooked grin.

The Jamaicans sang "Yellow Bird." All around them young white faces opened and lips formed the words, singing along.

Phoebe stepped to the edge of the circle and raised her voice. Tennis and riding had given her good lung power and a clear strong alto. She put everything into it, an octave above the melody, looking at the tangled tendrils and gray-eyed reflections of the chandelier. She felt flushed, hot; her thighs burned and her lips and earlobes swelled as her voice spread above her, a net to catch her love.

When the song ended Houston stepped next to her, clapping vigorously, touching her shoulder, charming her. "Terrific!" he said. "Haven't seen you! Loved that!"

He had an upper-class Boston WASP accent, slightly nasal, milder than the Kennedys'.

"Thank you! I'm Phoebe Bishop from Vassar." They uttered the key words: Exeter; Emma Willard. Did he know ———? Did she know ———? We live here . . . That's nice . . . There . . . Very nice. Blinky Mawson? Asheville? Beverly? That's very nice, too.

Phoebe's lovely, warm voice had snared another person she hadn't noticed and didn't now as she stood next to Houston, hips almost touching, smiling and nodding. This was a half-in-the-bag meatball who already had a date, Mark Randolph. He held two cans of beer, both for him, and stood flush-faced and grinning next to Blonde Betty from Skidmore, who was also a little shitfaced but held only one can. He was a Deke. He and Betty had run into Houston on York Street and Houston had touched Mark's shoulder, made his charming grin. "Rands! Come to Fence for the sounds!" Mark knew Houston from lacrosse. He'd been a scrub, tripping over his own feet and the stick, forget about handling the ball. Colorful, they called him. He was a meatball—fundamentally stupid, many thought—and from Chicago. But he had a friendly, doggy manner, knew people all over Yale, and had glimmers of feeling for those things he wasn't cool enough to handle.

Like Elizabethan Club. He'd been there once and spilled his sherry. It was this little fucking glass. Like a Master's party, where he'd told an outrageous dirty joke and hooted away, noticed others laughing nervously, and turned to see the Master's wife staring icily behind him. Like the time he got into yet *another* bar fight and found out, after being decked time after time by punches he couldn't even *see*, that he'd smarted off to a semipro hockey player on the Blades. This was the admirer Phoebe hadn't noticed.

He watched her clean, pretty, but strong face lifted like an Ivy League angel's as she sang, noticed her headband, her shirtwaist—yeah, her hogans—she was *so much* of that type that set the style there.

He saw her and Houston connect like Scottie-dog magnets. They must know each other. They looked like it. Houston in that frayed shirt, his loafer held together with white tape, she in that simple green dress.

A big blue-and-yellow form emerging from the crowd. A pudgy hand squeezing Phoebe's arm. Phoebe turning, startled. Ash Loakes's flushed face and glasses.

"Pheebs! Thought I'd lost you!"

"Ow!"

"Hi, Ash," Houston said, stepping between them, smiling, easily lifting Ash's arm. "Phoebe and I *know* each other. Come on, let's have a taste." He led Ash away, hand on shoulder, to the little bar in a painted alcove and bought him a drink.

They all stood next to each other. Houston brazenly said to Phoebe, "Come with me."

"I *can't*," she said, but she knew she would anyway. She saw Houston murmur a few words to Ash, saw Ash's eyes widen, his mouth open, his eyes shrink in pain.

"Thank you so much for dinner at Mory's," Phoebe said.

"Yes. Yes, of course!" Ash said.

Mark saw Ash turn away. Bird-dogged. Ouch. He knew Ash slightly. The guy pushed too hard. Ash liked Stan Kenton; he blared like that. Through the open window Mark saw Phoebe and Houston cross the terrace before the silhouetted spires and chimneys, saw Phoebe take off her headband and shake her hair flying. Houston kissed her on the lips and they laughed as they fled. He saw them a few other times over the weekend. There were parties all over.

"You have nice friends," she murmured to him, being cool, after drinks at one party, en route to another. All the things she'd heard about him. Keys—they'd passed the Moorish tomb. Torch. The letters. His family. Could she *catch* him? Anyway, she *liked* him, he was what she *wanted*. *Exactly*.

At the Taft Hotel she put up a decorous resistance. "You can't
stay, anyway."

"No, but, God, you're terrific."

"Mmmm—you're terrific, too, Houston. You're really not bad. I
don't think we'd better—"

They were on the bed anyway, clothes falling from them, buttons and hooks and snaps. Scents of beer, gin, tonic, sweat.

"Oh! Watch your *cast*, please!"

"Oh, Jesus!"

"Oh!

"God!"

What delicious calm. Then she'd felt awkward, sprawled over
the bed like some lurid paperback cover. She put an arm over her
breasts and with her Jaeger kerchief dabbed at her thigh. He was
worth it, so eminently worth it. "You have to go. We can't spend the
night. Now, what time are you coming back tomorrow, or do I have
to find my own breakfast at some awful deli, you bastard?"

The next morning, Saturday, Adams Crowther Lawrence Peabody III stood outside the cyclone fence behind Deke, Fence, and
Pierson College watching ugly privilege, class cruelty, and swinish
parvenus. It was Haunt Club—a horror show. At eleven A.M.

Haunt officers at the gate wore yellow slickers. Inside people
drank God knows what kind of alcohol and grapefruit juice from
paper cups. Haunt members wore maroon striped ties. Mark Randolph wore his, open collar, loose knot, laughing and gesturing, cigarette in fist. Betty filling their cups from the tub, laughing with some
other girl. Where was this Phoebe Bishop Carole was looking for?

A speaker in a window boomed the comic rock song "Western
Movies."

"She's got dark hair pulled back like this," Carole said. "And a
smile like this." Carole showed her upper teeth. "Why don't we go in
anyway?"

"I can't see her date," Peabody said, stalling. He didn't want to
spend two whole dollars—he wasn't a member—and then not find
them and feel he had to drink his money's worth, to "Get Slappy," as
the sign said. Money was a sore point with him.

The same song started again. Pistol shots. Black voices. The beat.

Everyone knew about him and money. He was sure they did.

His Mayflower ancestors, his mercantile, Revolutionary, and Brahmin ancestors, who'd lost their money while parvenu industrial families got Veblen rich. His mother and father, Radcliffe and Harvard, Depression radicals, marching for Spain, his father *finally* going in to fight the Nazis and dying in a stupid truck accident in Alabama, his mother marching for the Rosenbergs, showing up at Exeter (he was on scholarship) in her outlandish big shoes and turban. His *embarrassment* there. Being a bursary boy at Yale, working the Commons chow line in a white uniform, serving thoughtless arrivistes who had more money and less culture. He assumed everyone knew it because it pained and pissed him off so much.

But Carole liked his scene. She was so big, spontaneous, unself-conscious. He was small, dark-haired, his nose pointed; he had a mordant expression—perhaps, he hoped, a bit like Sartre's Mathieu. Eh? He affected dark plain shirts as European intellectuals did, wore black matador-frame glasses, had a book bag, stacks of those French plain-front paperbacks. He'd graduate with honors.

"I can *see* you drinking sherry in the common room and *talking* like that. It'd be so goddam *cozy! Stimulating!*" She *liked* in him what others might think—what he *himself* thought—musty, confined, and Eastern. She wanted to buy into his scene. She was loaded. And she had big tits. She even *called* them tits. Oklahoma City!

"That one's Mark Randolph," he said to Carole. "*He's* been out your way. Watch him—he's a real horror show!" Peabody was still nervous dating Carole and was impelled to seek humor by pecking at others. "He read *On the Road* and drove all over out there and never cracked a book here! Hyuk-hyuk-hyuk!"

Sophomore year at Silliman, his residential "college," or dorm, he and Randolph used to drink after a seminar. Mark told stories that enthralled Peabody, simple doggy accounts of chasing around, working odd jobs, being a barfly—all escapades Peabody had been sheltered from. Then Randolph had joined DKE, and now he was a member of Haunt, drinking in there, while Peabody, who was graduating with honors, was not.

Fraternities! Oak doors slamming in his face! Sometimes Randolph took him as a guest to DKE, but visiting it that way, as a kind of poor relation, angered Peabody almost as much as being excluded. Bits about fraternity secrets sometimes came out—a dazed pledge found naked, coated with molasses and feathers, Kotex taped over his eyes; a pledge master kidnapped and abandoned in the country—and from this silliness, only from the fraternities, a few of the loveliest or most dissolute members were chosen for Haunt, like Bridles and Randolph.

Peabody *did* belong to a senior society, the best underground society for serious scholars, Palimpsest. It was an honor but of course it was secret, so he couldn't talk about it. The bronze-haired god in there, Houston Bridles, who'd given him fits at Exeter, had been a shoo-in at the best old above-ground society, Scroll and Key. Even Randolph was in a society—an unserious one to be sure, aptly named Cups. He partied so much that in addition to Peabody coaching him through comprehensive exams, DKE and Fence combed through exam files, pointing him at answers (ring bell, pant, pant, bark, bark) to get him through. It was an ironic triangle that dogged his time here and perhaps would dog his life, Peabody reflected—Randolph having all the fun, Bridles getting all the glory, and no one knowing about Peabody's moral and intellectual worth.

"I see Phoebe!" Carole said. "That must be Ash! Whoo! Phoebe!" She grabbed Peabody's arm. "Against the far side!" She pointed over the huddle of madras and oxford and Beautiful Hair by Breck to a dark-haired girl with *not* Ash Loakes, but Houston Bridles.

"*That's* not Ash Loakes!" he said.

"She'll explain. Let's go in." She pulled him with her.

"Two dollars," the yellow-slickered snob said.

"Yeah." Bastards.

"Look! Phoebe!" Carole shouted. "This is Peas. Isn't he *cute?*"

A month later five of them stood on the terrace of Aunt Amanda's place on Park. Amanda, a thin, brittle-voiced woman in a slightly out-of-date Charles James silk dress, clapped her hands, raised her glass, and wished them well.

Houston Bridles had his arm around Phoebe. He had the lazy ease of a cat who's caught a juicy morsel. He and Amanda had hit it off well, playing "Who Do You Know" among the Lenox and Astor issue.

Amanda was active in the library. She gave Houston a little salmon-colored pamphlet called "Our Changing Moral Climate," put out by the library trustees.

"It's up to *us* to lead," said Amanda, "to make sure people don't *just* want bigger refrigerators and more cars. We have to get them to raise their sights."

"This is the problem of the Affluent Society," Adams Peabody said, scoring a seminar point. He and Carole leaned against each other. "You're getting along well," Phoebe had commented archly those last days at Vassar when Carole had come in with glazed eyes and disarranged clothing after seeing Peabody. Now Peabody and Carole were living together at her father's company apartment on Beekman Place. Two floors, terrace, view of East River. Peabody glowed in this material paradise. At last.

They all wore summer clothes and looked as glamorous as any group in sunglasses and ties in *Look* or *Life*.

Phoebe was so happy, so desperately happy. She smiled at all of them, felt bursting out of her dress. She'd given up her plans of working on the rue Madeleine as an apotheker, the odd name given women interns at *The Paris Review*. She could take photos as Mrs. Bridles if she could catch him; there were few women journalists anyway, and he was a real catch! And she was so happy Houston and Peabody had been civil. Carole had begged Peas not to say anything sarcastic. They'd kept their distance.

Down Park she saw the canopies in the evening light, the narrow bronze traffic lights, the gold-topped New York Central Building. A scene of eternal happiness.

She and Houston—oh, she hoped for so much!

Houston and Phoebe drove north the next day. She leaned against him and they sang and laughed. They drove up the seacoast north of Boston to the lovely town of Beverly with its village green tinted blue from the sky, houses sparkling in the salt air, then up quiet lanes hedged by lilacs, driveways marked only by small white signs painted with black letters. They entered the Bridles' long drive. Apple trees. A tall shingled house, its door shadowed.

In the doorway she saw a thin old man she felt she knew—a short face, wrinkled, pouched. Pale eyes, pale gray-white hair. Little curved ears like Houston's. A once-boyish face. He looked like Houston, but his expression was pinched, without any playfulness in his eyes. He reminded her as well of the squinting Mr. Magoo. She wanted so much to think of him as cute and loveable and wanted him to like her.

"Hello, Pa," Houston said.

"Halloo," she sang.

She didn't suspect that both men would bring her heartbreak.

New England
Summer

Two days after the funeral Phoebe rode to Loisaida with a crew to interview Lydia Acevedo in the Houses, tall blocks of brick the color of rotting meat, their ground-level walls sprayed with names and designs. Youths in leather lounged against a painted wall and watched them unload the camera and sound equipment from the car.

"The cop said he'd watch the car."

No working elevator. They smelled the urine before they entered the concrete stairway painted green and scribbled over in that wide flow-through pen she could never read. Their steps resounded. Chipped plaster in the corridor.

"Ah," Lydia Acevedo said, stepping back to motion them into the apartment. She was about five feet four inches, plump, with brown skin and soft dark eyes. They sat on tubular chairs in the kitchen while the apprentice looked for a plug.

The floor had a linoleum rug loose at the edges. In the small front room sat a large woman who said she would help Lydia talk. Lydia seemed shy. She sat looking at Pat, not Phoebe, and at the floor when Tom or Phoebe asked a question. When she said, *"No sé,"* I don't know, Tom put the question in Spanish and the large woman, whose name was Anna, amplified the answer.

"Angel was always a good boy," she said. "Until five, seven years ago. He hang out with bad boys, I can' do nothing with him."

On the walls were pictures of John Kennedy, and a Caribbean

Virgin shooting rays from her head and holding certain magic herbs.

Lydia said she had been born in Manhattan at 112th and First and had met the boy's father, whose name was Rafael García, on the street. "He come from Bayamón. Very pretty man."

She looked at the floor and at Phoebe. She said something to Anna, who said, "She maybe see you on television but she's not sure. They took her television when they break in. Before you call." She nodded at Tom.

"What happened to García?" Tom asked. "*¿Dónde está García ahora?*" He spoke enough Spanish to prep the story.

Lydia spoke rapidly in Spanish and Anna and Tom pulled out the story. García, her man, had had trouble and had gone back to Puerto Rico. Lydia had tried to find him; she'd had people look in Bayamón and San Juan.

"How old were you?"

"Sissteen. He eighteen."

The bright lights flooded the room with white glare and picked out every pore on Lydia's face and hands. She was years younger than Phoebe and was wrinkled. The lights put shadows behind a few crumbs on the Formica-topped table. Cellophane bags of chips and cans of food. Phoebe had never cared much for housekeeping either.

"I couldn' help it when the bad ones take him along. I say, 'Don' do it,' but he say he don' do nothing. An' he always good to me when he come home."

"Wasn't he arrested several times in the last four years?"

"*No sé.*" She shook her head.

"She doesn't know," Tom said. "She can't grasp he's in such deep do-do."

"I pray novena for him when I know he's in the gang. I buy special *paquete* for him for the Virgin."

"*¿Qué?*" Tom said.

Anna spoke rapidly and showed herbs in a packet from a *botánica*, a store that sells religious items and herbs used in Caribbean prayer and magic. "Seven Powers," Anna said.

"We should get this," Tom said. "Lydia, will you show how you used the herbs to protect your son?"

"It won't work on camera," Pat said. "You'll ridicule them." Phoebe thought she was much too earnest to be first-rate.

"Nonsense," Tom said, but Lydia put an end to it anyway.

She didn't look good, and she said, "I'm tired."

Christ, I'd be too, Phoebe thought. Man deserts her, kid's a killer, she's already sentenced to half-life in this Gulag of wasted memories the city fucked up: Let's fix poverty. Failing that, let's stick her somewhere, let's not see it. Inside she wanted to scream, but she purred comfortingly and reached out and patted Lydia's hand. "We won't rush it, dear."

Everyone knew Phoebe was as smooth and tough as they came, pretty as a gazelle, with a hide like a rhino. "We'll pick it up in a day or so *after you prep her better, please, Tom.*" And she gave him a glaring smile.

Fucking heartbreak. Killing. Where had the killing and heartbreak begun? They'd been going to solve all the world's problems. She and her bright-eyed young world-beaters. How much of this had she seen coming, this illiterate jungle, this Dark Age with modern conveniences?

Down the piss-saddened stairs. Away from the Dead Hope Project.

She remembered the Bridles' house on the shore in Beverly in July of 1962, and the white-painted wicker furniture in her second-floor room like the bones of a dream, and the wicker oval mirror showing her and Houston naked, framed by white filaments of summer memories. The upper porch outside her room led to another window, so she and Houston could meet at night, salt air thick as scented breath. Sparkling gray Winslow Homer days playing tennis on the green-hedged grass court, sailing past the club and orchards to what they called The Point . . . Houston, sitting in the bottom of the boat, hands on sheet and tiller, said, offhandedly, "That parcel is to come to me."

She ducked to light a cigarette and looked back at the land, green and rocky, shoving against the Atlantic. "Terrific," she murmured. They were both acting cool while boiling inside.

Every day sports and healthy air, seeing members of the family in sports clothes, all of them on the way somewhere else, sunburned, casual, yet studying her, because they all knew. It was fish life: sun, water, feeding, and then the pounding race upstream to spawn and float into darkness.

When had she leaped into the frenzy of love?—in the

moonlight?—as Houston panted and she moaned, and as he half slid, she half pushed his head over the moon of her belly between her legs and held him by his starlit hair dancing in the porch door trapped in ecstasy, in silver light, in wicker webs, over a painted sea?

"How do you feel about me? About us?"

"I think we should marry."

"I think so, too."

"That's swell, really."

Phoebe never saw what Houston did every morning when he stepped out of bed over clothes he'd dropped and left, heading to his wallet on the floor. She saw him as graceful, catlike, easy, was amused at his wearing old clothes like the pajamas of summer. She didn't know his grace was concentration and that he hammered his eyes devoutly every morning with the list of goals on the card he kept in the wallet.

GOALS

EXCEED $500,000 BY 25

$1 MILLION BY 30

THE STREET [by which he meant Wall Street]

FEDERAL APPOINTMENT

THE STREET [where he expected to make millions
    based on his government knowledge]

CABINET APPOINTMENT

. . . and a number of other specific goals. Some of the money he wanted was already in trusts. He would get it soon. He wanted to play the game and win his goals. He really was crazy about Phoebe—a racehorse! First-rate! A prize!—but he wanted her so intensely *because* he could see her standing up there, passing him the ball, helping him score!

"I knew some Airdley Bishops in New York, Penny—I mean, Phoebe. Forgive me," Houston's mother, Helen, said over a shore dinner.

"Yes, they're very distant cousins."

"Very nice." Helen was sunburned, busy, seemingly preoccupied, nibbling an ear of corn, putting it down. "And what are your plans?" Her hovering eyes settled on Phoebe's face for an instant.

Here it comes, Phoebe thought: Helen's prenuptial grilling. She'd played this game before, and returned the serve. "I want to take photographs. All over the world." In thinking of a career, Phoebe had always considered something she could continue after marriage.

"How nice. Very time-consuming."

Fault. Phoebe sensed she'd made the wrong answer. Helen was so vague Phoebe couldn't spot the error precisely. Time away from home? From other duties?

"Traveling takes *so much* time," Helen observed. "Your pa," she said to Houston, "has been on the go much too long trying to do too much." Pa had left for Washington a few days after she and Houston arrived. "It's Saigon again."

The Bridles, Phoebe learned, referred to important matters in this elliptical fashion. Pa Bridles was on some important advisory board at the CIA, or "The Agency," as the family called it.

She met other Bridleses.

Houston's Uncle Stu, a lanky, lively, sunburned sportsman who slapped Houston's back and called him Tony, was a New York businessman involved in Latin American affairs who had performed government tasks there as well. Stu was up for a few weekends to play polo at the Myopia Hunt Club; inside his elbow he had a purple cross-stitched scar from the tendon operation many players need after years of riding and swatting.

Houston's older sister, Edith Hicks, was there with her children, Melissa and Sam. She had separated from her husband, an alcoholic from Princeton, and had been trying to operate an antiques business.

"Tennis!" Stu called out one morning. She and Houston played Stu and Houston's nephew, Sam—a vigorous, sunny game, Stu loping, volleying hard at Houston, who moved like a cat sideways, racket held across his chest, always catching and firing back Stu's shots; little Sam, a skinny, shy kid, lunging and swinging, trying to put everything into his shots.

"Good game!" Stu said. "Quite a girl, Tony!"

Sam nodded, panting.

"I'll talk to Pa when he gets back from *this* trip to D.C.," Houston said. "It's Saigon again. He's due tomorrow."

He had told her, "No one ever *lives* here." He hadn't spent much time there or with them; he and Edith had had the nurse, and then gone away to school and summer camp and school again. "Really, I know coaches Harkness and Olivar at Yale better as mentors. So this is a visit for me too!"

They drove down to Boston for an afternoon. In the flat on Beacon Hill she saw a display case holding Houston's athletic trophies from Exeter and Yale and Pa Bridles's war mementoes case—he had been in the OSS and dropped into France, "as he will tell you," Houston said. Many pieces of furniture were covered with muslin. "They're not that old," Houston said. There was a framed photograph of a Civil War shoe factory. "We haven't been around that long—for Boston." They laughed about that. Did the past matter when they were so much in love?

It was a summer idyll, which means something different in New England, given the cruelty of its winter. A later lover, also a New England high WASP, told her how this worked: He described the love of summer, of freedom, the hot days as fruit growing between their legs, the sun running south and west, the mortal athlete, starburst nights touched with the cold breath of what lay ahead.

They were back in Beverly in time to sail before dinner.

"Tomorrow Pa comes back," Houston told her as they lay on salt-damp sheets, his hand light as silk over her full nipples, her ribs, as firm as bone over the wet silk of her hair.

"Tomorrow," she breathed.

Houston C. G. Bridles II, Harvard '37, ex-first lieutenant AUS (OSS), known to his family as Pa, stepped down the ladder of the Eastern shuttle Constellation, a radial engine prop job, much bigger than the Lysander he'd jumped from into France in the War, and thinking about aircraft and weighty new war matters at the Agency, he didn't watch others going across the hardstand through the narrow door into Logan Airport, which was still under construction.

He walked bent over, his face pursed like a smiling crabapple, through a wider door meant for baggage carts, where workers, shouting and flurrying around a cart train, didn't notice him. A perfect spy.

He walked down a service corridor, grasped he was in the wrong place, found an exit into the main corridor, and peered through the summer crowds. Lost. Dammit! Now where in hell . . . ? He was a quirky man, given to fits of temper, and like many absentminded and mistake-prone people, he grew defensive and truculent when he sensed he'd done it again. Goddam airports all look the same except the ivy-covered brick school building from which they'd walked over the grass (with Thompsons, .45s, grenades, maps) to board the Lysander in the clear night. He'd dropped behind Nazi lines into France with his OSS team to trip the Huns before D-Day. . . .

The PA announced Allegheny. No, no! He hadn't come in on that, no! *Where am I going? What am I supposed to be doing?*

Yet he remembered every word of the long meeting today and every word of the ones before. He knew the committee members—academics, businessmen, men of substance like himself with OSS backgrounds—better than he knew his own children, who were goddam headaches enough. Except for the goddam headaches in Saigon. That goddam ethereal twit Diem and his crooked brothers and bitch sister-in-law, who joked about Buddhists barbecuing themselves. Jesus. Briefings from Lansdale, Lou Conein; what could they do with Diem?

Lansdale and Conein had said he was our only hope—at least some important Vietnamese respected him: the upper class, the Hanoi Catholics who'd come south. Kennedy's shadow war specialist, Hillsman, wanted to know if Diem *could* stay.

He had the support of American Catholics who'd supported Kennedy, which complicated it for the President; but many other Vietnamese hated Diem; he was incompetent, vague, distracted by pseudophilosophical notions, given to rambling monologues like Hitler. A round-faced eunuch. But his brother, Archbishop Thuc, had clout here: a prominent American cardinal who—a secret Agency dossier said—was also a transvestite queen. But you couldn't tell that to the American people. And that bastard Nhu, Diem's older brother, was rubbing it in—he knew he had the Americans by the balls. Diem and Nhu were demanding more money and threatening to make peace with the VC if we didn't pay. That's what the meeting had been about.

If it were as simple as fighting the VC and paying off Diem's family, that would be tolerable, but the Agency was also pitted against the United States Army. The Army had funded the new ARVN (Army of the Republic of Vietnam) as a model mechanized force perfectly equipped to fight the last war. It was an army completely unsuited for fighting guerrillas—while the Agency was funding the American Green Berets and the Vietnamese copy of the Special Forces. The Green Berets were using tribesmen and killing VC efficiently in the areas where they could operate. Unfortunately Nhu had taken the Vietnamese Special Forces, on which the Agency had spent millions, and used them as his private extortion force—so the Pentagon was telling Kennedy the Agency couldn't pour piss out of a boot. "Look how they fucked up the Bay of Pigs," they usually added.

Kennedy, for his part, was only too glad to shove his lance into the Agency and break it off, while people Pa Bridles knew in the Agency would be glad to see Kennedy dead, given what they knew about his war record, his fiddling with the wrong women—a Nazi spy, a Mob chippie—and his father's Mob connections. But the American people couldn't know about—

"Good God!"

Again, Pa Bridles gasped that he didn't know where he was. He was surrounded by temporary plywood walls and could only dimly hear the PA. No crowds, no cigarette machines, no signs. He turned around and trudged back, head down, grousing, muttering, looking for some connection to what he'd seen before.

What are we going to do about Diem?

Suppose we lose in Vietnam? Or worse, what if the Army gets the upper hand running programs there? The Army can't run anything smaller than a multibillion-dollar program—he knew that from the War. Vietnam didn't have to be that big. He and his colleagues— JFK's Hillsman agreed—felt they could run it small and quiet, like an encore of that wonderful time in France in 1943–44. The Green Berets organizing resistance among the tribes, Air America dropping supplies—he fell into a nostalgic reverie so sweet, so sentimental, so unlike the chill around his withered soul. The kindest parts of his memory turned always back to that eternal summer of the War— working with the maquis near Clermont-Ferrand, tearing up Sepp Dietrich's Waffen-SS division as it raced north after D-Day— wonderful times.

He and a chum named Gerrity had jumped several Krauts and killed them all. Beat one to death with his own coal-scuttle helmet. The memory provoked a wintry smile even now, a relief in violence his life would not allow. S.O.B.'s head was nothing but a red pulp with an eye and a row of teeth. Amazing the amount of pornography you found on dead Krauts. Imagine telling *that* around The Gas House, his club at Harvard.

After Germany had collapsed, he and Gerrity were assigned to Counter-Intelligence Corps, interrogating thousands of German prisoners, pulling out the Nazis.

The government made deals with some of them to get information about the Russians or about communist movements in France, Italy, The Netherlands. Couldn't have communists taking over Europe after Americans had fought to liberate it. But these Americans must not know we made deals with the Nazis. Wouldn't understand. Pa Bridles didn't think the average middle-class democratic American could make *any* decision. That's why we have advisory committees and groups like the Agency, he thought. Why we have social classes. Harvard. Why we have New England.

He felt a twinge of discomfort remembering some of the Nazi deals, in which they pampered Nazi thugs who'd tortured maquis Pa had fought alongside.

The British officers, whose manners many of Bridles's pals aped, showed contempt for the Americans' Nazi deals. But at least the American *public* wouldn't know. Too complicated to explain. The American public must *not* know what a mess Vietnam was. No one knew what . . .

He saw a clock hanging overhead. Christ! A half hour lost. Then a man in black. Face he knew—pink pug nose.

"Mr. Bridles? It's Kelly. I was waiting at the gate—"

"Dammit, it's been a half hour!" Mr. Bridles muttered. "Looking around—" He gave a short, impotent gesture and stalked off, but slowed to let Kelly move ahead and lead him to the car.

"I couldn't see you, sir."

"I wasn't lost! I wasn't lost!"

Up the lilac lane to the house. Didn't like coming here, made him uncomfortable for years. Give Helen a big space and she fluttered around like a goddam moth. Blurs of white on the tennis court— Houston and that girl batting a ball. Edith's son—what's his name? Didn't matter, too young. Edith's son banging a ball against the bat board. Didn't like Houston bringing that girl up here. Screwing her all the time. Wasn't fitting. Wanted Houston to court the Mawson girl. Someone from here. Normal. Known. He saw Helen out on the side in her silly hat clipping flowers. Why in hell had he . . . ?

Because his brother Stu was going after her too. Always rivals, Stu going to Yale when he went to Harvard. Stu playing polo. Going down to New York simply *to pursue money*. Seneca: He had a talent for business and aspired to nothing higher. Stu's war record was nothing to brag about! Running around Latin America with Nelson Rockefeller while he was parachuting into France. Ha! Had time to come up and waste Helen's time, too. Shabby character—not like the Bridles who'd stayed in Boston.

The car stopped. As Kelly opened his door, Pa Bridles heard feet running on the gravel and tensed—then slowly turned and saw the sweating red face of his son.

"Pa, I'd like to speak with you."

"Moment," Pa growled, jerking his hand, facing away. He wasn't ready for any of them yet. *"Plus tard! Plus tard!"*

Houston saw trouble coming. He wasn't inclined to back off, but wanted to win her and needed Pa's approval to unlock trusts and get in in D.C. Pa's thin, angry voice signalled him like geese, crying that darkness and hardship lay ahead.

"No, I didn't talk to him about us. Kelly said he's been in one of his moods," Houston told Phoebe.

Phoebe raised her head and flared her nostrils. She was not quite used to this. "I don't understand. I didn't anticipate a problem. What is it?"

"He's funny. I told you we were somewhat strangers here. I'll try again."

Houston's inner sense, the ghost that told him when to shift for the ball, told him to wait till his pa calmed down from whatever had upset him in Washington. But his inner sense also told him Phoebe wouldn't stand for a lot of diddling around. The way she'd reared back . . .

"Pa?" he said at the library door some minutes later. Peering into the shadowy room, he saw his father—could that sour, hunched, scowling man really be *his* pa? Was that what *he'd* be? He vowed to write another resolution on his wallet card: If you're as dead as Pa, die first.

"What?"

"I want to marry Phoebe. She's first-rate, her family's flawless, and I expect we'll—"

"No." Mr. Bridles had barely heard him, didn't want the interruption.

"In a few months I'll be coming into the Fraker trust and I'll be on the Street anyway."

"Not with my approval."

"Why not?"

"You wish my help for an appointment. If you want my help, no. It's not time for any of this. You've not done anything yet. No war service, no business acumen. Simply to marry—it's too easy. Too—I shall not—"

What in hell's he talking about? Houston thought. He knew Pa was like a snake, unpredictable and dangerous.

But also he wondered if this was real life. Had this summer been too much happiness? He was conditioned to the notion of The Fall. That was the moral world he'd learned at school and college. He wanted Phoebe, but could he simply *be happy?* Were there not higher duties for him as a Fraker and a Bridles? Deep inside he didn't expect happiness throughout his life. Sports and school had been his lush summer away from the grumbling at home, the permafrost. He had his goals. He wanted public duties to beat out this withered man before him, for whom love and joy were merely memories. It's too bad, Houston thought, but it's inevitable, isn't it? Houston accepted, looking at his family face, Pa's mask of death, that youth, joy, and summer must be followed by hard, thin struggles.

"I shall not approve it now," Pa Bridles said.

I'm sure I can get around it anyway, Houston thought as he went back to the tennis court to see Phoebe. It's like shooting the gap—just keep your nerve! All the means he'd learned—a clear eye, risk, achievement . . .

He saw Phoebe, white, dazzling against the green, and his nephew, little Sam Hicks. Phoebe turned toward him—her dark brows and good pale eyes hit him in the heart.

She ran to him and looked in his face. She went cold, frightened. His lovely face was ravaged, his chin stuck out. A pulse beat at his temple. "It's bad," he said. "Bad news. Bad news."

"He's opposed to me."

"I'm convinced he hates me," Houston said. "I could kill him."

"But he didn't approve of me."

"He doesn't know his own mind. But he's got things tied up."

"Houston, I am not *at all* used to having someone who does not *know* me or my family presume to—"

"Phoebe, calm down, goddammit! I'll fix it!"

"You'll *fix* it?" She turned away. An iron clamp closed on his heart.

The door opened. Mrs. Bridles said, "Hello, Penny. Will you—"

"It is Phoebe, please."

"Yes, of course. Do forgive me."

"I'm sorry you never learned my name! Or had the manners—"

Mrs. Bridles breathed out through her nose.

"Phoebe!" Houston yelled, looking from one to the other. "Mother, listen— Phoebe, I'll fix it. They just don't know."

"I won't be here for dinner, thank you. Excuse me! Where is Kelly, please? May I please—"

"Phoebe," Houston said.

"May I *please* have Kelly drive me to the airport? *Away* from here?" Her face was squashed red and streaming. "Please!" And little Sam, his mouth open, ran to get Kelly.

As much as she cried and hated on the plane, she had no idea how much more heartbreak Pa and the others would bring to the rest of the country.

Far to the west of Phoebe's heartbroken New England summer, Mark Randolph was having a great, brainless summer near the Great Lakes—a physical, boozy, sunny idyll—but he was about to get ominous news, too.

To get in shape for the big test coming, he was working as a carpenter's laborer building flimsy but large houses on reclaimed swamp—since everyone had money and people were pushing out from Chicago to buy Better Lives in the suburbs. He carried stacks of lumber on his shoulders and slopped through mud from those August thundershowers, legs pumping and driving. He was a mediocre athlete but, like other men in his family, broad-shouldered and strong. As he skidded over sloppy clay and dodged holes, he panted in tune to the immortal Little Richard song, "Slippin' and Slidin'," red of face, sweaty of brow, beery of breath, laughing and calling out to all the guys on the project: "Hey, Carl! Vinnie! Joe!"

The carpenters were hillbillies from Tennessee, the plumbers were Germans from Wisconsin, the bricklayers were South Side black scabs under an Italian subcontractor. He liked to know everyone and be a pal. No one knew he'd just graduated from Yale—you don't tell them you're a college boy—but they knew he was going into the Marines and the ex-Marines told him what to expect. All the veterans gave him advice. It was part of his education, hearing tribal lore handed down, and it seemed more real to him than books he'd seen and cited but not read in college.

College! Oh, Jesus! I wasted my time! he thought in a seizure of guilt. All that fucking partying! Chasing Betty! Chasing nurses! Getting shitfaced! And I wanted—

At times he'd wanted to be a geologist! A poet! A theologian! A historian! A New Critic! And he'd settled for coaching from Peabody and the DKE and Fence exam files just to squeeze through. Slippin' and slidin'. *Whew!*

That sunny, hot day in mid-August he drove his battered Hillman wagon from the project over flat roads, past shimmering farms, into the hilly, tree-covered village of Barrington, and up a quiet street shaded by old elm trees, soon to die of foreign blight, to his family's house. It was a solid brick ranch with big picture windows. The long lot had seventeen kinds of shade trees tended by a gardener. He parked his Hillman, which was an unattractive and embarrassing shitheap, out of sight in a hedged cul de sac and went into the house. On the glass-topped Marshall Field's table was a big tan envelope. Black square letters hard as a rifle barrel:

DEPARTMENT OF THE NAVY
HEADQUARTERS, U.S. MARINE CORPS
TO: PVT. MARK H. RANDOLPH 1979064

Uh-oh, he thought. It had all seemed so unreal when he signed up. He pulled out the roster orders with an arrow by his name.

YOU ARE DIRECTED TO REPORT . . .

"I'm going to die!" he gasped in a gush of callow sentiment. He was given to surges like that, his heart blurting what it felt before he knew what was what. But sentiment ran in his family.

"Mom?"

"I'm here," she said sadly.

He found her in the living room on the big flowered couch by the picture window overlooking ten of the seventeen kinds of shade trees they paid the gardener to tend. Beside her on the inlaid marble tea table was a flat glass ashtray the size of a hubcap filled with cigarette butts. She was small, thin, and had big soulful eyes. She had just had her hair dyed the new silver shade. "I saw your orders," she sighed.

"Are you all right?"

"Yes."

"They're just orders. I don't want a horror show like Christmas."

"You won't get a horror show like Christmas," she said thinly.

Exasperated, he left the living room and stepped through the house, out of place in his dirty work clothes. He was afraid she'd go on the sauce again. He stepped into the pantry, checked the bottles of Scotch, bourbon, and gin—nothing consumed so far—and carried them downstairs to a closet in the knotty pine rumpus room. He locked the closet padlock, put the key in his pants pocket, and poked a finger in his shirt pocket, where he had several crumpled dollar bills—construction laborers kept their money this way for easier use in bars—and a pack of Luckys. He pulled one out and lit it with his Zippo.

Jesus, he hoped she'd be okay. But what could he do? She shouldn't drink. Actually, none of them was a drinking model. That was another fact he'd kept concealed, this time from his Yale pals— that he lived in a horror show and his family was falling apart.

But they put on a good front, yelling at any outsiders who slurred or even questioned the Randolphs or the Haweses, Mom's side.

A picture of them hung over the rumpus room fireplace. Dad— Henry—in a tweed suit, intelligent blue eyes wide, a broad red face, short white hair, that heavy-shouldered build he had given his sons; Frank, Mark's older brother, dark-haired, tanned, smiling confidently; Mark with his short brown hair, head cocked, looking straight into the camera; and Mom, smiling sweetly, hands folded in her lap.

They were an old WASP family, but not high WASP. Middle class. Commercial. Their ancestors had come from southern England before the Revolution and pressed out of the Virginia hills into Kentucky, Tennessee, and further west, always on the frontier, so they had cousins all over and relatives who'd been in every war and on both sides of the Civil War. Henry's grandfather had killed several Confederates and been killed himself. The family still had vociferous discussions about that war—heated, yelling discussions, scoring points—and on other subjects, too. Roosevelt. Kennedy. The New Deal. Eliot. The Threat of Modern Art. They would get choleric or empurpled without talking sense. Mark thought they resembled Tacitus's description of Germans living in the woods—intemperate, disorganized, high-colored, big-boned, given to fierce boozing and impulsive fighting and panic, not as artistic as the Celts.

Were Mom and Dad frustrated artists? This was one of the secret family questions—one Mark felt guilty about, believing his and Frank's arrival had denied Mom and Dad fuller lives. Mom had painted flowers but told them, "I gave up painting to have you." Dad had sung impromptu in places like Gus's and Ricardo's in the thirties and occasionally got paying gigs. They must have had disorganized lives because Mark remembered their binges in the forties, one time Mom and Dad quarreling and Dad throwing a jigger at Mom and bouncing it off her head, she turning away, saying, "Ohhh!", the jigger spinning and shining on the floor, the yellow-labeled gin bottle, and Mark and Frank holding each other and crying.

Later Mark had asked his father if he'd wanted to be a singer instead of going into business, and Henry said, "Not on your life! I love music—it's balm to my soul—but it ain't a living. I loved carrying on in bars. But I had to grow up. Understand?"

Henry had worked hard all through the fifties for a shipping company and made vice president and board member. The more successful he'd got, the more unhappy Mom got. When they joined Barrington Hills Country Club she couldn't make friends there. She became more isolated, and the family covered up for her.

Meanwhile Mark and his brother were going through high school. Mark was driven to make friends, be popular, go out for sports—anything to appear normal. His father took time out from work to come home early and watch him play football. Once in a JV game he made a tackle right in front of his father.

"Did you see it?" he asked later.

"I *heard* it," Henry said.

He took Mark to his office occasionally, introduced him to other executives, took him to Brooks Brothers and Marshall Field's and bought him suits, but they did not become pals. Something like a black rock sat between them: on Mark's side, fear and distrust of his father; on Henry's side, shame for what he had once done that he could not discuss now. As far as Mark knew, it was the same with his older brother Frank and Dad. But he wasn't sure. They didn't talk about such things.

Henry was out of town on business now. Frank was still in the Army, waiting to be discharged. Mark was here alone with Mom. He didn't want her to go on a binge like she had last Christmas. Because of the military orders. Oh, no.

Last Christmas they'd been three for dinner. Frank had been drafted into the Army after flunking out of MIT and was on garrison duty in Korea. This was eight years after the cease-fire, but when Mark said grace, in a gush of sentiment or maybe to see what would happen, he gave a tear-jerking, maudlin prayer for those on the edge of the world, in the icy mountains, defending their land—"the member of our family who can't be here—"

Mom howled and sobbed and Dad said, "Oh, Jesus, Mark, why—for Christ's sake—"

They'd all had several belts before dinner and during: sparkling burgundy, the rage of the Chicago suburbs that year. Mom passed out at the table. Dad wanted to go out driving. Mark tried to stop him by holding the Cadillac keys and they struggled up and down the modern fifties kitchen, bouncing off the curved chrome-edged counter, off the double fridge, against the sink by another picture window. Dad hit Mark's shoulder and face, blacking his eye. Mark didn't want to punch Henry because he knew he might damage his bridgework but finally shoved him across the room. Then he got pissed off and said, "Here! Take 'em! I don't give a shit!"

Henry drove out to the country club, bouncing off several varieties of trees en route and shedding chrome from the Cadillac, and Mark wound up in a roadhouse in Fox River Grove, looking for love and picking up a Czech girl.

The next day Henry was terribly hung over and abjectly sorry. He held Mark. Mark couldn't say anything. He struggled with emotions he couldn't voice.

He looked for fathers in other places. On the construction crew. Perhaps that's one reason he'd enlisted in the Marines. He didn't know. He hoped he'd do better with this than he had at Yale.

He showered, dressed, and went back to see Mom. God, she'd got small. "Are you okay, Mom?"

"Yes, Mark. You don't have to worry. I won't drink."

"Okay."

"You didn't have to lock the liquor."

Mark lit a cigarette.

"I'd like the key, please."

"We're not entertaining tonight."

"Please."

"You look so good now." He really wanted them to be like those Ozzie and Harriet families in the big well-kept houses.

"Please."

"No. Why don't you read a goddam book or something?"

"Oh, Mark, please don't talk like that."

"You don't have to get juiced."

"You're no prize. Frank's no prize. Your *father's* no prize."

"But we all take care of you. Remember when I was a Boy Scout and splinted your arm with *Life* when you fell down the stairs looking for a bottle?"

"I remember you and Frank *brawling!* And when you and your father fought—"

Shit, it was too much to go into; Mark couldn't cope with it. He was that kind of WASP, who could handle violence but not painful discussions. "Mom, I just want you to be good."

He kissed her and left. The house looked nice in the summer evening. He really wished they could—somehow—live up to their pretensions. And be *productive.* And sort of normal, not brawling all the time. Squabbles and fights and fierce uniting against outsiders.

Driving out to the bar, he saw one of those chain-wreck Midwestern accidents that went on for hundreds of yards of cornfield carnage. Way up ahead, two cars had collided, blocking the lanes; others had slammed into them; still others had skirted the wrecks, swerving onto the grassy shoulder, but one car had slid into the ditch. Then others had stopped, people getting out to help or—curious fellows—to look at the wrecks, standing on the shoulder. And then still more cars came along and hit the pileup or, swerving onto the shoulder, knocked people flying.

When Randolph drove by all the noise and blood and smoking metal, he saw bodies draped over barbed-wire fences and on mangled steel. He supposed a war would look like that.

His parents were so nostalgic about the War. Bing Crosby's songs, the olive-drab antiaircraft guns on the shore of Lake Michigan. He remembered hearing jets ripping overhead, frightening him, during the Korean War a dozen years ago. Communist menace. Fight for your side. The way the papers wrote up local boys in the armed forces; the joy you heard about when a neighbor's son was back on leave, wearing his GI T-shirt and khakis in the summer under the green elms. That healthy crew-cut look.

Life

Phoebe went to Aunt Amanda's in New York.

"Oh, what a bastard, dear," Amanda said. "I'm sorry. They're like that, you know.'"

Phoebe had no desire to go to where her parents had retired—Asheville. She didn't want them to know. It was too late to go to Paris now. She sat around depressed, feeling lousy and ugly. She did not want to brood; anyway, it was hard to sit and stew around Amanda, who kept asking, "Are you all right?" Amanda's husband had ditched her; Phoebe's misery comforted her.

She wanted to take photos. She took her portfolio to *Life* in its new chrome-and-glass building west of Rockefeller Center.

She filled out forms, met interviewers. A photo editor looked at her photos from Vassar and independent shoots. She went through sunlit big-windowed offices and saw people examining stacks of contact sheets and prints. The people were intelligent, detached, smooth. She wanted it. She had grown up with *Life*—the war photos, the great social drama photos. Margaret Bourke-White, Robert Capa, Howard Sochurek, David Douglas Duncan . . .

"Miss Bishop?" an editor said.

"Yes!"

"We can't hire you." No positions open, many on the waiting list, and they had stringers. But they took her to meet Sara Gelber, a short, busy woman with large dark eyes and gray-blue hair piled high on her head. She chain-smoked, looked at Phoebe's photos and clips, and offered her a job as a reporter. At *Life* that meant primarily research, but it was one of the few places then where women could work general assignment, not society or food, and already many *Life* women were on their way to being big names. Sara was nursemaid and doyenne of the talented *Life* women reporters. Phoebe started the following Monday, the last week in August. She was thrown right into it.

"Phoebe, check these post *haste*, please," Sara said, stumping among the half-partition cubicles called bullpens and dropping sheets of copy with names and addresses for Phoebe to check. Phoebe used *Facts on File*, phone books, an atlas and almanac on her steel desk, or went to the library. Sara checked her work and tested her mind to see if she was serious, not a spoiled dilettante.

"Did you check this?" she asked, her dark eyes searching Phoebe's face. "Check on this—wait, I'll tell you whom to call!" Sara said, swiveling in her chair. "Verify what I've marked," she ordered. "This stack," Sara said, handing over as much paper as in several phone books.

Phoebe plunged happily into work, staying late like other reporters, reading through back issues—those mesmerizing covers of New Deal dams, debutantes, war scenes—and the superb files. This was the most distinctive American magazine.

She also heard about other bits of the Luce empire. Her one-time and very brief date, Ashleigh Loakes, was an outspoken admirer of Yale man Luce and his formula for *Time* and its arch way of telling the news. (No rich boy he, scion of Protestant missionaries in China, Luce learned trade at oldest college daily, coined clipped style to speed, simplify stories.) Luce, propelled by the moral momentum of his missionary family and by Yale know-it-all certainty, personally distorted news coming out of China, suppressing stories of Chiang Kai-shek's military incompetence against the Japanese, Chiang's corruption, and the corrupting influence of Chiang's immensely rich Soong in-laws. Luce overruled fine reporters like Theodore White and concealed from American readers the hatred millions of Chinese felt for Chiang, so when Chiang was trounced by Mao's forces, millions of misinformed faithful *Time* readers in America were surprised, confused, and mad as hell, though they didn't know at what. The faithful readers were still misinformed and angry about Vietnam—but *Time* was supposed to make people angry and *Life* make them happy.

Phoebe found an apartment in the East Twenties, a third-floor walkup. The kitchen looked over a rubble-filled lot with an ailanthus tree. She bought old furniture and a KLH radio. She walked home tired and happy those shortening nights, buzzing with facts, words, ways she'd learned to get someone to give a detail over the phone, remembering pictures she'd seen and seeing city pictures—old brick fronts next to glass boxes, fire escapes, the last horse wagons hauling rags, lit-up venetian-blinded windows looking as if they were crossed by luminous bars.

Sara Gelber told her, waving a cigarette around, dusting her blouse with ash, about how Marian MacPhail and Murial Hall had made the department the best in the business and the best chance for a woman who wanted to be a serious journalist. "You'll learn more here than in Paris," Sara said. "Meet more people too."

After Phoebe had been at *Life* over a month and shown she was all right, Sara took her to the 3-Gs, a Forty-eighth Street bar in a brownstone where *Life* staffers had drunk from the first day of the magazine. She went to parties of people her age, dozens of them jammed into small apartments, sinks full of ice, open bottles on the tables, ashtrays overflowing. October in New York was delightful. The air was like champagne. You could stroll looking at street scenes or descend into the grimy subway and pay fifteen cents to ride anywhere on the new corrugated stainless steel cars or old green ones with high woven seats. You could go about day and night alone, which is how she preferred it then. She hadn't been too wise or lucky with men and felt it was better to make the scene as undated material, the way she'd hit parties last year, riding with Carole.

Carole phoned her. "Phoebe, Peas and I have moved in uptown! You have to come see us!"

A. C. L. PEABODY III
CAROLE ANNE TIDDENS

His card was from Shreve, Crump & Low, hers Tiffany's. They were pinned to the scarred door of a fourth-floor walkup, fire escapes in front, on 110th off Broadway. Student sounds and student posters on the way up. Peter, Paul and Mary. Odetta. Palestrina. Ski Austria. Interlaken. And, always correct, Paris.

Carole hugged Phoebe, the big blonde laughing, the shapely brunette acting cool and city-wise.

"And Peas! Look at you!" Phoebe said. "You *look* like a professor already!"

Adams Peabody beamed. He had grown a very good beard, thick and dark, fluffing over his open collar. He was still pale and wore a patched, threadbare tweed jacket he must have had since prep school, but his eyes were active, animated. His sharp nose and bright eyes looked good framed by the dark beard, and he was full of enthusiasm.

"I like it, Phoebe. We're doing real work here. It's not undergraduate! We're all—I don't mind saying it—we're all intellectuals here."

"And I'm taking Film!" Carole said. "At the New School!"

Their books were stacked together on the ubiquitous brick-and-plank shelves.

"It's very homey," Carole said. "We're living as man and wife."

"I'm free," Phoebe said.

Around his armchair Peabody had stacked Anglo-Saxons and moderns, C. Wright Mills and Michael Harrington, Weston and Frazier. "Look at these! This is terrific stuff! You have to read it."

A few times Phoebe went uptown when Carole asked her repeatedly to a party, promising it would be good, but the parties were different—the music, what people talked about, how they dressed. Already she and Carole were heading different ways. Sometimes at these parties, toward the end of the evening, Carole cried. She wanted Peabody to marry her and Peabody wanted things the way they were.

"It's because of his mother!" Carole sobbed. They were sitting on the fire escape, ignoring a thin, cold, autumn rain, getting relief from the smoke and crowd inside.

"If he doesn't want to leave home, fuck him," Phoebe suggested.

"It's not as simple as that!" Carole cried. "It's much *deeper* than that!"

"I've met her," Phoebe said. She was odd, Peabody's mother. Oddly dressed and with an air of noble suffering that drew attention to herself.

"Well, she works on his guilt."

"What guilt?"

"Adams's."

"Why?"

"It's hard to explain. She had to give *up* so much for her beliefs—their families cut them off because of their social activism and then, when Peas' father died, she brought him up alone."

"And made him feel guilty?"

Carole sighed. "As he says, 'We're a very complicated family.' "

"Carole, why are you advocating *his* part when he's screwing *you?*"

"Because I want to marry him. I want to be a New England professor's wife!"

"I'm not so hot on New England," Phoebe said.

"It's his mother."

"It's hard to fight family," Phoebe said. "Why don't you just bag it?"

"No! I *want* to *get* him! It's so cozy when things are right. We have dinner and read afterward. Sometimes he has a glass of Scotch and phones people and writes down *aperçus* and tells me about them and we laugh. He was so damn funny when he was calling Mark Randolph to razz him before he went in the Marines. 'You're not gonna sleep through an exam there!' he kept saying. 'Can't chase Bennett girls there!' It was so—well, I guess you had to be there."

Wham! Clang! Clatter whack-whack-whack! The galvanized iron GI can flew against steel two-decker bunks and spun down the linoleum while NCOs pushed over the racks, spilling scared skinhead maggots. "Up! Up! Up! All I wanta see is assholes and elbows!" Skinheads in skivvies, eyes wide as birds, quaking.

Cold-eyed NCOs. "Quit movin' around, you fuckin' *snake!* You wanta be thumped! Unsat! You're unsat!"

The captain had said, "We will drive you into the deck. If you're any good, you'll come back up."

A sergeant yelled, "You wanta be a marine officer? *I'm* gonna take *orders* from a puke like *you? Bullshit!*"

"Maggot! Puke! Pussy!"

"You're college boys," Staff Sergeant Boyce said in a low, bored drawl. He had been in Korea. "You don't show me shit."

Sergeant Smith asked, his voice rising to a bellow, "Clean? You call that *clean?*" He was a small, wiry black who grew and spread like a canopy of death when he got pissed off at numbnut maggots. "YOU WANTA BE AN OFFICER AND YOU CAN'T KEEP YOUR *GEAR* STRAIGHT!" He levitated over the maggots, bellowing, terrifying. An ex-NCO in the program said Smith had been Force Recon, the men who drop into forbidden territory, garrote sentries with piano wire, study enemy installations, and sneak out undetected.

"Oh, Jesus," Mark prayed. "Just let me . . . keep me from fuck-

ing up *again!*" One candidate was so scared he couldn't shit for a
week. They threw them out for dirty nails, voice breaking, misspell-
ing, breaking down. Randolph prayed to the globe, anchor, and eagle.
Each morning when the survivors fell out for rifle inspection, the
sergeants yelling that they were pukes, maggots, lower than whale
shit, they'd see something worse across the street on the grass outside
of Casual Company—a few shitcanned, broken young men in green
cotton utilities, all the white name tapes ripped off, now just privates
picking up cigarette butts. No one was yelling at them.

They took away the college graduates' names, degrees, home
towns, and gave them numbers: serial, rifle, rack, the rifle's and pistol's weight, chamber pressure, muzzle velocity, range, the steel
quanta of war. They marched among steel buildings, slapped hands
on rifles, slammed helmets in unison, became part of that loud, shambling engine larger than any individual. They knew they were getting
tough when Smith or Boyce yelled at them, crooned contemptuously,
"Oh, you great big steamin' turd," discussed their faults, ugliness,
and moral weakness, and they'd just stand there unmoved, letting it
roll off, perhaps admiring a vicious turn of phrase. There was a Marine Corps song to that effect sung to the tune of a Sousa march: "I
scarcely give a shit! I hardly care—" They learned something like
religious devotion, detaching themselves from insult.

Several weeks into training, one cold, rainy morning, the sergeants, looking mean, had everyone fall out with rifle, helmet, and
field marching pack, and they ran past the quonsets, across the parade
deck, up a slippery red-clay trail for miles and miles, maggots falling,
rising, and running to catch up, others wearing out, legs giving way,
collapsing, sobbing in frustration, knowing they were doomed. "Get
outa the way! Out! Pussy!" One candidate fell on his knees and
wouldn't get up as others slogged around him; a sergeant grabbed the
handle of the E tool on his pack and threw him off the trail. "Unsat!
You'r *UNSAT!*" Randolph finally was doing exactly what he could
handle, slopping through, panting, his legs cramped, about to collapse
but not doing it, keeping up, and when the wet, dark green, red-mud-
splattered column pattered into sight of the quonsets, he knew he'd be
commissioned. Even when Smith swarmed all over him at inspection
afterward. *"RANDOLPH! THIS IS THE FILTHIEST RIFLE I EVER
SAW! WHAT'D YOU DO—SHIT IN IT?"* Randolph stood dumb and
steady, looking into space, and bellowed back, "No sir!" with breath
that would stun a camel, causing Smith to recoil a millimeter. He'd

been broken down and reassembled, cloaked in new armor. Never reflective, he had blocked off more parts of his mind, but he was certainly tougher. This helped a few days later.

They ate off the usual steel trays in a mess hall decorated with photos of Marines past, cleaning M1919A4 machine guns in Korea, lining up horses in the thirties in China—pictures of the legend the candidates were to enter. After chow he sat on his footlocker polishing his boots, the smells of Kiwi and Brasso around him, when the duty NCO summoned him to the office. He ran, hammered on the hatchway, stood at attention.

"Get in here."

He ran in. The lieutenant and two sergeants were there. "Sit down," one said in a mild voice.

What the fuck is going on? He didn't allow himself to look in their faces.

"I'm sorry to say your parents are dead," the lieutenant said, and gave the details. Mark had got their card before they left to fly out to the Coast—in an Electra. This one had lost a wing and exploded all over a cornfield.

Mark talked on the phone with his brother, Frank, who'd just been released from the Army.

"Look, Mark, there's no need to come home," Frank said. "There's nothing here. The FAA's trying to identify people. There's nothing left."

"You can miss a day," Staff Sergeant Boyce said. "One day."

"Nothing to bury, sir."

But he flew out of D.C. Saturday night. The minister of the suburban white wood and brick church Mom had gone to held a memorial service Sunday. Frank drove Mark back to O'Hare in the Cadillac, both of them smoking cigarettes and saying little.

"Shit, they weren't very happy, were they?" Mark said.

"I don't know," Frank said. He was lean from the Army, taller than Mark, very bright; he'd settled down during his hitch and would go back to MIT soon. "The old man was happy with how things were going."

"What?"

"You. Getting through college. Even if it was liberal arts. And me *possibly* being able to get through Statics and Statistics this time. He was pleased."

Mark shook his head. He couldn't grasp it. Both Mom and Dad had been waiting for something else, disappointed, fighting. The way they'd get pissed off and hurt and not talk about it, glaring and sulking. Mom crying, singing songs from a time that couldn't have been all that much fun. What kind of life was that? What had his father worked so hard for? What had his mother been so miserable for? Riding a one-wing Electra, spinning into the big black. Nothing. Not a fucking thing on the other side. That's all she wrote, as the NCOs said, using the line from the country song. After the bad news there's nothing.

A few days later the maggots lined up for dog tags a clerk stamped on an Addressograph machine. "Religion?"

"No preference!" Randolph said. There's no God, just a skyful of accidents. It's all accidental. The only thing I belong to is this: the Marine Corps.

During this time the maggots were aware that no tactical jets were taking off from the airstrip across the way. They'd pulled out. The VIP helicopters were gone. The real Marines were on alert for something in Cuba, but no one knew much about it, and it didn't matter for them, the maggots. As Staff Sergeant Boyce said in his quiet, contemptuous drawl, "You can be shit sure *you* people ain't goin' in on the first wave."

The Missile Crisis was the first big story Phoebe worked on, gripping the phones, dialing and waiting, pushing for facts. Others rushed down corridors; photographers and reporters drew wads of cash for travel. She saw how the story broke, like all big events, in bits and pieces, little stories that could have meant anything: meetings at the White House, military bases on alert, no one talking. When Kennedy went on television, she was astonished. What a story! Especially if we don't get blown sky high! Sara had her phone bases all over the South. Phoebe quickly learned terms such as battalion, division, destroyer squadron; she also learned how military officers and bureaucrats could lie, mislead, or confuse the question. This would help her in covering the War later.

"Kennedy's trapped," Sara said. "He came into office with this young vigorous PT boat *shtick* to show up Eisenhower, and now every move he makes he's forced to be more militaristic."

They were at the 3-Gs drinking whiskey sours after another late night. "God knows where this is heading. And look at the way we're playing this." She meant *Life*'s eyeball-to-eyeball story. "We're playing us as the heros, the cowboys staring down the outlaws. *I'm* not a fucking cheerleader, thank you." She sipped her sour and licked foam from her lips.

"*Time* made a terrible mistake cheerleading for Chiang Kai-shek and the Soongs. It misinformed people. It helped them go crazy in the Cold War. It poisoned the way people understood Korea, even the Rosenberg case. The only way it kept credibility was going after McCarthy, later. Kennedy reads all the papers and magazines. I hope he doesn't make too much of that goddam cowboy business."

Adams Peabody probably had the clearest notion of what was happening because he opposed all of it, from the adulation Kennedy got in the vulgar media to the March-to-War busyness they showed on television—troops on alert, jet fighters taking off, destroyers knifing the waves like in "Victory at Sea." All the machinery of World War II propaganda cranking for what he was sure was a mistake. He didn't want thermonuclear war; he wanted to get his master's degree.

He brooded, bit his lip, walked, hands jammed in pockets, around the gritty streets and bland campus brick: thin, sharp-nosed, his dark beard and dark-framed glasses making him look like a man used to hard thinking. Here on campus students used to leaflet for fairness to Cuba. Now the rhinoceros was loose. War: where the boys are this year. He'd tried to call Mark Randolph but the base operators were impossible. "We were at *Yale* together," he'd insisted to some Southern woman who couldn't have cared less. It was in times like these that he wanted to talk with the Rands, hear stories, bullshit, crude humor—the lowdown. All he got was Southern accents demanding information he didn't *have*. He felt a withering, sinking sadness. Happy times were past. Cattails bending over cold water, fast gray clouds. The mob clamoring for war.

He didn't want to go. Simple as that. He wasn't a jock or a fool. *How much* trouble it saved to tell the truth—no posturing, no jut-jawed he-man excuses. The truth.

He knew how to say, "No money." It was so simple. He didn't have to agonize watching the swells. The truth! It makes you free! Free! The word tore like a cannonball around the vast library of his head, knocking off volumes of *pensées* and *aperçus*. Free!

But there was one truth that didn't make him free; it made him shudder. He was hag-ridden. Twice. Fought over by Mother and Carole—coerced, crowded, pulled, pressed, stretched, smothered. He was the ball; they each had one of his balls, pulling him each way, pressing him to act. Mother had taught him social history and Marxism while raising him. Carole fed him, cosseted him, suckled him. Mother approved of his living in sin but didn't like Carole. Carole liked the idea of marrying him but cringed at Mother.

The only way to protect Carole was to marry her, but that terrified him. Why? He already had sex, food, and a place. *Why get married?* But when Carole cried, her hot, pink anguish ripped open his soul, exposing raw nerves of guilt.

"Peas! I want us to go to any university you like! I'll help you! You know I have money!"

Eh? She *did* have money. And they did have terrific times in bed. Yet he had escaped one woman for another, hadn't he? And her *family*—Eisenhower Republicans. *Their* values versus Mother's values. *His* values. Could he be free and make this choice if it were distasteful to his values? He didn't have someone like the Rands to make good vulgar sense of it. Marry the girl, eh? He pondered, chewed, walked, squinting, searching, while the news photos on the stands showed erect missiles and lines of soldiers throbbing to be spewed over the earth.

The crisis ended.

Those rainy, sleety November nights Phoebe came up a couple of times for dinner or a drink. Carole cried and Peabody sulked. Finally Phoebe said, "I think you're both being stupid and I'm not inclined to come here anymore." Then, before Christmas, Carole called her at *Life.*

"I can't talk. I'm on a story."

"Phoebe, *please*, we have to *see* you!"

Phoebe put out her cigarette, smoke rising above the heap of butts and ashes. In the next bullpen they had photos of a Buddhist monk burning himself in Saigon, orange robe turning black, face serene in the transparent yellow flames. "I haven't got time to watch more bickering."

"You won't. We're getting *married.* And we want you to be in the wedding! You were so good to talk things over with us."

Peabody came on the line. "I'm so happy!" She thought that

sounded forced. "You've got to come! We can fix you up at the wedding!"

"Oh, brother," Phoebe said.

I don't want a boyfriend, Phoebe thought. I want my career. Yet she wanted a man—big hands, other hands cupping her breasts, flashing lightning in her empty nights. Maybe just a dumb, healthy, happy fuck, she thought. Carole had said Mark Randolph would be there too.

As the Electra thrummed west, over snowfields and gray rivers, Phoebe worked her way back to the john and examined her face—her domed clear forehead, her dark hair pulled back, her straight teeth, the way her good gray flannel shirtwaist fitted her body. *Somebody* had to notice her.

Carole and Peabody met her at the airport, Carole wearing a shining, soft brown mink full-length coat, her pink face glowing; Peabody more euphoric than Phoebe had ever seen him, smelling of good Scotch, a soft, expensive wool maroon-and-green madder paisley scarf around his neck. They bubbled, "It's a zoo there," and, "You won't believe all this."

Carole said, "She's never been in Oklahoma." They drove past black oil pumps bobbing on thin snowfields, on golf courses, on the capitol lawn. The houses were huge Tudor, Swiss chalet, Georgian, even Swedish cottage style, none old, surrounded by short scrubby trees.

"And there's where we'll have lunch tomorrow," Carole said, pointing at another big new house thinly screened by small trees. "There's a riding club down the road, Phoebe. They used to have fox hunts using coyotes."

"When?"

"Oh, years ago. When Eastern style was in vogue."

"Coyotes," Phoebe murmured. Maybe she'd appeared that provincial to Houston. She and Carole were closer than it seemed, she supposed. Yes, she'd ridden, jumped, had the tennis and dance lessons, but all in a small valley. Yes, an old valley, but two centuries younger than Boston, the Boston of Helen Franker Bridles, who wouldn't learn Phoebe's name, or Pa, who didn't want her around, or Houston, who didn't fight for her. Anyway, she had a new life now. She was free and a New Yorker.

They pulled into the driveway crowded with Lincolns and Cadillacs with bug screens. "Mmm. Nice house. I like Tudor." Many people were having drinks inside. A fire burned in the brick-and-brass fireplace. Would she get laid? Carole's mother, who had blue hair, walked up to guests, pointing to her cheek and saying, "Kiss me here."

The household had had a crisis when the colored maid, Etta, used the front "Whites Only" bathroom.

"Carole's parents agonized," Peas said, laughing. "They felt they should fire her to preserve apartheid!"

"Shh!" Carole said.

"But they need her for the wedding! Hyuk-hyuk-hyuk!"

"Shhh!"

Carole said she and Peas had been put in rooms a house-length apart, with her brother and parents in between, so they couldn't sleep together; they'd had to do it standing up in a closet.

Would she get laid?

Carole introduced Phoebe to a young man named John Taggart, who had been Carole's high school lover. His presence made Peas go into a scowling sulk, but by some perverse logic of the affianced, they tried to mate Phoebe and John. He was already rich, had oil land, skied Sun Valley and Aspen, had an AC Cobra among the fat cars out there. He was good-looking, strong-jawed, tanned. He had the self-conscious dignity of the very young man who is already successful. When he asked Phoebe why she lived in New York, she said, "What an astonishing question!" and offended him.

Mark Randolph made a grand busy entrance wearing a green uniform and carrying a big gray bag with his name stenciled on it. His head had been shaved at the sides and he looked fit. He yelled at Peabody, slapped someone else's back, plucked a drink off a tray, lifted his leg and pulled a cigarette from a pack in his sock—in his *sock*—and lit it with a match one-handed.

He didn't look bad in uniform. He wasn't like the West Pointers who came to Poughkeepsie. She'd seen him before in the right places, and familiarity made him All Right.

"Hello, Mark. We've met—"

"Phoebe! I heard you'd be here. It's good to see you!"

"You too. A familiar face."

"Hey!" he yelled past her.

"What's up?" another Yalie said.

She might have listened closely when he bantered with others about what he was learning, but everyone from the Kennedys to *Life* editors were talking about counterinsurgency. She had no presentiment that he'd become—briefly—famous, with photographs of him in uniform spread all over. Or that he would embody the violence that blew out in the killing that began this account of those times.

Randolph felt good. He'd ridden all night in a Navy R4D, the dependable, slow DC-3, and in a P-3V antisubmarine bomber, an Electra that *didn't* crash. It was so man's magazine, hitching a hop on a military plane, looking at all the gear, having a smoke and using ration cans for butt kits, thinking he might be a cool stud at last, even if he *was* a second lieutenant and subject to laughter from all but the kindest men in uniform.

"Can I get you a drink? We're both in the wedding—we ought to stick together."

"Terrific."

Organ music swelled over the crowded church. It was a huge, rich Baptist church. Adams Peabody, in morning coat, froze at the vestry door, stunned at all these strange faces and his life being chained. My God, what if her family shot *Wobblies?* Mark put his hand on his back and pushed him out by the altar. Phoebe smiled.

The altar was covered in shades of creamy white and silver gray. Carole wore white silk and was flushed pink. Peabody was pale. Phoebe thought Mark looked poised. At least he knew how to stand. The minister read the vows. She and Mark looked at each other. Their eyes met. Yes.

The reception had a champagne fountain pumping Taittinger like the oil wells outside. Carole and her mother quarreled. They scowled and spat angry words while the men looked the other way, Carole crying. The bride and groom left for France.

Phoebe and Mark went to the Capitol City Star Motel, where both had rooms. Mark had a bottle in his room. He took off his coat and sat in striped pants, starched shirt, and gray cravat. She took off her shoes and lifted the pink dress above her knees, putting her feet on the luggage rack. A cigarette. A warm, peat-fumed swallow of Chivas Regal. A few remarks about how nice this had been.

"I think we get along well, really," Phoebe said, a smoky quality coming up in her voice that Mark went crazy for. He kissed her. She slid her arms around him, her lips soft, and they kissed, tugged,

unhooked, unstrapped, unbuttoned, de-studded, slid out of and
dropped their clothes, holding each other hungrily. She raked her
nails across his back, clamped him between the strong thighs that had
controlled galloping horses, lifted off his dog tags, which were slapping her breasts. He clung to her, not knowing until then how much
he felt for her.

He kissed her closed eyes. Dark crescents. Mysteries. She
charmed him but it was beyond him to puzzle out why. Her body
wasn't as refined as Betty's—who as a person wasn't refined at all.
Phoebe really was a bit chunky below decks, but *strong*. But then her
voice was so . . . he didn't know what to call it. Her accent *and* her
pronunciation *and* its bell-like clarity. And her directness. But how
well placed she was, her position, her obvious breeding. That trick of
her right nipple. Her ambivalence and contrasts, her light and dark,
her perfumes and musks. It all baffled Randolph, hypnotized and
captivated him. In a burst of sentiment he thought he could die in a
plane crash himself and be happy. *No, as you were.* He had a chance to
go to the Mediterranean in a few months. And what about dying
gloriously in battle? Or coming back as the GI in his vision?

"Mmm?" She opened her eyes.

He lit cigarettes.

"Hold me. It's been a while for me, too."

When she got back to *Life* Sara had a treat for her.

"I want you to cover the Kennedy visit at the Waldorf." She said
it gravely, her dark eyes lingering on Phoebe. They both smiled at the
same time. She knew how Sara felt about the President and First
Lady—that they were sexy and powerful, yes, and therefore good
copy, but more. Sara had once told Phoebe, "I think Jack is making
the Presidency, and government, mean something alive and hopeful
for millions of Americans who'd been cut out before. Especially after
years of being practically comatose with Eisenhower."

Now she said, "He'll be asked about the civil rights marches and
Vietnam. See if he says anything new. Go have fun."

Phoebe walked over to the Waldorf from Sixth Avenue, showed
her NYPD Press and *Life* IDs to one of Salinger's staff, and went into
the high-ceilinged lobby, where she saw Secret Service men—fit,
short-haired louts. The outer part of the lobby was crowded with
news people.

A flurry beyond the big bronze clock, heads turning, and a neat,

slim, busy-looking man, Stephen Smith, one of the Kennedy husbands, came out with another one—a tanned and very handsome man
with large, clear features—Sargent Shriver, director of the Peace
Corps. Aides followed, then Robert Kennedy, the Attorney General.
He passed on the other side of a Secret Service man, who elbowed
Phoebe and stepped on her foot, grinding her instep to move her back.
Bobby was thin, athletic-looking, clear-skinned, with high color and
very bright blue eyes. He moved lightly. He wore a striped button-
down-collar shirt and gray suit. She hadn't been aware that he was so
small and good-looking; a warm, boyish, jocky magnetism pulsed
from him.

Then the President and First Lady, Jackie dressed for the afternoon in a soft camel-colored wool suit and matching hat and fine dark
brown gloves. Looking closer, Phoebe saw with surprise that she had
very large hands and feet. Her carriage was erect and she walked in a
dancer's flat, toe-pointing glide.

John Kennedy walked on the other side of Jackie, his fluffy hair
catching the light, shining flashes of copper and gray. Something was
wrong with the way he moved—when he turned toward Phoebe his
back and hips seemed stiff—but when his eyes met hers he made an
amused, expansive smile. His eyes, she felt, were cold—clear, gray,
penetrating, scanning, as if he could see inside her. He had lovely long
pale eyelashes. His skin had that same healthy flush as Bobby's. Jack
Kennedy opened his mouth and his eyes swept over her. She felt a
tremor, and, yes, she was sopping.

"Mr. President—"

One of the White House press corps. The President looked away
from Phoebe. The man asked a question about trade and growth.
Kennedy lobbed back a brief, graceful answer, his tone indicating the
man was not trying very hard, and looked away. He didn't maintain
eye contact. He seemed blithe in his self-assurance, as if part of his
attention was on something else, a private part in his charming public
persona. Whatever he kept in reserve made him playful with the
press.

Hugh Sidey of *Time* asked about new crises facing Diem and his
family. Another question about KKK bombings in Alabama and the
FBI's role vis-à-vis Freedom Riders. Another reporter asked why
Americans weren't being sent to Vietnam to "settle the issue decisively, as in Korea." Kennedy raised a hand to refute him. Strong,

blunt fingers. He had his phrases ready and served them. "We are making a vigorous response—" He looked as if he enjoyed all this and it was clear most of the reporters liked him. "We'll let the South Vietnamese direct their combat operations. They are prepared to do so. And they shall prevail." He was personal and charming.

"*Pheebs!*" She turned, and there in an expensive worsted suit and blue herringbone shirt, paisley tie, plastic cards on his lapel was Ash Loakes, grinning widely. Ash's bug-eyed photo press card showed the name of the great newsweekly.

"How *are* you, Pheebs? It's great to see you! I was delighted to hear you'd joined the business. Welcome aboard! Are you covering this for *Life?*"

"How nice of you to welcome me. Yes. One of many."

He chuckled. "Scores of staffers are on this! It's nice they let you out."

"They do occasionally."

He laughed. "No, I mean to get actual field experience. It's first-rate. Particularly with *him*. I've been on his tail for a week now! It's been amazing—absolutely amazing—covering the President."

Phoebe flushed, her eyes darkening. Just because he was a man—a flabby, conceited one at that—he got to cover the President. *And he is just so full of shit.* She said, "I've read about it."

"Oh, you must have read *my* stuff then. Anything about their visit to Hyannisport last month. That was mine. At least three grafs! Are you going on to Boston today?"

"No."

"Just covering here, huh?" His wide face assumed a sad, kind smile. He looked at the Kennedys and Secret Service men. "They're going! Have to run!"

Pa Bridles didn't like New York. Loud. Crowded. Rude people. Too many foreigners. But he stopped in Manhattan on his way back from D.C. that rainy February day to see Houston and push him into a slot in government. He had just met with cabinet officers and President Kennedy. Hours in the basement of the West Wing, Kennedy smoking those long, thick cigars, dryly asking questions, seeming so goddam bored and offhanded about the answers, except when his pale eyes fell on you. Cold and analytical.

"What assurance did Nhu give the Agency *this* time?" he asked.

"I can't say the American people have any patience left. Even *Asians* don't have that much patience!" His aides laughed.

"Sexy and powerful," they said in the press. Humph! Pa was powerful and *un*sexy. What Pa and his friends resented was the way Kennedy and his aides questioned their arrangements—like Diem in Vietnam, the U.S. companies that were Agency assets in Latin America, the mistakes the Agency wanted to bury: failed assassinations, lost airplanes, clients who took money and didn't deliver. The conflict was over who held the keys to appointments and money.

Pa picked his way, grumping, over the slippery slate sidewalks, brushing against *too many people*. Didn't like people. The People believed the press, all that bushwa about Style. Life was *meant* to be clumsy. Painful. Without all that sex.

Damp weather made his knee ache, the one he'd hurt in the ambush when they'd caught the Germans. Thinking of killing Krauts made him smile. Huns. They created execrable music, too. Deserved what they got. These people on the street, private citizens, didn't understand how it had to be.

He reached Stu's building. Walnut elevator. Building too tall. Stu's office: narrow, carpeted reception area. Plain walnut desk tended by a flashy redhead. Coppery red hair in a beehive, bright green scoop-neck blouse. Pink clavicles. Big smile. That was the word for Stu's operation. *Flashy*. On a stand behind her, a bronze modern sculpture showing a stylized map of Latin America.

Stu traded with Latin American players all over the Caribbean and Central and South America. Teak farms in Costa Rica, oil in Venezuela. He'd helped Agency officers working under commercial cover. Stu wasn't in the game himself, but by helping Pa's colleagues, he assured his company would keep operating with advantages. The keys to power. That was why Pa was stopping here—not to see Stu, but to position Houston in government to insure their side would continue to have power.

"Mr. Bridles?"

She led him down an office hall that he thought was a New York copy of a proper Boston office. Shiny fruitwood side tables—too new. English hunting prints. Houston's office. Houston getting up with a smile, hand out, gold cuff links, thick chalk-stripe flannel. He looked fit, handsome, muscular, hair shining red-gold. Proud of his surroundings. Fruitwood desk, team photos from Yale.

"Office's too big for someone so new," Pa said.

Houston ignored that. It was like lacrosse or football. Take the hit and drive on to your goal. He knew the old man's moods. What did he want today?

"Stu says you haven't done badly."

"No sir." Badly my ass. He'd put together multimillion-dollar bond issues for oil in Caracas and manufacturing in Puerto Rico.

"Seem to have gotten your feet wet," Pa grunted.

Houston nodded easily. He wasn't eager for Pa's next words because he knew the old man wanted him to do something, and he wasn't desperate for tasks. He'd succeeded with Stu's firm better than he'd hoped. He didn't need Pa's approval now. The old man had already wrecked his chance to marry Phoebe, whom he missed terribly, and as he'd told Phoebe that glorious summer, coaches like Harkness and Olivar had given him more warmth and attention than Pa.

But of course Pa had dozens of inside strings; occasionally he'd let slip a comment about someone like Harriman or Dillon that gave Houston an insight far beyond his years, so he respected his father as a sourpuss of wisdom. And because Pa was so bunched up in his crabby way, Houston amused himself by playing a step ahead of him. Pa seemed to be dragging out his next remark, so Houston jumped in, "Yes, Stu's given me a full plate! Very interesting, working with men of substance! Very nice. I'm going down to Venezuela again next week. Keeping busy. As you must be, Pa. Things going well in D.C.?"

Smartass, Pa Bridles thought. They *never* went well in D.C. Houston's insouciance—that's what pissed him off. No gravity. Nothing like his sober ancestors. That effortless grace. Didn't like it. But he had his agenda. "I have secured for you a position at Treasury assisting Henry Fowler."

"Pa, that's great! When?"

"June. Can you manage that soon?"

"It's a bit early. It'll put Stu in a bind—" Houston looked pained.

Pa Bridles smiled thinly, forming the words he'd use to taunt him: Can't handle it? Can't get your desk clear?

But Houston broke into a grin and said, "Of course I'll fix it."

Snookered. Pa grasped that Houston had been playing with him. Furious, he raged inwardly against the young man, *all* young, in words his Calvinist past had given him—Jeremiah, 4:4, "Take away the foreskin of your heart!" To Houston Pa muttered, "See that you do." He went out, down the print-and-fruitwood hall.

Alone in his office, Houston felt like jumping. "Terrific!"

He knew why Pa had sprung this, and it pleased him more that Pa didn't know what was on his own agenda and that he was one up on Pa. Assistant to the assistant secretary. Good move. He stopped exulting and watched the ball. Career moves. Whom to contact there, whom to look good for to leverage this appointment into that better one. He looked at a U.S. Government directory. He knew this man and that, had played against this other one, knew that one's son from school. Yes. Play it right.

He supposed it might seem terribly cold-blooded but he had his goals. He had left simple glory on the playing fields at Yale. He wanted power. And he'd hurt like hell since losing Phoebe. Yes, lost, admit it—lost. And he damn well better win something now. Phoebe was all right—the best, even. Lovely. Dammit! He opened his wallet and looked at his list of goals.

As usual after dinner, while Carole washed the dishes, Adams Peabody had a straight Scotch sitting in the worn green armchair and, like Luther on the toilet, waited for *aperçus* he could throw out in seminar or use in life. Unfortunately tonight's was one that had already occurred to him—that marriage had complicated, not solved, his problems. Now her unspeakable parents felt no compunction about meddling in his life just like Mother, and, unlike her, were ill-mannered and offensive. Furthermore, they'd been doing it since their wedding day, when Mrs. Tiddens had fought with Carole. She'd wanted to visit them in France *on their honeymoon!* And they'd been sending all those expensive clothes to Carole. He couldn't afford to take her to places she could wear them. Humiliating.

And all was not well with Carole. She *had* been happy: her pale hair draped about her face as she sang softly at the sink—she who'd always had a maid, he must point out. Now she cried when the subject of children came up. "I want to have your *babies*," she cried.

"Impossible! I haven't even got my *master's!*"

Even *thinking* of his master's unleashed a swarm of worries like Indian arrows falling around him, a cavalryman behind the dead horse of his Yale B.A. Yale was so rigorously faddish in criticism. In his time the fad was New Criticism: The New Critic was supposed to bend his mind to the text like a steel spring (Hulme), getting the exact curve of the thing (Eliot), regard the writing as a crystal existing out of time, out of social context, lit only by its own aesthetic rules. Peabody snorted. All those seminars with WASP kids talking about tenor and vehicle and thematic unity. Airless. Louis Martz had been the only Jewish professor. Here at Columbia you had Trilling and scores of intense Jewish TAs who told you to read Sinclair, Steinbeck, Wright, understand the struggle, breathe social context.

But where was he, Peabody, in social context? He was older, more sure of his mind, looked more as he wished, his hair full—a scholar's head—but it bothered him he wasn't acting on his knowledge in these times. Mathieu had shouldered a rifle. And you in the struggle? Eh? He'd open the pages of *Life* and see photos of Negro marchers in suits and dresses, sitting in with Dr. King. What he felt he must do was *join* them, go on a ride, be arrested. Phoebe'd seen that. She'd seen Kennedy. A more exciting life.

"Well, *did* your mother come to France?" Phoebe asked Carole. "I mean, I know you did it in the closet at home while they were scratching around outside, but to have her on your balcony in Nice—"

"No! She never got close!" Carole giggled. "We had it all out at the country club. When she called me a bitch cunt I had enough reason to sever communication. So they call *Peas* now. Daddy's trying to fix things. They're bombarding me with clothes and they've promised all kinds of money if we have a baby. You should get married, Phoebe."

"I'd sooner die. I don't have a love life and I don't want one. I'm working too hard. Work is more fun."

"You seemed to get along well with Mark Randolph," Carole said. "Why don't you marry him?"

Phoebe laughed. "Oh, shit, Carole—that must be the furthest thing from *his* mind. God knows where he is. That was months ago."

It was May, the most delightful season in the city, the window open on fresh air by Carole and Peabody's apartment fire escape, new little lettuce-colored leaves on the trees freshening the grimy street.

"I'm having the time of my life," Phoebe told them. "I was in Baltimore last week covering a sit-in at a lunch counter. I'm going to Washington for the civil rights march. This is history. I'm in the middle of it! I'm busy and I like it the way it is."

"Mark says he's having the time of his life, too," Peabody said. "Has he sent you any cards?"

"I doubt he has my address," Phoebe said, lighting a cigarette. Weeks after the wedding Mark had called from the South, terrible connection, and said he loved her. He was probably in the bag. Bar noise behind him. After that not a word, not a card. He'd said he was going to the field or something like what they said in the Gary Cooper movies.

He'd said, "I love you, Phoebe," while the jukebox played a tinny Brenda Lee song. She'd felt he meant it.

"I think you're very nice. It was fun." But it was impossible. Who was he, anyway? Look at Carole and Peas together on the worn couch: young and so—well—married-looking. Not for me.

"I want to be where it's at. But where *is* Mark?"

"Greece?"

Sawyer was trying to catch his breath; he had muscle spasms. His trousers were down. The corpsman, Doc Mills, was slapping Sawyer's face and jiving him. They were both black.

"Man, you beautiful. Nothin' wrong with you, we lettin' your ass breathe!" Sawyer had caught the clap in Palermo and his ass was peppered with penicillin shots. He was an automatic rifleman. His M-14 lay on its bipod on the trail.

Second Lieutenant Mark Randolph looked at others along the trail. It was hot and their utilities were dark with sweat. He could recognize every one of the forty, back, side, running, along way off, and tell his rifle scores and personal facts. They were on a hillside north of Kaválla. Goats nibbled scrub among the white rocks. You could smell wild thyme and oregano. They were close to the Bulgarian border. A small A-4 jet streaked up the valley below them. The ships in the harbor could shell Bulgaria. It was a show-of-force training landing. Later they'd have People-to-People, engineers and shore party running tractors and fork lifts, and troops humping stones and bricks to repair a church or bridge. The first sergeant called it Pecker-to-Peehole. He was a raspy-voiced red-nosed character who'd been a flamethrower man in the islands in World War II.

"My ass been assaulted and insulted," Sawyer said. Tough luck for Sawyer. Got to remember the three steps of the propylactic procedure. By the numbers. The government, or some general's wife, also said officers should recommend abstinence. Mark used the three steps. Skanky, hairy, Mediterranean whores—primeval! It was so much unlike Barrington, Illinois!

They'd had another landing in Turkey. The land looked like California with minarets and women in black and donkeys. Crete, Sardinia. He'd rocked to flamenco in Barcelona and grabbed a beer after a bullfight at a bar across from the ring, open to the sidewalk—it was like a bar near Wrigley Field. He felt at home.

"Will he be okay, Doc?"

"Yes sir. I froze it. It'll last awhile." To Private First Class Sawyer, Doc said, "You be the coolest one out here!" Others laughed. They all liked Mills. He was little, wore glasses, very fast with routines. Sawyer was a good automatic rifleman, a high school athlete, like many Marines. Someone said the Marines (unlike the Army, which drafted a cross-section of society) was made up of very tough kids and high school graduates named Percival. They were young, most of them. But not Staff Sergeant Owen Rinks Johnson, the thin black man with the funny boots crouching at the far end of the column. He had medical lifts for his bad arches. He was old. Everyone knew Johnson had been a steward—one of those colored Marines in white coats serving admirals on battleships—but in the Korean War Johnson took a demotion from staff sergeant to get into combat as a machine gunner. Proud, self-contained, angry.

He was one of the men Randolph used as a standard. Compared to Johnson, what did he know? What had he gone through? He doubted Johnson thought much of him. He'd been nowhere that mattered here. So many things Randolph had thought important simply didn't matter here. What did were unstated truths about who you were.

One night aboard ship off Crete, word came in about a speech Martin Luther King had made at the civil rights rally in Washington. Randolph saw Doc Mills crying in a passageway. "Lieutenant, what's gonna happen? What's gonna happen?" Randolph didn't know what the speech was. He fumbled for words. "Uh, we gotta do right, Doc. It has to be the same for everyone."

You couldn't be unfair. You had to take care of everyone's needs. It was so obvious. He wasn't the only one who thought so. All the younger officers had been stoked up to be hot leaders. They despised the segregation back in North Carolina—"Don't fuck with my men, grit"—and many entertained fantasies of hijacking a platoon of tanks and leveling Jacksonville, the base town.

Part of their lives ran parallel, like this, to what was happening on the outside, but the rest was its own world—traveling on-board ship, bivouacking ashore, boxing, playing soccer on the beach, and trading endless stories about legendary Marines like Jacobsen or Lay-'Em-on-the-Wire McGraw or about hard cases like the first sergeant, who gave a raspy laugh when he described his islands tour as "burning Nips out of bunkers."

They were backloading on the beach at Pylos and the first sergeant and the executive officer were watching the men while Greek vendors moved along the lines selling lemonade. One was a beautiful girl, angelic-looking, about ten or twelve, slender and with enormous dark eyes. "Gee, she's pretty, isn't she?" the earnest XO asked, and the first sergeant said, "Hrack! Another two years and she'll be fuckin'!"

"Move out!" Randolph stepped up the rocky trail, encased in helmet and pack, .45 and gas mask, K-bar knife and canteen, map case and glasses. His mind moved over details—range, number, temperature, condition of the men, frequencies—that military men use to step from one event to the next without thinking much.

Phoebe drove to Washington in August of 1963 with several New York staffers to help cover the civil rights march. She was given a room in an all-right hotel, for Washington—dingy and dark, near the Capitol. She had not spent much time in Washington. Most of it was old red brick from the nineteenth century or undistinguished twentieth-century flat fronts that looked like Oklahoma City. The heavy gray New Deal buildings and the classical Capitol and White House were the exceptions.

It was muggy, dark green trees drooping in the August heat. The streets were full of quiet black people in suits and dresses. King, who had absorbed Gandhi's ideas on using nonviolence for social change, was running the march as a religious mission, urging his people to be firm, quiet, peaceful, devoted to making their presence felt.

Phoebe and other staffers ate sandwiches at coffee shops, narrow, fluorescent lit, with old Formica counters, waitresses in white dresses. The city didn't have many real restaurants. A few bars served sandwiches, or oysters, and a few side streets had Southern-style lunch rooms showing half curtains in plate-glass windows. The buildings were all bare-windowed offices—law, insurance, trade group, union. She didn't see what you'd expect in a city, even a smaller one like Rochester: bright signs, shops, people.

"People here eat in clubs. Or at home," one staffer told her.

"What about the marchers?"

"Churches and homes are taking them in. Churches down here have always done it. Since slavery."

She was on the Mall when King gave his "I Have a Dream" speech. All around her marchers cried and called out, "You say!" and "Tell it!" as his voice rose to "Free at last! Free at last! Thank God Almighty I'm free at last!"

She was crying. Working through the roaring crowd, she saw Houston on the White House side of the Mall, his tie undone, sweating, tears in his eyes. "Amazing!" he kept saying. "Amazing!" He was so intense—as moved as she'd ever seen him.

They got away into the street. He pointed to the squat Treasury building where he worked, took her inside, got her iced tea. He touched her forearm and grinned at her. "It's so nice to see you! How about something tonight?"

"I'm not here to socialize."

"It's hot. There's tennis and a pool. It's just a thing a friend's having."

"No," she said.

He gave her his card anyway.

She was done with most of her work by late afternoon. Her hotel room was steaming. Out the window she saw an empty street. Other staffers already had dates. She called him. "All right," she said.

It was a nice party at a house by Black Creek Canyon. Houston made her feel terrific, introducing her and praising her before other young men she knew were bright and talented.

"Cobbs! Meet *Life*'s star reporter! Phoebe, say hello to Cobbs Moulton. He's at Justice. Phoebe, here's a man at State you'll want to know for a big story—"

They were Houston's age, their faces lively, interested in her, dressed more carefully than most newspeople, in narrow-lapeled jackets of seersucker or poplin, narrow ties in stripes or madras, or good sports clothes—linen shirts and madras shorts.

"Houston's doing well at Treasury," one said. "Have you known him long? Are you in the book in New York?"

The house was air-conditioned. A bartender in a white shirt

made highballs. People carried glasses around the pool. She and
Houston played a set of tennis. The wastebasket filled with empty
bottles. People laughed and yelled bright remarks, someone threw
someone in the pool, another. They turned off the pool lights and
others went in skinny-dipping. She and Houston kissed in the pool
and his hands, in an instant, found all she wanted him to remember.
They went to his apartment and made love.

The next morning she said, "Thank you very much. It was delightful."

"Look, I'd like to call you."

"No. No, thank you. Don't try. It's fine, but we're both busy."

For a moment she'd seen the flash, the flinching shock in his eyes,
but he took it well. He was unshakable. It wouldn't work—anyway,
she had no time. She'd been curious; now she knew. She wanted to be
at the center, doing what she was doing.

Pa Bridles visited Washington often that summer of Dr. King's
speech because his Agency board had several meetings about Saigon.
While thousands met in the open air of the Mall and heard passionate,
inspired calls to freedom, he and other intelligence experts met in
private, speaking in low murmurs and bureaucratese about saving
their asses and perhaps the fragile country of South Vietnam.

The truth and meaning of what was happening there escaped him
and his colleagues. He had been educated at Harvard, which more
than any other American university taught its students to see beyond
the obvious and think clearly. He had studied at Heidelberg—the
reason he was pulled into the OSS—and knew in the German manner
how to add up facts, *Tatsachen*. But all the facts out of Vietnam—
Army mutinies; Buddhists' anguished protests; villages refusing to
pay taxes to the Diem regime; Diem's sister-in-law Madam Nhu's
arrogant jokes about Buddhists barbecuing themselves; Diem's
brother Archbishop Thuc's persecution of scholars in Hue, the seat of
learning; the stealing of money by all Diem's brothers; and Diem's
miserable failure to stall the advance of communist revolutionaries or
provide his own people a government they could believe in—did not
add up to simple truth for Pa Bridles and his colleagues. The simple
truth was that Diem's government had failed.

Perhaps no American client could have succeeded, because the
Americans, who had looted Asia less than the European powers had,

were tagged as imperialist dogs since they'd supported the French fighting to win back Vietnam after World War II. The French had lost their magic in Vietnamese eyes because they'd collaborated with the Japanese, and they'd been racist exploiters before that.

It was far too late to ask why they'd supported Diem in the first place. They'd chosen him years ago, after the French war. He was the only Vietnamese of stature who didn't have any connection with the Viet Minh, the liberation forces, which were popular with the Vietnamese people. Possibly they could have chosen an ex-Viet Minh officer, for Vietnam had many people who'd fought to throw out the French and weren't doctrinaire communists.

But this was after China went communist and after Senator Joseph McCarthy, the Wisconsin demagogue, had harried out of government anyone who said anything remotely favorable to the Chinese revolutionaries. No one in government wanted to advance any Vietnamese with a Viet Minh past. McCarthy had purged and silenced the government's Asian experts.

If Pa Bridles had been the kind of Calvinist he purported to be, he would have searched his soul and asked, What are we trying to do in Vietnam? Can this government convince the Vietnamese that our way is better?

"Out of the question," he said.

"We've already had the cock," another Agency man said, using the military slang they favored.

"The point is," Pa said, "how do we handle this so the Agency isn't liquidated? If Diem's government falls apart, we're going to be out. Lansdale's too close to Diem. The Army will have it all on us and take over the show."

"Lou Conein's playing it both ways," Pa's chum Gerrity pointed out.

"But the Army's in stronger now. The President's listening to the Army."

"How's our information with the White House?" Pa asked, peering at the others' faces. "We don't have a good man there, do we?"

"The President's tilting military," Gerrity said. "Remember, before the missile crisis he used those photos Marine Recon took on the ground after jumping in."

"Hillsman uses our CI studies," Pa said. Roger Hillsman, Kennedy's counterinsurgency expert, had fought unconventional war in Burma. "Hillsman said the diplomatic picture will change when Lodge gets there."

Kennedy had just sent Henry Cabot Lodge as the new ambassador to South Vietnam. Lodge was an old, distinguished Boston WASP Republican, an ex-senator, ex–vice presidential candidate, highly decorated Army tank officer from World War II. He'd shake things up. But would the pieces fall in the Army's lap and not the CIA's?

"The President has it in for us anyway," Pa muttered. "That's the real point." And the feeling was mutual, he added to himself. Old Agency hands, particularly old WASPs and OSS types like Pa, simply didn't like the Kennedy family. They didn't like Joe and didn't like his ambitions for his sons.

Pa had heard from a Harvard friend about something Jack had said in Cambridge in 1946. The friend had gone back to Harvard after the war and had seen his classmate John Kennedy just out of the Navy. Thin, hollow cheeked, his eyes shadowed from the pain of his injuries.

"My father wants me to go into politics since Joe's dead," Kennedy said, meaning his older brother, a Navy pilot who'd died in the air off England. "I don't want to go into politics. I'd rather teach history at Harvard."

This is what baffled Pa about Jack Kennedy. He'd sat across from him many times, breathed his cigar smoke, faced his pale eyes and calm penetrating questions. The man was so graceful, humorous, obviously intelligent, gifted—but careless. He'd been careless when he'd approved the Bay of Pigs operation and then didn't grab hold when he had a chance to minimize the loss by bombing the beach. Careless about the women he chased and who knew about it. He'd slept with an Agency officer's wife. A Hollywood star. Even a mobster's girl when the Agency was using the mobster as an asset in Cuba. Such careless conduct didn't sit well with secretive officers at the Agency.

Furthermore, some hated Jack because he'd fired spies after the Bay of Pigs disaster. They feared for their jobs. Pa had heard they had it in for Kennedy because they felt betrayed. And somewhere down in Mexico or on the Gulf Coast were former Agency contract employees, ex-military snipers and raid-and-rally men who'd been hired for Cuba and then cut loose. They probably hated Kennedy. Some Army officers probably hated Kennedy for relieving General Edwin Walker, who'd given John Birch material to his troops.

The President had powerful enemies, but unlike Diem he wasn't hated by his own people. Americans loved his news conferences.

In the Irish, Jewish, and black parts of cities, Kennedy's picture was up on kitchen walls. Pa knew this by report. He did not have sympathy with the people.

One time he'd mentioned to the President, speaking in a low voice: "Mr. President, all these loose cannons, armed men in motion since the Bay of Pigs, might be dangerous to you."

Jack Kennedy leaned back in his chair. He was in shirtsleeves—a striped point-collar shirt. Unwrinkled. He changed them several times daily. He looked at Pa Bridles a moment. "You're talking about my slipping the Secret Service in New York?" He laughed. "Did the Agency have a tail on me?"

Pa Bridles made a wintry smile. He hadn't known about that but wouldn't admit it. "I state a general caution."

Kennedy shook his head, his thick cover of red-brown hair waving slightly; his pale calm eyes settled on Pa. "You've been shot at. You know what it's like when the slugs come in—there's not a goddam thing you can do. If they want to hit you, they will. If they're lousy shots, fuck 'em. We carry on."

Pa pondered that. Offhanded. Fatalistic. His style bothered Pa. God knows what will happen when things get worse. Pa knew they would.

"I want you to watch your tongue," he told Houston when he visited him at Treasury. "Hide your affection for any man." He looked at this smartass, fresh-faced young man before him and spoke in a low, tired voice. "Probably going to go to war. No one can stop it. It'll be a horseshit war. Stay out of it. I know you're so vain you'd want to fly a fighter and command a boat. Don't. You can do better here."

Houston's brow furrowed so gracefully, so sensitively, Pa Bridles was inclined to sniff it off as an act. He went on, "I've just been talking with my chum Gerrity, who's in a position to know. Kennedy's administration itself is in trouble. Make no mistakes."

Without waiting for a reply he left Houston's office, peering sour-faced at the terrazzo and marble.

"The people like him," Sara Gelber told Phoebe at *Life*. "Most of the people here like him—otherwise we wouldn't do so much on them. Jackie at the White House. Any of that. But the people who hate him really hate him."

                              *   *   *

The cold, damp night of November 1–2, when icy wind curled around the narrow brick buildings on Boston's Beacon Hill, Pa Bridles woke to the phone ringing. It was his old chum Ted Gerrity calling from the Agency. In circuitous sentences, because the line wasn't secure, Gerrity told Pa the bad news.

"Our Army friends took the moon-faced man's castle," he said in his flat mid-Atlantic tones. "Armor. Many rounds. Client hid in Chinatown. Open negotiations. A hand-over. Killed in a vehicle—APC. Both brothers."

Pa slumped in an armchair considering what Gerrity had told in those elliptical terms. The Viet Cong had people in the government, so they already knew what Gerrity had told him. But the American press didn't know. Jesus. The Army of the Republic of South Vietnam had attacked the presidential palace, firing tank rounds. Many officers hated Diem for promoting incompetent sycophants who could not fight the Viet Cong. Chinatown was Cholon, the Chinese yang to Saigon's yin. Diem and Nhu had surrendered. Undoubtedly they'd been driven away in the armored personnel carrier so the mob wouldn't jump them, but one of the officers took the opportunity to shoot them anyway.

Pa didn't doubt our Army had a hand in it. The important question was, Had the Army got the key position in the White House?

"I'm afraid so," Gerrity said. "They have the ball now. It's an Army show. He's got Taylor. McNamara. Won't listen to the Agency side." The Viet Cong had whipped ARVN troops in several battles but the Army had argued the South Vietnamese just needed bigger forces. Now South Vietnam was run by generals and American generals had the President's ear.

"Watch the balloon go up," Pa grunted.

He went back to bed not pleased, but at least reassured that the real world was just as bitter as his pessimism had predicted. It would get worse, all right.

Three weeks later, a beautiful sunny late-November Friday, Sara and Phoebe had sandwiches at Sara's desk by windows showing blue sky and chrome-and-glass buildings. It was beautiful weather all across the country—sunny in Dallas, where the Kennedys had just landed.

"Ugly reception there," Sara said. People who hated the civil rights movement, who hated progress, who hated Kennedy for relieving General Walker had met the Kennedys at the airport. The bureau in Dallas said someone in the airport crowd had spit on Jackie. Some waved hate signs.

"Hate feeds itself like war," Sara said. "He'll never please them. They're crazy."

"It's such a mild afternoon," Phoebe said. "I'm going to have to fight to keep from dozing."

Suddenly people ran through the office yelling and phones rang.

Saving the
Nation

This is history. More than ever I feel I am living in history. Even as a messenger, a phosphor, I am playing a part in history by delivering bits of it to other Americans. An American President slain in public in bright sunlight. They blew his head off. No one was printing it. Yet. His head exploded in pink spray in bright sunlight. It is bright sunlight today, three days later, and this is what Dallas looks like.

That Monday, November 25, Phoebe walked through the neighborhood where Lee Harvey Oswald had shot Patrolman J. D. Tippit right after Kennedy was killed. Low houses, screened porches, dry grass. She was trying to find anyone who had seen Tippit, Oswald, or had pictures of the police or ambulance outside the movie theater on Jefferson Boulevard. She walked up straight walks to neat little houses, rang doorbells, tapped on aluminum-and-glass doors. Usually women answered. Housewives in housecoats, permanents.

"Hello, I'm Phoebe Bishop from *Life*. It's about the Tippit shooting. Did you see anything?"

"No," said most. She could tell her accent put off some. Thirty doors. Thirty-five. She walked up more walks, knocked and rang.

"I heard the sirens," one said. "It's dry and I thought it was a fire, but I couldn't smell smoke."

"Did you take any pictures?"

"No."

One woman gave her a glass of water. They sat in a glassed-in porch that smelled of lemon wax. Phoebe was leaving when the woman said, "I never could make a camera work, but if you want pictures, my friend on the next block's son just got out of high school last summer and got laid off and he spends a lot of time with a camera. He's real smart, and she said he went to the sirens and took pictures of the body and whatnot."

Phoebe stopped in mid-stride, one foot off the ground, like a deer caught in headlights. She turned around carefully. "That would be terrific," she murmured.

She walked down the sidewalk past low trees and other neat houses. How many other people in there might have seen something? Might have seen Oswald, or Tippit, or Cubans? Oswald was a pro-Cuban communist, the police said. One of the New York reporters *Life* had sent out had looked over Dealey Plaza, and a witness who'd come back to reexamine the scene told him she'd seen someone fire a pistol up out of a sewer grate, hitting Kennedy in the head. The reporter said there were big storm drains there. "It's possible," he said.

Someone else saw a cop pick up a cartridge from the pavement there, an empty .45 automatic pistol casing; the witness said he knew guns, he had a dozen himself. War souvenirs.

Others said the shots and smoke had come from a slope ahead of the motorcade, away from the Book Depository. How many shooters were there?

It was the biggest story since Pearl Harbor. Incredible. All these people killed Friday and after. She'd been running for four days, electrified by the story. Everyone had.

Life had gone into its disaster mode that Friday. Sara sent Phoebe to Archives to get background from Lillian Owen on Dallas hatred of the Kennedys and progressive programs. Sara's boss, Marian MacPhail, the Director of Research, and Dick Pollard, the Picture Editor, stayed on the phones giving orders, sending people out. Staffers ran to the wire machines and ripped off yellow copy. Others listened to the radio as reports came in about the shots that sounded like automatic weapons, the motorcade racing to the hospital, Kennedy dying. The dead, horrible gloom that fell over the office. Particularly among the young. Out on the street people looked shocked. They stayed in the office digging for more facts on Dallas— hate, the Army's General Walker, Oswald's Cuba committee. They went to *Life*'s morgue, properly called the Bureau of Editorial Reference, and to the Mercantile Library nearby. The magazine took rooms in the Victoria Hotel on Seventh Avenue to put up staffers working round the clock, so they could get a few hours sleep. Few slept long. Coffee and sandwiches were brought into the office. News went through the rooms like electricity, people shouting over the bullpen partitions.

Phoebe worked all that Friday night. She saw on television Jackie in her bloodstained dress and Lyndon Johnson, the new President, back in Washington that night. She spent the next day, Saturday, in New York, checking facts on Governor John Connally of Texas, who had been riding with Kennedy and was hit in the same fusillade. Then she drew cash and got a Delta flight to Dallas that night.

She spent the dawn hours Sunday looking around back streets and the railroad tracks behind the grassy knoll. Witnesses said they'd seen puffs of smoke and heard shots from the grassy knoll overlooking Dealey Plaza—that more than one set of shots flew at Kennedy's car. People had described the shocking scene when John Kennedy was hit, grabbing his throat, jerking, his head blowing open, spraying blood. Horrifying.

Later that Sunday she stood outside police headquarters in the crowd waiting for them to move Oswald. Noise started. Yelling. Confusion. People cheered.

"Someone shot the son of a bitch!"

"No shit? Hey!"

"Yay!"

The police said Oswald was a peckerwood Commie loser who'd been under federal surveillance. The FBI did not want to admit this. Reporters saw police, FBI, and Secret Service men quarreling in police headquarters. Some cops and federal officers leaked bits to the press. One cop said the feds told him Oswald had tried to kill Edwin Walker, the right-wing general Kennedy had relieved. Had Officer Tippit been sent to kill Oswald, just to shut him up? Had Jack Ruby, a small-time mobster, killed Oswald to shut him up?

Two public executions in three days—it was too much to be believed.

Hundreds had seen John Kennedy killed, millions had been told what it looked like. A businessman named Abraham Zapruder had taken a color film that *Life* was buying. The images were already burned into people's minds like a dreadful icon: the handsome young President, sunlight on his coppery hair, riding in the Lincoln, being hit once, twice, falling mortally wounded. An American President slain in public, in a procession. And then the suspect, or scapegoat, an insignificant mousy loser, a defector—the opposite sort of person from Jack Kennedy, the sort of contemptible person you'd *expect* to strike at a star—being led out in another procession, surrounded by cameras, and killed with his face twisting in the lens. It was like an epode in Greek tragedy—a wrap-up—but it was too quick and neat.

"I don't buy it," Phoebe said. She had a feeling of terrible onset: demons of hate let loose in America.

Again and again she thought of the killings as she walked the sunny plain sidewalks. They had already become recurring visions that Monday. Here was the house of the amateur photographer the woman had told her about.

A thin young man wearing glasses answered.

"Hello, I'm Phoebe Bishop. I work for *Life* magazine."

"Well, that's fast. My aunt just called. I took some pictures."

"I'd love to see them."

Fair shots, some blurred, of the shooting scene. He'd used Plus X. Not grainy. A good one of a cop pushing the crowd back and Tippit's covered body being carried to the ambulance. She paid him $150 for two rolls, proof sheets, and prints. He said he wanted a job taking pictures for *Life* and she told him where to apply. She took the shots in and resumed ringing doorbells.

In the Dallas office Monday night Phoebe drank bourbon out of a paper cup, crowding with others on desks and chairs. They watched the news on television. The big, long face of President Johnson filled the screen. His sad eyes and long earlobes. His voice was thin, high, unnatural, churchy. The cameras also covered Kennedy in his casket lying in state, surrounded by military guards in the Capitol rotunda.

One of the others said television might get pictures on the air right away, but that we had text and intelligent shots.

Someone else said, "Yeah, but they had Oswald being killed on the air. You can't beat that."

"*And* commercials and snow. You can run a crowd for an hour and so what?"

"We'll have more good pictures," Phoebe said. "Look at all the people we have here."

"Yeah, but what's the story?" one of the old photographers said. "It's too complicated for pictures. It's too complicated for *television*. We don't know how many conspirators there were. What they planned to do. All we know is it's heartbreaking. How many contact sheets do we have of people crying? Of shocked expressions?"

Phoebe took a puff of her Viceroy, her fingers straight. "I keep thinking of it. Absolutely shocking. And what are we left with? He was truly different. You can't show the loss."

A young man said, "Yeah, they killed hope. That's how I feel. They killed hope. He offered hope to do something different and they killed hope."

"Can't show that in pictures, either."

"We should be in Washington," the old photographer said. "The funeral's the big story now. The networks are carrying that now and we're still putting the assassination together. Johnson's in D.C. now. Everyone's in D.C. That's where the story is."

Early in the morning before going to his Treasury office, Houston walked to the Capitol rotunda, the large, stone-floored round room under the dome, its rim lined with statues of dead politicians, its cold, still air clattering with ghostly echoes, John Kennedy's gray casket in the center decorated with flags, crowds waiting to file by. God knows what the dead man looked like. God knows what really happened. Washington writhed in rumors like a basket of snakes.

Sentries of all services in different blue uniforms slashed with red, white, gold, and silver paced by the casket, not looking at the people. They carried polished rifles. Their steps and metallic noise carried up to the dome and down to the crowd.

Some people cried. Many were shabbily dressed and some dressed up in cheap clothes. Some black people. Houston had never seen such a range of his fellow citizens. They were concerned, stunned. What had happened? To them, Houston thought, we, the government, absolutely must present the appearance of certainty, stability. How little they knew. It was panic over in the office.

At Treasury, the most patrician department, the correct style was to go about one's business quietly and quickly, not making too much of the thing, to avoid making false notes, and concentrating on the work to be done now—the status reports and updates President Johnson demanded.

All were terrified of Johnson. He was getting rid of people right and left, sending them away when he couldn't fire them. Alaska. North Dakota. Utah. Secretaries and higher GS-levels walked purposefully down the marble and terrazzo corridors carrying papers, mimeograph sheets, thermofaxes and the new Xerox copies, faces betraying nothing, watching what they said. Houston called people he knew and they called him—Cobbs Moulton from Exeter, Hill Blakes from Keys two years ahead, Blinky Mawson's older brother Win—to scope out what Johnson wanted and what his game was, much in the way they'd had preexam meetings at school and at Yale to guess the test questions.

In his desk journal Houston wrote: "Bad news! Cobbs thinks LBJ will zip all Eastern types—"

It was a curious trait of Houston that the more serious and far-reaching the crisis, the more preppie and parochial his diction became, and in this national and world crisis his journal was shot through with phrases like "We're in hot water!" and "LBJ seems big on this . . ." and "Holy Smoke!" and "X couldn't handle it, took gas. Sent to office in Utah!"

The desk journal was one of those monogrammed leather volumes, not small, which he'd started using the year before when Uncle Stu gave it to him at graduation. Its pages were to figure in a great *succès de scandale* when they were purloined and made public in the Watergate years.

"Face-off! This is *it!*" began his entry for November 28. "Chalk talk before LBJ himself!"

He had put in an all-nighter and was clearing out of the office that Saturday morning when the White House called demanding figures on the status of Batista-owned Cuban assets held in trust by Treasury.

Houston sent secretaries and clerks from the weekend postassassination emergency staff scurrying for the information. Then he called others into the game to find out what special angle LBJ might be looking for.

"He had a shit fit when he found out about all the, ah, CIA monkey business in the Caribbean," an acquaintance at Justice told him. He said, "We're runnin' a goddam Murder, Incorporated down there!"

Immediately Houston saw the big question, where the ball was going. LBJ wanted to know if the Agency was tapping government-held bank accounts, using impounded Batista airplanes and equipment. Why did he want to know? What did he intend to do? It didn't matter. What mattered was to demonstrate to the President that Treasury had done its job, knew what the score was, and could deny wrongdoing.

Uncle Stu had advised him to keep fresh clothes at the office. He shaved and changed into an emergency blue pinstripe and went to the Executive Office Building. Doom and Angst hung in the corridor outside the briefing room. A weary-looking middle-aged man left. As the door closed, LBJ's voice came through: "Dumb son of a bitch."

"Mr. Bridles?"

A young man in a blue suit led Houston over the heavy carpet. LBJ sat at a conference table with his hard-working administrative chief, Walter Jenkins, a thin man in glasses, his gray hair flying back from his high forehead. He blinked at Houston, his eyes bloodshot and weary. Also there was Johnson's chief counsel, Joseph Califano, a sleek fat man with full cheeks and shiny dark hair. His soft brown eyes looked as if they understood all. He wore an expensive blue suit. LBJ squinted at Houston.

"You the expert on Cuba?"

"On the foreign assets picture, yes sir."

"Good. Tell me about it."

Houston didn't let the pressure show. He opened his attaché case, took time deliberately putting papers on a chair by the wall, pulled an easel out where LBJ could see it, and wrote figures in a row across the sheet. Bright blue lines. He looked the President in the eye. "The status of Batista-connected assets claimed by Castro and held in this country is as follows."

He read the numbers, pointing to columns for bank accounts, movables, real property, leaseholds, accounts receivable, and miscellaneous, and gave a clear summary of disputed claims.

As he talked, LBJ leaned back in his chair, long legs folding, knees rising above the tabletop. He lolled and straightened, raised a big hand to scratch his long earlobe, looking at the ceiling, his attention still on Houston. He said, "Now, how're these bein' used? The bank accounts, for instance?"

"By law, sir, they are frozen. Interest accrues."

"And property like airplanes?"

"They are sealed and held at military installations. Eglin Air Force Base, the naval air station at Jacksonville, the materiel storage site in Arizona."

"Where the Agency was keepin' B-Twenty-sixes?"

"Yes sir."

LBJ leaned forward, his long arms braced on the table, eyes narrowed. "Now, I am your President and I want you to level with me. Who in Treasury has authorized the use of this property?"

"No one, Mr. President."

"You shittin' me?"

"No sir. Not at all."

"What about the other agencies? Can they get at this stock? Can they use any of those financial assets?"

"Not legally, sir. No one's touched the accounts. I have verified those. The balances are as they should be."

He leaned back. "And the other stuff?"

"The real property and movables?"

"The movables. The airplanes."

"We see no change, Mr. President. The military base commanders can release stock only on a court order. If another agency gets at the airplanes, it's forging documents and breaking the law. The seals are verified regularly."

"You haven't heard a whisper about the Agency usin' this stuff? Or D-oh-D?"

"No sir."

"You tryin' to fuck me?"

An unusual question. Houston kept his good-humored expression. "No sir."

The President looked at Walter Jenkins. "You check that with the Air Force. Call Goldwater. Go through that squadron you two are in. He has no patience with this horseshit either." He turned to Houston. "Good. I've seen you before."

"Yes sir. At Treasury last month."

"Name's Hugh-ston? Like Texas?"

"All compliments to Texas, but it's How-ston, Mr. President."

"Oh yeah. Good. You go on back and do a good job."

As Houston left he heard LBJ say to Jenkins, "Take this over to Treasury and get me an answer."

On Monday Houston found out he was not going to Utah. Mr. Fowler called him in and said he was being offered a spot on the White House staff.

Houston Bridles worked as hard as he ever had in school or on any playing field. It was a national and world crisis with a confused, timid, blustering Washington at the center. If Cuba or Russia, through

defector Oswald, had had a hand in killing Kennedy, then for its
honor the nation would have to fight! Wouldn't it? Or was it the Mob?
More than a few appointees and intelligence types knew about Agency
ties with the Mob for Caribbean killings. But it wasn't fitting at this
solemn national moment to speak of it. "There's a hell of a lot more to
it than you'll ever hear," President Johnson said.

"I want to put this behind us and get this country going again.
Startin' *now*. I brought in you young people to give us energy and
vision," Johnson told the new aides in the Oval Office. It was a week
after the assassination. Women still cried in the offices. Johnson
himself—a large, long-boned man with a long face, drooping nose, sad
eyes—looked especially somber.

"We've suffered an unprecedented national tragedy. John
Kennedy was controversial. But he was truly loved. We have an
obligation to carry on. . . ." As Johnson talked, his narrow eyes lit
up, his big hands caught the odd reflected light of that curved room;
his big form filled with energy.

What does he want from me? Houston thought, and in his preppy
terms put it: *Scope out the competition. What's the game?*

Most of the new aides in the Oval Office didn't look like Houston
or the New Frontiersmen with oarsmen haircuts and button-down,
narrow-tie, high-lapel briskness. There was Bill Moyers, a churchy,
promising young journalist from some Texas school wearing big
glasses and an odd-patterned coat. Richard Goodwin, a speech writer,
had gone to Harvard but had a furtive city look. Another Texan
named Bobby Sugg wore wide lapels and garish ties.

At first Houston and the other new aides took temporary offices
in the EOB while the Kennedy men cleared out of the White House
offices in the West Wing basement under the Oval Office.

Already some of John Kennedy's closest friends and admirers—
Arthur Schlesinger, Jr., and Theodore Sorensen—had complained
about Johnson's haste in moving into the White House. The Kennedy
men were fiercely partisan. Sorensen, who was rumored to have written *Profiles in Courage*, which won a Pulitzer Prize for his boss, was
especially ill-disposed toward the new President. Many New Frontiersmen had openly ridiculed Lyndon Johnson as a rube, yahoo, and
crooked politician from backwoods Texas. Houston soon got a chance
to hear Johnson's side.

It was a couple of days later, a Saturday. Houston was in his temporary office—an odd L-shaped room of stone molding and plaster wall on one side and partition on the other, a space unimaginatively cut out from one of those large, graceful EOB rooms—and he was looking at a list of Treasury questions Jenkins had given him, sitting straight up, sleeves rolled up, tie loose, fingers of one hand digging into his short pale hair, when he became aware of a bulky shadow at the corner. Another aide, he thought. All of them were putting in a weekend. But when he looked up, his eyes went up and up and up, and there was Lyndon Johnson in an open shirt and sport jacket, big fingers splayed around the doorframe.

His eyes crinkled as he grinned. "Well, you ain't watchin' the ball game, I see."

Houston had a genius for picking up the other person's mood and playing with it. He grinned self-deprecatingly and said, "No sir. I can't clear my desk that fast!" and this amused the President, who seemed to want to talk sports anyway.

"Now, you played halfback at Yale," he said. Obviously his staff had researched Houston. "You roll out much? Or take passes? How big your line run?"

Houston watched Johnson's eyes as they talked; narrow, shrewd, without illusion, they were framed in folds of flesh that drooped to magnify Johnson's air of sadness, or tightened up when he was in high humor. Houston answered easily and modestly. "After all," he said with a charming smile, "it's not Southwest ball!"

Johnson said, "Now, you tell me what you got at Yale that the Harvards don't." The big man smiled pleasantly at him.

That was the pitch.

Houston knew what he meant. He'd already heard the hints and rumors—that Johnson was ill-at-ease with Easterners. He was not dumb and did not lack charm—Houston had heard he was a hilarious storyteller, a talented mimic, a master of innuendo. But he didn't have Eastern graces and got stiff and unnatural when he felt he was under public scrutiny. Houston had heard LBJ was so socially insecure, so impressed by Robert McNamara, the secretary of defense, that when he saw McNamara having soup at lunch he changed his order to soup also. What LBJ wanted was the key to the Ivy League, Houston figured.

"Let me deflate the Harvard myth, if I may, Mr. President," Houston began, and gave one of those brilliant off-the-cuff talks that characterized his genius. He told something about Harvard and about who went to Ivy League schools. "We don't emphasize ideas at Yale. We're pragmatic. We emphasize winning. We call Harvard men weenies." This made the President laugh. "Since the War all those schools have changed anyway, Mr. President. They were filled with veterans on the GI Bill, not prep school boys. They're meant to provide people for national service now. Maybe they offer a wider world, and, sure, I know the accent's different—"

Johnson laughed. "Yeah," he said. "Okay—I have things I want you to do. Want you to work with people like yourself and get me answers." Then, gravely, he said, "Do you know what it means when a new President takes over?"

"Yes sir. It's a chance to change and revitalize government."

"It's a chance to run like a son of a bitch into a tar pool and get stuck and fall on your face!" Johnson said. "Because ninety-five percent of government *doesn't* change. We got the *same* people in the bureaus. The departments send—what?—four thousand memos and cables a day? How many are I or Jenkins gonna see? A hundred a day? Most of what I face is inertia. Or worse. Resistance. There are New Frontier people here that said terrible things about me in West Virginia." He meant the 1960 primary in which Kennedy had trounced Johnson. "I'm *still* mad about some of their lies, and I can't have any pissant resistance. Or officials who think they know everything, except they don't have the national interest at heart."

He grabbed Houston's shoulder. His hand was like a first baseman's mitt. "I *depend* on young people like you who *don't* think they know everything, who *try*, to get us movin' the right way."

Houston flushed. This man had power. He wanted to try for him. "I'm your man, sir."

"Good. You're goin' to be handlin' stuff you already have some acquaintance with. Treasury. And National Security. I know your daddy's connection with the Agency. You know people at State. I can't understand half of them. Defense. Most of these generals and admirals are no smarter'n they were in Korea. I haven't got time to mess around with them. You're going to help me and Bundy and Jenkins keep track of overseas, 'cause I got plenty of programs I'd sooner get started at home. This country drifted under Eisenhower— this I know, 'cause I saw problems coming up when I was Majority Leader in the Senate, and all Ike wanted to do was put them off so nothing happened on his watch. And Kennedy gettin' killed like that is a disaster. A shock. I want to rebuild what's gone to hell in this land, the way Roosevelt did in the New Deal." He smiled at Houston. "FDR was like a daddy to me. I was young like you when I worked on the New Deal. And I want my administration to do that much good for our people and land now."

The following week the new aides were assigned offices in the West Wing basement. Houston got one off the wide passage north of the barbershop, under the press lobby. It was only a few steps from the National Security Council meeting room and another few to the stairs that led up to the Secret Service room and the Oval Office.

He was assigned a young woman named Terry Menska from pool to be his interim secretary. She appeared about twenty-five, had straight dull hair, and wore black the first few days.

He was too busy to notice her for days after that. She moved briskly, typed eighty-five words per minute, kept his calls in order, and let him know what was going on.

"Mr. Bridles?" Miss Menska stood in the doorway holding papers and looking over them.

"Yes."

She smiled. She had a cute smile. The corners of her mouth went way up into her full cheeks. She was about five six; she wore a high-neck office dress. Under it, he sensed, she was robustly built, her breasts pointed. She had washed her hair; it was a strawberry-blonde color, pale and glossy. Dark brown eyes. "Hi. I typed these option memos, but if you don't mind me making a suggestion, the ones regarding State and Justice should be in another format. That's what I saw in pool. May I show you?"

"Yes. Come in."

She stood beside his desk and, leaning over, showed him an earlier memo to Dean Rusk about the first large group of Army advisors sent to Vietnam ostensibly as engineer relief forces after the floods of 1961.

"This was in the file. And I rememeber typing this." It was a 1963 reply to a Bobby Kennedy memo on organized crime. She leaned over Houston's desk. Her straight hair swung shining in pink-tinted strands. Her breasts *were* pointed. He noticed her perfume. Something flowery, not the Antilope-Fiji-Electrique musk he was used to smelling on women.

"How long have you been here, Miss Menska? Since 'sixty-one?"

"No. I came last January."

"Where were you before that?"

"With DNC." She meant the Democratic National Committee. "Here. And in New York."

"Oh, really. I worked in New York, too. And you, ah, you were with the committee then? Where?"

"Manhattan. I was a Kennedy volunteer?" She said it in a tentative way.

"Are you from Manhattan?"

"Brooklyn."

"Where?"

"Gowanus. Have you been there?"

"No. I've heard of it."

They looked at each other. She smiled politely and picked up the papers. "Should I put the memos in the other format?"

Her manner was so sweet and complaisant she could have been promising anything. He looked into her soft brown eyes. She gazed steadily at him. "I'll do it however you want." Her eyes widened. Hotter.

"Yes, ah, as you suggested, please," he said, the pulse in his temple pounding.

President Johnson was interested in all his young aides because he believed in progress and the future, and he seemed to find the sight of Houston especially pleasing. One afternoon he told Houston to go into his little side office off the Oval Office, a small room rich in highly polished wood. They drank Cutty Sark. Johnson asked how his work was going and they talked about the different ways the Kennedy and Johnson groups worked, the New Frontiersmen swarming over a problem like touch football players, Johnson assigning individuals to handle specific tasks. "I want a valuable hunk of humanity who can go there and fix it."

Houston began going to briefings at the Pentagon, State, and the Agency and sat in on second-level briefings staged at the White House. He gave some reports directly to LBJ, who roamed the corridors and sometimes impulsively grabbed an aide and demanded a rundown on a program. Other times he reported to McGeorge Bundy, Johnson's National Security chief, a hollow-cheeked, astringent man whom

Houston understood perfectly; he had a Yale degree and had been dean of Harvard College. Bundy had a way, when examining a report, of holding the paper away, wrinkling his nose and eyes, and saying fastidiously, "I am not persuaded by this" and "What is the premise of this statement?" He was sharp-minded, prickly in disposition, and rather bloodless, unlike the alert, hearty jocks the Army provided to brief Houston.

In one of the first, an Airborne colonel showed how superior American weapons were to the Viet Cong's. He projected a slide of a gray lump. "Look at this crude concrete mine. The Viet Cong's latest model!" (Laughter.)

Slide of new olive drab curved device on legs. "Our new Claymore mine, M-18," the Army colonel said. His shoes shone. His chest glittered with ribbons and jump wings. "It's one of the things we're providing to defeat the Viet Cong. This can wipe out thirty of them on a trail, day or night."

Because Houston was top caliber he could see quality in others but was not easily impressed, so despite his youth he wasn't snowed by the dog-and-pony shows. But he soon met a man who impressed him and whom he liked immediately.

"Houston?" said a tanned, fit-looking man in a good, gray sharkskin suit, glasses. "I'm Ted Gerrity. You're Biddy Bridles's boy. I know your dad. We dropped into France together. We blew up a bridge. Great fun. How is Biddy? Wonderful dry wit."

Even though Houston knew the Agency, with its customary perspicacity, had determined that *he* would be one of the ones handling intelligence and defense and had chosen Gerrity to play on his relationship with Pa, Houston still liked him. He'd played end at Rutgers! A pro, happy in his work. He had a family and sailed a catboat on Chesapeake Bay. He showed Houston photos of the catboat. Houston hadn't known his pa went by Biddy among his spook friends. It was either a play on Bridles or he'd always been a pisspants. Poor Pa! Houston looked forward to knowing Gerrity and learning more about Pa.

Gerrity gave him a *tour d'horizon* and a rundown on how the Agency really worked, as opposed to the conception given by James Bond thrillers, and told an amusing and mercifully brief, unlike Pa's, reminiscence about being in Austria in the summer of 1945 when a German general named Gehlen surrendered himself and his files on

Soviet forces and made a deal to set up bureaucratic procedures for processing information in Washington. "Which is why we work the way we do," Gerrity told him.

Gehlen provided accurate information on when the Russians were bluffing, as in the Berlin Blockade, and when they meant to be aggressive. "But in Asia the Agency had next to nothing," Gerrity said. "We had fewer OSS alumni from that theater and the McCarthy purges drove away many with area knowledge."

The only bright note was that the public remained ignorant, too, but unfortunately now too many newspapers and magazines were paying attention to Vietnam. The *New York Times*'s David Halberstam had won a Pulitzer Prize for describing the quagmire.

"I'm going to tell you some very startling things," Gerrity said, and did—about attempts to turn the tables on the North Vietnamese by dropping ARVN parachutists into North Vietnam. This failed because the North Vietnamese were extremely well organized and had not hesitated to kill thousands of their own people at any hint of subversion. He told about attempts to negotiate and about even worse corruption and incompetence in the south that the press, mercifully, had not discovered. It was always a heady thing to receive inside information, and even though he tried not to be impressed, Houston was. Gerrity put the red-stamped documents he'd quoted in an attaché case that he locked to a chain up his sleeve and slid the key into his heavy handmade brogan. Good God, this was exciting! Why couldn't Pa have been like this? Pulling off deals like Gerrity? Enjoying this exciting work! Poor Pa!

Two weeks after he joined Johnson's staff Houston sat through his first briefing by Secretary of Defense Robert Strange McNamara. In the soundproofed, soft-lighted theatrical National Security Council room with its rows of desks were two general officers, McGeorge Bundy, and the President himself.

Houston met McNamara before he began speaking. A big man, though not as big as Johnson, he inclined his head to look down into Houston's face. "Mr. Bridles," he said crisply. He wore the famous goggle-eye glasses. His voice was cold but he had a warm smile, and his skin looked hot—he flushed under the lights. His nose had scrapings of old sunburn. He often skied or hiked. Houston saw lights glisten on his slicked-backed hair when he nodded. (When Johnson first saw McNamara at a briefing and was impressed by his mastery of detail, he said to an aide, "Get me that one with the Sta-Comb on his hair.")

McNamara gave a brilliant briefing, gesturing dramatically with a pointer at columns of figures projected on the screen, touching it to two-day-old aerial photos of Soviet trucks and antiaircraft sites in North Vietnam, looking straight at Johnson, or Bridles, or Bundy, talking dispassionately about operational radii of aircraft, stay time over targets, surgical air strikes, factors of error for big bombs as opposed to small bombs—minima, maxima, and optima for air operations against the enemy and optimum man-hours on the ground of soldier patrols against insurgents. He was quite convincing, Houston thought. Extremely well prepared. His answers were much more definite than those from State or the Agency. One of the State people said, "Of *course* he looks good. He's got thousands of staff officers giving him statistics. And those photos—my God, he's got the *Air Force* shooting hot photos for him. And then he's got *eight extra minutes* to do homework in his limousine coming over from the Pentagon!"

"Our objective is to produce results using operations research and systems analysis," McNamara said. "Combat operations are repetitive, responsive to variable inputs of manpower and materiel, and follow models arrived at heuristically during our experience in World War Two."

Houston watched his feet. He had large feet and wore heavy black shoes. He planted his feet surely and then brought up his pointer. Not light on his feet or playful. Houston knew LBJ was impressed by McNamara. He grasped that LBJ relied on experts perhaps more than Kennedy, Eisenhower, or Truman would have— he depended on their special knowledge because he was unsure of himself in Eastern, social, and foreign situations. McNamara was a Westerner, from San Francisco, and had been in business. Johnson thought he could understand him.

"He knows figures," Johnson said. "He gives you a definite answer." State and the Agency talked about programs in Vietnam but Houston saw that most of the key decisions came from McNamara and the Pentagon.

This is not the winter of our discontent but of our self-betrayal, Adams Peabody thought as he sat with his Scotch after dinner. This is the winter of our renaming airports and expressways in lieu of remorse. He was depressed, felt personally hurt, deprived. His father had been slain by the government, now this. All the discontent before Kennedy's killing—that he wasn't moving fast enough, that he was listening to the wrong advisors—had been extirpated, amputated. They had no one now. Carole had cried and seemed just as stunned and angry as he. But her hard, grim-voiced father had said something tactless about the ceremonies.

He had been infuriated and helpless. Speechless. But now his doubts about their marriage, like electrons in acid, found a pole to vibrate around. He blamed her family and that oil-rich set for killing Kennedy. He didn't tell her, but it changed the way he felt about her, provided a ground for why he couldn't give to her. Perhaps they shouldn't have got married. One gets rid of her, eh? It all seemed perfectly reasonable. It was their fault! Her fault!

"First crisis!" Houston wrote in his journal January 10, 1964.

Terry pulled me out of meeting with urgent memo on Panama. On wire all day, classified messages about Panama flap.

Jan. 11
Americans burning Panamanian flag. Riots and shooting. Military and naval units alerted. <u>This is it!</u> Terry Menska said, "I'll bring you the op orders so you'll know what the ships and so on are preparing to do." Meanwhile the whys of the riot came in: Americans at a high school refused to fly the Panamanian flag with U.S. colors per agreement. Surely communists exploiting. LBJ furious.

Jan. 16.
Terry is guiding me through first crisis. Long work session. Terry typed some 40 pages in a little over two hours. Amazing. Terrific performance!

Houston was so impressed by her flying fingers, moved by her team effort, and intrigued by the soft way her hair draped, the way she formed her lips, that he kissed her. Not a peck on the forehead or cheek, but full on the lips. Her lips were soft and wet and her brown eyes wide open. When she spoke she sounded breathless.

On January 17 he took Terry to his apartment off Du Pont

Circle. She lay in bed looking up at him, mouth open, eyes shining in exquisite pain. She made sounds he thought were sweet and vulgar at once. Too sweet, perhaps—like her perfume. But she was a good kid. And a great worker! She told Houston, "Thank you so much. You're so nice!" He walked her downstairs and flagged a cab for her. What had she meant by that? What was she used to?

The next morning she didn't come into his office at first, but brought in reports about eleven. She made a civil smile and nothing more. Polite, but perhaps a bit servile, Houston thought—a bit self-abnegating. He'd wanted it to happen. She was a good kid.

One of the units alerted for Panama was the battalion in which Mark Randolph was now a company executive officer. They were already on board ships and heading south for training on Vieques Island, Puerto Rico, and the ships just kept going south. They had embarked in a sleet storm in North Carolina. Now it was warm, the sea was green blue, and dolphins played about the bows of the gray ships.

Sailors in gray helmets worked the 40-millimeter and 3-inch/50 guns, swiveling them against the sky. He smelled land. They saw a low green line on the horizon and wood and leaf flotsam from the jungle. The little steel speakers throughout the ship droned, "Now—General Quarters," and orders for the landing force to lay to stations. The small gray bow-ramp boats, called LCVPs, dropped into the water, motors blatting, and other ships opened sea doors to launch armored amphibious tractors and large craft holding tanks. Marines crowded steel decks with camouflage helmets and packs rigged so they could shed them if they went into the water. They tied lines for lowering black machine guns, green flamethrowers and rocket launchers, and worn steel mortars. Young men still in their teens sharpened bayonets. Green wooden cases of live ammunition and raw unpainted boxes of grenades came up from the hold—not the usual stuff, but specially marked, with lead seals—contingency ammo. Did it look serious?

Hot damn! First Lieutenant Randolph thought, but not being completely stupid, asked the first sergeant if *he* thought the balloon was going up. This first sergeant, a quiet, gentle man who had been wounded on Okinawa and then went, not home, but to China for the unpublicized skirmishing with Mao's troops, said, "The sergeant major said to close the unit diary," an order left out of all the John Wayne movies that means a unit really is going into action.

Randolph saw his drinking buddy, the antitank platoon commander, and gave him thumbs up. Hey, *we* are *badasses!* While the ships had been forming up in Norfolk, the whole battalion had raised hell and had fights all over Virginia Beach, from the colonel on down. Randolph had been in one and hadn't lost, he didn't think, and had fled the confusion, and his antitank pal, pursued by cops, had run up a flight of stairs, pulled a soda-acid fire extinguisher off a wall, and heaved it just right, crossways, hitting the cops chest high and bowling them down the steps while he dived out a window. Another lieutenant, a Social Register San Franciscan who was usually terribly civil, had called a naval ensign "an enzyme" and thrown him overboard. Yes, they were badasses. They'd even stiffed one of those stupid charity fund drives the base always ran, leaving envelopes with a few pennies and racing for the ships.

They watched the low green line of Panama in the muggy air. The ships' gun swiveled. The gray boats circled and muttered. A-4 jets raced for the land and roared low along the beach. Anyone could see the rockets under their wings. Anyone could see the landing nets over the sides and all the tracked vehicles.

They waited, and after hours the word came to cool it. Randolph knew nothing about the riots and Panamanian threats to attack the canal, but now they had petered out. "Secure the landing force." It was like clearing a rifle, racking the bolt, except Randolph and many others were all that much hotter to go in *some*where next time.

Houston was in bed with Terry. She said, "Is there, um, has the President made a decision to phase out all the New Frontier people?"

"No, Terry."

"Oh." She put her hands behind her head and looked at the ceiling. Lovely large red-brown nipples and a brown patch of hair. "You'd know, wouldn't you? I mean, you've been invited to the ranch. You must know as much as *anyone*, don't you?"

Her simple appeal touched him. "Don't worry, Terry. As long as *I'm* there, you're going to be there. You're tops."

"Really?"

"Of course. Don't you know it? You're remarkable."

"Thank you, Houston."

"Don't thank me. I look forward to coming to work. To being there with you."

She laughed. "That's nice."

She helped him pack for the flight to the LBJ Ranch. Houston, President Johnson, and a half-dozen others boarded a shiny green Sikorsky HUS helicopter with MARINES painted on the side and a white VIP top. The seats were soft, upholstered like airplane seats. It was Houston's first time in a helicopter. They flew to Andrews AFB and dropped onto the hardstand near the blue-and-white KC-135. Houston watched the crew execute Lyndon Johnson's strict instructions for departure. The starboard engines were running as the Presidential party reached the ladder. Johnson did not like to wait. As soon as he boarded, the port engines started. The aircraft was rolling before LBJ entered his special quarters. He wanted a crisp show.

What a swell layout! Rows of seats like a regular 707, work bays with Herman Millerish office furniture. LBJ was voluble, told them stories, and promised them good barbecue. They were all in a good mood because they'd got through the Panama flap without disaster. Houston had received a call from Uncle Stu praising the administration's work, too.

"You tell him for me he did a first-rate job," Stu said. "It was just and firm. His predecessor made the wrong impression with the Alianza."

Air Force One landed in Austin; the party transferred to a military VIP aircraft, and they flew onto the strip on the LBJ Ranch. Years earlier it had been designated Johnson City Airport. Johnson, then a senator, had got the Federal Aviation Agency to pay hundreds of thousands of dollars for landing lights and other improvements. Everyone knew how much clout he had.

At the ranch they ate barbecue, swam, and shot traps. Houston, a good bird shot, got further into the President's graces—so much so that LBJ took him with a few older cronies to the deer lodge he had on stilts like a Vietnam watchtower out in the scrub. It was equipped with armchairs and a refrigerator. They drank and told stories. Johnson told about his father, the local politician, and about illustrious Johnsons in the Mexican War. He was a marvelous storyteller, but Houston had heard that LBJ's stories—such as the one about a relative who'd been killed variously at the Alamo or the Battle of San Jacinto—simply weren't true, that LBJ lived, in part, in the realm of myth.

At the right time LBJ turned on powerful lights to freeze two whitetail, which Houston and one of the Texans shot. It was months out of season but no one bothered LBJ's shooting stand. He had ruined a Texas game agent who'd interfered with it earlier, when he was a senator, and no one in his right mind would mess with him now.

Except maybe the Cubans.

Another flap started, this time in Cuba, while Houston and the President were down at the ranch.

As usual, Mark Randolph, the cheerful pawn, didn't know anything about it. His battalion had finally got to Vieques and was training, shooting, running, and drinking. They had rations of ammo and beer to use up. He ran NCOs to the range for machine gun training, although he was a company executive officer—second in command of several hundred Marines—and presumably too lofty to do weapons classes. His first sergeant did most of *his* work and he'd taken up the M-60 as a hobby and had written a handout on it; he liked the low black slotted weapon.

Out on the ranges they fired all kinds of weapons. The Staff NCOs, ever shrewd in building relations, shot a stray steer and had a barbecue for the officers—perhaps not as power-dense as the one on the LBJ Ranch, but a pleasant time of drinking and chewing (tough steer) and swapping old stories like the ones about Lay-'Em-on-the-Wire McGraw and how Chesty Puller put Jacksonville off-limits. After being decorous and well behaved, the officers went up to their club and got *down*, drinking and singing and wrestling. In one free-for-all someone bit the colonel on the head. This colonel had been a rubber boat Raider and played guitar with a Django Reinhardt sound. Another lieutenant played Beatles and "Little Darlin'." And so they spent their time feasting and singing and firing ball and tracer until an earnest staff officer, a bare-chested captain, ran up the hill and said, "Emergency backload! Flap at Gitmo! Shooting on the fence!"

"I want you to go down and find out what the fuck the Marines did down there," LBJ told Houston. "You watch out for 'em. Marines'll give you fits ever' time, sayin' yessir this and yessir that and meanwhile doin' some damn fool thing like drownin' those boys in the swamp and you got to explain to their mommas and daddys why their son's dead an' there ain't even a war."

The President slapped Houston's shoulder and propelled him toward the VIP helicopter. Houston had VIP aircraft all the way down. At Guantanamo Bay he was given a plain green cotton uniform to conceal his status. Colonels and Navy captains briefed him. He saw aerial photos of Cuban tanks massed on the other side of the ridge. *They* were pissed off. A battalion landing team had just come in to reinforce the big barracks force here.

He flew in a helicopter—one like the President's but without the shiny paint or soft seats, just dusty nylon web slung seats and a worn interior—over American positions: troops and tanks dug into holes. Some holes were empty. He pointed that out to the colonel.

"What started it?"

"The Cubans say a Marine walked through the gate and urinated on their flagpole."

"Good God! Was there shooting?"

"A couple of warning shots. Not anything to speak of."

"What do you *mean?* When *do* you speak of it?"

The four-striper said, "Sometimes the sentries shoot at each other. Not to kill but just to keep the other fellow on his toes. The Cubans do it, too."

"Good God! Why?"

"They get bored."

"I can't accept that," Houston said. But it looked like the matter had been fixed, the right regrets and firmness relayed through the Swiss, the right buttressing on this side of the fence with combat troops. Houston, who was used to seeing the outstanding, tall, handsome guard Marines, did not know quite what to make of these battalion Marines in their wrinkled, unstarched uniforms. They were so small. They looked so young. They had such a mix of equipment.

He didn't notice his classmate Mark Randolph marching his troops along the road, but he wouldn't have recognized him anyway, and Randolph didn't pay attention to the man in unmarked Navy utilities in the back of the Navy jeep. He saluted the squid in the front. Houston went to the crypto center and sent a message saying all had been settled. He took off soon after in a VIP twin jet.

Power. They had applied force just right with the right words; force made the words credible. He knew all the criticisms of his boss, but LBJ unquestionably knew how to use power, and that was what Houston wanted, too. He liked being an emissary of the President of the most powerful country on earth.

Back in Washington everyone was pleased that the Cuban incident had gone flat fast. LBJ, much as he denigrated the brainpower of his Marines and flag ranks, was pleased that they had got into Cuba fast, and he saw the show of force as a handy foreign policy tool. "Hell, I got them in *now* and don't have to listen to all that crap from State," he told Houston.

Terry welcomed him back full of congratulations, proud of him for the way his star was rising; her soft brown eyes glowed. They drank gin and tonic, she fixed steaks, they went to bed, she clung to him, talked too much, and cried.

"I'm so happy to see you!"

Watch your step! his inner voice told him. Her slightly sour sweet scent. The teddy bears on the plaid bedspread. Her pronunciations of "water" and "coffee." No, no—it wouldn't work. She was a good kid, of course. Terrific! Good girl! But no—ease off. And he had the *power*. He could do whatever he had the *nerve* to do. She wasn't his type, anyway. He knew his type. By God, he'd made love to his type—Phoebe—and dammit, he wanted *her!*

He'd seen her name again, a haunting rebuke, a challenge on the scoreboard, when Terry, getting maudlin, had dragged out the worn Camelot issue of *Life*. There was Phoebe's name on the masthead. Her cool, high brow, her well-formed smile. Her *character*—she wasn't weepy like Terry. By God, she was all right. Dammit, he'd have her!

He made it a vow and copied it on the wallet card and looked at it daily to motivate himself. When Uncle Stu came down he told him about it at the Jockey Club.

"Yes, you should marry," Stu said. "It's time, and you need someone to stand up with you. A good wife will arrange your meeting others, set up the parties, keep track of names and relationships. Someone you know. Who fits in. Your pa always wanted you to take the Mawson girl."

"She's stupid, Stu. And besides, you know Pa wanted me to marry her to make our properties on the Point contiguous."

"Yes, of course."

"No, I want Phoebe!"

"She's all right," Stu said. "Of course she is!"

"I want to campaign."

"Good for you, Tony."

Of course he was the man to ask, Houston thought. Look at him—lean, sunburned, capable, perfectly dressed, a good athlete at all ages.

"A few words of advice, Tony. Press her hard. Be out there with roses, theater tickets, a quick trip. Make things happen for her. That shows her you're the man." Stu raised his eyebrows and leaned forward. "But *you* carry the ball. Don't be *too* kind, patient, or gentle. Women always say they want that, but they don't. They drive you nuts if you let *them* decide. You make your case and *tell* her: 'Join me and it's happiness. Don't and *tant pis.*' You understand? And if she doesn't go for you, go after someone else *immediately*. They'll run after you."

Honeymoon

It was December 16, four days after Angel Acevedo had killed the Yale VIP, more than twenty years since all the action Phoebe had been thinking about and *would* think about—her own heartbreaks, the war, the failed poverty programs that had made the streets a numbing pageant of cruelty, and her own lousy love life. The America she'd known shot full of holes and then its appearance re-created, painted over like a scene on a plastic balloon by President Reagan.

On the street outside their station wagon she saw a Puerto Rican wearing a sweatshirt printed with DON'T WORRY BE HAPPY.

She and Tom Hurley and Pat Mulkin were going down to Loisaida to shoot Angel Acevedo's gang friends and get more on the killer's background. Christmas traffic stalled them on Broadway, Macy's draped holiday lights attracting crowds a-gawking, taxis gridlocking, and a partridge in a pear tree. Tom and Pat were at each other's throats again.

"My car was broken into last night," Tom said. "Do you know how ruined this city is? I put a sign on the dash—'No Radio, No Radio' in big letters like a *Post* headline. They smashed in the windows anyway. Schools are so bad the little shits can't even *read* before they choose a life of crime."

"*Was* there a radio?" Pat asked. "It wouldn't be unlike you to lie."

"No radio, *comprende? No tengo radio.*"

"You're silly to have a car in the city anyway," she sniffed.

"Especially a BMW. You're just asking for it. But you can't help it, can you?"

"That's *typical!* No wonder this city went to hell. I worked for that! I should hide it? That's freedom? I have no faith left in democracy."

"That's why it doesn't work."

"It doesn't work because of people like you."

"Oh, *fuck* you!"

The wagon crept past the Flatiron Building. Phoebe's old neighborhood had become terribly chichi with the million-dollar lofts and neoclassical restaurants.

"Jesus, look at this!" Tom said a little while later. "We should have taken the subway."

Ahead on Canal two cars had smashed up and the drivers yelled while cars inched around them and crowds of pedestrians streamed along the sidewalks past bins of fish, vegetables, and pots under Chinese signs. Tom said, "You know what happens if you cross a Chinese and a Puerto Rican? You get a car thief who can't drive."

"Good light," the cameraman said. "A little dark on the vest."

He backed away from the gang president, who said, "That's not no vest, man, that's my colors."

The president was thin, about twenty-two, his skin brown, with a thin Fu Manchu moustache and long black hair in a pigtail; he wore a leather cap, black leather vest, and Levi's with the legs split over black biker boots. On his black belt were an 007 knife and chain and on his wrists, two studded cuffs. His vest, or colors, had an embroidered device of skull, bones, and dagger, and printed around them:

STREET WOLVES
L. E. SIDE

Phoebe said, "Paco Mangual, you know Angel Acevedo well as a member of the Street Wolves, the organization you are president of. What is he like? Tell us about Angel Acevedo the man."

"Yeah," President Mangual said, his eyes passing over her to the camera and onlookers. He arched into the tough-and-cool street pose, head back, eyes lidded. "Yeah, we all wan' to say Angel is a good man an' we're pullin' for him to get through this. They don' have no case—he din' do nothin'. We like to thank the people they come out for his defense."

"Could he ever have carried a gun?"

"Hey, guns on the street, man. Guns around. Maybe he pick one up. Streets aren't safe here, man. You look around?"

"Does your club have guns?"

"Man, this social club, man, we get along without no problems."

"Angel said he learned how to fight in this group. And his arrest record shows an arrest for manslaughter two years ago when the Street Wolves had a shoot-out with another gang. A three-year-old child was hit."

"They started it, man. They came here an' started it."

"But there were guns, obviously. Angel said he knew how to handle them. He's admitted committing several robberies."

"He din' say that to me."

"How many gang fights was he in?"

"I don' know, man. We got a war leader, the Wolves got a war leader like anyone else. I'm president. I don' pay no attention to that. You ask him who was where."

"Hold it." Phoebe leaned close to Tom Hurley. "I thought you had this shmuck prepped."

"It's a case of on-cameraitis," Tom said.

"Not much we can use."

"Let me try to take him over what he told me and we can splice it in," Tom said. "Mr. Mangual? Sir? When we talked before you told me you'd been on a shoot-out with Angel and he was a real *campeón*."

The president's flat brown eyes flickered over Tom's face. "Yeah, I said that, man. But I don' tell you no place. Did I tell you a place?"

"Can you tell me when, sir? Or at least how old he was, sir?"

Behind Phoebe, Pat said softly, "Oh, kiss his ass. . . ."

"Fourteen, man. We just formed outa the Ambuscaderos and the ol' Kung Foos . . ." President Mangual gave about fifteen seconds of good reminiscence about Angel the man.

Phoebe said, "Get some of that street. That wall. And the club-house." Behind Mangual was the Street Wolves clubhouse, a boarded-up storefront with a hand-lettered sign. The crew walked over. "Find the plug," the cameraman said to the apprentice who opened the door. Inside, youths in leather looked out at them.

"May have to use the battery pack. Got an outlet in here?" he said to a gang member inside. A plain room paneled with composition board printed in wood grain. Fluorescent lights. A pool table. "I found a plug," the apprentice said. Gang members watched the apprentice on his hands and knees putting in the plug.

On the avenue children played under the plane trees. The brick building fronts were screened brown with rusty fire escapes. Pat Mulkin came up and told them, "I found a bronze plaque to Lyndon Johnson not far away."

"How nice," Phoebe said.

"Give me a break. No, see? Angel was born then. You know, the War on Poverty? The Great Society?"

"They wouldn't get it," Phoebe said. The crew came out of the clubhouse.

Tom said, "I have something else."

"What?"

"I went to the *botánica* to check on the relics Lydia uses praying for Angel. The owner said he'd show us the spells."

They went around the corner to the *botánica*, a store with painted plaster Virgins and paper packets of Caribbean herbs in the window. The owner, a thin, animated man, went on camera and explained how faith and certain spells had helped many of his *clientes*. He held up one of the paper envelopes with its ray design and spoke a spell in Spanish, his eyes wide. It was a good shot, but that meant they had to get Lydia following up, showing *her* faith on camera.

"It's no problem," Tom said. "The establishing shots have her black Madonna and *paquete*. She could go voice-over."

"No, better to show her face. See her talk."

"We have good pictures of her face," Tom said. "Eyes show pain and concern."

"We'll see," Phoebe said. "I don't want to push it here with the Caribbean voodoo bit. The Hispanic groups got on Barry after that street-life segment, with the evangelists and sweatshops."

"It's a good human touch," Tom said. "The mother unable to cope."

"I know, I know, Tom," Phoebe said. "Now please shut the fuck up, will you? I know you have a taste for the sensational because you're young and decadent, and even though what you shoot is true, it might upset the average viewer, so you have to have a good reason for airing it."

"If you'll just take a few steps around the corner," Pat Mulkin said, "the plaque's right there. I think it's a monster visual. Look."

It was square bronze, camouflage-painted into the graffiti-sprayed wall. The raised letters told about the dedication of this neighborhood park in 1964, thanks to Mayor Wagner, Governor Rockefeller, President Johnson, and federal funds. Pat was pushing it because she figured Tom had stumbled. "No," Phoebe said. "That's ancient history."

In the car Tom said, "What did you think of Paco? *El presidente?*"

"Why do they use that title?" Pat asked. "The gang leaders?"

"It used to mean something," Phoebe said. Lyndon Johnson had trashed the magic of the name. Didn't everyone believe in more back then?

She remembered what she had fallen for when Houston had courted her in the spring of 1964.

First, a few white roses sent to her office—her bullpen.

> *Phoebe—up here for an hour on*
> *White House business and thought*
> *about you—and tennis, swimming,*
> *and summer fun.*

Nothing more. Tantalizing.

Another four or five days went by. She expected a follow-up. She anticipated. Nothing. She was slightly irritated. Then curious. Nothing. Days more. Then a small package. She opened it at her littered desk, her fingers carbon smudged. Georg Jensen. A small fat circle pin, silver in the shape of a dolphin curved in on itself. Not expensive, not tacky. An all-right choice for a man like Houston. Was he thinking of the silver moon on their skin, the smooth paleness? Or was it just a lucky shot?

This time he followed up with a call.

"Hi! Listen, I'm in and out of town all the time now. I'm the President's messenger boy to the Street!" They laughed.

He was *such* a winner—making a joke about it while letting her know how close he was to the Power.

"It's great, but I'm at loose ends at times," he said. "Great chance to see a show, go out. Look, I'd love to have you come along. You're probably blasé about nightlife there—"

"You know how it is," she laughed. Leaving *Life* at eight or nine with grimy fingers and a cigarette mouth to go to the 3-Gs with Sara. Or off to another bar. Or to see Carole and Peabody and watch their lives becoming more different. Of course she had met some interesting, well-off, talented men—husbands who wanted a little midtown nookie. And other young people *in* journalism—but perhaps she knew them too well.

"We'd have a swell time. I'm up for it, Phoebe."

"I believe it," she said. "Fine. Yes."

He came up the following week. This is what she saw:

His hair was perfectly trimmed. He looked weary—something about the eyes—but enthusiastic, full of nervous energy. His suit, a midweight worsted, was perfectly cut. Gold cuff links and collar pin. Handmade shoes. She had never seen him dressed so well—he'd been so casual and frayed that tumescent summer. He looked good. He was very powerful. That excited her. It was a feeling *she* had picked up, enhanced, in the business. She wanted to be near what he had and commanded, and she recognized that fact after he left, after the show. He hadn't asked to come in, said he had a plane waiting, a small Air Force VIP jet, so he could leave any time, but he had important work tomorrow.

"Wish I could stay, but—you know, ha-ha!"—and kissed her, hard. Her lips softened. "No, I have to go," he said.

She watched his cab head up the street of low brick flat fronts toward FDR Drive.

Part of her new fascination with him was wondering if she could make him stay. He was so abrupt, so sure of himself, so independent.

A week later he came back, they saw a play, they went to bed. Two weeks later she went to Washington and stayed in his apartment. She visited the White House, saw his office, the federal police, Secret Service, black cars, acres of white paper, the busy solemnity of Johnson's government, and she wanted to make that scene.

Houston went to the gray Navy CIA barracks by the muddy Potomac to say good-bye before Ted Gerrity took off on a fact-finding trip to South Vietnam. It was a lovely, sunny day and in his bare wood-and-beaverboard office, hung with sailing photos in plain black frames, Gerrity had opened a top window to let in a breeze smelling of new grass and river water. The trees were dusted with green. The terrible winter was over. Maybe they had a grip on it now.

Gerrity looked good, vigorous, grabbing acetate-tabbed folders and dropping them in his case—DOD briefings, EEI for the situation there. He wore horn-rimmed glasses, a blue button-down collar shirt, olive gabardine suit, and looked just like what he was—an executive of military force and civilian policy.

"Taking your tennis racket?" Houston asked him.

He laughed. "I should. The colonels are pretty jocky, you know. Not that many of them stay around long enough to get a court."

They bantered about all the screwups in Saigon, Minh and Ky and Thieu switching places, much to the discomfiture of American Army and State officers who'd been saying that a military government would at last bring stability to RVN and whip it into shape. And of course this made the *Agency's* stock rise, allowed Helms to say, "I told you so."

"That looks like it." He locked the case and hid the key. Houston walked with him down clattering wooden stairs and shook his hard calloused hand on the gravel by the gray Plymouth. Gerrity looked at him, a grin cutting across his strong tanned face. "Do a good job, Houston. I'll bet Biddy's proud of you." He squeezed Houston's shoulder and slapped his back, which pleased Houston immensely.

Far away from the imposing buildings and the mighty Potomac, a quiet little man squatted on his heels by a dusty footpath, watching people carrying baskets of beans and bamboo cages of chickens to sell along this other riverbank. A couple of black buffalo carrying baskets stood hocks deep in the mud, arc-horned heads swaying, dropping to drink the brown water.

Farmers in black wearing flat straw hats talked and argued, clucking, *"Duoc! Duoc!"* Crowds moved along rows of goods—baskets and bags, cans of American cooking oil for sale marked US AID—NOT TO BE SOLD, pigs, chickens, ducks, eggs, greens. Beyond the rows were the concrete walls of the nearly finished market enclosure and the low stucco buildings and tin and straw houses of Gia Binh.

The small man watched a couple of ARVN soldiers working in front of the new marketplace. They were wrapping telephone wire around a glass insulator on one of the French-style concrete poles. The little man had been an electrician and watched their technique. The puppet soldiers had already put up a platform near the new steel gate for notables to stand on during the ceremonies next week. Puppets and traitors from the provincial capital at Da Nang and from Saigon, even a long-nose official. The little quiet man was planning to kill them.

He wore gray faded cotton shorts and a shirt, middle-class country wear. His thick black hair looked as if someone had used a bowl to cut it in dim light. One ear was notched and scarred. He held the rank of major in the Main Forces, the Liberation Army of the *mat tran*. He was a *can bo*, a cadreman, organizing volunteers for direct action. His name was Nguyen Thuc Thanh. He had been reared here, in Annam, and had killed many *phap*, French soldiers, during the Great Patriotic Struggle and War of Liberation—the rapid-speaking *phap* who carried strong cigarettes, the red-faced, guttural-speaking German mercenaries in the Legion, the tall black colonials. Now he and his small groups, *chi bo*, would kill the long-nose *mỹ*, the new American enemy.

He had seen few Americans. They rarely came to the countryside, although lately they had put *mỹ* officers and senior sergeants with the puppet army units. But a *binh vanh*, a convert to liberation in the puppet government, said a long-nose AID official would attend the dedication. Everyone knew AID was the *mỹ* Central Intelligence Agency. Worth killing. Suitable for *dich vanh*, direct action.

One bomb. They had already stolen the ARVN jeep they would pack with C-3 and RDX and detonating cord and fuze with good new Soviet UZRG strikers on solenoids activated by radio. The new concrete wall would act as tamping, to enhance the brisance. Maybe they could destroy that, too, while killing the traitors and long noses. Maximum shock, maximum terror.

Major Thanh stood and padded up the path of brown dust, lighting a cigarette at the gate, ambling over there to the stand, ambling back, counting paces to make sure the blast would kill them all.

Houston's journal had a number of entries about what happened a few days later over that weekend in mid-May. These figured in the scandalous revelations years later about Vietnam and vile government.

Phoebe flew down for the weekend—a lovely warm sunny May weekend like the one in New Haven two years before. She saw some of the incidents that, as they say, made up the mosaic. But she was an action journalist, not a self-styled pundit like the pompous Ash Loakes. It was enough for her that something new was happening; and later on, she thought, who could say which event in that confused pattern of plots, coups, and deals was the one that sent Johnson into big mechanical war? It was all like sausage—which link mattered more? The air had changed when Kennedy was killed—everyone knew that—but where had the tailspin started?

Here is what she saw. Here is what Houston's journal recorded.

Houston met her at Washington National, hugged her, swept her out to a pool car with driver. They raced across the bridge and back to the White House—where Houston got out, scooting backward. "Du Pont Circle," he instructed the driver.

She let herself in with his key and waited. She was to get used to waiting for Houston because he was very busy, and she was and always had been very impressed with him. Besides, she was tired—she always worked hard at *Life*—and it was good to have time to collect herself. She was also curious and had never been stuffy about snooping. She looked through his apartment. A few rubbers. She used a diaphragm. No love letters, no pictures of other women. She was touched to find a few of her letters from two years before. He really *did* care for her.

She knew Houston lived for work but wasn't aware of what he kept at the office.

"Holy Cow!" his journal read.

IF I can keep stride—think Phoebe'll go for the bid this time! Meanwhile, back at the ranch, am having terrific time with Terry, trying everything—Lab 69! Some plays she's a bit shy about, but why not? What a balancing act—Phoebe's perfection and Terry's eagerness. Risky, but what *can't* you do if you *keep your nerve?*

This morning after she delivered the mail I locked the office door and ate her on my desk and let her return favor. Good thing the walls are so thick! I'm sure we sounded like a chorus of asthmatics. Terrific! (Sort of thing Stu has stories about. Others must have the same game here—fills long hours on watch. You can tell in their faces.) Then out of here fast to meet Phoebe at airport.

The next morning Houston got up especially early, kissing Phoebe, leaving a note of instructions about lunch. Gray light and long shadows on the grass. In the White House the early-morning smell of waxes and disinfectant and stale paper, the guards with that cigarette-fumed end-of-watch look. One of the communications clerks came out of the message room walking fast. Houston glanced in at the young Army clerks at their low gray crypto machines that looked like teletypes feeding out yellow paper. One clerk held a stack of black rotors, the fitting that scrambled messages into five-letter groups. They looked like thin hockey pucks. The machines clattered. Something was coming in.

He went into the office. Terry wasn't there yet. Good. He could get work done. She distracted him. In fact, she was a bit irritating sometimes, coming in not when they had a job but when, as she put it, "the coast was clear." How complicated could he let things get while Phoebe was down here?

Would Phoebe accept his proposal? She had to—she knew how good it could be! First cabin!

Terry brought him the message when she came in. Headed CLAS and PRIORITY and TOP SECRET.

Bad news! Houston thought. A terrorist bomb had killed Viet officials at an RVN civic function at Gia Binh (Thua Thien, Da Nang-Hue area). Houston didn't know the town. Not an important one. More to check for LBJ. . . .

He set to work on other matters and another message came in saying an American had been killed, too. An American survivor, an Army Signal Corps sergeant, described the ARVN jeep before the stand, the orange flash, the people on the stand being blown against, and through, the open-worked steel gates of the new market, the gates bending and walls crumbling. . . .

Houston assumed the dead American was some soldier. It wasn't until he left the office for lunch with Phoebe that the information came in about who had been killed.

Houston's note asked Phoebe to meet him at the West Wing entrance. He said he'd leave instructions with the guards to clear her. She knew he had something important to say to her because they had reservations at the Jockey Club.

She reached the West Wing entrance and was being passed

through by the guard when she saw Houston come through a doorway down the hall—not the one on the side of the press lobby but the one straight ahead to the Oval Office. He broke into a grin and waved; they walked to each other and kissed. They were pulling apart when Terry Menska came through the same door waving a paper.

"Mr. Bridles!" Terry called to his back, then saw him separating from Phoebe. Her eyes widened, her jaw dropped, she blushed. She handed him the sheet, shaking, and said, "It's bad. I'm sorry."

Houston's face had frozen. He looked at her. Terry. Phoebe. Back to Terry.

Phoebe glanced at her. Strawberry blonde, wide eyes, like a scared rabbit's.

Houston's lips pressed together as he read the paper.

Terry said, "You liked him, didn't you?"

"Yes!" he said angrily. "Don't talk about it!" Tears came to Terry's eyes. "Look, I'll have to see Bundy," he said to Phoebe. "Would you wait a moment? Ah, Terry, please call the Jockey Club and reschedule my lunch for one-thirty? Two persons." He turned and walked away. Terry blinked, looked at Phoebe, and went out through the door she'd come in through.

Phoebe waited at the paneled, quiet Jockey Club. Houston swept in and without breaking stride kissed Phoebe and guided her to the maître d', who turned and led them to the table. Not a second wasted!

"Sorry about the delay. Something sticky came up. I can't get into it."

"It's bad?"

"Yes. Not a disaster. Sad. Don't want it to spoil this, though. Drink?"

"G and T."

He told the waiter who had come up behind. They talked about *Life* and her work. The drinks came. More small talk. Oysters. No wine. Sole. Salad. He kept the conversation going lightly and she followed his lead. Coffee. He lit her cigarette.

"Good," he said. "Phoebe, you know it's a joy to have you visit and bad news when you leave. I'd like to—"

She reached across the table and put two fingers on his wrist. "Wait. What happened today?"

"Bad news, I'm afraid. I can't say much about it."

"Here or overseas?"

"Overseas."

"Europe or Asia?"

"Vietnam."

"Animal, vegetable, or mineral? Come on, Houston—I'm not going to report it."

"A friend of my father's was killed in a terrorist attack. I should say, a friend of my father's whom *I* had come to like and respect a great deal. That's really all I can say."

"I'm sorry."

"There's a lot to be done over there, Phoebe." His color came up and his eyes burned as he looked at her. "It's important and it's dangerous. Pa and I have never gotten along, but I've been amazed since joining the White House to learn how really important some of this unseen work is. There are always a very few gifted—extremely gifted—people out there working anonymously and taking major risks without glory. The last man before the goal line, so to speak, with no crowd to cheer him on. And this one bought the farm. He did clandestine ops in France in the War, and he bought it this time on an innocuous visit. Those people over there are sneaky little killers! Eisenhower didn't do much to stop them and Kennedy was just getting started, but finally I think this country's in a position to fight back and tell the other side they'll get flattened on the next play. It's a matter of will and knowing how to use the power. Johnson, of course, *breathes* power. He won't put up with this. But it's going to be a hell of a struggle. That's not what I want to bring up, Phoebe, but it's tangential.

"Look." He took her hand. "I'm not very romantic but I'll say my piece. I want you to marry me, Phoebe. You know I love you and think the world of you. Can't make this an event—we're both on the run. Don't even know your ring size, but if you say yes we'll, ah, satisfy that requirement."

He looked at her. She was flushed, her mouth open; it was like riding—the horse was on its way. She wanted him.

"Phoebe, I need you, for Christ's sake. This is big stuff we're playing with. You know how it is. You've got the brains and the grace of a— You'd be key in this."

"I think it's a wonderful idea, and you know I'm crazy about you," she said. "But I don't want another shitty breakdown like the last time." (Phoebe also had a question about that secretary. What *was*

that scene? But she wanted to be close to the power—it was centrip-
etal.)

"Deep-six that, Phoebe. I'm my own man now. In addition to my
position in the West Wing I have my own money, you know."

"But he's your pa. If he doesn't approve of me, where are your
loyalties?"

"He was wrong. We deal as equals. I outrank him already. Now,
back to the, ah, question on the agenda?"

"Yes."

He looked at her. "You'll have it?"

"Yes."

"Superb. First-rate. Oh, Phoebe, this is terrific."

"Houston, I do want to be sure we agree on some things
beforehand—"

"I think those arrangements are very sensible. I'm not a bit interested in *your*, ah, instruments and fiduciaries, I'm sure. Look, we
don't need to commingle—it's whatever you—"

"No, I mean I want to keep working for *Life* awhile."

"How long?"

"Some time."

"We'll hammer that out. Oh, this is great!" He looked at his
watch. They had to leave. On the way back he kissed and hugged her
in the car.

Back in the West Wing basement Houston looked at the papers
Terry had typed for him—lists of retaliation options and who had
proposed what in recent similar events. Houston's task was to run
between Bundy, McNamara, and the spooks and suggest the best play
to LBJ. He wanted to make sure the little bastards hurt. You couldn't
play it any other way. Others were muttering, too. He saw McGeorge
Bundy in the corridors. Gerrity himself had told him about Bundy
diddling over tiny details—like a Harvard dean (albeit with Yale degree!), not a staff chief. One time an American Army officer had got
friendly with a Laotian princess—terrific opportunity—and Bundy'd
been indecisive about whether the officer could travel with the royal
family. Now Gerrity was dead. Would Bundy be capable of pounding
them? Houston wanted them punished. "Send the big men into the
line!" he wrote in his journal.

At three-thirty Houston went into the Oval Office. LBJ stared at him. Houston made an impassioned speech. "This man was an authentic hero, Mr. President!" He talked about Gerrity outfoxing Germans. "He knew unconventional war, but he wasn't outwitted in a war like that—he was murdered by assassins. Dishonorable gangsters! Planting a bomb took no guts!"

"I'm meetin' with Mac on this," LBJ said. "I won't be the first American President to take shit from little rat turds like them."

"He was there to help build free markets, Mr. President. The Viet Cong want to destroy progress, and we better give them a bloody nose fast. To keep them honest. Like rapping the guy across the line!"

They discussed options. They couldn't attack on the ground— the ARVN wasn't reliable and the Chinese might intervene. The clandestine ops up north hadn't worked well. Houston felt the safest recommendation was Robert McNamara's surgical air strikes. McNamara *was* brilliant and these strikes were controllable. Not subject to ARVN misuse. ("Wisest recommendation," Houston wrote in his journal. "Whatever the intrinsic merits of air attack, wisest for *me* to recommend now.")

LBJ concurred, touched the miniature Silver Star on his lapel that he'd got after leaving Congress to go in the Navy and coming under fire in an airplane. He said, "We got the strongest air power in the world. I ain't gonna get trapped on the ground, and I ain't about to start World War Three or get the Chinese in there either. That cut off Truman's legs. I'm gonna control this thing. I don't—I swear to God—want American boys in there on the ground."

He looked out the curved window at the shimmering air and greenness. After a while he turned back. "That's all."

Phoebe flew to Asheville to tell her parents. They sat on the brick terrace. Phoebe's mother, Constance, wore an enormous hat and her father, Avery, a thin sunburned man with Phoebe's high forehead and straight nose, wore an open cotton shirt. "It's nice you are finally tying the knot," he said.

"Avery—" Constance said. She had the gray eyes and full lips that made Phoebe's face so attractive. "Houston is quite a *catch*."

"Oh, I know of the Bridles of Boston," Avery Bishop said. "Wasn't that the question before? That he didn't know of *us*?"

"I'm sure Phoebe's made certain he does."

"I take it you'll quit work?"

"After a while," Phoebe said.

"You'll have your work cut out for you, entertaining," Constance said. "Even down here, in this *quiet* place, I have my hands full." It was a pretty town of Art Deco storefronts and gardens and quiet parties.

"I'll try to finesse the entertaining," Phoebe said. "That part is silly, I think."

"What do you mean by that, please?" Avery said. He made a look—head back, nose narrowing—and Phoebe planted her feet, flushing, so that anyone who knew the family knew that Avery and Phoebe were about to quarrel again. But Constance laughed, "La la la," in her exhilarated, musical way, her voice rising, to jolly them out of it. "La—you two can't agree the *sun's* shining."

"I don't see why she has to work anyway!" Avery said petulantly.

"You don't think there's any kind of work but the law," Phoebe said. "Or banking."

"Well, they're out of the question for a girl anyway."

"La!" Constance said. "It's so *good* to see you down here, Phoebe!"

"You can see why I don't want to move here."

"It's really quite pleasant."

Phoebe was an only child. She knew her parents were bright, had coached her, provided her with tutors and classes so she shot ahead in school—but all she learned told her more forcefully that she didn't want to live like them. Her father had been away from the Southern Tier only to serve in the Navy Judge Advocate General's office in the war. Constance Louise Duikermann, her mother, had been one of the most charming "buds," as she still put it, in the 1935 season in the Genesee Valley. Phoebe felt it was too bad they knew nothing beyond where they'd started. This is why she stayed away from them and looked for what she liked: Big Events. Big Cities.

"You always wanted your head," Avery said.

"Yes, thank you," Phoebe said. "That's the way I am."

Back in New York, Phoebe put in for transfer to the Washington Bureau. She had ordered but not mailed the invitations and was on the phone several times daily with Houston, laughing about all the things before them.

Sara said, "I'd do the same myself. Even if the marriage doesn't last, you'll get good background. The White House!"

"I'll miss you," Phoebe said. "You've taught me so much."

Sara beamed, her hair straying from the pile on top of her head, her blouse dusted with cigarette ash, those dark bright eyes searching.

They went to the 3-Gs and sat near the dusty mural of Amalfi. It was another hot, muggy night—July 18. They talked about politics and the nominations. The Republicans had made an undignified shambles of their convention, right-wingers shouting down Rockefeller and ramming Goldwater in. Johnson had been pushing civil rights legislation through Congress. It was long overdue.

The next morning, a blistering day kept only slightly at bay by the air conditioning, Sara handed Phoebe strips of wire copy. "Check this. Something's going on in Harlem. It doesn't look like the usual kind of demonstration."

The wire said an off-duty police lieutenant named Gilligan had shot and killed a fifteen-year-old black youth named James Powell in Yorkville, the prosperous German-WASP Upper East Side district. Gilligan initially said Powell was in the wrong neighborhood, acting suspiciously, and had pulled a knife. Harlem was some twenty blocks—a mile—north.

Whether or not Gilligan had other clues to the dead youth's culpability and didn't mention them, community leaders seized on the "wrong place, suspicious behavior" remark and organized a march on a police station. Several thousand black citizens formed at the rally led by the Reverend Nelson Dukes. The police sent several thousand officers to block the demonstration. It was the beginning of the Harlem riot, the first big-city summer riot of the sixties.

Phoebe read wire copy about black leaders' demands, crowds forming, police barricades, fires being set in public housing, and officials' indecision. Mayor Wagner was in Europe. The police on the street didn't know what to do, while higher officers made the usual statements. She went uptown by cab, smelled the smoke by the Museum of Natural History, and ran into police barricades at the top of the park. Dozens of cops stood around shooting the shit but wouldn't let the press through. She needed a place to watch from. She had a brainstorm: Peabody's and Carole's apartment! She could watch the smoke from the roof, use the phone and toilet. A perfect lookout.

"Who's that? Jesus!" Carole barked. Phoebe heard her through the door. She couldn't have come at a worse time. She felt the blast of hatred in the kitchen—it flared at her as soon as she stepped into the cramped apartment. Carole, with whom she'd had so many hilarious times, standing oddly on the cracked linoleum, gripping the counter, her face like an itching wound. Peabody stood by the couch glowering, finger in a book. Carole had lost weight and her eyes were bright. Peabody's beard and skin looked dusty. But, Phoebe thought, I've simply got to have this story. "Halloo, sorry to barge in like this, but it's very important—" and explained.

"Terrific!" Carole said. "Jesus Christ, yes! I'll go up on the roof with you. I'll shoot film, fuckin' documentary."

"The chickens have come home to roost," Peabody said. "Malcolm X. I can smell smoke right here. Right *here*, can you *believe* it? Right next to a major university!"

Carole said, "Ignore him. Let me get a glass of water first, I'm so *thirsty*." She turned into the kitchen, head turning this way and that, hand scratching at air. "Fuck! Where are the fuckin' *glasses!*"

"You lose them," Peas said.

"Of course I do. I *wash* them all the time. Jesus!" She found one, ran water, gulped it, and led Phoebe to the roof. Tar paper, gravel, pigeon shit, sooty grooved bricks. They smoked cigarettes and watched black smoke and heat rise to the east. The air was like a dog's breath.

"You're not getting along," Phoebe observed.

"It's getting his paper finished and all the tension. We don't do it anymore, but I'm not depressed—I have plenty of energy. I have classes, too! Film. I know fuckin' well we'll untangle this the way chain does coming out of a well. You didn't see that, did you? Oil well. It'll be okay. Peas has a scholarship and TA-ship at Berkeley. We need a change of scene, new place. California's where it's gotta be. Bad winter here. I may shoot a film myself because of the sun."

"Are you all right, Carole?" Phoebe peered at her friend. Carole's eyes looked as if she had fever.

"Yes. Yes, we'll be okay." She made that self-deprecating *moue* Phoebe liked, pulling her mouth to one side and raising her eyebrows. "Fucked up, but okay," she said, and they laughed.

"I hope so," Phoebe said. "We've been through a lot."

"It's just his master's thesis. I know after he finishes that we'll be fine."

*   *   *

Downstairs, Adams Peabody sat rooted in his musty chair like Hightower in *Light in August*, unable to move, his mind, like Prufrock's, a pair of ragged claws scuttling over lives he'd read. I smell smoke out there, where real lives are struggling against oppression, mute inglorious Nat Turners. *I should be a part of the struggle. I have never even been at a sit-in!* Can I, like Lord Jim, Mathieu—*even Mr. Roberts*—this late join the . . .

His mind went on, far too active. Feverish. Was he going nuts?

His paper was on Djuna Barnes. He'd started with the notion of doing Hemingway or Fitzgerald, because he had traveled in France for his first time on their honeymoon and felt immediately he knew the country and what it meant to be an American following the literary paths of Americans in France in the twenties. Then aspects of twenties styles interested him and he read Gertrude Stein, who had coached Hemingway to use a bare, repetitious Dadaist style like hers.

He was intrigued that Hemingway—that handsome young supermale—became famous by stealing the voice of a fat middle-aged lesbian. That of course led him to Djuna Barnes, a wide-eyed bohemian whose *Nightwood* (so few know it!) T. S. Eliot thought was *the* work of genius in the twenties. Her voice was poetic, evocative, teasing, expansive. "One thinks of the vagina," he'd observed to Carole, and got a quizzical look.

Peabody always thought too much and got mixed up with his subject. He felt guilty about Djuna Barnes the way he felt guilty about not being in the riots to the east. *She* had interviewed Wobblies while *he* had married an oil heiress. Where were his ideals? Had he lost his bearings? Was he nuts? Or worse, middle class? But Hegel (that Adam-like namer of History's beasts) said the novel is the middle-class epic. What did Djuna say about—

"Halloo," Phoebe said, barging in again, now sweating and smudged from the roof. "How are you? How are you getting along? I'm so concerned about Carole—she looks so thin!"

"We have enough to eat."

"Are you really all right, Peas?"

"Yes."

His look startled Phoebe. She wondered if Carole had made a mistake wanting a particular *type* of man too much and trying too hard for Peas. But she had to phone Sara now.

*   *   *

She covered the riots for three days. Gunfire. Sirens. Youths threw rocks at police and police fired back. They fired thousands of rounds without knowing what to shoot at. Their service revolvers weren't designed for sustained firing and overheated. Few people were hit or killed. It wasn't like war. What it was, and what it meant, was the question. For Phoebe it was a terrific story—the first black riot of its sort, a citywide riot with sideshows in Brooklyn and the Bronx.

Race riots before had been white racists going into black parts of Chicago or Detroit with baseball bats to pound blacks who'd come up to take factory jobs during World Wars I and II—white trash hysteria. But the Harlem riot was a new play in the game, as Houston put it when he came up, or a new stage in the revolutionary struggle, as Peabody put it later when he himself became a revolutionary leader.

LBJ had Houston fly up to watch policy and find out if, as J. Edgar Hoover had said, communist agitators were behind it all.

"No," Houston told Phoebe, "but I'm going to finesse that question awhile. Hoover's obsessed—he hates blacks—but he's an institution and he has LBJ's ear." Houston *did* provide language from his school fund of lofty statements to describe the problem: "This was the cry of unaccommodated man," his report said, and "what discord follows."

What was the real reason for the riots? They had been so spontaneous, unfocused, no one could say, but newspeople thought it had something to do with all the noise coming out of Washington about civil rights bills, poverty programs, and new chances, and very little opportunity showing up on the street. Even at the beginning the Job Corps wasn't working. Trainees were using their pocket money for good times, learning nothing, and the government's only interest was to keep reports of program mismanagement and wasted money out of the papers.

Phoebe had such a great time on the riot she burst into tears talking with Sara one last time. *Do I want to go to Washington?* But she thought it would be better for her to go and was determined to get Houston.

Late in July government movers came up to her apartment, boxed everything, and hauled it away, and she flew down and moved into Houston's Du Pont Circle place. Her boxes arrived and formed a stack in the middle of the living room.

The riot delayed the wedding a week or so, but they got new invitations out and had it on August 7 at Washington National Ca-

thedral, then flew off to Maine, to an island owned by the family of
Houston's cousin and chum from Exeter and Justice, Cobbs Moulton.

It was a lovely, rustic place, one of those turn-of-the-century
high-ceilinged cabins with varnished wooden floors and gallery, huge
stone fireplace, and Adirondack stick furniture. They got blitzed on
gin and tonic and made love on the rug by the fire.

"Unfortunately," as Houston noted in his journal, "the sneak
attack at Tonkin Gulf has galvanized the government. Walter Jenkins
himself called. I cannot shirk . . . Phoebe cried more than I wished
but eventually was a good sport about it. . . . Appropriately, a military aircraft, a Coast Guard seaplane, came to pick us up to 'answer
the call to colors. . . .' "

In fact, Phoebe Bishop Bridles was shocked and stunned. She
feared she'd be shafted again. Back in D.C., she didn't have much to
do and became depressed. The cardboard boxes sat unopened in the
center of the charmless apartment.

"Houston, this is impossible. It's—institutional!"

Houston knew from the example of the President what it took to
be master of a situation. He had watched how the great man, facing
a problem, worked secretly and presented a grand solution—with a
flourish! In his heart of hearts, which he did not have to examine
because he was a Presidential aide, he thought LBJ was a bit over-
done, but what he did worked. Houston spent a couple of days in
preparation, then took Phoebe to dinner in Georgetown. It was charming. They walked along the rustic canal with its misty evocations of
yesteryear, ignoring the bats fluttering and feeding on bugs in the
muggy night air. They explored side streets of quaint little flat fronts
that had been slave houses but now showed pretty mullioned windows and print curtains.

Houston paused before one that had no curtains. It was gray-
painted brick with white trim. "Do you like this?"

"It's charming, isn't it?" she answered.

"It's ours."

Government movers came and took his things and her cardboard
boxes to the new place after she had it painted. The boxes sat on the
varnished floor. She was still depressed. It wasn't that she didn't like
the house.

Perhaps it was something about their sex. It wasn't like that summer two years ago. Perhaps he was tired from long hours in the White House basement and that made him seem perfunctory, but she was puzzled that he did things she didn't particularly like—a way of caressing her breasts, holding her derrière—that he hadn't done in lovemaking before. Why now? And he smelled different.

The *Life* bureau had plenty of work for her, but she couldn't get her heart into it. This was dangerous. It was risky enough being the new person, having everyone scrutinizing you. Simply not to care about the work was self-destructive. This was an election year. They had lots to do slicing and serving Barry Goldwater, William Miller, Lyndon Johnson, Hubert Humphrey, and their families. Look at their faces in the photos, the teeth and hungry smiles.

Goldwater was honest, personable, and backward. Black comedian Dick Gregory said Goldwater was so square he thought Johnson was an Ivy Leaguer. Johnson had a progressive message while personally being a liar and crook. Two of his cronies, Billy Sol Estes and Bobby Baker, had been arrested for fraud and influence peddling, respectively. Some Republicans called Johnson a murderer, floating the story that he had caused the death of two private pilots by demanding they fly to his place in bad weather and, after they crashed, trying to erase the records connecting him to the aircraft.

All the editors read the report avidly but none in the mainstream press wanted to print it because it had happened while Johnson was Vice President and it didn't somehow sit right to discuss the character of a President.

The campaign was busy with nasty stories. When LBJ's aide Walter Jenkins was arrested in a Washington men's room for making an immodest proposal, the Republicans found out this had happened before and Johnson had suppressed the story. Johnson distanced himself from Jenkins, and a Kennedy aide said Johnson had worked Jenkins to nervous exhaustion, as he did many aides. He may have used the previous arrest to whip Jenkins on.

"All right, all right," Sara said on the phone when Phoebe called because she missed New York. "Johnson is not an attractive person. But Goldwater? *Feh!*"

"What's he *doing* to you?" Phoebe asked Houston.

"I work long hours," Houston said. "It's important!"

Houston had told her he perceived his role as helping the President reach "people of our sort," but Phoebe didn't believe that. It was irrational, but she feared something dark and unstated—that under the surface Johnson was teaching Houston to be as ugly and power hungry as himself. It was as if Houston were having an affair behind her back. But they'd just married. He'd courted her brilliantly. But why was he so inattentive now, when she wanted attention more?

She was alone in a strange place and didn't feel right. She was more conscious of smells, more emotional, easily upset. At work and on the street she saw on posters the huge face of Johnson in the elections. It was the last chance people had not to elect him, if that choice was a chance. Goldwater? *Feh!* But she didn't even care much about that. Her face felt puffy and she had peculiar bruises under her eyes. Her breasts hurt. She told Houston, "I'm pregnant."

The Game

Mark Randolph didn't know Phoebe Bishop was pregnant. He didn't even know she was married. He was on a weather deck aft talking with the S-3 Air officer when a helicopter brought the mail. It hovered off the fantail, mailbag swinging on a cable. This Air officer was a young captain who'd already flown helicopters with SHUFLY, the Marine advisor squadron in Vietnam. He had a crew cut and a nonchalant manner. "Yeah, they shoot at you. So what?" he said, "You fly ARVN on strikes and move villages. People, livestock, everything." The sea was gray, with low swells.

"A little on the cyclic," the Air captain kibitzed the unhearing pilot who was eye level with him—they stood on an upper deck projection like a balcony. The helicopter hovering right there was a dark blue Navy Sikorsky HUS, the standard Navy and Marine helicopter, high and narrow, wheels on struts angling out, radial engine in a round nose below, pilots in a cabin several feet above. Mark looked through the Plexiglas at their faces, helmets, and orange suits. Mist came off the rotor tips as the HUS swung, nose down, and the bag swayed over the marker and dropped on. The machine lifted and banked like a bird, the ship's diverging speed making it seem to leap sideways at great speed over the blue waves.

They were heading back to the States after many adventures. French officers had hosted them at a six-hour lunch on Martinique. *Memorable!* Wines, fish, meats, cheeses, songs, droll stories illustrated with the usual hand and arm signals. Their mess beat the wardroom's Philippine steward's revenge—chopped whole chicken, bones and all. He ran into a French major later; they drank rum, and the major told him about fighting in the maquis, with the Free French, and in *Indochine*. *"Formis,"* he said; the communists fought like ants. And the usual swinish carousing in San Juan, except on the terrace of a good hotel Mark met a pretty girl from New York; she was short and had long black hair, lovely clear skin, and huge black eyes turned up at the outside corners. Her name was Natasha.

"I am studying music," she told him. She had a slight accent and gave equal stress to all syllables, apparently to enunciate clearly. "My father is a musician as well."

"I'm here to raise hell," Mark said.

"I would like to also," she said gravely, and then smiled at him, her eyes like black sapphires.

She was traveling with another girl. No chance in her room. They groped and necked. His ship left at dawn. "You must call me in New York," she said.

"Mr. Randolph," the runner said, "mail call." The trooper, green soft utilities, thin, eighteen, threw a salute and handed over the thick vellum envelope, which Mark glanced at enough to recognize Phoebe's round East Coast girls' school hand. Oh, shit! He knew what it must be. His guts dropped in the real person inside the starched shipboard khakis. He put the envelope down his stiff-front shirt ("Nothing in the pockets, Marine") and turned back to the captain, his face impassive.

"You should try it, Mark. Swing with the Wing. Best chance to get to Vietnam."

"This is true," Mark said. The few Marine infantry officers going there as ground advisors were outstanding and had more on the ball than he. The Marine Corps *Gazette*, the officers' magazine, showed the only combat medals being awarded now were going to airdales. He reached in his sock for a Lucky and the captain showed him how to light it in the wind, using two matches.

"Flight line trick. You could do it, Mark. You're running an H and S company now that's as disorganized as *anything* the Wing's got. You can handle S-2 and perimeter security. Swing with the Wing."

Mark walked to the wardroom, swaying and climbing like a deck ape. He looked pretty salty after these couple of years at sea and in the field, his brass and bars worn and polished. A competent officer. Thorough. Capable of running hundreds of men through live fire. Staunch. He got coffee in a heavy crock cup, lit up, faced the envelope bravely, and opened it. Reading it, of course, was like having a tooth drilled.

Mr. and Mrs. Avery L. Bishop announced the marriage of their daughter, Phoebe, to Houston F. Bridles in August at the National Cathedral. Goddammit. Oh, hell. Dammit! Perennially out of reach. How had she looked at the altar in Washington? He remembered how she'd looked in the church in Oklahoma, when her eyes had said yes. He had never told her how he treasured that—just gave her that dumb phone call from the slop chute bar. He sure as shit couldn't tell her now. One night in Oklahoma. He'd just been a hamburger on the road between her feasts with Houston. Unattainable.

"At Home," the thick engraved card said, and gave an address on Du Pont Circle in Washington.

Over the next few days he did his duties, checking paperwork, yelling and facing down people, shooting the shit, letting his mind handle the minutiae of military life, such as what the successive model numbers meant on flamethrower gun assemblies. Being fundamentally stupid, he knew how to repack a seabag but not his own life. He saw the battalion adjutant on deck.

"When's the next Wing quota for WesPac?"

"November."

"You think I can work it to Da Nang?"

"Probably."

"Put me on it."

Phoebe felt terrible and couldn't do anything about it. By October she didn't want to work and took leave. She went to New York for a few days to say good-bye to Carole.

The apartment door and windows were open, fall sunlight sparkling on dust over cardboard boxes of books and records Peabody had stacked on the windowsill. Phoebe hugged Carole. She burst into tears. Boxes. "Things aren't right with us, either," she told Carole.

Peabody turned away from the window. "We'll get out of here. This city's ruined. They killed Malcolm X. They caused the riots. We'll go west."

"We'll leave the bad here, baby," Carole said. On the street

Phoebe saw their car, Peabody's mother's old green Ford, loaded with
books and records.

At breakfast she told Houston, "I'm worried about Carole. Peas
is wrapped up in himself. It's the way he treats her that bothers me,
Houston. Do *you* think it's right for a husband to neglect a wife?
To forget little attentions? When she *needs* those things? Simply *responding* to—"

"At Exeter he thought he was too smart to play the game."

"Houston, I need you to be with me. I'm all nerves. Can't you
come home at least before ten?"

"Later, yes," Houston said. "But this is a crisis! National. World.
It's big."

It was a typical conversation for WASPs of their sort, neither
answering the other's questions, both making only oblique points.
Houston saw Phoebe was a bit upset, yes, but she was getting tiresome about it. After all, she'd joined the team! He couldn't understand what she was about now.

Houston could make great plays in the realm he knew, but anything he didn't, he finessed in a way that made many call him cavalier
or heartless. He'd used great passion and skill to win her but supposed
she should be like a ball in the net now, bobbling with him as he ran.

"I'm not the *only* one working late!" he said. Dammit, she was
crying again. He *wanted* to leave. He stepped out of the charming little
house and into the sedan the pool driver waited in. It was a *crisis!* She
didn't understand how delicate these operations were, Johnson trying
to make progress overseas while running for election with the Republicans and some of his own side picking at him. Like Phoebe crying on
the faded brick steps. He waved at her in hypocritical affection. Picking at him, not understanding. "Go straight to the West Wing," he
told the driver. Too easily upset.

Their chances for peace were too easily upset. Last spring they'd
tried an initiative to North Vietnam through a Canadian diplomat,
Blair Seaborn, on the International Control Commission. Seaborn
met with Ho Chi Minh. Until then the Americans couldn't make it
clear they wanted peace because both sides' foreign offices were putting out so much war propaganda. Houston had heard that *no* American Foreign Service officer wanted to go "out front" on peace with the
communists anyway, because of what the McCarthy purges had done

ten years earlier to other bright FSOs who'd recommended dealing pragmatically with Mao.

But the North Vietnamese threw out Seaborn's peace offers. The Americans had no bargaining position, they said; the North Vietnamese were beating the South Viet army in the field and expected to get what they wanted anyway.

Then over the summer Johnson himself asked U Thant, Secretary General of the UN, to carry an offer to meet Ho Chi Minh. Ho agreed, and U Thant offered to arrange conference facilities in Rangoon. But U Thant's message that a meeting was possible got lost between him, UN Ambassador Adlai Stevenson, and Secretary of State Dean Rusk, and another chance slipped away. Rusk was said to have killed the idea because the conference wouldn't have included the South Vietnamese, but Pa Bridles said Stevenson probably messed it up. "That's the trouble with liberals," he grunted. "No point of view." The Agency blamed Stevenson for blocking air strikes at the Bay of Pigs, making a bad operation a disaster.

In other negotiations LBJ had been trying to interest Ho in his idea to develop the Mekong Delta the way Roosevelt had the Tennessee Valley in the New Deal—a massive construction project to create jobs and provide power. Some in Washington had snickered at this. LBJ had offered money, supplies, equipment—but Ho wasn't interested. Pa had commented, "LBJ has to understand that Ho Chi Minh doesn't want to be a judge in West Texas."

Houston had been buttonholed often recently by Pa. "We know who killed Gerrity," he muttered. "We have a report." Pa and others from the Agency were sending volumes of CIA reports to show they had a handle on the situation, trying to reinforce their eroding position with paper, because everyone knew the military was carrying the action now, the Air Force and Navy bombing up north, the Army and Marines reinforcing their advisor units into combat support units.

It would have to be a bigger war, but they couldn't tell the public that because of the elections. Surely the Republicans would make the war worse if they got power—this was why LBJ ran the scare TV ad showing a kid picking a flower while a nuke mushroomed behind her. The Republicans had created the McCarthy hysteria and played to race hatred now. At the convention, just finished, in San Francisco, they'd let actors—*actors!*—such as George Murphy and that has-been Ronald Reagan shout down a civilized Easterner, Nelson Rockefeller. Right-wing crazies.

And they attacked LBJ for his use of Air Force jets to fly to political rallies. They tried to connect Johnson to the arrest of poor, broken-down Walter Jenkins. We have to win at all costs, Houston thought. For the country, yes. But most important for his career. He couldn't be connected with failure.

Phoebe couldn't understand.

Black cars were lined up at the West Wing entrance.

"Stop here." Down the stairs, stepping lightly, feet remembering the fields, jigging and cutting, into the nether air of cigarette smoke, dust, paper, autumnal darkness, the sweet-sour scent of Terry.

"Mr. Bridles?" She waited in his office door, her brown eyes molten, spots of red on her cheeks. "Nothing scheduled for an hour. The President is out for the morning. . . ."

As if he were hooking in the Bowl to see the football hanging in front of him, he envisioned her bush suspended in midair, waiting to be grabbed. If only Phoebe could be such a *team player!* Terry closed the door and locked it. "Fuck me, Houston. Eat me. Fuck me now."

"Terrific!" Houston's journal read. "LBJ won a true landslide . . . place in history assured . . . vindication from sniping." He was jubilant about his own triumphs, too. Stock high, child on way—First cabin! It was all coming out as he wished. With a child Phoebe would stop working and take on the kinds of social tasks that suited the wife of a presidential aide. He knew they could put on a better show than his competitors. *Take pipe!* He had a list of people they should entertain.

He'd encouraged her to monitor the unpacking—most of their things were still in those cardboard boxes—and had urged her to pick out their own china. "I don't know about these things—something that suits what I'm doing. But do it quickly!"

This hurt Phoebe as much as anything so far. Tasks she wanted to share, such as making a household, he was shoving at her. She felt trapped. And getting bigger every day. She chose the first set of porcelain she saw. Both of them didn't like it.

She threw up. Houston was crowing about the landslide and calling people all over the country. He told her they'd get The Point— that prime lot of shore property in Beverly—when she had the baby.

He wanted to go to The Game this year as a way of "showing his stuff" to his Yale friends and the Harvards, and wanted to take along some Texas couple who, he said, were perfectly nice and had the ear of the President.

"They're people we should know, Phoebe."

They flew up in an Air Force VIP jet. The other couple, in their thirties, had something to do with a construction company. Phoebe didn't care. They were terribly nice and curious about "how you did things up here." Phoebe thought the low pressure in the jet's cabin did something to her. She felt like she had a bubble inside.

They went to Soldiers Field. Houston was exuberant, calling to people he knew all over, introducing the guests and Phoebe. The Charles and the brick buildings were edged in Northern light. They sat among tan coats and striped scarves and watched a typical game, with missed passes, blocked punts, fizzled runs and fumbles. Yale men waved handkerchiefs to Beethoven's song.

They went to the Gas House and crowded against the bar with others in crimson and blue. Phoebe said nothing. "Loosen up," Houston hissed to her. She shot him an acetylene look.

They went to the Bridles' Beacon Hill flat, where the staff had laid a good smoky fire and served cocktails. She was standing by the window when she felt the bubble burst inside her and her legs went wet. She went into her room, reached in and—yes, blood. Tampax?

Houston came in.

"What's up?"

"I don't know."

"You're not very lively company. I want them to have a good time."

"Fuck you, Houston. I'm not a member of the Administration."

He looked at her quizzically and walked out.

She began changing clothes. Something wasn't right—the blood wasn't right. Some filmy tissue had come down with it. She didn't know what was going on in her own body. She found the traveling bottle of Johnny Walker Black Label and took a slug from the bottle. That wasn't bad. A terrible pain gripped her and she fell, screaming, holding herself.

Houston ran in. "What is it?" His coat was open. She saw his bright yellow braces under his impeccably cut flannel jacket.

She looked down. A tiny form. She threw back her head and laughed. Phoebe rarely laughed much but now she shrieked with laughter.

"What is it?" Houston said.

"What do you think! Jesus!"

In the bloody matter was a little identifiable shape.

"Are you sure? Isn't there something we can do?"

She shrieked with laughter. "*Jesus Christ, Houston! What do you mean 'do'? Who in hell do you think you are?*"

Later that night he brought her flowers and English mysteries at the hospital. He thought Phoebe looked very tired and wrung out. But the doctor said she'd be fine. First-rate staff!

She looked at him as she had once looked at a horse she'd wanted to kill after it threw her twice. His small nose and golden hair, his perfect bright-boy face. As unconcerned as a goddam beast.

"You mustn't stay, Houston. I know this other business is terribly important."

"Well—"

"No, just go. Good-bye."

Phoebe went straight from the hospital in Boston to Aunt Amanda's on Park Avenue. Amanda was used to having her stalk in from disasters with Houston. She felt weak. She called her father, a lawyer, who recommended another lawyer. That lawyer said the grounds would be extreme cruelty and Houston would be a fool to contest it. The property would not be difficult to separate. The lawyer sent appropriate letters four days after The Game. Houston called immediately. That is, the phone rang at Amanda's and an operator said, "Mrs. Bridles, the White House calling, just a moment please," and Houston's slightly high, well-composed voice came on.

"Phoebe," he began reasonably.

"I won't speak with you, Houston. I want to visit the house when you are out of it. I'll get a court order if necessary."

"You don't need a court order any more than you needed to sneak out of the hospital. For God's sake—"

"*I don't want to hear whatever you're going to say!*" she screamed, and then, more calmly: "I simply want to remove a few articles from the house. Fortunately so much is boxed up!" She laughed.

"Phoebe, you're acting like a fool."

"Yes, yes, yes—I know your boss will want to read in the papers about his high aide having a cease-and-desist order after Walter Jenkins and Bobby Baker and Billy Sol Estes had *their* day in public. He loves publicity like that."

Houston said something rude and she hung up.

*   *   *

It was December. She went to D.C. She had the cab wait as she went into the exquisite little house in Georgetown. It looked so nice. The cardboard boxes picked up the subtle blue gray from the walls and lent a warm cinnamon tone to the newly varnished bare floors. Houston wasn't there. She sent the cab away.

She listed and marked the few things she wanted to keep of the silver and crystal. Houston had left a note in a vellum envelope on the hall table. It was an appeal to reason. She tore it in half. Mail addressed to both of them sat in a several-days jumble on the closet floor under the mail slot. Houston, of course, would have ignored it. He had had his secretary and, briefly, her handling his mail, shirts, and shoes. She looked at the envelopes. He would tell his friends, she would tell hers. One of the envelopes was from First Lieutenant M. H. Randolph with a dozen letters and numbers afterward, postmarked FPO NY NY. He said he was on his way back from maneuvers in Spain and added he was about to be transferred to the Far East and would head up the coast saying farewells. Were the newlyweds receiving visitors?

She wanted to see him. She wrote a quick note that she had had a mishap, Houston was tied up on White House business, and she would be in New York and would love company. She felt like death— it was the death of her old life anyway—and she wanted to say hello and good-bye to somebody.

Mark Randolph didn't know what Phoebe's story was, but he arrived in New York up for a good time, euphoric anyway from a good time in Spain, and delighted he could see Phoebe. Alone! What was up? Was there hope for love? Would he get laid?

The impromptu maneuvers had been in Andalusia, where it was sunny and warm—some deal to show the Russians we could deploy fast. Then his ship got liberty in La Coruña, the Galician city on the Atlantic coast. He'd run into a Spaniard who'd lived in New York for years and years. The bars had that Atlantic feel—dark wood, people in wool. Cobblestone quays by the gray-green water. Now he was in Manhattan shlepping his fifty-pound ValPak across town, biceps aching and swelling, gawking with *On the Town* eyes at holiday windows, the richly dressed women leaving scents in the air, the—when the fuck did *this* start?—numbers of young men with long hair dressing down in GI field jackets. He wore wrinkled flannels, an old tweed jacket, and a beret he'd bought there perched flat on top of his head, but his white sidewall haircut, if not the gray bag with its USMC stencils, told who he was.

She'd said she'd had some kind of mishap. With Houston?

Several Marines had been killed in a helicopter crash and a truck accident on the deployment. They were in another regiment. Phoebe's mishap—whatever it was—was unknown and distant in that way.

Park Avenue. Marquees. Here. He couldn't help glancing at the doorman's uniform and appearance. Tsk-tsk; awful. A small fussy lobby. He knew those—like the Drake Apartments in Chicago. Little walnut elevator. Three doors. One opened. Dark hair, high forehead—Phoebe? He kept his face impassive, though he was shocked. She looked terrible. He forced a grin and hugged her. *"Good to see you!"*

Phoebe saw his face over her shoulder in the girandole: *He knows I look like death.* "Good to see you, too, Mark. Come in."

For him it was a treat to be able to sit in this New York room with its escritoire, bow-back love seat, and striped chairs, and have coffee in a porcelain cup and smoke a cigarette. Take your fuckin' pack off. And try to be cool. He liked little comforts. And to see Phoebe—this terrific girl he'd thought about so long. He looked at her, smiled, tried not to look as if he were studying her. Well, it was like other things when you got analytical—she looked different.

"You've been through a rough time."

"I have, but tell me what you've been doing. You look terrific. So tan." So simple and healthy, she thought. So full of simple doglike affection. "I've been inside for *days*. Let's go for a walk."

They walked to the East River and stood by an iron rail watching a tug dragging a barge upstream. The cold wind scratched white scallops in the iron-gray water. Phoebe told Mark about her miscarriage.

"It was perfectly *dreadful*, Mark—I have never been so desperately—"

He was rapt by her Eastern pronunciation and the sound of her voice, not getting the meaning of the miscarriage. It was like a ruptured cartridge, right? She didn't look too lively. But he had this shining vision of her, remembering how she'd been, and hoping for her. He understood easily why Houston had acted that way—he knew him too and knew how he operated. Hadn't Phoebe understood that? Because he'd grown up emotionally damaged in some ways, and used to cruelty and shock, he couldn't trace out exactly how she'd suffered, what she'd hoped for and she'd seen destroyed, but right here he could see her bravery and anguish. She burst into tears. He held her. She had a shawl around her head like a Mediterranean woman and her polo coat collar up.

"Let's get out of the wind."

They went to P. J. Clarke's and ordered cognac. She looked more composed. They didn't talk about her crying. He felt good enough tasting the coppery bite of the brandy, sniffing its sharp fumes, dragging on a cigarette and looking at her against the dark wood—her stately face; high forehead; intelligent, direct eyes; straight nose; her lovely lips that he'd tasted; her arms and breasts that he knew, under the soft tan cloth. She looked so right. He said, "I have to tell you I love you."

"No."

"Yeah. Affirmative. I mean, if I buy it over there, you have to know. What if you never knew? That someone loves you?"

She held his hands. "Oh, Mark, I guess in a way I love you. You're—loyal."

He kissed her mouth. Her lips were soft and warm. Should I? He tried a little tongue.

"No, it's impossible," she said. "You're nice. Too nice, really, for me to be any— It's too complicated. Anyway, you're going off— It's stupid." She began crying.

"I know why I'm going. It's not stupid."

"I mean if *we* got involved."

"Yeah," he said.

"You can leave your things here," she said at the apartment. "We can provide a bed, too. Aunt Amanda said she'd be delighted to help a serviceman." Amanda had told her about helping the Boys during the War.

"Thanks. That's really nice."

"You should look around. Enjoy New York. I'm sorry I'm so tired."

Mark left his ValPak and wandered off. From a bar off Fifth he called Natasha, the girl he'd met in San Juan.

"Oh, hello—I hoped you would call."

She'd been in class—cello, composition, theory—all day. They went to the Russian Tea Room, which he'd never heard of. It was warm and quiet.

They had vodka and sweet tea and leaned back in the booth,

looking around the room and at each other. She looked so unusual but pretty. Her face made him feel good—her full cheeks and bright dark eyes. Her black shiny hair was piled high on her head, but even the top of that was below the level of his shoulder. She had small soft hands and thin forearms covered with fine dark hair but full round breasts under her blouse; he supposed she was a bit thick in the middle. Will we? She told him about her classes. He smiled. She smiled. They talked about San Juan and Spain and she said something about her father's visits to Barcelona from France that suggested how recently he'd come over. He was fascinated by her accent and the look of her lips and kissed her.

She said, "I will take you to my place."

At her apartment in Hell's Kitchen she fixed them an omelet and later they went to bed. It wasn't a very tidy place but Mark wasn't very neat either and was used to field conditions. They screwed all night long. It was like wind sprints. He was dehydrated.

"You thought I was a virgin?"

"Oh, no."

"I like it very much. And I don't masturbate. You are really in shape. I have never known a Marine before. Anything you want to do we can try."

She came from a quiet musical family. Yale produced talented musicians, but he knew nothing about that scene either. She had something beyond, another dimension she felt and worked in that he didn't quite understand. And was it necessary? In time of war, with all the other stuff going on? He'd longed for Phoebe. Even though they were a couple of social classes apart he felt he could understand her because they were WASPs, and everything with Phoebe was right out in view like her forehead and the time she'd stepped out and sung.

The next day they went to the Village and visited coffeehouses and a bookstore. While Natasha was in class he called Phoebe. "Found a place to stay. How are you?"

He was in yet another good dark wood bar in midtown. The smoke of the Scotch threaded through his head and her clear alto voice hit him again. "It really was so nice to see you, Mark. I really feel so much better just seeing a familiar face. I *am* sorry I was such a dud."

His heart leaped. Was she . . . ? Was this . . . ? "Great seeing you," he managed.

"Will you be coming by?"

"Of course. I want to see you."

"I want to see *you*. And for you to call me," she said, which puzzled the shit out of him.

Natasha came into the bar, her dark eyes like burning incense, and his pecker lurched: He was yanked this way, toward this woman he didn't know but obviously had made friends with, and that, toward the woman he'd admired and dreamed of.

"It is cold," Natasha said, looking up at him. She wore a floppy black velvet cap and her eyes shone. "Have I kept you waiting long?" This woman so unlike anyone he'd known, but so comfortable. Smoking in bed with her, ash tray by her copy of *La Chute*. Phoebe's clear Eastern voice in his ear. His past hopes to have her, to live her way.

"Of course I'll call," he said to Phoebe, skating. "Gotta go now. Can I bring you anything?"

He and Natasha went to a foreign film—nothing too taxing for him, *les parapluies de Cherbourg*—then a coffeehouse. Espresso! Just like the Med! The dark thick coffee of Natasha; the light, aromatic coffee in a porcelain cup of Phoebe.

In bed he told her about things he'd never have told Phoebe: about Mediterranean prostitutes, how they rouged their cheeks and rimmed their eyes black and used spots of blue paint. "And they shave their"—he cast about for a more sauve word than *pussies*—"uh, snatches." He told her about all his sexual weaknesses and follies and exaggerated a few. He wanted to warn her off.

This stuff didn't faze her. "I've heard of that," she said, and "Oh, yes! I know of that." She had never known anyone like him, she said. A meatball? A Marine officer? The bits she hummed and other parts of her world lay beyond his understanding; at best, like a well-trained dog, he tried to be appealing company and maybe that was what she meant. At the Museum of Modern Art they saw *Guernica*, the gray chill light of the air-raid siren, the faces like voice balloons, the terrified horse. He was going to an air war.

He saw Phoebe for a drink at the King Cole Bar. She cried. They vowed to write. He left her at Aunt Amanda's and carried his ValPak down Park. He spent the night with Natasha and in the morning they vowed to write. Natasha cried. He lugged his ValPak away and began his long journey.

Po—Peeling Off

Carole Peabody called Phoebe after Christmas. She was agitated. "Peas left me."

"When?"

"Just—he—it was when we reached Oklahoma. Last fall—"

"That bastard! Why didn't you *call* me?"

"I didn't want to believe it. I thought it was just a thing—a mood—and we'd get back together—"

"What happened?"

"I don't *know!*" she cried. "Look, I'm in a bad way! He *didn't* come back, even for the holidays. I need— Can you come out here, Phoebe?"

"I can't, Carole. I don't feel so hot myself and I'm just going back to work at *Life* here. I can't leave now. Didn't you get my card?"

"Yes! Oh, I'm sorry, Phoebe." Both of them cried and commiserated and agreed Carole should come back to see Phoebe.

She arrived the next day, her face puffy from grief. They sat by the window above the passé holiday decorations and talked and cried. Across Park someone slipped on ice.

Carole burst into tears. "I thought everything would be better. We were going to have a nice drive. I'd imagined our trip west in Ford cinematography, the blue George Washington Bridge receding. Farms and silos. 'Clichés!' he said, and got nastier. Sulky. When we reached Oklahoma City he asked my parents, 'Have you assigned us separate rooms this time, too?' He was impossible talking to Etta about the Harlem riots. He said, 'I want to apologize to you as a whitey—' *I* was going around making excuses for him. 'He's really brilliant,' I said. 'It's his way of telling the truth.' Then one morning I knew something was *really* bad."

"What happened?"

"He was up when I woke. It was one of those chilly, ugly days. He was lying on his back looking at the ceiling. He said, 'I'm unhappy.'

"I didn't want to try to reason with him before I brushed my teeth, but when I came out he was packing and talking to himself. 'Money,' he kept saying, and 'It doesn't matter!' and then he went off on this tirade about freedom. 'Have you noticed,' he said, 'that we always cause our worst disasters by wanting what we shouldn't have?'

"Daddy and Bucky were at the door and I was going, 'Shhh! Shhh!' and telling them we were all right, and then Peas pushed right past them carrying his suitcase. You know what his good-bye was? 'I'll separate your LPs in California.' "

She began crying again. Phoebe cried. What a sorrowful afternoon that was. What *shits* men can be, they agreed: Either they want to kill strangers or be killed themselves or they want to hurt women.

"You're better off without him," Phoebe said. "Look what you wanted—some little preppy church mouse who'd take you to faculty parties and give you sherry and learned remarks. You're free!"

"That's just it! I'm not! Look at this!" She scrabbled in her bag and came up with a letter. "Look at this! *He's* free! He says *he's* free! He said he was free first! That puts it on me, the son of a bitch!"

Phoebe unfolded the letter. It was fine linen stationery, a spiffy A.C.L. PEABODY in red. He did have expensive tastes, as much as he'd been deprived. Phoebe read. "What crap!" she commented, taking on the tough-critic shtick she admired in Sara. "Preachy—'I am paid to teach young students, not ourselves.' Oh, brother. 'I am taking Aspects of the Revolutionary Novel. London, Sinclair, et al. Substantive, seminal, innovative—a good deal more authentic (in Trilling's sense), I must say, than those film courses you are so proud of.'

"More authentic!" Phoebe said. "If that isn't a short-dick remark!"

"Read on," Carole said.

Phoebe read:

Today I walked out in the sunlight and stood in Sproul Plaza, surrounded by mild greens (sixty-eight this afternoon) and sanguine brick. This warm pavement is as important as Smolny Institute's frost-silvered masonry. This is where the Free Speech Movement stood up to police only weeks ago. Students distribute literature now, police circle them. I am taking my place in a drama that (I am ashamed to say) I have hitherto only witnessed. You were not interested in it. Your parents are the racist exploiters who killed Kennedy. No matter. Forget about Freedom Riders, forget about the power of industrialists in the vicious East. I am from Berkeley now: *ICH BIN EIN BERKELEYNER!* The ruthless oppression endured by the "nigger," the Indians, and the Cubans is now trampling students here! I join their struggle! I spare you the hardship.

Phoebe folded the letter. "What hardship?"

"That's just it! I didn't *care!* I wanted to be with him."

"Jesus, were you ever wrong."

Carole burst into tears again. "I've always been wrong! Clumsy! Graceless! Doomed!"

She wasn't ready to stay by herself at Beekman Place, so Phoebe put her in the side room.

Carole stayed a few days, going to foreign films and museums she hadn't had time to visit before. One afternoon when they met for a drink she looked less depressed. "Remember the dexies we took before exams?"

"Yes."

"I have speed."

"I've never tried it. What does it do to you?"

"It helps you lose weight and gives you lots of energy," she said. "I was using it off and on here before."

They were in a dark booth, so no one saw Phoebe tap a few shakes of powder into her glass of beer.

"I don't feel anything."

"You won't. It just gives you a boost."

Hours later they were at their fourth bar, not drinking much but talking so fast they were very thirsty. When they went back to Aunt Amanda's they talked for another hour. Carole's face was flushed and her eyes were bright. They saw it all so clearly—how men used them for whatever they wanted and that they simply had to be strong enough to make it their own way. Even being hurt didn't matter if you kept going, the way Houston said you played the game. And Phoebe could understand—it was so *clear*—how she'd gone along with getting pregnant and Mark Randolph, that amiable fool, didn't question going to war. The drug took layers of film from her nerves, eyes, and mind, and Carole was laughing for the first time in months.

Carole left the next weekend for Oklahoma City, came back with more clothes and money, and took an apartment downtown. She flew out to the Coast a week later for a few days, didn't tell Peabody she was there, and scouted Berkeley. She said she wanted to see it on her own. It was easy to hop a 707 and change your mood.

Phoebe examined proof sheets—glossy eight-by-tens of whole rolls of film showing all the shots without magnification—and prints and blowups of Vietnamese villages, old women, chickens, helicopters, and copy about American know-how moving primitive villagers away from communist threat—"And land they have farmed for centuries," Sara commented—to defended areas. Photos of bitty ARVN soldiers wearing big American helmets, holding oversize M-1 rifles.

"The monks aren't burning themselves now," Sara said. "But I don't think anything's changed much since Halberstam started writing about it." She said George Hunt, the managing editor, had been a Marine in World War II and wanted coverage in the World War II positive way.

"I want to cover it," Phoebe said.

"Who wouldn't?" Sara said. "I wouldn't bet on a woman getting there."

Houston Bridles put down the glossy pages of the *Yale Alumni Magazine* and shook his head. This on top of everything else. Phoebe having a miscarriage. Pa sniffing, probably gloating, that he didn't have to sign over that parcel of land, the Point. The humiliation of Phoebe walking out *and* the shit she'd spewed at him two days ago.

He had stood on the brick sidewalk in Georgetown in front of their house. Their charming house he'd *bought* for her! He'd nipped over when he found out she was making another trip down to get her things. Her eyes had burned. She'd yelled, "Oh, you *bastard!* I was *sooooo wrong* when I thought you had half a heart! You're a killer! You tried to *kill* me, you—"

She was screaming in the cold canal fog, which deadened her sound like pistol shots in damp wool, others on the sidewalk in that decorous and dignified neighborhood glancing and hurrying on. That had been a mistake, going over—but he'd had to make a move because LBJ knew his marriage was breaking up.

The President had snoops everywhere, looking at his own staff. He encouraged snoops "to keep on top a things," as he put it. The President himself had made a jocular cutting remark: "You better get that woman back under your roof if you want to show any couples around."

He had to be on top of it! He was running ragged now, trying to stay in the game. He'd had a joyless Christmas working; "the lights burn late at the White House." And now at this glum end of the year he was partaking of the New England sacrament of Taking Stock.

Was Presidential appointee. Had ear of President. Three trips, no less, to LBJ Ranch. Special missions, too. *Had* won back Phoebe.

Debits: Lost her, too.

On the other hand, in the women category, *had* deftly solved the problem of Terry—her demands, her innocent (or not so innocent) attempts to console him. He'd called Boots Martin at Treasury, told him all she could do, including eighty-five words per minute, and had her sent over there in an afternoon. Terry had cried pitifully and got mad at the end, but it was a promotion for her—and relief for him. She reminded him of too much.

Much on the plus side was on the pages in his hand, the class notes in the *Yale Alumni Magazine:*

Anyone who's seen pictures of President Johnson signing those thousands of bills must have seen HOUSTON BRIDLES behind the desk handing up pens and paper (and presumably Light and Truth!). He went from the Yale backfield to the Oval Office background. "I had no choice!" Houston reports. "Goss Brewster and Harry Cain were taking over Wall Street and someone had to go to D.C. to balance the Harvard weenies!" Houston was a key aide to Treasury Secretary Henry Fowler before being tapped. . . .

He'd called Cottie Billings, the class secretary, and gone over the information with him to make sure he got the right tone of jolliness

and sobriety. After all, they had an impressive class, even outside of
Keys and Bones. In the same notes were announcements that two men
his age had formed their own companies and he knew several who'd
passed into seven figures, by no means largely through inheritance.
One merited an article in *Forbes*. So he wasn't the only hot one.

But it was the entry farther down that disturbed him:

From Boston the sad news that First Lieutenant USMC
Tewkes Beveridge, one of Yale's great oarsmen, was badly
wounded while serving as a ground advisor to a Vietnamese
unit. Tewkes lost his arm and is recovering at home. For
God, Country, and Yale! Others there or en route are Jim
Dawes, flying Navy carrier jets, Pete Newbold, with the
Army JAG in Saigon, and Mark Randolph, with a Marine
helicopter squadron in Da Nang. Show them the winning
spirit, guys!

Poor Tewkes. He was one of the truly outstanding, a thoroughly fine
man. Family absolute tops. Unquestionably. Houston remembered
seeing him on campus once or twice in dark shirt and pants for Naval
ROTC. Hadn't been aware he'd gone in the Marines. Navy, one
could understand. To be disfigured and crippled in what Pa said
would be a horseshit war was a bad business—well, it went beyond
sacrifice to thankless waste, didn't it? Tewkes had had such a wonderful world waiting after Yale. Sculling meets. Someone like Mark
Randolph was another story. A meatball; it was a war for meatballs.

Imagining what the Rands was doing made him smile. Bennett
girls? Beer? It was a relief from sadness to patronize someone else.

In a way he'd lost a limb, too. Phoebe, you know. He'd heard it
was that way—you still felt it, thought your foot or hand was
itching—and even now, weeks later, he thought of things to show her,
tell her, anecdotes from the White House he thought she'd— But
dammit, she hadn't *liked* it at all down here.

What had he done but make her cry?

For all his certainties, he was baffled. For all his quick grasp of
facts, he was confused—but determined he must not confuse himself
further by brooding now. The loss of someone he'd loved and fought
for might have crippled another man. Knowing he had pushed and
shoved his love and killed it might have driven another man to de-

spair. But Houston was held up now by the armor of tradition, family heritage, and duty. Other Bridleses had got through nasty spots and, frankly, Phoebe had chosen not to—

He withdrew into self-assurance.

She'd let him down. He'd put the word out about her in press circles, too. He'd seen how LBJ called editors. Dammit, it was a war. The Gulf of Tonkin. Confronting a shadowy enemy.

One, at least, of the shadowy enemy was known to the American government. His name was on the list Pa Bridles had waved before Houston after Ted Gerrity was killed. "We have a list," he'd told Houston. "We know who planted the bomb."

The Agency's paper said Nguyen Thuc Thanh had been born in Hue in 1928, height 162 cm, weight 63 kg. It noted the notched scar on his left ear from big, slow shrapnel (U.S. Mark II grenade, action against French at Tourane, now Da Nang, 1953). The National Police file told how Thanh had coordinated cells for this *dich vanh*— direct action—blowing Vietnamese and American VIPs to rice-size matter and leveling the market gate.

A VC defector to the *chieu hoi* (open arms) repatriation program had told how Thanh worked with Main Force staffs and the political interzone committee on special tasks. But the National Police and the Agency didn't know where he was now. The *mat tran* had many *can bo* the police couldn't track, but the South Vietnamese officials knew who the men were. In many cases they'd fought alongside them in the Viet Minh against the French years earlier. But they didn't know where Thanh was now.

In fact, Major Thanh was wearing the uniform of an ARVN captain—tailored green fatigues, three round brass collar pips, stiff cap—and driving an ARVN jeep he didn't plan to blow up. He drove to the gate on the Air Force side of Da Nang airfield and exchanged salutes with the *Quan Canh*, or MP, as he drove through and turned left on the long perimeter road, shopping for targets. A few brown VNAF H-34s and silver T-37s—forget them. *Duoc!* An inviting array of U.S. Air Force targets—little C-123s, fat-bellied C-130s in camouflage, and F-100s, F-105s, and other types the imperialist swine used to bomb the Democratic Republic. A few ARVN soldiers watched him driving. He stopped at the south end of the runway and without hesitating walked to a puppet bunker, stooped in, and barked at the frightened puppet soldier to *didi* his ass out of the way. The country kid cringed against sandbags. Thanh scanned the interior. Blocky gray steel American .30-caliber M1919A4 Browning machine gun, olive drab rectangular can of link belt ammunition next to it. He crouched and looked along the barrel. It was set to fire across the front to block an attack upslope from the Tourane River. "Is this on its correct mission?" he yelled at the scared puppet. "Where are the connecting fires! Point to your connecting guns!" The soldier pointed. Thanh snorted angrily, making the soldier relieved to see him go. *Duoc! Ja phai*—now we know the bunkers to knock out if we attack this sector.

He stepped back to the jeep. The puppets were lax. No sergeant to notice him, the privates too uninformed. As he got into the jeep he sighted up the length of Da Nang airfield. All those *mỹ* Air Force aircraft parked in a row presenting a gunner's dream, an enfilade target, one silhouetted by the next, all the way up, like dominoes. *Ja phai!*

He drove around over sandy open ground to the Army and Marine side, a couple of dozen green and brown helicopters and fixed wing, not very far apart, but scattered over a macadam hardstand by a forties stucco building. A few sleepy puppets on the road and long-nose pigs on the flight line, carrying tools, pulling carts. It was after the rainy season, when the air was clean and cool.

The pig *mỹ* used the cool thick air to put heavier bomb loads on their cruel airplanes.

The interzone committee had directed cadres from neighboring areas to assist their comrades in Da Nang to develop plans to attack long-nose airplanes and stop the bombing.

UNITE PATRIOTS FROM ALL COMMITTEES TO DRIVE OUT
THE FOREIGN AGGRESSOR!

Thanh had come down from Gia Binh. His cells would provide support for the attacks. Surrounding districts always provided volunteers for dozens of tasks when the Liberation Army gathered to attack.

Look at this. What had been bean fields and a pine grove, he remembered from 1947, when he had visited Tourane in phase two of the Great Patriotic Struggle, was now concertina, steel containers, sandbags, a small compound for *mỹ* Special Forces and Army pilots, a Marine motor pool of green trucks. He turned west toward the green hills and drove over scrubby ground past a battery of white Hawk missiles the long-noses had just sent in, fearing the brave pilots of the Democratic Republic.

He stopped in the dirt near tan stucco buildings with tile roofs and watched men in green cotton and flight suits walking among the buildings. This is where the Marine helicopter pigs stayed.

Nearby was a thicket of palm bushes and a cluster of tin and straw shacks. He stepped down the shaded path. People watching out uncovered windows, staying back. Of course. They feared puppet officers. He tapped at the flimsy door of a shack of flattened tin cans. A woman answered. His manner changed, he assumed modesty. They sat on plain chairs in the dirt-floored room. She was a tired city woman recently enrolled in the struggle's *Hoi Phu Nu Giai Phong*, the women's group. Her man had been drafted into the puppet army. Thanh had been directed to her by the local committee coordinating reconnaissance here. *"Ja Phai,"* she said, "all soldier families here, all not content. We have not been paid. The officers pocket the money in the fighting among colonels . . ." It was the power struggles between Ky, Thi, Minh, and Thieu. *"An cap,"* she said. The long-noses gave the puppets the money for their payrolls, but puppet officers took the money to finance their bids in the power struggles or to get rich in the chaos; they were bad puppets, as the joke said. "Many here will join the *mat tran*," she said. "Do you know what the long-nose pig Marines call this *ap*?" She waved her fingers at the cluster of shacks. "Dog-patch."

Thanh's skin darkened and his nostrils flared. Dogpatch! Stepping back to the jeep, he glanced over at the French colonial stuccos, *ouai, vrai française*, with their broken tile floors and glassed windows. He had been in there many times, with many covers; most important, *memorable* that wonderful night of the long-nose *phaps'* Christmas Eve, their sun and star birth feast, when he had gone in with Viet Minh special assault teams and slit the throats of drunken Legionnaires only a dozen years ago.

A couple of officers came out of the BOQ. He had been in there—tile-floored rooms, steel bunks, wooden armoires, and the usual air crew weapons hung from the walls, revolvers and gray stubby M-3 submachine guns with wire stocks. One officer he knew, long time here, the brawny one with a moustache named Black. Cap-

tain of rifle troops, now intelligence, S-2. The other was young and he
didn't recognize him—cut-off khaki shorts, T-shirt, cap with a silver
bar, boots, knife and automatic pistol on a belt. The lieutenant saluted
and ran off, getting exercise. Taped name tags swung on his chest.
Pilots carried revolvers. Ground administrative officers didn't tape
their tags. This one might be rifle troops, too. More long-nose pigs.
He watched the long-nose pig trot. Strong, but look at him sweat! He
must weigh eighty-one kilos! Swine's turd! *Duoc!* He hated long noses!
Red skin, foul odor, sweating always, cruel ugly faces, oyster eyes.
Kill them all!

DOC LAP! LIBERATE OUR HOMELAND FROM LONG-NOSE TYRANTS
AND THEIR PUPPETS!

Mark Randolph didn't know that the man in ARVN captain's
uniform was a spy or that Major Thanh termed him a long-nose pig,
since he didn't know about Vietnamese racism, but he was as happy
as a pig in shit. He was in Asia on the edge of a war. So far he'd seen
beautiful Vietnamese women in their *ao dais*, the flowing slit-sided
dresses over tight pants; the short, wiry men in shorts and straw hats;
the tin shacks and stucco buildings with French tiles—smelled the
Asian smells of sour rice, cooking oil, human feces used as fertilizer in
the paddies. He'd seen old women in black pajamas carrying the stuff
out in honey buckets swaying on shoulder poles. It was as exotic as
the "Terry and the Pirates" comic strips of his childhood. He was
staffing a war of intrigue against communists, the boogiemen of his
school days in the fifties.

Randolph ran between the BOQ and messhall and cut behind the
thick-walled stucco-and-brick headquarters building where Buck
Black had his S-2 office. All the intelligence papers were in strong-
boxes and steel file cabinets that had cylindrical gray incendiary grenades wired to their tops. All Captain Black, or Mark, or the clerk had
to do if the VC took the compound was to pull the pins on the way
out; the grenades' magnesium compound would burn down through
the steel and set off the papers inside.

"Yeah, next we'll booby-trap the door," Buck Black had said.
"Ain't this a bitch? They can shoot their way in any time." Buck had
opened a box full of submachine guns, thousands of dollars' worth of
short gray-and-black weapons, dull finished, some with narrow green

web slings. "Here—you want an M-Three? Got no Thompsons, those are worth their weight in gold. You ever try a Swedish K? MAT-Forty-nine? French tried to copy the Thompson in nine millimeter. It's blowback. Too light." He jerked his head up, his big moustached face turning to indicate what any qualified small-arms user knew about rifling causing the muzzle to climb right.

"We were trying submachine guns in the LZs during SHUFLY." This was the name of the old Marine aviation operation in Vietnam, a few aviators testing helicopter techniques under fire for the first time since Korea, when the Marines had pioneered the use of helicopters as combat vehicles. "The copilots wanted to fire submachine guns going into LZs up in the bush," Black said. "Put a few bursts in the grass around the edge if they got fire coming in. You know, the book says hit it with fixed wing, but sometimes we didn't know the LZ was going to be hot, and what the fuck, a Marine wants to shoot. But one hop—let's see—yeah, last year, the pilot got hit going in and here's the copilot trying to stow his SMG and take control. So we went to a door gunner and I got the submachine guns. You should have seen it *then*, though. Those guys were salty. We had just a few birds down at Soc Trang and Quang Ngai. AvGas in drums."

Captain Black was salty, too—his uniform today was utility trousers and old-style high shoes called boondockers, trousers flapping free, a T-shirt, and a Naval Aviator's black baseball cap embroidered in gold with his name, rank, and MUV for Marine Unit, Vietnam, the current name given this ad hoc bunch of pilots, drivers, and now infantry that were supposed to be advisors but had become combat support for the ARVN. You got salty fast here, Buck said. To be salty—experienced, seasoned, handling the job without looking as if you were on a parade deck—was at the heart of being a Marine. Like that film they showed of the field at Tarawa, palm trees shot away to ragged poles, sand kicked up by Japanese machine gun fire, and a Marine sergeant walking across, being shot at, giving the finger to the Japanese.

Randolph ran along a dirt road past a couple of other small American compounds—secret, surrounded by concertina, green ship containers filmed with dust—and on to the flight line. Most of the Marine aircraft were gone, except an HUS, the tall, stilt-wheeled standard Marine helicopter, being worked on by two mechs. The round clamshell nose covers were swung open to the sides, exposing its big radial engine under the high windshield of small panels of Plexiglas. The green-painted sides of the helicopter were punched with several bullet holes and black smoke stains streaked back from the engine. It had taken fire and had some cylinders knocked out but had chugged on back.

The Navy name for the machine, HUS, meant Helicopter, Utility, Sikorsky. It had been designed in the fifties for antisubmarine duty, dropping sonar buoys and dragging sensors, but it handled many jobs well. Randolph had seen the one dropping mail in the Caribbean. The Army had a few of the same aircraft, which it called H-34, but it was giving its H-34s to the Vietnamese on the other side of the field while it got new jet-powered UHIE's, or Hueys, made by Bell.

On the other side of the field a low silver Air Force B-57 took off, roaring, its underside and stubby wings thick with bombs and fuel tanks. It used the whole long runway getting up. It would bomb North Vietnam.

He ran back along another lane behind a truck park by a rudimentary wire barrier that marked off the American compound more than it protected it. Anytime the VC wanted to hit this place hard, they could get in. The ARVN who were supposed to protect it weren't even around every day as troops mutinied and generals staged *putsches* to grab power.

"So *we'll* fight—what the fuck," Captain Black had said. "That's why I asked for another Oh-Three-Oh-Two." He meant Randolph, another infantry officer, referring to his Military Occupational Specialty number. The Marines, at times a mystic group, used the magic number three for its most important specialty. As he ran, Mark checked the wire and soil surface down in the southwest corner of the compound. This was the route they'd take if the barracks were hit and the aviation officers, enlisted mechanics, avionics techs, cooks, and drivers were changed by the magic of fire back to what they'd been as new Marines—riflemen. No breaks in the wire. No digging. No footprints.

He saw the same ARVN captain watching from a patch of palm bushes over by the shacks, but thought nothing of it, and after washing off his sweat in the BOQ, using a green plastic bowl, the ubiquitous plastic basin of Asia, he put on khakis and headed for the

Officers' Club to have a drink with Captain Black and work on him. Randolph had something he wanted to get from Black that was more important than an M-3 submachine gun.

The O Club looked like a bar you'd see in a movie about war in Asia. French tile deck, bamboo bar and tables, men in khaki flight suits or green cotton utilities or khakis, like Mark, drinking under overhead fans. At the door a bamboo planter holding coils of web belts, .45s in black leather holsters, aviators' .38s in brown leather shoulder holsters. A sign on the bulkhead said, SOUTHEAST ASIA BUSH PILOTS AND MERCENARIES ASSOCIATION.

There was Buck Black at the bar. Mark got to the point right away. "Buck, I gotta fly some."

Captain Black looked at him, leaning on the bar, thick necked, calm, his eyes amused, his mouth lifting a little under his moustache. "You just got here."

"Yes sir, but it's an air war. I'm an Oh-Three. I gotta get blooded."

"Oh, you'll get blooded," Buck laughed. "We might *all* get blooded, har-har-har."

"I've had command—"

"Watch Charlie put a couple of assault teams through here the way they did with the Legion, there'll be enough fuckin' heads to make a parapet, har-har."

He *was* salty, Mark observed. Great sense of humor for gore.

"Yeah, listen, Mark. I'll get you blooded. Don't worry. You know what I did in Korea when I took guys out on ambush. Mortar men—guys like that. We'd cut down the Chinese and I'd have the troops walk up and look at the dead and see what their rounds did. Takes the impersonality out of it, har-har! You want to fly, I can get you up there—you gotta see ground fire anyway for the reports. But that's the *fun* part. You'll take collateral duties first. Shit details. You're the man in the barrel. You just got here. You take payroll?"

"Yes sir."

"Laundry?"

"Yes sir."

"Chaplain?"

"I'm an atheist."

"Okay, crypto."

Next to them at the bar was a Navy AD Skyraider pilot who'd made a strafing run up north with rockets and cannon. His aircraft was a 1945 vintage prop bomber. Talking to him were a couple of Marine observation pilots who flew small Cessnas called LOEs. When the VC began shooting at them they'd responded first by firing their .38s out the windows, later by bombing them. They'd put an M-26 frag grenade in a bar glass. The rim of the glass held the lever down. They'd pull the pin and drop the loaded glass into the bush where the shots came from. The glass would shatter and the grenade would blow. But soon the club ran out of glasses, so that tactic stopped.

Over in the twilight on the other side of the wire Major Thanh, in ARVN captain's uniform, took a last look at the Marine compound as Marines in faded uniforms walked back to their squad bays at the end of the day. He stepped down the path to his jeep, ready to report on places he thought the Liberation Forces should attack to destroy the long-nose pigs and their aircraft.

Just as you could jump on a 707 to change your mood, you could go into a store and change who you were. Carole and Phoebe consoled themselves with what they could buy or handle in the square mile from Aunt Amanda's apartment to Maison Glass to Bergdorf's to Altman's and back up to Bloomingdale's, with stops at Saks, Cartier's, Tiffany's, Steuben, and Georg Jensen, looking for that flashing winter sunlight on expensive store windows like Bedouin seeking the shine of water.

Phoebe spent well beyond her *Life*-salary, which at best was never as high as what apprentices made in television, but she had trust funds her parents had set up and the Duikermann fund, which had devolved on her at twenty-three. Carole had an arrangement in which her father transferred funds to the Bank of New York.

Silk scarves, plastic belts, short skirts, high stockings, silver pins, gold buttons, Italian bags, silk underwear. Sometimes they wore no underwear, showing nipples under silk blouses. They stood in aisles, in viewing rooms, before mirrors. "Is that you?"

"It should be."

"How much?"

"Does it matter?"

"You'll need a new coat with that."

"I don't see why not."

"That looks *sooooo* good on you, Carole. Now that you're skinny."

"I owe it all to my little white friends." She made her silly face and Phoebe laughed. It was fun again.

They'd go to stores speeding and try on things, like them, buy them. It didn't hurt. They could afford it. They wanted to change who they were because they were failures. Yes! Failures! It was their duty to marry, assume smiles, and grow lovely white families like pots of gardenias. Instead of the embarrassing messes they'd been slapped with.

Phoebe could still hardly examine what Houston had done to her six weeks earlier. She called it the Dark Star. The miscarriage, her tiny dead fetus, her marriage crashing, her hopes collapsing as she realized this hotshot was a self-centered prick—all depressed her the way a dark star pulled everything including light into itself. Thinking about it pulled her in to nothing, outside to inside, with no eyes or ears, like a navel—but her feelings blossomed and she brightened with a little dash of speed powder in a martini. They found it made them feel better to move in glossy midtown channels to the St. Regis, Côte Basque, or Sherry dressed in simple, expensive clothes, wearing jewelry. In the Maisonette with Mr. K's delicious piano or the Palm Court they'd talk a mile a minute about why happiness had eluded them and whose fault it was.

"It wasn't just that Peas was a prick, Carole. You wanted him too much."

"He humiliated me, Phoebe. I didn't provoke that. He had a political obsession."

"A money obsession."

Carole watched a waiter in a short jacket carrying a tray around a palm bush, brushing spiky fronds with his shoulder. "I thought it was *my* fault. For who I was."

"He *wants* you to think that."

"But why? I thought we were special. I *treasured* him."

"I keep being reminded of how *un*special we are," Phoebe said. "Remember White Angels? And sherry after chapel? I was brought up to believe I was better than town girls, cheap prick teases, but I wish I'd known how to work that way. Let's face it—we always learn by watching someone cheap. They're like lion tamers—they know how to move the beast."

They were in the big, busy room with the high ceiling and columns that went up a story above the tables of people talking and waving for service. Phoebe listened to the buzz, feeling dissociated impulses, so she shrank to a dot like an eye and then swelled to the size of the room and sought herself inside like what she had lost. This is

not useful, she thought, this speed and Sybaritism. I have to work and
produce. But I lost something, she remembered, and the Dark Star
pulled her in again, and she found herself crying. "Why did I let
Houston do that to me? Twice! I was cheap! I threw myself away!"

Carole looked at her, blinking, and suddenly waved, jerking her
hand. "No! No, no. I've got it. You weren't cheap, Phoebe. I know!"

"What?"

"You're a jockfucker."

Phoebe stared.

"No, listen, Phoebe—when someone is in the center of the action, then you can't help yourself. Your vein starts throbbing. You
said it yourself. Remember senior year when we were chasing parties?
You wanted to be where it was. Even if you didn't *screw* people, you
wanted to feel the center. You— Don't you see?"

"No, I don't, thank you very much." Phoebe didn't like that at all.

Carole said, "Well, I remember what Reverend Bray said before
the wedding: 'Let your heart be a cornucopia and be brave and giving
and *for*giving.' God, was he full of shit! When I went out to Berkeley
I saw the crummy stucco Peas gave as an address and I felt just
terrible he had to live there—I should have given him *money* when he
walked out so he'd *live* better—and I knocked on the door and waited,
and didn't hear anything. I wanted to help him even then. What a fool
I've been!"

The people at the next table got up. Over at the entrance two
college men in ties stood with their dates, who had on nice dark
dresses. Phoebe and Carole looked at them. The young women looked
so hopeful. The young men looked so sure of themselves.

"Bastards," Carole said.

President Johnson announced the Great Society in his State of
the Union address. Phoebe knew it was coming since Houston had
mentioned it those last days in the bunker of their marriage; it was to
be a grand American-style upgrading of the War on Poverty with
chrome and fins, without the social vision of the New Deal. Aid for
schools, community grants, billions for highways. Houston had con-
tributed language. *Life* got floods of government photos on all the
whirlwind would bring—gold-tinted satellites, astronauts in silver,
blacks in class, and LBJ beaming by the red-white-and-blue flag, head
tilted. Some of the group shots showed Houston, too.

*   *   *

A Radcliffe woman a year younger than Phoebe said she'd tried the most interesting tablet in a psych class up there. "Take this." It was called lysergic acid. The best—Sandoz LSD, perfectly legal; Cary Grant and dozens of other insiders had tried it. They talked all night long while Phoebe watched a plaster wall dissemble into melting wax and running water. She felt fine the next day. She and the stoplights were friends, like trees in a forest.

One of the photographers gave her pot and she liked that, too. Carole said she'd found a source of pot and hash among her friends at the New School. They were barely a month into 1965 when they were flitting like big-eyed songbirds all over the inside of this circus tent called the Great Society, listening to *Fantasticks* and Beatles and Herman's Hermits. Phoebe told Carole about the Mao and Che Guevera books Mark Randolph had read. She looked through Mao herself, and Carole produced a small green book, the *I Ching*. They smoked pot and threw coins and asked questions.

Carole said, "Okay, we had lousy marriages, you had a miscarriage—what's the next phase in our lives?"

The answer was Number 23, Po—Peeling Off.

As they studied it, they knew it was true.

"*Look* at this!" Carole said. "Yes! Po! Goddam, yes, look! You have the mountain, Kên on top of K'un, the woman!"

"That's par for the course," Phoebe said.

"And it says, 'The weak alter the strong; there is no goal which can be sought with advantage.' "

"After what happened to us?"

"Look at that candle. It's dancing."

It was the time of Po. They were peeling off from agony to depression to schizophrenic detachment to manic running. So much was going on in such a short time. No one saw it all. Phoebe and Carole thought Houston and Peabody and Randolph had got where they wanted to be, while they, the women, had been abused, tortured, and discarded. Bombs were falling and people shooting regardless of the landslide vote for no war. What was agreed on, hoped for, promised, comprehensible blew every which way. Po.

Adams Peabody was falling apart, even as he wrote his exultant letter to Carole from Berkeley. Like many moving from a temperate climate to California, he became depressed once the novelty wore off. Bright sunlight irritated him. It illuminated too starkly what he had done: marrying Carole for her money, taking her money and still doing nothing to aid civil rights after all his high-minded talk about freedom. She'd wanted to give him more than money, herself. He'd ditched her messily. He couldn't stop remembering how she'd looked—shocked, as if he'd shot her, the blood boiling to her face as she cried and asked, "Why? Why? Why?"

He was frightened of himself. He had the power to hurt. He felt guilty about that. He had freedom and he was caged, trapped in a noisy aviary of guilt, birds of self-rebuke screeching and beating their wings around his head. This is what was going on inside his mind, hyperbolic images shorting out, while outside he looked like the old Peabody, in California style—thin, sharp nosed, his dark hair grown longer and a bit ratty. He now wore gold-rimmed Trotsky glasses. He'd seen others wearing them on Telegraph Avenue. And he wore a T-shirt and Levi's jacket, the trappings and suits of Berkeley, while within he writhed in woe. He had trouble concentrating on the work he had to do; he thought not coherently but in those vivid images that exploded from his fears and worries. His verbal reasoning, formerly his strongest power, was *kaput*.

He began staying in bed later and later, missing classes. He had a cheap flat in a stucco off the Avenue. Someone knocked on his door several mornings—was it Kathy? She was a girl in his department doing her dissertation on political themes in Edgar Rice Burroughs. He didn't answer. He thought about suicide. What an irony—to get through Yale, the leading suicide college in America, if not the world, where students had to get reservations and take turns to dive off the library tower—to go from that big league of Wertherian bathos to an obscure fizz-out in *Berkeley!*

He dragged himself from bed to Student Health and got counseling. The counselor, a full-bearded man named Weiss, listened to his worries, suggested changes in his diet, and talked him out of despair. "It's never too late," Weiss said. "If you want to get into the civil rights struggle or any struggle, do it. What about Free Speech? What about Cuba? Just do it."

"What about grades?" Peabody asked.

"What are other students doing?" Weiss answered. "Haven't you always been unhappy because you felt you had to work while others did these group activities? What's your life been? Work, work, work. Has it been good? You've done it for yourself, you think, but has it made you happy? No. What have you done for other people? You talk about others who have more recognition or more fun. Why not do it yourself? Do what you must do."

Peabody went outside into the sunlight. On Sproul Plaza he talked with students leafleting against the bombing of North Vietnam and the so-called advisors in the South. That night he went out with them and put up posters. He had Mark Randolph's address in Vietnam; he wrote him, telling him to keep his big Midwestern nose out of other people's politics. He put peace leaflets in the envelope going overseas.

After exams he took part in his first teach-in, giving the facts to small groups around the campus. He dressed carefully for his first class in a new style—old cowboy boots, faded Levi's, plain shirt, bandana. "Come over and listen, friends."

Younger students sat and took pamphlets, turned their clean, tanned western faces up to him.

"The government that killed Kennedy says we're sending advisors to Vietnam to defend freedom. Here's what we've done to that country since nineteen forty-five. . . ."

When he made a funny point he laughed in the loud hyuk-hyuk-hyuk his old friends would have recognized. "We don't have allies over there," he said. "We're not rescuing France from the Nazis. The Vietnamese want to be *free* of colonial domination. The only people we're helping are stooges of our military industrial complex!"

First Lieutenant Randolph did the shit details and got to fly—at first in the back seat of an LOE spotter plane, the high-winged Cessna. It had tandem seats and was almost as narrow as the width of his shoulders. It had big windows all around. Like many military things, it looked shiny and freshly painted on the outside but was worn inside, the tubular frame scratched, the brown cloth seat pads faded, stained, and torn. Flying at night over the hills toward Laos, they saw red glows where woodsmen made charcoal and VC camped. The LOE drew fire—white-orange muzzle flashes and orange tracer streaks. The communists used orange tracer, the Americans red.

He flew as an observer on routine resupplies and air strikes in HUS helicopters. On resupply one or two birds carried cargo into dusty strips the French had built in little towns of stucco and tin on the rice paddy flats along the coast or inland where farmers raised beans. They ranged from Quang Ngai and Qui Nhon in the south up through Elephant Pass north to Gia Binh, Hue, and Quang Tri near the DMZ. On strikes they carried ARVN troops into landing zones to surprise the enemy.

Military aviation was as old as aviation itself, and the morning routine before a strike could have come from fifty years and two or three wars earlier—aviators eating puffy eyed in the mess hall, no one talking, boarding trucks to ride in the dark to the flight line, ungainly wheeled aircraft silhouetted in the dim light as crewmen checked the hundreds of parts; the sweet smell of AvGas, engines coughing to start.

Mark was learning that this was a war of primitive appearances and sophisticated realities. The Americans and South Vietnamese presumably held Da Nang, but around Christmas they'd lost two Marines there—mechanics—believed snatched. Buck Black told Mark he assumed the VC had sent spies into all American compounds and had *binh vanh* turncoat informants in most South Vietnamese units. Sometimes the ARVN or VNAF tipped off the VC before the Marines flew ARVN troops out on a strike, so all that noise and gasoline went for nothing. To keep secrecy, American ground advisors planned strikes with Marine air but didn't tell the Vietnamese where they'd land. Then, when the strike *did* get to the LZ, sometimes the ARVN troops refused to get out of the helicopters or, once out, fired back at the Americans.

If the VC *were* caught when the helicopters went into the LZ, they fired on the helicopters. The first time Mark experienced this he saw the crew chief at the big open door talk into the wire mike on his flight helmet, then swing his black M-60 machine gun on its pintle and fire down. Meanwhile little points of light appeared in the thin magnesium bulkhead, holes the size of a pencil. Mark went into hot LZs by Quang Ngai and on the Batangan Peninsula and got out to listen to what the VC were shooting—the *whap! knock!* and *pop-pop-pop-pop!* of different weapons. Down on the ground he moved and observed cautiously, by the numbers—but running back to the bird and lifting out, seeing the receding ground kick into gray puffs, he felt gushes of sentiment. Goddam! This is living! He'd light a cigarette and suck in smoke, exhilarated watching the shooting.

A pilot named Page, a part-Indian from Arizona, got a primitive kill in an LZ. A local guerrilla, a *du kich*, ran out of the high grass and fired an old Sudayev burp gun, not directly at Page's sitting helicopter, but a few feet in front of its nose; obviously he'd been told to lead the aircraft. Page took off and flew at the man. The helicopter wheel hit him in the chest and killed him.

This story caused much head-shaking and laughter in the club. Behind the appearance was the sophisticated reality. Mark and Buck knew that better automatic weapons were showing up with better instructors. They knew from Naval Intelligence that cases of Soviet RPD light machine guns were coming in by boat and that the VC would soon learn to use them against aircraft. The VMO pilots in the spotter planes knew from flying up to Laos that the Ho Chi Minh Trail—which may at one time have been a tree-shaded path for *du kich* and *bo doi*, regular soldiers, wheeling loaded bicycles—now was wide enough to take trucks. The People's Army of the Democratic Republic—what the Americans called the North Vietnamese Army, or NVA—sent down antiaircraft crews with twin and quad machine guns on wheeled mounts called ZPU Twos and Fours.

DEFEAT THE AGGRESSOR IN THE AIR AND ON THE GROUND! read the mimeographed sheets Major Thanh gave people in the hamlets. He showed them clips from *Nhan Dan*, the party paper, with pictures of crashed American jets up north and the new Soviet long-barreled guns firing high explosive that had blown the jets out of the sky. Thanh gave his talks in the center of each hamlet around Gia Binh. Head back, arms straight at his sides, he shouted slogans. "Use all means! Listen, comrades, we won at Ba Gia!" He told them how a *binh van* ARVN soldier had warned that Marines would fly into Ba Gia. "Our Liberation Army mortar gunners were ready! They fired high explosive into the landing zone as the helicopters sat down, killing many puppet soldiers and long-nose pigs and destroying two helicopters! Two others flew away smoking and are ruined!

"We have long-nose prisoners!" he shouted, and told about the two unlucky Marine mechanics who'd been snatched in Da Nang and now looked out through the bars of bamboo cages as they were taken from hamlet to hamlet for propaganda.

For propaganda also, just after the lunar new year, Tet, Thanh had organized cells to support a Liberation Army raid on a district police station. His *du kich* local volunteers secured roads and cut phone lines. The Liberation Army light machine gun and rifle teams shot up the stucco building, causing the police, the white mice, to cower inside, and assault teams ran in throwing grenades and firing submachine guns, killing all the police, capturing puppet files, and delivering to Thanh those most valuable weapons of this war, two typewriters and a mimeograph machine.

DISSEMINATE NEWS OF THE STRUGGLE TO ALL! Thanh thought in his sloganeering way. All his thought and passion went into The Struggle, *dau tranh*. Words were as important as bullets. Mimeographs would produce newsletters to motivate people to fight—and, propitiously, the newsletters could say our patriots had killed puppet police at Tet, the time of new beginnings.

Ground fire was getting more intense. Mark's and Buck's reports went to Wing headquarters at Iwakuni, CINCPAC(Air), and the Navy's bureaus. Directives came down. Paper up, paper down.

To suppress ground fire the Army was arming helicopters with rockets and machine guns. (The Army did this because, despite what it said on paper, the Air Force wasn't providing enough close air support to the Army; air politics was yet another thing MACV never could get worked out.)

The Marines had used helicopters first in combat, as troop carriers in Korea, and didn't want the Army to be one up, so at Da Nang they experimented with arming the slow, durable piston-engine HUS Sikorskys. They called them "Stinger Bees"; they had racks on the sides for machine guns and rockets, and one carried a 20-millimeter automatic cannon under the belly between the wheels. The aircraft weren't stable gun platforms. None crashed, but they didn't hit anything, either. Later they got armed Hueys like the Army.

Already reports from hot LZs suggested that both high-silhouette Sikorskys and squatty jet-powered Hueys took fire better than anyone had expected a year before, and the old Sikorskys took fire better than the Hueys. A bullet in a jet engine blew it up. The VC could shoot a piston engine and knock out a cylinder but the bird could still fly, blowing oil and smoke, for several miles. On the flight line mechs mounted tetrahedral steel plates, like double chins, under the HUS's round noses to protect the engines.

"Enlist people of all ages to drive out the foreign aggressor!" Thanh said in a night class in a palm grove for volunteers who themselves would go out in *dan van*—action among the people—to bring others into the struggle.

Thanh faced the fifteen volunteers, men and women: a jeepney driver here, a boatman, a poultry-selling woman, a clerk for the puppet police. "Use each person's skill! Country women to plant trail mines! Men to spy and run! Children to drop grenades! All join the struggle!" His dark eyes flashed.

He told them the way of Mao Tse-tung, a history professor-turned-general who had mobilized country people to fight aggressors. Mao's teachings had been shaded for Vietnamese by another history professor-turned-general, Vo Nguyen Giap, the genius who had outwitted the French and destroyed them at Dien Bien Phu. The essence of the People's War was to mobilize the people—arouse passion, focus hatred, give tasks to all. "We will fight and share victory!" Thanh shouted, arms out, including them all. "Go out in *dan van!* Build our Liberation Army! Our *quan du kich* grows! Our Main Force grows! Look—as our armies approach Da Nang, the puppet soldiers flee!"

At Da Nang that February of 1965 Buck Black and Mark Randolph walked the perimeter wire and figured where to put machine guns, of which they had plenty. Engineers flown in from Okinawa built fortifications.

In Washington Houston sat in on several tense and bitchy National Security Council briefings. He had taken to wearing plain blue suits like LBJ, but with round-collar striped shirts and gold collar pins. His clean boyish features had been rasped by lack of sleep over this goddam thing that had been going on forever—the constant crisis in Vietnam—always a battalion of Marines from Okinawa floating offshore.

"But this time it's the end of the string," the Agency man said. "The VC can overrun Da Nang. The second-largest city. Our ralliers say they have five Main Force regiments—ten to fifteen thousand men—and enough mortars to pound it."

"Your ralliers haven't always been right," the Pentagon man, an

Army colonel, said. The Army didn't like the CIA having men in the bush producing field intelligence that contradicted the Army's field intelligence.

"Fat lot of good *your* clients have done," the spook said tartly. "The ARVN haven't stuck *around* long enough to count VC noses! After you people paid them millions. They're probably halfway to Australia and still running."

"Fuck you!"

Bundy looked away, nostrils narrowed.

"Are these data correct?" McNamara asked.

They talked endlessly and solved nothing. Should the garrison fight to the last man? And should they tell the press about it? Rally round the flag, Americans! But what if the press finds out about the ARVN deserting and the CG of that area, General Thi, demanding more money?

"I'm not gonna be pushed around by some ratty-ass guerrillas," Lyndon Johnson said.

In the end, because it was too complicated to untangle, Johnson said to land the floating battalion.

The day of the landing Captain Black told Randolph to take on an intelligence function in town. "Don't get snatched, har-har-har!"

Very funny, Mark thought as he drove in, using the battered International pickup with Navy markings no one else wanted. Still, he tapped his .45 magazine to make sure it was seated. Everyone knew the CIA ralliers had spotted those two snatchees in cages with the agitprop teams out in the hamlets.

He drove to a bar on Doc Lap Street. Dim inside. Clean, dusty tile. Grenade screens. Illuminated tigers on black velvet. Two girls—quieter in the daytime. Nice faces, almond eyes, *ao dais*, small breasts.

"*Chao, trung uy*, you buy me drink? Like company? Boom-boom?"

"*Chao, co, phai khong*—no. Where is everybody?"

"Duty! You no alert, *trung uy*? Land today. China Beach."

"Army?" Randolph asked cagily.

"No, *phai khong*, Marine! Like you! Don't know? Marine Nine Regiment, one battalion. Support elements, boocoo!"

Buck had wanted Mark to see who knew what. If you ever want to find out about troop movements, ask a bar girl. Some security.

He drove to China Beach. A half-dozen gray ships in the bay under Monkey Mountain, amtracs and boats chugging in, troops dropping kapok life vests and taking flowers from the girls as they crossed the beach. All the vehicles—tanks, amtracs, mighty mites, trucks, 105s—crowded the road, so he had a bitch of a time getting back.

He asked Captain Black when he could transfer to the 3rd Division. "I want to go to the field with the ground forces. I'm an infantry officer."

"Never volunteer."

Major Thanh went to the First Interzone Committee meeting to discuss the Marine landing. They met not in the bush but in a big white French stucco in Gia Binh. It was the safest central location because the puppet army and police had been meeting, too, and no one was watching the streets. *Bo doi* hiding automatic weapons sat in scooter trucks and Citroen *deux-chevaux* by the approaches.

"We outnumber the Marines still," a Liberation Army colonel said. "They have only eighteen hundred ashore."

"An attack is not authorized," the liaison from the central *mat tran* said. "We could destroy them, but their leaders would become more furious and irrational and throw in more men."

"The *mỹ* changed the nature of the struggle by landing their own rifle troops," Major Thanh said.

"*Ja Phai,*" the liaison agreed.

"In *dan van* we will say they are clearly aggressors and the puppets *viet xian*." This term for Vietnamese traitor held so much contempt that the Americans and their puppets had tried to turn it around by forming the similar-sounding name Viet Cong, Vietnamese communists, as a label to throw back.

"The *mỹ* are clumsy," the liaison officer said. "Look at all their trucks and tanks. They will make more patriots for us by blundering. We will go back a phase, gather intelligence, harass them—then a decisive blow!"

In Washington Houston sat through more meetings of the NSC, more Pentagon briefings, more tense and angry conferences in the Oval Office with Lyndon Johnson railing against "this bitch of a war that's killin' my Great Society." He didn't recognize that once he had landed the battalion of Marines he began a landslide of a sort he hadn't anticipated and couldn't stop. The Marines were there specifically to hold Da Nang airfield, but the Army wanted to land its own elite outfit from Okinawa, the 173rd Airborne Brigade, because the ARVN was pretty weak downcountry. The Marines wanted long-range artillery, so landed Force Troops. The Army wanted straight infantry and armor. The Marines opened a second airfield at Chu Lai further south. The Navy had ideas for river patrols. Hundreds of thousands of men were on the way.

LBJ became increasingly somber. He went on television many times during that March and April of 1965, his big face sad on the screen, reassuring Americans that he would control the situation and protect freedom. Houston liked LBJ but he liked him less watching him on television, his voice unnaturally high, his personality choked and corseted in by—poor man—his provincial notion of good manners. Houston saw him in private.

"You come have a drink."

They went into LBJ's side office and the President poured stiff shots of Cutty Sark in the heavy crystal glasses.

"I'd sooner take a whipping than see this bullshit go on every day," Johnson said, letting his long, loose form sag into his low leather chair. "I just got done talkin' with McNamara and Wheeler about why we can't have five hundred thousand men ashore and *Dirksen* calls up—" LBJ imitated Everett Dirksen's warm bass voice, which had got him named the Wizard of Ooze. " 'Mr. President, we have American boys there who *need* the protection of American tank units. We have Marines who need that antitank machine Allis Chalmers makes out where I call home—' And then Sandy *Sanford* calls. Shit, I thought he was in my column!" This was the Democratic congressman from Southern California. Houston had noted in his journal, "Sanford is one of those fluffy-haired Kennedy imitators. Wife an attractive blonde who looks bored. She went to Mills."

LBJ said, "Sanford wants the generals to pay more attention to some goddam aircraft rocket they make in his district. Everybody wants a goddam piece of this war and I want it fixed and gone!"

"What does SecDef say?" Houston asked.

"He says, 'We have all the conditions in place now.' " Even slumping, Johnson roused himself to imitate McNamara's crisp, antiseptic delivery. "He knows more about it than anyone. I got to ride with him. But we ain't turned it around."

They drank for a while. Houston had to say something to cheer up the President, so he delivered the obvious. "Don't worry, Mr. President—this is the strongest nation in the world. We have the most brilliant strategists and we beat the Japanese. It's inconceivable we'd lose."

"Yeah," Johnson said glumly.

In the bullpens at *Life* someone had a little Japanese TV and they watched President Johnson when he came on every few days to talk about Vietnam. Photos showed the thousands of Americans flooding into that hypnotic, violent, picturesque land. "I have to go there," Phoebe said.

In his journal Houston noted, "Landings threatening to reverse the game for LBJ. Totally unexpected!" The President had treated the war as a promising pork barrel, but now his clients and beneficiaries were turning it around on him. His friends in aerospace demanded massive bombing. Lobbyists wanted the Army to use their equipment over there—no matter that it was meant for European war. Dirksen and Halleck, the ranking right-wing Senate and House Republicans, demanded decisive action to protect our boys. The right wing kept whispering that Kennedy and the Democrats had abandoned Brigade 2506 at the Bay of Pigs.

"We can fight on two fronts or three fronts at once," LBJ said. "My ancesters settled the frontier with one hand on the plow and another on a rifle, fightin' Indians and bandits and makin' our land rich. Now, you go on over to the Hill and tell Charlie Halleck I'll cut off his balls if he don't walk with me on this."

Houston worked closely with Johnson, carrying in classified cables, seeing the man tense, angry, harried, and seeing that when Johnson tried to relax, to reassure and consolidate himself, he told stories like that about the pioneers. But that was myth. Houston knew—anyone who read knew—that we hadn't won the war like that and that pioneers hadn't plowed and fought simultaneously in one Hollywood scene. Houston knew LBJ was a great teller of tall tales, a populist who believed—had to believe—in the heroism of The People. But wasn't he grabbing at wishful fantasy now? Houston thought LBJ was nearing exhaustion. In his diary he noted: "LBJ could be dangerous. Grasp of reality tenuous." Then with his usual confidence he added, "But I can handle him."

*   *   *

Adams Peabody signed up for a minimum load for summer, taught four teach-ins, and demonstrated at the Presidio, various Navy docks, and Travis Air Force Base, from which large numbers of servicemen flew MATS to Vietnam daily—busloads of short-haired kids and mean-faced older men wearing baffling insignia. He and Kathy went to the gate carrying signs and leaflets. The police shoved them, broke their signs, and finally arrested them for disturbing the peace and unlawful assembly. Peabody laughed hugely, his hyuk-hyuk-hyuk resounding over the small-town court's parking lot. "I'm a political criminal!" he yelled at a motorist looking for a spot. "Stop the war!"

The numbers of demonstrators grew from a half dozen (passersby yelled, "Kooks!") to fifty and more, which got more respect from hecklers ("Fuckin' commies! Go back to Russia!").

Adams felt as exhilarated as he had—God, when?—when he was a boy playing sports, before he'd realized he was mother-ridden, unjustly impoverished, and out of step at prep school. Riding back with Kathy, laughing with others from history, psych, all of them carrying papers and ideas, he felt a sense of wonderful anticipation, the opposite of that guilt he had been issued with his first tweed jacket. He would educate, lead, witness. He had a great purpose and mission.

Phoebe sent requests to *Life*'s hierarchy and other journals to get an assignment in Vietnam. Everyone said no. Sara pulled her aside. "Your ex-husband has been using his office to spike your reputation. Editors say they don't pay attention to squawks from on high, but don't bet on it."

"Thank you." For years afterward Phoebe treasured the memory of how Sara had looked steering her from being betrayed. She felt the black core of hatred Houston had shoved inside her. "I'm going anyway. I'll go as a stringer. I can afford it."

She told Carole over martinis at the St. Regis. Carole went pale. "You're out of your mind!"

"No. I'm going."

"Phoebe, no! Don't be silly! You don't have a job there!"

"I don't need one! I'm free! Why can't I just do it?"

"You're being a jockfucker! You just want to get there!"

"I am not!"

Others looked their way.

"No. I'm going."

Phoebe waited for a cab under the bronze marquee. She would show Carole and everyone else. Anyone nearby on Fifty-fifth Street would have seen a pretty, full-breasted woman with dark hair and a high forehead, wearing an expensive white linen sack, pacing this way and that, sweating a little, biting her lip, but very determined to get her way.

In May on the full moon Da Nang Buddhists celebrated Buddha's 2,002nd birthday. They marched behind monks in saffron robes, people waving little flags, signs, and a big banner of pale blue, yellow, red, and white squares. They marched around the now crowded American base and chanted suggestions for them to go home.

President Johnson authorized free mail and a new GI Bill. Buck Black said, "More people we get ashore, the better chance we got of having infiltrators among us."

The Marines were talking about funny things on the wire at the new base at Chu Lai. Black men in Marine uniforms with gunnery sergeant insignia had appeared at dusk on the other side of the wire and quizzed privates. "Where are your mortars? You got recoilless rifles?"

"No accent," Buck said. "What do we got? Americans? Black radicals? Black VC? Kids the Senegalese troops left?"

Scuttlebutt had it that an Air Force C-123 crew, flying resupply in the hills, had landed at one ARVN fort, kicked out supplies, taken on Vietnamese in green uniforms waiting by the runway and flown them back to Da Nang, and *then* found out the fort had fallen the day before and that they'd flown a squad of VC back for liberty in town.

Major Thanh was summoned to a zone committee meeting and ordered to provide volunteers to hold a trail open and guide radiomen and others down from bases near Laos for *dich van*, direct action against Da Nang airfield.

A few nights later, on July 1, 1965, Mark Randolph was on the flight line talking with the sergeant of the guard. The hardstand was blacked out so all you saw were silhouettes of helicopters, rotors drooping, and sentries at sling arms. Lights shone over on the Air Force side where an all-weather, meaning night, photorecon jet was

taking off and crew worked on big multiengine aircraft. You couldn't
see the Ninth Marines troops on the perimeter. Captain Black said the
CIA field men had indications the VC were going to make a move.
They usually pulled this stuff around midnight.

Mark's Timex said midnight. He heard a couple of choked coughing shots—the peculiar sound of the M-14 rifle the Marines used.
Then a *braaaak pop-pop*. *That* was Soviet, the high cyclic rate of fire.
More *cough-cough braaaak pop-pop*. It was southeast, near the river end
of the field. Then a good-size white flash and *whoonk!*—the sound of
a mortar being fired. More rifle shots and more flashes and *whoonk!
whoonk! whoonk!*—what the fuck?

Where were they sending those mortar rounds, which were arcing way high, slower than a .45 slug and about to turn and drop,
speeding down? At us? Hear them sigh—Jesus Christ! Orange flashes
marched up the line of Air Force bombers and C-130s, then big
yellow flashes and the *Crump! Boom!* explosions—half the Air Force
flight line was on fire. People ran around over there—shadows,
silhouettes—and the Air Police and VC shot it out, little rattling M-16
rounds and blatting Soviet 7.62.

Randolph called in the report.

"Get back here. We're forming up."

In the compound every swingin' dick, pilots to cooks, was in
helmets and armed. They took defensive positions. Nothing happened.

At dawn they saw what the VC had done. One small stamped
mark in the earth downfield by scattered Red-bloc brass. No bipod
dents. The VC assault team had used the inner ring of the baseplate,
held the tube, put a dozen shells in the air, and split before they
landed. The falling shells enfiladed the line of big targets. American
troops were taught to respect the communist forces' skill with
mortars—the Chinese had been deadly in Korea—but this was a vir-
tuoso performance of freehand searching fire. Millions of dollars in
aircraft destroyed with perhaps two hundred dollars' worth of mortar
shells.

Already the American command, to put the best face on it, was
calling the VC raiders "a suicide squad."

"Some suicide," Buck Black said. "*They* got out. If they got a few
killed they still had enough to do the mission."

The Air Force had one killed, an Air Police staff sergeant who'd had the balls to charge the flashes and open fire with his .38. He'd been cut down immediately.

"It's like no one remembers a fuckin' thing about war," Black said. "You look at photos of flight lines in World War Two, they weren't bunched up like this."

Two days later—the same day Phoebe Bishop got on her Pan Am flight to Hawaii, Tokyo, and Saigon—Mark was summoned to S-3. Two lieutenant colonels he didn't recognize were there, but new units were coming in all the time. Buck Black was there, too. He gave an I-know-something leer under his walrus bristles. "You're going to the field, Mark. See? You didn't have to volunteer. We're dispersing the helicopters. MAG-16's going down to Marble Mountain. *You're* taking a party out by Gia Binh to secure an expeditionary field for MAG-86. They're coming in from—get this—Santa Ana."

One of the lieutenant colonels said in a smooth, calm voice, "My name is Charles Mason. I'm the S-Three." He was a muscular man with a gray crew cut and a bomb tattoo on his forearm. He went on, "This is Lieutenant Colonel Curtis Thomas, the CO of MABS." Thomas nodded vigorously and put out his hand. He was tall, thin, and birdy-looking; his hair went straight up like a rooster comb.

Colonel Mason said, "And you've done CP deals like this?"

"Yes sir."

Colonel Thomas said, "I was an Oh-Three before flight school. In Korea. No one's set up a field this way. We'll probably be harassed and probed. But you know how to do the whole thing? Patrols? Obstacles? Listening posts? Defensive fires?"

"Yes sir," Randolph said.

"Good. No one knows what's out there."

Doc Lap!

Major Nguyen Thuc Thanh walked the few kilometers up the path of brown dust from the market town of Gia Binh to the hamlet of Ap Nhac Muoi. His orders were to organize the hamlet to destroy the *mỹ* airfield the long-noses had just begun. The interzone committee had a number of *binh van* patriots—men in the puppet forces—telling of the Marines' plans and the movement of helicopters.

He saw the straw and tin roofs by the river. The hamlet was separated from the enemy camp site by a low (ten-meter) ridge. The path was screened by palm bushes. At gaps he saw a half dozen enemy in green working with a tractor, leveling earth, others in ones and twos digging holes and setting up squad tents. He walked without turning his head but kept his eyes moving under his straw hat in case puppets or long-noses had scouts in the bushes beside the trail.

He looked for boot prints in the brown dust, broken vegetation, for the puppet army sent out platoons to round up suspects and take away conscripts. *Though they are vicious and eat the livers of patriots, they are cowardly and move only in large units.* None today, though. Thanh saw a patriot woman he knew carrying two jugs swaying on a shoulder pole. It was Mrs. Huu, about fifty, an old woman. Ba Huu's husband raised rice; Thanh had passed him in the paddy off the curve of the river.

"*Chao, Ba Huu!*"

"*Chao, Ong Thanh. Di Gia Binh?*"

"*Ja phai! Co gi la khong do?*"

She laughed, her teeth red from betel. "We are all at work! *Ja phai*, work while we can! *Khong xian*—no traitors are about. *Duoc!* Ba Linh will surely have her baby this afternoon."

This was important. It was auspicious to begin organizing on the day of a birth. Thanh assured Ba Huu he would help. She looked beyond, making sure they were alone, and told him about the enemy.

"*Duoc!* Long-nose *mỹ* troops, including black troops. The first Americans I have seen! First a green helicopter came with white letters on the side. Long-noses got out and looked around. Then a green truck came from Elephant Pass and more long-noses took off bundles. *Duoc!* There aren't very many. Then one of them walked over here!"

"Who? What rank?"

"I don't know! He had a silver sign on his collar. And a pistol. A green cap. He smiled and laughed but he didn't fool me. I hate all long-noses! He wanted to snoop and spy!"

"Where did he snoop?"

"All around. He walked across right into our hamlet. Right into Duong's store! He bought cigarettes and looked at things, and squatted in the dust, and offered Duong a cigarette, and idled there a good hour, trying out Viet phrases. And *phap* words!"

"When was this?"

"Two days ago the first time. Yesterday again at noon."

This was troubling information. The American officer must not sniff around the hamlet, for anyone with sense can tell when a hamlet has normal routine or tension. Especially if it has traitors to warn the *mỹ* officer. Thanh was professional and dedicated, though, and had been doing this so long that each change of situation, like a throw of dice, alerted him to select correct, proven measures to master it. In this case, it was to proceed—no error! He resolved firmly to organize Ap Nhac Muoi for the struggle!

The path took him over a slight rise—again he could see the long-noses—then up the lane of reed mat and wire fencing between bean patches and pig yards. Dogs barked as he cleared the rise. He went straight to Ong Duong's store to find out about the enemy.

Ong Duong was a patriot but not a member of a *chi bo*, a unit. He had fought in the Great Patriotic Struggle and killed many *phap*. His store was on bare earth in the center of the hamlet, where paths cross in the shade of low, wide meeting palms. A simple, modest store of flattened tin cans, without garish signs. A *Vietnamese* store, Thanh thought. Like many Vietnamese, he disapproved of the Chinese merchants who dominated trade. One side of Duong's store was hinged to swing up as a dry and shady overhang, letting light in, showing shelves and tables of goods for country people: *alumettes*, red *vung bac*—"uncle money"—for the shrines, kerosene and lamps, cloth, plastic basins, canned food. The floor was packed earth and sand. Ong Duong waited in the shade watching the trails, peering through his round glasses. "*Chao*," they greeted each other. Thanh paid for cigarettes with a hundred-dong note and asked in a low voice about the Americans.

"Not here. Not today."

They squatted out front and watched the cross trail that went over the ridge to the flats the Americans occupied. "What have you seen?"

Ong Duong traced lines in the brown dust with his finger. "They came with a rifle squad but are getting a few more every day. No machine gun, no mortar. Small unit. But the tractor runs from here down to there. It will be a big camp."

"The long-noses want to put a helicopter base there," Thanh said. "Our fighters destroyed their airplanes at Da Nang. They will move some over here."

"It will ruin the hamlet. That land was supposed to be distributed. We had cutting rights there, to dig roots. Then the puppets gave it to the *mỹ*."

"The Americans will be killed," Thanh said. "They will die and their airplanes will be destroyed."

"They are very rich and strong," Duong said after a moment.

"They die like the *phap*. We have killed one already here, when the *mat tran* set the big bomb at Gia Binh market last summer. Did you know a big *mỹ* in a tan suit was blown *through* the gate's grating? His necktie was wrapped around the steel bars and bits of his bones and flesh were vomited all over the earth inside. He was not so strong then!"

They laughed about this. Duong held his glasses with one hand and his side with the other and they laughed and laughed. "Not so strong! In pieces he was not so strong!"

Thanh asked about Ba Linh and the arriving baby, offering to be of use.

"They will appreciate it," Duong said. "The Linhs need help. Linh Tu had to put in the rice seedlings alone since his son was drafted. They'd hoped the Phams, their cousins, would help, but they can't because all *their* sons are being called up for the puppet army."

"All three?" Thanh asked, hoping he had the number right.

"Yes."

"One is barely sixteen, I think."

"All," Duong said. He dropped his voice and looked this way and that. "Ranh volunteered them."

Ranh was the hamlet chief appointed by the puppet army. He had disagreed with the Phams and other families. "Ranh is a criminal and a traitor," Thanh said.

They had to keep their voices down because a friend of Ranh, Thac, lived across the square. The little hamlet, which looked so peaceful, had rivalries and hatreds like any other place.

"Where is Ranh now?"

"In Gia Binh. He spends all his time with puppets and whores."

"I say to you now that we shall change this, beginning today. But you must help your *xa*, your hamlet, and your brothers."

Duong smoked for a moment. The hot breezes from the flatlands to the river moved the fronds of the meeting palms. They heard the distant *whop-whop-whop* of a helicopter. Duong said, "I will fight again."

Women made noise up the path at Linh's. Ba Pham called others to help. Thanh glimpsed Ba Linh inside, squatting on a blanket on the packed floor, hands squeezing the roof post, her dark hair down over her shoulders.

A girl tended a fire under the black pig pot and others carried basins of hot water into the house. "*Chao, Co Pham,*" Thanh said. "Save your eyes from the smoke! I will tend this!"

"It's very kind, Ong Thanh."

"An honor for me."

He squatted by the hot glowing pine knots and charcoaled roots. Ash dusted the black pot set on bricks. Children watched Thanh, the man who did not live here but visited. As he poked the fire he told them about their brothers who lived in the hills upriver, who made charcoal and raised beans and pigs because the land away from the coastal plain was too steep for rice. The children listened to these tales of people so far away with wide eyes and open mouths.

He told of heroes and patriots among the charcoal brothers, who cut out brush in hollows to make camps for *bo doi* soldiers in Liberation Army units "and for volunteer *bo doi* from the north who are coming down to help our struggle.

"No matter how hard the task or how suddenly we are called to it, our charcoal brothers work tirelessly for *Doc Lap!* Some who are very brave bring arms and explosives for the struggle down the trails to our flatlands and guide *bo doi* who do not know this area to assembly points for attacks on traitors! Some bring new grenades! Would any of you like to see this powerful new grenade?"

"*Ja phai! Ja phai!*" they sang, nodding eagerly.

"Perhaps soon you will. You can help the struggle. But you must promise to say nothing now."

"We know," one said. "We are not *Viet xian* here!"

Motivate all ages for the struggle!

"Now!" a woman in Linh's house said. "Now!" He saw Ba Linh's hands reaching up, squeezing the post as she strained.

"Here." A hand held out betel. "Take this." Groaning.

"*Ja phai!*" one called. "Here baby comes!"

"Water now!"

Mrs. Linh screamed and the woman clucked, "*Duoc! Duoc!*"

"Aiee!" Ba Linh's voice broke.

"*Duoc!* Here! A strong boy! Good! A strong boy!" His thin wail came through the window.

A boy was very auspicious for the struggle here.

Women came out for water. Children were allowed to look through the window. Thanh sat with Duong and planned tasks for the struggle. "When does the traitor Ranh come back?"

"Day after tomorrow."

"And the long-nose officer?"

"I don't know," Duong said.

"Please describe him."

"He wears a bar like a *phap* lieutenant bar but silver and shorter."

"That is a senior lieutenant of *mỹ.*"

"*Duoc.* He carries only a pistol and acts unconcerned, and talks and laughs, thinking to make friends, but always his eyes are searching and counting, looking in house windows. When we squatted I saw him looking low over the trail dust, obviously examining footprints. He must know how to tell a column of men from only walkers."

"I would like to know if he is intelligence or *quan canh. Police militaire.*"

"No," Duong said. "He is rifle troops. I watched him ordering riflemen here and there. Dropping to sight along the ground. Setting a principal direction of fire up this trail. Another along the axis of the low ground for grazing enfilade fire. What's more, I know his name!" Duong grinned. "It must be pronounced 'Muh'!" Duong drew in the dust: MH RANDOLPH. "It was inked above his shirt pocket. With some eagle sign. Muh!"

"No," Thanh said. "Remember the *phap?* Long-noses put their family names backwards. He is *Trung Uy* Randolph, Lieutenant Muh Randolph. We will kill him and destroy the camp. But first we must kill the puppets and traitors here so we can operate. I will come back in two days when Ranh is here."

The trick was to keep them from guessing anything, Randolph thought. The terrain had hummocks and low spots, pine scrub and palm bushes. The green Cat scraped a flat runway, but now you saw only a couple of nine-by-twelve tents and pallets of supplies. A marsh over there to anchor a flank on, and the other way that low sandy ridge with the hamlet on the other side. Beyond the hamlet he'd seen paddies and the Gia Binh River. A big area. He'd read about a similar airfield defense in World War II.

Out here now were Lieutenant Colonel Thomas, the base squadron CO, and his adjutant, a fussy captain named Shick; a couple of squads of engineers operating the equipment for rough grading, setting it up for a construction company; and his squad, platoon, company, or defense battalion, whatever you wanted to call it—a dozen bodies heavy in rank. They were crash crew and drivers. Crash crew were the badasses of the Wing. They ran up to burning airplanes and pulled people out. Staff Sergeant Rodriguez, who was crash crew now, had been a machine gunner in Korea. Rodriguez had a Brooklyn accent. He was a big, slump-shouldered man with hairy forearms, a growling voice, and one thick eyebrow that ran across his forehead like a black rope.

Mark and Rodriguez knelt by the CP hole. Mark drew lines in the sand. "Looks like this," Mark said. "Too big to wrap around, right? So we put machine guns here, grazing fire across. Rifles. British did it like this at Myitkyina. Peleliu was similar."

Rodriguez nodded. "Kimpo, too." He put his fingers on the sand downrange of the hypothetical machine guns. "It's not ideal, but, yeah, beaten zones here, here."

"We can put observation down that low ground."

"Right. Trip wires, too. We got wire. Fifteen hundred meters and no troops. What a lashup." He laughed once and shrugged. "Looks okay to me."

He bought the plan. Good. Mark had been off-handed talking but he wanted to be sure Rodriguez was convinced. "I don't want any machine guns out in daylight. Cover them with ponchos. Work out range cards at night. Keep the guns secret."

"Yes sir."

"Listening posts and screening patrols later. I'll put them in. I want the experience." Anyone could cover a place with lots of people. This would take some ingenuity. He'd read all the tactics books—it was 180 out from his skating through college. He knew the VC organized to a gnat's ass before they moved. Somewhere out there the VC must be— Well, what would they be doing?

That morning Major Thanh walked along the river trail from the hills toward Ap Nhac Muoi. Behind him were six other regular soldiers, *bo doi*, of the Liberation Army, all wearing green cotton uniform shirts with shorts or black pajama pants and rubber truck tire sandals. They had weapons and green web gear. They crouched under wide-leafed palm bushes when a helicopter passed over.

Downriver another element of the strike force came along another path from Gia Binh, hiding when aircraft passed, and more troops and a special unit came from the southeast, Elephant Pass.

Senior Sergeant Dau, crouching behind Thanh, carried an old green PRC-6 hand radio, provided by the puppets, to communicate with the other forces—not by talking, but by pressing the radio's talk button to interrupt the rushing noise in a dot-and-dash code. Thanh carried a prestige item, a Soviet staff officer's slim Tokarev automatic pistol, 7.65 millimeter.

At noon they were in position on the trails surrounding the hamlet. A hazy blue sky. The birds, usually noisy, had stilled. Thanh saw the blue cloth that patriot Duong had hung on a bush to show all was ready. Dau keyed his mike button.

"Now," Thanh said.

They moved quickly up the path about fifty meters until they cleared the paddy and had dry ground on both sides, then men moved in action teams over the grass and fenced patches to block this side of the hamlet. Thanh trotted past them up the path into the hamlet, the path turning into a lane. A dog barked. A man's hand reached out and yanked the dog into the house.

Beyond the houses Thanh saw other elements moving into place—*bo doi* bending over assault weapons trotted to their positions. Coming down another path, the *tuyen truyen*, the agitation-propaganda team: a woman in black, with long black hair, carrying a new Kalashnikov assault rifle, and two men, one carrying a guitar and M-3 with silencer.

Duong had dropped the front of his store. Thanh reached the dirt square in front at the same time as the *tuyen truyen*. Thanh knew them—Co Thi, Hao, and Kiem, training to be *can bo* like himself.

Thanh pointed at the chief's house. "Get Ranh."

Bo doi moved down the trail to cover its flanks and the *tuyen truyen* walked into the yard.

Next door, farmer Thac yelled, "Ranh! *Di di!* Ranh, go!"

A *bo doi* ran into Thac's house and smashed Thac across the face with his Sudayev.

"Bring him out," Thanh said to the soldiers at Ranh's house, and raised his voice: "People of Ap Nhac Muoi! You are quite safe! You are now free! *Doc Lap* is here! Come see your puppet chief!"

Kiem played chords on the guitar while the soldiers dragged out the puppet chief Ranh, hands tied behind him. He was small, wore glasses, and had a chief's brass button on his short-sleeved shirt. A scream from the house: Ba Ranh knelt at the door, wailing after her husband as the *bo doi* led him away. She formed her hands in the prayer gesture and screamed, "Release my man! Please release my man!"

A *bo doi* kicked her in the stomach and she stopped. They took the puppet chief to the center square. "Come out, comrades!" Thanh called. "Come out, brothers and sisters. You're free now. Watch your liberation." Doors opened, and people stood at the doors and windows of their huts.

"Come, brothers and sisters, this won't take long. You'll be back in the fields in a few minutes!"

Bo doi from the action detail moved among the houses pulling people out, shoving some with weapons. Thac was tied like Ranh but kept to the side. Most came without pushing and assembled on the dirt by the store. Co Thi played a struggle song on the guitar, and she and the others sang the words about not fearing when all served the struggle. It was a rousing song, and for those who had fought the *phap*, it raised true passions of pride and worthy hatred.

"Brothers! Sisters!" Thanh yelled. "Here is your puppet chief! Where is the puppet army to protect him? You know. You have seen. They now ride around in long-nose helicopters with the cruel-faced *mỹ*, looking for liberation forces! And where are we?"

"Here!" Duong yelled. "Under their long noses!" People laughed.

"Yes! Here! To liberate you! You do not have to be afraid of the puppets! They are lazy, vicious cowards. Look at your puppet chief!" Thanh poked Ranh in the gut and knocked off his glasses. "You will read no more conscription orders!" People laughed. Thanh turned to them and said, "You need not fear any puppet. You need not fear the *mỹ*, either. What have you heard about the *mỹ*? That they are strong and big and have cruel faces? So did the *phap* we beat in the Great Patriotic Struggle! Do the *mỹ* have machines? See them now! The *mat tran* will show you! See them now! See the strong Americans!"

Bo doi crouching up the trail strained against their shoulder poles and stood, lifting the two bamboo cages. The cages swayed as the soldiers walked. The American prisoners inside huddled in the center as they had been taught.

One had long pale hair, the other brown. Their whiskers covered their chins. Their boots had been taken away but they still wore their green uniforms, tattered, wrinkled, and stained with urine and shit. They were the ones captured in Da Nang before Tet.

The *boi doi* set the cage of the blond on top of the cage of the dark. "Look!" Thanh said. "*Mỹ!*" He pointed his Tokarev at the blond, who looked away. The dark stayed in a crouch, looking at the ground.

"There are your masters, Ranh. The one on top tells you what to do. Greet him." People laughed. Kiem swung his weapon at the backs of Ranh's legs and knocked him to his knees. "Greet him!"

Ranh, on his knees, looked at Thanh and the *tuyen truyen* singers. Kiem gestured with his weapon and poked Ranh in the ear with the muzzle. "Say what you say to the puppet district chief, snail turd."

"I don't know what you mean," Ranh said.

Co Thi, the slim young woman, whacked him on the head, a grave insult in this conservative Buddhist village. "Tell him you are honored to report to his felicitous presence, pig's anus!" Tell him you have collected taxes from the people to pay the puppet chief's whores and have drafted sons who would be working with their families to go into the army of puppet cannibals instead! Bow down before the long-noses, snail slime!"

Thien brought his automatic around behind the puppet chief's head and knocked him flat on his face. "The puppets must be concerned about their monkeys."

"Gibber," Co Thi said. The captives stared at her. "You know what to do." She pushed her barrel between the bars and poked the brown-haired American. The prisoners made a high squeaking noise listlessly. They had done this many times. "More spirit!" she yelled. "Aren't you concerned about your puppet?"

"The *mỹ* will abandon their puppets," Thanh called out. "Our group will tell a story about it."

Co Thi played her guitar. The *tuyen truyen* sang the song about the water buffalo boy who outwitted and captured the tiger.

Thanh stepped to the center and called out the promises of the future. "Liberation and democratic rule!" he shouted, dark eyes flashing, holding both hands out to the farmers. "Improved rice, bean, fowl, and pig production! Plastics and bicycles!" Looking at them all, gesturing to the children: "Schools! Classrooms so that young men instead of being drafted will study higher subjects! Each at his own desk!" He reminded them that the vicious *phap* had built only one school for all of Vietnam but that Giap, hero of Dien Bien Phu, had educated himself as a boy by tending his livestock near the open window of a country school so he could hear the lessons inside.

"Morally we are better!" Thanh shouted. They clapped.

"They are strong in materiel but are wrong. We are weak in materiel but morally strong!"

"Ja phai! Doc Lap!"

They sang the marching song. The *bo doi* had the people file by the cages and poke sticks at the American prisoners. One shoved the stick into the blond man's eye, causing him to scream. Others spat on the men's filthy uniforms. They gathered around the cages laughing and poking sticks from all directions so the prisoners couldn't fend off the blows and huddled and flinched. One person shoved hard and got the other *mỹ* in the kidney, causing him to throw out his arms and groan. Thanh stopped this because if the American started pissing blood he would probably die soon, and the performers needed the prisoners for shows along the coast.

After a few minutes both were battered and trembling, arms over their heads. Watery red stuff ran from the pale *mỹ*'s eye down his chin, and the other writhed to one side for his kidney.

"Now, brothers and sisters, we have seen how powerful the *mỹ* are. They can make machines fly over us, but they cannot fly from their cages!" People laughed. Some yelled, "Fly, long-nose!"

Thanh said, "Let them watch the government of this *xa* change, too."

Old Ba Huu poked her stick at them. *"Écouté!"* she yelled, mimicking the *phap* oppressors. *"Regardez l'officiel!"*

Kiem grabbed Ranh by the back of his collar and yanked him to his feet. People stepped back. No one was standing on the other side of Ranh. Thanh took his pistol, put the muzzle by Ranh's ear—the man blinked—and fired, the shot making little noise. Ranh's head yanked away and his shoulders and legs swung like sticks on a string. He fell on his side, bright blood welling from the hole in his skull.

"Kill the puppet's puppet, too." He pointed at Thac, Ranh's friend.

Co Thi took Kiem's M-3 with the perforated pipe silencer. She shoved the short gray weapon against Thac's chest, reached across the top to lift the safety cover, Thac's horrified eyes on her small hand, and fired a burst, the weapon coughing, Thac looking skyward and falling on his back. Thac's wife screamed but her voice was cut off.

Thanh put the death notice on Ranh's body, a paper listing his crimes. He looked across the way at Sergeant Dau, who held the radio to his ear. His men were watching the paths. All clear. The Americans were working a few hundred meters away on the other side of the low ridge but were unaware of anything.

"Kill the others," Thanh said. This was also the signal to clear out in five minutes.

Co Thi threw back her head, her long hair flying, her eyes flashing. She raised the blue shining AK with its pale stock over her head, saying, "New weapons not from the *phap* or *mỹ!*" She shoved it against Ba Thac's chest, thumbing the lever, Ba Thac raising her hands before her face and making the praying gesture. She fired a loud, ripping burst and Ba Thac flew back and skidded on the dust. She turned to Ba Ranh, who was crouching, holding her abdomen, and fired again, Ba Ranh shivering and curling up.

Kiem pointed his M-3 at the prisoners in the cages and one shouted two syllables again and again, "Kill me! Kill me! Kill me!"

No one understood English. Hao shoved his barrel and rapped the enemy's face, splitting his lip.

"It is time for us to go now," Thanh said. "You are liberated. Even with the Americans over the ridge, you will meet in *chi bo*. We will be with you night and day, and you will join the struggle and throw out the long-nose enemies!"

Co Thi slid her AK around her back on its sling and played chords on the guitar, and the performers and cage carriers filed out of the dirt square. The people sang and clapped as the *tuyen truyen* and *bo doi* walked down the brown dusty trail between palm bushes to the river.

Phoebe Bishop reached Saigon that August keyed up, impatient to get her career going, to get The Big Story. She'd left a jittery, muggy New York that was expecting another riot. People had war jitters, too. She'd been in a midtown bar with other news people watching CBS showing Marines sweeping through a VC village on Batangan Peninsula, men in camouflage helmets walking spread out as in all the war movies.

"Go, Marines!" some of the news people cheered.

Then the camera showed this startling shot of a Marine using his Zippo to light a grass shack. Immediately the atmosphere changed.

"Oh, no," one said. She saw people's attitudes change because of that shot: It was the opposite of the World War II icon, the GI giving candy to the European waif. "Oh, no!"

Heat blasted her when she stepped onto the ladder. The sights and noise jangled her—quonset huts, signs, olive drab, odd-looking jet fighters painted camouflage. She caught a cold at once, sweating and chilling, going from air-conditioned huts to glaring heat and back to cold. Already she wasn't inclined to believe the MACV briefing officers. She'd seen hundreds of shots of men in the dirt, eyes ringed with dust—stock war shots. Here she saw crisp, clean officers in those French designer fatigues (dramatic slanted breast pockets, nipped waist to accentuate the powerful shoulders, swollen thigh pockets to show pumping legs) that were starched, which couldn't have been cool in this climate. She had an advantage as a woman; she observed right away how uniforms gulled male correspondents, particularly American males.

She found a 1-2-3 flat, three rooms, very similar to a New York railroad flat, on a side street near the train station—which ran few trains now, because the VC blew them up—the busy market, and Tu Do Street, the boulevard of hotels, whores, and old hands. She observed the cyclo cabs, girls in *ao dais*, soldiers and hustlers. She burned far beyond what the sun poured into her. *Dammit! I'm going to do it!* she vowed. She'd had her apprenticeship, she'd missed Paris. Forget about love and marriage—she was going to crack open the business right here!

Phoebe's street had a white mice police post at the corner. This didn't make it safe but, as the old hands said, if you saw them running you knew to get down.

Her immediate worry wasn't a VC terrorist attack but the American jerk next door who stared at her on the sidewalk—a squat red-faced man with yellow-gray eyes. She saw him through the open window, his shirt off, drinking beer. He was a supervisor for RMK, one of the contracting firms the American government used.

"Get on here, both of you!" he yelled one night. Phoebe heard it all through the walls. He had two prostitutes in his room and they were laughing. "You *titi* cock, you *nhac muoi, mỹ!*"

"I guess I am, huh! I told you I'm good!"

From his doorway he stared at Phoebe. "Hey! You American?"

She looked away from him and went into her place, seething. She wanted to be left alone; she wanted to get her work done. She'd need someone to protect her, dammit—or a gun.

One small bare footprint in the clay-streaked sand.

First Lieutenant Randolph, who had been up all night with his riflemen, peering dutifully into the dark, raised his eyebrows and bent down to the Sign of the Intruder like a dog sniffing spoor. The tiny footprint's edges were sharp in the dew damp.

"No shit," he said.

Staff Sergeant Rodriguez, shambling downrange from the parked Cat, his bearish arms swaying, nodded at something else on the ground. "Knee marks. Little fucker crawled up."

When He Tires, We Attack

Phoebe went to the hotels favored by news people, the Caravelle and the Majestic. She sat on the Caravelle's balustraded terrace in a sensible cotton dress with many pockets, watching soldiers, prostitutes, American tech reps, engineers, spies in short-sleeved shirts streaming by on the street. She had read some of Ash Loakes's purple war copy—it made her *fume*, his fat male corn about "snarling warplanes on the tarmac" and "grunts from upcountry" and particularly *his* account of drinking at the Caravelle: "*You look for an officer in dirty fatigues who's been out in the bush. His eyes mirror the agony of combat and political doubt. He wants a drink, and you want information. . . .*"

She saw a few officers, none dirty, and many newsmen combing each other for quotes.

"You're new," an English voice said. He was a bearded sunburned man in his thirties.

"Not as new as you think," she said.

"Who are you with?"

"I'm a stringer."

"So am I. Who else are you with?"

"No one."

"Good. I'd offer you a drink anyway."

"Who says I'd take it?"

"You might." He had this way of leaning back and studying her. Dove-gray eyes. Not cold or warm, but calm. Pale lashes. His hair and beard were sun-bleached. She could tell right away he had *virtu*, or what the Chinese call *chi*.

"Yes."

"Take gin. It's safest."

His name was Jim Robinson. He said he sold stills to *News of the World, Bunte Illustrierte, Stern, Oggi,* and *Look.* He had plenty of work.

"How nice for you," she said.

He also took footage for the BBC, Canadian Broadcasting, sometimes American networks, and sometimes even did voice-overs. "Of course my accent's less marketable to Americans. Have you ever worked with film? Perhaps we could work together on stand-uppers?"

"That would be terrific!" she said brightly.

All news people exaggerate, so she took time during the next day or so to see that he was who he claimed to be. Sara had warned that Saigon was full of poseurs. He was okay, her contacts said. She watched for him at the Majestic.

Major Thanh came padding into Ap Nhac Muoi in late afternoon from a meeting upriver of the zone committee, *lien khu,* that coordinated political and military action in the lowlands between Da Nang and Hue. All action went through the *lien khu,* whether it was sending a Liberation Army battalion to attack an enemy base, having two local *du kich* plant a mine, or putting leaflets and workers in a village for *dan van,* action among the people. To the *mat tran* all the war was political, while to the Americans it was all military action with no political thought. At least Thanh thought so *that* afternoon—helicopters all over the sky—and not troop lifts, either—single ones going here, there, like Da Nang traffic. Did they fly *everywhere?* He'd wasted hours under palm bushes waiting for the sky to clear and was sweating and tired when he came to the reeds by that last creek where he could see the rooftops up on the ridge.

Duong had left a yellow Buddhist streamer, this week's all-clear signal, on the late chief Ranh's gable.

Thanh waded over, followed a paddy dike, and plodded up the hill, watching still, not trusting just the streamer. But women clucked in the houses, children played on the paths, and there was Duong under the overhang, his little round face behind his little round glasses, looking not a bit like the fierce warrior he had been—and would be when they attacked again.

"We have penetrated the camp!" Duong said, and gave his report. They had three cells, *tieu to*, of volunteers—River, Road, and Lightning. Ong Linh, the proud father, had gone in crouching. The Americans hadn't seen him.

"They are blind and stupid. Pham goes tonight."

"I will go along with you to the release point," Thanh said. "I'll stay here tonight."

Thanh moved around. He had safe houses in Gia Binh and Da Nang and in a number of hamlets; he could stay in the *mat tran*-held areas upriver, but had business all over down here—*chi bo* and meetings. It would be good to watch here tonight.

He spent the evening talking with families, going from house to house, accepting a bowl of rice here, a bit of pork there, a cup of tea, a cigarette. He squatted with men on the porch, talking while the sun dropped behind the hills into Laos. From the ridge he could see the American camp, the men sitting and eating out of green cans. Using binoculars he watched the big senior sergeant and the talkative lieutenant mouthing and pointing. All they had was riflemen, Linh said. The lieutenant and the sergeant had been constantly on the move last night, checking men in holes. Linh had crawled to one side while the lieutenant thumped up on the other, the riflemen turning toward him.

Duong said the lieutenant had come thumping over that afternoon of *Doc Lap*, too—fortunately they'd had time to throw the bodies in Thac's house, kick over the bloody dust, and pick up spent cartridges before he arrived; he bought cigarettes and talked but noticed nothing. The bodies went into the river that night and were either past Gia Binh or being eaten by dogs and pigs now.

The houses had gotten quiet, children inside. A few pigs grunting, children already asleep. The smell of cooked rice, beans, burning kerosene from the lamps. Little halos of yellow light through the unglassed windows. He liked a country hamlet. His Bac Thuc, Uncle Thuc, had lived in such a one. He and his father, who worked on the boats on the Perfume River, used to go up to see Bac Thuc and the family and listen to country tales, all the ways people were connected through family and work and friendship and rivalry in the *xa*. "It's time, Comrade Thanh."

It was 2300, completely dark.

He and Duong met Pham on the porch of the late Thac's house and discussed Pham's route and what they wanted him to notice. He was in shorts, shirtless, barefooted.

"Let's go."

They walked down the soft dark paths, crouched, and stepped among palm bushes till they came to the gully. They watched the American tents lit white by gasoline lamps. They could not see the riflemen in holes in the dark. Pham, a stocky man in his late twenties, duck-walked along the gully into the darkness.

The first volunteer for listening post was a crash-crew lance corporal named Lindahl, a big-jawed stud.

"He's okay," Rodriguez said. "Steady."

Randolph crawled out with him part way, hauling his coil of wire; Lindahl crawled on, cradling a rifle, sound power phone in his shirt, trailing wire, into the low ground.

The wild card in night observation was how new men saw shapes turn into people as their fears took living forms. Men in the holes had seen moving shadows the past few nights; but Rodriguez and all the body of sea stories told everyone to expect this and disregard that sudden gut-dropping panic. "You sit tight," Rodriguez told them. "You'll see the difference soon enough."

Lindahl had only just got into position when he called in, whispering that he heard noises.

"He's not excitable," Rodriguez told Randolph. "He may have something."

"Twenty meters west of the lone bush," Lindahl whispered. "In the gully." They had a system for marking sectors.

"Stay down," Randolph said. He fired one round from an M-14. The cough was loud. The flash, because of the slotted suppressor, only a little blue finned wink. "There?"

"Affirmative." Pause. "No noise."

In the gully under palm bushes Thanh and Duong heard the peculiar cough but weren't sure about the muzzle flash. They waited. Had the long-noses hit him? They would have to get his body. Then they saw the shadows as Pham came back, mad.

"Swine!" he hissed. "Dogs!"

Pham had not been in the patriotic war so didn't know the reactions one had when being shot at. Thanh said in a kindly voice, "You are upset, Brother Pham. First you're startled, then you're mad. Don't dwell on it. They missed. Tell us what you saw."

Thanh marked his map and made notes of what Pham said. He hadn't got very close. Perhaps the *mỹ* had night-vision scopes. There were ways to tell. "Good, Brother Pham. We will bring in more support for this."

Jim Robinson was a true war correspondent. When he called at Phoebe's flat the first time he said, "You must have excellent observation up there." They went to her roof and looked at the firing across the river miles away, tracers in the blue-violet dark, the dim white flash and rumble of artillery.

"They're landing quite far," Jim said. "You'd hear the rounds hit otherwise. Cigarette?"

"Mmm."

He took out a half-pint bottle of gin. They sipped.

"I like covering wars."

"Were you ever in one?"

"No. Wrong age. Malaya had just ended and the government had done away with National Service. But I went to Suez. Then East Africa. I know how a war works. The generals say one thing, their staff officers embellish it with asides on the principals of tactics, then you go to the field to see the truth, which is all bloody confusion and chance. Crucial details you wouldn't have thought meant life or death. Human error. Life sliced open. Good job to make sense of it. I like looking at the way war moves across the face of a land, turning over customs, lives—the lot. See everything in the people then—horror and greatness. Couldn't stand city journalism. I was in Saigon in 'fifty-nine when Diem fought the river gangsters, the Binh Xuyen, and again in 'sixty when his army mutinied. Didn't think you people would stick then. Went from here to the Congo shooting. Prefer Asia to Africa, though. People are more interesting. Asian societies more complex. They know more about war than we'll ever learn. They taught cavalry to the Europeans, and now People's War. Fascinating. After all, it's half of public life. Something I like about having a drink while the rumbling's going on. And you?"

"This is terrific," she said. "But aren't you scared?"

"Of course. But it's exhilarating seeing what might get you. Not the anonymous funk of civilization. Don't you know the odds are about the same? War and accidents at home?"

She went to bed with him because she was lonely. He smelled

gamy. Even in this climate he didn't bathe often. In this climate she was enervated, so it wasn't a torrid affair. But they became intimate colleagues.

The fat redneck saw them together and backed into his hole.

"This is it!" Houston wrote in his journal. "LBJ wants me to go to Saigon! Intense briefings! Mekong Delta Development & Power Authority, aerospace clients, carrying water for President. He gripped my shoulders—'I want you to make sure the goddam television doesn't get another Zippo shot! We're there to defend freedom!'

"Met with Sandy Sanford . . ." This was one of the score of Kennedy-style congressmen who had longish, blowing hair and used phrases like "This isn't acceptable." Sandy had a Southern California district that was part dovish flakes, part General Dynamics and Northrop. He was stuffy but his wife, Marty, could be a lot of fun. Houston hoped.

"Facts for Sandy about his district's war products used in the fighting to defend South Vietnam," he wrote, putting his eye back on the ball.

Evening two nights later. Thanh studied the Marine camp with binoculars. The usual after-work routine, the long-nose pigs in T-shirts eating out of cans. A flash of sunset light: the lieutenant studying the ridge with binoculars. Thanh was under a palm bush. He crawled back and talked to the four Liberation Army soldiers who'd come down to help. Two carried rifles. Two had a tool that farmers or longshoremen would recognize. Or butchers. It had a T handle and a long, curving steel hook, sharpened at the tip to grab into whatever was to be hauled away.

Twenty-three hundred hours. The volunteer *du kich* this time, Brother Tuc, a rice farmer from the upriver edge of the hamlet, moved off easily, crouching, stepping, waiting. The Liberation Army troops crept about ten meters behind.

That night a Marine in a hole heard Brother Tuc crawling. This one was a motor pool corporal as green as anyone else (except Staff Sergeant Rodriguez) but old enough not to be hasty. He knew you imagine things at night—but hearing dirt scrape and smelling *nuoc mam?*

He called in on the loop line.

"Fire one round. Aim low."

He did. *Cough!* No sound.

In the hamlet another *du kich* was burning mad. The shot hadn't been *that* close, but it was the suddenness of it, the *whack!* flinging dirt on palm bushes and his arm. Dogs!

"No night scope," the Liberation Army carry team leader said. "We can check that later by using one of *our* night scopes, but I'm sure he fired by guess at a bush he'd sighted before."

"The long-noses do this?"

"Some units."

"We will go in through the low ground tomorrow," Thanh said.

Two mornings later the riflemen in one hole found tiny footprints in the low ground. That night First Lieutenant Randolph took out a screening patrol.

"I turned back," Brother Linh told Thanh not long after midnight. "I saw at least four of them out here"—he pointed on Thanh's map—"deployed over the low ground. The middle of nowhere. I smelled them."

This was a new dimension. Thanh reported to the zone committee. The orders came back: Proceed. Gather information.

Lieutenant Colonel Mason, the S-3 Operations Officer, came out to look over the scratched-out camp that was supposed, eventually, to take a group of eighty or so helicopters now in transit from the States. Mark walked with him over the dug-up terrain. Mason stumped along, squinting, turning, squinting. He wore a black baseball cap with scrambled eggs on the visor and a khaki flight suit and shoulder holster. His sleeves were rolled up, showing his bomb tattoo. He hopped easily over the plowed ground, Mark at his left. He was irritated.

"Goddamit, they didn't cut that pad right. I don't see drainage." Then, to Mark: "You have holes on both sides here. Certainly the strip is a clear division. Why not assign separate squads?"

It probably was an innocent question, but it pricked Randolph and he answered heatedly. "One unit, sir! Got to enfilade that avenue of approach. One squad's responsibility."

Mason looked at him a moment and nodded. "Lieutenant Colonel

Thomas has done this before. I have not. Although I saw the deal at Peleliu."

Shit, Randolph thought. This was like meeting one of the apostles and bitching to him. At Peleliu the riflemen had shot it out with Japanese at the edge of the airstrip while Marine attack pilots took off with full ordnance on their wings, didn't even raise wheels, and bombed and strafed Japanese positions just beyond the end of the strip. And he'd been impatient. With a colonel who'd done it. Fuck!

They stepped over furrows and down and up ditches. "What about that hamlet?"

"I've walked around there, sir. The people aren't friendly."

"What do you mean?"

"They're not like the people around Da Nang. They don't come out of the houses. The intreps I've read say that means someone's working them. I'd like the ARVN or police to count noses. There might be cadre there."

"I'll put it in." They walked. After a moment Mason said, "It's a madhouse down there. S-Two isn't set up yet. We have all we can do tracking down aircraft and boxes. Be tougher to get any administrative work done here."

In other words, cool it.

They walked back to the tent camp and exchanged salutes. Randolph was pissed off at himself. He'd heard earlier Mason had sunk a Jap ship, too.

The following week Thanh sent out night probes by volunteers from River and Lightning cells. The American patrols got better, quieter, more odorless and invisible. Every evening after dark the four to six men lined up in that peculiar patrol rig not shown in John Wayne movies because it doesn't photograph well, the men's trouser legs unbloused and taped tight, sleeves down. They wore no belts or metal, their rifles had no slings. They carried a couple of magazines, a grenade, a compress in their pockets. They appeared featureless because their faces and hands were blacked out—no mouths, no noses, tiny eyes.

They were to be astonished later by the even more bizarre outfit the enemy assault teams wore.

Randolph had his taped-down, blacked-out shadowy men jump several times—no noise. "Lock and load," he told them. They filed into the dark, moving slowly, bent over.

By now the patrol members, who rotated every few nights, and Randolph, who went out every night, had developed a refined sense they hadn't got in training—a hunter's sense. When they waited, absolutely motionless, for ten or twenty minutes, lying in a rough arc, ready to fire, something stilled inside them and removed caution from animals around. Rats and sand crabs started crawling again, bats fluttered, frogs peeped, and the Americans' senses triggered alarms when someone *else* moved into this field of sensing and caused the animals to quiet.

This night Randolph's neck hairs went up and, turning his face toward the gray shapes of palm bushes and dark slashes in the earth, he felt a warm spot out there and saw his left flank man, Corporal Hollis, a crew chief, observing the same. Others turned toward him. He slowly lifted a grenade so they all saw it, seated the lever in the web of his hand like a .45 grip, eased out the pin, and threw it.

Pfft! went the fuze as it flew. *Ding!* went the lever. *!Crunch!* went the little charge of Composition B, red streaks spinning out in the dark—wire shrapnel, going *whit-whit-whit*, and the *yeep-yeep-yeep*ing of the ear-damaged bats flying away.

In the morning, near the white starburst where the grenade had gone off, they found footprints, all right—several sets—but no blood.

"He heard the thing activate," Randolph said. "Okay, next time, Hollis, you fire a burst at the spot and I'll throw during the noise. When he puts up his head again maybe the shrapnel'll get him."

Phoebe was catching that Vietnam thing you couldn't be vaccinated against—blasts of image, touch, and smell that stayed in the back of your awareness, the intense greens, blinding blues, the worn and cynical whites of old stucco and dirty cloth. Beautiful faces, strong faces, ugly faces, busy people pedaling cyclos, hawking beans, chicken, fish, begging. A middle-aged woman held a dead baby near the market and begged. A few days later she was begging in the same place with a different dead baby. Arrogant soldiers and police shouting, waving thin arms gracefully. Buddhist monks in orange robes, Viet priests in chocolate-brown cassocks, the smell of ginger and fish. Slim, dark-eyed, snake-moving fuck-me-and-I'll-rule-you women whose *ao dais* trailed in the steamy air. Sometimes a car bomb went off and killed surprised American clerks who thought they had safe air-conditiond duty. Live or die now. Jet fighters painted like trees and black water buffalo pulling wooden carts. Barbed wire and flowers. She took pictures.

"Good," Jim said, looking at her proof sheets. "I'd have composed this differently—an editor can pick it up cropping but not all would see it."

Jim took her to a bistro called Givral, where correspondents drank with old French *colons*, spying for anyone; Vietnamese officials; and the Saigon intellectuals who called themselves the *attentisme* because they could only watch as their country was dragged through war and chaos. Many of the correspondents she saw there went on to fame covering the war and what happened at home later.

She photographed a Cao Dai in robes and brass spangles and chains, wearing a fantastic tall hat that was a hollow column peeled back down the sides like a scallion crudité. He was a priest in an armed sect that believed God is an eye and used teachings from Victor Hugo and Winston Churchill. She photographed Hoa Hao, another armed sect of mystic faith healers in black, wearing machine gun belts and straw hats. Jim said the Catholics up north had been another armed sect and had the only power base the Americans could have allied with then.

She visited government offices built like French summer-white bureaux or glassy fifties American-style boxes with dusty chandeliers and bullet pocks from some coup or mutiny. She talked with officials who were charming, positive, well spoken—but, as Jim said, "Don't ever believe them. They're on the fiddle."

"The take?"

"They call it the *an cap*. It's everywhere."

A police official requested extra uniforms, which he sold. A Viet justice official was issued U.S. supplies of cement and lumber for building jails and used the materiel to build apartment houses like her 1-2-3 house. ARVN colonels trusted with payrolls kept the money and let their troops go ragged. Combat units sold artillery rounds to the VC, who made them into mines that killed American soldiers. It was the *an cap*.

She talked with a Chinese financier. Chinese handled most of Vietnam's financial affairs, import–export trade, rice brokering, and currency exchange, because the Vietnamese male considered his proper role to be that of a poet, scholar, or soldier. This Chinese had dealt with Americans earlier up in Taiwan.

"Your government officials are fools," he said, speaking with an unsoftened, unsweetened directness that meant he respected her intelligence. "They insist they don't bribe. Anyone who does business bribes but your officials don't. Yet your officials don't count the fish when you hand out aid. You let people steal you blind. You *expect* them to steal. They do it up in Taiwan. The National Air Force stole parts all the time. Chiang sold your howitzers to Mao and they were fired at you in Korea and at the French in Dien Bien Phu. You do it to yourselves. "These *yuen*"—his word for Viets—"are stealing you blind."

It was 2000, time to go out again, the twelfth night of anxious probing on both sides. Lieutenant Randolph lined up the men in their taped uniforms and inhuman-looking blackface—except for Dobbs, a new man two days in-country. He was black, a quiet young man from Mississippi, a machine gunner by MOS. They'd been getting more O3s, trained infantrymen, off the drafts, so Staff Sergeant Rodriguez had less to worry about running hole watch while Randolph crawled out there.

The men held out rifles and the shotgun and submachine gun. "Shake 'em," Randolph said. "Jump up and down." And: "Grenades." They took the M-26s from black cardboard and metal packing cylinders and checked the levers and pins. "Tonight we try the grenade drill. Listen up! Fragments go out and up in a flat cone like this. You keep low and cover up this way."

They crawled out and waited. It was hot and windless. No smell of rice sweat. A light in the hamlet. The scent of kerosene lamps. A mosquito. Randolph had to piss. Waiting.

A sense in the dark. They were all wolf-apes, feeling the pack danger-prey signal. Heads slowly turned. Hairs up on necks, hearts pounding. A couple of men slowly putting out hands, pointing. They knew. They all knew. Randolph gestured to Hollis.

Corporal Hollis was a short, strong, red-faced, gritty man. He operated a machine gun in the door of the bird and had been a machine gunner in Division before, though being a crew chief meant he had to know everything else about the aircraft too; from wheels to rotor hub—more complicated than a machine gun.

He was a country boy from Kentucky. Two months before, going into a hot LZ, he'd caught a metal piece in the nose from a shattered slug and now his nose was split down the center, though you couldn't see anything with that dead-black face—just his eyes and the short pipe of his submachine gun. No sound as he lifted the safety cover. He fired. Randolph threw. No flash suppressor—a huge pulsing flash, another vignette of sound and light: *pop-pop-pop-pop-pop*. Pause. *Crunch! Whit-whit-whit-whit*, *yeep-yeep-yeep-yeep*, *flutter-flutter*. Ears ringing. Then unmistakably, someone groaning, feet running, scraping earth.

"Up on line!" Mark shouted. "Move out!" They crashed through the palm bushes, chasing. How many feet? Couldn't tell. Where now? Couldn't hear after the shooting. Couldn't see after the flashes. "Move on! Keep moving!" Nothing.

At dawn bare footprints, sandal footprints, scrapes where someone had dived or fallen—but no blood. "Not a fuckin' sign! What's goin' on? Shit!" Mark had read about this in Bernard Fall's *Street Without Joy* and the Malayan accounts. We have to try harder, he resolved. He saw himself as fundamentally stupid. He couldn't think of a way around. He was baffled. Push harder.

In Ap Nhac Muoi that dawn, Major Thanh squatted in the late Thac's house and examined Ong Thuy, who was sweating and perhaps dying, but not in great pain. He was in shorts only and sand clung to his sweating skin. Barely visible under the coating of sand were the tiny puckered slits where the *mỹ* grenade's wire fragments had gone in, but you could see where he was bleeding inside because his skin was swollen over brown-purple patches. Brother Thuy opened his eyes and closed them. All he had said was *"Mỹ!"* and "Suda! Suda!" He'd thought the SMG was a Sudayev, which patriots used in the Great Struggle against the *phap*, but Thanh, who had been watching from a gully, knew it was the American grease gun, a cheap throwaway. But the new *mỹ* grenades were very powerful and deadly. Brother Lam the other night had been cut and shaken, and one of the *bo doi* on the recovery team had been cut on the face and disoriented and now had trouble holding his balance. If a wire had penetrated his skull he would likely die.

The big round holes in Brother Thuy's calves were swollen shut where they had sunk the meat hooks to pull him out of the low ground; then they'd grabbed each end, one clamping Thuy's mouth, and trotted back.

Sergeant Thien of the Liberation Army touched Thuy's forehead and used his thumb to curl up the wounded man's lip to look at his gums. Turning blue. He glanced at Thanh. Too bad, but they were, after all, full-time soldiers, and many had already died and been crippled.

Ba Thuy had howled and shrilled for her husband and had already been taken away.

"The long-noses did this!" Thanh told the hamlet people outside. "They must be driven out! *Liberate our hamlets! Achieve an economy based on* xas *and labor!* To do this we must probe their camp, see it day and night, so on *that* night we can kill them all, destroy their machines! When they advance, we withdraw! When they tire, we attack!"

He spoke of history and doctrine, then said, "The *mỹ* are like children. They learn a trick and think they know everything. This is a clever trick, this cloud of small patrols. Tonight we will send lightning into the cloud! Lightning, *tieu to!*"

"No patrols tonight," Lieutenant Randolph said. "LPs north and south."

After they were in place, Randolph smoked cigarettes and drank instant coffee in the CP hole. Nice to sit on your ass for a change, he thought. He didn't handle idleness well. Couldn't think profitably. He'd sooner be out there in the dark facing simple fear and sneaky people. He wanted to outwit death.

He'd had a premonition from time to time of a white flash sparking across the inside of his skull—*zap!* Catching a slug in the gourd. What would it be like being killed? The shots in the HUS going in the LZ, those first night fears patrolling.

Dead was all she wrote. He didn't believe *anything* happened after the white flash—that's what made it all so important now. He'd been brought up in one of those white-steepled suburban churches that offered perennial optimism. Think positively. Rise above death. Bullshit. Look at Mom and Dad—a lifetime of suburban striving, paint and hedges, booze scenes, unhappiness, and when they're supposed to take the big vacation and be happy, what? Black dead nothing—blacker than a moonless night on patrol. At least there your night sense and purple comes in your retinas let you make out something, but dead is absolute zero. Life was to fight for the living, carry out the job and take care of your men. In a ground operation, if you don't fight full out, balls to the wall, you lose everything. But don't look for contact. Don't ask for *nothing*.

He'd known outstanding officers, hard chargers who asked for it. About one, a Ranger/Recon officer, his old drinking buddy the AT lieutenant said, "He's great to train with, but I wouldn't want to go into combat with him. He'd trade a seabag of dogtags for a Navy Cross." Randolph was at heart a follower of hotshot leaders, one of the pack; he wanted to do it right and be sort of a stud but not stick out. He wanted to see what this stuff was like but survive it, for bar talk later, shooting the shit, which is what he did now with Rodriguez: "How'd the Chinese do it?"

"Go for the obvious weak points."

"Were they quiet?"

"Yes. You could smell 'em, though. They weren't completely quiet. You know that story about Lay-'Em-on-the-Wire McGraw."

"Yes."

They watched yellow lights go out in the hamlet, listened to distant shell fire and small arms.

Pretty soon he was alert. It was near midnight. The listening post off Six called in on the radio. It was broken ground down there, so he had a small PRC-6 hand radio. "I got men. Motion. Fifty, eighty meters bearing one niner zero."

"Sit tight, Marine," Rodriguez said.

Randolph called the rifle squad in that sector and told them to hold their fire. He didn't want them to show their positions. "Coombes," he said.

A thin, very young Marine with big feet stood holding his M-79 grenade launcher. He couldn't have been over seventeen but swore he was eighteen. He'd come off a draft that morning and had fired the grenade launcher at 1300 to get used to it.

They trotted down a plowed ditch, crouching, out of sight. Coombes ran, gangly and eager, elbows out, swinging the short, fat-barreled M-79. Randolph dropped to his knees and Coombes skidded to a stop beside him. Randolph talked into the PRC-6.

The LP man whispered, "Two, possibly three vector south southwest now crouching five to ten meters east side of large mound, range five zero."

"Interrogative you in cover? Over."

"Affirmative, gully, defilade."

Randolph crouched beside Coombes and made sure he had the right target. Coombes fired. Pause. A little orange crunch.

The LP reported, "Fucker yelped, sir. Over."

"Stay down."

Coombes fired several more—*ponk-crunch, ponk-crunch*—orange flashes skirting the mound. Randolph lifted the radio and— What the fuck? Muzzle flashes twinked, his guts dropped, the shots went *rrripp, whap! flutter—way* high. Shit, are *they* lousy shots!

"Silhouettes moving!" the LP hissed. "They're diddy-boppin' due west!" Coombes fired again and corrected on the LP's adjustment. After it was quiet they walked back. Coombes was so excited he could shit. At boot camp and ITR they hardly saw an officer, and look at this—on his first day in-country one took him *shooting!* "Goddam, sir, this is decent," he blurted. "What are we gonna do tomorrow?"

At dawn they found short shell casings probably from SKS carbines.

At Ap Nhac Muoi Thanh was furious. Three men wounded, two of them *bo doi*, cut in the same way by the little wires. The levee of volunteers had said nothing as they carried the wounded up the river trail. But the way they had looked at him meant they believed him less.

"Where are Ong Thuy and the other soldier?" Ba Huu said, chiding. And another farmer, Dinh, always faint-hearted, said to Duong at the store, "How do we know the Americans will be like the *phap?* They haven't fired at the village. They don't act like the *phap*, no *écouté moi!* No grabbing people to work on levees. They wave their money around. Of course they are fools, but all they do is spend money and make noise. And they are big and well armed."

"We will beat them," Thanh said. "Remember, slow reconnaissance, slow preparation, slow rehearsal, slow movement into position, fast attack!"

"The father of our sons was killed for nothing!" he remembered Ba Thuy shrieking as they carried her upriver to get her away from the others. The Struggle couldn't show doubt.

"We will outlast the enemy!" Thanh shouted. "When he advances, we retreat; when he tires, we attack!"

Many looked at the ground.

*   *   *

In Saigon Houston Bridles pushed the President's idea for a TVA on the Mekong. The way State and Vietnamese Foreign Ministry officials listened—frowning, lips forming objections, eyes glazing over, or asking what was in it for them—Houston could see it was a dead duck.

He listened to Vietnamese bitching about all the Americans there—a quarter of a million and still coming—and what they were doing to the economy. "We pay them in MPC," Houston said. "The Army's putting everyone out in the remote areas." Still the GVN officials wanted other considerations—i.e., money.

He was hustled from one briefing to another. The same play-offs he'd seen at NSC. The Army had a lieutenant colonel who later became a White House aide in another administration. He was short, dapper, wore a crew cut and four rows of ribbons. He had a trick when looking at you of winking, so he seemed mischievous, or a good guy, or maybe he appealed to queers, Houston thought. He flashed black-and-white aerial photos of wide paths taken under trees and odd shadowless photos, infrared, taken at night, showing convoys of canvas-topped trucks.

"The Ho Chi Minh Trail, gentlemen. It's not a *trail*—it's as wide as three-oh-one between Washington and Baltimore!" He winked; all laughed. "Maybe years ago the enemy wheeled stuff down on bicycles, but those deuce-and-a-halfs aren't bicycles! [laughter] They were made in *Volgograd!* [laughter]."

"The NVA's flooding down here. There's no guerrilla mystique to it, gentlemen." He looked at each of them, including the CIA liaison, a thin man wearing glasses and a short-sleeved white shirt, a Princeton graduate who was interrogated later on television. "It's not guerrilla war; it's Asian war. The enemy moves in small groups at night to avoid our air. He stashes supplies. The Chinese did all this in Korea. He uses atrocities to distract us. But there's no mystique. Look at these, please."

He ran slides overlaid SECRET and TOP SECRET. Photos of North Vietnamese soldiers under packs and pith helmets. Shiny weapons labeled AK-47, RKG, RPD, RPG, SKS, ZPU-2 and -4, and photos of tanks and things that looked like tanks—PT-76, T-54, JSU-100, and JSU-122. Houston gleaned that PU and SU had something to do with the gun mount. Other briefees were high-level Defense and

Congressional staffers used to this kind of detail; they went "Oooh!" and "Ahhh!" at the right moments. Houston didn't bother with it. His eye was on the ball. What will the Army ask for? Who gets less?

"What we intend to do, gentlemen, is put our big units in the boonies where the NVA is coming in and knock the shit out of them! [laughter] The communists have buffaloed the American press into thinking it's more subtle than that. . . . [laughter]."

An Air Force full colonel stood and said little other than responding to recurring charges that the Air Force and VNAF were bombing indiscriminately and killing women, children, and farm animals. "I must remind you that these missions are flown against VC territory and the Vietnamese themselves identify the targets as enemy." A Navy captain said the crew of the North Vietnamese torpedo boat that had attacked the *Maddox* in Tonkin Gulf was still being held in a special brig at Da Nang and that none had talked about their orders. Both the Navy and Air Force officers gave the numbers of air crew dead or held prisoner. The North Vietnamese antiaircraft fire was better than the American people should know, Houston thought; our aircraft losses were too high. Enemy fighters were shooting down a lot of Americans, too—"although some of these pilots might be Russian, Chinese, or Warsaw Pact," the Navy briefing officer said.

Houston took notes. This was the dangerous stuff—not what was happening to the American flyers, but letting the public know the Soviet weapons were effective. The Americans had stopped making antiaircraft guns after Korea because defense planners, generals, and industry leaders agreed to use airplanes to knock down enemy airplanes. Building airplanes made more jobs. This is what he'd gone over with Congressman Sanford while making eyes at his wife. The Americans had air defense hardware like the Hawk missile, made by Raytheon in Houston's home state, but not the array of machine guns, automatic cannon, big guns, and rockets the Russians made. As one of the Defense staff said, "We can't let the people know they have all this and that for them it works. We'll have too many people meddling in what we're trying to accomplish!"

Houston followed the Marine guards from the glassy embassy to the CIA quarters in a *belle époque* French house nearby. He paid no more attention to the press outside the fence than he did to the straggle of pickets that sometimes stood outside the White House with their silly signs about stopping the bombing. He didn't notice the bearded British correspondent in shorts or the sweating dark-haired woman in shades.

The Agency briefing was handled by a thin, elegant New Yorker named Harry Beechwood. The name caused Houston's social antennae to quiver. Very well connected, well married. Beechwood gave an amusing little talk without as many visual aids as the winking colonel. It was still the same Army–Agency pissing match, though.

"The longer we are here, the more incidents we blunder into," Beechwood said. "Thus the more opportunity their *can bo* have to form *chi bo*, or local groups of volunteers, formed into three-man cells, *tieu to*, which they regard as toes, as on the feet of a marching peasant"—he raised his eyebrows, and Houston laughed—"and the cells execute direct action. Atrocities, bombs, little boys who don't know they're going to die carrying grenades into crowds. These *horrors* make others recoil in fear; they conclude the Saigon government can't protect them. Vietnamese are survivors. They bend before force. So they accept the *mat tran*, the NLF."

Beechwood looked at each of them in turn. "Military action is of course one of their phases—the *khoi nghia*, or general uprising, at the end, and the armed struggle, or *dau tranh vu trang*, on the way. But each of their violent acts makes a political point. They want to slap us not *only* to hurt us but also to make *them* look braver, and stronger, for taking on a giant. The more stuff we have here, the more targets we give them.

"The political war is where they're killing us. The Special Forces, and some Marine units, work with local volunteers. They try to build trust. Most don't. The cadres are working the hamlets and building cells. Only by good, tough CI—police work, local surveillance—can we stop their political work." He smiled ruefully. Houston smiled back at him. *I understand you, old fellow.* He remembered Gerrity fighting the good fight before he died, that day outside the gray wooden barracks.

"Mr. Bridles, would you take a few minutes to speak to some high-ranking officers?" It was a brisk gray man from the embassy staff.

"How long will it take?"

"They're in the building now. Most of them have recently arrived in-country and are taking over commands here. MACV's been briefing them, but you know how a word from the President would pep them up."

"By all means, by all means."

They came to attention when he entered the room. They didn't look so high-ranking—most were colonels or lieutenant colonels. He took a moment to shake hands and get a feel for them. A Navy captain. "Christenson, RAGS." Ditto. "Shuford, MedAct." Marine. "Foster, Three MAF Staff." And a thin, quiet one with a damp handshake. "Dillis, MAG Eighty-six."

"Good, good," Houston said, grinning. "I'll give the President your best wishes. Please sit down and I'll relate, on top of what you've heard, what the *President*'s concerned about. What the American people are concerned about."

He winged it awhile, talking about the peasants—"They're *key!*"—but he got a little mixed up on the intricacies of what Beechwood had said about violence and close local surveillance, so settled for the President's worries: "You must be aware that CBS showed Marines burning a village with a Zippo. You can't let that sort of thing happen. Or be *seen*. I should remind you there are rules of engagement. Your men must challenge and be very careful about shooting." He was thinking that troops on the ground could be photographed, but the Air Force or VNAF—well, if you do bomb a village, you can finesse it. In any case there were the Harlem and Watts riots, touched off by police shooting. "Just stay out of trouble," he said, grinning, and got a laugh. Good for them to think of the President as a friendly, all-seeing presence.

Lieutenant Randolph talked over the ground situation with Lieutenant Colonel Thomas in Thomas's office—one end of a squad tent. The furniture was green folding fiberboard field desks and wooden mount-out boxes. Thomas sat on one in a T-shirt, his hair sticking straight up. He'd been to VMI, one of the best schools for Marine officers, but was one of the oddest-looking field grades Mark had ever seen. Too obviously intelligent. On the post was his office sign, Thoreau's quote about some men marching to a different drummer. Thomas said, "The rough grading's done. The civilian construction company's coming in next week."

"That's going to create an internal security problem."

"Yes. They'll be near the work areas, and we'll have birds on the ground. Colonel Dillis may have questions about that when he flies in this afternoon."

Dillis was CO of the helicopter air group, several squadrons, moving into Gia Binh.

At 1300 a Huey helicopter, one of the few the Marines had in-country then, landed whistling and raising dust off the scraped earth. Out came a tall, thin full colonel—Dillis—and a shorter lieutenant colonel—Pym, his XO. Dillis squinted against the sun. The skinny was he'd just got here from California. Randolph watched Lieutenant Colonels Thomas and Mason talking with the two. All of a sudden there was more silver than Randolph had ever seen in one place in his time in the Corps.

What were they talking about? They pointed here. There. Dillis pursed his lips.

"Lieutenant Randolph?"

Mark went over and saluted. He looked the colonel in the face. Colonel Dillis seemed worried. He had pale, kind eyes. "The picture Lieutenant Colonel Thomas and—ah—S-Three, Mason, are giving me doesn't square with what I'm told at Wing. This is supposed to be a clear area. I'd expected we could put up a series of walking posts! The ARVN are up the road!"

Lieutenant Randolph was astounded. Where had this man been? He expected a bird colonel taking command to know more. The colonel looked like—well, he looked like a fifty-year-old man— pleasant, kindly, tired, hot, thirsty—a man in Marine utilities, but not a Marine colonel.

"It's a tactical situation, sir. The VC have people probing here most nights. We have—"

"I *know* about the footprints." He looked at Thomas and then at his own XO—Pym. "What if they're just taking a walk? Or looking around?"

"If so, they should be shot. It's after curfew. That's SOP, sir."

"Those aren't *our* rules of engagement. I've just been at a Presidential briefing in Saigon and *I* know *that*." He looked around, frowning, and said to Lieutenant Colonel Pym, "I'm not happy with this."

Thomas said, "The intruders shot at Mr. Randolph's LP and grenadier, sir. We have the brass."

"How do we *know* it was enemy? And not lost ARVN?"

"Seven-point-six-two Kurz," Randolph said. "At Da Nang they have all sorts of diagrams to identify ammunition."

"I'm going to get a reading from Wing," Colonel Dillis said, and as he walked back to the Huey, to Pym: "They fired *grenades*. I want—" The door slid closed, Colonel Dillis looking straight ahead. The helicopter whistled and took off for Da Nang.

"The skinny is Dillis was high up in Wing logistics," the adjutant, Captain Shick, said. "G-4. He flew R4Ds. No combat. Had the clout to get this command."

Blood

Phoebe and Jim Robinson walked along the Saigon River under the trees by Ben Bach Duong, the boulevard that curved along the bank. Other streets with what Jim called "smart" shops and cafés butted into the *duong*. The grass, trees, and river made it a pleasant place to stroll. Vendors with pushcarts and shoulder poles offered snacks and a restaurant in a tall white boat downriver sent pleasant smells to them. Others strolled too. She and Jim snacked on strips of dried fish bought from a vendor. From another they got rounds of bread fried in garlic oil, covered with small shrimp, crisp and tasty. The air was cooler as autumn approached. Phoebe stopped to photograph boats in the brown water. Jim took shots of gray Navy ships, decks loaded with containers. Guarding them were sailors butting rifles on their hips or swinging them in slob-macho style. Jim said he was surprised the VC hadn't blown up more ships. They bought hot spiced fried rolls at another stall. Phoebe felt something happen to the air, saw a bright flash down the river bank, and heard a sharp loud *!Crunch!*

"Bloody hell," Jim said, pulling her flat to the ground. He covered her head. "Stay down—it falls for some time." Nothing fell their way.

"Let's go," she said. People were still turning to look as they ran toward the gray smoke hanging in the air, dodging people who were running away, screaming. Whistles. National Police in white moved

across the grass toward the riverbank. She saw the white My Kanh
floating restaurant and what looked like tattered rags on the gangway.
Bodies. A wounded woman writhed and screamed on the grass, bright
blood like red silk shining on her white blouse. The dead lay jumbled
up, punched all over with red holes. White and green paint chipped—
otherwise no sign of damage to the boat. An ambulance hooter
sounded behind and an American-made three-quarter-ton army ambulance with Vietnamese markings pulled across the grass.

She had never seen a group of dead. Terrible, her manners told
her; but fascinating. She stared at people in death and agony, in
images more startling yet prosaic than she had ever imagined. A
policeman grabbed her arm and said, *"Ba di-di!"* and added, "Get the
hell out of here!"

Jim was already taking pictures, clicking and cocking, shifting to
a new position, shooting again. She sniffed a bitter smoke smell.
"Claymore," he said.

"What's that?"

"An American mine that throws steel pellets." He pointed at two
policemen squatting by a length of wire. "That's where they set it off.
They aimed it up the walkway when it was full of people."

She used her Rollei. The wounded woman was still screaming.
Phoebe swung toward her. The light wasn't so good, but she had Tri
X in the Voigtlander and took a close-up hold on the woman's face.
Looking through the viewfinder, she saw blood well from the wom-
an's mouth. Phoebe felt so detached. She clicked, then brought up the
Rollei, which had Ektachrome 200 in it, and took shots with that.
Perhaps the color would come out—that bright red.

It didn't hit her until later. She shuddered and kept seeing the
same images.

MACV and the Vietnamese had handouts about the bombing the
next day. They said it was the work of a few terrorists who would be
caught.

At Givral correspondents bet Saigon had *beaucoup* cells of terrorists ready to hit other targets. They had parked a car bomb in front of
a hotel used as a GI rest center and blown away the front. Most of the
correspondents didn't feel good about drinking at Givral; it was simply a French café, not well protected from the street, and could be
blown in by *plastiquers*.

"The war is everywhere," Brian Beechwood said at Givral. He was a thin young man who'd already sold a couple of articles to good magazines. He'd gone to Amherst. Like Phoebe, he'd won a *Paris Review* internship, but he had actually gone while she had been having her heart broken in Massachusetts. He was very stylish and well connected. She'd asked where he was staying; he evaded, then finally admitted he was staying with his father, Harry Beechwood, a high officer in the CIA station.

She couldn't get out of her mind the images of blood and screaming; the worst thing she had ever seen, yet she had observed it coolly through the viewfinder. "That's the way it works," Jim said.

She sold the My Kanh shots to the *Life* bureau under the agreement she'd made as a stringer with the magazine. Two days later she got a cable from Sara saying she had seen them and they were excellent. It was her first important sale. The money wasn't so important as breaking the barrier. She didn't go out drinking to celebrate, either. Some of the correspondents had opium, and she and Jim smoked it with them in a flat. Each had a little brass pipe and lit the little ball of tar and sucked in the burning sweet smoke. She wasn't sure how the others felt, but she felt suspended in oil. Another thing she liked was that it didn't make her horny. It calmed her. They talked awhile and just sat there. At least they weren't in a bar someone could bomb to riddle them with shrapnel.

Opium was a word you could hum, leaning back in a cushioned bamboo chair in a dim room, faces of acquaintances floating in shadow, sounds outside strung together in smooth fabric, the cyclos, singsong voices, *"duoc duoc, khong manh gioi,"* even the *wham!* of the artillery guns and the *tok-tok-tok* of the machine guns in the distance and the *whop-whop* of the helicopters. Poor people out there starving, the *nha ques*, the coolies, the beautiful, tough lipsticked whores of Tu Do Street, the poor soldiers in the helicopters and the VC in the shadows, all doomed to die—for now it didn't matter. She accepted the constant sounds. The war was everywhere, as Brian Beechwood had said.

Several officers lunched on the deck of Lieutenant Colonel Thomas's tent, opening cans and pulling out the cookies and date-nut rolls; spooning up the stews, ragouts, and *potages;* and setting aside the canned bread, dense as football padding, and the vomitous ham and eggs, scrambled. A lot of brass in a squad tent—Lieutenant Colonels Mason and Thomas, majors and captains, and three or four lieutenants other than Randolph, who sat near the door.

A few hundred meters away RMK Construction was putting down pierced steel plating. Vietnamese laborers, American foremen. Stoop. Lift. Stoop. Lift. RMK had told Lieutenant Colonel Thomas it guaranteed the security of its workers. Sentries watched them anyway. A few helicopters were on the pad, antennae and radar were off to the side, and some bunkers held MAG-86's secret weapons.

The helicopters were a couple of dozen H-34s—the Sikorsky the Navy and Marines had called the HUS until Secretary McNamara ruled that everyone use the Army and Air Force terms, which told much less about where the aircraft came from and what it was supposed to do.

"If you think *this* is bureaucratic, you should fly with the Air Force," Mason said. He held up thumb and forefinger two inches apart. "They have to file this much paper after each mission. Particularly ground fire and ordnance expended."

"How is the ground fire?" one of the new captains asked.

"Getting worse," said Captain Shick, the MABS adjutant, who was a pilot, didn't fly much, but enjoyed upsetting the new fish.

They had just got here from tract houses in Southern California and were appalled to be living in tents God Knows Where. They'd already heard about the infiltrators diddy-bopping through the camp, measuring them for mortars and coffins.

The rest of the group's squadrons, dozens of helicopters, had been diverted to Da Nang and Chu Lai for some operation taking elements of the 1st Marine Division, also just arrived from California, in strikes around Chu Lai. The First MarDiv was *the* legendary formation. It had Guadalcanal on its patch. It had destroyed Japan's Sendai Division so decisively that Tojo lied about it for three years; it tore up ten Chinese divisions at Chosin Reservoir. Mark wouldn't mind being *in* it, but he didn't have the energy to ask for it now. Mark had wanted to be in such an outfit—once. But he was exhausted now.

The strain was telling on him. He had a tic and a hoarse voice and his bleak attitude was like black obsidian inside him, reflecting everything he saw in clear, sharp, dark images. He was tired from all the patrols, day briefings, little sleep. The routine of patrols and checking ground was boring. But he had to do it thoroughly because a mistake could be fatal. He was up day and night. It was hopeless. The best he could expect was another night without an accident. Maybe hitting an infiltrator, filing a report, knowing it would be ignored by Colonel Dillis. He had decided Colonel Dillis was a pussy.

He cocked his head and asked innocently, "Will Colonel Dillis be out today?"

Thomas looked at the tent beam. Mason said, "He's in Da Nang today."

Like a dog who feels life is all good or all bad, Randolph felt Dillis was all bad. Of course, the colonel had reasons to stay in Da Nang— getting his group assembled, keeping track of squadrons arriving in-country and detached to Chu Lai. But Mason, his Operations Officer, was out here, because Mason knew this was where the action would be that would call for his decisions. The squadrons down south were under operational control of that task force anyway. Dillis didn't want to sleep out here. He didn't like the squalor of the Vietnamese. Mark noticed Dillis's pained expression when he saw Vietnamese crowding the trash heap near the road, the discarded, uneaten cans. Randolph had heard he'd had a staff meeting to decide if it was better to let them have garbage, because they were hungry, or to destroy it because their rooting for garbage was unseemly.

The colonel *certainly* didn't want to deal with the sticky problem that wouldn't go away—the footprints, shots, scramble marks, and now, one or two small blood spots by the drag marks after the patrol had tossed a grenade in a burst of fire. Blood on the ground was a sign of something, whether or not the colonel could face it.

Noises in the ether, too. The communications officer, an ass-kissing but diligent regular, Lieutenant Szabo, had noticed a mike keying and other noises on the group's local defense net. Part of Szabo's job was listening to the air. No other friendly units had the group's frequency. The odd noises meant Charlie was listening. "They aren't primitive electronically," Szabo said. "They have the gear."

"Well, how do you know for sure if some guy is VC?" one of the new aviators asked while opening a can of fruit cocktail, twisting his opener like a man with good motor skills.

"If he's shooting at you," Mason said.

"One of the mechs said ARVN shoot at the aircraft leaving the LZ."

"Some of *them* are VC," Szabo said. "They've been *binh van*ned."

"They don't even have to be converted," Thomas said. "If they've been shanghaied into the army and aren't paid, they're pissed off enough anyway."

"The elite units are as good as any," Mason said dutifully. "The Black Cat Company." He didn't want the new fish to be disillusioned.

At the door of the tent a handsome red-faced, black-haired sergeant appeared. He had the muscular, shy manner of a Li'l Abner. He was Sergeant Vernal Luke Pearl, an ex-DI and machine gun instructor from South Carolina. He threw a salute. " 'Scuse me, gentlemen. Mr. Randolph—reckon you're needed on the field."

They walked over the broken ground and cat tracks, Pearl falling in step on Randolph's left. Pearl was a squared-away Marine, Mark thought.

He'd got Pearl and a skinny, tall, ex-seagoing sergeant named Lawrence off the same draft. Both unfortunately had made the faux pas, when they reported to the CP the first night, of wearing camouflage utilities undoubtedly bought on impulse from some Indian merchant in Da Nang, thinking they would give them an instant salty look. Randolph had been gentle about it—"You won't need those, they're no advantage at night"—while Lance Corporal Lindahl, who *was* salty, choked down a laugh in the background. Randolph knew his own appearance must have startled them, with his tic and the stiff way he moved, since he spent as much time crawling as he did walking.

Pearl told Lawrence he thought the lieutenant was like a fifty-year-old man, wheezing and grunting as they walked in daylight. But when they patrolled at night, Randolph and all the others had been quieter than Pearl thought round-eyes could be, feather-footing and floating over the ridge onto that trail by the paddies. So alert they smelled others, Vietnamese, out scouting. So disciplined they all got quiet as the dead in the night.

"You're good," Randolph told him. And a little later he grabbed Pearl's shoulder and leaned toward him, eyes locked on. "Whatever happens," he said, "*you* make sure all these gunners know that fuckin' machine gun backward and forward. Range cards. Night firing—" He named off hoarsely what drills he wanted. "Defilade fire. The VC are rigid. They passed up a howitzer when they hit an ARVN camp a few months ago—it wasn't noted on their plans, so no one took it out and the ARVN used it to break up the attack. Everyone says they base their attacks on detailed reconnaissance and rigid orders from the top. So we keep the guns hidden and *you* train me gunners who can come up and get fire superiority all of a sudden. You're the instructor."

"Aye-aye, sir." Pearl was surprised how personal and intense these officers were here.

"I best tell you what happened," Pearl said as they patted over the PSP, the pierced steel plating used for runways and hardstands, to the scene where a Viet laborer lay on the ground and a pissed-off civilian foreman glared at the sentries. "That'n on the ground tried to snoop in Bunker Four," Pearl said; the sentry buttstocked him, sending him rolling like a croquet ball, gibbering in pain. The slope didn't see the poncho-covered gun or tripod legs. Meanwhile *another* slope had swung the surveyor's transit to aim at the antennae over the comm bunker, and another Marine knocked over the transit and then aimed his M-14 at the man's nose and said, *"Dung lai,"* meaning "Freeze, motherfucker," which caused the man to crouch, bowing, hands steepled in the praying gesture.

Antennae aren't supposed to be examined by strangers with calibrated optics. This surveyor had no need to look at the comm bunker. The fact that he did was suspicious. It was the kind of thing ferrets did in ports, which is why warships shroud their antennae going into harbor. Randolph didn't trouble to explain this to the foreman because he didn't trust *him*, either. While the man complained, Lieutenant Randolph's face grew cold and set; he stared, his eye going jump, jump, jump. The foreman's voice ran down.

"Who in the fuck you think you are? You're lucky my troops didn't shoot you. I don't know if it wouldn't be a good idea. At least tie your ass up and fly you and your pals here to Da Nang for interrogation—"

The foreman recoiled. "You can't do that—"

"Bullshit!" Randolph exploded. He advanced on the foreman, wheezing and ticking, telling him where he wanted these laborers to face and how they would be shot or worse.

Lieutenant Colonel Thomas arrived, eyes gawking, a soft cap on top of his straight-up hair; he questioned the foreman himself. "What *were* you doing? You know the terms of the contract regarding supervision."

Thomas had much better manners than Randolph but an even

shorter temper, and after a few exchanges he told the RMK man *he'd* shoot the next asshole looking in the wrong place. "We don't need you to do this," Thomas said. "We have engineer troops." His voice rose. "You don't think I can do that?" He grabbed a Marine's M-14 and threw an offhand hold on the transit man, who sank to his knees and resumed praying vigorously.

"Goddam," the foreman said, dry-mouthed. "You don't gotta—"

"You keep that transit off our gear!"

Then Lieutenant Colonel Mason arrived, swinging along in his flight suit with rolled-up sleeves, his bomb tattoo, and his baseball cap. He saw the Vietnamese on his back, the other praying, and the Marines ready to thump the foreman. He put his hands on his hips. Behind him came several captains and majors who had nothing better to do. And then the captain on Operations Duty Officer came up behind them and said Colonel Dillis was on his way and would land in a few minutes.

Mason turned to the foreman without hesitating and said in his smooth, cultivated voice, "You and your firm could be in deep shit, my friend. Our colonel can make a big stink with Contracts. He won't stand for this."

Thomas looked skyward. Mark took it in, staring. What a great line of shit! If this grit only knew what a snatch the colonel was.

"No, sir," the foreman said, "meaningly they wasn't no tryin' to—"

"I suggest *you* get back to work and keep your slickie boys out of restricted areas."

"Buttstock 'em if they get *close*," Mark grunted to the sentries.

Then the colonel's Huey flapped into view.

Several hundred meters away, Major Thanh watched the round-eye fire drill through binoculars from a hole in the mat side of Thuy's house. So the *mỹ* had caught our *du kich*. But they hadn't shot them. They were softer than the *phap*, who liked to "make examples." Indeed, the Americans were indecisive. All the *binh vanh* patriots in the puppet forces said that.

They said one *mỹ* officer will be concerned with showing figures of progress—missions flown, patrols run, patriots killed—and another will be concerned only not to disturb, to avoid bloodshed or blame. Thanh, who had been made moralistic by his Confucian thinking and more so by his Giap-Mao-Leninist training, repeated the axiom "They are rich in things but morally weak." They are indecisive because they do not know what is right. The Will of Heaven is against them.

But when Brother Bao, the patriot who operated the transit spying for the Struggle, reported to his control that the long-nose pigs had anticipated every innocuous trick and reacted immediately, Thanh was bemused. They were confused; he was bemused. They reacted to some conditions, ignored others. Long-noses were incomprehensible.

This outburst of officers, for instance—a lieutenant colonel grabbing a rifle, or that lieutenant taking out patrols, chasing and firing his pistol, yelling. The *phap* lieutenants had done it, too, but it was so typically *long-nose!* In the *mat tran*, officers stayed back, for only they knew how to balance *dan van* and *dich van*, political and violent action, leaving the execution of attacks to sergeants. Command in the Quan Doi Giai Phong, the Liberation Army, was like a pyramid, with the officers at top center making military decisions informed by political sensitivity; they passed fighting authority by strictly defined orders down to NCOs in contact with the enemy. The sergeants' orders were carefully spelled out, each step and nothing more.

Of course, it was true the long-nose officers could make decisions on the spot—he had heard Randolph on the radio, ordering special illumination, or changing his units' positions unpredictably. Anyway, soon enough liberation forces could mortar the base, RPG the trucks, and assault the positions and kill everyone.

"Dear Houston," began the letter from Harry Beechwood, Brian's father, the CIA station officer Houston had met in Saigon. "Please regard everything in this billet-doux as Top Secret and dispose of it accordingly. . . ."

It had arrived by pouch. Chatty. Sometimes arch. Houston imagined Harry Beechwood's meaningful glances, eyebrows high, the way he had talked in Saigon.

"I wanted to let you know about something intriguing that's probably been lost in seas of paper there. . . ."

Houston was reading the letter after lunch while the corridors buzzed because LBJ was having a shitfit about what the press called "peaceniks" and "vietniks," playing on the public's amused image of beatniks. They usually came out by the fence after lunch. Probably slept late! Houston thought.

They had that same lost, shaggy, lumpen bohemian look of beat-niks, too. Peaceniks, ha!

"Whose fuckin' side they on?" the President asked. The sight of his big shambling leader, ego-wounded and dangerous, made Houston's instincts warn, "Heads up!"

"Our friends in Sofia," Beechwood wrote, "last May Day showed an item of military equipment that, our sources here say, is now in-country and will affect the military picture. Mark you, I said *our* sources, not the Army's. What I'm talking about will show the Army *can't* make it by slugging it out. . . ."

The message Harry Beechwood was putting so coyly was that the CIA's men in Bulgaria, following standard procedures, had photographed Soviet military equipment during the May Day parade, the red military's day to show off. Bulgaria, Russia's closest ally, usually got new stuff. This year they showed what appeared to be an automatic antiaircraft cannon—that is, a gun that fired high explosive shells as fast as a machine gun. "Radar directed, we think," Beechwood wrote. "The photographs are very grainy."

Houston knew these trench-coat guys took the pictures at curb-side, using trick cameras concealed in arm casts, lapel flowers, etc.

"It appears to be no bigger than a jeep," Beechwood wrote. When he said "in-country," he meant that Agency informants in Vietnam believed this odd weapon was in South Vietnam. Finally, his remarks about the Army meant that he thought the Agency had more reliable field intelligence than the Army, and that this weapon could knock out the air support the Army depended on; which meant, in turn, that the Army could not win by using Westmoreland's strategy of seeking big battles.

What the devil does he intend by this? Houston wondered. Does he want me to tell the President the Army's wrong? People in the *Army* think the Army's wrong, for God's sake.

One recent flap had resulted from a retired general telling the *New York Times* the Army was throwing away all charades of coun-terinsurgency and deploying the mechanized Army it used in Europe simply to "blood" it—season its officers and NCOs—and try out equipment.

This meant that sooner or later the Army would move to attack across the DMZ, which gave Johnson fits because military and polit-ical intelligence agreed the Chinese had five divisions north of the DMZ to protect Hanoi.

"I sure as shit ain't gonna admit the Chinese got people up there," LBJ told them at an NSC briefing. "This fuckin' talkin' by generals is what cut off Truman's legs in Korea."

Houston was troubled by the way Johnson talked now.

"I ain't gonna have my legs cut off!" he said querulously. Another time he said, "I'm paralyzed."

Houston could tell he *was* paralyzed because he relied on experts and didn't know how to challenge them. He wasn't versed in foreign affairs. He wanted to create the Great Society and let the generals and McNamara produce results overseas. But would they?

"I quizzed those goddam admirals and generals in Congress," LBJ said. "They'll mislead you to get their own ends. But they won the War and Korea and who in hell's goin' to do better?" Big as he was, LBJ gave out that sense of power locked up. He was suffering.

This was when his manner went from imperious to strangely overbearing. He was known to demand that visitors accompany him to the toilet so his time wouldn't be wasted while they continued the discussion. Perhaps it was a way of imposing his will on others when he was helpless in bigger matters.

Houston wondered if Johnson was getting tired. It wasn't a question of competence. Johnson was brilliant, much more aware of some aspects of politics than any of the old crowd of Eastern WASPs in office since Roosevelt. Indeed, it was people like the Dulleses of Princeton and Bissell of Yale who had fumbled so badly overseas. The question was one of appearances—dignity, Houston thought. One of *us* certainly wouldn't have done that.

"The other thing I thought you should know especially, Houston," Beechwood's letter continued, "is that we have *political* information, not snapshots taken at a parade, that our friends in Stockholm"—by which he meant they weren't friends at all—"are selling a kind of radar to the Russians for use by North Vietnamese troops. The Swedes, as you know, play neutral but always toady to the closest bad boy; they allowed Nazi troop trains free passage across Sweden to Norway so the SS could fight British commandos, and they let the Nazi prisoner trains out the other way. They toady to the Soviets now. They provide the radar, the NVA uses it, the Soviets get credit for superior technology."

A handy fact to salt away, Houston thought, since one of his rivals on the staff was a tedious young liberal—a Stevenson admirer, in fact—and this could block him. But he couldn't see value in telling LBJ any of these facts now. The man was innately suspicious. His eyes narrowing: "Who told you this? What's he want? He tryin' to fuck us?"

Houston knew to follow his own career plan of government, Wall Street, and back to government and not get caught in side deals. The aircraft hardware deals, for instance: He massaged people LBJ had always served without making his own deals. Everyone knew Lady Bird had a strong position in Textron, which meant Hueys. He didn't get caught in discussions about one product or another. He was an appointee and had future appointments to win. Congressman Sanford of California said much the same thing—"Take their money but don't get trapped in harness." For all Houston knew, Sanford was a closet dove. He *did* know Sandy spent too long mending fences because he'd become very friendly with the congressman's wife, Marty. They had a regular room at a hotel on K Street.

He did the same calculating dance with construction men who called LBJ—keeping them happy and praising their public works, but not getting too close.

Out of the question to tell LBJ what Beechwood had told him about new weapons the NVA was getting. LBJ had enough of a wild hair up his ass with the demonstrators out there.

Phoebe was at Givral when she found out about the captured terrorist. No one had bombed Givral yet, so the press had decided they wouldn't ever because so much information traded hands there. "It can't happen to us," they agreed, and went back about the time *Life* ran her photos of the huddled dead and the dying woman.

Jim was off drinking with an Army officer. She'd been smoking bhang and got to the café at dusk after a ride in a cyclo and a view of tracers fired for who-cared-what reason like red confetti flung across the violet sky. Would the Romans, who took omens from flights of birds, read tracers in the sky? That was where her head was. She ordered Amer Picon. She saw Brian Beechwood.

Most of Brian's Vietnamese friends were *attentismistes*, young professionals not in government, but in the group tonight was an older man whose manner suggested he didn't know the others well. Brian said, "He told me he wanted to meet you."

"I am with the Ministry of Justice," the man said. "I can arrange for you interview with bomber terrorist we captured, who killed so many at restaurant." There would be a consideration, he said.

"*Bien entendu*," Brian said. The *attentismistes* laughed.

"For the interpreter," the government man said.

"I will interpret," Binh, Brian's lawyer friend said.

"You cannot get into prison."

"Your government's threatened me with it," Binh said, laughing.

"Why me?" Phoebe asked dreamily, stoned.

"Because you had story and photos before."

"There may be no story," Phoebe said.

"No, I assure you, he killed many. Killed Americans, too."

That would attract editors, she thought cynically; American deaths were local interest. She haggled and struck a deal for a thousand piasters—a hundred dollars.

The following day the government man picked her up in a gray Peugeot and drove her out Le Van Duyet and the Bien Hoa road to an unmarked brick building surrounded by concertina and guarded by ARVN soldiers. She was checked through the gate and past two checkpoints inside, down a corridor that smelled of urine, shit, and Lysol, into a plain room with tables and chairs, the walls painted tan. A flat tin ashtray made from a U.S. ration can sat on the table. She lit a cigarette. A soldier opened the door and led in the terrorist—a man in his thirties, about five feet two inches tall, with pouched brown eyes. He glanced at her and looked at the floor. He wore cutoff fatigue pants and a T-shirt. His stiff black hair went up in a bush on top and was cut to short bristles above his ears. An interpreter in khakis came in. The fixer left. The interpreter smiled and nodded. "I speak English French. Either better."

"Try English."

The terrorist sat with his elbows on his knees, staring at the floor.

"Identification," the interpreter said. "*Ten ong la gi? Ten ong la gi?*"

"Nguyen Lang Minh," the terrorist said.

"Probably not his real name," the interpreter said.

"Where are you from?"

"Saigon," he said, pronouncing it Shy-gonk.

"How old?"

"Thirty-four."

"How long have you been with the Viet Cong?"

Minh yelled, "*Phai khong! Khong Viet Cong! Viet Minh! Mat tran!*

Toi la nguoi nguyen!" He sputtered and yelled words she'd heard, repeating *mat tran*, which she knew as NLF.

"He say he's with the communists since eighteen."

"Why did you join?"

Minh spoke rapidly. Then he lapsed into his torpid slump, staring at the floor.

"He say family very poor, father work groundskeeper club, mother laundry. Family nine children, only three boys—bad luck. He say good family, not kill girl babies. He too poor to go to school, French hurt his family."

"How?"

"Father lose job. Mother sick. Sisters go to city but can't find good job. He works unloading trucks. Then go with communists, *cong-san.*"

"What doing?"

More talk.

"He carry messages. Then place grenades. Communists have young boys ride bicycles and drop grenades in crowds. Many die, but he very quick. Then French go away and he work to save money to buy own truck."

"Did he?"

Minh loosed a torrent of words, repeating "Diem," which he pronounced Ze-yem, and *"an cap."*

"He say he lost all money. Paying taxes."

"He said *an cap*. That means corruption."

"An cap!" Minh cut in, his dark eyes flashing. *"Ja phai, an cap!"*

"Didn't he say something about Diem?"

"Diem! *Ja phai*, Diem no-good motherfucker," Minh said, agitated.

"He not like Diem," the interpreter said.

"Whom do you hate more? The French? Or the Americans?"

Minh looked at the floor and spoke dully. He used the word *phap* and the upward-toned *me-yee*, and the interpreter said, "He say French very bad. Steal. Shoot in villages."

"The Americans?"

"Not hate all Americans. Soldiers and white-shirt men have too much money, he say. Degrade women."

"He hasn't said anything about being angry that the war has killed his friends. Unless none of his friends were killed."

"Oh, yes, yes. He say friends killed, too."

The government was trying to sell her a talking-horse routine; this is what the horse means when he nods his head. She said, "Unless you tell me exactly what he says, without changing it the way your supervisors want, I won't use this. If you tell me the truth it will advance you."

"Wait one please, thank you." The interpreter left and stood in the doorway speaking with the government man. A high-ranking cop. The interpreter came back, grinning. "Okay." While Minh stared at the floor, the interpreter told the missing parts of the story.

"Man say two things, always two things, contradict, also we investigate background. He come from very—incorrect family. Unrighteous. Not work. Not think. Father not follow right conduct. Father disgraced family. He say mother go away often, stay by self, never call children to her. Father shout, beat children only, not give correct guidance as fatherly duty. But then he say they good family, it is fault of French. Or Diem. Or Americans."

"Which is true?"

"They do not know. Officer here say he grew up to hate." The interpreter looked at her. "This without merit—not good to hate, our custom not to hate. To act correctly regardless."

"Among Buddhists?"

"No, all."

"But Christians hate. They say it's bad but everyone does."

"No, not in Vietnam," the interpreter said. "Catholic not matter, most still practice Vietnamese custom. Very strict rules on what is right behavior." He laughed. "Like army."

"That's unreal," she murmured. "I don't believe it."

"No, true."

"I'm sorry," she said, standing. "He's uttered nothing I can use."

"You not come back?"

"Not unless he talks and you level." No one tried to stop her when she went out to the car.

If her flat she looked at Vo Nguyen Giap's "People's War, People's Army," the Viet Minh commanding general's short pamphlet about the war against the French. She ran across a phrase others had mentioned: "We are weak in weapons but fight for a just cause. They cannot win and we cannot lose." It had that irrationally intense obsessive conviction she sensed in Minh. And in the interpreter speaking non sequiturs. Was everyone here nuts?

At Givral she saw Brian Beechwood and Binh, his lawyer friend, at the table they liked near the door. Brian winced as rude laughter exploded from a group of American civilians who had taken over two tables and were drinking whiskey, which was extremely expensive and probably fake. "Look at this fuckin' joint!" one said.

"I can't make sense of this bomber," she told Brian.

"What about him?"

"He doesn't respond like a person. More like a robot. He drags himself in and answers in a monotone, but blows up at terms like Viet Cong."

"Well, of *course*," Brian said.

The lawyer smiled. "It's an insulting phrase. Also theft of a proper term to use Viet Cong, which is a play on *viet xian*, Vietnamese traitor."

"So it's name-calling."

"No. It's not hard to understand Vietnamese ways—the French did—but you must first be able to understand ways not your own, like learning another language. One aspect is the value of correct terms. We carefully identify things and assign correct terms. Have you read Confucius?"

"A few analects."

"No, plunge in," Brian said. "You have to detach yourself from argument and counterargument and accept ambivalence."

Binh said, "Confucian ways are strong here. Even I, I understand European ways, but we do not think that way. A poor uneducated man has no notion of European ways."

"The bomber also uttered a string of false pieties," Phoebe said.

"What?"

"How he didn't hate Americans, when obviously he did; how his family was so good, when he obviously hated them."

"No, that's Confucian too," Binh said.

"How?"

"The values must be observed. Instead of saying he hates the Americans—which he must—he says he hates their presence, or soldiers, or workers, so he's still able to kill any he sees. And he honors his family because family is at the center of everything. Without the family you die. We don't have an idea of self—not like the Western idea. Certainly not the American idea of self, where you stand alone and leave your home and go anywhere. We exist as parts of families, so when one of us has a specific duty toward his family, he must practice the right conduct. That means showing the right emotions. If it isn't right conduct to hate all Americans, you say you just hate the bad ones."

"Like these boors," Brian said, nodding toward the loud whiskey drinkers.

"Sounds schizo to me," Phoebe said.

"Yes," Brian said.

"No," Binh said. "Not here. To us duty is more important than freedom. Freedom is chaos, the stars out of their tracks. We are all part of something else. If playing our parts means controlling a facial expression, better that than chaos. The family has the Will of Heaven. Pieties express the will of heaven. Do you know, Diem was hated not because of his cruelty, but because he claimed to have the moral authority of a Confucian ruler, the Will of Heaven, but he had not. Our people can endure the worst oppression if they believe the ruler has the Will of Heaven, but if they perceive he does not, everything changes. They fight against impossible odds to destroy him, because they know in the end they will win."

"That's what Minh said."

"Of course. The Viet Minh said it about the French because they had been defeated by the Japanese and collaborated with them, thus losing dignity. The *mat tran* loses no chance to say it has the Will of Heaven."

Brother Duong squatted beside Major Thanh on the porch of the dead puppet's house. They smoked cigarettes and watched night fall. A scrape of metal on dirt as volunteers dug behind the ridge and down in the paddy.

"Ba Huynh is all right?" Thanh asked.

"Yes. She will go away and come back later."

"Huynh is really all right. He needs a few days to heal."

He had been hit with a shotgun pellet and gone down, but had bad wounds in his legs from the hooks. "Perhaps they were hasty, but they had to get him out fast," Thanh said. Unfortunately they had left noticeable blood marks on the ground.

Duong smoked awhile and finally said, "Some of the patriots are not happy with it, frankly."

"I know."

They both knew too many patriots had been hurt already and

one killed. Another upriver would probably die. Thanh knew people were saying the darkest things about Huynh's chances.

Duong said, "I must tell you forthrightly some say the *mỹ* aren't so bad. Their helicopters aren't so noisy."

"Wait till more arrive."

"They hand out money. This they say in Gia Binh, too."

A few women from the hamlet were doing laundry over there.

Thanh said, "The *chi bo* in Gia Binh tell me any decent family's daughter is forced to be a prostitute for the *mỹ*. The puppet soldiers run the whorehouses for the long-nose pigs to defile our daughters!"

They both knew people in Gia Binh liked all the money the Americans pumped in, to say nothing of all the *mỹ* equipment people stole and put to use in town.

Duong said, "It was that lance corporal today who fixed the people's bus."

He and Duong and Sergeant Thien had been waiting for a patriot to arrive on the jeepney, a brightly painted jeep carrying long benches hanging out behind. They traveled the roads to Gia Binh, Da Nang, Hue, Quang Tri, carrying honest country folk and their goods. This jeepney also carried radio dry cells that had come in from the sea by fishing boat and been carried to Gia Binh, where the patriot, Ba Huu, received them. She had twenty kilos of batteries covered with dried roots in her heavy sack. The jeepney was crowded and overloaded, and the engine stopped when the vehicle was a half-kilometer up the road. They had to get the batteries. Ba Huu couldn't haul her heavy sack even that short distance. Three men of military age couldn't run out. They saw Ba Huu yanking at her bag, cursing, trying to drag it anyway.

A long-nose jeep came up behind, the driver wearing goggles. He looked under the hood of the jeepney, made a carburetor adjustment, got the engine running, and shot in fluid that blew black smoke out the rear and helped the jeepney run smoother. He was laughing and showing off for the passengers.

"Ba Huu said she hates long-noses but he seemed like a nice boy."

"They are children," Thanh said. "Children are charming but savages. Some here like the long-noses because of their garbage. Disgraceful! This is not how we fight the struggle! I will talk to them again!" He was getting tired of this. Of course he had to motivate them. But he would have *bo doi* covering them now. The zone committee was counting down now to the battalion attack on the Marine camp.

Phoebe went back to see Minh. She still couldn't believe the bomber had no self, no will of his own. She asked him about sex.

"What do you do for sex in your camp?"

He looked at Phoebe, wrinkling his nose.

"He say no sex in camp," the interpreter said. "Say all work for Great Uprising."

"Are there no women?"

"Yes. But they work for revolution, too. They not decadent, he say. Men and women not together."

"Do the fighters masturbate?"

Minh made a sour face. "No. It makes one weak."

"Is he telling the truth about all this?"

The interpreter shrugged. "Communist women, very serious." He laughed.

She stared at Minh. His face was empty of feeling. "Make sure you translate exactly." The interpreter nodded. "What do you feel like when you kill?"

Minh answered dully.

"It is for the *mat tran*, he say. It doesn't matter."

"But you killed Vietnamese at My Kanh."

"Puppets."

"But you would rather kill Americans?"

"*Ja phai!*" Minh shouted, eyes blazing. He understood that much English. He slumped back, muttering, looking at the interpreter.

The interpreter said, "He saying, 'I do not hate Americans, only that they are oppressors. If they leave I don't hate them.' "

"Tell me, is it creative, or ingenious, for you to devise ways to attack a place?"

"He doesn't devise. They give him plans. Always same."

"The plans?"

"Yes. Always same."

"How?"

They spoke briefly, and the interpreter said, "He answer question many times. Plans always same. They send scouts to place. Not him alone—many—*bo doi* and volunteers, *du kich*. They wear uniform or right clothes. Police station, military office, even American Embassy. Always same."

Phoebe sent queries to *Esquire* and to someone Jim knew at the *Sunday Express* and used the same material in different form for both pieces, which the editors bought. She packaged the bombing shots and mugs of Minh with a couple of inches of copy for *Stern*, which was buying gore and serving it with moralistic comment about warlike Amerika.

That summer Adams Peabody moved in with Kathy Dunlap, the ebullient, freckled, curly-haired girl he'd met in the department when he first arrived. She often said, "Bitchin'," wore T-shirts, and was doing her dissertation on politics in *Tarzan* and other Burroughs works.

They went to teach-ins and helped form the Ad Hoc Graduate Humanities Against the War. At a demonstration at Port Chicago (ammunition shipments) a deputy sheriff rapped Kathy in the teeth, knocking one out, and said, "That'll give you something to remember me by."

She spit blood all over his khaki shirt. Other sheriffs moved in to beat her with nightsticks and Peabody and several other AHGHATW members formed a ball, blocking the sheriffs. They arrested everyone but didn't know what to do with them. "You fuckin' peace pussies!"

Adams and Kathy met with other students from Health Sciences for Peace and Science and Engineering for Peace. They formed a loose coalition. Some members were student government types who'd been in the Student Non-Violent Coordinating Committee working for civil rights before the black majority voted whites out in 1964. Others had been members of Students for a Democratic Society since the Port Huron Statement, an activist manifesto issued in 1962.

"I'm not a student government type," Peas said, "but, man, we have to do something now!"

"I want to fuck up that cop," Kathy said.

Peas worked on a demonstration on the Bay Bridge. Someone in the coalition asked him to work on the Golden Gate Park demonstration. Without having political ambition, he found himself taking charge, forming work parties to hand out leaflets and put up posters. They always did this at night, from a car, with lookouts a block up and back for cops.

He was a monitor at several demonstrations, wearing a color-coded arm band, and a speaker at several as well. He had become a leader. He didn't doubt the value of what he was doing, so it seemed perfectly rational and natural to act now, to be a part of one's times; Mathieu against the Gestapo, eh?

He assumed some of the characteristics of leaders. In front of groups he limited his speech to clear, simple statements no one could confuse. "Big business wants you to fight for it!" he shouted. "Don't die oppressing others!" He wore more colorful clothes, a funkier and more faded and tattered Levi's jacket, brighter bandannas, wilder hair. The style now was not to wear a watch, but he paid close attention to time. He had meetings to make.

He must have met old leftists, communists, student socialists, and outside agitators during all these coalition activities, but no insidious serpent with a red star seduced him, the way J. Edgar Hoover said in his report to LBJ on the Bay Area antiwar demonstrations, the first big ones in the country. Houston saw and initialed the report but didn't notice Adams Peabody's name on the list of communist leaders. Houston was not a detail man, and he was paying attention to what the demonstrations meant to LBJ's fantasy of consensus.

Adams Peabody hadn't sold his soul to the horned Marx, but he did do something that gave that appearance. He was talking with a community organizer from Oakland in a storefront office on a paper-littered street of flat-walled buildings near the waterfront.

"Pamphlets. Leaflets," the man said. "I have stock shots *now* from activists over there. Have you read 'The Peasants of North Vietnam'? It's French. You know what kind of suffering they're going through?"

He gave Peas photographs of North and South Vietnamese peasants in villages holding weapons. "Look! An armed peasantry—no different from our Minutemen! Those guns were captured from the South Vietnamese! And here are liberation soldiers. You can use these in leaflets." Most of the photos appeared also in *Vietnam Vietnam*, published a few months later in Berkeley. The Humanities committee decided it should put out leaflets since, as Kathy put it, "Communications arts are Humanities' bag."

The committee produced two—a broadside manifesto proclaiming the American war illegal and a leaflet telling about the justice of the liberation cause, with photos of the people at war. Peabody mailed samples to Mark Randolph in his camp at Gia Binh airfield with the enjoinder, "Read and think! This is truth!"

Unseen Fighting, Buried Conflicts

When Mark Randolph got Adams Peabody's peace leaflets two days later—mail service was faster between Vietnam and the States than between American cities—he stared at the offset-printed sheet and snorted. He was furious! Does Peabody really believe this stuff? That *I'm* oppressing villagers? I can't even get a census! What had happened to Peas? First that odd letter, then this off-the-wall leaflet with its distorted facts and blanket accusations.

They'd had some good times at Yale, shooting the shit after class. Peabody had been so much a pale, cramped, sheltered scholar, wanting to hear stories about the world out there—high school and cars and cheerleaders. He'd shown Peas townie bars where you could get shots and beers and—what else?—shoot the shit. It wrenched Mark's vanity, understanding he had probably been a specimen this guy consulted—the vulgar theme in our fabric of thought. Anyway, Peabody was full of shit.

Randolph threw the paper to another lieutenant, an aviator named Polchuck, in the same tent. "Look at that shit!" It was the photo of the Vietnamese Minutemen with weapons; the cutline read, "Captured from Americans and their hirelings," but the weapons shown were clearly Soviet carbines, ancient Mossin-Nagants (which had, in fact, been made by Remington for the Czar), and World War II SKS gas-operated semiautomatics. They were so *clearly* foreign in shape. Mark felt like a scholar pouncing on an inapposite footnote—Ah-*ha!*

"Who's he?"

"Guy I knew in college." Mark didn't mention Yale much in the Marines. The schools that mattered most here were the academies and VMI. "I don't even *want* to go back to the States. Isn't anyone challenging assholes there anymore?" He was thinking also of Colonel Dillis, their surburban CO, and all the twats who'd come out here. One, a major in MABS, the base support squadron, actually got on the net when they had a contact and were trying to chase a man. Or the twats who thought up the rules of engagement, particularly the one who you were supposed to challenge on patrol at night. In English? Excuse me, are you an eentsy bit hostile? He felt his hackles up, spine strapped down, locked into the pattern in that way of stone military men, rejecting all that was unnecessary, uncertain, incorrect, civilian. He was ready to commit murder anyway, stepping down from the decked tent's plywood platform, strapping on his holster. He drew his .45 and moved his hands over it quickly, thumbing, turning, shoving the muzzle, checking the magazine and safeties.

Sergeant Lawrence, the tall ex-seagoing Marine, saluted him and fell into step on his left. It was overcast that afternoon. Rains coming. They walked over broken ground and met the corpsman, a sailor in Marine utilities carrying a big green shoulder bag and a .45. A baby-faced second lieutenant and two clerks carrying rifles, and an ARVN sergeant interpreter. They were going to visit the hamlet to hand out medical care and look around. The lieutenant was an intelligence officer by specialty—Ned Montross. Since he wasn't infantry or an aviator, Randolph didn't regard him seriously. He'd said he'd been in the best fraternity at UCLA and got *Esquire*, if Mark wanted his old copies. He raised his hand and grinned now. "Hi." The ARVN sergeant standing next to Lieutenant Montross saluted Mark.

"*Chao, Ong Tu!*" Mark said to the sergeant, and to Montross: "Look, Ned, you won't need your clerks as extra riflemen on this visit. I want Sergeant Lawrence to scope out the place casually, as if we're not on guard. He's got EEI to look for." He meant essential elements of information—clues to a VC presence in the hamlet.

"Will we be safe?"

Mark looked at the clerks. They were as new as Montross. Maybe less fatuous, since they weren't second lieutenants. "It's not cool to go in heavy, Ned. They can cut us down if that's their game." He laughed. "It'd give us a pretext for flattening the place! We wouldn't have to dick around so much, screening." Sergeant Lawrence smiled. The clerks went back to their office tent.

They walked down the dirt road. Ahead was the ridge of squatting bushes. Also squatting man, taking a dump in his yard. They did that here. Sanitation was terrible. That's why they were going over on this medical visit called MedCap.

Second Lieutenant Montross asked again, "Well, what *if* there's an incident here?"

"You mean if they shoot us in the backs?"

"More or less."

"Rodriguez'll come over and shoot some and haul the rest away for questioning and we'll find out who lives here, since you guys can't."

"The ARVN doesn't *know*," Montross said. He looked at Mark with wide kid's eyes. "I don't want to do anything here I'll regret later."

Randolph snorted. "Later?" Who has the luxury of thinking about later?

"You have to understand how sensitive people are back home."

"Fuck 'em."

The corpsman smiled.

"I walk over here alone anyway, just to see how they react."

"I know. The colonel isn't happy with that."

Mark glanced at Montross. Was he being dared to say, "Fuck the colonel," too? Instead he said, "I have my own thoughts about this hamlet."

They followed the narrow path to the dirt square. No one was out. A woman's face in a window. "They ain't lively today," Sergeant Lawrence said.

The store's front tin wall had been swung up to provide an overhang and the small dude with glasses inside looked stonily at Randolph and the MedCap party. Randolph grinned, blithely greeting him, and motioned Ned in. "Hey, Ned, look! Good tobacco they got. *Pâté dentifrice!*" He bought cigarettes and offered the storekeeper one and lit up. They were like Gitanes.

Randolph's sense of danger had improved. This guy wasn't a bit inscrutable. Look at him. He hates me. Hates us. Randolph wondered if *he* was the cadre working the hamlet.

Nothing to pull out his .45 and blast him. Not now, though. Run over, no insignia, a mask, run out. Have a good man covering him. Shotgun? Automatic M-14. Did he have the balls to do it? Would it pay? It was one of the great Marine Corps legends—how Sergeant Hanneken put on blackface, walked into the Haitian bandits' camp, and shot Charlemagne Peralte. The BAR man covering him, Corporal William Button, had two Medals of Honor—one for the Boxer Rebellion. How salty can you get? Legends.

All he really wanted was to sit well in the memory of his men, which meant taking appropriate action where necessary, like greasing the cadre setting up the attack. Since there was no afterlife, none of this wishy-washy Christian transcendental vaporlift to take you over The Abyss, you had to grab the fucking threat like Grendel and kill it or die right so the survivors thought well of you. Someone who fucked that up was damned in memory. On board ship Navy officers still told stories years later about the skipper of the *Missouri* who had ignored subordinates warning him, one after the other, and ran the battleship aground. And there were plenty of legends about men who delivered and saved their shipmates.

"*Dan nguoi Ap Nhac Muoi!*" Sergeant Tu yelled, calling them out for free medical care to cure them of hating Americans.

It wasn't that Randolph was terribly warlike by nature or family. His father hadn't even been in World War II. Maybe that had directed his impulse to join this. But his ancestors had fallen into occasional wars, like the Civil War, and left notes and diaries. One had written: "I got even on the damned Rebs. Killed five today." Each man has to do it sometime—get even. That remark by Second Lieutenant Montross: "I don't want to do anything I'll regret later." Typical.

Free medical care! Sergeant Tu offered.

A few women came up, some carrying children. Randolph gave out the cigarettes he'd bought, grinning and using the few phrases he knew, glancing at the storekeeper. Had the dude poisoned the cigarettes? Sergeant Lawrence, who in addition to being tall had outlandishly huge ears, strolled aimlessly around the paths, acting dumb and friendly, looking for digging marks, men of military age, traces of comm wire. Women, children, and old people came up the path from the paddies. A few more shacks down there in the brush, someone working in a dry paddy. A woman with sores held out her limbs to the corpsman. God, these were benighted people. She had a pus-welling sore on her ankle you could stick your thumb into. Another who'd come from the river had one on his elbow. His legs were clean where he'd waded across the creek.

The corpsman checked children with infected eyes. An abcessed tooth. Boils. He looked at the ears of kids with earaches, listened to an old man's stomach complaints. "Tell them to cover their food," the corpsman told Sergeant Tu. Flies all over yards, open bowls of food in the shacks.

The people took their APC's and iodine swabs and walked away without a thank you. *Jesus, are they sullen.*

"Looks like that about does it," Second Lieutenant Montross said. "We can go back now! Boy, a beer will—"

Randolph said, "I want to go down by the river. Couple of houses down there—maybe they didn't get the word."

"Is that okay?"

"Yeah. Come on."

They walked downslope, Mark aware of that storekeeper staring at him. That one's got to be the cadre, he thought.

At the bottom, Sergeant Tu yelled again. A woman came out of a straw building leading a child. An old woman in black came down a paddy dike path. In the dry paddy a man in a flat straw hat kept working, bent over, ignoring them. Mark walked closer. How old was this dude?

The man straightened and took an off-balance, swinging, limping step toward the flat basket of sets, leaning on his digging stick. *Jesus, look at that!* His hip and leg swung like an almost-severed head. The man pivoted on one foot and scowled back at Mark. Nothing inscrutable about this dude, either. He must have stepped on a mine years ago. French mine. American mine. He sure hates us now.

Major Thanh bent over, touching the rice sets in the flat basket. Under the beginnings of fruitfulness—*Increased rice production and equitable markets!*—he had his slim, dark blue field grade officer's Tokarev. Kill the long-nose pig lieutenant of rifle troops! But not as self-indulgence. We will kill them if they see anything. Sergeant Thien had men waiting in the palm bushes, in the houses, ready to shoot if this deceitful medical mission blundered onto anything. The empty houses had holes dug in the dirt floors. Men hid there.

Other holes waited under palm bushes, covered with poles, mats, and loose dirt. The long-nose *mỹ* were clearly spying—but so far they'd seen nothing. That lieutenant was staring at him. Continue work to avoid suspicion. Thanh took a handful of sets, limped back, poked, stooped, planted. The long-noses stood on the paddy dike, which was honeycombed with concealed holes. Patriots working at night had buried grenades, mortar rounds, boxes of 7.62-millimeter Kurz Chinese ammunition wrapped in black plastic sheet, shoved in holes in the earth bank. Thanh saw bits of the shiny black plastic sticking out.

Farm folk gathered around them. A tall sergeant at sling arms looked at the path surface and the brush along the trail, where men would hide if they weren't two steps ahead like Sergeant Thien's *bo doi*. *Look down and you will all die, long-noses.*

They didn't. "Secure," Randolph said. They walked away. None of the Vietnamese thanked them.

Good, Thanh thought. The *bo doi* stood ready to discipline any too friendly with the *mỹ*.

In 1965 the rainy season, which was well named, began in Gia Binh in October with overcast days and dark nights. They'd crawl to layout positions and wait, feeling the change of air, the cool wind that brought smells of kerosene and shit, watching over rifle receivers, listening. Then: *Pat. Spat. Drop.*

Maybe it won't come down. *Pop. Drip. Drop. Braaa-patata-tatatata,* and it was like lying under a fucking shower. You could see the silver spatter glow on men's heads sinking lower as their uniforms turned black, the air dropped 20 degrees, and the ground cooled, grew sticky, water seeping through T-shirts and skivvies, forming a cold puddle along your spine, racing like a river down between your cheeks and wrapping icy fingers around your balls. And it kept up like that for two or three fucking hours while they lay, freezing. The patrol troops lay without moving. Hollis, Pearl, Coombs, Lawrence, Dobbs, Lindahl. They were good troops.

Sometimes it rained so hard rat holes flooded. Once a rat crawled onto Randolph's lap, maybe seeking warmth, and he debated absolute silence and the value of his nuts before he swatted it one way and leaped the other. Maybe there were no VC out there anyway. They *had* to have more brains than the Americans. But sometimes they were out anyhow.

"If you think you got a wet gas cylinder, bring your muzzle up like this before you fire." In the wet, a rifle shot sounded more choked and blew steam, smelling of oil and lubriplate, the white grease they put on operating surfaces before going out.

When they came back at dawn they always had red mud and sand plastered over them, paint and soot streaked on their skin, which was soaked through, so wet you couldn't pick up a cigarette to light it. The water streamed from your skin and when you touched the cigarette it soaked through and crumbled. If you were a smoker, what you really wanted after all those hours in the mud was a smoke. Your lungs twitched like a pussy. Your balls had shrunk to BBs and your skin was chilled, but most of all your clean rain-washed lungs needed tar and nicotine. What the base troops saw as they carried their mess kits over to chow in the gray drizzly dawn, or worked on the rows of H-34s and Hueys on the PSP, was a file of filthy, soaked men at the guard bunker turning in grenades and one of the dry Marines putting lit cigarettes in the wet men's mouths as they walked past, the men sucking and exhaling, puffing smoke clouds with the white cigarettes stuck in their streaked faces. Even then your face was so wet you could only get a few drags before the cigarette fell apart all over your chest. It couldn't burn you, though.

At the bunker, Staff Sergeant Rodriguez said, they had a rat the size of a small dog that lived in a hole under the bunker and got big on ration scraps that fell in the dirt. When it rained hard the rat came out on the side of the mound the bunker sat on and made a squealing noise like a high-pitched fart. They couldn't shoot the beast—they didn't have a clear shot because there were tents and gear beyond. "I'll get that fucker with a grenade," Rodriguez said. "I'll fill the hole with napalm and blow him out."

Toward the end of October Wing G-2 sent down a report that Gia Binh and other airfields along the coast probably would be hit— Phu Bai, Da Nang, Marble Mountain, Chu Lai. A *chieu hoi* defector from the VC told the story. Wing sent a few more men off a draft. Colonel Dillis, who had been upset by Lieutenant Randolph's reports because he didn't want to believe his field would be hit, was even more upset by Wing's suggestion that he might have to fight for it.

"All I wanted was walking posts," he told Lieutenant Colonel Mason. "We didn't have this in the Pacific." But as Lieutenant Polchuk commented, in the Pacific Dillis had always flown his transport planes into islands already secured. He'd been rear area resupply. There *was* no rear area here.

"I have to keep aircraft available," Dillis said when they were going through the crash plans. "I'm judged on aircraft available. I can't have mechanics sitting in holes all night in the rain and expect them to work without mistakes the next day."

In other words he wanted someone else to do it for him or he wanted to fight the problem. He was just a nice, middle-aged man in an uncomfortable position. Randolph despised him. But he was a Marine officer. Mark dissembled in the way you do to jerk a senior's chain. He saw Dillis on the officers' field head, plywood, ten-holer, green. Colonel Dillis looked extremely uncomfortable sitting in the elements, on rough wood open to the view of underlings, especially in such a barbaric setting.

"Good afternoon, sir!" Mark said cheerily, grinning as if he wanted to bubble into conversation.

"Hello," the colonel muttered glumly, and withdrew into himself.

"Listen up!" Staff Sergeant Rodriguez told the two ranks of new men at the CP bunker while Randolph and the others were getting ready to go out.

"You're goin' into position tonight. Some of you say, 'What if we're attacked?' No ifs! We probably *will* be attacked. Some of you say, 'What if they shoot at me?' So what? They might not hit you!"

Rodriguez looked into their faces, head forward, black brow low across his hook nose. "Some of you say, 'What if I get hit?' So what? Where in the fuck you think you are? You get hit, you may not die. I got hit twice. You're Marines! There's no other question except are you gonna tear their asses off if they *do* come in? 'Cause it's you, Marines! You're the only ones who's gonna save your own asses!"

Rodriguez and Pearl had them drill on the M-60 machine gun in a way not shown in movies. When the gun sits on a tripod the gunner aims by clicking handwheels on the heavy steel elevating-traversing mechanism at the rear of the gun under his chin when he's in firing position. Each click moves the point of aim only a few inches so the gunner can make fine adjustments, read the settings, mark them on a card, and return the gun to the settings at night or in fog to hit targets he can't see. The real thing about the gun or gunner wasn't the flash or noise or the gunner's biceps as he waved it at the camera, but having the gunner stay low, think coolly, and put out steady, accurate fire to block out an area.

Rodriguez told the new men the story of Lay-'Em-on-the-Wire McGraw, the legendary machine gunner in Korea.

"He's in the hole one night. *Hordes* of Chinese creepin' close to his position. 'They're gettin' closer,' he whispers into the phone.

" 'Wait,' his gunny says.

"They tiptoe over the trip wire and start *slitherin'* over the concertina. Shadows. Noises. Finally he gets the order to fire his machine gun.

"It was an A-Four," Rodriguez said. "You seen 'em. The old one. Had a heavy receiver, perforated barrel. He's lined up on the Chinese on the wire. He *squeezes* the trigger—and *click!* Broken firing pin!"

Rodriguez hunched his shoulders, glaring at them, conjuring shadows of enemy and McGraw on the gun. The new troops' jaws dropped. "What's he gonna do! It's night! They're all around! He's got an M-1 and a BAR in the hole with him and his busted thirty air cooled. Is he up shit creek?

"Nah! McGraw *lifts* the feed cover, *clears* the belt, *lifts* out the bolt—that kind had a big square split bolt—pulls out the old pin, drops in a new one, replaces the bolt, belts and closes the feed cover *all in seven seconds!* And he opens up and cuts down so many fuckin' Chinese they're stacked up like this. They're caught on the wire. They're trippin' over their own dead and wounded. *One* fuckin' thirty-caliber round can go through three, four men, and the first couple of guys it hits it throws like a car hits 'em. Breaks bones. Took 'em by surprise. Screamin' all over the place. You read me? He waited, he knew his stuff, he cut 'em down. Now, you go out there—"

A few days later Rodriguez rotated back to Crash Crew, the fire and rescue unit he usually served in, and Randolph got a new Staff NCO, Gunnery Sergeant Homer Hamlin, a short, calm man who never raised his voice. His specialty was aviation ordnance, the same field as the Mad Bomber of New York, who'd been an aviation Marine in the thirties. Gunny Hamlin had helped rig gun racks on the experimental Stinger Bees, the armed H-34s the Marine advisory mission had experimented with a few months before, when it was another war. In the days remaining before the attack he showed the troops how to rig explosive devices in the beaten ground before their positions.

*   *   *

At the five o'clock follies on that day in Saigon the starched officers presented material about the new Army helicopter division operating in the Central Highlands. Jim Robinson told Phoebe, "I heard in town the Americans are going up against North Vietnamese there. It's the kind of set-piece battle you chaps are saying you'll win. I think I'll go."

"I will too," she said.

It was the First Cavalry (Airmobile) Division. Robert McNamara had conceived of an all-helicopter division as the way to defeat the guerrillas. The Army had balked at its expense but in the end had refitted one of the best infantry divisions with helicopters and sent it over, giving it the designation of the division on garrison duty in Korea. The fighting had started near Plei Me, where earlier the Special Forces, while still classed as advisors, had raised an American flag to fight under when attacked by well-armed troops.

Army protocol assigned correspondents the rank of colonel for priority on aircraft. Jim and Phoebe got seats on an Air Force C-130 to Qui Nhon and a smaller Army bush cargo plane into An Khe, the Air Cavalry headquarters, the pilot banking sharply and lurching to veer around a mountain near the runway. It was a bald, recently cleared camp chopped out of brush, roads bulldozed and leveled, pallets of supplies, tents, and containers, men boarding dusty brown helicopters and high-wing Caribou of the sort they'd arrived in.

An Army officer drew with grease pencil on an acetate-covered map and explained how North Vietnamese regiments had occupied the Chu Pong massif and how units of the Air Cavalry had had brushing engagements while moving overland, had located the enemy, and now were pouring in force through Landing Zone X Ray. The Americans met stiff resistance, attacked, and knocked the regular NVA units back. It was called the battle of the Ia Drang.

They stayed up there several days in November, flying over Route 19 and the shocking battlefields littered with cardboard and shell casings—hills torn and shaved by gunfire, trees stripped of leaves, splintered into stumps. Shell craters in red clay.

More correspondents flew in. They met and traded information. The Americans had had hand-to-hand fighting everywhere and were killing North Vietnamese everywhere. One correspondent said it looked like what he'd read of the Battle of Chancellorsville. A trooper showed his broken M-16 rifle, explaining he'd shattered the plastic stock beating an NVA soldier to death. They saw green plastic body bags and unbagged American bodies in green fatigues darkened by blood, stiffening on ponchos, what had been young men looking old in death, jaws jutting open like old people's. An Army officer explained how the Air Force provided shipment containers—that is, aluminum coffins—to take the bodies stacked on forklift pallets to what he called CONUS, the continental United States.

The First Battalion of the Seventh Cavalry Regiment, Custer's regiment, had walked into an ambush because they followed the Army practice of leaving off flank security. They took hundreds of casualties but held tight and outshot and routed their ambushers.

Jim said the men he talked with were quite pleased with the new rifle. "They keep saying it kills them by shock." Phoebe saw red-eyed, weary men who, she became aware, must have been five years younger than she. Many had the Playboy bunny stenciled on helmet covers and armor vests.

"This *is* decisive," Jim said. "The Army's proving an all-helicopter division works, and it's proving Americans in conventional units can take on the NVA. Of course it pays you to fight big battles." He was exhilarated by the scent of blood.

One of the correspondents was Chick De Vore, a gross character Brian had pointed out at Givral. He said, "Hey! These people aren't from the real First Cav! This is the Second Infantry Division. The Army renamed it to send it over. It took the flags from the original First Cav in Korea! And you wanta know what *really* happened? The Army wanted the First Cav to go into action to win back its glory. It got mauled in Korea. It lost its colors. That's why it couldn't come home."

"Is that so?" Jim asked. "They don't do that with British regiments."

"Yeah, it's a fact. I been around awhile."

Phoebe noticed that American male correspondents liked to exude a blasé Bogart air about the spectacle but seemed more credulous than she when some officer with a shirtful of jump wings, combat infantryman's badge, and Ranger patches talked to them. Newsmen *were* odd, she knew—close to power, denied power themselves, fascinated by it, jealous of it; some of them would act out power fantasies later, when the war drove everything crazy at home, too.

She saw North Vietnamese prisoners—small, muscular men with bowl haircuts wearing limeish-khaki uniforms.

"Why is this called an insurgency situation when they're using regular troops?" Phoebe asked a major.

"They're aiding the insurgents," the major said without missing a beat.

"Is it an invasion from the North?"

"What MACV calls it is up to them. We're taking on enemy units, that's all."

"You mean it's a political matter?"

"I guess I mean I can't answer that, miss."

She got stills of prisoners and American dead. One long shot with no depth of field, the dark helicopters heading at the camera nose to tail like pallbearers coming in over the brown earth stacked with body bags.

A lieutenant colonel press officer took them on a Huey ride to LZ Albany, where the latest fighting had been. A forest had been burned and blasted. A large blackened area was covered with a ghastly carpet of dead NVA soldiers and equipment where an entire company had been trapped, napalmed, and wiped out. She smelled the gasoline.

The colonel said the point of this battle was to prove the NVA couldn't hit a remote place like Plei Me and expect to slip away in the classic Mao-Giap way. "If they're out, they can be hit." The Americans mopped up. She heard machine guns and rifles fire in the distance and saw American soldiers running.

She learned to pick out the different sounds—the slower American machine guns and light popping, cracking M-16 rifles and the fast rasp of the North Vietnamese Kalashnikovs—but she could see very little, just dirt kicking up here and there, some orange and red streaks, and she couldn't pick up anything through the lens. The field was too wide.

At An Khe another lieutenant colonel said, "This was a big battle, not only for us but for the NVA. They haven't had anything this big since they fought the French. This one they lost. They were routed. We took everything they had and tore them apart. We know already that they had the Thirty-second, Thirty-third, and Sixty-sixth regular regiments. We killed over two thousand. These were seasoned troops and we beat them. Now we're blooded. The NVA's in for a rougher time than they thought."

Jim asked the colonel if he thought the North Vietnamese planned to split South Vietnam at the highlands.

"No, they won't mass like that. Their doctrine calls for a general push and the Main Force and locals coming out to hit secondary objectives. They have this expression—*khoi nghia*—the great uprising. They're not ready for it yet and may have to revert a phase—go back to their earlier tactics of small night actions."

To Phoebe it was upsetting up there, not because she was squeamish—she was that kind of horsey WASP who can look anything in the eye as long as she was correctly dressed—but because she was unused to the clash and ambivalence of death in life. War and death had not been part of her life before, and, like many Americans, she could not accept that death part of life all around us—the edge of the campfire light, the end of the party. She knew there were thousands of deaths and saw bodies on bodies, but she also saw young Americans laughing and grabbing a smoke and young Vietnamese prisoners sitting in safety. Death in life and life in death. It seemed unreal because she, the American, was unused to them.

The officers and soldiers were more plausible than the starchy Saigon briefers. The cavalry soldiers were incredibly dusty, brown-red powder over their uniforms and cloth-covered helmets and bunny silhouettes, down their necks, their eyes red with it. Men coming out touched their weapons, glancing this way and that. They didn't move in that ramroad military way but in a manner both natural and frightening—loose-limbed, watchful, manic, turning quickly to face everywhere.

And the variety of clothing—men slung with medical bags, ropes and tools, bags of explosives, drivers wearing dusty goggles, aircrew with Plexiglas-front helmets.

Men carrying black machine guns had rubber bands around their helmets with green cans of oil stuck in them, the oil staining their dusty helmet covers. They had copper-and-black belts of ammunition draped over their shoulders or slung from their necks in thin cotton pouches. All around she heard the jet-whistling helicopters, whopping and shrieking and blowing up dust, and the startling boom of artillery firing, and the distant rumble of B-52 strikes. You couldn't see the bombers, because they were ten miles high. You just heard the rumble.

She was vexed trying to photograph fire fights. You can't get it all in one composition—the teams fire from dispersed and concealed positions—though you do have plenty of noise, bullet strikes, and screaming. She had trouble grasping what a fire fight was supposed to accomplish.

"It's an exchange in the process of another maneuver," Jim said.

"We attempt to get fire superiority over them so we can move on them," an Army captain said. "But sometimes either side will break off."

"Did they have them in World War Two?"

"They've always had them," Jim said. "Robert Graves gives a good account in *Goodbye to All That*."

"Fine, but that's World War One. You can't ask a reader to understand something that long ago."

She was not only trying to picture it, but also, following Sara Gelber's advice, trying to get a picture understandable to readers who knew only about GIs advancing on a European town with a steeple. This kind of battle was brushing engagements, fire fights of great intensity, since every man in the NVA had an automatic fast-firing Kalashnikov plus light machine guns and plentiful mortars and grenades, and the Americans had their automatic M-16s, machine guns, mortars, artillery, gunships, and bombs, so a thirty-minute skirmish could denude the landscape of leaves and leave bare trunks and bodies. The hills blew up with sharp, nasty engagements like that.

Since none of the photographers could get it on film, they settled for shots that became stock over the dozen years of war. Silhouettes of door gunners, men running among trees, etc.

"Big bloody battle," Jim said. "Biggest *I've* seen anywhere. Biggest to date this war, too." He grinned. He had had a fine time collecting a bagful of good pictures. He was a picture himself with his bushy pale hair and beard and his chest slung with cameras and ID cards. He loved wars. He was a connoisseur of them.

At An Khe several correspondents sat together to "syndicate" the story—that is, they compared notes and tried to make sense of what they saw, or at least come up with dovetailing descriptions of the chaos. This was so their editors wouldn't say, "How come X and Y said this and you're saying that?"

"You gotta call it a victory right off," Chick De Vore said. "We kicked the shit out of them. People at home were worried about that, and we gotta put them at ease." You could see why he was a staffer on a big chain. He worked the office tents, plodding and breaking wind, his short, dumpy body in jungle fatigues that should have been loose but clung to his sweating flesh, asking elementary, obvious questions, the ones his readers wanted answered.

Jim said, "The NVA'll be studying this to see how to change their tactics."

"NVA's willing to take losses," another correspondent said. "The French beat them in battles, too. I think this is an unlucky victory for the Army. It beat the NVA so well on the field, it won't have to look at the political war."

"Yeah, but look at all the stuff we hit them with," De Vore said. "Any sane man'd get out of our way."

"They have," the correspondent who remembered the French said. "It's going to be a yin–yang thing. We won here fighting mass to mass, and they're going to pop up somewhere else with little attacks to nibble us, the *van dong chien*."

Phoebe thought of the death-in-life paradox she felt among the men and corpses younger than she. Someone said the little attacks were already going on in the flatlands at bases and airfields along the coast.

The VC hit Marble Mountain airfield down the coast and a few days later threw mortar rounds and RPGs into Da Nang and Chu Lai. Wing G-2 told Colonel Dillis to expect a shelling. The colonel had a deep bunker near his office roofed with runway Pierced Steel Plating and sandbags.

The listening posts and riflemen noticed brief yellow lights. One flash, then, a few minutes later, another flash several meters away. The lights were shielded and aimed back at the hamlet ridge. It took the Marines about three seconds to figure out they were the X in this trigonometry exercise. Sergeant Lawrence, the ex-seagoing NCO, was using binoculars, which gather light at night if you don't have a star scope, to peer into the night, when he saw the man's silhouette before he saw the yellow light eighty meters out. Lawrence grabbed a rifle and fired. The light dropped and lay shining on the ground.

They'll grab him, Lawrence thought. He dropped to his knees to deliver grazing fire. He put out three more shots and heard the men grunt and scream, then the sound was choked off. Another Marine said, "I heard that fuckin' slug hit meat!" Someone covered the light and the *du kich* fired a burst.

The next night Lieutenant Randolph took a patrol out in front of the only area that had not yet been probed. He was exhausted and nearly fell asleep once they were in position in a bowl of scrubby palm bushes. Then his guts dropped and his hair stood up. Crouching men a few yards away! So close he couldn't believe they were enemy. They sank out of sight. He moved to one side and grabbed Hollis's shoulder. "Anyone out of position?"

"No."

"Fire!" He fired his autromtic M-14, the others opened up with rifles, M-3, and shotgun. "Grenade!" Shit! If he'd just opened up, he could have got two, maybe three. "Up on line!"

They ran through the palm bushes, heard footfalls and groaning. Coombes put M-79 rounds out. More groans. Near the south end of the hamlet a dog barked, then gave a canine scream as its voice was cut off. Footsteps. Scurrying, leaves brushing.

"On line!"

A scrape, tinny clatter and bang, and a silver flash. Corporal Hollis grabbed Randolph's arm and pointed to where it came from—a dark mass of bushy shadows.

"Fire!" Mark said. Small arms flashed and then Coombes fired, the grenade startling them because it detonated so close.

"Cease fire! Move up!"

He heard crying. What? The silver shine was the tin of a house. A kerosene lamp came on. The door opened. Randolph looked in. A man in shorts lying on the dirt floor. A woman in black on the bed. A girl about ten holding the lamp and crying. Furniture. The Buddhist shrine on the chest of drawers. The girl crying. A baby curled up on the floor, motionless.

He had killed him, her, it—he had destroyed a family. He didn't want this. He was horrified. He wanted to die. He imagined the oily taste of his .45 muzzle. But he had too much pride to do that—he had to finish the goddam thing. He felt as if his skin and guts had been stripped away, felt the physical pain of self-despair. But he had been well trained.

"Put our security. Quick! All sides!"

"Should we pursue down the trail?" Hollis said. "I *know* they got more fuckers down there—the dog was killed that way."

"What?"

"They must've dropped him off here or he crawled up," Hollis said. "Look." He pointed at the dying man. "Look at all the sand on him. All the sweat. Blood's dryin' on him. He got hit out there."

"No pursuit. This is fucked up enough already. Besides, they could be set up anywhere." He'd wanted to bring the son of a bitch in on a pole. Not all of this. The dead. The girl crying.

He called for an ambulance and corpsman and radioed a report to Lieutenant Colonel Thomas. The new asshole major broke into the net and Thomas told him to shut up.

He talked to Thomas and Mason in the MABS tent the rest of the night. They sat on boxes smoking cigarettes and stubbing them out while he reported. Thomas looked at Mason. "Backlash report."

When Mark hit the rack at dawn he put his hands over his face and smelled blood. A few hours later that morning Thomas called him on the phone in his tent. "I reviewed the guidelines. You probably acted correctly but I urge you to get a lawyer. Call Wing."

"Now's the time to get a census over in that 'ville."

"Colonel Dillis won't hear of it. Anyway, they're demonstrating. Look over there."

He saw people massed by the hamlet, waving signs.

He walked to the men's tent. Corporal Hollis told him some officer had been trying to get statements from them.

"Don't say a goddam word."

Then he saw Coombes, who though haggard still looked seventeen, and Coombes said, "That thin captain said they's gonna charge me 'cause I fired the grenade."

"Bullshit! You acted on my orders. Corporal Hollis, you take all of these men and go lay by somewhere." Mark walked to the adjutant's office, fuming. It wasn't the men's fault. *He'd* been a step behind all night, *he* was wrong, but he wouldn't concede *that* to these goddam airdales, either.

Captain Shick, a thin man with a prominent Adam's apple, looked startled when Randolph walked in, his face grim as murder.

"Captain, those are my men! You want to charge someone, you come to me!"

"That's not necessary, Mark."

"We still in the Marine Corps? You're trying to hang a trooper to make things look right? I want to see General Walt, Captain. I want to talk to an infantry general."

Lawyers flew up from Da Nang and convened a hearing in the mess tent. Colonel Dillis was not to be seen. Randolph tried to figure which way Lieutenant Colonels Mason and Thomas would jump. Why had Thomas called on the phone rather than sending a runner? Did he want someone else to witness that he was sending a warning? He didn't know if he could trust them, but he knew he couldn't trust the CO. Both Mason and Thomas told the inquiry they would only speak about the tactics. "This was an authorized operation," Thomas said. Mason concurred. Randolph and the men refused to speak. The investigation ruled that no crimes or breaches of naval law had been committed.

Lieutenant Szabo, the comm officer, said Colonel Dillis would have been happier if they could have hung Private First Class Coombes—after all, he was the lowest-ranking man—but no one wanted Randolph to go wheezing and ranting in a general court. Dillis didn't want infantry generals scrutinizing a Wing operation.

"Assholes!" Randolph said. "Assholes!" It was a filthy business. Even if you got through, it wasn't right—it didn't set things right. It was no damn good. The girl crying, the baby, and no one wanted to know who backed the guy they'd chased and killed. And why try to hang *Coombes?* Coombes, for God's sake—he wasn't even full grown, except for his feet. Although Lieutenant Randolph still believed he was fundamentally stupid, he discerned a glimmer of light through the unexamined images of flag, home, and honor in his sentiment. What kind of war was this? It was us against them. Not just the VC, but also against officers like Dillis and that major who kept coming up on tactical radio, and Second Lieutenant Montross, all of them so ignorant and self-interested they had no idea who they were threatening, what they were ruining. It was like what mortar and artillery crews did now, putting aiming stakes front and rear so they could fire in a circle because of the threat from all sides. The only thing he could try to do was protect *his* Marines, particularly the new fish who were even more credulous. The rest of it was pointless—there was no honor to it.

The next morning he collapsed in his tent. He had chills, fever, the runs, and didn't give a rat's ass. The corpsman said he had dysentery. He passed out again in the sick-bay tent. He came to in late afternoon when Mason came by. "Someone's got to run the show tonight."

"Gunny Hamlin can do it."

"The colonel wants Lieutenant Timme to handle it."

"He's not qualified." Timme was a motor transport officer, a nice young man who'd come over from California.

"Well, we might just be shelled anyway," Mason said calmly. "I know and you know he can't conduct patrol operations, but we have a case of nervousness here. If we're just shelled the yield of patrols is marginal."

"He better put out LPs," Randolph said. "Hamlin can do that."

Mason nodded, calmly. "You don't know what I mean by nervous."

After Mason left, Mark looked at the canvas. His grudge was set like a charley horse. Dillis didn't want to protect his own command.

He passed out and dreamed of white flashes and black rectangular solids of immense density: Death. What he'd feared all along. His family had died for nothing. The family he'd killed had died for nothing. His grief and fear were for nothing. The ashes the airline had given his brother were probably just charred upholstery and in-flight magazines. Feverish dreams.

For Major Thanh, the cruel killing of Brother Linh, Ba Linh, and the baby, leaving little Co Linh Tho an orphan, though sad, was as lucky in its way as the birth of the little Linh boy these many weeks ago.

"*Drive out the long-nose colonialists and their traitor puppets!*" he shouted to the people the *bo doi* pulled out of their houses. "It is the long *hang chien!* Now the main struggle!"

Again they were getting mad and could be roused to action. Before the killings, the people had been losing heart. None wanted to go out in the rain. "Why are we doing this?" even Ba Huu asked. "Yes, their helicopters are everywhere, but they do not come here to take work levees, like the *phap*. They pay good money. They throw away enough for us to lack nothing."

Many resented the long nights of hauling grenades and mortar shells up to the pits from the boats. They resented him and the *bo doi* he had used to push Linh to go out last night.

"This will be the last reconnaissance," Thanh had said. "We attack immediately."

Brother Linh, who was thirty and had not fought in the great liberation, had looked at his wife, and at the ground, and sighed. His wife had said, "I worry. I will wait at the door until he returns." She had been killed at the door.

Thanh had watched the lieutenant beating the bushes and yelling. He had watched from one of the trenches everyone had dug and concealed in preparation for the attack. After the Americans left he had plenty of people ready to shout and hold signs for his demonstration, but the long-noses hadn't even sent anyone to look. A patriot on the RMK crew told him the *mỹ* were having meetings instead.

That night elements of the 3rd Independent Rifle Battalion, 1st Sappers, and signallers of the 117th Rifle Regiment (People's Army) arrived and took up positions on the trails and roads to isolate Ap Nhac Muoi and Gia Binh airfield.

Khoi Nghia!

The Will of Heaven, and the charcoal sellers, brought young Private Linh to Major Thanh a few hours before the attack.

The charcoal sellers had come down the river trail with heavy bags strapped to the black water buffalo. Linh walked among them, dressed in gray and khaki. He was thin and scared-looking, not very bright, Thanh thought, but not disrespectful.

"He has been in camp with us," the leader of the charcoal men said. "Two weeks."

The charcoal men removed bags from the carabao, and sullen hamlet people, watched by *bo doi*, carried the explosives and ammunition to cache holes.

"And you are from here?" Thanh said. "You are a Linh from here?"

"Yes! We know him! Poor boy!" Ba Huu said.

The youth looked at the ground. "I am Linh Van Giang. I was drafted three months ago by the *viet xian*, the traitor puppets." Prodded by Thanh and the charcoal leader, Linh told how he'd been shanghaied.

"We killed the puppet chief, Ranh," Thanh interjected, making his point to remind others nearby.

"The Army gave me a few weeks training," Linh said. "But I wasn't paid. Our captain pocketed all the money and told us, 'You aren't ready for pay yet.' Then a major of truck transport came to us and said, 'I will pay you for a task in uniform.'

"We rode in one of his trucks to the American supply base in Da Nang and loaded it with bags of concrete and rode to a place where the major was building an apartment house. One of the others said the major was rich because he rented apartments to Americans and Indian merchants.

"We worked very hard. The major swore us to silence and gave us piasters and passes. I had never had so much money before. I walked through Da Nang. I had never seen such a big city before. So many trucks! People wore wristwatches! There was a huge market! I bought clothes and threw away my puppet uniform. In the market someone said I could buy new papers. It was one of the charcoal sellers. I went with him."

The sellers had taken him to the *mat tran* camps in the hills, where he had been trained.

"He is reliable," the charcoal man said. Thanh looked into the young man's face. Yes, he looked like his late father and a bit like his mother.

"Let us go to your family house," Thanh said. "But I must warn you—"

At the sight of his family's empty house, young Linh fell on his knees and wept by the shrapnel-punched door.

"You must help us avenge them."

"Yes, I will."

Linh's orders were to guide the assault teams to the right gullies and then to help position the assault battalion that even now was dispersed among hamlets and the town of Gia Binh and would assemble here after dark.

He looked with longing over his *xa*. Could any place be as sweet as home or as sad as this? "Trouble!" old Ba Huu said.

At dark radio technicians from the People's Army, men who spoke with a different accent, set up an antenna on the ridge and a radio in the deep hole behind the crest.

The people pulled dirt-covered mats and boards off trenches they had dug.

Linh watched in amazement, for he had never seen so many soldiers, even up in the camps. The officers handed out big white pills called *thic con thuoc*, a stimulant that made you not feel pain. The men swallowed them.

Major Thanh moved from group to group, wearing black and his field-grade officer's Tokarev. He gave short, intense speeches. "Drive out the long-noses!" he shouted to the *bo doi*, and to the people who were assembled in work parties guarded by other *bo doi*, he shouted, "This is *khoi nghia!* The great uprising! We kill them all and win *Doc Lap!* We destroy their machines! They are naked and poor and beg us!"

Before midnight Linh guided a light machine gun team among the palm bushes to the concealed trench and gully overlooking the south end of the camp. For a moment Linh watched the foreign town of tents and machinery that had dropped onto the ground here. Lights shone all over the tents. A few white lights among the rows of helicopters where mechanics worked. Down the trench the *bo doi* set up an RPD Degtyarev light machine gun on its bipod and other riflemen knelt and put Kalashnikovs and short SKS carbines over the parapet. He went back to the radio hole to serve as a runner.

In the hole were the Liberation Army battalion commander, signalmen from People's Army, and Major Thanh.

"Sappers on the way."

Linh heard the radio reports as the sapper teams crawled to the American lines. No American patrols out. A little flurry of shots as the sappers ran in. When the first helicopter blew up and burned, its intensely bright magnesium light showed sappers running down rows of helicopters, pulling strings from wooden-handled Chinese grenades and tossing them into helicopters.

Linh saw a Marine sentry running down another lane toward the explosions. These were the ones who had killed his family and beaten patriots. The *mỹ* ran into a sapper running across; he shoved his shotgun into the sapper's stomach and fired, pumping and firing many times, so the sapper fell to the ground in two pieces. The sapper radioman called back that he heard screaming from a burning UH1E marked with a red cross and they supposed a medical worker who had been in the aircraft was burning to death.

Other assault squads called in that they were attacking the rifle bunkers. Linh crawled to the crest and saw grenades going off in some. Scattered white flashes came from the American rifle positions. Then the People's Army signals sergeant pressed his instrument against his ear and said, "They're changing! Something's changing! I can't understand it all! They're calling out numbers and orders! New tactics!"

The sergeant and Liberation Army commander exchanged a word. Meanwhile red streaks came out of two of the long-nose bunkers, then from another, then all of them were firing. The red streaks made an X pattern moving sideways across the low ground where the Liberation Army attack platoons were forming. Another machine gun shot streaks along the gully where they used to get gravel for the chickens. One of the assault squads was in there.

Sergeant Vernal Pearl heard a loud *!Crump!* and knew they'd hit a bunker in his sector—Corporal Kane's, Three. They were firing, then stopped. Pearl ran bent over downslope to where Three faced north and unlocked his rifle. Where were the VC? Nothing moving around it. What'd they hit it with? He didn't fire. Behind him other Marines were firing rifles and machine guns, and the air boomed from helicopters blowing up—big orange flashes and white fires. Then he saw across the low ground where the lieutenant's patrol had killed those people—a line of white flashes. First time he'd faced it, been here only a few weeks. Well, goddam, you taught it, didn't you? Enemy troops on line, firing into the camp.

His sense told him there wasn't anyone hiding in the bunker; he dove in, his knees feeling the damp sand. His eyes stung. Ammonia smoke from the high explosive. Kane and Hayes flat out, gun knocked on its side. VC threw in a concussion grenade and ran on.

No time to check Kane and Hayes. Mission first. He was just aware of their dark shapes over there, musty smell of sandbags. Pearl pulled the tripod back to its stake markers, brushed sand off the gun, opened the feed cover, cleared links, checked the feed pawls attached to the camming groove that twitched side to side, pulling in the belt when the bolt went back and forth, pulled back the bolt, reset the belt, closed the cover and made sure it locked, while he looked along the left side of the barrel and worked the elevating-traversing mechanism handwheels and checked his sights. It felt like two minutes but it was about fifteen seconds. Fire. An orange-blue flash pulsed from the flash suppressor, and his tracers, speeding red dots, hit the right of the VC firing line. He ran a swinging traverse, not even stopping to burst. *Run it on; she likes to go.*

The mechs said they did it all the time goin' into an LZ. *She's got a chrome-lined barrel, fire it out.* If he had to get fire out, now was the time. One long traverse. Fuckers over there ain't even firin' now. He stopped. They opened up. Flashes, *whack! whack!* Flutter. They didn't have the range. He fired again, putting red dots a few inches under their muzzle flashes. *This here NATO round can go through thirty inches of white pine, a couple of sandbags, a parapet—chew that parapet down, cut them fuckers down.*

He knew he had fire superiority already, bursting and watching. Bitter smoke drifted from his receiver. He felt around to his left, still firing bursts, and found another ammo can. He grabbed Kane's foot. Kane groaned. Alive, anyway. Goddam. He fired bursts and, groping, found the EE-8 field phone and cranked it and called in. "Heya, gunny, Three's up, send some more men." He put another burst on the enemy muzzle flashes and they stopped. *Goddam, we* can *fuck 'em up. Well, shit.* Marines.

Lieutenant Randolph was in sick bay dreaming he was Mark Randolph somewhere sane when he woke startled by the *pop-pop-pop-pop-pop* and *braaap* of the AKs and the crunch and boom of the helicopters blowing up. Corpsmen were flat on the deck. He jumped into boots, trousers, and a shirt, couldn't find his cap—*Fuck it*—grabbed his .45, and rolled out onto the sand. He trotted bent over between tents, readying his pistol, looking around. Small arms fire whacked canvas overhead. Men yelled. *Get the fuck away from them.* Colonel Dillis had no plan. He ran across open ground, plenty of light from burning helicopters, and dove into the back of a bunker. Private First Class Dobbs and Private Curran were crouched at the embrasure. He put his hands on their shoulders. "We got no orders, sir," Dobbs said.

"Fire your mission." Randolph got on the phone. "I have command!" He identified himself as Six Actual. What in the hell had Lieutenant Timme done? "All hands take on targets, gunny you copy, section leaders check in." Dobbs was firing a PDF down a gully, the slugs grazing about ten inches off the ground. Others opened up, tracers going out in the classic interlocking bands, working over every route in, except these were double and triple the allotment of machine guns for this space, and they had never fired machine guns from the bunkers, so they had surprise fire on the enemy. They had guns on the mound and scattered around the pad working over the VC positions, which he saw as sequined lines of muzzle flashes among the palm bushes and straw and tin-can shacks, now lit up brighter than daylight. Shit, you could see their NCOs crawling and running to check their riflemen, casting shadows. They probably hadn't planned on that. Rounds worked over one line, Randolph saw a man go flying.

"You said there were no machine guns!" the Liberation Army battalion commander said.

Linh watched the assault squad huddled in the gravel gully. Machine gun fire came down their column. He heard bullets hitting flesh like mallets pounding earth. Tracers whipped and spun before the trench he'd led the light machine gun team and riflemen to. The signals sergeant told the Liberation Army colonel, "Squad leader's hit. Assault team leader's dead." The People's Army translator who was listening to the long-nose pig radio and telephone talk said, "The lieutenant of rifle troops is back. He's telling them to follow his orders and no one else's."

"Too late to put a patrol out," Thanh said, sniffing. It was the Will of Heaven that the services lieutenant, whom they had as Terence J. Timme, twenty-four, of Garden Grove, California, married, always in supply services, probably cautious, had not put out listening posts or patrols. The machine guns would be a problem, but they had never lacked for heroes. "The assault teams must move all the faster," Thanh said.

"This Randolph has a voice like a dead man," the People's Army translator said. "Wait! He's moving! He told the gunnery sergeant he's going to Three."

Thanh stepped this way and that in the long revetted hole. The circumstances bothered him regardless. He had told everyone the enemy had no machine guns and was terrified and clumsy. He turned and said, "I know their numbers! He's going to First Platoon's firing sector! Have the RPD saturate that sector while he's moving!"

The colonel glanced at Thanh and nodded to a captain. A moment later one of the Degtyarevs fired, and right away two machine guns fired right into the RPD. They didn't even adjust. They were on. Liberation Army riflemen fired and *mỹ* machine guns traversed their line, the rounds thudding and kicking dirt up toward the command hole, ricochets making that quick buzz-whistle, patriots in the trench flying back, falling. Linh heard one make a terrible sound as he clutched his chest.

The signals sergeant said, "Sappers running to break out the south end."

"Fire on the south end!"

Sergeant Marion Lawrence came from Evansville, Indiana. He had played football (end) and basketball (center) there. He was six feet two inches so went to sea duty out of boot camp, guarding nuclear weapons on a carrier and keeping squids in line on a cruiser. Once a big sailor came after him with a long wrench—a sloppy, ugly blivet, the kind of skuzz-bucket hair ball who keeps a seabag full of pussy pictures and smells like toe jam and has a big mouth like Bluto in the Popeye movies. This sailor was swinging steel at Lawrence and Lawrence sank his nightstick endways into the man's gut and then whacked him *real* hard across the shins—so hard they heard it two compartments away—and it hurt the squid so bad he fell on his face and curled up crying.

Lawrence had always been in a lot of fights. In Indiana he fought because of his first name, his lip, and his looks—he was skinny and his ears stuck out like catchers' mits—and in the Marines he fought just for drill. From sea duty he went to Marine Barracks, Philadelphia, and fought more squids and street blacks, who were gutless unless they had five to one, and then he got orders to Vietnam. He'd never served in a line outfit. He had taken the correspondence courses on tactics.

He was hot to be a "grunt"—a term that had just come into use. When he arrived off the draft with Vernie Pearl, he'd used the term "grunt" in front of the lieutenant, and it was like when he and Pearl showed up in those dumbass tiger stripes. The lieutenant pulled up his lips and made that kind of face, shrugging, "Grunt, huh? Grunt!" Probably didn't know how much *he* wheezed. But things got cool after Lawrence shot the gook with a flashlight—the lieutenant laughed his ass off when he described the light dropping to the ground and shots hitting meat. Put his face close, challenging: "Your men going to *fight* for you? You got them *drilled?*"

Lawrence wanted to look good here. He was a professional, and he'd been good at some of the most demanding duty before. You got to have a clear idea of what they call right and proper, what's an appropriate military manner and fashion. Then you jam things to conform to that.

So when the AKs opened up and the HE went off, he was up right away with his checklist in mind, telling one gunner, "Fire your secondary, that low ground," and then running to the other bunker in his sector, on the way seeing the other lines of gook riflemen firing. Sure, he was scared, but he was excited as hell seeing how it fit what he had been told already, the lines taking shape, reading the situation. The enemy had several bases of fire, two on the ridge, sounded like another north, against Pearl.

Then he saw the sappers running on the pad, silhouetted by burning helicopters. *Those assholes were naked!* They were running *hard*, not trotting like Marines, sprinting like they were in a fucking football game, reaching into bags on their legs, pulling out wooden-handled grenades and flinging them, reaching for another, a couple flank men running, holding AKs kinda funny across their middles, barrels level or down, letting off bursts—sure, take the ricochets off the PSP.

Fuck it, why not?

Lawrence dropped to one knee in the soft earth. All he was carrying was a .38 he'd cumshawed off the Navy. Squids didn't count their weapons anyway—deserved to lose them. He hadn't heard about the Air Policeman who got killed trying a .38 on sappers. It was at least eighty yards. He was a good shot, though. Two-handed police grip, cock it—.38 threw different from a .45—hold high. Gook running toward him, axis of path over axis of fire, bare yellow skin lit up against dark sights, notch cradling post, squeeze.

The cylinder flash bleached out his picture, but look! Sapper on his knees, shaking his head, others running on. Mission, he thought, and I can get a rifle in the bunker. He ran on, not even shifting gears when the small arms fire started hitting around the bunker, kicking up dirt, and *loud! Whack! Whack! Whack!* He hit the deck and scuttled like a jet cockroach the rest of the way in, grabbing his gunner's shoulder. "Traverse that line! See it? Fire away!"

Lieutenant Randolph ran crouching over the low ground behind Three, where he saw Pearl and the new men. Over there was Five. No fire coming out. Were they dead? He ran toward it. The ridge lit up and he saw right into the firing barrels, the bright fire—*This is yours, roundeye!*—and felt them coming in, whacking and jarring. He wanted to live! He leaped nose first into a cat track and crawled like a sperm, feeling all that shit whack and bite at him, wanting to dissolve into molecules and disappear into the earth. He was sure some were going *under* him into the hopping ground, a little quieter now.

There was Five. He yelled at the back of the bunker that he was coming in.

Corporal Lamont, just off the draft, sitting there. "Good evening, sir." Smooth talker, scared shitless, afraid to draw fire. Two men watching.

"Fire your mission. And keep it up." Randolph put his face next to the corporal's, glaring. Not an embarrassing word, just let him know you'll destroy him if he doesn't hack it. The gunner opened fire. Randolph called in on the loop line. Gunny said, "Six says he's hurtin'."

"I'll go there now."

Flat ground well lit from burning helicopters, VC firing on the ridge—all *over* that ridge—palm bushes, houses. Have to put more fire up there. He saw the silhouette of the bunker, Six. Regular bursts of machine gun fire shot from it, steadily working over part of the ridge. He ran to it.

A couple of dead sappers lay outside the bunker. Naked except for some kind of jockstrap, black rubber sandals, grenade bags. The sand and dirt clung to their sweat—natural camouflage. AKs on the dirt.

Corporal Pike sat with his legs out, leaning against the sandbags, rifle across his legs, looking relaxed and casual.

Pike had arrived a month ago. He was from Wisconsin. Randolph had taken him on patrol a couple of times, saw he was good, thorough, steady, and made him a squad leader. He was also from the Sixth Marines. He said he remembered seeing Randolph around the barracks. He'd come straight from the Dominican Republic. He told Randolph a captain named Nickles had screwed up everything landing his company. Mark didn't laugh out loud but rejoiced at the triumph of truth—this Nickles was one of the bare-chested captains the lieutenants despised because he kissed ass, ranted at underlings, and didn't know tactics. He was from that post-Korea Eisenhower-era group of officers who with no war experience tried to advance their careers by having the most men subscribe to *Leatherneck* or having their barracks lights go on all at once in case some colonel was watching. Kennedy, everyone said, had demanded the services have more realistic training, but this Nickles hadn't read his manuals and had got his platoons tangled coming ashore in the Dominican Republic.

"There was a lot more shooting in the Dominican Republic than the papers told about," Pike had told Randolph one night. "Lot more than I see here."

"We'll see," Mark said. "Are you ready? Will your men fight for you?"

"Yes sir."

Here was Pike leaning against the bunker in firelight.

"What's your situation?"

Pike opened his mouth and shook his head. Now Mark saw that what had looked like shadows on his clothes was blood. Ribbons of blood ran out his ears.

Inside the smoke-filled bunker he saw the machine gun firing, orange-blue flame at the muzzle, the black linked brass stepping in, gas, brass, and links out the other side, bits of smoke. The bolt shuttled forward and back, its roller camming the feed cover track, pawls pulling in the belt one cartridge at a time, feed, fire, feed, fire, 550 rounds per minute, and there was the crew—two Marines huddled flat, heads close together behind the gun. Joseph's hands were on the trigger and E&T mechanism but his face was turned toward the ground. How could he see to fire? The A-gunner, Bonner, fed the belt with one hand and yelled in Joseph's ear. "Add two! Right two! Add two!" His other hand, the one on Joseph's back, was bleeding. Joseph couldn't see and Bonner couldn't move and they were firing their mission. Pike was deaf and crippled, dead VC he'd got beside him. Selfless, devoted—Randolph was choked by rage, love, passions he had no time to contemplate.

Outside he found a dazed naked VC crawling over the sand, dragging his mangled leg; Pike had shot him point-blank and the NATO round had blown his knee into bone dust, so his calf and foot were hanging on by a tendon the size of a little finger. The young man's face was twisted in pain. He made a sound like a cat. Randolph grabbed him by the hair and dragged him back to the PSP, where the truck he'd called for was speeding up, swerving around wreckage. Beyond the pad Mark saw explosions among the office tents, mortars. The truck slid to a stop, new Marines ran up to the bunker with Sergeant Pearl. Randolph and one of the new men carried the wounded back to the truck. "Is this hotter than the Dominican Republic?" he asked Pike, lifting him on, his face next to Pike's bleeding ear.

"Yes."

The corpsman put compresses on the men, checking them rapidly, noting their wounds; he slapped the prisoner.

"Leave him alone or I'll shoot you," Randolph said quietly. "I want him to talk."

"I'm sorry, Lieutenant." He taped the prisoner's mangled thigh and taped his wrists and eyes. "Take off!" he yelled to the driver. "Angle around this side." You could see the mortar rounds and muzzle flashes in the tents and hear the cough of M-14s—the leaderless troops were doing God knows what over there. Randolph ran to his CP to get back on the phone.

The Liberation Army battalion commander sent Linh to carry a message to another firing line. He looked over at the camp as he ran. Everything was lit up like day, even some of the tents burning. In the trench many men were wounded.

He ran back to the command hole. The People's Army translator NCO said, "The lieutenant's calling for specific machine gun teams to take specific targets. We don't know the numbers. Wait—"

"There weren't supposed to be any guns," the Liberation Army commander said.

"He's saying, 'Fire missions'—some designation. Can't hear—ahh—he's calling for defilade fire."

"That's us," the People's Army signals sergeant said. "We're in defilade."

"They can't do that," Thanh said.

"I think so," the Liberation Army commander said.

"What does he say now?" Thanh asked.

"He says, 'Read your fucking range card!' "

Linh crawled up to the crest and saw the bright muzzle flashes—then everything became very confused, loud whacking and dust flying. The air popped against his cheeks, dirt flew into his nose and eyes, splinters of wood, sap-smelling, and bits of leaf showered over them in gusts as in the hardest of the rainy season, the falling never stopping completely but coming heavily and waning. In the danger all surfaces had silver edges like the light of the moon of death, the tin shacks shining, the trees seeming thicker. Would he die now? Men yelled that they were wounded. Linh crawled against the side of a low bank by the trail, where Ba Huu had her fence, and with his cheek on the dirt saw the enemy machine gun bullets arcing over the reverse slope and kicking dirt and wood, combing through shacks, over the trench lines and trail, hollow tracer rounds bouncing off the dirt and spinning, burning bright red. A tracer set fire to Thac's straw fence.

Clusters of machine gun bullets fell along the trails on the reverse slope, where carrying parties and reserves waited. It happened so fast. Many were wounded. Soldiers were bent over and crawling. Not only *bo doi*, but many of Linh's own people, from the *xa*. He saw Duong writhing on the ground, holding his stomach, and Ba Huu face down in a paddy.

Yellow flashes lit the brown dirt where the mortar crew pumped shells over the ridge into the enemy camp. The machine gun fire did not reach them.

"It's bad," the Liberation Army commander said. "They have fire superiority."

"Linh!" Major Thanh yelled. "Linh! Get up here!" He told Linh to follow the store trail to the chicken-craw gully and guide back a People's Army corporal from the assault element. Linh sprinted and crawled down the gully and found the corporal, who had been shot in the upper arm, which flopped at his side. He had lost his Kalashnikov.

A Liberation Army officer quizzed this man.

"There are more rifle soldiers than we thought," the corporal said. "Many were panicking in the tents and shooting each other, but others were running and looking for us, falling into blocking positions, and I saw the lieutenant from the patrols running between bunkers."

"Why didn't you shoot him?"

"I didn't know it was him then. He was bareheaded. I thought it was one of the Liberation Army NCOs. When the machine guns started we were all hit—"

He said another squad had got hit on the way in and that he saw the lieutenant and an older officer in a flight suit and black cap with gold braid going over the wounded from that squad, separating dead from wounded and kicking grenades out of the way. "They were very fast," the corporal said. "They'd step on the man's hands and use a big knife to cut away all his bags. A rifle bullet must have hit one of Sapper Dinh's grenades and set it off, because when the old officer grabbed Dinh's wrist to pull him away, only his arm and head came up. He walked away, thinking he was dragging the body, and turned around and started, seeing the rest of it stretched out behind him. He and the lieutenant burst out laughing. They laughed very hard. A puppet NCO started interrogating the wounded right there."

"Did you have any grenades?" Thanh asked.

"No."

"Did any of your team have grenades?"

"Oh, yes."

"Why didn't you throw any?"

"There is no excuse. I was shocked to see Dinh's head separated from his body. The fire was very intense then, and I didn't think we could move."

"You did not do your duty," Thanh said. The officers spoke among themselves and one took the corporal to Thac's yard and shot him in the head.

Linh carried messages. Between trips he heard the signals NCOs and officers talking about the attack being stalled. The Liberation Army commander said his orders stated he was not to go into the assault when three conditions were lacking; therefore he would withdraw. He said to Major Thanh, "The reconnaissance was not adequate."

Can bo Thanh said nothing. Then he said, "Linh! Go tell the carry parties to come up!"

Linh spent the rest of the night guiding carry parties, taking away wounded and dead *bo doi* from the low ground and the ridge and then the hamlet wounded and unused ammunition, but they could not get it all since so many carrier volunteers had been wounded and *bo doi* had to cover the others. The People's Army signals sergeant was angry that the assault teams had lost brand-new Soviet radios and RM-114 field phones that foreign advisors had given out only last month; he said he himself had talked with the Russians. They did not look like *mỹ* or *phap*.

The battalion and attached forces began falling back by platoons. Some headed south. Some went up the river trail. Dawn came soon enough.

Linh watched from the riddled house of his dead family. The Americans started the few helicopters that weren't heaps of white ash on the steel plating and began flying wounded out. Burned-out tents smoked in the camp. "We won," *Can bo* Thanh said to Linh, Ba Duong, and the other few survivors. "They are crippled. Look! They are going to evacuate."

He handed over his binoculars. By the enemy radio antennae a fire flared up. A pale, thin older officer and a short-haired officer and clerk put papers on a fire on the ground before a sandbagged tent that Thanh said was used for cryptography and classified storage. The old officer held his hand at his mouth and his cheeks puffed out. He looked at the papers and nodded for others to drop them on the fire. He looked uncomfortable.

"That is Colonel Dillis," Thanh said. "He's their leader. Look at him, he has no stomach for it. They are burning records and will leave! You see, we hurt them enough anyway! We drive out the long-noses!"

Linh watched the intense man. He was so sure of himself he must be believed. Linh had nothing—no family, no home; this man knew something. The few other villagers said nothing. Thanh turned to them. "We will go upriver and regroup and occupy this area!"

Linh heard a noise, a dull hammering. It grew louder. Brother Duong's widow pointed. Low on the horizon, dark shapes appeared and flew close. Helicopters. Green, flying in echelons of four. They put down on the runway, the last place not littered by wreckage. Their rotors stopped. On their tails was printed MARINES in white letters.

"No troops are lined up to get in," Linh said. "The drivers are getting out. The *mỹ* just sent in more helicopters. They must have endless riches and numbers." He did not want to look at all these things that did not belong in his *xa*—the foreigners in tents over there, this big-city *can bo* here. He went inside his lost family's house and sat on a stool. He felt a light touch on his arm. Thanh. Linh said, "They died for nothing. The long-noses are still there."

"No. We will drive them out."

"I don't care. All I ever wanted was to come back here, to help Father sharpen his mattock and knife-sickle and watch Mother cooking, to gather knots for her fire. My life is over. How I miss them! How I miss them!"

Nguyen Thanh saw the young man's face crumple in grief and felt as he had not in years the weary heartbreak of the struggle. This house, like his poor uncle's, killed by the *phap*, this unformed young man, lost. One feeling gave flight to another like birds taking off—how many mothers shrieking over slain children, how many men groaning in pain, crippled or dying, knowing their families will go hungry because they have fallen to enemy fire, how many young men like Linh pulled one way by the decadent government and the other by the right demands of the struggle, how many millions of his brothers and sisters suffering over thousands of years fighting the invaders, the *nha ques*, coolies, prostitutes, farmers, mandarins, and bonzes, being beaten down and rising again? It was too much for one man to feel. But he was not alone. Neither was Linh.

"You have a home, Brother Linh. Your home is the *mat tran*. Our life is the struggle. Come with me. We will kill them all. They cannot win and we cannot lose."

Linh got up and they walked over the crest down to the river trail and moved in the shadows up into the hills.

Fire in the Sky

"Phoebe Bishop, war correspondent" was the cutline under a shot Jim took of her squatting to pee in floppy green clothes with cameras hanging from her neck. She supposed Jim had no higher compliment. Their Ia Drang shots had come out well. Now she had to sell them. Would this be her big break?

The battle had run a week. Newsmen who'd gone up and come back immediately with any film at all, such as helicopters taking off, had a beat on the rest of them, who'd stayed around to see what was happening. "It's the industrial nature of the thing," Jim said. "Quality goes up and down, but they have to have pictures." She took her work to bureaus in Saigon and sent sheets to editors in the States.

She bought a Yashica and experimented with it on the streets of Saigon and Cholon, the Chinese city, and out in the countryside. She and Jim hired a car and driver and went to the Delta to shoot color. They drove hours along straight, crowded roads through fields of low crops, trees, along dikes above wet brown and sky-blue paddy whiskered with green shoots. On the roads and lanes into tall grass were Michelin trucks going to property the French still owned, brown ARVN convoys, psychedelic-painted jeepneys full of Vietnamese riding between villages with crates of chickens and ducks, baskets of beans and eggs.

They also saw U.S. Army tanks. She said to Jim, "I suppose some general said, 'What the fuck, I want to use them anyway!' " By the end of the outing she had the hang of the camera.

In Saigon the mail said no one wanted her photographs.

". . . Phoebe, this is nice, but we've run work like this . . ."

". . . we already know what this war's supposed to be . . ."

". . . the body bags are good, but don't think we can run them now . . ."

"Oh, that's utter bullshit!" Jim said. They were at Givral drinking *pastis* to drown her sorrows, which were considerable. "Damn disappointing," he said. "After all, your first battle, and a good one at that. *Lovely* battle, absolutely first-rate shots, bloody bastards!"

"They'd buy worse from a man," she said, crying.

"Of course they would. And it's hard enough to get combat shots. Nothing wrong with your work. But what they're saying has some weight. You probably can't sell strong stuff to America just yet. Don't think your readers want to be upset. My people are buying gore, but that's because they think the Americans can't bring it off. Yours must want more of GIs giving gum to kids."

"Don't be asinine, Jim. There weren't any up there."

"Quite right, but you can see they don't know how to treat it back there—they don't know if it's a balls-up. Mark you, they must suspect it, because look at the interest in stories like the Zippo Marines. But body bags would be an escalation, wouldn't it?"

He said he'd send some of her work to his European editors, which stopped her crying, but she wanted that American breakthrough. They ended up on the roof of her building smoking what he called cannabis and watching shellfire and flares.

Then she got good news. In New York Sara had mentioned her to a *Parade* editor who wrote asking her to do a feature on the new Vietnamese Air Force, which was made up of young men trained in the United States. She interviewed several young pilots and visited them and their families in their small houses and apartments near Tan Son Nhut.

These were the most Americanized Vietnamese she had met. Some chewed gum. They talked about "these hot machines"— the Grumman F8F Bearcat and Douglas A-1 Skyraider—and what they would do in their new F-5 jets. "Yeah, I'm a fighter driver, babe."

One major, Nguyen Lang, who grinned constantly, said, "I'm made in U.S.A." He used expressions like "Keep it cool, baby." He said, "You ready to Christmas shop? I saw two Christmases in Texas. Even saw snow." He laughed. "They had a big PX there. Bigass PX."

"What was the difference," she asked, "between training under the French and training under the Americans?"

"Full one-eighty. Everything. French didn't train. Didn't train. We have *pas de finesse*, they said. They only trained a few pilots at the end and made a big deal of it. Marshal Ky was one of their first. But when my buddies and I go to Texas, it was SOP—they crank us through U.S. government-style."

"What did you do in Texas when you weren't flying?"

"Bitchin' time. Beer parties, happy hours, swimming-pool parties. Drove all around. Bitchin' time. I like America."

She took shots of men in scarves, of families at home. The Vietnamese were pretty people, and the pilot's furniture and wall hangings, some of it American, were so middle class the VNAF families couldn't have looked exotic even to Sunday supplement readers.

She sent the story and was working on a picture feature on the Cao Dai when *Parade* wired back, "Sold." She went with Jim to Givral that night for a celebration and saw Brian Beechwood with a few young intellectuals of the *attentisme*. She told Brian about the VNAF pilots and their American slang.

"Oh, the fighter pilots!" he giggled, waggling his fingers over his head. "They just fly *around* up there! Well, *you* can go mass market, Phoebe, but *I'm* doing a think piece for *New Republic*. You'll see—it's about all the carpetbaggers here, the ugly Texas construction men Lyndon Johnson sent over, and the arms makers *drummers* and tech reps, the generals *lusting* for some way to use their pet weapons on this quivering form, and anything made by a company they want a director's seat on, and *us*, like little birds picking their teeth for stories. Really, it's more of a jungle war than they thought! *This* is the jungle! Saigon! And the important part of the story's already happened as far as *history*'s concerned."

"What's that, d'you think?" Jim asked. The beer he'd been drinking soaked his beard and moustache, so he smacked his lower lip over his whiskers while gazing at Brian. "What's the old story?"

"Quite *obviously* that the political people were pushed out of the picture. That Johnson chose the impossible way of trying to win a political war using soldiers. Draftees. Even the *French* didn't use draftees here. He's supposed to be such a pragmatist and political genius and he doesn't know what these people are *about*. The North Vietnamese must have *welcomed* us ashore because it's simpler to fight us."

"It's a war, still," Jim said. "I cover wars. They're good copy."

"Vivid," Brian said. "Not much content." He and his friends laughed.

Just before Thanksgiving 1965 she was sitting on the terrace at the Caravelle watching Tu Do Street's prostitutes and young Americans and saw someone familiar. He got out of a Peugeot taxi with two other men, one a short white and the other a young black. All wore slacks and short-sleeve shirts and had shaved heads. They were laughing, tossing their heads, pointing back that way; they scanned the street. The one she knew looked over the terrace. His eyes went past her and came back.

"Mark?" she said. "Where have you been?"

"Wait," he said to the men. "Phoebe? I hardly recognized you."

"He's with the Marines in I Corps," she said to Jim.

"Come on through," Jim said. "Have a drink with us."

She watched them work through the open-sided terrace room and among tables. Awful quickie-shop sport clothes; she remembered Ash Loakes's engorged copy about men coming straight from the bush to the hotel terrace still stained with the smoke of battle. These had that scrubbed look American troops have—and the same difficult manners. When they ordered beer they told the white-coated waiter, "Open it here."

"Don't sweat it, man."

"*Ja phai, ja phai*, do it anyway."

"It's really quite okay here, Mark," she said.

Mark introduced the men, a sergeant and a corporal. The black corporal watched the street. Phoebe noticed the gun, a small wooden-handled police model, under his shirt in his belt. The black corporal looked very young. The sergeant had a New England accent. She noticed the tic in Mark's eye and where a front tooth had broken off and was stained at the break.

"I was *wondering* about you. I hadn't heard since last summer," she said in her throaty, compelling voice, leaning across the table toward him.

Oh, yeah, he thought. Still, old feelings hit him, but strangely—like putting on wet clothing. He peered at her. "You look a lot livelier than when I saw you last. How are you?"

"Fine. I loved your letters. While you sent them."

"I got busy."

"So did I."

"So I see," he said, glancing at Jim. "It's nice to see you." But she looked—*different*. He compared her handsome dimensions and reddening, large-pored skin with those fine, wiry, brown-nippled, speed snatched, fox-fuck Vietnamese whores—she was like a retriever to whippets. Still, he remembered the taste of her lips and more distantly the power of her back bridging off the bed, and dimly how she'd lifted her face and sung Calypso at Fence, though he had not been aware at all she was singing directly to another man, Houston Bridles, whom she had seen and wanted to lure.

Phoebe thought Mark had that slightly manic, addled look, officer's version—in command, but ready to lash out. What was he doing with NCOs here? "Aren't you due to go home?"

"I still have a month to go—as you were, six weeks—but I extended a few months on top of that."

"Why?"

"Had a chance to do something with a colonel I knew from Gia Binh. He got a squadron up at Phu Bai. I'm his S-Two. I just made captain."

"Good for you! But you want to stay here?"

"I want to get even."

"What *did* happen at Gia Binh?" Jim asked.

He snorted. The men laughed. She and Jim asked a couple of questions but couldn't get much. The story among the press was that it was a sharp little action not worth more than an inch since there were so many like it. Mark sniffed around Jim to find out where he'd been and what service he'd been in, if any. They ended up talking about Africa.

The black corporal, Dobbs, said, "We got scuttlebutt them peace demonstrators kill a soldier comin' back at San Francisco airport. That happen?"

"People *are* terribly concerned," she said.

"Concerned! I'll say concerned," Randolph hooted. "Kill some poor SOB trying to get home. Very peaceful of them. That's yet *another* way you don't want to buy it—being stomped by asshole civilians!"

"Some of the demonstrations have a point," Phoebe said.

"I miss it."

"Yes, you do."

A whore came by on Tu Do and called across the balustrade at them, "You think you badass GI fucky sucky titi pee—"

"Ahh, shit! You again?"

"Fuck you! *Didi mau!*"

"Go blow a water buffalo!"

She wore a black slit skirt and peasant blouse and had full painted lips; she kissed the air and gave them the finger as she stalked away.

Sergeant Kane said, "She's boocoo trouble. We had trouble with her."

Dobbs said, "She's tryin' give us grief in that bar downriver— that's how we seen the captain."

Randolph said, "I had a cab. I saw them through the glass—the bouncers were holding the door closed. So I attacked."

The sergeant and corporal were laughing. "Good fight?" Jim asked.

"No, we just split!" Dobbs said. "*Dove* into that car. And *gone!*"

The men laughed hugely at this. Phoebe didn't think it was so terribly funny. "It's a shame this war is making so many whores," she said.

"Some women want to be whores," Mark said.

"You really ought to get your tooth fixed," she said. "It looks terrible. How'd you do it?"

"Falling down. You've gained weight, haven't you? I guess that's what looks different."

"It must be harder to see with your eye twitching."

"Sidearm?" Mark said to the NCOs, and to Jim and Phoebe, "Want a shot of brandy? And then we must go. I'm going to the Chinese opera in Cholon tonight." The waiter brought brandies for all of them. Mark and the NCOs stood, raised their glasses, said, "*Semper Fi!*" and threw them down. Kane and Dobbs walked down the sidewalk, shaved heads turning this way and that while Randolph settled into the front of the cyclo cab, keeping one leg out; she saw the .45 under his clothes, too. She had heard there was an MACV order against taking weapons to Saigon on R and R, but few obeyed it.

Christmas came. Robert McNamara, the organizational genius, had said at the landings that the boys might be home by Christmas, but absent his projected optimalities, no manpower retroflow obtained. Happy New Year 1966. A few weeks later Jim and Phoebe celebrated Tet with Brian and his lawyer friend, Nguyen Binh, in their houseboat, one of a row of barges and graceful double-enders with arched bamboo cabins. They had a barge. Wooden jetties ran out from the reeds between boats. Vietnamese on both sides kept cormorants—graceful long-necked diving birds—to fish for them. The thick air smelled of mud, fish, *nuoc mam*, charcoal, tobacco, oil, and the sweet musk of opium. They drank gin and beer and ate garlic shrimp, chicken, roast pig, fish wrapped in leaves, fruit, rice pastry, and candy. Small fireworks popped and occasionally artillery boomed and white flares puffed. The official story was the Americans had called a cease-fire for Tet.

"*We* don't know if they're observing it," Brian said, "but if there's noise of firing, they can claim the *mat tran*'s violating it."

Binh brought out the red and gold paper called *vung bac* and burned it in a wide ceramic plate. It meant "uncle money." *Tet* meant "holiday" or "feast," and the Vietnamese year had a lesser tet at autumn, but this lunar new year celebration was a time of shedding old troubles, starting new successes, and honoring family and ancestors. On top of a wooden chest of drawers Binh had a family shrine, a little box open on one side showing small scrolls and a copper cup of ashes—not of people, Binh said, but of *vung bac*. "Ashes are part of Tet," he said.

"There's a sweet, sad story about it," Brian said.

He and Binh told it. It began with a woman who was happily married, but whose husband beat her when she didn't produce children. After agonizing about her duties, she left him, wandered the trails, collapsed, and was taken in by a kind farmer. They lived happily for years and never discussed her past. One day she saw her ex-husband, looking wretched and starving, begging along the market road. She took him in, sheltering him in a straw shack at the back of the plot. The kind farmer came home and, needing ash for his field, went straight to the shack where the ex-husband slept and, without looking inside, set it afire.

She looked out of the house and screamed. The shack was already burning furiously. "No!" she sobbed. "No!" She ran across the field and, overcome with remorse, threw herself into the flames. The kind farmer ran after her to try to pull her out but the flames were so furious he too was overcome, and he died with the unfortunate spouses. "All three ascended to heaven and were made spirits of the hearth," Binh said. "They watch over the welfare of Vietnamese households."

Overhead the ripping sound of an artillery shell. They looked at one another. Then a soft pop and white flarelight made the reeds' shadows sway in the mist.

"Good," Brian said.

"They love sad stories," Jim said.

"Yes, it is lovely," Binh said.

"Quite. I mean the characters suffer however they choose."

"Family doesn't mean the same in our world," Phoebe said. "My ex-husband and I are better off apart. I don't think I'd enter an unair-conditioned *room* for him."

"We're incomplete either way," Brian said. "We see no beauty in devotion. We have destroyed the beauty. Where are the paper goods, Binh?"

He brought out paper hats and a paper carp, which they burned, the smoke going up to the Jade Emperor, its scent hanging in the misty air with the dark smell of the river and the smoke from other boats. They heard the rapid *braaaat* of a communist weapon and saw thin orange streaks far over the reeds.

Binh said this part of the river had been controlled by the pirates known as the *Binh Xuyen*, the first faction Diem fought and beat in the fifties when then-Senator Lyndon Johnson had called him the Churchill of Asia. Bodies had floated downriver then, too.

At Hue/Phu Bai the squadrons were billeted in decked tents next to a dinky little field. The air was always dank. The gray sand was packed hard but was sticky. Duckboards and bits of PSP ran among the tents as walkways.

The 4th Marines had already secured the area, so the atmosphere wasn't screwed up like at Gia Binh. Nor was there a Colonel Dillis here. For a time, Captain Mark Randolph felt it was like Basic School or a big fraternity with live fire—working days and drinking beer and shooting the shit at night. Maybe going on a strike, but no day and night strain and no pussy field grades.

Lieutenant Colonel Mason ran the squadron well. Everyone thought he was hot shit. How many other Naval Aviators had been on Peleliu, pickled ordnance down the stack of a Jap ship and sunk it, flown close air support in Korea, had two or three fixed wing shot out from under them, and then kicked around in ground fighting? Mark had this picture in mind of Mason, with his short gray hair and wide eyes, watching and walking around during the fire fight phase, not flinching at sudden noises, acting like an officer. When he had grabbed the dead VC's arm to move him and the guy's body had come apart, so he was holding the man's upper half and a trail of guts, the legs over there like a mannequin, they'd laughed so hard Mark thought he'd faint or shit from the dysentery. It was the funniest goddam thing he ever saw.

Then Mason had said, in his smooth, cultivated voice, "I don't know what we're laughing for—they blew up our birds at the cost of a few dead." For some reason that was funny, too.

One night at Phu Bai after chow a few officers were standing around watching across the way where a Marine Huey was taking fire from VC in brush. The VMO squadron had only recently got machine gun racks for its Hueys, and the pilot was flying in a circle— sending down red bursts, adjusting rudder to bring his nose inboard, firing, adjusting rudder—while the slope sent up long orange streams. Charlie Mason was on the steps of his tent drinking bourbon out of a sturdy glass.

"Pay attention to that, gentlemen," he said quietly. With his melow authoritative voice he could have been an executive on a terrace in Winnetka talking about golf. "You work a point target like that in a figure eight. Around, straight run, around. You always have your guns bearing."

Mark saw the younger aviators looking, nodding. It made instant sense. Here was a guy who extrapolated something from his old fixed-wing experience and applied it to the lashed-up rotary-wing tactics of Vietnam. He made *sense*. And he was *believed*.

He was so much better than those shitbird officers and old Staff NCOs every service had to suffer here—the ones who talked about how much they knew about the *last* war, and *wouldn't* listen, and fucked up details. Mark, who needed a leader, admired Mason as much as any officer he'd met. As much as the Escape and Evasion instructor who'd escaped by killing North Korean prison guards by breaking their backs, as much as the Medal of Honor winners he'd met, as much as the hot officers in the 6th Marines. He didn't question it when he saw Charlie Mason himself clumping over the PSP walk late that evening.

"Mark—get all the information you can on Sat Ong Valley."

"Aye-aye, sir."

Randolph was already on his feet, putting on a shirt. Mason started to walk on but turned back and said quietly, "We have a rough night. Briefing's at twenty-three hundred."

Mark went to his office tent and unlocked file cabinets. He had a notion what was going on in Sat Ong Valley. Fragments of information had come in over the past few weeks. The NVA 324B Division had been moving around there. Elements of other divisions, too. That high ground—the valley led up into the Laotian plateau—was where the NVA moved men and trucks. They could truck men down from North Vietnam in a couple of hours and they had thousands of men in sanctuary in Laos. The Main Force units stayed closer to the coast. The Main Force were supposed to be locally raised, but the 4th Marines had been ambushing Main Force units and finding dead and prisoners from North Vietnam as well, some down just a few days.

Sat Ong Valley had a Special Forces detachment that used montagnard tribesmen and mercenaries to ambush North Vietnamese traffic on the trail. Sometimes Mason's squadron, HMM-865, flew supplies and men up there. Mark had seen tribesmen like the Meo, who had tattoos and scars and wore jewelry and smelled of fetid alcohol and wood smoke, or Nungs, wandering ethnic Chinese hill people who looked like something out of "Terry and the Pirates." Gold teeth. Black pajamas. Crossed bandoleers. Little caps. They carried U.S. M-26 frag grenades with the pins out, just a rubber band holding the lever to the bottom flange. In a fire fight they could snap and throw as fast as any NVA pulling string jobs. They liked to carry old, pretty, blue-steel Thompson submachine guns with the stocks chopped off. They took their sons—even little bitty six- to ten-year-olds—along on raids so the kids could learn the business. They hired out to the NVA, too, but they always filled their contracts.

They were mercenaries, not guard troops. Boarding aircraft, they straggled and mobbed at the door, all in black and webbing, grenades and Thompsons swinging, gold and brass flashing, kids yelling and holding on to Daddys' hands.

Not that the Special Forces weren't strange models themselves. Blood brother scars from ceremonies with tribesmen. Odd black bracelets. Odd ways of speaking. There was much to amaze Captain Randolph.

Outside he heard officers thumping out of the tents, boots on wood and PSP, aviators shouting questions and jibes—"Fuckin' mission!" and "It's a shit sandwich!"

He unlocked a thick wooden grenade box and took other papers out. Grenade boxes were good to stow papers in. You could bury them. That's how he'd got out of Colonel Dillis's range and got to this squadron with Charlie Mason, the one he wanted to follow.

It had all happened in the confusion after the raid on Gia Binh.

"I was afraid I'd be investigated," Colonel Dillis told Mark in his office tent.

Randolph was astounded. Did this man understand what he said and to whom he was speaking? Dillis was afraid *his* conduct would be examined. After he'd wasted so many good Marines. After he'd failed to engage the enemy. He *should* be investigated.

Randolph was seeing the colonel because the day after the shooting, while mechanics were poking through the wreckage to see what could be salvaged and EOD was blowing all the dud Chinese grenades, lucky for us, Randolph had gone to Lieutenant Colonel Thomas with a simple memo: "I request mast with the Commanding General, III Marine Amphibious Force. I wish to discuss this matter with an infantry general."

What he had was his own carbons of all the enemy contact reports he'd submitted to Colonel Dillis and all the requests for an ARVN census of the hamlet. He had buried them in a grenade box.

Lieutenant Colonel Thomas, who was a shrewd officer, encouraged Mark without making it look so. He blinked, nodded, his spiky rooster crest bobbing. "I'm sure if, as you say, Lieutenant Szabo and others destroyed documents, and you think they're the ones you have carbons of, by all means General Walt ought to know of it. We don't like to have helicopters blown up or our own troops shot up, do we?"

Colonel Dillis, that slim, frail, white-haired man, sat slumped at his fiberboard field desk. "I was afraid I'd be investigated."

What about Pike, Josephs, and Bonner, bloody and crippled firing their mission to protect your stupidity? What about investigating your own Marines, trying to hang that eighteen-year-old wonder,

Private First Class Coombes, who had feet the size of sandbags and had been so excited about his first enemy contact?

Dillis hadn't had the guts to go after Mark; he'd tried to get the lowest troop, to keep some asshole happy topside. This misguided man who two months before had been in an air-conditioned office in California and whose memory of war was years ago, when his airfields were one island away from the shooting. "I'd just like walking posts," he'd said. And then he'd ignored shooting reports and betrayed his own troops.

For an instant Mark had the image and feel in his flesh of pulling his pistol, arming it while the man's sheltered, ignorant eyes widened, putting a round in his pink face above those wide, watery blue eyes. He could feel the good grip in the web of his hand, the lifting recoil, see Dillis's head jerk, grow a hole, blood and goop hitting the dark canvas behind. Of course he was capable of killing this nice, normal, well-meaning middle-aged man, this incompetent leader. Mark had no virgin's inhibition—it was a matter of decency and intelligent choice. It wouldn't be intelligent to kill Dillis. Aesthetically it wouldn't be right, either. The man was one of those weaklings the instructors had a name for—"Oh, you great big steamin' turd."

Randolph communicated none of this. He stood at parade rest. "I wish you'd think it over a few days," Dillis sighed.

This is where Randolph made an error by complicating his plans. He wanted to destroy Dillis to get even but a day later he realized he also ought to cover for his men, make sure they got awards he'd put them in for, make sure subcaliber officers like Dillis didn't pick on them. He thought, What's going to happen to Sergeant Pearl? Lawrence? Kane? Dobbs? Coombes? He'd had a heated discussion with Captain Shick about the wording of the citations: ". . . when attacked by superior enemy forces. . . ." Finally he'd yelled, "Fuck the aircraft! My men stopped a battalion! The prisoners said so!"

Second Lieutenant Montross, who didn't want to do anything he regretted, slapped a couple of prisoners until Randolph stopped him, then ordered a corpsman to shoot them with pentathol, and they'd told many stories about the battalion's plan to sweep through the camp and being stalled because they didn't know about the machine guns.

He'd have to stay close to be sure they got their awards, since Dillis was known for burning records.

And when he saw General Walt, what would he ask for anyway? That Dillis be tried and executed? Relieved? Dillis had had connections to get the command. How could he hope to get even with the pussy bastard?

Then he heard Mason was taking over HMM-865. He'd seen Mason a few times in the aftermath and knew he was on the horn to his own friends at Wing. He also knew Mason had little regard for Dillis. He guessed Mason had his own copies of the contact reports that Dillis had ignored and burned later. Mark supposed Mason didn't want to torpedo Dillis; they were both aviators and had to serve together. He guessed Mason struck a deal to get 865. It was a prize billet, command of a squadron far away from higher authority. Mark, the incurable optimist, thought he was cool enough to strike a deal, too—to take those men who wanted to go with him and send others to Division or wherever they wanted to go, where they'd be safe from unworthy officers.

"When's the fuckin' briefing?"
"Twenty-three hundred!"
He assembled maps and airmen's charts and int reps on mimeographed sheets. The Marines hadn't got a Xerox capability in Vietnam yet. To get the latest he walked to the comm tent. Behind it was Crypto, a sandbagged steel ship container where the communicators got messages in five-letter groups. He sent a priority interrogative to Wing G-2 and smoked a cigarette. Outside he heard aviators' boots, mechs cursing, trucks and mighty mites running up and back. The reply came in. Jesus.

The message, marked SECRET, said the Sat Ong Valley was the site of an intense air battle over heavy ground fire—not just a helicopter trap, which the NVA had been running for months, but a fixed-wing trap. At the center of the trap was the Green Beret post. The tactic was to isolate the American unit, occupy the surrounding high ground, and set up antiaircraft weapons and shoot down all support helicopters and now, obviously, fixed-wing attack aircraft. The NVA units there, over a regiment, had destroyed elements of an Army aviation company, two Air Force squadrons, and a Navy VF/VA squadron. ". . . Largest combat air engagement in-country to date . . ."

Electronic monitoring reports had come in from Air Force and

Marine aircraft and Army and Navy ground installations—clusters of masts, poles, antennae surrounded by tons of concertina, where the clerks were pale and big-eyed from life under sandbags, listening with earphones. The electronics watch reported heavy traffic on NVA frequencies and heavy radar activity on several bands of the spectrum. One of the radars used a phasing not encountered in-country before.

This radar, the electronics people said, was probably not made by the Russians or Warsaw Pact designers. Its electronic patterns resembled those of Swedish gear. Wherever it came from, the NVA had it. They were well equipped. G-2 concluded the NVA had the capability and intention of destroying as many strike aircraft as they could. But how? Mark wondered. What were they using? What can I warn the aviators about? What the fuck am I going to tell Charlie Mason?

It was 2245 and he heard the heavy growl of the AvGas truck and the cough and chuggle of H-34 engines starting, being tested.

It was close enough to time—he had to talk to the man at G-2, even on an insecure line. He'd talk around it. He had the Comm Watch Officer put him through and sat on a box holding the handset of the canvas-wrapped EE-8 field phone.

"Okay. I know who you are," the major at the other end said. It wasn't a bad connection. "We got a debrief on someone just back. Tell your boss it was Spatsy."

Spatsy was a lieutenant colonel Charlie Mason knew in G-3. He'd been on Shufly. Mark had met him once—a tall, baggy-eyed man who looked something like John Huston. He'd flown bombers in World War II.

Spatsy spoke slowly, picking his words to imply what he couldn't say in clear. "Listen very carefully, young man. I was in an LOE observing from two to three thousand yards east. Conditions: darkness. Muzzle flashes both sides of valley, also fighting around camp. Before I arrived, the Army'd waved off Hueys. They lost a couple at one thousand feet and couldn't send in more VFR. Too dark to follow the ground. Other observers said they blew up in the air. A big orange ball—HE and fuel."

Mark had seen helicopters crippled in the air, even go haywire when a round hit the main or tail rotor and the bird lifted and rolled, bucked, spun like an eggbeater, men doing God knows what inside, while the fragile green contraption nosed over and plummeted and crashed and burned. But what kind of weapon could it be that blew them up in the air?

"I observed the Air Force send in two flights of F-One Hundreds to lay cannon and napalm on the rim. I observed pale yellow or white tracers, fat streaks, and saw two A-C flamed. Out of eight. The Navy sent in F-Eights to suppress radar but"—he paused—"sustained damage." He couldn't say the number.

"Then the Air Force sent in Puff the Magic Dragon." This was a C-47, the stable, slow DC-3, fitted with Gatling guns that fired thousands of rounds per second and could reduce a treeline to toothpicks.

"I flew in trace of Puff. He was at two thousand at a steep bank, one hundred knots, and fired like a son of a bitch. Nothing but solid streams of red working over Charlie. When they opened up, young man, I have never seen anything *like* it. Streams of orange fifties and that goddam thing with the pale tracers. I figure at least a half dozen ZPU twin or quad fifties and this automatic cannon—"

"Cannon?" Mark asked.

"Correct. Firing HE. That's what it's got to be. Some kind of automatic cannon, radar directed. Maybe a thirty-seven." The 37-millimeter was a standard Soviet and Chinese light cannon round, like our 40-millimeter.

"But listen—I tell you, this thing locks on *fast*. The shell must arm at two hundred meters out or so, and it's dead on. Puff took, I'd estimate, three hits right off. It blew up in a big orange ball, both wings, and the *ball* was catching HE rounds!"

"I copy." Mark ground out his cigarette and took the information to the briefing tent. By now the PSP teemed with men in soft caps walking fast, shielded lights, mites and trucks moving slowly, and aviators in flight suits at the lit-up tent door.

What was the mission? Be pretty hairy to resupply the Green Berets with all that fire in the air.

He understood why Marine helicopters were being sent. It was a night operation. The Army pilots weren't trained for all weather and night flying. Their helicopter pilots were plenty brave—crazy, in fact. He'd seen gunship pilots go twenty feet above a woodline to work it over—but they weren't trained to fly in all conditions. The Army took privates out of basic training, sent them to a six-month school, and made them warrant officer pilots. They were hot, brave, and died young. Naval Aviators started older and had years of training in subjects like night navigation. And the Marine H-34s were fitted with electronics that, while not ground following, at least allowed them to get around at night.

The Air Force had lost six attack aircraft there. That was a lot, but the Air Force was notorious for lining up its aircraft and sending them all in on the same vector. Simplicity of operation. They had balls but they took terrific losses.

Mark went into the tent, which had a plywood floor, rows of folding camp stools, and a map stand lit glaringly, like *Guernica*, by naked bulbs. Aviators took seats and lit cigarettes. Charlie Mason came in, squinting, and got coffee from the green jug. One of the aviators said, "Colonel, who's leading this mission?"

"I am." He took .38 rounds from a tan box and put them in his shoulder holster loops—copper ball and red-tipped tracer. By now the tent was full.

Mason spoke quietly in his clear, smooth voice. "We are being handed a hot potato. Our mission is to evacuate the Green Beret detachment in Sat Ong Valley—"

Aviators looked at each other. This was truly a shit sandwich.

Mason talked about the intensity of the fire and who *hadn't* got through. "Mark?"

Randolph told what he had heard, showing the ridge lines around the valley, reiterating what they knew about the enemy ZPU multiple fifties, spelling out what Spatsy had said about the secret weapon, this automatic cannon.

"We will go in low," Mason said. "Very low to get under the cannon, and fast to cut the ZPU's arc of aim. Two hundred knots at fifty feet. I will lead in the first flight." He looked at them. "Gentlemen, this may be the last time we fly together. It may not. I don't have to tell you other aviators have flown other aircraft into heavy fire and it wasn't the end of the world. We got this mission because we're Marine aviators. Whether or not the Army could fly this mission, at night, is beside the point. It's why we are Marines. Now *listen*—"

He jabbed a finger at them. Mark thought he was going to torque up the motivation, but he said, "Make sure of your avionics. Calibrate your instruments precisely. MACS-8 will give us vectors. We are going in on radar right off the ground; watch your wingmen, watch your altimeters. Lead flight: Buckley. Del Campo. Matteson—you're going in with me." He named Wilfong, a captain who had just got there, to fly right seat with him.

Almost as an afterthought he turned to Mark. "Captain Randolph, that's a ground situation there. You better come along as liaison with the Army."

Mark's guts dropped. He'd thought he was just going to be an office pogue—sit on his ass and answer questions. But he managed to show nothing. "Here I am, Colonel!" The thing was to lie like hell and look cool. His hands shook once, twice as he lit a cigarette. His last? He could die tonight. Better not think about it.

Out in the dark ordnance men and crew chiefs stocked the helicopters with machine gun ammo, flares, and grenades. The air was sweet with AvGas.

Mark sat by the open port aft. He saw Mason's boots in the instrument glow forward; he could look up the little passageway to the high flight deck to see boots and some controls.

They did a rolling takeoff and climbed into darkness. He remembered how the ground came up going toward Laos.

He went to the open door to piss and stood by the crew chief, Corporal Barry, who sat, hand on machine gun, watching and listening to his helmet intercom. Wilfong was flying it now while Mason talked on the radio; Wilfong's boots shifted on the wide, worn aluminum pedals. Mark looked in and saw his hands working the control levers—the cyclic, which tilted the rotor mast to take you forward, hover, or flare out, and the collective, a complicated sleeve on a stick you twisted for throttle and lifted or let down to set rotor pitch. You had to have bite and power matched or you stalled out or oversped.

It was too noisy to hear what Mason was saying into the mike but Mark knew he had several nets to listen and talk on—artillery and gunfire going in, attack aircraft hitting the target, and his wingmen and the rest of his squadron. Above them out of sight flew Willie the Whale, a Marine A3D, a tubby fifties-vintage jet loaded with electronic gear. Willie was there to jam and monitor. In the ether were radio beams from MACS-8 to vector them onto target.

Out the unglassed port he saw the high, round-nose silhouettes of the other three H-34s, flashes of light showing a wheel, a strut, a Plexiglas windshield, and the dark thing under the nose like a double chin, a bolted-on armor plate to protect the engine. He could see the red glow from the engine nostril.

He saw the air battle up ahead. Oh, Jesus, yes, it was all over the fucking sky! White parachute flares, red tracers, orange tracers, a weird band of red streaks that must be Puff Number Two. You could sense how thick the trees were and the peaks and valleys in the gun flashes. Corporal Barry motioned him to strap in. Mason's hands moved to the controls.

Mason dropped the aircraft fast. They were *diving*. Mark gripped the tubular seat frame, atheist though he was, saying to himself, *Oh, God, save me. I didn't mean to volunteer. I'm a dumb shit for wanting to get even. I don't want to buy it.* They flared out right above the trees. He saw feet moving forward, Corporal Barry swinging around and firing the M-60, tree silhouettes under the wheels, limbs and leaves lit in flashes, muzzle flashes, ripping lines and jigger points, tracers every which way, the helicopter lurching and hopping as Mason dodged the treetops and jigged for the hell of it. The bird on the left, Del Campo's, took a stream of orange, slugs sparking off the armor plate, ricocheting off wheel struts, sinking like orange needles into the fuselage while the gunner fired long bursts under and ahead. Then Matteson's bird, two left, gave a jump and veered off.

They were flying into daylight, into a sky of white flarelight. Mark saw Barry jerk and wheel away and fall, sitting, on the floor, held by his leash strap. The bird gave a lift, an upward lurch, bouncing bumpety grinding bump like a car hitting railroad ties, loud crashes and holes splayed *up* in the deck. Shit! Mason's hands and feet moving—it was machine gun fire into the engine, fat ropes of oil smoke boiled back over the wheels. Oil stench filled the cabin. Mark crawled to the door gun but Barry motioned, palm down, no fire, because just then they cleared the edge of the Green Beret camp and were diving in much too fast. Out the door he could see it was all lit up by flares and burning canvas, a long isoceles triangle, sandbags lit yellow green, Special Forces men in helmets running toward the landing zone. Barry hit him and motioned arm over face, crash position, the flimsy metal deck dropping away from them as they fell.

The wingman, Captain Del Campo, saw Lieutenant Colonel Mason's aircraft drop, rotors spinning, gray smoke pouring back, into the center of the camp triangle while mortar shells also landed in orange gray puffs. He told debrief—what was left of his squadron staff at Phu Bai and Spatsy from Wing—that Mason had yelled "Waveoff!"

into the radio when he was going in, that his helicopter hit very hard, the nose bouncing and dropping, the struts crumpling, and that it burst into flames.

"It was lit up like a flashbulb while I climbed out," he said. "I didn't see anyone exit, but I was trying to get clear fast."

As it was, the other three birds in the flight were damaged, Matteson's junked.

No one knew for several hours what had happened on the ground, and then they saw the NVA had overrun the camp.

Betrayal on the Ground

A Special Forces Sergeant First Class named Loomis was the first to reach the burning aircraft. Men fell out while it lit up. A pilot in a khaki flight suit swung out of the high window and rolled away from the bobbing rotor blades; a captain in jungle poplin pulled out the crew chief, who had blood all over his flight suit. The H-34 went up fast, first the magnesium fuselage, then the gasoline, machine gun ammo, and flares, blowing and popping. By then they were in the bottom of the trench.

Loomis put a compress on Corporal Barry's arm—shattered humerus, big exit wound. Lieutenant Colonel Mason, gasping for breath, said a captain named Wilfong had gotten it in the face on the way in. "He was monitoring radio traffic. I heard him groan on the intercom and looked over. That's all she wrote."

The other captain, Randolph, said, "Better get pots on. Got any spares?" He put a lit cigarette in Barry's mouth.

"I'll get Major Byrne," Loomis said.

Major Byrne, the detachment CO, Sergeant First Class Loomis, Randolph, and Mason met in the command bunker while others dressed and splinted Barry's arm. Byrne, who looked tired but was full of energy, explained the situation in bleak, clear terms. "We're cut off and surrounded. They're digging trenches up now, but they've got about an hour and a half to go. We've put mines and hosangs out there. Claymores." He added that the NVA had started closing in last

261

week. Between explosions you could hear the shovels scraping and clinking.

"We have a string of outposts. All tribesmen. We use Sidgees close in, on the wire." He was talking about CIDGs, Vietnamese Civilian Irregular Defense Group employees funded by the CIA. "A couple of our outposts were picked off. NVA knew just where to find them. An ambush went bad. Then we heard them digging up. So we knew we'd been compromised."

"By whom?" Mason asked quietly.

"Sidgees," Byrne said. "New bunch we got in hasn't been reliable. We isolated them—they're on the wire, firing out, but meanwhile the NVA's on the way in."

Sergeant First Class Loomis told in a few words how he and other men had gone up on the trails and snatched a couple of *bo doi* and interrogated them back in camp. They gave much useful information because the People's Army, as part of its motivation, gave a lot of information to its troops, and also because the Americans had wired a EE-8 to the *bo dois'* balls and made them scream, and played Buddhist head threats, offering to separate their skulls, the seat of the spirit, from the rest of their bodies so they would be isolated forever in the spirit world. The captives cried and bobbed, trying to bow, and told what they knew.

"A large proportion of the NVA up there in the hills are signals, radar, AA, generator mechanics—their mission is to fuck up the air," Major Byrne said.

"They did," Mason said.

"Do you think it's possible to get another flight in?"

"Not that many crazy aviators left," Mason said. "Unless we can knock out the fire."

Major Byrne showed Randolph on the map where the trenches were. It was a standard People's Army slow attack. "We've had the cock here, Colonel," Randolph said. "Better haul ass. You're SOPA, too." He meant Senior Officer Present Afloat, or, as the gag went, Awake. Marine officers were presumed to know all about ground operations because every Marine, excluding Colonel Dillis, was a rifleman.

"Which means I'll hang for it," Mason said dryly. "Needless to say, I expect your best advice. All right, Major Byrne, you're the CO of ground troops. How do you propose to get us out of here? What's your strength? How many in the breakout force?"

"We've lost five killed," Byrne said. "We have twelve of us and twenty Sidgees. We all go. It's out of the question to leave them."

It is? Mark wondered.

They huddled over the map and aerial photos. Then Randolph, Loomis, and a Special Forces lieutenant went around the wire, running over the ground and crawling along the trenches. The mortar rounds coming in made rising sighs just before they hit. Randolph was so ragged from the flight in, the impact, the noise, the fear, it was just up-and-down panting. Around the camp Green Berets put thermite grenades and gasoline cans on anything they didn't want to carry. A couple of avenues of approach had tilted 55-gallon drums facing down them, the hosangs, incendiary mines. The drums were filled with napalm, wrapped in detonating cord, sitting on TNT blocks to make them spray fire when the enemy came their way. The men showed Mark other surprises. He kept nodding, saying, "Yeah?" and "No shit!"

"Yeah, one of the prisoners knew about that cannon you talk about, Captain. Didn't know what he meant, then. Said they called it Firedragon."

"Soviet?"

"Affirmative. Said the foreign advisors, Russians, call it a ZSU-twenty-three. Gotta be like a twenty-mike-mike."

"Be good to know how high the shell arms." It was too late to ask the prisoner.

"You was under it or you wouldn't be here."

They were in the bottom of another trench with that creosote smell of sandbags, oily clay, sweat, the sharp smell of new nylon on his vest, and the iron smell of blood from whomever they'd taken it. The background noise was constant hammering of machine guns and rifles, desultory shells and shrapnel whispers, and the American mortar *Poonk!* going out. Then Mark heard a jet high above and the groaning, creaking sound of its controls. Only Willie the Whale sounded like that—the slow, straight-wing A3D the Marines used to read and jam enemy electronics.

Mason came out with an Army radio of a sort Randolph had never seen and talked in an air strike. Two Marine A-4s skidded across low like gray bats in the flarelight, firing cannon and laying napalm and HE but didn't get the Firedragon cannon. For all their expensive gear and McNamara genius procedures, the Americans didn't know how to take out a radar-directed gun. It wheeled and sent a stream of yellow-white after the attack aircraft, hitting nothing but showing it owned the air here.

Mason said, "Okay, let's walk out." He grabbed hold of Mark's shoulder and looked in his eyes. His were weary, clear gray. He still wore his baseball cap under his helmet. "You okay?"

"Yes sir."

"Be sure you know what's up and keep me informed."

Corporal Barry's thin, sharp-nosed face looked dreamy from the morphine. His arm was in a sling.

A Special Forces radioman. Riflemen. M-79. One machine gun with assault pouch and bipod. More riflemen. They formed a column along a trench, dropped their helmets and vests, and slipped out over part of the wire. Sidgees and Green Berets in the security team picked up the firing while the column departed. The security team set off some of the thermites. More firing. They were leaving a pile of radios booby-trapped: pressure plates, pull devices, mousetraps in grenades, and land mines around the stack in case the NVA walked around to study the problem.

Corporal Barry's upper body was stiff—he must have been hurting—but he didn't say a word. Randolph watched Mason. Every word and gesture was calm. He listened to facts, asked Mark to explain an element he didn't understand. They did all this while moving a few steps at a time, breathing softly, speaking *sotto voce*. This was an outstanding officer. Holding roots and rocks, they dropped down a ravine through brush and followed the creek trail while the rear guard in camp fired out all the machine gun ammo. They moved a few steps and crouched and moved on, keeping in touch on the air. Mason talked in a low voice on the radio, hands cupping the mike. They heard Willie the Whale. Mason made a signal moving his hand like a dish, meaning the NVA had boocoo radar.

They crouched and waited. And waited. Like a delay on the subway. Word came back that the point had seen an NVA guard and knifed him. They stepped past the body.

By now the security team had fired out the machine gun ammo. In the column they heard a few loose shots. The last Green Berets were slipping out. The column waited under overhanging brush about one kilometer from the camp. The first claymore went off, *crunch*, then two more. Then the *whooomp!* of the hosang's napalm showers. Screaming up there. A few men grimaced at the humor of it.

They stopped again when one of the flanks radioed that the NVA were moving along another trail up the slope—but the NVA were climbing to observe the camp from this side, so the Americans moved on very quietly under them. They had picked the right trail out. The column dropped again.

The flank called in that they saw Chinese advisors up the slope. "Same kinda uniform we saw on Chinese in Saravane," Loomis murmured to Randolph. "Leather straps. Darker green cloth. Definitely not NVA." But these Chinese were headed back where the Americans had come from.

Now they could go over the ridge and try to get clear. They climbed the leafy, brushy slope and heard Vietnamese yelling. Higher up, they heard an engine and smelled diesel exhaust. The generator for the radar units.

"Go on down more," Mason said. "When we get to an LZ we have to get out fast before they lock on to us." A couple of thousand meters more.

Loomis was listening to the radio and heard the rushing noise break in regular pulses. He touched Major Byrne's sleeve. "Something's wrong," he said. "Someone's keying a mike in code. And it's not our code."

Byrne listened. He told Mason. Mason waved to Randolph to join them. "Gotta find this man fast," Loomis said. "We come through all that shit, this fuckin' *binh van*'s gonna call them in on us anyway. And they'll be able to see soon."

By now the sky was pale, but it wasn't a normal dawn. No birds sang. Too many people moving around. The brush was over their heads so they were in darkness, but they could make out fingers and feet on the shadows ahead. Several hundred meters away they heard metal clanking. NVA search parties. Whoever'd keyed the mike gave the NVA a clue to their location. The *bo doi* were coming after them. How much time did they have?

Mason in his flight suit and baseball cap with the scrambled eggs had a quick conference with Byrne, who told Loomis to move along the column and get all PRC-25s turned off except his own. Meanwhile they kept moving over the ridge and into a hollow. The man who'd taken over Loomis's radio was listening to the rushing noise. He signaled Byrne. The column stopped. Then a commotion back in the brush and a Sidgee handler and a Green Beret sergeant dragged up one of the CIDGs, a big oafish one they called Hoss, holding him by the arms. "He and JoJo had a PRC-6 hidden. They were the ones," the sergeant said. Others dragged in the one called JoJo.

"Separate and interrogate," Byrne said.

Randolph watched them work on Hoss. He was a very surly, angry man; after the Americans slapped and struck him he came apart, yelling at them, so they had to gag him. "They were going to kill his family, he says. His family's shit, past Quang Tri. He should have been screened. They're not catchin' this shit," Loomis said.

JoJo talked right away, begging and praying. His reasons for treachery were the same.

"The question is," Mason asked Byrne, "how many others are there in this bunch?"

"I wouldn't bet," Byrne said. "We can cover the rest of them now. One move and we chop them down. But it'll be hard to move with these two tied up."

Mason asked, "Can they be tied and left?"

"Yes sir. The *bo doi*'ll find them soon, though, and they know a lot about the way we ran our camp, how we set up patrols, and our signals equipment."

Mason looked at Randolph. "Mark? What's your idea?"

"They're spies in friendly uniform, Colonel. They can be shot out of hand. Remember that law-of-land-warfare memo Colonel Dillis sent around for initialing before we were hit at Gia Binh? We better get rid of them now and fast so it's clear to any other converts the VC has with us." *Look at these bastards.* American uniforms. One scowling, one begging. He hated them. He hadn't wanted to ride along on any of this and they were trying to kill him.

Mason grunted. The sky was light now. The only dark they had was in the shadow of the brush. They could hear Vietnamese calling and clattering weapons. "Make it fast," Mason said.

They huddled in the clearing—the two CIDG suspects, interpreters, Major Byrne, Randolph. Mason told the Sidgees what the hearing was about. The witnesses repeated what they'd said. Hoss spit at them, glaring. JoJo looked at his feet.

"No doubt about it?" Mason asked.

"None," Byrne said.

"As SOPA and tactical commander," Mason said, "I judge you guilty and sentence you to death." The interpreter, Sergeant Fraser, repeated it in Vietnamese. Hoss spat. JoJo tried to lift his hands to pray and beg.

"Okay, how?" Major Byrne said. "NVA's had reveille—we have to be quiet."

"Break their necks," Randolph said. Mason glanced at him and nodded. Mark looked at Hoss. Rage filled him like hot blood. Swinging his shoulders, he stepped past Hoss, spun and punched and felt his fist go through, bone giving way. Hoss grunted so you couldn't hear his spine break, but his head and shoulders flew back flopping while his trunk sagged forward. His legs kept kicking. He shit, too. Randolph rubbed his fist and looked at the dead man, not feeling any better.

JoJo, who was blindfolded and gagged, grasped what was going on and squealed, struggling. Major Byrne stuck a knife in his throat, which sent a shower of blood in front of him until Byrne threw him on his face.

Lieutenant Colonel Mason looked at the dead and in his smooth, composed voice said, "All right. Let's go."

Some distance further Mason came up on the air and asked for a strike. First Marine Air Wing had air on station. A-4s came in firing cannon and dropped napalm. Black smoke and flames came up beyond the ridge. After that they couldn't hear the generator. The NVA didn't have many men down the creek. The point killed another *bo doi* on road watch.

By 1100 they had reached a clearing 10 kilometers away, out of range of 120-millimeter mortars. The men set up in the brush and Mason called for air extraction. H-34s came in and flew them to Da Nang for debrief.

In the aircraft on the way back they drank water and sucked in cigarettes. Mark was far past understanding this experience. It was imbedded in his nerves like fused elements, sights and smells, sensations and gouts of emotion, so that he couldn't untangle it and, in the interests of his own mental health, wasn't inclined to.

Got through that one, he thought. What's next? Are we heroes? The crew on the extraction and the debrief officers, Marine and Army, said they were heroes.

Another opinion came in a few hours later, when a pale, diffident captain from Wing Legal walked into the Casual Section Officers' Tent where Mark was lying on his rack, smoking a cigarette and staring at the canvas overhead.

"Captain, it looks like you're being charged with murder."

As usual, Mark showed little. In fact he was too exhausted to feel much. Oh, shit, he thought. Up on charges again. Promotion, charges—what the fuck am I doing here?

"Hello, Houston," Congressman Sanford's wife said down the phone line. Her California voice was flat and slightly nasal. "I'll meet you at four." She paused. "In splendid tan silk." Her sibilants caressed his ears the way her tongue did.

"Five-thirty," he said.

"Five. We have a full evening."

"Wonderful. See you then."

Houston carried on the affair while cutting and dodging through the backfield confusion of the Great Society White House at War. Confusing it was indeed. President Johnson was obsessed by the war, hated the war, saw the war as a bitch that bit the ankles and balls of his Great Society.

He'd told Houston, "FDR was like a daddy to me," and another time: "History's gonna look at me—" He wanted to stand in history as a President like Roosevelt, as a great domestic father and triumphant war leader. Houston had nodded, grinning open-mouthed, while calculating, like a defensive back gauging yards, the distance between this man and Roosevelt.

FDR was, after all, a patrician, a patroon family, Groton and Harvard—not a scholar, but knowledgeable of the world. Pa, Uncle Stu, and their friends who had known Roosevelt said that, though he was maddeningly illogical, his mind was organized. He always had a list of things he wanted to do and deals he wanted to make, and knew at all times what these deals would accomplish and how they would look. Perhaps it had something to do with having been an athlete and then working around his crippling illness. They said FDR had dealt with problems patiently, like a fisherman, as when he played Joe Kennedy, patronized, then got rid of him. He could be quite ruthless, as any leader must be, but didn't let many see it.

But Lyndon Johnson, Houston thought ruefully, was quite another character—uneducated, socially insecure, driven by embarrassments from Texas, demanding attention, presumptuous and posturing. He pushed too hard, outraged many, and did not know how to focus his mind to solve complex problems, like this bitch of a war.

Johnson, McNamara, Bundy, Rusk, the aides, the Agency men, all talked about it constantly, but they couldn't cut to the heart of it, made no decisions.

The Army wanted to invade NVA sanctuaries in Laos and Cambodia, to say nothing of North Vietnam. LBJ listened, studied, and ruled it was politically unacceptable.

Military critics said McNamara was brilliant, perhaps, but fatuous, citing his TFX jet and other ingenious screwups similar to those of Milo Minderbinder, the supply officer in *Catch-22*. Johnson kept McNamara because he was the genius of Camelot. Still, almost pathetically, Johnson wanted the good opinion of Camelot.

Others, including generals, said Westmoreland didn't have a grip on the war and was ignoring the VC's political progress. But Westie was married into Douglas MacArthur's family and was well connected in Southern and Army politics.

Tuesday was the "Vietnam Lunch" and NSC briefings, so every Tuesday and Wednesday the White House had Vietnam craziness—aides leaping like chickens off their perches, squawking and flapping to implement the President's latest bright idea to end the war, and then settling down for the rest of the week.

But today was Thursday. Houston got a pool car to K Street and walked down the block to the hotel. Ah, Marty! Mrs. Sanford walked down the sidewalk toward him, beautifully dressed in city tweeds. Despite the gray day, she wore large square violet sunglasses, which she did not take off until she walked into the hotel room, undoing her buttons.

She wore tan silk as she had said. The fullness at the sides of her breasts. "It's all these dinners," she murmured, and: "See what it's done to my thighs." She showed him, moving aside the crotch of her tan silk panties. "Don't do that, Houston, I'll come too quick."

He didn't answer.

"Oh! Say! Oh! Houston!"

She pulled him to the bed and they bounced, chewed, grabbed, coupled, came, collapsed. This minor explosion, Houston thought. But we're in a hurry. She lay with her head up on the pillows, waiting. She still wore her tan silk chemise. She was a dark blonde and had cute features, a small nose, kissable full cheeks, a couple of years past ripeness in her thirties. "That was our fastest," she said.

"Do you keep time?"

"I think a lot about . . . screwing . . . with you, yes. Don't you think we're . . . something special?"

"Ah—of course."

" 'Ah—of course!' You are *such* a New Englander, *so* East Coast." She batted her eyelashes. "My family's been in California since . . . before the Gold Rush. You're not the only patrician around."

"We aren't patricians," Houston said. "Not even Brahmins."

"Well, *Sandy*'s family are patricians. They're from Pasadena. He went to Ojai." Her brown eyes stuck out slightly, not her best feature, though eyeliner helped, and he wished she would shut up. She simply talked too much. But there she goes again—this was her charm. She moved the silk aside just a bit with her fingertips and moved it back.

"Sandy spends *so* much time at the office. I know I've . . . told you this. We had a patrician marriage." She moved the silk again. "At times I'd get raunchy in his office, but—"

"It's a shame he doesn't know better. I find you damn attractive."

"He's very devoted to helping others. Of course I want to help, too."

"You're helping him by standing up at these things and smiling and saying hello. You are, ah, charming, you know."

"Thank you."

He moved the silk aside and kissed her body and sat up, caressing her. "I had hoped my wife would do that—stand up."

"Were you going to run? Was she going to help?"

"I'm sorry?"

"Run for office? Congressman from Mass?"

"Oh, no. I am an appointee. My family are appointees."

"Nevertheless we're all human beings," she said. "It must have been . . . sad."

"It's a lot of work here. Well, ah, of course I'll console you."

"We're going about this in a grown-up way—aren't we?"

He would have preferred she shut up. But he said, "I'd like to be."

"What?"

"Grown up."

"What do you mean?"

Capable of moving ahead without second thoughts. Regrets. "Ah—don't you, when all is said and done, tire at times of public life? Being out, under eyes, under the gun, all the time? I need to—"

"We have these . . . private moments. You've helped me wonderfully. We can help each other."

"Yes. I think we understand," he said.

"You'll let me know, too, what he's got in mind. Programs? So I can help Sandy?"

"Yes, of course. He's got clear sailing, you know. It looks like the war will be increasingly technological. McNamara wants to use electronic sensors and remote-control guns to block the Ho Chi Minh Trail. Lots of gadgets. That can't hurt Sandy's district."

"No. He doesn't like it, though. 'There's something incomplete about it,' he says. The bombing and shooting."

"But that's just it," Houston said. "No matter how many guidelines we send down—and you should be in the cockpit with me. I've seen these things, instructions *this* detailed, *pages*—and yet the ground troops still keep causing *incidents*. Face-to-face killing. Of course it's, ah, ugly—and when the press finds out it ruins us. So we *have* to use something—foolproof devices—to make it remote."

"Some of Sandy's constituents are upset."

"No, I know. You should see how confused it is on Tuesdays, when we *respond* to concerns. Nothing's ever quite—"

"I know." She opened her thighs as a dark blonde suggestion and rolled her chemise up above her full pink-pebbled nipples. "Let's hurry."

Houston knew it was dangerous but felt all things were possible if he kept his nerve.

Phoebe Bishop, Jim Robinson, and a half-dozen other correspondents flew up on the Air Force C-130 mail run to cover the murder in Da Nang. The story had come in to all the press hangouts. Cold-blooded murder. Officers. No one knew anything beyond that. MACV and the Marines weren't talking. But given the crude violence all around, the fact that this involved officers made it as appealing as society scandal.

"What happened?"

"Something about Marine pilots and Green Berets. And espionage."

"Yeah, my readers'll go ape shit," Chick De Vore said, scratching his leg and lifting up on one cheek on the C-130's webbing to break wind.

"You have to watch out for the Marines," the AP man said. "They act very friendly but they'll feed you all kinds of impossible stuff."

The ramp dropped and heat poured in. Across the airstrip were gray-painted Marine fighters and green stacks of supplies. They hitched a ride from a six-by-six truck driver and rode around the field to the Marine headquarters compound. Other newspeople were already there in all styles of overseas reporter garb—tailored khakis, fatigues, white cottons. They stood on the dirt street in the shade of tan stucco buildings and a couple of trees. They couldn't enter the buildings. Marine MPs in red-and-white helmet liners stood by the doors. Clerks typed *rat-a-tat-tat* in rows of tents, a reassuring office sound. Phoebe saw Ash Loakes, wearing fatigues and a camouflage helmet cocked to one side, strap undone, plump and red-faced. "I've been down at Pleiku with the Cav!" He winced and shook his head. "Rough."

Other correspondents arrived from Saigon, Quang Ngai, Hue. Two flew in from a carrier. They traded rumors.

"The Green Berets were running patrols in *Laos!*" one said.

"The VC had a *helicopter trap!*" another said.

"Two Vietnamese spies!" Ash Loakes said. "They killed them without a trial! They beheaded one of them. A Marine told me. Then another one said, 'No, it was NVA scimitar shrapnel.' "

"What?"

"They said the NVA were using a secret weapon up there and this sergeant said it was scimitar shrapnel—the charge blows little razor crescents out sideways and they take people's heads and limbs off."

"Oh, horseshit," the AP man said. "Don't swallow that—the Marines told me they had three-story bunkers here and I filed it and got no *end* of trouble from my boss."

"You can't keep blades oriented coming off a charge," Jim said. "There's nothing to give them directional stability." He looked at Phoebe. "Scimitar shrapnel. Right. Sure."

A correspondent said, "Those are the ones from Legal!" Marine officers came out of the tan stucco Wing Headquarters building and correspondents lurched toward them. They're runningggggg—Chick De Vore pumping his short legs, Ash Loakes bouncing under his helmet like a fat Yalie, Jim and Phoebe legging it, cameras flying, others galloping in the brown dust.

A couple of MPs double-timed out to form a line between the correspondents and the officers.

"Hey, officers!" a correspondent yelled. "Hey, sir!"

"Sir! General!"

Phoebe saw the ranks: Lieutenant Colonel, Lieutenant Colonel, Major, Captain, First Lieutenant.

"Who got killed! Hey, what's the story?"

"Hey, Colonel! Captain, who'd you kill?"

The short-haired captain wearing a cap set low over his eyes turned to face the newsman, hand on his black holster. Phoebe looked into Mark Randolph's face, as cold as anyone she'd seen. When he saw her he looked like something momentarily gave inside; then his face set again.

"Mark?" Phoebe called. He turned away.

"Hey, Colonel!" Chick De Vore said.

"Is that Mark Randolph?" Ash Loakes said. "I knew him at Yale! What's he doing here?"

"No statement now!" said the press officer, a lieutenant colonel. "Give us some space, please." The MPs leaned and urged, separating the newspeople in motley clothing from the suspects in clean, pressed green cotton uniforms.

"So who'd they kill? What happened?" Chick De Vore asked one of the MPs.

"Nobody. Don't know," the MP said.

"Are they under arrest?"

"Negative. Take a look. They're under arms."

"What's he mean?"

They stood in the dirt street and smoked cigarettes, dropping butts everywhere, neat officers probably seething at them behind office windows. Jim walked away and looked at an eight-inch self-propelled howitzer behind a row of pines and came back. "Nothing doing here. I'm going to pick up other work."

"What?" Phoebe asked.

"American fighters use a British ejection seat. Bread-and-butter story. I'll go chat up some Wing boffin." He walked over to the Wing press office and she saw him talking to Marines there. It was easy to pick out Jim in that cluster of green cotton. He wore grease-stained shorts and a camping shirt and had that wiry, pale bedspring hair and shaggy beard. He wasn't posing self-consciously in a costume, like Ash Loakes. You could see the Marine officers took him seriously after wincing first at his accent and then at his rank smell. He turned to one and another, talking in his low voice, his pale eyes and raffish coyote face showing interest, expectation, humor—probably laying on the Brit drawl, too, she guessed.

"Of course, old chaps, seen this before. Tell me about the Mark Twenty-five Mod Two Alpha—" He knew how to chat them up, could talk about other wars he'd seen; he got along easily with other men. She studied his gift to help her career.

Phoebe didn't see Mark or the gray-haired colonel. They had slipped into the array of stucco and metal buildings. Jim came back and pulled her away with him. "Had a nice chat with a staff light colonel named Spatsy. He said this Charlie Mason's quite a bloke. And you know this Captain Randolph?"

"We slept together once. You met him in Saigon."

"Yes, of course. Let's play it right—we may have an in for an exclusive. Play along."

They went to a tent office on the grass next to Wing HQ, met a few majors and lieutenant colonels, and a minute later in came Lieutenant Colonel Mason, Captain Randolph, and a major from Wing Legal, a young man who wore black-rimmed glasses. They sat at a small table, Marine officers on one side, press on the other. "We're speaking background," the major said. "I enjoin you not to press them."

"Agreed," Jim said. "Remarkable story, the walkout. Like what you chaps did on the Hump." He raised his eyebrows and gave her a look with his bloodshot eyes, meaning, We'll winnow the story out of them anyway.

Phoebe turned toward the gray-haired man with the silver oak leaves. "I'm so *delighted* to meet you! I've heard so *much* about you. You've flown combat in *three* wars?"

Jim worked on the major, whose name was Nachtleben, and Mark Randolph. Phoebe heard him chatting them up—growl, Brit drawl. "Quite right . . . Sixth Marines? Know you chaps. D'you think the ground fire you encountered was—"

Phoebe tried to look breathless and available pulling facts out of Lieutenant Colonel Mason. He really wasn't bad-looking, she thought. Really not that old, either. And well-spoken, if you overlooked his too-smooth voice, which didn't square with his bomb tattoo.

As he told bits of his story and she put it with what she had heard, she knew he was an authentic American hero. Not an ace, which is a fighter pilot with five kills. He'd flown single-engine bombers. The Japanese ship he'd sunk. The aircraft he'd had shot out from under him. His coolness in describing it, speaking slowly and clearly, using his hands this way and that to show aircraft.

"Very nice," she murmured. "Then you used your engineering background to understand how far you can push the plane." I am such a *slut*, she thought, for she was grinning at him, murmuring, trying to charm him, yet the more he talked, the less *interested* in him she became.

"The machines respond differently to certain stresses," Mason was explaining, moving his hands. "When you put a helicopter in this attitude, for example, you're putting stress on the rotor hub—"

What he did was exciting but when he talked about details he seemed so prosaic. Her conception, certainly the public's conception, of a hero was much different. Flashing teeth. Tales of Sinbad. This man was so self-contained; in a way she resented him for the same reason she knew some male correspondents resented the men who did the fighting.

Jim was asking Major Nachtleben about aspects of the murder case.

"Y'know, I don't quite understand how these chaps *did* die," Jim said. Mark Randolph stared at Jim's shaggy head.

Major Nachtleben said, "One had a broken neck and the other had a throat wound." He leaned forward, smiling, clasping his hands. "It was a very dark night, marching on a steep trail. Also shell fragments from the NVA attack. So it's hard to say just what might have happened. An unfortunate fall, for instance—"

"A good job if they can stick to that," Jim muttered to Phoebe. "Let's see if we can winkle them out."

Phoebe nodded. They might have, too, except at the same time Jim was muttering she saw Mark leaning across and talking behind his hand into Lieutenant Colonel Mason's ear. He said hoarsely, "Don't waste your time, Colonel. I've had some of that. Stick to slopes."

She colored and stared at him. "Mark, that was *totally* uncalled for!"

"Cool it, Mark," Mason said.

"Yes sir."

Jim laughed to try to deflate the moment and jolly them. "Bit of a balls-up, it seems to me—not sure Headquarters knows quite *why* it's investigating this, d'you?"

"No," the major said, standing. "But it's time to go."

"Shit," Phoebe sighed. She and Jim walked back to the dirt street.

"The point of the inquiry," Jim said, "seems to be that Wing Headquarters object to killing these chaps in daylight, before they were lifted out. 'You were almost there,' they seem to be saying, and 'Look how it appears.' "

"Well, who did the killing?" Phoebe asked.

"That's what infuriates them. This Mason said he'd debrief on the operation but not on the killing. So also your friend Randolph. The Special Forces major isn't talking either. Further, the Special Forces detachment isn't doing anything. I rang up one of their chaps. 'So what?' he said."

Jim and Phoebe stayed in Da Nang another day, hanging around with other correspondents, trying to put together a story. They stayed in the white stucco press building by the river. No one at Wing HQ would say anything. "Except I heard this," Jim said. "A colonel named Dillis apparently has a grudge toward Mason and Randolph from Gia Binh."

"What?"

"Don't know. I inferred this from something Spatsy let slip and he sidestepped immediately. Now, the number of directives these headquarters boffins cite suggest your government's terribly keen on making the war look very legal at every whack. Hence this hearing. And the headquarters officers are all the more eager to get the boot in, to stick something on the field men and establish that the staff have properly passed on orders. Egyptian Army did much the same at Suez. Sign of a losing mentality."

"The weak succeed in altering the strong," Phoebe said.

"What's that?"

"Po—Peeling Off. From the *I Ching*."

Other correspondents came in with rumors of dissension in the command, of quarrels between commanders and staff, of disagreements about policy and the rules of engagement—ultimately about what the field troops were supposed to be doing. Brian Beechwood had said in Saigon that the Americans couldn't run their affairs in the common Aristotelian sense because they couldn't agree on what was good or bad and therefore what must be done. At the press building no correspondents discussed the Aristotelian ground. They had the killings, whatever they meant. This had to be a story. Everyone's gut said it had news value. A hell of a story, as Ash Loakes said. And they couldn't get it.

Nevertheless, Captain Mark Randolph, like White House aide Houston Bridles before him and Adams Peabody afterward, got his moment of national and world fame: the photos in newspapers and on two magazine covers of a grim, scowling captain in plain, black-stenciled Marine utilities and the cutline "Hero or murderer?"

By the end of the second day it was clear the Marine staff had reached some kind of impasse. Mason and Randolph and the lawyer came out smoking cigarettes for ten minutes, then went back in and came out for another break, while officers in starched green cotton, with black-inked USMC stencils on their shirts or dark, sewn-on Navy tabs, carrying attaché cases and folders, entered and left the building. Finally Randolph and Mason came out in the dirt street and both showed by their posture that something had been resolved. They didn't seem angry or jubilant, just tired.

"Yoo hoo!" Phoebe called in her most musical voice. She tried to hit that throaty timbre that she knew had caused Mark to gasp before, but a six-by went past and killed the tone. "What happened, Mark? Can't you come over and talk with me?"

He looked at her as idly as if she'd been a parked jeep. "Can't make it. Sorry." He and Mason went between buildings to the bar, where correspondents were not allowed. MPs made a sign that they were not even to cross the sidewalk that way.

Jim found out from a clerk that Wing Legal had dropped murder charges against Mason and Randolph for lack of evidence and because of a concern that the Green Berets down the road might snicker at them. Lieutenant Colonel Mason, the clerk said, had been put up for a Navy Cross for taking out the Green Berets. He had flown attack aircraft in two other wars, had had mounts shot out from under him like a movie cavalryman, and had done well in ground combat against great odds. The clerk said Mason wouldn't get his Navy Cross, "but then he won't be court-martialed for murder, either."

Vietnamese stories are sad.

*   *   *

In Saigon at an American Embassy reception Phoebe met the most interesting Vietnamese woman, Ba Ma Thi Dinh. She was a pharmacist, an important and lucrative profession there. Like Western druggists, she dispensed pills and bottles, but she also listened to symptoms and prescribed Asian remedies—roots, herbs, powders. She was in her forties, thin, and wore huge French glasses. She spoke French and English.

"It is wonderful you do this," she told Phoebe. "In our society women have more status than in China or Japan. We are expected to run daily affairs while the men write poetry and wage war—but you, Phoebe, you make picture, you present the statement? And you travel where you wish. You are not bound."

"No, I am unbound."

She had a daughter who was finishing school here and wanted to study in the States. She asked Phoebe to visit, to talk about her strange land.

Ba Ma lived in a white stucco house near the Thi Nghe Bridge. Spiky pale-green palm bushes screened the columned porch. Phoebe arrived wearing a linen dress. She had been in sexless fatigues and sports clothes so long she felt terrific just dressing decently. Ba Ma greeted her on the porch wearing an old-style long silk coat. A servant brought tea and an inlaid mother-of-pearl box on a tray of leaves. Ba Ma opened the box with her long delicate fingers and took out areca nut, which she sliced and wrapped in betel leaf. They chewed and swallowed the tongue-tingling juices, which caused a mild euphoria. They sat talking comfortably about politics and limits and what one could say and do and what her daughter might face in America.

The girl's education sounded as if it were a bit too classical for her to be accepted anywhere in the States. Her education would be appreciated in France, of course, but the only Vietnamese really accepted there were the very rich ones in Versailles.

Phoebe realized that they had been talking for some time and Ba Ma said it was the betel and areca. Leaning forward, she said, "I tell you a story about this. It tells how we value friendship and family here."

She told about a mandarin many years ago who had two sons devoted to each other. The mandarin and his wife died in a fire and all their possessions were lost, so the boys had no home. Another mandarin took them in. He wanted one of them to marry his beautiful and talented daughter. She could not choose. "To solve the problem, she prepared a feast for the young men and brought out only one set of chopsticks." Ba Ma laughed and, though she formed her lips delicately, Phoebe saw streaks of dark red on her teeth. "You follow?"

"Of course," Phoebe said. "We try to avoid being forced to make choices that way."

"But our people are not rich and we have gone on long time by making choices. Now the daughter and devoted brothers face the problem of one pair of chopsticks. The younger gives the sticks to the older—duty to the elder, you see?

"They marry and begin a beautiful life. The younger outgrew his love for the girl in the name of family duty. But the older neglected his devoted brother—he was so involved in love for his bride and their times in the garden. The younger suffered alone, his heart broken because his brother neglected ties of blood. Finally he left the house, torn by that most excruciating of pains, the loss of love of one's own, for whom he had sacrificed.

"They did not miss him for hours. He walked down the trails of brown dust and came to a river he could not cross—the current this way, the path that way. He sat, dejected, languished. Death came to him. He turned into a chalky white rock.

"Finally the older noticed his brother's absence and at once understood. He set out walking, reproaching himself. He came to the same river bank, could not cross, and collapsed by the white rock. He died there and in his place sprang up a tree with a straight trunk and clusters of leaves and nuts.

"Now the bride knew something was wrong. She too set out walking, reaching the riverbank exhausted, and clasped the tree trunk until she died of sadness. She changed into a creeping vine around the tree."

Ba Ma moved her fingers to form the world as it must have been then, with villages and elders and forests of spirits. "Now the people of that district knew these three had led beautiful lives of devotion and sacrifice, so they put up a pagoda inscribed, 'Brothers united, husband and wife devoted.' "

They sat a moment. Phoebe felt the buzzing of the betel and that sadness refined in the taste. "That's very sad," she said.

"Oh yes, and there is more," she said. "Later a terrible drought killed all the plants but the tree and the vine, so pilgrims crowded that pagoda. The king visited and was told the story of the tree. To test its truth he powdered the white stone in a *mortier, comme ça?* With vine leaves and nuts. The mixture turned red, like mingled blood—proof of the spiritual power, the king said. He had areca nuts and betel leaves distributed to the people to chew to keep their mouths moist. And that is why it now is the beginning of a good conversation."

"How long has your family been here?"

She laughed. "Oh, not long. Only a hundred years. Saigon is not that old. We are from Annam. They were there from the time of the Trungs."

They talked for hours. As she sat there, aware of time passing but aware that it didn't matter, either, Phoebe felt in bits, glimpses, and tones how much there was to Vietnam, how many families, rules, lines of obligation, sadnesses, rivalries, conflicting goals. How many families are there in Vietnam? How many villages? A few blocks away in the typewriter-clacking offices and car-filled streets, officers and bureaucrats and newsmen wanted to think of it as something they already knew, calling it a nation, an ally, a source of stories to be packaged.

March of 1966 was a terrible month. Jim and Phoebe went to My Tho. The Army said it was going to sweep out VC units so people could tend crops. My Tho is a provincial rice-trading center in the Delta—flat all around, lush green, low buildings. Armored vehicles, brown Army tanks, armored personnel carriers.

Using her camera, she zoomed in on the backs of the tanks to get the shimmering black fumes and pollution to underscore the ugliness. At home smog and pollution were becoming good copy. "Why are you using tanks in this paddy land?" she asked the Army information officer.

"These don't bog down. Charley's here in force and we're going to blow him out. Watch."

Some vehicles had sandbags and claymores wired to the sides. They drove into the brush; when ambushed from the sides, they blew their charges, leveling the brush for forty yards. Through her long lens she saw a figure in black writhing on the ground.

"Fire fight on the right flank!"

They were at least five hundred meters away. A trail smashed flat by APCs led into the brush and soldiers hot for it ran and yelled, "Motherfuck! RTO—send up the fuckin' RTO!"

As the radioman trotted up the trail, Jim said, "I'm going to get pictures. You stay."

He loped behind the radioman. He wore a fatigue shirt and boonie hat and shorts. The sun was copper on his beard. He ran with his elbows out, holding his Nikon in the center of his chest. She could see his back moving a hundred yards up. She saw his arms fly out as he fell on his face. He didn't move.

She screamed for minutes. They wouldn't let her close. The soldiers had dived to the side, were regrouping and firing at something she couldn't see. It was outrageous. Silly! He hadn't needed the shot. He was already known as a first-rate correspondent.

Phoebe took his body to Saigon and made arrangements. She sent a telex to his wife signed P. Bishop, *Life* stringer. Mrs. Robinson must have known, though. No one had secrets in this business.

Phoebe didn't know what to do. She couldn't say she and Jim had been in love, really, in the way it should mean. They had been quite matey, and he had helped her and showed her how to do things, and she must have cheered him up. She shipped his body air freight in dry ice to be buried in England. There weren't that many arrangements to be made and they were more logistical than spiritual or emotional. She didn't know why he had gone after that shot without a preface.

It was better to stay busy. By now she was selling her work regularly. Jim's editor at *News of the World* asked her to send on any film, which she did, and agreed to look at her work, too. She didn't want to hang around Saigon. She spent days at a time traveling by C-130, C-123, Army Huey, Marine H-34 and H-46, from IV Corps to I Corps.

The ARVN General Thi led a mutiny at Da Nang and Hue. Thi was crooked but one of the best field commanders. He demanded more money from Ky and the Americans and drove self-propelled guns into position to shell Da Nang. The Marines flew ARVN troops up to quell the mutiny and put jet fighters into the air with a threat to strafe the mutineers.

Chick De Vore flew up to cover it. "Ha-ha-ha—ya know what happened?" He lifted up on one cheek to break wind. "The ARVN said, 'We're going to adjust our one-five-fives.' And the Marines said, 'We see your one-five-fives and we'll raise you two F-fours.' They were on the approach run with rockets and napalm. The ARVN backed down."

·

At Givral she met kids who looked like freshmen—a woman from San Francisco, two bearded men from L.A. They were "film people," they said. They were going to be stringers. "What fuckin' *action*," one said. "I saw them napalm a fuckin' field. I got it on thirty-five." None had read *The Quiet American*. "Hey, that's from the fifties," one said.

They wanted to go out on the roads, where the convoys were blasting open the routes. "I bought a Honda three hundred," the girl said. "You better *believe* I can cover ground."

One night the drunken construction boss in the next building hammered on Phoebe's door. "Lemme in," he said. "Ahmo teach you somethin' about American men." Phoebe didn't have a gun but she told him she did and said she'd blow his balls off.

Summer came in May. The heat went from merely oppressive to intolerable. It had been four years since she'd first seen Houston at Yale and ruined her chance to go to Paris. Houston was probably at the LBJ Ranch worshiping power. Four years since she'd first seen Mark Randolph, laughing and gladhanding, now a bitter survivor of wreckage. It was bizarre. Maybe she had stepped into the wrong movie. What had happened to those times? Whoever would have thought a President would have his head blown apart in public? Or Americans rioting, burning, New York and Los Angeles? Or in a city at war, Saigon, these crowds of clean, office-working American sailors and soldiers strolling and spending money? Enough money so that by Gresham's Law all women were regarded as Tu Do whores? She felt, as one soldier had said, that she was at the bottom of a great sewer.

She'd begun sending her credits and good photos of herself to television stations in America and in August she got a letter from Rex Bisbee, the news director at KLQA in Hollywood. He was interested. He knew Sara Gelber and Chick De Vore. He said he had women newswriters and wanted one with Phoebe's experience. "I'm always looking for new talent and bright, new, innovative approaches to news," he wrote. "I note you've done stand-uppers for foreign outlets. Here in Los Angeles we are very much on the cutting edge and I think we are ready for a woman on camera doing hard news. Let's do this—send me a few film clips and air checks. I'll let you know right away. I expect a busy winter and next year."

She had one already—a minute-thirty bit on cyclos with a foreshortened zoom of a mass of them, gray green, drivers' legs pumping, and her voice over and talking head. Jim had shot it; another of his gifts to get her started. She asked another cameraman to shoot her giving thirty seconds of official statement in front of the American Embassy.

She talked with the network bureau chief, who had offices on Cong Ly Avenue. "Bisbee is pretty innovative," he said. "And I think you can trust him. He probably wants to change the appearance of his show. He's had women on camera doing fashions, but hard news would be a bold step. Do you know about Bisbee's fashions?"

"Not at all."

"You'll see if you go there. He has, I think, a thirty-five share."

A few days later, Rex Bisbee telexed Phoebe to phone him. She did. The connection wasn't bad. He had a smooth announcer's voice. "I'm offering you a job," he said. "It's AFTRA." He explained about the salary and AFTRA scale, and payments for pieces aired. "How soon can you start?"

Phoebe
in the Soup

Newsmen are great kidders.

When Phoebe opened her desk drawer at KLQA TV News that first day, she found a box of Tampax Super and a jar of Midol. She looked at the other half-dozen desks in the long room. Two women newswriters typing. Four men in shirtsleeves staring studiously at typewriters. Another two, field reporters in jackets and ties, stood by the "A" and "B" wires, ostensibly reading copy. Sunny Beinfleischer, the receptionist showing Phoebe around, flashed a smile at the men. "You guys are all assholes!" she yelled.

The white-haired man typed furiously, the fat bearded man swiveled a few degrees away, and the men at the teletypes laughed.

The assignment editor came into the room and said, "Cool it!" and a minute later Rex Bisbee came into the room.

Rex Bisbee was one of the nation's top local television newscasters: a lean, tanned, handsome man in his fifties with a friendly, fine-featured face. His family was an old Los Angeles family. He had large, deep-set eyes which could have caused him trouble on camera, if the light dropped shadow over them, so he had developed the habit of lifting his face and widening his eyes when he spoke. He did it off camera, too.

"Hello, hello, hello, hello," he said in his warm, low voice, lifting his face and widening his eyes.

"Hi, Rex. Hello, Rex," every chorused.

"Ah, Phoebe. Settling in. Any questions?"

"No, thank you. Everyone's being lovely."

"Good, good," he said. "Excuse me, won't you?" He made a little nod and stepped into his office, a large soundproofed space with a window to the newsroom.

He and Freddy Walburn, the assignment editor, held up long yellow sheets of wire and script packet flimsies to work out the news day. A list called a "budget" came out from a local wire service each morning showing the day's events and news conferences in the Los Angeles Basin. The AP B wire also carried local news or national news with a local peg that KLQA might want.

The two reporters at the door were waiting for Freddy to send them somewhere. Three others were already out. These two—Mort Blair, a thin gray-haired man, and Ned Pittman, a handsome, jut-jawed beefcake with a crew cut—were at the bottom of the ladder, Sunny said. "That's why they're afraid of you. Mort's a nebbish but he's been around forever. And Ned's *so square* he'd go to a love-in and say hippies must be poor 'cause they're sharing cigarettes. He's got good camera presence, but he's like nineteen fifty-five, you know? And we don't have surfers in our share."

"Phoebe," Freddy Walburn said. He was short, pink, plump, with quick wet-looking eyes, very cool and professional. He handed her a strip of the budget and a news release. "Cover this. Any questions, call on the radiophone. Chop-chop."

"Check your makeup," Mort said as she left. Ned giggled.

The newsroom had two women newswriters who hadn't had the break Phoebe was getting. Maggie Lane had spent years doing Society and Home writing for a newspaper. She was in her late thirties, and though she sometimes did lead-ins for fashions, she probably wouldn't go on camera for most stories. Elaine Rodgers was younger than Phoebe, had a journalism degree from SC, had a gorgeous, sexy figure that Sunny said drew endless lewd comments from men, but her face wasn't pretty so she probably wouldn't go on at all. Phoebe was the guinea pig.

She walked down air-conditioned corridors into the parking lot roasting with smoggy heat. Around the asphalt were other cinder-block buildings and dry gray palms. Cast members of a soap crossed between cars, makeup bright in the glaring light from windshields. Phoebe got into the station wagon. "Hi, fellas."

The driver was an apprentice cameraman named Jerry, a kid. Len, the cameraman, was in his fifties, short and gray. Chuck, the sound man, was her age.

"What do we got?" Len said.

She looked at the slip. "Black Arts new conference, Watts Towers, One Hundred and—"

"I know where it is."

They drove past the guard, down palm-shaded streets onto the hot, smog-smelling freeway, where you could see the scope of endless dry ridges dotted with houses and little trees, lowland covered with boxy stuccos and lines of gray palms.

"What were the Watts riots like, Len?" She thought the question would massage his ego. "They were big, weren't they?"

"Shit, *big* ain't the word," Len said. "Like a *war!* Smoke all over the place. The National Guard was firin' machine guns. The cops had a real defensive line to keep the spearchuckers down where they belonged."

"Yeah, that's no shit," Chuck said. "We both worked it. They had *tracers*."

Freddy Walburn had warned her that the men would resent her having been a war correspondent. A woman war correspondent at that.

"I mean, it was like *Vietnam!*"

"Yeah, fuckin' shootin' *everywhere!*"

"Yeah!"

"LAPD doesn't fuck around," Len said.

"This is really a different place out here," Chuck said. "Like, most of the people who moved here don't like it back there."

"People here don't *give* a shit what they say back east," Len said.

They drove into Watts, which at first glance looked okay—little pastel-painted stuccos on little lawns or bare-scraped yards. Not the three-story tenement squalor of the east, but some buildings had smoke marks, broken windows, littered yards, and the streets held old battered cars—in L.A. a sure sign of dangerous attitudes.

"Fuckin' Africa down here," Len said. "Look at 'em. Rugheads."

"They *deserve* to live like this," Chuck said. "I mean, they were the ones who burned it."

They were your usual liberal bleeding-heart newsmen.

The news conference was held by a black writer in an Afro and a maroon-and-yellow dashiki. He talked in that mix of sweetness and power some blacks do so well. A white middle-aged screenwriter said a few words too. One other TV crew was there. They shot the same skyward shot of the lacy eccentric pipe towers decorated with glass.

"Do you have enough, Len?"

"They'll recognize the towers."

They went to the next thing, a small demonstration at a federal building in West L.A., no more than a dozen housewives from Women's Strike for Peace walking in a leisurely oval, carrying signs about stopping the bombing and napalm. When they saw the news crew they accelerated their walking and shouted and waved their signs at the camera.

"Fuckin' dykes," Len commented.

"Women are half our share," Phoebe said. "Halloo!" she called to a marcher. "Will you help me?"

"We want them to at least reduce the level of violence," the woman said.

Phoebe watched Chuck's light. Maybe he wanted to fiddle with the sound and ruin the story as she interviewed the middle-aged woman from Encino telling why they were against the war, but he didn't—probably because he knew he was being watched.

They went on, an air-conditioned station wagon full of jealousy, resentment, and bitchiness, from one so-what story to the next, breaking for lunch at a hamburger stand in the blinding light. They covered a gripping announcement by the Veterans Administration, then another nothing story at UCLA. Back at KLQA they put the film in the soup, long troughs of developer. The station used tape, but only on network stories fed over telephone lines.

Air time. They sat in the newsroom smoking cigarettes and watching Rex Bisbee's face, jaw high like FDR's, listening to his smooth voice. Rex had devised the winning format for local news, one that other stations copied nationwide and use now. The opening tease—today a snippet of film showing cops, flashing lights, and a covered body—then the titles and Rex talking stories and leading into film, tabloid-level gore and commercial-pretty fashions with music over, novelty cars, a tearjerker about children or hurt animals, and commercials in between.

"Good going, Phoebe!" Ned Pittman called across the newsroom. "You can do fashions tomorrow."

The next day, appalled, she did do fashions. The third day she got nothing on.

"The men are poisoning Rex's mind," Maggie told her. "I think *he's* telling Freddy to send you to stories that won't upset the others. He's an old Angeleno and what you've already done might make him defensive. And he knows the others. He doesn't know you."

"But he was the one who hired me," Phoebe said.

"Yeah, but who knows what's really on his mind? He's quirky. I think you have to hang in there."

The next day she had a story on refuse at City Hall, a storm drain opening in East L.A., and a neighborhood story about a freeway pedestrian overpass. She knew nothing would air. She hated L.A., the smoggy air, the bigoted crew, the resentful males.

You have to hang in there, Maggie had said. Maggie was a good newswriter, knew everything about film, but *she* couldn't get on camera.

I'm absolutely furious, Phoebe thought. This place is *so* out to lunch. And yet I'm twisting myself for it. Why?

At two-thirty the worst possible thing happened: They got a real story with not enough time to catch it before air time.

It came from Freddy on the radiophone. "Midair over the San Diego Freeway. It could be the top of the news. You're the closest, Phoebe."

They raced down Pico Boulevard past crummy bars and stores— the freeways were already blocking. Sigalert, the radio said. Two light planes had been approaching Santa Monica Airport, Freddy said. One went down onto the ramps of the San Diego–Santa Monica Freeways interchange, the other went into a residential area where Palms, Mar Vista, and Culver City ran together. "There!" Columns of black smoke in the smoggy sky.

Len said, "I shot TAs around here. I know the streets."

"It's your story," Phoebe said. "It's going to be visuals or nothing."

Jerry drove side streets to the first wreck—the burned plane tail high, nose buried in a side yard. The wing had broken open and sprayed burning gasoline over bushes and trees, now black, and set afire a stucco home. The housewife, a woman with bobbed hair, in a blue muumuu, was crying next to the firemen.

Len got the wreck and panned across to her while Phoebe questioned the housewife and a fireman, who said the body was still in the aircraft. Len zoomed to the open door. You could make out a blackened lump, possibly a skull.

They jumped back into the wagon and sped toward the other crash—by now it was after three—and saw crowds, cars, police, highway patrol, and flares. They jumped out, carrying equipment across backyards, and climbed the freeway fence and bank, slipping on crunchy ice plant, a succulent used on road shoulders. Phoebe fell and ruined her skirt but it didn't matter, Len could shoot her chest up. They clawed through the crowd, Len and Chuck shouting, "TV Crew, let us through!" They shot a few feet, some too raw. The firemen were pulling the bodies out of this wreck, which hadn't caught fire, and one of the victims had been torn open so that when they tilted him his bright blood poured from his chest and caught the sunlight in crimson sparkles.

"Zoom back," she said to Len, who grunted. They had about ten seconds establishing the ramps and stucco houses. *Tick-tick-tick*. She got a short quote from a police sergeant—Chuck's light stayed steady for that, too—then she stood before the crash site summarizing the story.

"Let's go!"

They trotted and stumbled through the crowd, over the fence, and met Jerry, who drove a crazy route east, jigging up dinky side streets under parched palms until they were past the freeway tie-ups; he got on the freeway and hit ninety on the way back. "Don't sweat it," he said. "All the cops'll be out on the crash." He swerved into the lot, braked hard, and ran off with the film to throw it in the soup.

While it was developing she went to the newsroom and looked over her notes so she would know how to cut the story. She remembered what quotes were good. The thing was to make them into a clear, visually interesting two- to three-minute story.

The other reporters were back—Page Barrett, a big, handsome middle-aged man who some said would be an anchor soon; a young aggressive man named George Moore; and a quiet, cerebral political reporter named Gary St. John. She wasn't a threat to any of them, so they ignored her. She told Freddy Walburn what she had.

"You *got* the crashes? Gosh, that's wonderful! We could have a beat! We could have a beat. Rex, Phoebe says she has the midair!"

Rex Bisbee had been sitting sideways, his neck stretched up, reading air copy he held out before him—he had a fine profile but the way he held his head looked odd. She supposed it was for the camera, too. He swiveled around and looked at Phoebe, smiling sadly. "It must have been tragic."

"Yes."

"How much do you have?"

"About three minutes."

"Is it good? Freddy, is it good?"

"I haven't seen it, Rex. It's in the soup."

"It could be the top of the news."

"If the others have it, *they'll* have it up top," Freddy said.

"This is up to you, Phoebe," Rex said. "Make it good."

One of the film editors came into the newsroom. "Who's doing the air crash?" He was a kid in glasses.

"I am."

"Come on."

In the viewing room he ran film on the screen—the sky shot, the street signs, the burned tail and sobbing housewife. They could have "benched" the film—run it through a movieola, a small bench-mounted viewer, to take out what they needed—but lately when the crews had been covering love-ins and demonstrations, they'd been letting Bad Things through. Body-painted hippie girls with bare breasts. People flipping the bird or mouthing "Fuck you." It had only started in the last year or so, and as the editor said, "They can show a traffic with blood and gore everywhere but don't let a bare tit through, because that's dirty."

She watched the film and minute counter and marked cues, which looked like:

:45	woman	". . . lost my house!"
1:32	up on fireman	"The aircraft was observed . . ."
1:53	zoom charred head	". . . still in the aircraft."

In the standupper she looked all right and the whole thing came out in 2:50. She still had time to cut the other stories and just before air time Freddy said, "The editor tells me it looks good."

In the newsroom they all watched the screen as the tease came up—Len's startling shot of sparkling blood pouring from the body before the wrecked airplane and cops, all so fast they shocked you like city life, and Rex's voice-over: "An air tragedy above our freeways today . . ."

The MJB Coffee commercial showing lines of people crowding to move across the state line into California. Sound up, sirens and yelling, housewife sobbing, the blackened tail and the rest. In the sum-up her hair was blowing and she seemed breathless, which Freddy said "made it all the more immediate and dramatic."

Later Sunny said Ned Pittman bitched that a man should have got the story and that she must be some kind of dyke or ghoul. It was good to get on the air on top that way, but Mort Blair and Pittman sulked even more. She had made her first dangerous enemies.

That was a colorful time for television news—love-ins, demonstrations, flower costumes, mass shows like the Monterey Pop Festival. But it was also a dangerous time; enemies lurked among the flowers and growled under the great music.

Over the winter into 1967 Phoebe covered Los Angeles and learned to handle everyday television news in that screwball city in those screwy times. Individuals who would have been called outrageous a year before were the usual faces now—General Hershey Bar and General Waste More Land, two clowns in soldier suits hung with church keys, bottle tops, and tinsel to mock the head of the draft and the head of MACV-Saigon; and Max Rafferty, a glittering-eyed, hysterical conservative who, like so many hawks, was found to have ducked military service himself. Suburbanites of the Sexual Freedom League stood up in their poplin suits and shirtwaists to discus cunnilingus, fellatio, and the repeal of Penal Code 288. The Women's Strike for Peace put nice middle-class matrons out on the streets picketing with signs. Bikers in leather vests and greasy pants, smelling of gasoline and piss, were considered glamorous by some. Anyone who was vaguely hip wore long hair. Plastic hippies worked at straight jobs all week and put on wigs to hang out in coffeehouses on weekends. Phoebe filmed them.

God, Los Angeles! she thought. The coffeehouses weren't *real* coffeehouses, like Borgia or Feenjohn's. You just got *coffee* or spiced tea, for heaven's sake. They were so machine happy here, but they hadn't even heard of espresso machines.

But she filmed it all—the hippies in motley flower clothing at love-ins and concerts by the Nitty Gritty Dirt Band, Big Brother and the Holding Company, the Mothers of Invention, and a half-dozen other groups that became big names. She had plenty of images to catch and talk over because it was such a visual time and a time of visual extremes—primary colors, bold black-and-white op art, people painting their faces and bodies, ringing their eyes with blue, green, black, and white, guerrilla-theater actors in masks, middle-class white boys and girls in Indian headbands singing to the sun in Topanga Canyon. They called themselves priests of the tribes, druids, and witches.

In Venice UCLA students opened storefront community centers to help the poor get counseling and aid. They had some Great Society money to pay rent, but the counselors were working cheap or free. They wore long hair and sandals and truly did want to help others. The counterculture was in place.

"Terrific visuals," Freddy said when Phoebe came in with a local color piece on bikers jumping choppers on the arched Venice bridges or a heartwarming poverty piece showing poor blacks filling out forms. Rex wanted to show a bit of everything but pitched to the average Angeleno. Sometimes they'd do a middle-class sentimental tearjerker about a hurt horse or an abandoned dog; sometimes they'd go into radical territory and feature hunger in the ghetto—but Rex spaced these carefully because he knew his audience. He didn't explain the audience to Phoebe, but Freddy did.

"Phoebe, understand this about Los Angeles. When you get away from the kooks and freaks and bikers and health-food eaters and women with bass voices and religious visionaries, what you have here is Iowa with palm trees. A good part of our viewers is always *shocked* about what they see here. They hide on their patios. All we want to do is titillate and hint at what's out there. Otherwise they get *mad*."

He was right. After the hunger feature the phone buttons lit up and *everyone* fielded complaints and impassioned cries. "Hey!" one man yelled down the line at Phoebe. "Lay off that stuff about *chow!* Y'hear?" Others who didn't know there was hunger in this paradise made impassioned cries. "What can we *do? Where* can we send money?" They wanted to change the picture. The people were besieged on their patios, depending on the tube for their vision of the world, and this is why they reacted so emotionally.

All of them in the newsroom knew they had great power, the power to conjure the world, and like magicians or artists they played tricks to make reality more simple, vivid, or palatable for the viewer—zooms, freeze frames, jump cuts, split-screen images framed in black; sped-up film like Phoebe's one minute of a county fair with people double-timing among blue-ribbon hogs, gobbling cotton candy, a Ferris wheel spinning fast, all to Flatt and Scruggs banjos.

Gary St. John, the political reporter, had a way of filming a woman he called The Iguana—a large self-important dowager on one of the city boards. She was always calling news conferences and burbling on about some do-good project, and Rex liked to run her for Civic Pride. She had a mannerism of shooting her tongue out to lick her lips between sentences, so St. John always worked in a side shot to show her tongue dibbling the air. He did a similar thing with Mayor Sam Yorty, having the sound man pick up every grating note of his Nebraska accent when he called the city Loss Ank-ell-ess. When they watched St. John's stuff in the newsroom, the writers and reporters looked for twists he'd concealed and laughed hugely at tricks few viewers out there understood.

Others did their comedy bits, too. An old star who played lovable codgers died and Rex sent teams to Forest Lawn to cover the outpouring of grief and huge motorcade. The cameraman took establishing shots of Forest Lawn's copies of famous statues and chapels, and Ned Pittman did a clown act on a grave, dancing, singing, holding a mike over the earth. "Tell me, Mr. Smith, what's it like down there?"—and holding his nose, replying in a nasal wheeze, "Let me tell you, it sucksssss!" Ned pulled people out of the newsroom to watch it while they were waiting for their own film to come out of the soup.

"Come in and see this!" Ned said, laughing. "It's a scream!"

Phoebe also handled national and war news, which came in at three over telephone lines and she viewed in the tape room as the stuff rolled onto big aluminum reels on the shoulder-high consoles: footage of helicopters or soldiers or Lyndon Johnson's sad-dog face. Often she would do a story right there while the editor backed up and fed one reel to another.

The war as much as anything galvanized viewers to complain about what they saw.

"Why did you show *that?*"

"Why don't you show Americans *helping?* Aren't we giving them food?"

"Why don't you show my husband's company?"

The more the caller depended on the tube for news, the more cretinous and hysterical his comments. It was hysterical comments following the next major event in the war at home—the first massive demonstration against Lyndon Johnson and his war—that got Phoebe fired.

Houston Bridles's famous journals, which were to figure so splashily in the Watergate years, had scanty entries now in the *Rubber Soul* and *Sergeant Pepper* years. He was busy, didn't have time to reflect, and exercised such great power he didn't have to remind himself of goals. Furthermore, it was dangerous to set down too much on paper. The war and the Great Society were turning to worms, and he was busy fixing appearances. He was fucking Congressman Sanford's wife. And his father and other spooks were telling him things it was key to know but he couldn't admit knowing.

"Hot potato!" he wrote earnestly. "Distance self from this!"

Pa made a remark suggesting that the Agency backed New York Congressman Allard Lowenstein, a left-wing Democrat, in his Dump Johnson movement. That was one dangerous thing to know. Another was military disasters.

Even though General Westmoreland was suppressing news of his many fizzled operations, officers talked and people knew. People knew from outraged pilots and shot troops about equipment failures like the TFX/F-111 and the M-16 rifle. One infantry officer said the M-16 rifle "is worth a division to the NVA. It jams. It gets our men killed. You never see *them* picking up *our* rifles."

But what was important about the rifle from Houston's point of view was that it was a Colt product, meaning jobs for New England, and connected through Air Force and aerospace politics with Lyndon Johnson in a way he did not deem it wise to delve into. His long-term goals included winning a Cabinet appointment, not blowing up at some minor play in the game.

The rifle and the TFX/F-111 could be hung on Robert McNamara, who had gone ahead with both projects over the specific objections of some old warhorse officers. McNamara distrusted the old warhorses because they did not give quantifiable criteria. This was why, in a lesser-known move, he created the Defense Procurement Agency, replacing some two thousand low-paid military officers with some twenty thousand Civil Service employees at an administrative cost of hundreds of millions. That was one of the items on the bitch list Houston had to clear up when President Johnson sent him to Los Angeles that June of 1967 to mend fences and prepare for his visiting there.

The only people unreservedly supporting the Administration now were hawks in the aerospace and defense industries and the kind of peculiar right-winger found in California. These did not believe in big government. They had just made Ronald Reagan governor. They thoroughly approved of spending billions to bomb Vietnamese but didn't like any government agency growing tenfold.

The last sticky business Houston had to explain, as he had up in New York the day before, was how Johnson would treat the *Liberty* strafing. During the Six-Day War two weeks earlier, in June 1967, the Israeli Air Force had hit an American electronics ship in the Eastern Med, F-4s laying cannon fire and napalm not in one mistaken pass but deliberately over several hours, killing more than thirty American crewmen, while the Americans were forbidden to fire back.

The President had seen the terrible incident in political terms. "I don't want an anti-Semitic backlash to fuck up my support in the cities." So far, most of the facts, which were appalling, had been kept secret, but Houston's tactic in L.A., as in New York, was to let McNamara be the lightning rod for that, too. It was a slightly different game out here—not quite as many Jews as in New York and the *goyim* right-wingers more blatantly anti-Semitic because many were oilmen with Arab ties—but, as always, he met with them in separate small groups at the California Club, the Jonathan Club, and at country clubs and hotels.

To Jews who were hawks on Israel but didn't like the Vietnam War he said, "McNamara's studying ways out," and told them about the memo McNamara had circulated in May, asking for reports that became the Pentagon Papers. To decent American hawks concerned about bloodshed, he told about Operation Arc Light, McNamara's expensive plan to put electronic detectors in the jungle so we could fight the war by remote control. To right-wing *machers*, he pointed out how bomb tonnages and enemy-killed counts had gone way up and spelled out what this meant for companies that made wings, bomb racks, arming devices, and thousands of other weapons components in California. His meetings went off without a hitch.

"Talked sense to the sensitive and stroked hawks!" he noted in his journal at the Century Plaza, a showy new glass box on land 20th Century-Fox had sold to pay its debts from *Cleopatra*. Houston was in the hotel to examine it for LBJ's visit the following week. The President wanted to tell the California Democrats who, as he put it, "was buyin' their groceries on me, I'm spendin' billions in their fuckin' districts. I want them to shut out them peace hippies and get on my team." The biggest antiwar protests had taken place in California. These must stop. "I'm spendin' fifty million dollars at GD, Pomona. Eighty million at Douglas, Santa Monica. Christ *knows* how much Lockheed's gettin' between the Air Force and the fuckin' Agency on those black airplanes."

"Sandy has to kiss their asses, too," Marty Sanford had told him in bed. Houston would meet her later, but now he and Congressman Sanford stood up at an awards ceremony at the new federal building downtown. The two of them and an Army officer read citations and pinned Bronze Stars, Purple Hearts, and Soldier's Medals on young men while their families watched.

This is America, Houston thought. White Moms in stiff dresses, butterfly glasses; black Moms in curious shades of orange, blue, brown; Dads in suits or featureless shirts and pants, pens in pockets; the young men in uniform, short-haired, wary, most of them smaller than the Marine or 3rd Infantry guards in Washington.

Houston stood in front of one scared young soldier, caught his eye, and smiled engagingly. "This is from your President. He sends his best wishes." He pinched the fabric above the man's pocket, pulled it out so he wouldn't stab him, and slid in the pin on a thin brass bar from which hung the ribbon and medal.

"Thank you, sir."

"The nation thanks you." He stepped along the rank, not crisply as a drill-trained man would, but with his natural lightfooted grace, and caught the eyes of a black soldier. "This is from your President—"

In the next rank, or row, he saw Sandy Sanford's fluffy brown-gray hair bobbing. He was talking too long between punches. *Come on, Sandy, you're not at a shopping mall!* He and Sandy had fifty-seven of these damn things to hand out and he had calls to make. Marty.

One of LBJ's strategies to win was handing out blocks of medals by congressional district. Houston, other aides, and LBJ himself sat

down with these congressmen and local party chiefs, like members of
the California Democratic Council, and told them how many awards
they were getting and how many dollars in defense appropriations,
how many jobs, how much for highways and government buildings,
how many positions for Head Start, Job Corps, and other Great
Society programs.

"And you're going to raise shit about a war no one understands
anyway?"

Even so, too many had begun wavering. Before playing Pin the
Medal on the Private, Sandy had made some silly remarks to reporters. "Credit where credit is due in this unfortunate war," he'd said
with a sad smile and a fluff of his hair, and one of the television
reporters, someone named St. John from KLQA, had followed up,
asking questions, and Houston had to remind Sandy of the time.
When the President himself came out to meet the CDC, he'd undoubtedly kick ass and get people in line.

Houston met Marty Sanford later at a curious place on the beach
in Malibu. It was all driftwood and timbers on the outside. The dim
cocktail lounge was lit by big windows facing the beach, but the
booths were isolated by glass-bead curtains. Rooms waited down a
dark hall; it was a *cinq à sept*. Marty wore bright California clothes and
shades and mouthed, "Fuck me, eat me" between sips of her marga-
rita.

In bed he said, "Surely Sandy can see the value of sticking to his
guns. With the President."

"I know it's important," she said. "For appearances."

He had flown out commercial because the Air Force had a pinch
on VIP aircraft now, due to the war, and the DC-LAX route offered
plenty of seats anyway. He preferred to fly VIP because he had so
much work, so many memos to consume, so many ploys to rough
out—or he could stretch out and sleep. Anyway, this was a late flight
and wouldn't be crowded. Good to move among The People a bit.
The faces of the young soldiers in the medal pinning. Something in
their eyes—what it was hung at the back of his mind. He was, of
course, comfortable with all kinds of people. And he didn't kid himself that with some, like the soldiers' parents, perhaps—he told a few
small lies, for the greater good. But something under the surface

pained him—like a lost splinter, a charley horse. Better not dwell on it.

The black government sedan stopped in the lane by United. Houston saw people crowding the door, long-haired kids flying youth half fare, soldiers, seedy-looking cowboys heading somewhere else in this vast West. Maybe that was it. His instincts told him there was something powerful, something to watch out for, in these people. Don't trust them. Yes! That's what bothered him. Too much space in front of that glass hotel for people to gather. He must write a memo on the plane. *Don't let the President be confronted by the people.*

The driver was getting his luggage out of the back and handing it to the skycap when Houston saw a low, dark Lotus roadster pull up fast in the wait lanes, slowing on downshifts, *chirp, vroom,* and twitch into a no-parking zone. It was some distance away, and it took a second before he recognized the face with the moustache—Mark Randolph. Was he still in the Marines? Houston didn't have time to talk and the last time hadn't been too good anyway, when he had seen Mark in New York last summer. Houston stepped through the glass doors and checked in.

But a few minutes later, riding the conveyor belt to his gate, he thought of it again. He'd gone up to New York on his own to brief Stu about the business forecast and at the Yale Club saw Crotty Powers, who'd tried out with the Steelers—not bad for Ivy League—hurt his knee, and now was selling space for *Sports Illustrated*. Powers, a Deke, said the Rands was getting back from Vietnam, had come this way around the world, and was going to see some of the guys here. They met next door at the men's bar in the Biltmore—a half-dozen Dekes and a couple of Fencies, most of them dressed for the office in good suits, and Mark in a wrinkled poplin suit he said he'd carried in a seabag all around. His teeth were stained, one was broken, and he smoked foul-smelling foreign cigarettes.

"What was it like? What's Asian pussy like?"—it was, after all, a Deke crowd—"How could you tell the difference between VC and allies?" Some of them had seen the news photos of Captain Randolph and the murder cutlines. "What *did* happen? How many people did you kill?"

Mark drank shots and beers and told a few stories in his loud, hoarse voice, including some funny tales about traveling through Iran and Turkey on the way back, but he was clearly tired and irritable.

Between remarks he settled into repose, saying nothing, eyes bottomless; and at some questions, like those about shooting and being shot at, he shot the questioner a sharp look before answering. He shot one at Houston, which ruffled his feathers.

"But how many did you, ah, actually account for? How did it feel?" Houston asked—he'd access to the best military men in the world, but of course this was someone he'd known in college—and Mark gave him a sharp, incredulous glance.

"You mean myself? Or morally? I'm an officer. I put a lot of fire out." And he dismissed the rest. But when someone else asked about the VC moving among the people, and Mark told about old women laying mines, and little boys dropping grenades, and how some new American fish were too slow, trusting, and dead, he said, "Other guys just had it. They'd shoot a man on suspicion. It got personal with them. The thing's got a dynamic of its own."

Houston had felt it his duty to put the best face on it—after all, these *are* classmates and they all know *his* position—so he said, "The government *does* have rules of engagement, guys. I think what he's talking about is a few enlisted men. Some of them are really bad news!"

Mark shrugged.

In his heart of hearts, which he did not have time to examine, Houston had been a bit put off. Mark was rather shaggy, after all; there wasn't much to be high-hearted about regarding the warrior returning home. And the facts, always the facts it was better everyone didn't know about, weren't clearly glorious and made one a little uneasy.

Captain Randolph didn't see the presidential aide, Houston Bridles, at the airport, but he did see the government car and in the slightly addled paranoid way he had learned scanned the route out and other surroundings. Security officers from Defense and State had been doing the usual background checks on him; some time ago he'd thought about working for them in a civil service job that had to do with security and weapons and had put in the paperwork. Buck Black, who ran the school where he taught tactics at Camp Pendleton, told him the feds were around. Buck had asked Headquarters Marine Corps to send Randolph to him out of Vietnam. Black looked the same as ever—the moustache, the loud, confident manner. "You got a lotta stuff to get across, Mark! Night work! Air operations! You could make major here!" Buck had been a captain as S-2 of the lash-up in Da Nang but had just made major himself, even though he was one war ahead of Randolph.

The black car pulled out and no one else was standing around. It was funny how you remained as paranoid after you left Vietnam as you had been there. He didn't see any of the strange guys with shades and golf jackets, either. These were men in their thirties and early forties who hung around San Clemente, Oceanside, and Laguna Beach, recruiting Marines from Camp Pendleton or the Santa Ana Air Facility; they never came up to you cold, but through someone else you knew. A captain Mark knew who'd been in heavy tanks on the east coast called up and said someone named Joe or Fred wanted to talk. Mark had coffee with one and they talked in his car, an unremarkable air-conditioned rental. They were recruiting experienced infantry officers, NCOs, and chopper pilots for fifteen hundred dollars a month for operations in a warm climate—not CIA contract work; that was handled another way. These were private mercenaries recruiting for Africa or Latin America. Maybe they had government funding, too, but that never came up. Mark thought about it a few seconds. He believed himself to be fundamentally stupid but he wasn't that foolish. He thought, systematically: Who else is doing this? Who's on your right and left? What's your medevac operation? And: Do you pay now or at the end of the month? He still had that silly urge to be a cool stud, but how cool is dead by someone else's mistake in a totally strange place?

The fact was, he didn't know what he wanted to do with his life. Buck Black wanted him to stay in the Marines. "Look, so you ran into a bad airdale. It'll always be better than that. You're an O-Three, you got an excellent rating coming out of MAG-Eighty-Six. I can get you language school."

Mark shook his head. He couldn't answer, couldn't respond. He knew this guy was reaching out to him, and all he wanted to do was turn his back.

The glass doors opened and the woman he had a date with came through, a stewardess he'd met in Istanbul and traveled to Rome with. He supposed that was part of acting like a cool stud, meeting someone somewhere interesting. They didn't have a very interesting weekend—they went to the beach and drove around San Juan Capistrano, but he was preoccupied and she must have used all her smile muscles to put up with him.

He began his work week riding into the base on a motorcycle. All the instructors had sports cars or muscle cars and several had motorcycles. He dressed up small Marines in black pajamas and straw hats like Vietnamese and put them in the hamlet of straw shacks by the dry creek bed. The NCOs ran other Marines through the hamlet while some of the combat surrogates begged and cowered in front and others popped from trenches behind, aiming rifles and throwing dummy grenades. "You're dead!" the NCOs yelled. "You're dead, too." And "Asshole, watch it, *you're* dead!" Mark ran a class through the hamlet every few days. He wasn't aware of it, but it got to him, reliving the goddam thing every few days.

Or at night, in his apartment in San Clemente, when he went out to sniff the air, seeing the flash of artillery firing toward Fallbrook and hearing the rumble. He wanted to leave that crap all behind. In his heart he had that memory of the GI next door come home in his clean T-shirt—and the only mechanical sound you heard was a lawn mower. He clung to that memory like a dog with a smelly bone. And what do you have here? Night firing and Tijuana Brass.

He'd pictured in his mind what homecoming would be like and for a time had felt real joys—arriving in Florence on a cold morning and having espresso and a cigarette watching traffic on the cobblestones before the Uffizi, playing darts and shooting the shit with USAF and RAF men when he got a hop out of England—but touching down in America just wasn't right. Seeing the guys at the Biltmore—their questions were silly. How do you answer questions like that? Or a piss-ant comment like Houston's? He'd sooner be with his patient, devoted, courageous enlisted men than most of the guys he'd known before. That was the thing—he felt the only guys he could talk with easily now were Marines, or at least military. It was one of the effects of the war—guys couldn't shoot the shit across the board anymore. You had to know who you were talking with and what he knew—what he *really* knew.

He couldn't handle other kinds of relationships. Didn't know how to handle his memory of seeing Phoebe in that yapping pack of correspondents; didn't even know how to handle Natasha, who'd always been so gentle, kind, intelligent. He'd stopped writing her during the rainy season, when he was busy, and hadn't felt right afterward. She'd called him in San Clemente a month after he got back. "I—I got your number from the base locator," she said. "Is it all right? Are you all right?"

"Uh—" he said.

"Mark, are you all right?"

"I'm in bad shape," he said.

"Can I do anything?"

"Leave me alone."

She gasped. Perhaps he'd meant he felt he wasn't ready for civilized society yet. He didn't know what he meant. He'd uttered a truth without understanding it and didn't do anything about it. It remained inside him, this memory of Vietnam he could retreat into.

Sergeant Kane had written him with news from the old group. Pearl had made gunnery sergeant, very fast; Lawrence had gone to flight school; Coombes had been killed by a kid with a grenade while waiting for the liberty truck in Gia Binh. A horrifying story that a mustang major had come in bragging about his past war experience and then got a Marine killed because he set up a patrol wrong; then the major went batfuck in another crisis. Unforgivable. It was because of fuckups like this, by a few incompetent officers, that Mark had decided he had to get out. This was his only home, he loved these men, but his heart was broken, he couldn't trust the whole because he felt passionately about a few weak links. He turned his back on Buck Black, on Kane, Pearl, Lawrence, the officers he'd known before; he turned his back on Natasha. He didn't think of the future. He had a few memories, he had a motorcycle and sports car, and he didn't give a damn about much. Some guy he'd run into said he was a good talker and ought to go into sales with this oil company. Mark couldn't see why not.

He came in from a day at the beach the next weekend and heard about the big peace riot up in L.A. but it didn't mean anything to him.

The Century Plaza Hotel was a big, curved metal-and-glass building. Its front driveway was filled with people, its windows lit up. President Johnson was upstairs. Secret Service men in dark suits with enameled buttons in their lapels walked around the entrances and press lines grinding newspeople's feet to make them stay back.

The demonstrators formed a hundred yards away—young people with short hair and Kingston Trio clean looks, others with long hair and beards, mothers with children, housewives, members of the UCLA Health Sciences Committee Against the War, Women's Strike for Peace, the San Fernando Valley peace groups, and others from up north. They held signs about stopping the bombing, the napalm, and the war—*now!*

Along the periphery of the group were monitors, men and women wearing arm bands, some carrying megaphones or electric loud hailers. They walked up and down, kept people in line, and gave last-minute instructions. Phoebe recognized one. "Peas! Adams Peabody!" It had taken her a moment to make out his sharp nose and quizzical eyes among the metal specs, beard, and long hair.

"Phoebe!" They didn't have much time to talk. He was excited, happy, keyed up. He didn't mention Carole Tiddens. "This is the real fuckin' thing, man. This is where it's at now." He turned away and called out, "Berkeley! Oakland! Watch for these arm bands! Kathy and I will be on each side! Keep looking straight ahead! Don't stare at the police! Don't provoke them! We're here to witness for peace!"

In front of the hotel were several ranks of LAPD officers in blue creased uniforms. They had taken off their chrome name tags and some their badges. They wore black Western police leather—thick tooled belts, ammunition pockets, handcuff pouches. Their nightsticks were not hanging from their belts but in their hands. Some wore black gloves. A sergeant said through an electric bullhorn, "This is an unlawful assembly. Disperse or face arrest under Sections Two-oh-nine and Four-fifteen of the California Penal Code!"

The demonstrators kept walking, looking straight ahead, the monitors moving along the flanks and calling instructions. One yelled on his megaphone, "We only want to make a statement to the President!"

"Batons!" the police commander ordered, and the officers brought up their nightsticks, holding them horizontally with a hand at each end. The demonstrators marched closer, some singing. The police stepped forward. People lurched offsides.

They got it all on film—the signs bobbing and tilting and falling, the fights breaking out on the fringes, the nightsticks coming up high and dropping, men cursing, women screaming, mothers crawling away clutching screaming children—and they had time to race back to

Hollywood, put it in the soup, and lead off with it at eleven o'clock.

The switchboard lit up right away, before the show got into the second commercial, and most of the calls were complaints. "Why did you show *that?*"

"They're communists! Didn't you see how they looked?"

"He's the *President!* Why'd you show the *mob?*"

And threats to Phoebe. "That broad is a hippie! Fuckin' Red!"

By this time she had settled into a one-bedroom apartment on Hollywood Boulevard and bought a Rover sedan. The apartment had off-the-shelf plastic stickups and one set of earthenware plates from The Broadway. The Rover had air-conditioning. She had her hair done and spent a good deal on cosmetics because of the ultraviolet photochemical atmosphere and was anything but a hippie, though she liked to film them. She didn't feel any joyousness at that time, any membership in a tribe, any flow of love. All she wanted to do was take picture stories, coolly and truthfully, showing what was there. When she smoked marijuana, which she did just before bed, alone, standing on the balcony looking at the millions of lights in the basin, she didn't feel cosmic visions, just relaxed. She listened to *Sergeant Pepper* often and the songs that meant the most to her were "She's Leaving Home" and "A Day in the Life." She remembered John Kennedy, and Jim, shot, lying on his face in the dirt near My Tho. The only life she had was news. She wanted to be an eye on the ceiling, as she had when speeding at the Plaza, but because of her nature, parts of her blood that didn't come out in work, she caused things to blow up around her anyway.

Things blew up in the newsroom. All the newspeople had been instructed to respond civilly to all calls, no matter how stupid or hostile, and to trip the beep recorder when threats came in. They recorded many threats against Phoebe. "She's antipolice," one said. "I saw her talking with demonstrators. When I see her again, I'll play catchup on her gourd."

"That sounded like a cop," Sunny said. "They talk like that."

Page Barrett said Rex would be pretty concerned.

The next day the L.A. *Times* reported the demonstrators had provoked the riot.

Rex called Phoebe in and looked at her, his expression solemn. He stretched his neck—she realized now he did it to lessen his dewlaps—and, speaking softly, said, "My family has been in Southern California since the days of the Spanish aristocrats. We have always regarded this place as special, not like the corrupted cities elsewhere. Our public services are more efficient. We do not have organized crime. Our police are among the best in the world, Phoebe. And I'm afraid this story of yours slanders this wonderful city and its fine police and drags it down to the level of a Dallas or even a Selma. It *can't* have been that way. The *Times* isn't playing it that way."

He smiled sadly and shook his head. "This was unprofessional and cannot be tolerated. I'm afraid you'll have to leave."

"I stand by my story, Rex. What I shot you'll see others showing."

"Perhaps. But the accusations on these calls are serious. That you encouraged the demonstrators."

"That's a lie. I wasn't close."

"You were seen talking with a monitor."

"Of course. I knew him years ago. He was backgrounding me."

"Freddy took the precaution of taping the general complaint calls so we'd be able to examine their substance, and I must say *many* allege you slanted the story."

"May I hear them before I clean out my desk?"

"Of course."

Phoebe listened to the calls. People were really ticked off at her and at the story. But she noticed something. Many male callers used the same language about camera angles and "comsymps." Some sounded like the same voice, and that voice, a nasal wheeze, sounded familiar. But she couldn't figure it out.

She was in the audio room by the door, just leaving, when she heard Mort Blair and Ned Pittman joking around. Ned said in a fake announcer's voice, holding his nose, "Big New York star Phoebe Bishop cleans out her desk—" and Mort giggled. She'd had it.

She went to the editors' room and got the outtakes from the beloved codger's funeral at Forest Lawn and played Ned Pittman's clown act. That was the same voice. Then she played complaint calls claiming she had encouraged the demonstrators. *That was the same voice!* She should be able to find Blair's voice on the tapes, too. She played through again and found a hoarse, fuzzy one, obviously disguised, that still sounded like Blair's intonation. She went into the newsroom.

"Rex? Freddy? May I play something for you?"

Rex listened. "Hmm," he said. His face showed thoughtful concern. People who are on camera act like this. "I'm troubled by this," he said.

"It's unethical to hype your own newsroom," Freddy said.

"I'd like to sleep on this," Rex said. "In any case there are other things to consider. It *is* a hurtful story."

Hitherto only the L.A. *Free Press*, an underground paper, and KLQA had said the police started and escalated the violence, but by midweek people in the business heard there was a newsroom revolt at the *Times*. Among themselves reporters had been saying what Phoebe had shown, but editors had overruled them. *Times* reporters were threatening to go public. One called Maggie and asked to be put on the air with Phoebe's associates. He didn't care what happened at the *Times*.

Then the *Times* did an about-face and printed its reporters' versions of events, that the police did riot. This raised a police protest and comment from Mayor Yorty that the press were *all* radicals and militants. Rex Bisbee called her in again.

"You're staying. Pittman and Blair are going."

Rex had called it paradise. She covered a story out in the warren of flimsy blue-collar Okie apartments in Vernon-Bell Gardens-Cudahy, where local cops, certainly less professional than LAPD, hit the wrong apartment on a drug raid. One plainclothesman—she saw him in his Sears tie and cheap jacket, talking to other detectives—had been drinking and for some reason carrying an M-16. He had an accidental discharge and his round went through the flimsy wall into the next apartment and killed a father walking his baby.

Disneyland turned away hippies. The tape feed brought the Detroit riots, with scenes of American soldiers pouring sustained machine gun fire into houses. An American tank with the high slotted back she knew from Vietnam ground up before an American house and fired its big gun, blowing the house to toothpicks. They had more from Vietnam showing big operations named Cedar Falls, Junction City, Greeley, Hickory, Union, Malheur. The Black Panther Party carried guns into the state capitol in Sacramento and intimidated the legislators. Blue Cheer, a proto-heavy metal group, played in Santa Monica at 110 decibels and rendered young people deaf, possibly saving some from the draft.

Phoebe was sent to cover a Black Panther–police shootout on Century Boulevard and reached the scene before the ambulances. Many LAPD black-and-whites were there. No one talked. LAPD cops stared at her. They wore all-dark uniforms and mirror shades. One said, "Wait over there." The others ignored her.

A detective in a tweed sports jacket came up. "Phoebe? You are Phoebe Bishop? Okay, will you move your wagon and crew?"

"Will you talk with me?"

"We don't know much. Try moving the wagon."

"I'll take it all. Jerry, please move the wagon."

This detective had a sense of humor. A smile played around the corners of his mouth. High color flushed his brow. He said, "Do you want a standupper? We don't know how many there were at the beginning. A carload. Some split. They may still be running. Three of them were hit but we don't know if by their rounds or ours. One and a half are dead." He grinned.

"Was this a confrontation? Who are you?"

"*I'd* call it a confrontation. It wasn't planned. I'm Sergeant Ed Donahue, Seventy-Seventh. It was a random incident. They got hinkey and shot and ran. They might have hit a streetlight. Didn't hit any of us. It's not an equal battle, you know. They have no discipline. They can't shoot. They can't clean a pistol. They just got a lot of mo' fo' jive. And they're losers. A con's a con. You're not talking about SC versus UCLA here. They're wrong and we're right. What do you have against cops? You treat all these things like Monday-night football and act as if the teams are matched ethically." Again that playful smile. "I hope you're shooting this."

"Using it's another matter."

He shrugged. "Just the facts, ma'am. Dum-de-dum-dum."

"Maybe we can use this. You're a live one."

"What do you expect? This is California. Where you come from cops are blue collar. They call a watch a shift. Dey don't like da job. We aren't stiffs here. We can think. They pay us to think."

"Well, what do you think?"

"I think you were wrong to stick it to us on Century Plaza."

"But you beat up people."

"They should have dispersed."

"It was a worthy cause."

"So's peace and quiet."

"That's outdated."

"That's *typical*," he said. "What are you people? Truth or fashion. Right is right. Situation ethics is one of the scams *no* one's going to benefit from."

"It's true your department's insensitive to black people and poor people."

"Society is. Don't you watch television? It's society, not us." He jerked his head. "Do I get a break because my own family was poor? No way! It's *picturesque* poor people you want—someone who's got a bone in his hair or makes quilts in Appalachia, not the ones we got here. Let me tell you, we *do* care about poor people—we have to clean up after them. You drive the freeway? What do you do when you see someone coming along in a shitheap with dents all along it? You *know* what you do. Your instincts tell you: This dude's looking for his next I-couldn't-help-it wreck. You steer clear. We're the ones who have to clean up after these goddam slobs who can't do anything right for themselves or others. We clean up after they beat their wives and abuse their children. We clean up after their cuttings and murders, after a family fight drinking cheap beer. Most of our goddam *problems* are caused by a small group of poor slobs who can't take advantage of what we have here. Look at L.A. It may not be paradise, but it's clean. There's work. It's not rat city like where *you* come from. If someone skates here he's askin' for trouble."

"It's their fault, you're saying."

"It's not ours. Ask any insurance actuary. Ask a priest." He laughed. "Ask a newsman. Where do you find cuttings and shootings and all this activity that gives sob sisters their thrills? *They're* not victims of society. They make society *their* victims. Besides that, why listen to sob sisters? They're opposed to anyone in authority. But if you don't have people in authority, society's institutions collapse. Then the sob sisters'll have plenty to talk about. Maybe soldiers aren't heroes now, Phoebe, but I'll tell you, cops are the only thing between you and— Huh?"

A uniformed sergeant said something in his ear. Over his shoulder he said, "Thanks," and faced her. "Okay, one dead suspect's name is—take your choice—Rufus, Roosevelt, or Tyrone. He had three IDs—"

He gave her twenty-five seconds.

"When will you show my sermon?" he asked.

"We probably won't."

"Can I buy the film?"

"You know you can't. Have you thought of acting? You don't speak badly. You argue well."

"Jesuit education."

"Here?"

"No. Back east." He laughed. "I hope you'll show this to your colleagues. My wife'll think I'm a hero if I can do something to give cops an even break."

"I doubt I can. Why don't you write a letter to the editor?"

"Yeah, yeah. You can't fight city hall."

One night after the show Phoebe lit a joint and opened her *Book of Changes*. Her question to the *I Ching* was self-interested and professional. What message does the city give that she should carry to the people in order to advance and go to New York?

She threw the coins and got a hexagram of five female lines and a male on top, looking like a lintel gate. Again it was Po—Peeling Off. There is no steadfastness. Misfortune. One is left without friends. We lose contact with those above and below. She will be close to a terrible misfortune, yet ultimately she shall be free from blame. The Superior Person will acquire a carriage, meaning the support of the people, but the mean man will lose his own house and be found useless for anything.

Po. Peeling Off. At present there is no goal or destination that can be sought with advantage. She was to contemplate the ebb and flow, the emptying and filling changes that are the ways of heaven. She settled for sitting on the balcony, stoned, watching the ebb and flow of car lights in the dark white-spotted basin.

A couple of days later Adams Peabody called.

"What's happening? We're going to change things! We're forming a new political party, Phoebe—I'm coming down, I'll tell you about it! The times are changing! We're going to be a new voice from California to the nation!"

Saving the
Pentagon

Lyndon Johnson raged after Century Plaza, that summer of 1967. He sulked, sputtered, turned narrow-eyed, hog mean, and more paranoid. He chewed out Bobby Sugg, the churchy Texas aide, and humiliated him until he was on his knees in the Oval Office, crying and praying for Momma Sweet Jesus to save the President as a sign of his faith. Johnson spent hours with J. Edgar Hoover going over names of the communist conspiracy organizers and fellow traveler com-symps. Hoover had shots of dovish Congressman Rudy Fain (D-Indiana) going down on a known KGB whore.

"Hah!" LBJ crowed. "He didn't learn *that* in Indiana! I'll ram his program up his ass!"

He had taps put on the phones of newsmen and other suspects. The man who claimed to be a populist had become as suspicious, remote, and vindictive as Stalin.

"A narrow escape!" Houston wrote in his journal. The only thing that saved his ass when LBJ rampaged was that memo advising against Century Plaza and urging better security. Still, Houston thought it key to finesse the White House for a while because Johnson, like a bull shot in the nuts, went on howling rages when he remembered being reviled by thousands and prowled the West Wing yelling at people he could bully.

"*July 2. West Wing Basement*. Hit the road, Jack, and grab support for the President."

One of the wisest sources suggested he see a great man and go south, where Stars and Bars Democrats were prepared to support any war, but Houston chose to go northeast and visit college campuses and faculties. One thing Houston noticed in the FBI report was the number of university-connected peace committees. "Carry the ball onto the campuses!" he wrote.

Houston was so sure of the moral and intellectual preeminence of the Northeast that he wrote in his action plan: "Visit schools that are unquestionably the best—Yale, Harvard, etc., perhaps Williams, Amherst . . ."

He also had repair work to perform in Hartford, which he got out of the way in the morning. It was one of those *contretemps* the White House staff was used to but others found difficult to accept. A delegation from Hartford—insurance executives, engineers, some officers from United Technologies, a helicopter maker—had called on the President when he was in one of his insane moods and Johnson had had them ushered into the Presidential toilet, where he was taking a dump.

"His attitude," one Hartford doctor said, "was quite clearly 'You need me more than I need you, so take this.'"

Most of the Hartford people were Houston's sort, so he was able to smooth it over (bad day, President in a hurry, and we *are* buying your helicopters), and then he flew down to New Haven for a delightful visit with Uncle Stu and Uncle C. Moulton Fraker, a little wiry bald man with the Fraker freckly red skin and pale eyes.

"And a Yale man!" Uncle Stu said, laughing.

Uncle Moultie had retired near New Haven after a long career in the Foreign Service in Latin America; he'd been Berzelius and Chi Psi. Stu was Fence and Book and Snake. They planned to call on class-, club-, and tomb-mates to win support for Houston's play. They discussed it over lunch at Mory's, having many drinks and much laughter.

Anyone who walked through the low-ceilinged rooms hung with oars and team photos would have noticed their sandy-hair similarities and vocal differences: tall, broad-shouldered Stu, red-faced from his martinis; compact, catlike Houston; and the elfin Uncle Moultie. Houston's voice came over a bit high, the way he'd learned to speak at Exeter; Moultie's had the clipped rapidity they taught at Choate; and Stu had that hoarse low growl of Boston prep schools. But they were all Yale men, joking about the presence of *women* in Mory's (summer hours), laughing with good-natured pride about Yale accomplishments (Crotty's stint with the Steelers, Cy Vance as Secretary of the Army), and discussing some others they knew whose son and daughter had met and betrothed at Yale Law School, about which Uncle Moultie drolly commented, "This is a marriage made, if not in heaven, at least in New Haven!" And their high, clipped, and gravelly laughter bounced off the wood.

Uncle Moultie also gave Stu advice about a glass factory he had in Bayamón, Puerto Rico, near San Juan. Stu had built it on the site of a run-down subsistence farm. It was doing well, employed about thirty people, and had "a sound future," Stu said, but its ten-year tax break period was ending soon and this would cut into its margin, now close to 40 percent. Should he pull out and start another enterprise? Where could he get a similar arrangement? Venezuela? Argentina? The question meant more than tax law, as Stu said. "It's a guess at the business future of the Caribbean. You know all about that, Moultie."

"One of the luckiest moves I ever made," Moultie said, "choosing to handle unglamorous, peculiar Latin America while others took *glamorous* posts like Italy. Or China. Where you could be dead wrong."

He told about the poor chaps who'd put the wrong things on paper before the McCarthy years "and found themselves stamping passports!" Laughter. "In small cities with muddy streets and irregular electricity!" More laughter.

"Of course, that's why your boss is in such a bind now," Moultie said. "The old Asia hands were purged."

"He won't listen to the experts he has," Stu murmured.

"Bad thing to have a parvenu touching foreign policy," Moultie said. "Advantage of the Republicans is that they don't *do* anything, they just want to make money and they leave you alone. We used to handle so much business on horseback. At polo. Particularly in Argentina." Uncle Moultie had been a five-goal player. "Kennedy nearly ruined that kind of understanding. The *Kennedys* . . . do not know horses." He looked at each of them and nodded, having made an important pronouncement.

He gave Stu his advice about closing the Puerto Rican factory and named academics he'd call on to speak in favor of the war.

"Boston next!" Houston wrote. "Harvard weenies! White House fellowships! Surely the best students want us to have a winning team!"

He had never noticed in the FBI lists of communist conspirators at Century Plaza the name of his classmate Adams Peabody.

Adams Peabody showed up at the KLQA newsroom in faded Levi's, a cowboy belt with silver turquoise buckle, sandals, and a burlap shirt with a peace pin saying

VETERAN
CENTURY PLAZA

His hair had just been washed and it fluffed out in the breeze from the air-conditioning.

"This is amazing," he said. "It's like *Day of the Locust*, all these *show* characters in the parking lot, hyuk-hyuk-hyuk. Do they discuss current events with you at the commissary? Do they call it a commissary?"

"I usually eat on the road," Phoebe said. "What's the story on this new party? Why are you down here?"

"Organizing. We're going to have the founding convention in San Luis Obispo. And I want to see the Century Plaza trials. We have people up on charges. Are you going to cover it?"

"I doubt it. It won't come across visually."

"But the people need to know! The police and White House are trying to make something else of it!"

"We covered the march, as you know. The truth wouldn't have come out unless we'd shown it. But people aren't going to watch what we can film of a courthouse."

"They ought to look anyway," Peas said. "They have to be told over and over that this is a criminal war and the authorities are committing criminal acts to keep it going. They've lost legitimacy. That's why we're forming the party."

Peabody wanted her to cover the organizing meeting in Venice. Because he was inflamed with his mission, he assumed any friends in the media had to carry the gospel.

"I'll give you a ride there anyway," Phoebe said.

They drove over blistering freeways, thin gray-tuft palms sticking up through the afternoon's orange smog, onto cooler streets near the ocean to a Venice storefront used as a community social agency. It was filled with young people, most of them white, talking in groups, from time to time one jumping on a desk to make an announcement, others coalescing into new groups, cigarette butts piling up in cans and cups.

Most were in graduate school or had left not long ago to work for the communities. Some had short hair and wore short-sleeved shirts and pressed pants, but most had the look Peas had—flowing hair, flowing clothes, jeans and loose pants. When Peas's friend Kathy Dunlap showed up, she looked more efflorescent than the month before, her thick dark blonde hair fluffing out around her, her body swelling against her top and short skirt, her thighs full and curved, her breasts free, nipples poking, bouncy and elemental as an R. Crumb Kupkake.

"We want the blacks to form a caucus and give us input," Kathy said. "It was a tactical error for SNCC to kick whites out—we're bringing black students in. We're going to get understanding and racial justice here and stop the violence overseas."

"We have to get on the ballot for next year," Peabody said. "Sixty-eight is the year. Dumping Johnson is only part of it."

"I'm handling West Side registration," a bearded young man told Phoebe. "Are you on a committee?"

"She's news," Kathy said.

"Is that okay?" He look worried.

"She's okay," Peas said. "She told the truth about Century Plaza."

Some other young men and women talked among themselves, looking at Phoebe. She saw them mouthing C-I-A.

"Oh, wow, what if they *film* us?"

Kathy said matter-of-factly, "Some of the kids are afraid of any cameras. They don't want an FBI-CIA purge."

Phoebe heard a few talking about police–Black Panther shootouts in Oakland and Watts. "It's genocide," one kid said.

Another said, "Governor Reagan and Mayor Yorty have a propaganda campaign to *discredit* the Black Panthers in addition to *killing* them. No, listen—the police say the Panthers use *foreign* guns and in these shooting struggles the guns jam because they're *dirty!* I mean, oh, wow, isn't that *anal?*"

"Oh, wow, foreign guns."

"Dirty guns, man." People laughed.

"It's *racist*."

Phoebe thought it was going to be an interesting battle of fervent, sheltered students like these against tough, quick street cops like Ed Donahue and really bright, ruthless pricks like Houston and his crowd. Compare them to the *mat tran* bomber she'd interviewed, a real revolutionary. The innocents were going to bleed.

Peabody went south often those weeks after the Century Plaza march, as the loose march and antiwar committees tried to form an apparatus. Most of the time he moved on the Fairfax-Westwood-Venice axis, but once he called Mark Randolph in Costa Mesa. The Rands drove up in a sports car. Wearing shades and a short-sleeve, button-down-collar shirt. Oh, wow. Peas had intended to lay Marcuse on him but the Rands wasn't up for shooting the shit anymore. They drove up along Mulholland Drive and Mark put the car briskly through curves and esses, shifting and popping, watching the tach, obviously a master of this mechanical thing. "I got a motorcycle at home, too," he said. "I like speed and a little risk, man."

"Oh, wow," Peas told Phoebe. "He had his shades on and looked *grim.*"

"Is he married?"

"He's living with some girl. I didn't see her. He wasn't very outgoing. We went to a couple of bars. Barney's Beanery."

"I know that one," she said.

"We had shots and beers, and finally he said what was on his mind. 'You sent me that *peace* literature about the time we're getting hit,' he said. 'And it was bullshit! It's all wrong!' He was *boiling.* He wouldn't even talk about the politics. 'I don't give a shit,' he said. 'I'm back. I don't give a shit. I don't want to watch the war on the news. Just don't say crap that isn't true!'"

"He was pretty mad at me, too," Phoebe said.

That summer of 1967 Peabody often called Phoebe with tips and so did some of his "kids," but the more often they called, the less their news was worth. They hammed it up. They overdramatized nothing stories, like the signing of petitions. But the movement was their life. These young people didn't date. They went to meetings and became friends with members of the opposite sexual party. Perhaps they fucked between meetings, but they didn't "focus on each other," as Kathy said.

Peas was charged with energy. It flowed from his hair. He had
that kind of build that meant nervousness anyway, and he had his
share of nervous gestures—that hyukky laugh, biting a thumbnail,
squinting through his glasses and hair and leaping to make a point,
and when he was making the point, excitedly rocking his bushy head
from side to side; all things you couldn't do in the cool medium, he did
with absolute conviction and carried you along.

"We are the truth! We're what's comin'! We are the future! With
the truth on our side they can't stop us with their computers and
wiretaps! The liberation fighters in Vietnam are using bicycles against
our jet planes, and we're using signs against police cars! We're going
to stop the war and create a just society here!" He shouted from a
desktop, and committee kids raised their fists.

"Tell it like it is!"

"Hey, man!"

"We have right on our side!"

Of course, Phoebe knew about his rather strange upbringing and
the way he had taken it out on poor Carole.

"I was wrong," he told Phoebe. "Wrong in intent. I didn't understand her, didn't love her or myself. I deliberately hurt us both."

"Would you go back to her?"

"God, no—she's politically *compromised!* I was wrong to want
her! It was her money!"

"How politically compromised?" Phoebe asked.

"Her parents killed Kennedy." He had that ability to say the
most farfetched thing with utter conviction. "The important thing is
how it's made me *grow*," he added. "The broken part heals stronger,
Hemingway said. Part of my growth process had been distancing
myself from my mother—God, the country isn't *wide* enough! Hyuk-
hyuk-hyuk—but not from her *ideas*. They aren't really hers anyway.
We're all turtles crawling out of the mud and I'm years ahead of her."

Leaping into the center of a crowd during a demonstration at the
L.A. federal complex one time when Phoebe had a crew covering
them, he said, "Listen, brothers and sisters—we're all from *liberal*
families, aren't we? And they're shocked we're making all this distur-
bance now? What do they say?"

"You're going too far!" Kathy shouted on cue.

"Yay!"

"I say, go all the way!" Peabody shouted.

"Yay!"

"Yeah, they're not liberal *enough*—that's their problem! We're their sons and daughters! If they honor justice, we'll create it!"

"Say it, man!"

"I say there are no heroes, only suckers! Do you want to be maimed or killed?"

"Oh, wow!" Laughter.

"We all know veterans, don't we? Are those heroes? Bullshit! They're *lost!* We're the ones who'll save our brothers and sisters!"

"Yay!"

He flowed with energy. Perhaps Carole had been right that Phoebe was a jockfucker, because Phoebe tried to get Peas interested in putting his fire into her, but he didn't "focus." They'd talk a minute, Phoebe'd ask him a question, touch his leg, sometimes they'd kiss and trade tongues, but then he'd pull away and rush to make a statement. He and Kathy made it, but she was her own avalanche of energy, wrapping up her dissertation on the political themes in Edgar Rice Burroughs—she was a year or so ahead of Peas—and interviewing for jobs on campuses while hitting committees and demonstrations.

The political kids moved all over by VW and cheap air, recognizing one another by hair, bumper sticker, and pins on flowered shirts, pushing the Movement. They spent a weekend at San Luis Obispo forming the Peace and Freedom Party.

It was a time of splinter parties, since government wasn't working. KLQA also gave air time to George Wallace's radical right party.

"You covered fascists," Peabody complained. Phoebe told him testily that he didn't own the air and the FCC had rules about equal time. Peabody fired back one-two-three that LBJ had corrupted the FCC, that Marcuse rightly said totalitarians shouldn't be allowed free speech because they'll take yours away, and that fascists perverted the media to create heroes; this got him reminiscing about Houston Bridles at Exeter, where Bridles had been a terrific athletic hero and where Peabody had learned to hate him.

"No, it wasn't any one thing," Peabody said. "It was just that he was always so *graceful* and *forgiving* being around me, when my odd mother showed up on visiting day or when he noticed that I, who came from families that were important in Boston in Hawthorne's day, had holes in my tweed jacket. He was so kind, so tolerant of and bored by people who didn't measure up to his world. He embodied all those *fucked* establishment values of team and money and force and pointless grace and suspending your *own* thoughts and feelings. After practice I used to sit on the bench in the locker room and beat my fists against my knees and cry. Yes! Hyuk-hyuk-hyuk—hot tears rolling down my schoolboy cheeks! Why can't I be stronger? Why can't I be faster? Like Bridles! Will we beat Andover? *Andover!* Hyuk-hyuk-hyuk!"

That fall when he came south to assemble signatures, he talked about a trip to Washington. All the peace groups were going to picket the Pentagon. It was an idea that had come up virtually overnight.

"You have to come, Phoebe. It's going to be big!"

He had no idea how the business worked. That irritated her. Also it irritated her because it really would be a big story, the network would cover it, and she wasn't at network. It put her in a snit.

By October of 1967 many talked about the Pentagon March, an event like King's march four years earlier or Monterey that spring or Woodstock two years later, events that became great because people together felt passions and hopes that lifted them out of what their lives had been and showed them other hills to climb.

Adams Peabody confronted Houston Bridles on that Pentagon weekend.

In Washington in September, Houston saw the FBI reports, now a stream, on the upcoming march on the Pentagon: the formal FBI memo sheets in boilerplate with RESTRICTED top and bottom and the scraps, tatters, and snapshots J. Edgar Hoover brought over as toilet gossip for President Johnson.

In those days Houston was a harried young man. Never fat, he had lost weight, he was pale, his boyish face had already begun to wrinkle, and he had a squint. His patience was thin.

"I cannot abide Hoover's insane conspiracy connections," he wrote in his journal. Hoover linked groups like Peace Action, People's Forum, Popular Front, and Peace and Freedom and insisted P-combinations were radical code. The Director also said the recurring phrase of the young, "The Emperor has no clothes," was a code for radical collusion.

"This is appalling," Houston wrote. "This strange man, who wears high shoes, lives with another man, and delves into *God knows what*—" He railed in the proper fashion for a liberally educated Yale man, but also like a Yale man he concluded: "Hoover *does* possess immense power. Don't run afoul."

He was thinking about his continuing dalliance with Marty Sanford and the chance that some gumshoe would blackmail them. She *was* helping to keep Sandy in line, to support the President's war as long as money flowed into his district. Of course, he couldn't and wouldn't want to do that with all congressmen's wives, but she also told him, in her way, what the truth was.

"You know and I know, darling, nobody with a brain in his head thinks Johnson's any good anymore." Houston, smiling ruefully, looking over his shoulder, had to agree with her.

He'd seen all the intelligence reports on the breadth of discontent. Not just the war. Doubts that Great Society money was going to the people who needed help. Most of all, doubts about the Kennedy assassination: the accusation in the play *MacBird* that Johnson and a Texas cabal had killed JFK. The hatred cutting through Paul Krassner's vignette of Johnson committing necrophilia on Kennedy's corpse. What Houston heard, in visits from his stooped, pinched, grouchy pa, who kept saying, "The Agency had no *policy* to have Cubans and mobsters operating here," and "We did not *run* Oswald," meaning he knew more than he had said, and probably knew who *had* run Oswald and the other gunmen.

So many witnesses had died. Houston was inclined to believe rogue agents and mobsters did it, but he was damn sure he'd never say a word about it himself.

Even LBJ, one time over Cutty Sark, said, "There's a lot more to it than anyone's gonna *want* to know."

The rumor around the West Wing Basement—and among the discontented young, according to the FBI reports—was that a rogue agent had killed Adlai Stevenson, too. The UN Ambassador and leading liberal, the man who'd begged Kennedy not to use air strikes at the Bay of Pigs, had been walking down a street in London when a man collided with him and poked him with an umbrella. Stevenson's body showed the symptoms of heart attack. That could be cyanide; Ted Gerrity had told him about that kind of hit years ago. Nothing seemed too strange these days.

In October just before the demonstration, reports came in from the FBI that California Druids and Diggers and East Coast Yippies intended to chant and perform a magic spell to levitate the Pentagon from its foundations.

"Oh, wow—what are *they* smoking?" said one aide, herself a plastic hippie.

"Very funny," Houston said. "Zany."

But then a Defense Intelligence Agency liaison came over and told them about Soviet magic spells. DIA handled strategic weapons information. The little wrinkled man with wet-combed hair said, "You know the Soviets are experimenting with ESP to send messages to their cosmonauts in case of radio failure."

"No, I didn't," Houston said. "My purview is—"

"It doesn't matter. But the CIA is funding *some* ESP experiments at Lockheed in California to see if *we* can use anything like that. There's a center at UCLA for parapsychology—not just telepathy, sending messages, but telekinesis, using mental force to move objects."

"And?" Houston looked at this ordinary bureaucrat talking such off-the-wall plans.

"Well, suppose the Russians know something about this that *we* don't know? We know goddam well their agents are all *through* the Movement. Suppose these hippies *can* raise the building? I'll tell you, Mr. Bridles, there are colonels and generals over there who are frankly *worried*."

At times Houston was so astounded by the egregious zaniness of these times that he could only stretch to attempt to perceive it, as you would to bat down a pass—and then he'd shrink into reflex, with the answer he'd learned at Exeter and Yale, the tried and true Loss of Innocence.

On the eighteenth Houston received a call in the office from Adams Peabody, of all people. He had not seen him since cocktails at Phoebe's aunt's place.

Without preliminary, Adams said he was coming to the Pentagon March and asked for a place "to crash."

Good nerve! Houston thought, but said yes; he might learn something. Get down to cases. Houston was a true WASP in that he preferred to talk with someone he'd known before, even someone whose actions were so extraordinary and bereft of team spirit as Peabody the Peace Marcher. *I'm going to work you over, Peas. I won't shelter you as I did at school, thinking about your wretched circumstances and eccentric mother. You're responsible for your own actions.*

Peabody's speech on the telephone was shot through with "hey, mans" and "fucks." He didn't mention Phoebe, yet Houston knew they must have been together because Peabody openly admitted he'd been on the Century Plaza March and Houston had seen Phoebe's name on FBI intelligence reports about Century Plaza that quoted Los Angeles police intelligence. Houston knew more than he cared to about her outrageous behavior in Vietnam and since. No sense of propriety whatsoever; yet she'd told him years ago what she wanted.

"Can't brood! To achieve, look ahead!" he wrote in his journal, and "Now to face Peabody and tell him he and his peace pals will accomplish nothing."

Here is how his journal recorded the Pentagon March, the East Coast follow-up to the Century Plaza demonstration, which together showed President Johnson had lost the Will of Heaven.

2 Nov 1967 West Wing Basement

The demonstration is over—that is, the last long-haired visitors seem to have flown and driven away in their cars and vans. The ones left, in long hair and beards and shawls, chanting at the White House fence, are some kind of permanent haunting group.

Hey, hey, LBJ, how many kids did you kill today?

Stop the bombing, stop the NAY-palm!

Adams Peabody arrived Friday. Normally I would have worked til 8 or 9 but fortunately got to Du Pont Circle at 7. Found him sitting on a car hood outside like a vagrant, with a six-pack of beer on his lap. Had to peer to recognize his sharp nose. Long hair, beard, faded jeans and denim jacket, a red headband. From his mother he seems to have cultivated knack of being outrageous, from his first comment about Du Pont Circle to his "right on, brother" handshake to his "what's here to drink?" as soon as we stepped inside.

"Very Fence Club," he said as he looked around boldly. "Oh, wow. Hunting prints. Oh, wow, leather chairs! Cattle died for these. Brass lamps."

I gave him a stiff taste and took one myself and put it to him. "What *is* this act, Peabody? You look silly. We're at war. You don't knock your own side."

He didn't blink—any connection he might have had to old loyalties, to God, Country, and Yale had been severed. "War is another kind of exploitation, Houston. *You* wage it, *we* fight it."

"No, you don't. You're not in uniform."

"Neither are you. The poor and powerless are, and I'm fighting for them!" He launched into a long-winded rhetorical harangue, using the terms "morality" and "self-determination" more times than I care to count. Some statements simply hysterical: "America is deliberately bombing indiscriminately to make money!" and, "You are using the draft to get rid of black people!" And, "Ho Chi Minh is the George Washington of Vietnam. He admires the Declaration of Independence!"

I told him Ho Chi Minh was hardly an enlightened gentleman like our founder, pointed out how he ruled by suppression, and told of the massacre of 1956, before we were in the equation, when Ho killed 50,000 in Nghe An province in the north, including 2,000 landowners.

"Of course!" Peas riposted. "They were oppressing the poor!"

"Two thousand? Fifty thousand! This is government, to kill your own people in those numbers? Peas, get *sane!* You can't use *our* words like liberty and our heroes like Washington when you're touting a dictator who uses mass executions and concentration camps."

"It's their own country!" Peabody said. "Let them adjust matters themselves and sort out whomever wants to copy our ugly system! And what about the Indians?"

"Let's talk about now," I said. "We have a war. This means all self-respecting men have a duty to fight it or at least support it."

"It's a totally unnecessary war. We get nothing from Vietnam. It's done nothing to us."

"I thought you were so bright, Peabody. You ought to know what the point is; we *are* protecting ourselves."

"From what?"

"We're denying Russia warm-water harbors."

He stared at me, incredulous, then burst out laughing. "That is so fucking *dated!* The British said that in the nineteenth century!"

"Yeah, laugh, asshole! You want to be too fashionable to fight, and then we'll all be walked over! You'd have done the same after Pearl Harbor!"

He snorted. "If it had been World War Two I'd have gone in. I'd have carried a gun." He looked at me. "And I'd have shot people."

"Come on, Peas. Don't be a simpleton. You wouldn't have shot anybody. At Exeter before practice you'd talk about how you'd flatten someone across from you and then you'd miss a block and skid along the turf while footsteps pounded past you. See here, Peas—we have free speech, to be sure, but each speaker's words have different *value* because some speakers, like you, simply don't know what they're talking about."

"Elitist!" he shot back, and went into another harangue, an academic lecture, on heroes and what he called "American myth."

"We are *not* decent liberators," he said. "I have proof our GIs bayonet children! Americans are the most violent people on earth! For God's sake, Houston, what about *napalm?*"

"We have always been decent," I said.

"That's propaganda! What about the Indians?"

"Our history has always been one of decency."

"History is the verdict of the victors!"

"That's why it's better to win than to lose!"

He sulked at that.

"See here, Peas—what do you think this kind of demonstration does to our men overseas?"

"I hope it encourages them to mutiny!"

I stared at him. "You don't care if they do? You don't care about loyalty? Honor?"

"I do care. About life. And justice."

I found myself back in the attitude I had at Exeter: poor fellow, he can't help it. "Have another drink," I said. I went to bed.

*   *   *

Saturday morning I went to the Pentagon to monitor for LBJ. All tense in corridors—federal police, MPs, officers talking about "being under fire"; from tenor of comments I intuited they never had been, like me.

Then in key corridors downstairs had startling sight—paratroopers of 82nd Airborne in battle equipment sitting on floors. Unsettling—men five, eight years younger, many combat experienced, handling weapons with familiarity. Bright brass ammunition, green and gray grenades by these painted walls, bulletin boards, linoleum floors. Men's young faces, old eyes. Smelled gasoline. Young paratrooper with flamethrower on back. "*What* are you going to do with that?" I asked.

He shook his head slowly. "I *hope* I don't have to do *nothin'*."

Upstairs, officers worried. Nervous jokes about levitating the building.

One of UnderSec Def staff said Robert McNamara had had a terrible taste of the protest already—he had been in Manhattan the previous night (Friday) with Jackie Kennedy at the Picasso show at the Museum of Modern Art when approached by a young art student who screamed, "Murderer!" and asked how he could defile this life-affirming greatness with his presence. Secret Service man said the student raved on; McNamara froze, flushed, his arms came up stiffly, jaw set, eyes glittered as if having a seizure. SS man took student away. No arrests. Mrs. K cool throughout. McNamara much upset; whether doesn't like accusations of murder because he's a Quaker or because they challenge his *amour-propre* is another question.

I joined others on Pentagon second floor and watched above steps of river entrance. Mob of young people crowded barricades, MPs and soldiers held. Young soldiers had clean, unschooled faces; clearly a case of the more privileged making fun of the less. More pushing, then the mob broke the barricades, and police moved in to arrest them, dragging them to buses. A thick crowd, thick as the Civil Rights march. Saw Norman Mailer—short, gray curly hair. Some

demonstrators very determined, clinging to poles, barricades, while police clubbed them, tried to pull hands loose.

I saw Adams Peabody in handcuffs, yelling and waving
his manacled wrists as if he'd caught a pass against Andover.

News cameras everywhere. The people being arrested
were depicted as heroes—not a word about the government's
restraint. LBJ pale and drawn during this time. To find a
crowd of a quarter million against him must have been painful. (D.C. police, responding to cue, gave lower figure.)
Bobby Sugg told me LBJ had all the televisions running,
getting reports, chewing on insides.

Spent night with Marty Sanford at my place. She
showed me an intriguing process with small brass globes
called Ben-Wa balls. She said before demonstration Sandy
called counsel to see if congressional immunity protected
him from arrest. Also had staff checking to see if *should* be
arrested. Would it look better? In any case Congressman
Sanford went to demonstration, walked through barricades,
was taken away, can claim solidarity. Marty says LBJ thinks
he can zap Sandy's district but doesn't know what Sandy
knows about the votes now.

We got out of bed to watch late news. She was disappointed Sandy wasn't shown but said he'd arranged for staff
to photograph him anyway. She was incredibly horny and
so was I. But we must both be careful.

As a presidential appointee like Pa, Uncle Stu under
FDR, Grandpa Fraker under Wilson, Horace Bridles under
Arthur, in this great Republic, to grasp that I must exercise
more than reasonable discretion to guard against FBI agents
watching for adults fucking is appalling. Disappointing. Degrading. And to understand that the President is ignorant
and barbaric is disquieting. This is not *lux et veritas* but a
charade with a yawp. Yet one can't bail out. Like riding a
bad wind, tide. Pa said he had to endure ignorance under
Truman when he was helping to form the Agency, and more
under Eisenhower, who wanted everything swept under the
rug—no disturbances on his watch. Some of our problems
now are ones Pa colluded in concealing. We are beginning to
pile up large numbers of our aircrew known as missing or

prisoners of North Vietnam. Opponents like Wallace point to these. Eisenhower had far more, some 8,000 men missing after Korea, yet was able to finesse them, let people go back to sleep. Must learn how he did it!

The capitol is very grim. Few parties, no splashy ones, even now as holidays approach. This deadly war hangs over us. The only ones who looked like they were having fun were the demonstrators.

Houston met with FBI agent Curlew some days later. A tense, pale, overweight man in his fifties. Houston made small talk to see what he was about, asking where he was from and so forth.

"Denver." Agent Curlew also said he had been in New York, which made Houston brighten, but Curlew explained acerbically that he had been sent there on church work and that no one had listened to him. "Filthy," he said. "Filthy place."

Houston asked what church and Curlew said, "LDS" several times, finally explaining, "Mormons. Mormons!"

Houston later noted in his journal that he "met all kinds *here*, too"—but for the nonce he told Curlew he was concerned about an acquaintance of his, Adams C. L. Peabody, who had been a leader in the Pentagon March. His picture—being carried away, manacled hands high, hair flowing behind him, bearded face split in a triumphant laugh—had run front page in the *Post*, *Times*, and had been shown on NBC. He had given an interview to the San Francisco *Chronicle* on his return. He had used—it infuriated Houston to read—every damn cliché they had all learned at Exeter and Yale, including "We have lost our innocence," and the media had lapped it up! As if this weenie were an *oracle!*

"I want to make sure you are square on these New Mobe ring-leaders," Houston said.

"I think I've seen his name in our files."

"I should have known he'd turn out this way," Houston said. "His mother was a strange *declassé* radical." As the pale, flabby man wrote, Houston wondered if he knew what *declassé* meant.

RFK Shot!

Once more the boys weren't home for Christmas and then it was 1968. Phoebe covered Tet in California hospitals, interviewing wounded who came back through the government's enormous medical facilities.

When the Viet Cong and North Vietnamese began their attacks all along the country in late January, about 400,000 American ground troops and thousands of Australians, Thais, South Koreans, and Filipinos were based there. The Americans lost thousands killed and wounded in a week. This seemed to be at last what the *attentisme* at Givral had called the *khoi nghia*—the great uprising that would free the country.

Over the tape feed they got great pictures of American paratroopers fighting house to house in Saigon, machine guns and grenades peppering little stucco buildings and palm-shaded alleys. They had long-range shots of fighting around the American Embassy, Marine guards running across the lawn, bodies of VC on the grass, American paratroopers at the fence firing rockets into the building and assaulting under machine gun fire. Fantastic—more than they could use. At last television could get clear pictures of a fire fight because it was contained in the width of the low building.

What did it mean? General Westmoreland called it a victory, saying we had broken the VC. Hedley Donovan of *Time* called Westmoreland not very bright. MACV claimed the suicidal attacks depleted the Main Force units and that the American counterattacks destroyed them. Ho Chi Minh told a sympathetic Italian correspondent, Oriana Falacci, that the liberation forces had lost a half million killed to date and over a million wounded. But that didn't play as an American victory because Lyndon Johnson had been telling everyone he had the situation under control, and here the stations had clear pictures of armed VC running around an American embassy. It was unthinkable that Americans would lose an embassy.

Meanwhile North Vietnamese regular units replaced the *mat tran* and local committees. In some cases North Vietnamese *can bo* liquidated their VC rivals. The power shift mattered to intelligence officers but didn't play to the viewers.

A network stringer sent pictures from a Huey flying low over the streets and alleys of Cholon, the Chinese city next to Saigon, where the remaining VC had gone to ground; his sound pickup got the shots and shouts as soldiers and police shot the stragglers.

Phoebe interviewed an Air Force man who'd been blinded. He described rockets coming into Tan Son Nhut. As he talked through his face bandages she remembered the sheet metal huts and buildings and imagined what they'd be like under fire, and the splatter of fragments hitting all those fresh-painted white office signs.

A soldier from the Delta said that when he was hit and evacuated he begged his buddies to make sure his dope was in his personal effects, but he passed out, and when he came to in Japan: "I felt around. Where's my *dope*, man?" He was perhaps twenty. He said the VC they were killing had little dope pipes, too.

A Marine who'd been at Hue told about the North Vietnamese tank attack that had destroyed the ancient city. He said he and his company, down to platoon strength, had spent a week in the rubble of buildings, coming up to shoot into the backs of passing NVA units. He said downriver a cut-off antitank platoon had used its Ontos vehicles against NVA tanks. They drove the little machines at top speed down alleys behind known NVA positions, slewed around corners, fired all their guns, and got out before the North Vietnamese could react. He said a number of Navy boatmen were among them because the river had been cut off.

At the end of it an armored relief column of Marines and Army drove back into Hue. When he was being evacuated, the Marine said, he saw a company of limousines that General Abrams had brought north for the staff officers planning the counterattack.

One afternoon they got gruesome pictures over the electronic tape feed. The Marines who went back into Hue discovered mass graves of thousands of petty officials and neutral citizens massacred by the NVA and *can bo* during the few days they had held the city. The pictures showed Marines and ARVN with faces covered and military earthmovers pulling the rotting rags of people from the brown earth.

A producer named Chet North later told Phoebe that the network didn't know how to play the Hue massacre. It was an atrocity but it wasn't in line with how most of the newswriters perceived the communist revolutionaries. All of them knew the communists were supposed to be like fish in the water, helpful, enlightened, pointing to the future.

North said, "The massacre *did* show that, just as the VC were saying, the government could not protect its own citizens, so we felt it, too, was part of the VC victory. But we sent along the pictures in case the stations wanted to make something else of it."

At KLQA, though, Rex didn't like to go over 3:30 on war news, so they didn't go into massacre details.

Everyone had pictures of General Loan's famous shot. Loan, head of the National Police, had put a revolver to the head of a Vietnamese in a checked shirt and shot him. It was a current-events icon. This man was said to be a VC who had shot up General Loan's office and killed Loan's wife and daughter. Few newswriters mentioned that. You saw the general in uniform and the man not in uniform, his cheeks blowing out as the bullet went through his skull. That image played hundreds of times and everyone recognized it, whether or not anyone knew what it meant.

Along with other good news, the North Koreans captured the U.S.S. *Pueblo* without a shot fired. Phoebe got an interview with the mother of a crew member.

"I don't know what they're doin'," she said. "They said he's got to go, now they don't know what to do."

In Washington Houston Bridles knew less about the military picture than Phoebe did because so much exculpatory information was crowding the official channels. Westmoreland's reports said, in effect, "If you can overlook losing Saigon and the American Embassy, we did just fine."

"He's so fuckin' *stupid!*" Johnson raged—but didn't fire him immediately because Johnson *himself* didn't know what to do. He'd kept

Westmoreland there because he had been a shrewd political choice, a Southerner married to Douglas MacArthur's family, a yes-man and a bureaucrat. "*I'm* runnin' things," Johnson had said. He couldn't evade responsibility.

Los Angeles lost tons of weight that winter. Hillsides descended in mudslides in the rain and Phoebe Bishop, KLQA woman-on-the-spot, was out there getting drenched, freezing her ass off, holding the mike and talking about the tasteless cheap houses you could see sliding downhill over her shoulder. She thought Rex wanted her to cover the rains so she'd have a wet blouse on camera. They wouldn't let a bare breast go through, but a wet, color pricktease would be okay.

Her emotional life was still shit. She was making good money, which she spent on clothes and cosmetics. Frequently someone would introduce her to a lawyer, doctor, stockbroker, and they'd have a few dates, then she'd find something lacking—the man would be too cocky, too dull, not interested in what's happening, not interested in photography, hadn't traveled, hadn't grown up, was hung up on politics, was snotty-social (in *L.A.!* she marveled), wanted her to quit news and have children, or sniffed his fingers after sex. She dated producers. They developed rivalries. They were too close in the business. She had achieved a good deal and couldn't communicate with many men. The good ones were already married or proven pricks like Houston.

She worked. She filed stories. Network didn't notice them. Mama Cass Elliot sang the leaves were brown and the skies were gray. She listened to *The Magical Mystery Tour* 500 million times and used "The Fool on the Hill" during one Hillside Home Lost in Tragic Mudslide story.

That winter Rex Bisbee developed a fixation about germs. He fumed at one of the newswriters for taking a newspaper to the men's room and bringing it back where others might touch it.

L.A. television had a forerunner of Morton Downey, an insulting fascist named Jack Needles, who interviewed and sneered at guests. Ned Pittman had gone to that show. The "Needles–Pittman News" held a live question-and-answer forum on Vietnam and Jack Needles addressed a crippled Marine in a wheelchair who said he couldn't understand why he and his friends where shot up.

"You can't take it!" Needles yelled.

Ned Pittman, the handsome toady, added, "It's a good thing you weren't around in World War Two!"

As for Houston, if all the Tet traffic wasn't a blow to the nuts, Marty Sanford's conduct was.

"Why?" Houston said at the French Embassy party. Marty looked gorgeous, desirable in black, her blonde hair shining, fluffy, the sunshine copy of her muff, but her face was not the face that had urged him on. She was distant, distracted.

"I can't and I won't talk with you now. Sandy has his career. I'm pushing him. And *you're* the one who's wrong. Please don't be *difficult!*"

Not long afterward, the FBI called Houston. "Floyd Curlew. Remember me? Good. I think I'd better tell you about this in person."

Agent Curlew very kindly explained that Sandy had been talking with French diplomats who were carrying messages for the North Vietnamese. "Some kind of peace overture," Agent Curlew said. "It certainly looks suspicious to me. Better steer clear of her."

George Wallace's American Independent Party and the Peace and Freedom Party got on the California ballot. Martin Luther King, a true saint, was shot and killed in Memphis. It all came over the daily network tape feed like the tank firing in Detroit and Hue and the *Pueblo*—King's intense dark eyes, the fuzzy gray official photo of the ship, the cities burning and tanks rolling and machine gun fire.

One of the editors made fancy film of the twenty-five-second bit of General Loan shooting the VC suspect in his checked shirt. It was a loop to music. You had Loan in fatigues, hatless, and the man in his sports shirt, and the hammerless short police revolver kicking, the man grimacing, eyes closing, cheeks puffing out, bright blood welling from his head, *wham!* forward and *wham!* backward, the man's cheeks going in and out, the revolver tilting up and down, to the rasping music of the Velvet Underground, Lou Reed's "Angel of Death."

Television was the magical mystery tour. Phoebe had to get to network somehow, to New York.

In February Uncle Stu called Houston with an edge in his voice. "Look, Tony—most important. You *must* schedule several people in to see LBJ soonest. He's got to know something."

"What?"

"I will tell you when I arrive."

The next day Stu came to Houston's office in the West Wing Basement. Stu was tanned, just back from Puerto Rico, and pleased he'd got out of the glass factory. Otherwise not buoyant.

"It's bad news and we're going to bring him, Tony. He's suffered too many military reverses, and the economy's going out of control. He's not kidding anyone, using paper to fund this, and he hasn't cut back on his welfare programs or put in price controls."

"He doesn't want a war footing," Houston said. "It'd be socially disruptive."

Stu laughed. "You are a good man, Tony. You truly are. But don't waste your breath. He's not in command and you know it."

Houston nodded. For all he knew his office was bugged.

Stu said, "We're simply telling him he has lost our support."

Houston thought and felt, in a flash, like seeing a ball carrier surrounded by defense men, how Lyndon Johnson was trapped, scrambling in sunlight, and how he would be hit, blocked, stopped—and power taken from him.

And then he thought of Lyndon Johnson's face, his peculiar, pouchy, sad-eyed American face, so quick to smile, to swell and stretch in rage, to squint in suspicion of subjects he didn't understand, to gaze, hopefully, listening to experts.

What had we told him? What had McNamara told him? McNamara's consistent certainty that Air Power and Operations Research and Logistics and soldiers in helicopters could defeat the primitive enemy, his bloodless displays of numbers as proof, and Johnson drinking it in. LBJ was like those poor rustics who went to see the Wizard of Oz—and the Wizard confessing, at the end, that he had no magic powers. McNamara himself had told others months ago, when he resigned, that his heart wasn't in the war. Poor LBJ couldn't imagine *not* winning, and had pressured others to provide winning fantasies. Everyone knew what he did when he got information he didn't like.

"He'll hit the roof," Houston told Stu.

Stu shrugged. "His own party's deserted him. Al Lowenstein got Congress against him. McCarthy and Kennedy are running against him. He won't fight. He's proven that. He's a bully, Tony, and a coward. He's not a toe-to-toe slugger like you." He gripped Houston's shoulder. "Set us up, will you? *You'll* always be afloat."

After making the appointment Houston put in a call to John Lindsay, the Kennedy-style mayor of New York. Houston reminded the mayor of having met him with Stu last fall and said he would be available to take a job with the city. "I know where the federal money is."

A few days later Houston saw Uncle Stu and other financial leaders pull up in their limousines.

LBJ was uncommunicative afterward, prowling corridors, jumping on underlings.

Stu told Houston about it at the Cosmos Club.

"He couldn't seem to understand how far behind he was," Stu said. Stu thought a moment and laughed. "All his old plays were there when we talked, you know—he slapped backs, wrapped his arm around my neck. I thought he was going to kiss David Rockefeller's ear—but when it came time to count cards, he was talking about growth and jobs, as if Kennedy were still alive stoking the economy. I think he's into the sauce a bit now, too—have you noticed it?"

"He's not completely rational," Houston said. "But he keeps most of the aides at a distance now."

"Hmmm. Yes." Stu put his big hand flat on the table. He turned his head to see who was close, but the nearest man was reading a paper in an armchair across the room. "In any case, we told him the bad news, and his reactions were instantaneous. He narrowed his eyes. He was suspicious. He said, 'That queer Lowenstein been talkin' to yer people, too?' and when I said, 'We only read the graphs, Mr. President,' he positively glowered and it seemed he was about to try to bully me. Of course, I won't be pushed around by a . . . contemptible . . . Texas . . . crook, as you know. So we looked at each other awhile. I stared him down. I don't know what he was thinking, but of course as a bully he has that side of cowardice. He moved to being quiet and reasonable. 'Come let us reason together,' he said. 'Who've you got to replace me? *Hubert?* Gonna have *Hubert* run the country and the war?'

"We said nothing. It sunk in. He won't fight us, but you can look for a storm here."

Houston saw the storm the next day. Johnson summoned the aides to the Oval Office and stared coldly as they filed in.

"Now," the President said, "I want to know which o' you people been fuckin' your President and your country. Hah?"

No one spoke.

"Which o' you been to the news tellin' em this administration is in trouble?" He stood and curved his arm out in an unathletic but menacing gesture. "This administration *is not in trouble! We have prosperity 'n jobs at home an' we're tryin' to defend freedom overseas! Sugg!*"

He turned on the wide-eyed young man. "*Get out front here!*"

"Yes sir." Sugg was pale. He stepped out in front of the group.

"What's the big idea of tellin' the Houston *Chronicle* I didn't have no stomach for a fight? Hah?"

"Sir, I didn't."

"Don't tell me what you think you done! They quotin' people callin' me *weak* for not *invadin' Hanoi and startin' World War Three!* Now, where the fuck were you when this was bein' printed? The fuckin' Chinese got five divisions up there! You supposed to know all them people down there and make sure they don't get it wrong! They don't know what *I* know!"

LBJ walked into the center of the room, and the aides shrank to the sides. He glared at each in turn. "*I'll* say they're on a rebellion. They don't care if we win or lose there and don't even put up a fight. *They* don't know government like I do *or* war. *I won the silver star!*" He touched his lapel and dropped his big hand to his fly, which he unzipped; his big hand flew in like a pigeon and emerged holding his thick, gray-yellow penis. Sugg glanced at it and looked at the ceiling. The President's hand held his cock in four fingers, pointing its eye at them. "I'll tell you one thing, Ho Chi Minh ain't gonna get *this* and neither are those goddam shithead pigwallowin' fruitfuckin' editors who think this war's gonna go away. I been there! *I been there!*"

President Johnson turned toward Houston, pointing his cock at him. "Now, what kinda *queers* you been spendin' your time with, Bridles?"

Sugg laughed.

Houston looked LBJ calmly in the eye. His voice rang. "Mr. President, that remark is beneath you! And beneath the dignity of the room in which we stand!"

"Don't you tell me— You tell me how come that queer Allard Lowenstein, who's tryin' to torpedo this war, *and* this President, has been to talk with your daddy and your uncle and David Rockefeller and all those *New York bankers to undercut* my *Presidency? Huh? You tell me that!*"

LBJ's face was red and he was squeezing his cock so hard it was red too.

"No, Mr. President. I have talked with Stu about economic indicators. He and Lowenstein aren't close."

"He doesn't like Jews, does he? All you people are anti-Semitic." He walked across to the side door and into the toilet; he shed his coat, dropped his trousers, and sat. "Get in here."

Sugg looked at the others. Houston said, "Good-bye, Mr. President." He turned to walk out. Others went with Houston.

"You're fuckin' traitors!" Johnson yelled. He leaned forward over his bare knees. But with his trousers down he couldn't chase them. *"Traitor! The FBI'll nail Lowenstein and you traitors!"*

They all left. Houston walked downstairs, where he had his secretary, an efficient middle-aged woman, put in the call to Mayor Lindsay's office. "I'm ready to start work," Houston told the mayor.

All spring Phoebe turned over ways to get to network. That big story. What would it be? Los Angeles had more crime, love-ins, rock concerts, hippies, demonstrations, but those were everywhere. What story could she possibly get that would break things open for her and make it, "This is Phoebe Bishop in New York"?

In May and early June of 1968 the California Primary was big news. Robert Kennedy, who had seized on peace after Eugene McCarthy had challenged Johnson with it months before, used the California Primary to show he had more appeal than the oddball, quirky McCarthy.

Bobby made good appearances. He looked serious, handsome, his cornflower blue eyes dazzling. Someone had coached his voice out of its Bugs Bunny squeak. Gary St. John covered him most of the way, but at the end of the primary, when it seemed Kennedy was winning, Phoebe was sent with a handful of other field reporters to help cover the victory gathering at the Ambassador Hotel, a tree-shaded brick building west of downtown off Lafayette Park.

Gary had a live hookup with video cameras and sound to Rex Bisbee. He was in the big ballroom with the balloons and revelers and interviewed California and party officials near the podium. He got Bobby's pleasant, hopeful victory remarks.

Phoebe had an ear wire and mike to connect her to St. John. She, Len, and Chuck were in the kitchen getting color from the Mexican dishwashers and other workers about what Kennedy's victory meant to them.

"He is a great man, he has feeling for the people."

They were shooting film. They couldn't remote live from the corridor.

You know how it is in a crowd—it's like water; people push before you know what's happening. They felt the commotion as Bobby and his party came down the corridor lined with stainless-steel cabinets and racks. Len was standing on a box. Rosie Grier's big Afro head stuck above the others, but Bobby was short. So was Sirhan Sirhan, a thin Palestinian. People shoved, yelled, "What the—" Little pop shots sounded, and the men around Bobby piled on.

Len got pictures of Rafer Johnson and others crushing Sirhan while the crowd went frantic. She couldn't get a word out. Len shot the faces: Kennedy staring at the ceiling, eyes protruding and twitching from the bullet in his head, his two upper incisors showing in the light, and the hands on Sirhan.

"He Mexican?"

A dishwasher said, "He no Mexican, he don' speak Spanish. We say him go, *va*, he didn' understand. A minute ago, only."

He didn't work at the hotel, someone said. Cops pushed in. Phoebe yelled, "Is he dead?"

"No!" a cop yelled.

She pushed into the ballroom. People crowded, yelling that Kennedy had been shot. The floor director stood by the camera, which was on Gary St. John, who looked on top of things—tall, thin, wearing the black-framed glasses of a man of the world. Phoebe waved and Gary's voice came into her ear. She told him Kennedy had been shot in the head and she had film.

Gary looked at her. The director broke in. "Stand by. Rex wants to know."

"Phoebe," Rex's smooth voice came into her ear. "What do you have?"

She told him. "Stand by," he said. "Give it live."

The camera swung to her, red light on, the cameraman's hand adjusting the zoom. In her ear Rex was telling Los Angeles viewers they had a report from the scene.

She faced the camera and told it quickly. Rex asked a question. The camera cut away to catch the crowd. Shocked expressions, people crying. Party ribbons, balloons adrift. In her ear Rex described the "shocked and sad confusion of this—what was to have been, sadly, a happy—" Then the ear gave her Gary St. John arguing with the director about the story. When Gary looked across the room at her, though he was fifty feet away, she could see his eyes incandescent with hate.

"*I'm* the political reporter," he said. "You call to me, I'll *get* the facts from her. Phoebe, are you up? Tell me what happened. Who shot him? Have the police ID'd him? For God's sake, what are the *facts?*"

Rex's voice came into her ear. "Phoebe, stand by. You're going to give it to network. For a national viewership. Be sure to clear up details like where the hotel is, what's known about the shooter. Where is the film?"

The director cut in and said the film was on the way, an apprentice had left a minute ago after Len got the last shots of the shooter and Kennedy being hauled away.

"Stand by," Rex said. A network producer spoke in her ear. The network director came on. She faced the camera and told a nationwide audience what had happened in the corridor. She looked into the black and glass probe and gave it all her intelligence and sensitivity, as if she wanted to charm it to fuck. She told about the mood of the crowd, Kennedy's appeal and the euphoria around him, the commotion, the shooter, the shots felt by people who'd brought Robert Kennedy to victory for a clear chance at the Presidency. "A chance, these citizens believed, to lead us out of the heartbreaks of the last five years since his brother was slain. Now they grasp that their hopes have been destroyed." She paused, her face brave, lovely, composed, not innocent. "This is Phoebe Bishop in Los Angeles."

The network producer, Chet North, said, "That was very good." Rex came on and said the same.

She went back to the corridor, found other witnesses, got more, and when network wanted an update, Rex had her go on again.

"Good," Chet North said. "How long have you been doing this?"
She told him.
"Are you available to work the conventions? For network?"
"Yes."
"Plan on it."

Fun Cities

Phoebe counted the hours until she could leave Los Angeles for the conventions in Miami and Chicago. She blamed the entire vast polluted basin for killing Bobby. Maybe he wasn't America's only future, but he'd offered a different future than what they got—more years of shit. L.A. had turned mean and nasty. Before Robert Kennedy was shot, she and others felt America had a chance to swerve. Even after King was shot? After Tet? After losing the *Pueblo?* Perhaps. But Bobby's killing proved you couldn't hope for a better future.

She saw anger. Demonstrators provoked the police now. They knew the police would lash out with nightsticks and the news would show it. People in news were angry. Print and on-camera reporters were generally liberal and went out of their way to show cops and politicians looking awkward, and the off-camera techs, usually less tolerant, tried to embarrass "freaks." Len the cameraman didn't like blacks, hippies, and students. At UCLA he filmed a bearded student eating grapes, which were taboo because of the farm workers' strike; when the student realized he was being filmed he yelled angrily and Len filmed that. Len said, "The secret of these goddam students 'n' hippies is they got enough money to sit on their ass 'n' talk poor." People's class resentments boiled up in clots of words. Mayor Yorty talked of "radicals 'n' militants," by which he meant black people who wanted to walk north of Wilshire Boulevard. Richard Nixon, soon to be named the Republican candidate, spoke of "law 'n' order," by which he meant

Stop Blacks From Demanding Their Rights. George Wallace, the short
Alabama governor who had stood in the doorway at the University of
Alabama to stop a black student during a famous standoff against Attorney General Robert Kennedy years earlier, now used "law 'n' order," "left liberal," and "pointy-headed intellectuals" to stir up anger
and support for his splinter American Independent Party. His vice-
presidential candidate, General Curtis LeMay, suggested that the way
to end the war was to bomb Vietnam back to the Stone Age.

The summer before, she had filmed people talking about flower
power—the 1967 Monterey Pop Festival, flower children coming to
California with flowers in their hair. Even last fall she'd seen demonstrators sliding flowers into the muzzles of soldiers' rifles. But 1968
was the year of anger and confusion.

Confusion in the newsroom. Most of the newspeople weren't
sure how much truth to tell and how to rationalize what they didn't
tell. From network they got BBC footage of the Cultural Revolution
in China—Red Guards smashing stores, whacking scholars on the
shoulders, shooting from barricades at bourgeois elements. It was a
civil war but Rex didn't want to call it that, since he and Freddy
Walburn, the assignment editor, felt it would sound too much like
fifties anti-China news; Rex didn't want the truth of the news to get
in the way of the image he wanted to project. And then there was the
distressing truth of Vietnam. Network took foreign footage from BBC
or Canadian Broadcasting when they showed an American atrocity
like a surgical air strike on the wrong village and innocent women and
children killed.

"There's a very simple reason why we do it this way," Freddy
said. "Lyndon Johnson has been calling stations and threatening to
pull their FCC licenses. And he *owns* the FCC. So we'll let the British
and Canadians tell the truth for us."

When they did run the truth, the switchboard lit up and outraged
viewers said, "Why did you *show* that? Don't you know you're helping
the communists?"

The Peace and Freedom Party, the splinter on the left, nomi-
nated child-care expert Dr. Benjamin Spock for President and black
comedian and civil-rights activist Dick Gregory for Vice President.
Gregory had campaign handouts showing his face on a dollar bill. He
quipped: "It's time we had a black face on the money. We ain't even
on a penny!"

The splinter parties, another sign of anger, divided the vote even further. Before she left L.A. to cover the conventions Phoebe saw that one of the tape engineers had a Nixon sticker on his console.

It was about this time that Rex said people on camera should smile more. "The news *is* terrible. Grim. I think our viewers would like to see a smile and hear us occasionally say, 'Have a nice day.' "

You could buy plastic stick-on flowers in the stores in those neon colors of yellow, lime green, orange red. Some of them had printed mottoes: "Have a Nice Day."

Mark Randolph's life in 1968 became increasingly bounded by circumstances and details, yet he felt these details were increasingly unreal to him. He was a couple of years out of the Marines and Vietnam, yet Vietnam's green-, blue-, and brown-dusted scenes, its night fire-streaked visions, its echoes of voices clucking and meowing, its smells of blood, smoke, and sweat still gripped him more than his sun-sterilized air-conditioned surroundings in Orange County. Here are his details in 1968:

He had grown a moustache and sideburns for work—as a marketing rep for Mobil Oil—wore slacks and a short-sleeve shirt and tie, leaving his jacket on the seat of the car, so that he looked like several million other young business drones of California's vast, teeming, motorized population. He drove from his thin-walled stucco apartment-with-patio in Costa Mesa to a number of Mobil stations—huge asphalt areas with rows of pumps and sometimes pots of flowers, and small, prefab steel panel buildings for the lube racks and offices. He talked with dealers about ways to move more thousands of gallons of gas, more hundreds of quarts of oil, tires, wipers.

"Okay, Bob, let's try double stamps to help your summer tire special." In those days gas stations offered trading stamps to attract buyers for gasoline at forty cents a gallon. "You win the wiper promotion, Jimmy, you'll get a two percent override. That'll give you that cash you need for that Winnebago you want, won't it?" They had a sight on the American Dream.

He strode across the asphalt gas pump aprons while his body remembered striding across asphalt parade decks. He learned about his dealers' needs, desires, business situations, families, ambitions the way he'd used to remember his troopers' details. He planned details of his visits, concentrated on driving techniques to waste no time be-

tween stations scattered through Santa Ana, Laguna Beach, Garden
Grove, municipalities vaguely defined by freeways, shopping centers,
and the few remaining orange groves. He remembered from an earlier
trip during college how many orange groves there had been, the Disneyland mountain sticking up out of green; now the gray cone rose
above endless parking lots and stucco buildings. When he drove up on
the heights in Costa Mesa or Laguna Beach his eye saw relief—the
glittering Pacific. And on the other side of that, Vietnam. All those
characters there were concerned with numbers like frequency range,
fuze delay—numbers that meant something: lie or die, laugh or
scream, drink or bleed.

He did his hundreds of miles of daily driving in a range of cars—
the Lotus, when he was traveling light; the big Ford station wagon
he'd got for work, air-conditioned, engine three times the size of the
Lotus's. It used twice as much gas, which pleased the dealers. He
liked the Lotus because it was crisp, pure; he could drive it hard. But
this was a different life now. The other car in their three-space carport
was Judy's, his wife's. She was a cute blonde a year older than he. She
had full lips and a quirky hoydenish smile. She worked for Mobil,
too, in Accounting. She had been divorced not long before from a
man in Legal who, she explained, made more money than Mark, so
she was doing him a favor. Her car was a blue four-door Toyota. She
had told Mark about her mother, a fussy woman who wore a wig and
said, "Always get a car with four doors!" Judy said she spoke in strict
rules like that. " 'My land!' " Judy imitated. " 'Who'd want a car with
two doors!' "

Mark hadn't known Judy well before they married. "I haven't
even told Mom you have a *sports* car!" Judy laughed. "She'd be hysterical! I won't face that!"

Judy had left Indiana right after graduating from DePauw. "I
packed my bag and left home while they were at work," she said. "I
knew how they'd carry on. But then I called them up after I got work
out here." She'd done the same with her first husband—walked out.
"I don't like confrontations," she said. This wasn't quite true, he'd
found in a few months. She did like to cause scenes, but didn't like to
quarrel in private. When she caused scenes in public she looked over
her shoulder to get approval from others.

A couple of times when he'd run into guys from Yale, she'd
resented the amount of talking they did. When Peabody came down

she said, "Is his accent *real?* He says *'awnt'* for *'aunt'!*" She over-dressed and her idea of style was what television personalities wore. In short, he found her vulgar, peevish, and tiny minded. Why had he married her? He hadn't given a shit, he supposed. He'd thought it was time he got married. She'd seemed okay. He'd grabbed her, hastily, to fill a job, WIFE, in the quick way he'd learned in the military—but he hadn't intuitively weighed her character as he'd learned in the military. Danger signs: the catch in her voice; the way she wrinkled her nose and put an edge in her laugh implied vengeful narcissism. He'd seen the same fleeting expression in bad NCOs. But could you judge civilians, particularly *women*, by the same standards? This was one of many things he did not know.

In Vietnam he'd seen death and learned the range of powers people have. He'd been, as Martin Luther King said, to the moun-taintop. But once down he'd forgotten what he'd learned. His view of life had got so purified there, so bleak, that he could one minute help a good man with his gear and in the next consider shooting an enemy like that hamlet storekeeper or Colonel Dillis. Now his range of choices had to do with speed limits and stamp options.

Today he had had one hell of a lot of driving—a meeting in L.A., racing up and back, splitting traffic, drifting on the ramps; then visits in Tustin and Fullerton and many more. His tires blistered the free-way as he pushed the wagon along at 75 and 80 miles per hour; the Highway Patrol didn't use radar, so had to clock you from behind, and he'd got used to scanning the shoulders and mirror. He'd done 120 and 130 with the Lotus and loved the feeling, in a sports car or Detroit iron, of streaking flat out, belly down, concrete and posts whizzing past in a blur—and he liked going flat out over the grass on a dirt bike he'd borrowed. The fascination of speed was thinking constantly of wheels, angles, traction, rpms, pushing it harder—details that could kill him or save his life but weren't morally or culturally important.

Dry grass a blur, 80 miles per hour, over the rise, check for cops, the glittering Pacific; he slowed the big wagon down curves to Pacific Coast Highway, T-Bird engine muttering.

He pulled over at a bar called the Sandpiper. It was a Marine bar, mostly for pilots. Squadron and Group patches hung over the bar—those oddly austere designs Marine aviation used, geometric figures and forties-style letters. It had dark plywood surfaces.

He played darts with a couple of new aviators in a heavy helicopter squadron going over to Vietnam from Santa Ana. One was a
big ballplayer named Collazzo. He had a badass sarcastic streak Mark
liked. The squadron CO, it turned out, was Major Shick, who'd been
MABS-86 adjutant when Randolph was there. Many aviators were
being sent back.

"Yeah, and is *he* pissed off!" Collazzo said.

"Well, he had one tour."

"Don't *we* know it! We heard about every day of it! He jumped
sideways about four times to land in heavies 'cause he thought we
wouldn't ship out for a year!"

"What kind of bird is it?"

"CH-Fifty-three. Big single rotor, twin jets. They have a lot of
lightweight Kevlar armor and fifties at the doors."

"They were getting the Forty-sixes with fifties when I was short,"
Mark said. "That Kevlar's amazing."

"Sure as shit."

It was easy and comforting to shoot the shit about something you
thought you knew and sound like an old salt.

"You don't want to ship over, do you?" Collazzo said.

"Horse*shit*," Mark said. "Never volunteer. Sorriest sight I saw at
Pendleton before I got out was a guy who'd come back in, a captain,
O-Three. Left his job and family. He'd kept his blues. They didn't
quite fit. He had to hold his neck up like this. *I* don't want to go back!
I don't want to waste any more time! *Never* volunteer."

"Yeah, yeah," Collazzo said. "We're all fish anyway!"

They laughed hugely—that kind of humor that has Death on the
other side.

"Hey, Division's gettin' some shit at Khe Sanh, isn't it?" Collazzo
said.

"Yeah. Con Thien must have been a shit sandwich, too."

"They'll have the One-twenty rockets blasting our airfield off the
map," Collazzo said, and laughed. He was dark haired and had a
gleeful, bloody-minded expression.

"Yeah, you know one thing I never could figure out," Mark said,
"is why they're sliding all those units into fixed positions. All the time
we were training before the balloon went up, the instructors kept
saying, 'You have to forget what we did in Korea,' like, you know,
none of us had *been* in Korea anyway. They said, 'This will be a war

of traveling light, lots of patrols.' And now they have fixed positions getting the shit shelled out of them."

"Shick says the Army wants it. That's another reason he doesn't want to go back. Army's fucked it up bad."

Mark felt for the guys in the smelly bunkers. Remember crawling in the sand, muzzle flashes, wrapping fingers around a grenade? It sounded like a conventional war now, a pounding match. Had he been a dumb shit for believing the war would be guerrilla/counterguerrilla or were the generals full of shit now? Got me.

He drove home. He had the radio set on easy-listening music. Sometimes it soothed him. But then he liked rock pounding in his ears, Velvet Underground or Stones, when he drove fast. Maybe he should get a motorcycle. He had six calls tomorrow—Placentia, Fullerton, Santa Ana. He knew Judy'd give him shit for stopping at the Sandpiper, shooting the shit about things less boring than her—she got jealous of things he'd done beyond what she knew. But he drove home. Gotta have a home.

He was in a yin–yang nowhere orbit, his life and marriage full of mistakes, missing a war that was no good, driving pointlessly for sales and points and stamps, down off the mountain but he forgot what he'd learned there.

Phoebe covered both 1968 conventions, the Miami shoo-in of Nixon and the circus riot of Democrats in Chicago. In Miami she got air time with Nelson Rockefeller and various delegate chairmen, who explained why Nixon would win.

Between conventions they were pulled to New York to go over procedures for Chicago, which was expected to be a spectacle. The Yippies, or Youth International Party, had been founded two years earlier and had staged happenings around the East, such as skits mocking commuters at Grand Central Station. The Yippies promised to sing, dance, and stink bomb the Democratic Convention.

Of course, network could not show dog shit in living color when Yippies threw it at Chicago cops, nor could the affiliates run the tape feed of Chicago cops using nightsticks on Yippie faces, breaking noses and knocking out teeth.

When someone hits someone in the face with a nightstick, you see a basketball-size spray of bright blood and then more blood welling over lips and chins, down shirtfronts. If you can do slow motion, you see eyes bugging and sinking, cheeks distorting, and the blood in crimson strips arcing through the air. Those didn't air.

She got three minutes of a bewildered IBM executive named Philip Wayde in a blue cord suit and button-down-collar shirt waving his hands and blinking, trying to see, as he told how he'd been maced. He'd come out of a bar on the Near North Side when the police were chasing Yippies down the sidewalk. They were macing everyone and zapped him. "And I never gave a shit about politics!" he said. That didn't air.

Hubert Humphrey ran around to every reporter he could find, pleading in his hoarse voice that he truly did "*bleeve* in America! I *bleeve* in our promise! I *bleeve* poor people need a *piece of the action!*" He aired.

In Lincoln Park one afternoon Phoebe saw a familiar face in a group of people on a blanket. A large blonde in jeans and a cowboy shirt and a headband was looking at her as she lit a cigarette. "Phoebe?"

"Carole!" It was Carole Tiddens. She ran over. They hugged. "I'm working. What are you up to?"

"The Movement," she said. She looked radiant. One of her friends stared at the camera and Carole said, "She *is* TV news. Not the FBI."

"Stop anyway for a second," Phoebe told the cameraman. "How *are* you?"

"Wonderful. Really, Phoebe. This is fuckin' outasight. We fucked up two carloads of pigs last night. We got them to chase us up a one-way street. We're running and they're *speeding*. We had oil on the street at the corner. They spun out and did this *wham bam* into each other. They were so pissed off. It was like Keystone Kops."

"What are you doing otherwise?"

"I've been traveling a lot," she said. "Look, can you come back without those? Are you working all the time?"

"I'll have time later," Phoebe said. "I'll come back." But when she went back she couldn't find Carole. She asked others for Carole but nobody knew where she was, or wouldn't say.

At the end of the convention Chet North told Phoebe she could work the campaign if she wanted. The team would be run out of New York but would be on the road much of the time. "Could you do that?"

"Yes."

She followed Edmund Muskie and sometimes Hubert Humphrey. They had reports Richard Nixon had telephone boiler rooms
operating before election time with volunteers calling voters and telling how Humphrey was "soft on communism" and would appease the
Russians, who had invaded Czechoslovakia that April. They had reports he packed Humphrey crowds with long-haired demonstrators.
They couldn't confirm either. Nevertheless, few newsmen trusted
Nixon. After the election Chet North said network wanted her in
New York doing local news and being on call for national features,
and would she mind terribly moving to New York?

"I'd love to!"

When she got there Phoebe found the man she hated most in all
the world, Houston Bridles, and in time began planning to get even
with him.

She left KLQA in mid-November 1968 and went to Asheville for
Thanksgiving. Her father had lost more weight. He had loose red skin
and his hair was silky white. Her mother had wide freckles over the
backs of her hands from gardening.

They had settled into a decorous, lovely life that didn't appeal to
Phoebe one bit, enjoying their terrace, visiting the shops, going to
parties and giving them, visiting Charleston, Savannah, and Palm
Beach.

"We don't intend to go up there," her father said, meaning New
York. "It's probably ruined."

"Amanda says it's *just fine*," her mother said, clenching her jaw to
mimic Amanda being defensive. "She's always been stubborn."

"You will stay with her?"

"For the time being."

"Be careful. Even Park Avenue isn't safe now."

She went up the following week. The network and WNQY's
working offices weren't in the big office building with the logo near
MOMA but in a warren of yellow and red brick buildings, one-time
garages, on the West Side. To get there from Amanda's she had to
walk or take a crosstown bus and still walk, listening to the new
freedom of speech:

"Hey, you fuckin' bitch, shake you ass."

"Spare change."

"Pretty black hair, white bread, white bread."

"Fuck you, cunt."

The street talk had changed in nuance and texture from a few years ago. This had been an Irish, Polish, and Puerto Rican neighborhood but now groups of young angry blacks ranged through fighting and yelling. Nice people saw their conduct as a *cri de coeur*. She was making enough to take cabs whenever she wanted.

Not long after she reached New York she got a mysterious letter from Carole Tiddens, addressed to her c/o Aunt Amanda on Park Avenue but with no return address, postmarked Chicago:

Phoebe, I'm sorry I couldn't get back in touch with you in Chicago. It wouldn't have been a good idea then. Others were watching. I know you're okay, but government goons might have been tracking you. I didn't want you to risk my friends inadvertently. But I'm writing so you'll understand now.

Do you know how the Movement bifurcates after every crisis? How SNCC kicked out whites, who went into SDS, and SDS and Yippies and Peace and Freedom bifurcated after Chicago and the elections?

Phoebe, it's so *clear* the whole process is *rigged*, Daley pigs beating up everyone, the Democrats refusing to seat blacks and choosing that asshole Humphrey so Nixon could win after L.A. oil money killed Bobby Kennedy—it's so *fucked!* All the straight parties work for The Man.

I'm in what's called Weather. You'll hear about it. Think of Dylan's line that you don't need a weathervane to see how the wind is blowing. Phoebe, this is my destiny. It's in Bakunin, for Christ's sake. Have you read *God and State?* Didn't I mention it in New York? Maybe it was after you left for Vietnam. I'm sorry we fought then. Here's what happened to me—I was watching a lot of Eisenstein, Renoir, a lot of film about the end of the old order, and it was so *clear* that the answer for me is the Movement. The system's wrong, Phoebe, or we wouldn't have been treated so cruelly. If someone on the left of the Establishment like Peabody could be so cruel to me and go *unpunished*—so I'm here to destroy The Man.

I can't tell you where I am (the Midwest now, but I move around a lot), but you're going to see interesting

things from us, big as a prairie fire. I'm not here for Peace
Love Tie Dye—that's the shuck record companies use to
market our times and most people *want* to be jerked off
like that. We're going to bring Freedom and Justice. And
Fire. You'll see. When you hear 'Weather,' think of me.

Love ya—
C.

Phoebe thought she understood what Carole was saying but
wasn't sure. The other thing she flashed on, but couldn't analyze
then, was how their lives seemed to go in a spiral circle to the same
places at different angles—Carole from Midwest money, now somewhere out there planning to shatter the houses of money and power.

WQNY had a large operation with a couple of dozen on-camera
reporters handling local and some network stories, including three or
four women, so a little less cheap crap for Phoebe. The assignment
editor was Donna Gaffney, a pale, quiet person who chain-smoked
and made very quick decisions. She had soft brown eyes and nicotine-
stained teeth. She spent twelve-hour days at the assignment desk. She
said, "You probably know the city well from your days at *Life*," and
gave her a string of city stories to check her out.

When Phoebe was crossing the lobby of City Hall, a narrow,
graceful Federalist building, she saw Houston. He stood by the bottom of elegant stairs to the Mayor's wing, talking with a well-dressed
black woman. He wore a dark suit and held papers. His hair looked
copper blonde in the light, wavy and shiny; his face had not got puffy
or strained. He seemed, as usual, to be on top of things—a word to
someone passing by, a nod to someone else. He saw Phoebe, raised his
eyebrows—*So you are here, too, in my city?*—and smiled and waved her
toward him.

He went through the steps quickly and gracefully: "Hello, how
long have you been here?" and "Merreleese, say hello to Phoebe
Bishop. This is Dr. Merreleese Fuqua, who's the Mayor's Special
Assistant for Social Programs."

Dr. Fuqua leaned back an inch and breathed out through her
nostrils, looking at Phoebe. She was as tall as Houston, her head and
hands large, her forehead broad. Her skin was silky black brown, her
lips painted salmon pink. She wore glasses with enormous frames and
a brown-and-black suit. Her voice was low and pleasant. "How nice

to meet you," she said, her eyes running over Phoebe. As they talked about nothing in particular and her hand touched Houston's forearm, Phoebe knew they were sleeping together.

Houston had been having this affair for several weeks. It came to him like all his other games of love, not completely by chance but when he could do it right, like picking a ball out of the air.

They didn't work in the same office—he'd learned that much—but they did have adjacent spaces in City Hall and in the administration building a block away. She had briefed him on "The Social Picture."

"Hot Stuff!" he wrote in his journal. "The black oak!" It was never strictly business from the start; she had a smoldering way of looking at you and that trick some black career women had of trying, when they could, to challenge your self-esteem. "A B.A.?" she echoed. "But everyone else here has a B.A. just to start."

Houston smiled serenely. "I know you have a doctorate from, ah, Wayne State?"

Solves all your problems!

"You were allocating Great Society megabucks in Washington and they sent you up here only four times?"

"Of course Washington *is* a city, too," Houston said, grinning patiently.

Her nostrils flared, her lips moved powerfully like the flexing muscles of Valkyrie horses.

"Well, ah, you *are* an expert on all this, the poverty picture. I won't fake knowledge I don't have. So tell me." He put his hand on her shoulder, grinning. "Do it over a drink."

She drank Johnny Walker Black and soda.

"Let me *horrify* you to see how strong you are," she said. "Babies gettin' bit by rats. Young men throwin' someone else's baby out the window or beatin' their own to death 'cause they can't stand it cryin' in some shithole apartment—you hearin' me, Houston? Family breakin' their toilet to pieces in the *housin'* project and lettin' the water flood the rooms downstairs 'cause they so *mad* and frightened and penned up. Poor people don't lead happy, simple, carefree lives—get rid o' that shit—they are mean and scared and *confused*. Where do you cash your paycheck?"

"I, ah, have it deposited at the Bank of New York."

"If you poor, you can't *have* a bank account. A bank won't take you without a couple hundred dollars. You *get* a check, you pay twenty-five percent to have one of these shylock money shops cash it. Poor people get fucked over, extortionate rates, they gonna want easy money to get it back."

They had a couple of favorite places downtown off Park Row and they had a place they liked off Columbus Avenue. She lived at Amsterdam and Seventieth. He lived on Sutton Place. The building had a doorman. They made love at her place.

"I smoke pot with her," he wrote. "I like it."

"It's natural," she said. "Any Third World village has better highs and music than Chrome City." But she was every bit as aware of dress and hierarchy as he was. She had the right kind of attaché case, the right kind of office dress, the right kind of African rig for visiting the ghetto.

Her apartment was furnished in catchall middle-class academic—books and more books, records, a dowdy couch, Colonial armchairs—but she had good framed photos of blacks on the streets, Haitian appliqué, African carved wood. "You know blues?" she asked.

"I've heard some." He told her about going to the New Golden Gate in New Haven. "You were just a tourist," she said. She told him about griots—call-and-response slave songs—the pentatonic scale, and prison terms like "the midnight special."

Houston's mind was quick but thin. He didn't store information. She did. She was a tireless classifier, a taxonomical beaver. After Phoebe ran into them at City Hall, Merreleese spent the evening—indeed, became tiresome—classifying Phoebe.

"That's yo' ex-wife? She's not Locust Valley. Hudson Valley I can see. Doesn't try to be cute. Probably athletic. Did they have horses? Father's in the professions. Sure of herself. Only chile, right? You see how she hates you?"

"I saw nothing of the sort," Houston said.

"She smiles like she hates you," Merreleese said. "If you don't notice it you must be used to insincere people." And that was not all she said.

Houston's job as Assistant Deputy Mayor to John Lindsay was subtitled Projects Facilitator. He went over new programs with project heads, figured where money would come from, and got it somehow. The city at the time had what some considered a huge budget—a few billion—but with it Lindsay was trying to make New York the model city, the city where the American Dream could be realized, a city where people grew and the arts flourished.

God knows other cities didn't work—racist Birmingham; angry, tasteless Los Angeles; brawling, bigoted, corrupt Chicago, epitomized by Mayor Daley yelling, "Fuck you, ya fuck!" at Abe Ribicoff at the clownish Democratic Convention. In San Francisco, cops busted artists. New York welcomed them. In Detroit, cops beat up poor blacks. New York welcomed them. Indeed, the city agencies sent scouts south to encourage poor blacks to move to New York, where they could be safe, vote, and go on welfare.

"More grassroots control!" community activists demanded, in keeping with the Mao style of the times, so Lindsay formed community boards to watch over neighborhoods. He decentralized education so community school boards had a say in administration and curriculum.

"I want to take power away from the power brokers and make our city serve everyone," Lindsay said when he was first running for office in 1965, when the big war was just starting. New York was to be Fun City, the city of the American Dream.

What had happened by the time Houston got there was what had happened to the American Dream elsewhere. Immediately after Lindsay took office, vowing to break the hold of the power brokers, Mike Quill led a transit strike that tied up the city. It cost billions in lost business and wasn't settled until Lindsay gave out increases costing $70 million.

Quill, an Irish-born warrior, thought that Lindsay, a Yale-educated lawyer, was just another Ivy League twit. He called him "Linsley," deliberately mispronouncing his name.

It may have had something to do with the way Lindsay walked through Harlem during the campaign in Topsiders, wash pants, and open button-down-collar shirt, blazer slung over his shoulder; or it may have been Lindsay's referring to his time at Andover as "high school." Or it may have been another element of the times—racism. Quill hated Lindsay because he was a WASP; hated him so much he had a heart attack.

The old Irish leadership of the unions was inherently racist. The building trades union referred to blacks as "eggplants" and wouldn't hire them. Blacks, Hispanics, and others demanded a share of the Jewish bureau, the Board of Education. Police, firemen, and sanitation men, inspired by the transit workers, struck in turn and got more money. Although cops, teachers, and other public employees tended to be middle class, they used the confrontational tactics of the poor and desperate to get a bigger share, which put more pressure on the eggplants, which in turn caused their leaders and demagogues to threaten more fire next time.

"One of the things that was cool about New York was ethnic politics," Merrie said. "Let a black man like Jack be borough president, let the Greeks run the coffee shops, Italians handle garbage, blacks run numbers—but we got more voters now, and someone's got to move over, someone who's already moved to the suburbs."

The city's Job Corps program lost $10 million down the tubes. It trained no disadvantaged youth. Many used the money to score dope. The city's program to help apartment-fire victims wasted millions. Welfare families knew they could get a $6,000 grant to replace furniture and clothing lost in a fire, so they torched their apartments.

A term used in those days was "open-ended commitment." It went back to John Kennedy's stirring promise: "We shall pay any price, bear any burden. . . ." Another disappointment to the high-minded. The expensive programs weren't working and it wasn't Fun City. The parks were dangerous, the streets more so. The Patrolmen's Benevolent Association defeated Lindsay's efforts at civil service reform so that bad cops couldn't be thrown out; one was promoted and killed an eminent psychologist in front of Aunt Amanda's. The transit union was ready to strike again, regardless of the damage it would do to the city or its own image. Houston saw the situation as old thirties labor leaders fighting their old battles like Pa, without even listening to a voice from the present.

"But, like Pa, they should just be endured," he wrote in his journal. "It's unthinkable to try to break a union."

To find the revenue to pay all the bills for welfare burnouts and community board salaries and city worker wage hikes, Houston looked for tax revenue allocations, federal revenue sharing, and the kind of money New York was using more often these days, paper—Bond Anticipation Notes, Revenue Anticipation Notes, and Tax Anticipation Notes (BANs, RANs, and TANs)—issued like shylock loans in advance of money coming in.

The paper was not only shaky but spurious. Many times the city issued notes for more millions than it could rationally expect in taxes. Businesses weren't paying taxes. They were fleeing because the city was too dangerous and expensive.

Another gimmick the city and Houston used was the magic window, the month-long gap between the ends of the state's and city's fiscal years. This allowed the city to roll over some debts. Houston worked with Abe Beame, then comptroller, on ways to pace the application of paper. One way Houston used that would have horrified his New England ancestors: raiding capital—using capital funds meant to repair streets for paying current welfare expenses. But on all sides people demanded more money from any source to alleviate suffering. "Get it from the Department of Defense!" one city councilman screamed. "We have people *starving* while they waste *billions* in that immoral war!"

"It is the will of the people, and if not the people, the Mayor, to do this," Houston wrote in his journal. "And I do not intend to blow my chance for appointments by caviling over the source of funds when the game is already being played this way. God knows Horace Fraker must have found it calmer in Chester Arthur's administration."

Anyway, he was running the notes through Stu's chums so the handling and carrying fees, which were enormous, millions, went to members of the financial community to which he expected to return. "A good arrangement all around!" he wrote cheerily.

"I saw your ex-wife on the TV last night," Merreleese told Houston at City Hall.

"Yes, I suppose she's getting on a lot."

"You still feel for her?"

"She ticks me off royally," Houston said.

"She's bright."

"I know."

"You must have made quite a couple. Vassar and Yale. Did you *think* about bein' part of a set?"

"I assumed we were."

"Why we doin' this?"

"Ask yourself," Houston said. "I get a kick out of you. I love your dark passion. Baudelaire had the right idea. I like your art, Merrie. I like what you know, what you tell me, your, ah, grasp . . ."

He liked her *chocolat-amer* color, her slightly rough skin, the trail of wire hairs from her navel and her conical breasts that shot out like the ogives of rockets, the depth of her power when she came. Others paled by comparison. He liked her intelligence.

She batted aside what he said, her calm brown eyes on him, and said, "So what do you want from me?"

"I want to grow up," he said.

"I suppose you mean that, too. I can't understand what the *style* is you get in the Ivy League, all you men cuttin' your hair like little boys, dressin' like prep school boys, talkin' squeakin' like little boys."

"Watch what I do," he said. "I have the moves. John doesn't have *anyone* who can move through committee and funding boards faster."

"I know. That's what I want you to show *me*," she said.

That was the game. They were *machers* on the way up to being mandarins and she was great fun in the meantime. "Fine woman," he wrote in his journal. "So fine."

Her father was a minister in Detroit, her mother a teacher. Merrie was *big*. She weighed 135. At times her passion, her emotional force, was so heady he felt he'd lose balance and tailspin into—what? He'd heard it had happened to white men before, particularly men like him, always on view—he could go crazy in passion for her, lust, hedonism, dope and music, those nights on the copper-satin covered bed, listening to Otis Redding—except she was a career woman too, so they always had to get up and ride the subway down to City Hall.

In the flat gray light of city business he noticed her prickly public traits, which irritated him all the more since he was such a smooth public man—the way she used bureaucratese out there as opposed to her colorful, direct private speech, strong as black coffee. The way she tried to win points by the force of her considerable personality.

She loved to start scenes, banking that most men would retreat, murmuring politely, rather than be shouted at in public. One scene she started was about a meeting he'd called that she wanted rescheduled, so she argued in public.

"Why didn't you give me advance input on this?" she shouted after him in the polished corridor upstairs, by the Council Chamber; she pursued him, her shoes clattering. "You got to touch base! Coordinate! Wait!"

Houston had stayed cool facing louder roars in the Yale Bowl and looking down Lyndon Johnson's big mouth. He wouldn't be perturbed and threw it back at her in her own bureaucratese. "You were properly minuted! Check the routing ladder!"

The scene that blew it started in City Hall and carried across the grass and down Park Row. She yelled at him because she'd suggested a trip to Martha's Vineyard; *he* said he didn't want to go because it was too middle class; *she* said, "That mean they have trouble with *me?*" and *he* said, "No, I mean it's dull middle class. Cutesy and dumb."

She said, "Okay, but *I* wanta go there!"

"Impossible."

It was his calmness as much as his refusal that touched her lioness nerve. *"Who you think you are?"* she yelled at him on the sidewalk under the plane trees.

He crisply said, "I'm your lover man, but I still don't want to go!"

They yelled, they kissed, they yelled again.

Old Pa Bridles was beetling his way along toward City Hall, cursing the world since 1945, and heard the rich black voice running the scales of desire and anger, but he had other things on his mind. Nixon was in office, and though he was not an ignorant yawp like Johnson, he had another agenda and his own supporters. He didn't trust Easterners, either.

Didn't rely on Agency advisors. Had his own friends. Dangerous ones. Erlichman, Haldeman, threatening some people with dismissal or postings to Canada or Australia. Dangerous.

It upset him a good deal.

He saw the couple arguing ahead. Decline of decorum, dignity in public conduct, nothing taught in the schools anymore, black woman making far too much noise, statuesque—he squinted, making out her structural magnificence—and the white man, sandy-reddish hair, crisp high voice. Kissing—separating.

My God! Houston!

His blood rose, roaring in his head and throat. His legs and arms didn't respond. He watched the ground come up and felt it smack him in his pinched face before he went out.

Adams Peabody was crossing Sproul Plaza in the sunlight when he saw the girl handing out peace leaflets. She wore a simple granny dress with small pink flowers. She had pretty features, a high forehead, honey blonde hair pulled back around a bone. She was thin, girlish, and had a catch in her voice.

"Take this, w-will you *please?* It's very i-important."

He thought the catch in her voice was disarming. Appealing. So sincere, honest, warm. Genuine. She *believed*.

"It's important to *me*, too," he said in a low voice, the way he reassured students on the right track. "But I know that one by heart." He smiled at her, the sun picking out the wonderful tangle of his beard and mane of hair, glinting on the brass shapes of his heavy belt buckle, on his round, brass-framed Trotsky glasses. "Like, I've been busted for this."

"You *have?* I-I'm just a freshman!" she said.

Her name was Kimberley Sutton. She was from Sacramento. "I-It's an o-old California family," she said. She was very impressed to learn who he was, and to connect with news photos of him being carried off at the Pentagon.

"P-People like you are why I wanted to come to Cal and not Mills. Or Scripps."

Peabody's nose for people who had money twitched at the mention of those expensive private schools. He asked her discreetly about her family. Her father was a lawyer. They had land. She wore elfin little high shoes of glove leather that must have cost two hundred dollars.

"My family's been in Mass awhile, too," he said. "But the East is fucked, of course. I want to teach here. Spreading the truth is more important than making millions with *IBM*," he said.

"Oh! Yes! I u-used to *ride* and I was pretty good at dressage? B-But that's *so* expensive! Selfish. It's all *behind* me now." She nodded. "I believe in the s-struggle."

"Yeah. It's war. Look, do you want to get a pot of tea somewhere? Or a glass of wine?"

Phoebe Bishop got the envelope on good gray rice paper addressed in calligraphy with plum-dark ink. The invitation was calligraphy, too:

ʼΑΓΆΠΗ

Witness

Share Our Vows and Celebrate with Our Union

Kimberley and Adams

Noon

March 10, 1969 [ye ram]

The Flower Meadow

Cerro Verde, California

Participatory

Phoebe decided to go. She had nothing else to do that weekend, her emotional life was still shit, and she supposed it was her kharma to see things twice in the sixties. Two Peabody weddings, two Kennedys shot, two great black leaders shot, two city riots, etc. She hadn't heard from Peas for months; both of them had been busy. She didn't know Kimberley. She'd called to get directions and Peas said, "She's from an old California family."

That was a California name, all right—she didn't know about Sutton, but Kimberley as a first name. She'd seen so many California girls given trade names like that: Tiffany, Morgan, Avis.

Looking down before the wing, she saw winter green on the breast-round hills ribboned with freeways, squared and glittering with parking lots. She hated California. Back a second time. King and Malcolm X.

They landed at Oakland. She was met not by one or two revelers but a VW van load—Peas and this pretty, dainty girl in a flower dress, speaking in a soft voice with a catch; a loud, long-haired professor named Bracken, who had a fierce grin like Teddy Roosevelt; two undergraduate women friends of Kimberley and another couple from California State College, where Peas had just begun teaching; and in the back of the bus, Mark Randolph and a dark-haired woman in some kind of graduate school sack clothes and leather bands. It took a moment for Phoebe to recognize him behind a moustache.

They drove a long time, laughing and bantering about the wedding, the charm of Northern California versus Southern California trash, courses, quals, Nixon the fascist, and the university.

"It's a g-groovy place," Kimberley said. "They have r-rap groups instead of structured *classes*. It's not l-*linear*."

"They're cool about lots of things," Peas said. "They know we younger faculty are in the Movement and have constituencies and they give us a platform."

"T-They're just landscaping the c-campus *now*."

They drove into a small dusty town shaded by eucalyptus, live oak, and ambar, and stopped at a small wooden green-painted twenties house with a porch. Other revelers sat there. Glasses of wine stood on the rail. Fat-leafed jade plants in wooden buckets. Wind chimes. The music was Crosby, Stills, and Nash. Phoebe flashed on the terrace at Fence seven years ago. The man at the center now was Peabody, the bridegroom shining in his well-brushed, wondrously flying beard and hair, his glasses and tight shirt, heavy buckle and faded jeans, and his delicate, pretty girl bride, the hero of many demonstrations, ready to settle down teaching.

Phoebe was an incurable snoop but had been brought up so well no one noticed. She murmured greetings, smiled, played modest to someone who *did* recognize her, and slid inside to use the bathroom.

It was a lovely cottage, and no academic poverty about it. A heavy low teak table, good fiber wall hangings, Indian throw rugs. In the john she opened drawers and saw Peabody's English razor and wooden hairbrushes and Kimberley's generous collection of little bottles of scent and splash. The john reading was Hinton's *FanShen* and Fanon's *Wretched of the Earth*. Inside the door, under a rough cotton robe, was a red-printed broadside titled "The Berkeley Manifesto," calling on all the poor and oppressed like Peas and Kimberley to take over the system from the capitalist exploiters.

This would certainly be a different arrangement from Peabody's other wedding, but so many of the elements were the same. She doubted she'd get laid but didn't feel like it anyway.

She joined the noisy group lounging on the floor, couches, and cushions listening to music, drinking wine, passing around joints, talking. Peas told about his dissertation.

"It's called *The Long Barrel: A Study of World War Two Fiction*," Peas said. "It's a—I *hope*—the *definitive* look at the myths that I'm sure led to our fucking outrages in Vietnam—"

Phoebe noticed that when he talked about it, his voice deepened and he became, not passionate, but pedantic, arch. He sounded as musty as he had years ago at Columbia.

"The title's a play on Styron's Long March, of course, but alludes also to the, ha, *phallic* obsession of the fascist colonel in *The Naked and the Dead*. Of course, Fenton's anthology—he's another Yale man—

tells us about the social and political implications of the Army. For instance, *New Yorker* stories made it part of the New Deal, a home for lost souls. And Harry *Brown*—also a *New Yorker* writer—has men *vying* to take command as sergeant in *A Walk in the Sun*. But this was all before we saw *all* ground for elitism and heroism *destroyed*. There can be no military heroes now—"

"H-His *father* was killed in the war."

"You should read Che Guevera," Peabody said. "He does *away* with sergeants' ranks because they're petty tyrants."

Peabody seemed so sure of himself now, and Kimberley was such a believer. The others were laughing and getting ripped.

They pinched out their joints when Kimberley's parents dropped by and resumed the party with a succession of small munchie dishes. Mark Randolph and his girl, Jeanie, cooked some of them. Mark stayed in the kitchen. Phoebe saw he wasn't eager to talk to her.

Peas told her, "Mark's marriage fell apart. He's going to graduate school nights and working at some sales job in the daytime. The GI Bill. Do you know what he gets? A hundred dollars an hour! Jeanie's in Psych."

The loud one who looked like Teddy Roosevelt, Bracken, told a hilarious story about all the times he'd been busted in the Army and sent to the stockade. "I told this officer, 'Fuck you!' I had a master's! I wasn't going to take shit from someone with only a B.A."

"What do you think about that, Mark?" Peas said. "Mark *was* an officer," he explained to the others.

"I think I'm glad I wasn't in the Army," Mark said.

Someone said, "I heard from this one guy who was over there. He said he was *stoned* all the time."

"He probably was," Mark said. "I heard from a lot of guys who were stoned all the time. One time this other ex-Marine who'd been at Hue and I listened to a guy talking about how he was always stoned. He said, 'Oh, man, I was, oh, man, so *stoned* and I walked through this LZ and mortar rounds were landing and I was so *stoned*—' The other Marine looked at me. We're trying to figure out why this dude's alive. He said, 'I wouldn't do that,' and I said, 'Neither would I.' "

"What's he mean by that?" one of the others said.

Bracken was talking radical action and Mark said, "Hey, Bill, I wouldn't be in uniform with you 'cause you sound like a shitbird—but suppose you wanted to topple injustice. Would you give a talk or blow up a police station?"

"Waste the pigs," Bracken said, laughing.

"You better get someone who knows how to do it, then. Amateurs blow themselves up or get shot on the way in."

No, Phoebe wouldn't get laid. Her period started. She didn't guess it until it was too late and she'd spotted the couch. "Oh, shit!" she said.

"Cut your hand?" Bracken said, giving his Teddy Roosevelt grin.

"Here," Jeanie said. "Come with me."

From the john she heard Randolph saying, "I had a black NCO who called Kotex 'beanos.' "

"Beanos? Why?"

"Be no sex tonight," he said, heehawing with laughter.

"Oh, Jesus," Jeanie said.

"Have you been with him long?"

"This term," she said. Their eyes met. "He's my rehabilitation project."

"Is it much work?"

"Well, you must have noticed this male cultural and experiential bias. We were at a party and a with-it sort of minister asked him what he'd done in Vietnam and Mark said something about infantry, and the minister pointed his fingers like a kid playing guns and went, 'Agkagkagkagk?'—and Mark said, 'How do I answer *that?*'

"And I told him, 'You just have to understand no one's going to explicate or integrate it for you. Don't blame him.' I have him reading *Civilization and Its Discontents*, too."

"I'm ready," Phoebe said. They went out into the big room.

Someone complimented Jeanie's empanadas. Jeanie said she'd been in Ecuador hiking and listening to Indian music. "I dressed like Peace Corps," she said. "You know—black sweater. But I *wasn't*. I still feel guilty about that." This made Bracken laugh.

Phoebe helped Kimberley make cookies. When heat flooded from the oven, Kimberley blew air up over her forehead and looked at the ceiling—a self-conscious pretty gesture, Phoebe thought bitchily. She's a *tchotchke*, a trinket. Peabody's gone from Trotskyism to tchotchkeism.

It was like summer camp, staying up late and talking and snacking.

In the morning Phoebe woke to the chatter of many voices. People were laughing and singing outside. It was sunny and mild. They had coffee and no-preservative sweet rolls, which were stale, and worked outside plaiting cut flowers into a long chain. The men wore clean faded Levi's and flared trousers and long shirts, the women long dresses and miniskirts or Sergeant Pepper dresses with frogs and braid.

Kimberley said, "One of the d-definitive parts of Peas's dissertation is his treatment of u-*uniforms*."

Peas said, "Men won't have anything to do with military stuff now, but women can wear the old nineteenth-century Sergeant Pepper things as nostalgia for the light opera times before the Somme, before Owen and Sassoon. Before the Fossalta and Hemingway. Before the machine of war. Armies didn't take industrial-strength casualties then."

"Heavy line, man," Bracken said.

"If they'd only try to reduce the l-level of *violence*."

"It's time," Peas said.

They got in cars and vans and drove up a valley to the next town, the pretty village called Cerro Verde. The meadow was on a hillside by a line of live oaks. The Unitarian minister wore a blue turtleneck.

Kimberley and Adams walked to the center of the meadow and the rest of them carried the ten-foot-long plait of flowers and stood around them. One of the women played a medieval piece on her recorder. Peas and Kimberley recited vows they had written.

"You kids," Kimberley's mother said. "Joe and I wish *we* were your age in this time. We hope you'll have freedom and love and all the things in 'Desiderata.' "

"I pledge to love Kimberley and work for justice and peace," Adams said. "It is a year after Tet. Our brothers are still in chains."

Jets from Travis Air Force Base or Livermore Naval Air Station blustered across the sky far overhead.

"We can all work for peace and justice," the minister said.

"We want to work, l-live, and l-love, just as F-Freud said."

"You are so lucky to have found each other, to give and receive love," Phoebe said.

Mark said, "May you have peaceful and untroubled lives."

"And love and happiness," Jeanie said.

Phoebe flew back to New York that night. Her emotional life was still shit. She couldn't understand why. She'd chased the big events.

A jockfucker, Carole had called her. But the men of events had treated her terribly or the events had themselves. Houston, her star, had kicked her in the teeth. His miscarried baby had been the Dark Star that pulled her into severe depression. Her family went funny like that, brooding, developing delusions, shrinking, narrowing, like Constance in Asheville bustling about her garden parties and remembering her time as a "bud," or Amanda in New York talking about a luminous time that may never have existed.

Were those black street dudes right when they rapped "white bread" at her? White bread, inbred? So used to the kind of boy she'd met in dance class and school that anyone different had seemed unacceptable? Mark Randolph had been all wrong, too simple once, too crude, too bloodstained now, lost. Jim Robinson had been exotic, unsanitary. Dead.

She knew from the hints her body gave her that she could only respond to a certain kind of man now. She wanted a man who wasn't going to push on like Houston, Mark, Jim. Someone she could keep. What kind of woman was she? She thought in a flash of Freud's American patients; Eliot's lady in the portrait, unloved; Prufrock's unsatisfied women.

Her salvation was work—or was it? Most of the time she did daily stories, trying to chop the truth into daily segments, even though events and big stories developed over long periods and ran on and on. As always, she loved the big events, pulsed to what was happening— but feared the kind of man who'd take over the events. Wanted a man, needed, hoped, feared; cramped in work, unfettered and empty by herself. Christ! She smoked cigarettes and drank coffee from the plastic airline cup and watched the lights of unknown cities below.

When she went back to work the next day, Donna Gaffney, the assignment editor, gave her the assignment that broke open her life.

"I want you to cover the spy dinner," Donna said.

Old Spooks' Soiree

It was the annual dinner of the OSS alumni. "Is this dinner a social fossil?" Donna asked. "A fraternity dinner? See if you can get some coming out drunk and have them comment on intelligence disasters now, like losing the *Pueblo.*"

"Bay of Pigs?" Phoebe asked. "Some of them must have been in on that."

"Try it." Donna's fingers were stained with nicotine and her eyes were red. "I had half a bottle of Scotch last night working this out. You're the one who can get it, Phoebe. They won't talk to a man. You can distract them. They'll want to impress you. You have the right voice and accent. Dress for it, keep the crew back, then rush in and shoot."

It was black tie at the Waldorf. Correct, businesslike, not the absolute best. These were well-connected adventurers. Houston's father, as everyone knew, had been one and had parachuted into France.

They rode in a wagon to the Park Avenue entrance. She had the crew wait in the round vestibule while she scouted the blue Art Deco lobby and side rooms. She saw the black flock ahead and stalked down the carpeted corridor in impeccable green silk, smiling and murmuring throaty, well-bred, you-might-be-able-to-fuck-me greetings to the middle-aged men in black with gold studs and watches, their eyes—spy eyes, strategy eyes, killers' eyes—turning toward her.

They were the most bizarre group of men she had ever seen.

One was very tall and wore a French "smoking" with one empty sleeve pinned up. Another had an eye patch. One was short and jovial and talked like a Rotarian. Some had the dry, watchful expression of bureaucrats with lethal powers and watched her suspiciously. Some had the smooth, healthy skin, good hair, perfect tailoring, and easy gestures of the rich. Some looked like thugs, black tie or not.

She gave her widest smiles, acted as if she knew someone there, jostled this one and traded remarks with that one, let all of them get ideas. They were having a break between the fruit and the cigars, port, and brandy. She saw Mr. Bridles hunched over by the end of the corridor, making a vague, wintry smile, and guessed he couldn't see or recognize her. She thought he was in the bag.

A pleasant, bald-headed man who'd been in China and now taught history said a few words on camera. A red-faced man with a silky voice, now a banker, said into the lens, "It remains to be seen whether the American government has the spine to manage its destiny as it did in our time."

"Do you mean in Vietnam?" She'd been trying to find someone to comment on the OSS mission that aided Ho Chi Minh when the Viet Minh rescued American aircrew and spied on the Japanese and Vichy French.

"I mean everywhere. But we're here to celebrate a victory— something *we* did right."

"Hear, hear," another said.

She heard conversation in German, French, and what she believed was a Slavic language. It looked like a banquet for Fencies, Porcellians, and European gangsters. She got two more quotes, not very good, a thin story, but two minutes, thirty seconds' worth, when one of the men in black tie approached her. He had well-cut hair, well-tended hands, tanned skin. Grasping her as if shaking hands, smiling, he firmly propelled her backward, past the Waldorf's display case, moving so deftly the camera couldn't pick up his force, and his speech couldn't be aired, either.

"Private function, my dear—don't carry on like a barging slut, please." As he pushed her back, the French doors closed on the spies in black sidling to their tables.

"She's no barging slut!" a young man said off to the side. "She's my Aunt Phoebe!"

The polished bouncer nodded to him. "Perhaps you can escort

her, then," he said, and wheeled about and walked into the banquet.

She looked at the kid in the alcove—a boy of nineteen or twenty in black tie, skinny, his face radiant, with loose long blondish-reddish hair curling softly around his ears. Her stomach dropped and her skin tingled. Her earlobes and lips swelled. Indeed, her nipples popped and rubbed deliciously against the green silk enough to show on camera and her pants went soppy. Her toes curled. But who *was* he?

He grinned, one side of his mouth higher than the other. On a tennis court. Against green. "Remember me, Phoebe? Sam Hicks. Tony's—Houston's—nephew."

"It's okay!" she called to the cameraman. "Don't shoot him. He's not a spy." She blushed. Surely he could read everything running about inside her the way she could read his curiosity, his confidence, his recklessness.

"What are *you* doing here?"

"I'm baby-sitting Grandpa. Did you see him?"

"Down the hall." She couldn't be cool with him—he was too *young*. She leaned toward him. She was flushed and knew her eyes must have been feverish. "You *can't* think I'd say hello to him?"

"He wouldn't recognize you," Sam said. "He's had a stroke."

"I'm sorry to hear that."

"I'm sorry to hear that, thank you." His eyes were mischievous.

"Oh, shut up. When did he have the stroke?"

"Months ago. He found out Uncle Tony was shacked up with a black woman. It was intense for a while. It took the pressure off Ma and me, though. She'd wasted another wad of money and I'd got in trouble with drugs."

"Were you arrested?"

"Don't be silly. Bridleses are not arrested. There was a disagreement about a lid in the beach house and Ma ratted on me. And she'd *used* some of it! Look, are you doing anything now?"

"Oh, no, Sam, I always walk around hotels with a camera and sound man. I have to put this together. For the eleven o'clock."

"Let me watch."

A man in black tie stood blocking the French doors, a good backdrop, and she stood by him and gave a quick stand-up summary.

"Listen, I'll come to the studio," he said. "Grandpa'll be in bed by then. He can only stay a few more minutes. I'll drop him at the Harvard Club and be over."

He was very breezy and sure of himself.

At that time she had an apartment at Eightieth and Lexington. It was a brownstone walk-up, no doorman. This is absolutely silly, she thought as she opened the front door and led this kid up the stairs. A door opened in the hall, the woman in 2-B looked out, saw her—whom she knew on television—with this skinny boy in black tie, and smiled and closed the door.

"I can offer you a drink or a joint," she said.

"I have some terrific stuff," he said.

She put *Chicago Transit Authority* on the record player and lit a candle. He had that young grin. "I like a big-band sound," she said.

"Let me help you," he said. She wasn't doing anything that needed help. He just put his arms around her and kissed her.

"Hey. Do you know what you're doing?"

"Yes." They went to bed.

They listened to records. He showed her the plastic bag trick, a silly bit of psychedelia, tying it in knots, lighting it, and watching in the dark as flaming drops fell with a moog sound. He opened a window because the fumes were dangerous, and the cold air refreshed them. He told her about Brown, which he called Camp Bruno. He was a sophomore. They made love again, and early in the morning, just before dawn, while the men clattered garbage cans, yet again he pressed into her.

In the morning they were just grinning at each other. What was the basis of their relationship? She didn't want to think. It must have been lust between appropriate people.

And she couldn't be afraid with him, could she? He was too young, untouched by ugliness.

"I have to get back," he said. "I'm driving Grandpa back at eight."

She walked with delicious difficulty that day. She was sore all the way up to her tonsils. He called her that afternoon from Boston. They met the next weekend. He had guest privileges at the Harvard Club—they had drinks there—but stayed at her place. They walked all over. He wore jeans and an army jacket. She wore jeans and big shades and a black El Gallo hat so no one would recognize her. They walked in Central Park, smoked a joint, took a carriage ride. He had his hand under the blanket caressing her as they clopped past the Sherry Netherland. She didn't care; it was all new to her.

He was so thin, so nonmacho, so pleasing and cheerful. Perhaps he was the only man she could have loved.

Houston's Journal, April 8, 1969, Boston

> Visited father today. Looks very bad. Trembling, chewing lip, speaking in a stream of fucks, motherfucks, German oaths, and strange bits that must have something to do with the Agency—phrases about Cuba and mafiosi and killing Kennedy—though he didn't say specifics and I certainly don't want to know. No one in the family should know.

"It must be lust," Phoebe said.

"Don't analyze—your superego's too strong," Sam said. "Use it to dominate me." He was lying in the bathtub and she was giving him a bath. "Just do what you want." He put his hands behind his head and looked at the ceiling. "Oh, Jeez, do more of that! Ohhhh!"

She watched him thrashing like some fish she'd caught and couldn't stay analytical. She climbed into the tub with him. They put an inch of water on the floor and the woman downstairs knocked on her ceiling.

"You sang," he said.

"What?"

"This time you sang. I used to hear you and Uncle Tony. On the shore. When you came you'd hit a high note."

"Oh, brother. Where were *you?* On the porch?"

"No. In my room. Keeping pace with you. Like this."

"Sam."

"How do *you* do it?"

"I don't want to shock you."

"You won't."

"This way. And that. And sometimes, this. . . ." His eyes widened; her instincts worked as they did on camera. After all, she was a performer as well as a bearer of information. "And a little of this, and then . . . this!" He leaned forward. She felt power knowing he was going gaga, his mouth open. She could have been Aphrodite before a mortal worshipper.

"Oh!" he moaned, made a little sound, and fell on his knees. His arms surrounded her and his tongue shot into her like fire.

"How loud was I, Sam?"

"Loud enough."

"I mean then. Did anyone else hear?"

"I think so. Not Grandpa. His ears went bad parachuting into France. That's how he became impotent, too."

"He did?"

"That's what I heard obliquely from Ma. Helen—Grandma—probably hasn't had a good lay since before Tony was born."

"Do you come from a happy family, Sam?"

"I come from an important family."

By now they were lying on the new bed she'd got, on the soft vicūna Indian-weave spread, and he was stroking her with a peacock feather. He gave her a sugar cube and said, "Take this."

"I don't trust acid anymore. The mob's ruined it. They adulterate it with smack and speed. In *my* day you could get good acid."

"It's not acid, it's THC."

"I've never tried it."

"It's fine."

"I don't feel anything," she said. Then it was like stepping into another room. Suddenly they were up there. "How long have we *been* here?" she said.

"*Hours*," he said.

"I have brownies in the refrigerator."

"Let's send out for Chinese," he said. "I can answer the door in drag. In your underwear."

The Chinese man didn't think it was funny but they were rolling on the floor.

She didn't know what Sam learned about psychology at Camp Bruno, but he seemed to know everything about sex, drugs, and rock and roll.

"The thing is to stay away from mob drugs," he said. "Pot is power to the people. That's why the Mafia doesn't like it—they want alcohol and smack put out, addictive stuff, so they can take over the suburbs. They're all Republicans. We have sunshine vitamins here."

They smoked rosebuds and ate morning glory seeds. They chewed magic mushrooms that he got walking over cow pastures after a rain, and felt stoned and short of breath, so they panted at the window, watching people walking like turtles on Lex. They smoked varieties of cannabis from tarry hash, which burned their throats and made them soar like eagles, to Indiana Ditch that left them coughing and hyperventilated and Sam cursing the classmate who'd sold it to him.

She provided high-grade Jamaican ganja that one of the editors sold. Sam brought in a few pills, too—yellowjackets, reds, and dexies—but they stayed away from pills. Pills were for suburbanites who fumed about long-haired people using drugs.

They dressed up and went out on the town. She wore black and shades to the Russian Tea Room, and nondescript shawls and jeans to the Village and to walk across the dangerous jungle of the park to the frightening, rundown Upper West Side to look at old buildings like the Apthorp—wow!

One time they were walking around Murray Hill in shades and hooded jackets, when Sam pulled her into a doorway. "Shhh! It's Ma!"

Across the way they saw Edith, Sam's mother, in a long opera cape and shades, skulking out of the Hotel Tuscany like Anna Karenina, looking both ways.

Sam laughed against her shoulder. "Hah! She's been having a *cinq à sept!*"

"Why's she sneak around?"

"John, my father, will zap her child support if he thinks she's playing around. He's a real prick. He wants her to use a dildo. She does, too—I found it. She really got mad about it."

She watched Sam's mother striding past the narrow brick townhouses in shadow from the weak sun, looking around while trying to maintain dignity. Her hair, bound with a headband, was shot through with gray.

"Who's her boyfriend?"

"God knows. She can't keep them."

Phoebe pressed his hand against her breast. "It's cold," she said. "Let's move." She was afraid.

That spring WNQY got its first minicams, even smaller than the ones used at the convention. Now they did most stories on tape, which meant they could shoot up to just before time to get back to the studio. She could figure her cues in the car and edit the tape on the console if it were hot. For big stories they'd have a van on the scene and could dump there or use its power and go live remote.

Within a certain range, you could cover any city story right now

faster and better than newspapers, and between work and being in
bed with Sam, sometimes she felt real life was stepping through television screens. They'd lie in bed and watch Phoebe on tape if she had
a feature over the weekend, or they'd see President Nixon talking in
his heavy-browed faggy gangster way, and more on the war, always
the green-brown pictures of things she'd seen years ago still going on,
and Sam, watching intently, and city stories of shootings, fire, black
awareness, Puerto Rican pride, hard hats beating up peace freaks,
Mayor Lindsay announcing programs to give communities autonomy,
to increase welfare entitlements, to provide grants for people in
burned-out tenements, and Abe Beame, the comptroller, telling where
the money would come from, this issue of notes or that magic way of
delaying payment, with the approval of Governor Rockefeller, who
also came on the tube, announcing new, megabillion-dollar programs
for the state universities, highways, and buildings in Albany.

Sometimes Houston was on camera looking over Lindsay's shoulder as he signed a directive setting up a program. So was Dr. Merreleese Fuqua, his mistress. Sam said that when Pa Bridles stroked out
seeing them kissing, "he was probably *jealous*—you know Boston
WASPs have *fantasies* about having black mistresses, and Tony's got
the balls to do it. I don't think Grandpa ever kissed *Helen* in public."

"Why'd they get married?"

"I heard he wanted to get even with Stu. Stu had taken her out.
But he was off touring the West, playing polo. And either of them was
a good catch, so Helen took what she could. The Frakers wanted to
marry one of us anyway because we have contiguous lands on The
Point. Have you seen The Point?"

"Yes."

"Grandpa told me I'm going to get it. We should go sailing this
summer."

"Sure."

He leaned over her. "What's the matter?"

"Nothing."

"Well, then, let's go sailing this summer." He looked so vulner-
able. He wanted her to say yes, as in a pretend game. He had been
sheltered, and he showed a hothouse nervousness when he didn't have
a clear role. His pale hair fluffed out all around his head, like an
angel's, light, his eyes wide open. "Phoebe! What's the matter? Why
do you have that tone of voice?"

"I don't want to go up there."

"It's not bad."

She had been there nearly ten years before. "Sam! I'll be thirty next summer."

"So what?"

"You know perfectly well so what!"

"I do not. People live beyond thirty."

"Look at this, Sam." She opened her robe. "Look in the eye of the camera, Sam. *This* doesn't change but only *we* know. *These* change. They are changing already." She held up her hands. "These change too. My eyes change. My face changes. I am hanging heavy and ripe on the tree, Sam. I will fall."

He shook his head.

"Sam, why are we in love?"

"We feel every limit of joy."

"We get stoned and eat each other and try new ways to come."

"We talk. We watch Nixon!" His face flushed. "Phoebe!"

"I don't want to be cruel," she said. She was crying. "I don't know why I'm saying this."

"You don't care!" He was mad and crying too. "What is it? Ma doesn't give a shit about men—she uses them like back scratchers and wonders why they shit on her—and you're a fuckin' bitch! Why do you—you were—why do you *change* on me?"

"Sam, I'm sorry."

He didn't say anything. He held on to her. It was the first time she knew he needed her. Still she was afraid, and she didn't want to be hurt again.

Is any love conventional? She loved him, she knew how unusual he was, she knew how they matched up in ways as common but singular as fingerprints. She was frightened. How much time? How many periods? She worried about herself, feared the future, became bitchy. When she bitched at Sam at first, he didn't know how to take it. He was hurt. He hadn't expected to see that. His voice caught, his hands fluttered. He was a sheltered bird. But after discovering it, he fought back.

"Break my balls, will you?" he said the next weekend when she said something bitchy.

"Break my balls?" she asked. "Break my balls? That's a vulgar Italian expression! What happened to your class act?"

"I'm around showbiz, you lush whore."

"Fuck you, you little prick! You'll never see this at Brown!"

"I'll have a hotter *time* at Brown! We have class breaks." He smirked. "Two minutes of ecstasy behind a tree. We're young and quick to come."

"Class breaks? You bastard! *You fucking bastard!*"

People were turning to look at them outside Rizzoli's, and she adjusted her shades. Sam said, "Oh, let them see. You look like hell today—they'll never recognize you."

"Fuck you!" she screamed, and stalked away. She crossed to the St. Regis without looking back, stepping left through the marble-and-bronze lobby into the bar, where she sat pouring cigarette smoke into the air, fuming, a good, dry, clear and brittle martini in front of her. She expected he'd come in and he did. Perhaps they wanted to act out theater. He stood beside her table, grinning down.

She stared at him. Was he going to apologize? Be endearing?

He said, "I'll take you home. Let's get a cab."

The way he looked intrigued her.

Out front they got a cab driven by someone who could barely understand English. Sam told him to go to Park and Ninety-first and then east. They settled back against the hard imitation leather that smelled of cigarettes. He had such a strange, youthful leer. She wasn't a bit surprised. She wanted to be outrageous with him.

He didn't even kiss her, he just talked and grabbed her. She insulted him and grabbed him. They snarled and bitched. He pushed her sideways. She had a foot out the window as they went up Park. For all she knew, Aunt Amanda saw into the cab. Her face had the memory of snarling but her body had melted, changed, she was upside down like a tree, limbs and foilage burning against her climbing trickster, her flesh stretching and exploding into a million pieces all over Manhattan and coalescing around him again. It was about 200 degrees in the cab and smelled like lust. The driver groaned along, peering over the wheel rim. They were smoking cigarettes by the time he looked around and turned onto Lex. She tipped him ten dollars.

Sam and Phoebe stood on the sidewalk looking at each other. The heat steamed through them. She'd have thought the sidewalk was pink.

"You think you're so goddam cute, don't you?"

"You looked better in the cab, upside down."

"Class break, you bastard. You couldn't last that long."

They went through moods like trees in varying winds: They pulled apart, twisted, yet rooted, grabbed back at each other, became fierce or languid. "It must be inexhaustible lust," she said.

"Blow me," he said. "My back's tired."

She felt. She thought. She feared. It was a doomed relationship. It couldn't last. She felt too old, too old, passing ripeness now. She would be withering when he became a man of the world. They were too passionate. She was too public. Who was he? A scion. An heir. She hated his family. She could never present him to a member of her own family as a lover (though they saw Aunt Amanda at MOMA and Amanda chatted on to Sam in her vigorous blind way about Hickses *she* had known and Brown and Pembroke and Providence), but because Phoebe and Sam knew and feared their disparities, they seized each other more desperately, wringing out all the emotions, playing nasty, affectionate, athletic, passive, while Mayor Lindsay and Houston and Richard Nixon and H. R. Haldeman and General Creighton Abrams and Henry Kissinger acted out the large dramas that were supposed to be our world, with its shrines for vaguely stated beliefs and our icons of John and Robert Kennedy and Dr. King stamped KILLED and General Loan shooting the flinching Vietnamese man and Jane Fonda sighting her North Vietnamese antiaircraft cannon at the American bombers and Richard Nixon vee-fingering crowds.

"That's our world?" Sam said. "No way. That's *their* world. That's your place of employment—they're doing it all on television. Fuck this global village, that's Disneyland, that's McLuhan's campus. It's all made up—they probably have it all in studio sets. They probably use Chinese busboys in the three-minute war scenes. *I* don't believe it. Here, sniff this."

"What is it?"

"MDA."

"Oh, forget that. I outgrew speed years ago."

"I need it."

"Then take it."

Central Park was a good place to watch ad hoc demonstrations. Washington Square had them too, but Union Square, which traditionally had been the scene for radical demonstrations, was now territory for knife muggers and junkies. Tompkins Square, a little southeast, was completely Junkieland now. They rode by in a cab and watched them lying on the ground and crawling over one another like seals on a rocky beach. Graffiti had not been scrawled over the city yet, but the streets and parks had grown their own living helplessness, people going on the nod, people screaming in groups, in anomie, none of the headlines and stories connecting except they were all the same unraveling: Po—Peeling Off.

One of the producers let her use his place in Sag Harbor, and they took his sailboat, a small daysailer, to go out in the harbor and around Shelter Island. It was very pretty out there, all pastel grays and blues. They wore shorts. Sam looked slim and leggy and graceful—totally free of that bunchy-jocky look she had come to fear. She told him how pretty his legs were, and noted the slimness of his back as he set the jib, and somehow he connected something and squinted and said, "Do I remind you of Uncle Tony?"

"Oh, fuck Uncle Tony. No you do not. Not in the least."

"We haven't done anything you didn't do with him."

"Oh, yes, we have, asshole, thank you very much. You don't know."

"What do you mean, I don't know? Do you think I was inexperienced before you?"

Of course, he was so young—he couldn't spend two days of comfort without pulling something here, pushing something there, turning something else over just to see what would happen.

"Do you loathe my family? Or hate it? What's your temperature?"

"Oh, Jesus, Sam. What can I say? How do they figure?"

"They have to. You can't ignore them. Subconsciously. They're there."

"Or are you projecting?"

"You see, you're transferring now."

He wanted to pick at something. She didn't want to get into it but he wanted, she felt, to blurt something. They were on a run now sitting in the bottom, facing each other, and he said, "Uncle Tony is probably only Cousin Tony."

She stared. His eyes did not have a touch of mischief. Pleading, if anything.

He continued, "Grandpa's sure Uncle Stu is Tony's father. He was out of the country that month going to Heidelberg and Paris. He's sure Stu diddled Grandma. They always were rivals, and Helen Fraker was the tops then. Stu would have—he's a rogue."

"Don't you think Helen would have had something to say about it?"

"Yes. And she never has. She's too clever and well balanced to be lured out, too. It's preyed on Grandpa ever since. Not being sure of his own wife."

She wondered if it ran in the family but said nothing. He wanted to unload. He watched her closely. To shock? To test?

"Grandpa has terrible rages," Sam said. "He hates Tony."

"Because of that? His suspicions?"

"Yes. He didn't really want him to go to Washington. Ma said Grandpa began to get impossible when Tony was winning trophies at Exeter. She says Grandpa's only big deal was the war. And his Agency consulting. He's always been in a snit that Stu makes so much money. And he can't help crowing when Stu takes a bath."

They came about and took a nice hard tack up toward a white house; the wind sang across them; Sam and she sat next to each other, knees together. He had the tiller and she huddled over and lit cigarettes and they clipped along, the smoke whipping out over the bubbling blue-and-white wake.

Sam said, "We were rather relieved when Grandpa stroked out. I don't know how Tony feels about causing it by having his *affaire africaine*, but he did the family a great boon because we were concerned Grandpa was going nutso, which some of us have, and the stroke gives him an honorable out. Otherwise we'd have to put up with him raving on in Boston and find some other excuse to hide him."

She opened her blouse and cupped her breasts toward the sun, beaming at the sky.

"You don't care about this, do you?" Sam said. "I'm trying to tell you about nuts in my family. They were shits to you before—I'm trying to tell you what *else* is wrong with them."

"My family has a few squirrels, too," Phoebe said. "You'll find them in any family if you keep track. It's one of the perils of education, knowing what your relatives were really up to."

"No, I mean *really*," Sam said. "We're different. Listen—" And he told her how nuts he thought his family was, talking in his flushed, excited, birdy way—the old nineteenth-century Bridles men's fascination with black sex, one mill owner and selectman's black mistress in Boston; another, an appointee, who became a prick to all his youthful friends and died hated. Some Bridleses who were repelled and hysterical at the suggestion of incest and others who practiced it . . .

He was *such* a Bridles, she thought. His family had to be the best, and different, even at being screwy.

"But I'm part of a larger picture, Phoebe."

"What? Psych majors at Brown?"

"Oh, fuck you! No! The New England syndrome! You know what it is—the insincere wholesomeness in youth, the sentiment about summer, the sadness as you age, clinging to memories, being an absolute prick to people you meet after age twenty, the ones who are outsiders. I know all that. Justifying utterly monstrous behavior on the most pious grounds, the lower the loftier. The xenophobia and the assumption that if you do hurt others it doesn't matter to them as much. Let me tell you—I don't want to grow up to be like Grandpa. But he's the only man around. Tony left. John—Pa—left Ma. Stu left years ago. They put me in that rat maze. *I* don't want to come out like them!"

"You won't."

"You're too serene about it."

"I love you and I know who you are. I'm not serene about them, though. I was badly hurt by Houston, you know—I had a miscarriage and he did nothing. It interfered with his plans. That was the main thing that bothered him, I think."

"It's worse than that. You know what Grandpa was bruiting about?" He looked intently at her. "After you left Houston? No comment about your miscarriage. Grandpa suggested you were having an affair and that's why the marriage blew up."

"That bastard. I'd like to kill him! What did Houston say about it?"

"He wasn't in contact. He was too busy. We didn't even see him until a year or so later. But I suppose it'd be possible to find out what he thought and felt."

"How?"

He didn't look at her. "I can't let you know."

"No, tell me."

"I'll let you know. I can't tell you, Phoebe, really."

That had been a nice sail over an enameled gray-blue Atlantic, seeing sunny whites and summer greens ashore, and later eating shore food, and grasping each other on the sea air-damp, salt-smelling sheets, her nipples burning and lips swollen, chafed from damp clothing, their skin burning. Sam's pale eyes glittering, his face changing from frenzy to surprise to a Botticelli enchantment, celestial and lascivious at once, her voice erupting in a high note and her toes curling.

He was right about the New England syndrome; that was the height of summer, 1970, and she was to find out what he meant about Uncle Tony's mind.

The newsroom went crazy. Bells rang on the AP machine. Kissinger had announced peace negotiations with the North Vietnamese and then there was a shootout and a demonstration in Harlem an hour before deadline. She was at her desk frantically piecing together notes for a voice-over when her phone rang.

"Phoebe?" the woman's soft voice said. "It's K-Kimberley. We're in New York from Europe and wanted to touch base w-with you. How *are* you?"

"Too busy to talk!" Phoebe snapped. She asked them to come to the studio after the show. They did. Peas wanted to go up Broadway to bars he knew from his days at Columbia, but of course the whole Upper West Side had become dangerous, and no one went up Columbus or Amsterdam at all, and Broadway was safe only in daylight, so they went to the bar across from the studio and ordered beer. "Where did you go?"

"All *over*," Kimberley said. "I have S-Spanish and Peas has French and G-German, so we had *carta blanca*." She leaned across the table. "We went to Rome, Florence, Venice, S-Salzburg, Vienna, Amsterdam, Paris, and S-Stockholm, and we talked with the *people* everywhere! We met nice people traveling, too, ones who really appreciated w-what they were seeing. Students."

Peas said, "We went to the riding school in *Wien*. Kimmie analyzed their dressage."

"I was seriously thinking about going there, y-years ago."

"She's giving up her riding medals. Aren't you, Kimmie?"

Kimberley nodded. "I'm s-sending them to Nixon to protest the w-war. Peas is organizing the rejection. H-He's sending back his letter f-from *Exeter*."

When Kimberley went to the john, Phoebe said to Peas, "What's with Carole? Have you heard?"

"Not a thing. You didn't have to wait until Kimmie left, you know. We have a completely honest relationship."

"Carole sent me cards from France, Spain, Morocco, and Germany."

"How long has she been there?"

"Months. Since last winter."

Peas scowled. "She can afford it. Her trust funds. Her family doesn't even know what European culture is and yet she gets to live there."

"Apparently it agrees with some members of her family. Her younger brother's in Amsterdam and is marrying a Dutch girl."

"They're probably doing drugs," Peas said. "It was embarrassing seeing so many stoned-out American kids hanging around American Express waiting for money. Kimberley sewed maple leaf flags on our backpacks so we could pass for Canadian because of the war, and when we got there and saw these drugged kids, I was doubly glad. Of course, it's not their fault this country's gone fascist. The West is dying. You should have seen all the police and paddy wagons in Paris. And those hypocrites talk about Czechoslovakia!" He looked at her. "What *is* she doing? Carole?"

"I don't know. Her notes were cryptic. But you know after I saw her in Chicago she sent a note saying something about Weather. One of her cards said she saw Mark Randolph over there."

Peas shrugged. "I wonder what *he's* doing for money."

"She didn't say. When did he go over?"

"Months ago," Peabody said. "He'd gone from that oil company job to some other sales job, bullshitting all the way, and getting *money* for graduate school, and then he punched out his boss. He was on the sauce. He had a *motorcycle* accident. He could have been killed. He slid under a truck. 'Nah, I made it,' he told me. 'It was a good laydown.' He was on *crutches*. Completely out of control. The next I heard he'd bailed out of everything. He called me and said, 'Fuck it, I'm going to Spain.' Listen, can we crash at your place?"

"Yes." Sam was at Camp Bruno.

"We're flying out tomorrow and I don't want to spend any more than necessary in New York. They don't pay me enough to stay at the *Plaza*."

When they went to Eightieth and Lex, Peas looked around and made a comment about the Upper East Side and how much money Phoebe must be making and she had to soothe him by telling him it was rent-controlled.

"I'm a professor," he said. "I have responsibility fo· the future and I'm paid less than a *sanitation* man here—someone who cleans up the *past*. I've been *reading* about your salaries here. It's obvious where our values are. It's all sensation and convenience and throw it away. Education simply isn't revered."

If he had one raw nerve it was money.

Kimberley didn't believe she could find vegetables in New York but did. She made a salad and brown rice soup. "This is v-very nutritious," she said.

Peas said, "We had squid in its own ink—"

"*En su tinta*," Kimberley chimed in proudly.

"—in Spain. Most people would be too squeamish for that. Spain suits the Rands. It's a fascist state. The police carry *machine* guns. But why does he get to live in Europe and not me? He never read *The Sun Also Rises*."

They had begun to wear on Phoebe. It was either their academic parochialism or their California brashness that made them so grating. Or maybe she was a bit jealous he'd married and won the kind of life he wanted. Or irritated that in spite of his luck he still bitched. Or maybe she felt distaste that after leading demonstrations, struggling in great events, and speaking passionately on great issues, he'd married not someone vital like Kathy, but this seagull-brained loveliness. From Trotskyism to tchotchkeism.

Or maybe it was because he wasn't news anymore.

From time to time Peabody called her. He had formed a rap group at his college that he wanted to develop into a Center for Freedoms and he wanted coverage. He wanted coverage on the way Nixon and Reagan—"He has henna hair!"—were raping state higher education. "They're destroying free access! They're trying to cover it up! It's like My Lai!"

She had other worries by then.

The war had always been there but for her it was distant, another story she'd already done. She knew newspeople who were still there, of course, and it was still going on under different methods of violence. People far younger than her age group were going over and older ones were going as part of their careers, but it had lost immediacy for her.

Sam and she had talked idly about what might happen when Nixon changed the draft from its system of classifications and deferments to a lottery. After Thanksgiving Sam called with the real results.

"I got a low number," he said, and laughed. "That's it. I'll have to chop off my foot."

"No!"

Of course, the government couldn't take him. His family was too important. But his family had no power with the Nixon administration. It was only a number. He might not be selected. But he had a low number. They all knew what could happen.

Death Comes for the Archbishop

Houston Bridles had no idea his nephew was seeing, let alone fucking, his ex-wife, or, as he still put it, "playing Hide the Salami." He didn't know Sam was in New York that often (since Brown was farther away than Yale), and the depth and passion of their love he wouldn't have understood anyway because it wasn't a "match."

But he *was* concerned that Sam had a low number. He didn't like a Bridles to be subject to a blind mechanism. Surely there was a way out. Edith had called and demanded he do something. He was a bit put off by her demanding, but he'd get to it.

"I'm working on an issue," he told her. "As soon as that's set . . ."

The issue was a mixed bag of short-term notes and bonds. Stu had suggested Houston give a treat to friends at an old investment house and, as Houston noted in his journal, "What a surprise! Whom should I run into but another Yalie?"

In fact, the man was a Fencie from the class after Houston's. "Old Bates Tomkins—good man! A real wild man!" Houston wrote.

I think G & T—some underground. Bates *looks* like G & T—small, thin, active, quick jokes. Played squash. Not top athlete, but went into Navy and flew jets over there. He brought a friend, also an aviator. We went to the Downtown

Club. Drinks downstairs by the big fireplace. Business went
all right but rather rough byplay. . . .

Bates's friend was Mario Collazzo—very *now* for that
house to hire an Italian—big, dark hair, played ball somewhere out West. Had been a Marine aviator flying what he
called 'heavy helicopters.' Handsome face, but thin, sarcastic smile. He and Bates got into a game against me. . . .

Houston, as always, was charming and upbeat, smiling, touching
an arm here, waving to the waiter there for drinks, and he felt especially buoyant talking with aviators just back from Vietnam. "The
best!" he wrote. He always wanted the best; he knew that tradition of
oil-painted DKEs and Fencies in uniform with their biplanes, or that
friend of Stu's—Bates knew him, too—who had buzzed Boston garden parties in the thirties in *his* biplane and then flew missions from
England. Houston assumed he knew a good deal about Bates's and
Mario's flying "from *my* time in the cockpit in the West Wing Basement" —but right away he made a foot fault. He said something about
"fighter bombers," what he assumed Bates flew, and Bates said, "Oh,
shit, Howze, that's a term McNamara coined. He wanted to sell using
fighters on ground targets. That's why we've lost so many. Dumb
term."

"Ah," Houston said.

"Ask Mario about ground fire. He flew six hundred fifty missions."

"Isn't that a lot?" Houston asked, remembering the fifty missions
Pa had muttered about.

Bates said, "No, several hundred wasn't uncommon in World
War Two. Americans didn't do it, but the Russians and Japanese flew
on that scale. And Germans. It wasn't like what you might think—tell
him about your last mission, Mario."

"Your six hundred and fiftieth," Houston said.

"Fifty-first," Mario said. "I didn't file the paperwork. I didn't
give a shit."

"What were you? What was your rank?"

"Captain. Marine captain."

"And where were you?"

"I flew out of Hue/Phu Bai and Marble Mountain—but I wrapped
that up last June. I was short, I had about a month to go, and I had
a bad case of hemorrhoids."

"Occupational hazard," Bates put it.

"And I was too difficult for the pussy who ran my squadron to deal with," Collazzo said calmly. "This guy had an emergency landing anytime someone shot into the air. He didn't lead strikes. From a leadership standpoint he was suckin' hind tit and he knew I knew it, so since I had plenty of hours he sent me to Wing and I looked at maps and marked targets and got wasted at the club every night. I was as safe as I could be, four stories underground on Freedom Hill, or under a table at the club, 'cause I was short. *Two days* before I'm due to fly out, as usual after drinking till three or four, I was passed out in the rack and some second lieutenant's pushing on my shoulder.

" 'Captain Collazzo, Captain Collazzo, get up, there's a briefing, you have to fly a strike.' 'Oh, get fucked,' I told him. He kept pushing. 'I'm off flight status,' I said. But it was true. Big lift, every swingin' dick was flying.

"I was so drunk I could hardly stand up straight. I staggered into the briefing. We were supposed to lift the Fifth Marines up one side of a ridge while some mob from the Americal Division attacked up the other side. They said the NVA had all kinds of fire at the top.

"I went out on the flight line to meet my co-pilot. By now I was only half-drunk, half-hungover, and before I could say hello I had to turn my head and puke. Good morning, *braaaaak!* Then I looked at this co-pilot. Oh, no. He was a first lieutenant I'd known before. He had about two combat hours; he'd kept finding ways to be transferred back to Okinawa. Somehow he'd got down here again and drawn this strike. I told him, 'Good, you have plenty of company. You take it off. I'm going to sleep.'

"We're hardly in the air before he's looking around for ground fire. This area was secured three years *earlier*—"

Houston said, "What were you carrying? Troops?"

"Yes. About twenty-five from the Fifth Marines. Helicopters all over the sky going there. The words comes over the net that LZ Parrot is real hot. This scares him more. 'Hot LZ!' he says. 'Hot LZ!' We cross our line of departure to go in and he drops into an attitude like this—" Collazzo tilted his hand sharply this way and that.

"Bang! All of a sudden I was sober. This asshole couldn't fly. 'I got it,' I said. 'Hand over.' I brought it out straight and meanwhile chewed him out. 'What were you trying to do, you stupid shit!'

" 'Hot LZ,' he said. 'Evasive action.'

" 'You *twat!*' I said. 'We weren't even in range! You don't fly evasive action with your wingman right there! Watch the radio!'

"He had two nets to monitor—one for air traffic crossing our flight patterns and the other for artillery and naval gunfire coming in. All kinds of shit was hitting the ridge then. We came in low toward the LZ and I was just about to make my run in when, *Bam!* the goddam helicopter practically flipped over and this F-Four burns on ahead on a strafing run—you could see right up his pipe. He was about eighty feet off the deck going *uphill* and strafing. His turbulence nearly downed us. I pulled the goddam helicopter straight and we sat down and the troops are running out while I'm chewing the asshole first lieutenant out. 'You idiot!' I'm screaming. 'Why didn't you hear the *net!* You stupid turd!' The crew chief was listening to me chewing out this dumb-shit officer instead of pushing out the troops. 'Why, godammit, why?'

" 'I was listening to the artillery,' he said."

Collazzo shrugged. "What can you do with a helpless pussy? We took off and in the air we got the word. The Fifth Marines had taken its side of the ridge. The American Division's stalled down in the low ground on their side—someone was shooting at them and they didn't want to move. We have a few thousand Marines hanging on and close to being surrounded. We have to fly in supplies and ammo fast. We went back and lifted several tons of ammunition.

"Now the NVA are *really* pissed off and they're shooting at everything in the air. We're supposed to drop our load on the ridge, and on the approaches the gooks are shooting the shit out of the underside of the aircraft. They're firing like mad, I'm trying to watch all the tracers *and* my gauges and the terrain. We were above a goddam slope machine gun position. My door gunners had their fifties working it over just to slow the fuckers down. 'We're hit! We're hit!' this asshole beside me yells. 'The ammunition will go up!'

" 'If we survive this fuckin' flight I'm having you court-martialed,' I said, and that scared him enough to make him get hold of himself. When we sat down and dumped that load, the crew chief counted fifty-eight holes in the fuselage."

"Why didn't you go down?" Houston asked.

"The heavies have a new kind of Kevlar armor," Collazzo said. "Our fifties will go through it, but theirs usually don't. The older helicopters they shot down in hundreds, though. Thousands. Ours you have to hit the pilot or knock out an engine. You can let a heavy down right on top of a gook position and have your gunners depress and pulverize them with fifty-caliber fire. Our fifties will go through the tops of their log bunkers."

Collazzo grinned, a sardonic leer. "Sometimes I'd switch onto the gooks' net and hear them yelling while we were coming down on them. They'd jabber away faster and faster and I could hear our machine gun rounds hitting and them screaming."

He and Bates laughed at this. "You are a piece of work, Collazzo," Bates said. "Finish your mission."

"Okay," Collazzo said. "Fine, I thought, now I'll fly back and get drunk and go home. But in the LZ I get the order—take these five people and fly them to LZ Shrike. Oh, Jesus, I thought. Shrike was a shit sandwich that day. They'd waved it off four or five times. It was getting mortar fire, which could get me topside."

"Anyway, who wants to fly through it?" Bates said.

"That's right, it was a shit sandwich. The crew chief said they're aboard, we take off, and I fly to LZ Shrike, and it *is* a shit sandwich. You can see flat gray flowers spreading out on the ground, mortar rounds hitting. I came up on the net and said to give me some slack, and the FDC got counterbattery out. I think. At least they said so on the net. I was listening to the fire net then in case Sweetheart messed that up, too. We flew in. Nothing hit us.

" 'Wait,' the order was. These five passengers walked over to the edge of the LZ, where a machine gun was dug in. Two of them stand by it and a third takes some pictures. It was some dumb deal with correspondents. That's all it was—some press deal."

Houston stared at Collazzo. Could this be—what kind of attitude? Bates was smiling mirthlessly.

"Now it's time to go," Collazzo said, "and as we lift off, a sandbag flew up and caught on the intake of one of my jet engines."

"Where are they?" Houston asked.

"Over my head. Two ducts on top. I saw the thing go up there."

"You mean an empty sandbag."

"No, full," Collazzo said.

"But that weighs—what? A hundred pounds?"

"About eighty."

"How can it pick it up?"

"You've seen helicopters land, haven't you?"

"Of course, I've seen them countless times on the White House lawn."

"The thrust down, which is your lift, equals the weight of the aircraft. Several tons. So it can pick up a sandbag. It can cause all kinds of things to fly around."

"That's one of the things that's dangerous about a war," Bates said.

"Then what happened with the sandbag? Did it go in?"

"No, it was hung on the edge and I thought it had just blown past. I flew away. Fuck it, I was going to haul ass back to Da Nang. And go home. We flew—that's a twin-jet aircraft, we're unloaded, so I really moved coming out of the hills. Over the Tourane River I dropped down to come in and, *pow!* the aircraft shudders and slews sideways—the shift in attitude and airspeed knocked the bag loose and it went into the port engine and blew it up. I have starboard thrust only, the fucker's going to go whipping this way, so I poured on power and rudder enough to jump it straight. We're about fifty feet off the ground, my co-pilot Lieutenant Sweetheart is chewing his socks, and I cut it and dropped onto the dirt. *Bam!* Destroyed the gear. We tilt. The rotor caught and broke. All the blades stack up. One engine's blown up and the bottom's shot to shit. It's a wreck. I puked. Co-pilot Sweetheart is gibbering. He went straight to the adjutant to be removed from flight status on account of nerves." Collazzo grinned fiendishly. "That was my last mission."

Houston wrote later, "Most of the time I have felt thoroughly at ease among men, whatever their abilities or accomplishments, but my feeling with these two was like school—being the new one who's going to lose his pants. Their apartness quite palpable. What Collazzo described with these armored helicopters blasting bunkers is a far cry from the escapades of lightly armed helicopters at the start of the war. . . ."

At the time, though, Houston wanted to keep things upbeat, and said, "Amazing! Do you think new equipment like this will give us the edge?"

"No," Bates said. "Can't win from the air."

"Air power's like a ratchet," Collazzo said. "It keeps you from losing, that's all. We don't have a plan to win. We're just shooting to shoot. My six hundred fifty missions were for no objective. Look, these slopes are revolutionaries. They know what they want. Organize this village. Take that district."

Houston said, "I'm sure My Lai set us back."

"Oh, fuck My Lai," Collazzo said. "The NVA massacre every town they go into in I Corps. They massacred thousands at Hue. The point is they know what they're doing."

"Yeah, we have rules of engagement and they have total war," Bates said. "They use the weakness of our culture against us, 'cause we don't know how to fight for what we say we want. You want to know why we're losing attack jets faster than the Israelis?"

Houston said, "Hanoi has newer antiaircraft weapons."

"Yeah, but there's one thing the Israelis do on a strike that we don't."

"What's that?"

"They blow up the radar site before they go into the target. You have to knock out the eye of the giant before you kill him. We weren't allowed to attack radar sites. You know that. Your boss picked the targets himself. He didn't want radar sites hit."

"Certainly not the ones in population centers," Houston said.

"Of *course* not. It kills people. That's why the North Vietnamese put them there," Bates said.

Houston noted in his journal:

This was the last lurch as our boats, as it were, drifted apart. I could see it in their eyes. Bates I had known under entirely different circumstances "at New Haven" in an atmosphere of camaraderie and gentlemanly tolerance. The fact I'd been a Presidential aide, *instead* of carrying weight with them, indeed condemned me. I, like the emperor, discovered I had no clothes. I would rather have flown in the war, and it was too late for me to get in now—it was too stupid, too obviously misguided.

Houston nosed around draft board appointees to find out what he could do about Sam's low number. At this point, nothing.

Sam was in Boston for his birthday and got his draft notice there. He called Phoebe. "I have to go in next week."

Edith called Houston at City Hall. "I don't want him to go in with all those *others!* You *have* to do something! Pa can't! He's incoherent! You have to!"

"Please pull yourself together," Houston said. "I'm sure we can do this."

He asked Uncle Stu in Stu's office, dim even with its three windows, the honey-colored pearwood hutch, the hunting prints, and photos of Stu playing polo. He and Stu sat in leather armchairs. Stu's big hands made bridges and steeples pointing down.

"This will be a tough one, Tony. The fact is, *we* simply don't have the kind of clout we did. Nixon's appointed Californians and they want to go out of their way to play hardball with us. No favors. The lottery is Nixon's revenge on the Ivy League."

"Can't we go over their heads?"

Stu thought for a moment and said quietly, "Agnew takes money. Let me see."

"Phoebe? It's Sam. I'm in Boston with forty others waiting for the bus. They just swore me in. I showed up in drag and they still swore me in."

"You'll do okay, smartass."

"I'm *horny*, Phoebe."

"So am I, darling."

"Let me tell you what I'll do for you. My tongue—"

"Not now. Who dropped you there?"

"Kelly. But Ma and Grandma and Grandpa said good-bye at breakfast. Grandpa drooled and struggled to say something. It was important, he said. He strained and said, 'When you get to the school, tip the batman ten shillings and you'll be sure to get tea.' " Sam laughed. "I'm going to have an accident as soon as I can."

"No! Don't! I don't want you hurt! *Please* be careful, Sam. I love you."

When Sam had talked about the New England syndrome, he'd anatomized the process he called Transcendence When You Are Caught in Shit. "There's always a lofty out you can grab," he said. "It's called 'missionary work' when you massacre natives and 'keeping harmony' when you betray someone."

When he called Phoebe again he said, "I'll think of a way to transcend this. Can I call it a need to meditate if I desert? I don't think they shoot deserters anymore. Oh, balls, I'm a Bridles—I can't desert. But already, Phoebe, I'm the most reluctant soldier they've seen, and I've got a lot of competition."

Phoebe knew what men had told her about basic and she felt serene. After all, it's only training; he's sure to get a safe job. And they had weekends anyway, though she missed him very much.

She kept busy covering no end of zany and violent stories. A welfare family had been put up in the Waldorf by the city. Nixon was encouraging hard-hat construction workers to beat up peace demonstrators, playing on class hatred. What they could not catch on tape were the bricks and two-by-fours ripping flesh and breaking bones. One hard hat grabbed a young man by the throat with big channel-lock pliers and led him around like a calf.

Aunt Amanda and Phoebe had a drink; she bulled on in her usual obtuse way about Sam being drafted. "They *must* have the sense to use his education. I'm sure he must have administrative ability. I've never been to Brown. I'm told it has a *very* pretty campus."

They sat on the two cream-and-burgundy-striped satin chairs by the tiny tea table, Amanda's back straight, knees together.

"I'm told by *many* that Brown is preferred by young people now. Sam's lucky to be pulled into the Army. That lieutenant friend of yours from the Marines—what's his name?"

"Randolph."

"Yes. I *shudder* to think about what the Marines did at My Lai."

"No, that was Army."

"Oh? Well, the Marines are much too warlike anyway. Surely the Army couldn't do anything to hazard Sam—he's a *Bridles*. Does Brown put on those disgusting half-time shows? I was talking with Meg Bloor about what the marching bands did at Harvard–Dartmouth and I understand others are no better. Why does *everything* have to be sex?"

"Youth, I think, Amanda."

"It's *so* degrading—they call older people hypocrites because we try to show restraint."

"Honestly, Amanda, I can see why they accuse older people of hypocrisy. When—"

"*I* most certainly don't," Amanda said, interrupting. "I have *always* been liberal. I have always been decent to black people and they like me. But certainly *no one* can abide these black people who *sing* that way or talk that way on the street, or the whites who *copy* them. That's not how *any* of us should act! At Saint Bart's we— Look at this, this is what I mean!"

She left the room and came back with the *Times*. "Look at this survey of sex among *high school* and *grade school* students! They"—she rattled the paper—"they *know* things *we* didn't know—and certainly didn't *talk* about! Fifty percent have touched the other person's—oh!" She shook her head. "And this! Thirty percent of all experienced oral sex in high school! In high school!"

She walked to the window and looked out on the avenue. Her shoulders shivered. When she turned she had tears in her eyes. "Men force it! Even young schoolgirls!"

Phoebe hadn't known how sensitive poor Amanda was, and could only guess what had happened to her because they didn't discuss these things in her family.

"That goddam stupid fool!" Stu barked. "I gave the money to Agnew *right in his office!* And then they got Sam's identity wrong! Some other Sam Hicks, probably black, was released from Fort Dix and this two-bit hustler says he can't do it again!"

"I better go down there and see if I can call on old acquaintances," Houston said.

He flew out on the next shuttle, which was crowded and filthy. No Air Force VIP jet now, he thought ruefully.

He went first to the CIA—not the wooden barracks where Gerrity had been but Langley itself, the big American motel/hospital-style glass-and-masonry headquarters among trees and parking lots. They took his picture and put it on a plastic pass card clipped to his coat. He met with a briefing officer he'd known from the White House, one of Gerrity's assistants. Houston said, "I know it's a bit to ask, but I'm sure others have—"

The Agency Man, in his forties, nodded, nodded again, and winced when Houston reached the point, getting his nephew out of the Army or at least Vietnam.

"The only way we could do that, you understand, is to put an Agency hold on him, as if we're going to use him later. I don't know if from what you say about him—he showed up at the induction center in a dress?—if that would be credible. Let me check." He left.

Houston found a cigarette and lit it. He was in a waiting/ conference room of government Danish modern, the long table vinyl walnut veneer, two splotchy watercolors. The second-string room. He didn't have clout anymore. He couldn't wander around. The kind of card clipped to his coat limited him. This fellow was only humoring him, he supposed.

The Agency officer came in with an envelope.

"I haven't got an answer yet but in the meantime I have something you might like to know. I'm cleared to tell you."

"Yes?"

"It's about the terrorist, the cadreman who killed Ted Gerrity."

"Oh? Ah, yes. Good."

"We've known all along *who* he was—Nguyen Thuc Thanh—and much of the time *where* he was. For instance, we knew he was organizing in Thua Tien province after setting that bomb that killed Gerrity. Our ralliers got a defector who told about his *can bo* work in Gia Binh. He set up an attack on a Marine airfield—"

The man droned on, looking at documents. "We know Thanh was political officer of the Hundred Ninety-eighth Independent Rifle Battalion and was probably wounded in the Tet attack on Hue, probably sent to a hospital in Laos, and when he got back found his Interzone Committee run by northerners.

"As you remember, the NVA fought it out with local cells after Tet. Said they'd made a mess of it. The attack pretty much killed off the Main Force units."

"Yes."

"What we *didn't* know was the extent of the bloodletting among the committees. The Tonkinese always thought they should run things. They want the Dai Co Viet, the big state including Laos and Cambodia. They say the southerners were too slack and interested only in fighting for the south." He shrugged. "Well, all Vietnamese are contentious. I don't know whether they're worse as allies or enemies."

"They're both anyway," Houston said. He had assumed the eager, patient expression he'd learned so well.

"Yes." He pulled out a report and looked at it. "Thanh committed ideological error. They threatened him. He went into hiding. Tried to organize *chi bo* around Da Nang, convinced the Annamites could take back their area. The NVA got after him and he went on the lam, probably hiding in villages upriver until it blew over. Then he started a new life. He moved to Hue."

He handed Houston a piece of flimsy. "Our ralliers grabbed a charcoal seller who was carrying the original." Houston looked at the government manual typewriter text and Agency translator marks.

"It's a letter to his brother in Quang Tri."

Beloved Brother Tu,
 May this reach you before too many weeks. The charcoal seller assured me he would seek you diligently.
 I write out of love and filial duty to keep you informed, that you may remember me to our beloved family and tell them they are in my thoughts always. As you know, I have been involved in the struggle for our land, for Annam, for a new nation, and for our people. This is not like the Great Patriotic Struggle against the French. This is a crueler and more confusing war. The long-nose Americans offer money, deceptions, and huge destruction. It is easy to lose our bearings, like those who have been under B-52 raids and, even though protected 20 meters underground are still so shaken by the blasts and heaving of the earth that they come out trembling, incapable of speaking, never quite the same. In such a way though protected by the righteousness of our cause and the Will of Heaven yet we become confused. At times we must run and be harried by those on our side. Yet we are all patriots.
 Should I die please know I die honoring my family, people, and land.
                                   Your Faithful Brother,
                                   Thanh

"See? This guy was a True Believer. Even with his work of twenty years condemned, his own wounds discounted, the sacrifices of his comrades ignored by his nominal brothers in uniform, this guy still believed. Amazing." He shook his head. "The charcoal guy talked enough so we could locate Thanh."

"Where was he?"

"Running a small electrical shop in Hue, Binh Luc district. He repaired radios, rebuilt those old French cylindrical light switches. Fixed a lot of stuff the Americans threw away. Slept in back of the shop.

"This was perfect for Phoenix—in fact, Gerry Lankers, who knew Ted, monitored the job. A few of our Vietnamese ralliers isolated the street for a minute—they just stood in the middle and showed their Swedish Ks—and Gerry's contract agent, a cop on TDY from Kansas City, walked in and got a make on Thanh.

"Thanh looked up from a radio on the counter. He was easily identifiable, with those burning eyes, stiff hair, and a notch in his ear. Our man put five rounds of thirty-eight in his face and left him slumped behind the counter. Walking out, he yelled to onlookers, *'Toi sat Viet xian!'*—'I kill Vietnamese traitors.' Just so they knew what's what."

"Good!" Houston said. "Terrific!" He was greatly pleased our side had scored back—but what about Sam?

The man left and after several more minutes returned.

"Listen, I'm very sorry, but just can't. Can't find a credible ground."

"That's too bad," Houston said thinly.

"But you can try this—see our DIA liaison in the Pentagon. *They* may have an out."

Houston drove his rental car at top speed. No red-light escort now, no clout to get him out of a speeding ticket. He had plenty of money, and would make *millions* when he got clear of government, with what he knew about paper, but he didn't have that power that meant "You don't have to wait."

The expressway wound through trees, mist and sunlight, over a rise, the Potomac basin, majestic sprawling buildings, an airliner hanging in smog, the Pentagon. Shit; no VIP parking, either.

The Agency man had said that since Nixon had the Army doing surveillance in domestic activities, DIA might be able to pull Sam into that. He'd given him a contact and said he'd call.

Houston walked up the steps and through the multidoored river entrance where years earlier he'd seen Adams Peabody and Norman Mailer arrested while on floors above colonels worried that hippie Druids would use Soviet parapsychology to levitate the building.

"Wait here," the guard said.

This time he didn't even get to a long-table waiting room. The short fat DIA man who met him in the corridor said, "Out of the question. We can't do that sort of thing. For one thing, I don't acknowledge we're *doing* what he asks about. For the second, we wouldn't take just anyone. I never talked to you about this. Sorry. Have a nice day."

"Fuck you, too," Houston said. This was an age of lousy manners. Nixon had poisoned the air.

From the entrance he called an Army lieutenant colonel he'd known as a briefing officer and this one gave him a few minutes in his office—*promotion!*—talking easily about the war, the new SOGs, and General Abrams's punishing raids, but no dice on Sam.

From a pay phone he called Boston. "No luck, I'm afraid."

"No!" Edith said. "You must! Please!"

"What about Fraker Chillingworth?" Ma said on the other extension.

"What about him?" Houston asked.

"He just got out of Harvard Law, he's in the Army, and Pookie said he's in the Pentagon. Surely *he* can do something."

Lawyers started as first lieutenants but the guard, leafing through his directory, could find no First Lieutenant Chillingworth.

"I'll try the legal locator."

After several phone calls the guard said, "He'll be down."

Can he do it? Surely one of us can do it, Houston thought. Perhaps he's a captain. He saw a familiar pudgy shape walking toward him, Fraker's round face with an Army haircut, his collar shining brass. Major? No, discs. On his sleeve were Spec 5 insignia. Houston frowned. An enlisted man?

"Well!" Fraker said. "Let's sit down!" He led Houston to an empty conference room and dropped into a steel chair.

"Well! I hope this is all of government service *I* ever see! It's quite enough!"

"I didn't realize you were, ah, in—"

"They drafted me," Fraker said. "Of course they offered me a commission—I was in the top of my class at Harvard Law—but that would have added years, and I told them, 'You can have your pound of flesh, but I won't go one single second beyond the two years—' "

"But what do you *do*?"

"I spend most of my time giving free trust and will advice to colonels about to retire," Fraker said. "In my off-duty hours I do draft counseling."

"Wonderful! Then you can help with Sam!" Houston explained the situation. Fraker pursed his lips.

"Well! He's already in, you see, that's another—he'd have to initiate some action. Go for CO, get injured safely, discover a chronic back problem—but that's risky. Make no mistake about it, this is an enormous war—much bigger than anyone wants to admit. The Army's sucking hundreds of thousands of men through, even stripping units in Germany, sending them TDY."

He sniffed. "And then General Westmoreland, of course—you know he's assigned here; he doesn't have much to do, he's been kicked upstairs, and he's crippled by dysentery—but he prowls the corridors and if *he* sees a soldier with his shirttail out, he personally makes sure the man's sent to Vietnam."

"Can Sam be pulled out of training? Or sent here?"

"Of course."

"He's college educated. Brown, but still—"

"Well! A college education, you know—the Army fears it now. You know the First Battalion, Third Infantry?" This was the honor guard at Arlington.

"Yes."

"Some time ago the commander observed that soldiers with college time were sharper for his purposes, more articulate and smoother answering tourists' questions, so he brought in more college draftees. Eventually the unit had the highest numbers of college men in the Army." Fraker laughed. "But when antiwar demonstrations became common and the honor guard went out to defend government buildings, the commander feared his soldiers would sympathize with the protestors, so at demonstrations he's been putting a second line of noncollege sergeants behind the line of college privates!"

Both of them laughed rather uneasily, Houston sensing they were, after all, civilized men in the den of the beast—a beast that had grown enormously.

At the end, Fraker said, "Well! I'll see what I can do. Insure he's in a noncombatant MOS, try to keep him out of the Vietnam quotas."

"Wonderful! Terrific!" Houston said, shaking his hand, squeezing his soft shoulder. "Great! First-rate!"

Phoebe missed Sam. He had been fun and full of all the hope, certainty, exuberance, and open delight that she'd learned to regard as uncool in the fifties and that had led to heartbreak in this decade, when whatever looked hopeful was expelled, shot, or burned. Even though he'd been gone only a few weeks, just across the Hudson, she thought of things he'd said and the way he'd made her laugh, imitating Phil Ochs's one tune or Buffy Sainte-Marie's tremolo, the way he took on all WASPs as well as his own New Englanders: "We don't like to show money or emotion. You know blacks in any class don't take no dude serious 'f he don' show *passion*, man, 'f he don' *feel* and *show* it!" Sam's eyes flashed and his head flew and somehow his lips thickened. "Got to *feel it!* But we envy those who can do and feel the things we can't without committing a grave social error. We've become parasites, like mistletoe."

You know how it is in love—you begin seeing and feeling life not only your way but also your lover's way. Phoebe reacted to dumb-

WASP comments from Aunt Amanda, noticed New England tricks like Boston naming a Combat Zone, as if Sam were touching her elbow, snickering in her ear, making her laugh again.

She remembered a line Peabody quoted from Robert Bly's war poem: "Your gaiety will end up in Asia."

Houston had a notion to ask someone at the meeting at the Century about getting Sam out. Certainly enough important people were there.

That night was cold and rainy, so he felt comfort and assurance immediately in the Italianate building's understated stone vestibule—a strong shelter—the graceful stairway split like ram's horns leading up to the lounge with its leather chairs and bookcases, the staff in gray coats gliding up to his elbow to take drink orders.

McNamara looked tanned and fit from time outdoors. Schlesinger with his grinning gnome's face, the sober Bundys, Cy Vance putting his glasses on and taking them off. A few Yale faces. Perhaps Yalies aren't great theorists, but they're the ones who toil in the corridors of government, carry spears—the grunts, Houston thought. It pleased him to think of policy-making in battle and jock terms.

The point of the meeting was to see what enlightened leadership could salvage of this moral shambles, our country.

The question indeed, Houston formed in his mind in case he was asked, was not only "Whither America?" but "Whither us?" He put what he knew was under discussion—government, atmospherics, goals, facts, and observations—into the patterns of New Haven common-room chats, Our Moral Duty, a nod toward expedience, a clever, possibly self-deprecating remark (but not *too* much, to detract from one's dignity), culminating in a proposal that reflected Sweetness and Light and Our Interests.

"The fact is, Nixon's using his madman tactics," Schlesinger remarked. "And he's running with them. He's already promised to pull out of the war, but he's committing cruelties to make it more acceptable to the people on the right who buffaloed us."

One cruelty after another. Not only the Phoenix program, killing off cadre, but the Special Operations Groups the Pentagon officer had told him about—Army elite troops who wore boots soled like Ho Chi Minh sandals and used foreign weapons, who dropped into Laos and Cambodia and killed headquarters staff. General Abrams's lightning attacks that killed and captured numbers of NVA. *Their* draftees were sixteen- and fifteen-year-olds now. They used drugs to numb their privation and terror.

This is unspeakable cruelty, Houston thought, beneath us, uncivilized. With his cat-quick reflexes he saw but knew better than to utter the corollary: "Nixon's getting even, you see. He's pleasing the bloody-minded. He's appealing to the public's worst instincts. And how rotten it will be for us if Nixon *gets away with it!*"

He found himself sitting next to McNamara in armchairs by a low oak table. McNamara's glasses glittered and his tanned, sunburned nose was peeling. His eyes fell on Houston. Recognition. Measuring of present and former status. "Hello," he said with a moderate degree of warmth.

"How do you like it at World Bank?"

They talked about debt awhile. Houston wanted to broach an idea Stu and others had for developing rain forest into cattle land, but a professor whose name Houston couldn't remember came up and mentioned what a few insiders had heard about, McNamara's documentary study of all the miscalculations that had led Kennedy and Johnson into the Vietnam mess. McNamara licked his lips. "Yes, yes," and cut it short with his hand.

"You are the savior to us," the professor said. "You've been sensitive at least to—"

"Yes." McNamara cut him off crisply, but others were there and McNamara could not avoid speaking for a few minutes about Vietnam, about "repairing the ravages" through the World Bank. He also said, with a peculiar expression on his face, "I did at one time think of running for an office. But that's impossible now." He seemed distracted, couldn't talk as forcefully as Houston remembered, and jogged his thoughts by doodling on a cocktail napkin.

A few talked about whom they should put out as a spokesman, indeed as Presidential nominee, but they could settle on no one. Bayh, McGovern, Tunney—all had something wrong. They didn't want to make a mistake. As Bundy noted in his usual astringent way, "We are not used to making mistakes!" (Laughter.) They couldn't settle on a promising name. Houston thought of the strange time when Kennedy was alive, when Pa was going back to D.C. for Agency meetings, when they couldn't settle on someone to run Vietnam.

Should he ask McNamara about getting Sam out of Vietnam? He saw him twisting the napkin, fingering his lips, obviously not quite at ease. He consulted someone else, who said, "Don't. He got caught getting a friend's son out while he was SecDef. That was one of the things they yelled at him when he was mobbed, when he was trying to rest at Aspen and up on the Vineyard."

If he couldn't do any good, he couldn't. Barbarians had taken over the government; they did not speak the same language. *I hope Chillingworth can pull Sam's name.* . . .

As they left, Houston looked back to see if he could pick up McNamara's napkin and read what he'd noted on it, but the genius had put it in his pocket.

"Bad news," Fraker Chillingworth said on the phone. "I was pulled in for questioning by CID for my draft counseling the day I was to do the deed, and I find now that Sam's on a draft to Vietnam. He does have a clerk MOS, which is something, and I'll try to get him shunted to a big rear-area base. They have hot and cold water and television."

"I'm a g-gourmet cook!" Kimberley said.

"I know you are."

"I don't see w-why you did it! I'm better looking! She w-wears glasses! Even w-when she can afford *contacts*. She speaks precisely. Fascists are *anal*, and you—"

"Kimmie, I'm sorry. I'm sorry."

Peabody was in trouble—with Kimberley, with the dean, the other faculty, and for all he knew with Reagan's and Nixon's secret police.

The tension in the cottage was dreadful. Kimberley faced away from him, stirring the ratatouille. She was hurt—hurt in a blind, helpless way Carole had never been because Kimberley had always been *here*. Sheltered here in the land of happiness. "It *snows* back east," she'd said. "The buildings are so grimy and old." She had no defenses. He felt terrible—chilled, withering. But he had to be free.

It had begun over money. The dean said the room he was using for his center would revert to general allocation when his grant ran out. That was the problem with soft money. The government holds you hostage. Peabody argued, "I have a constituency!" But others on the faculty said they had more students interested in other interdisciplinary pursuits, such as structuralism. People were talking about *structuralism*, an insidious, nonactivist, masturbatory quote game using Diderot, Foucault, Levi-Strauss. It required no political commitment! No Marcuse! No Fanon!

It was money. He suspected the California State College system had become a tool of the real estate developers. He called Phoebe, demanding she run an exposé, but she sounded strangely uninterested.

What he wanted to expose was the trivialization of colleges as radical centers, the "boutique-ization" of the small dusty town by the new campus. Last year there'd had been a storefront poverty center, counseling for migrant laborers, draft aid. Now there was an earthenware and thong shop called Norwegian Wood and an arch, snotty café called Au Petit Gourmet. Suburban housewives ate there. A tiled walkway. Flower pots. He'd seen realtors' ads proclaiming that Cerro Verde was going to be "Another Palo Alto!" Another Westwood! Another Irvine!—a capitalist trick of sticking fashion onto ferment. Marcuse would be livid.

But it was the girl that did it. It was Nixon's and Reagan's plan to undermine the campuses. They brought in Vietnamese exchange students to talk about *South* Vietnam and why Americans should support the war. They were always of the upper classes. Of course you knew what they were going to say. Miss Hoa Hoa Thi was a ringer, the ultimate Mata Hari.

She told Vietnamese folk tales at The Trees, the new timbered-atrium student union building.

They were the most lugubrious tales Peabody had ever heard—tales of love thwarted by obligation, betrayed by war. And militarist propaganda, like the tale of the Golden Claw, which must have concerned fighting the Chinese. Yet Peabody became fascinated by her forceful and delicate gestures, leaning this way and that, forming her hands to tell the story.

He had intended to shout her out of the rap bay, to have students from his center interrupt her, since Marcuse said you cannot have free speech if the speaker is a totalitarian. But he couldn't get his followers together and, as he watched her delicate hands and earnest face behind her big glasses, he decided to wait and study the enemy in Maoist–Giapist fashion.

Hoa Hoa Thi said, "I tell you now story about a lute girl who played in common tea houses, who took in a poor, starving orphan student and nursed him back to health. He came from a good family but had no inheritance."

Peabody felt what freshmen wrote along the margins of moving poems: *"Me! Me!"*

"The woman loved to play lute for him and to listen to him tell of things he study."

My *aperçus!*

"They live together a few years while the student regain strength and study for his mandarin examination. He passes with honors. . . ."

Adams Peabody stared, practically open-mouthed, as the slender, lovely bookish girl told how the new mandarin was offered an important magistrate's post in the province and how, with news of his success, a family friend turned up and offered his daughter's hand in marriage. He said the young man's father and he had discussed this. The young man was pulled between love for the lute girl and duty to his family.

Hoa Hoa Thi arched her back, reached up, imploring. "His lute girl said, 'You must take her.' "

"And he said, 'I will take you with me.' "

" 'No, you cannot,' she said. 'I cannot be seen in magistrate palace. You must do your filial duty. But I can see you in processions and I will know we have shared this friendship. I heard your learned speech selfishly and now all the people will hear it.' "

Peas shook his head. *No! I reject this!* She says this to argue that despite its class oppression Vietnam is all one people! Claptrap! Propaganda! It's like the Disney–Rockwell propaganda in World War II, an attempt to portray us as a *happy* society when we were *deeply* troubled and hypocritical about Russian sacrifices. I *must* argue with her.

Hoa Hoa Thi widened her eyes and looked from one face to another. "Many years passed. The magistrate become very important, a governor, with power over a wide territory, and one day while inspecting his villages he sees two beggar women on the road. Why are they here?"

"He has them brought in for questioning. One of the women looks familiar. She was the lute girl who help him years earlier. The older is her mother, whom she's leading in the last, painful years of her life."

There! Peas saw the flaw! The whole thing was shot through

with Confucian family propaganda, the discredited ideas the Maoists were overturning in China. All art is political, to be sure, but this was filled with premises about that mandarin, *elitist* society, and informed with Erich Segal sentimentality about loss, so it's bound to have vulgar appeal. Must challenge!

Perhaps Hoa Hoa Thi noticed his agitation, his questioning, for she faced him when she resumed. "The good mandarin took her and her mother in and put them close in good quarters where they can visit the garden and the lute girl can sing when she feels like it. Sometimes when he works at his desk he looks up from his scroll to hear the sad notes of a song of distant love."

Peabody pulled his beard and nodded. I *see* what she's trying to do. Anything about obligation in that sweet, sad vein is hypnotic. A sense of obligation is neurosis. Fascists use it to hold people down. Doesn't she know *human beings* are *dying* in that immoral war?

"I must talk with you," he said when she was finished.

"Yes?" She looked up at him, her features delicate, eyes so exotic, obviously intelligent. Cute glasses.

They met a few times. He gave her wine. They spoke French. Of course she came from a well-off family and had gone to a French school. He quizzed her on where she was coming from. The French school. She must know that most Vietnamese didn't have *access* to those things.

She insisted her country shouldn't be abandoned, she wanted Americans there. She admitted how ugly we were, our soldiers brutal, libidinous, free spending, and they discussed the French and the larger aspirations of colonial peoples, but she insisted her government needed protection. "We are too new," she said. She was crying. She wanted to be held.

He tried to screw her on the couch in his office. He pulled at her clothes. She cried.

"I have been dishonored," she said. "No!" She covered herself. Peabody was trying to see if her hair was like what the GI's said. "No! *Cochon!* Boor!" She shouted insults as she ran down the hall, clutching her clothes. Her thin bare back . . .

He felt less than heroic about this. He kept saying to himself, *No! Guilt is a bourgeois device! I am getting even, like Shaw's "Sailor Off the* Bremen." *I am not* guilty.

But the girl complained to the dean and left school. *Strike one.*

But not before, dammit, Hoa Hoa Thi had confronted Kimberley and, crying, told her she'd been dishonored.

"Peas, that w-wasn't *fair*," Kimberley said. He couldn't bear to be diminished in her eyes. *Strike two.*

And then there was the veteran who tried to disrupt the center's leafleting in front of The Trees. You saw them standing there, the veterans. It wasn't what they wore—it was that odd, old, *different* expression on their faces. The college was attracting them because it was a nice setting—warm, sunny—and someone who wasn't serious about what Peabody considered the real issues could just take easy courses and bask. The campus had an office to handle GI Bill payments. It was part of the Nixonization and Reaganization of the campus, to put in these veterans. They had money left over for beer. And the disabled veterans could fly free on government aircraft! Could a wounded veteran of Century Plaza?

Peabody was out by the center when the weirdo veteran came out to hang around again. He had long hair but wore a fatigue jacket. His eyes were hollow. You could see a mile into them. He was on aluminum crutches. One Levi's leg was pinned up. He gave some of the kids the creeps. Peabody asked him not to hang around. "It's just not cool, man—give us some space."

One thing Peas knew he could do was talk to people in their own language. "What's goin' down, man? Bummed out on Nam?"

But the weirdo said, "This handout's callin' me and my friends murderers. We didn't murder no one. I lost my leg."

"Yeah, man," Peabody said. "That's cool—but you lost your leg for nothing. We're trying to get that through to people, that it was all for nothing. It's fucked, man. There it is."

He gave Peabody a look—Peabody didn't know why veterans had that look they gave him, as if they were the only people who knew anything—and turned and crutched away.

"He complained to the dean," Adams told Kimberley.

"About what?"

"About me saying he'd lost his leg for nothing. I was just making a statement, for God's sake. What was I *supposed* to say? Should I have lied? How many are shot for no good reason? What about Prince Andre being shot in a field *waiting*? I was making a *statement!*"

The dean was very insensitive.

Was this strike three? What could he do?

His thinking ran from the loftiest moral choices to academic rat cunning. He was on a tenure track—but could he get the axe? He better look around! What was in the *Chronicle?* Was there really a radical campus forum? At Yale they hadn't even rioted, just rallied off-campus for Huey. Antioch? But it *snows* there, as Kimmie said. What if structuralism and boutique-ization took over here?

His world was changing. Was there really a lute girl? Carole, whom he'd despised, was nevertheless in *Weather!* Had the Movement passed him by? He'd be judged just as a teacher! He'd never hack it on his teaching alone. He'd better publish. But publish *what?*

"You know, Kimmie, I saw where someone's doing a dissertation on frog imagery in Dickens. Hyuk-hyuk-hyuk-hyuk! We learn more and more about less and less. In the Renaissance, when the human spirit was exalted, we had big gobbets of time. Now we measure it by milliseconds. We're like the rats psychologists dose to make them run faster and faster in smaller and smaller circles. Hyuk-hyuk-hyuk."

She came over, wooden spoon in hand, and kissed the top of his head. "I k-know you've had a l-lot on your mind."

Phoebe got a call from Kimberley. "Please tell m-me what's up w-with Adams's first w-wife?"

Phoebe stared at the phone. But this was a time when Cayce and Bishop Pike talked with spirits. She guess she could take a question off the wall, long distance. She told Kimberley the few things she knew about Carole and their marriage.

"D-Do you see her?"

"No. She's still in Europe, I think. Why?"

"Peas been saying 'C-Carole' in his sleep. Could sh-she be *calling* him?"

"I doubt it. Carole hates him. Does he mention her otherwise?"

"No. Not exactly."

"Well, what?"

"He's j-jammed up 'cause uptight people are trashing him here and h-he thinks he's *nowhere* and, like, he admires her for being in W-Weather now and that's something I won't—I don't—I just can't accept any kind of violence. And he has photos on his wall of—" She sighed. "Well, J-Jane Fonda and Buf-fy Sainte-Marie and—and Frances Fitzgerald! I know he admires them and I do too, but the w-way he *looks* at them hurts my feelings, and—"

"I wouldn't worry," Phoebe said. "You have him under your roof. Safe and sound in America."

Sam met Phoebe at the studio for their last night together before he flew out. She had expected him to be in a depressing Army uniform but he wore a wrinkled blue pinstripe suit and black army shoes. His blonde hair had been cut close at the side but still stuck out on top. His eyes were glazed. "I scored some boo."

"What time's your plane?"

"Eight. They'll have to beat me up and throw me in the stockade. Beat me! Oh, it's wonderful! Okay, we need a cab. *Phweeet!*" The great two-fingers preppy cab call; Phoebe knew girls who'd married men for that.

He looked even more long-legged and gangly dancing out onto Broadway to stop the cab. "Harvard Club," he told the driver. They settled onto the hard vinyl seats and he put his feet on the jump seat. "We'll have a drink there." He kissed her full on the mouth.

They had a drink in the game room downstairs, among the backgammon addicts, then went to a small room off a second-floor reading room and smoked a joint.

They caught a cab in the spangly lights to Rockefeller Center and went up to the Rainbow Room and had a drink looking over the city. It had that early-winter metallic-blue glow sparkling with yellow and red lights.

"It's pretty," she said.

"No sentiment, please. I'm going off to war. I'll hide there."

"You better."

"Shit," he said.

She was crying.

"Look, we're WASPs. No emotion. I can't help it. I'm a WASP. I'm a New Englander. I'm a Bridles. I'm being dragged off to this stupid fucking war and I can't stop it. But just remember the tragedy so many women faced in World War Two, seeing *their* men off and thinking, 'If only I'd blown him one more time.' "

"You little shit."

"Do you want dinner?"

"No," she said. "I want to go to bed. I don't like to think about your going overseas. I won't be tiresome, Sam. It's just the diseases you'll catch."

"I'll jerk off. I've been practicing."

"I hope not today."

They went to her apartment, smoked, made love, watched candles, made love. At two o'clock they were exhausted and sore.

Your gaiety will end up in Asia.

She watched his clean face, his ears, the puppy softness around his nose and lips. How appealing; despite all they had done and tried, how untouchably innocent.

He looked up at her, his eyes surprised. "I don't think I can."

"Let me try."

But he fell asleep, and in the morning there was no time. He left the suit on the floor and put on a drab green uniform. His face was that of a boy soldier. He could be anybody of any class.

He would take a cab to New Jersey. As he left he handed her a package wrapped in brown paper. "Something for you. For your work. Don't open it now. You don't know where you got it."

The cab left.

She cried looking at the space in the street. They had had fun, such sweet, loving silly times in this ugly senseless mess.

She opened the package hours later. It was one of those expensive leather-bound large-page desk journals filled with Houston's small, neat writing—his notes on the great and his big ideas.

Sam had put a note in front: "This was on the floor of his office, where it's been for a month. You know how careless he is." Indeed she did—the S.O.B. *always* dropped things for others to pick up. "Please copy and return discreetly. I love you. Sam."

Sam sent postcards from Travis Air Force Base, Hawaii, and a free letter from Cam Ranh Bay.

> *I'm a clerk here. Only 363 days to go. Good TV reception, dumb programs. And the rock they play is no good. Got to have tapes. Will you send?*
> *. . . This is like a bad motel. Remember when I said it all happened on a television set? Still, you have the smells.*
> *. . . Must get out. Can you come to Hawaii?*

The next letter was from another soldier.

Dear Phoebe Bishop,

You don't know who I am but I was close to Sam Hicks for a short time and he wanted me to tell you if this happened. He was killed last night. This is the fifth time I've started this letter. I'm sorry. Sam was a good man. I know he was crazy about you. We liked each other from the start; I guess we'd been picked up by the same random scoop and put where we didn't belong. I went to The Hill and was drafted out of Princeton last year. I was pre-med so they made me a medic, which made more sense than the Army traditionally has. Sam was in S-1. He read every AR he could get his hands on to find a way out.

We smoked a number last night after dinner and he said he thought he'd found one. I don't know what it was. The rockets came in after midnight and he was running to the trench when he got a splinter in his chest. I must tell you this so you know. I tried all I could, blocking the wound, but he was filling up too fast. I could see his color changing. I told him, "Sam, I can't help it, you're going to die."

"Fuck!" he said. And then he said, "Phoebe." And then he said, "Come on, I don't feel that bad." He tried to joke. "You sure you know what you're talking about?" Then he couldn't talk. He just went out.

I'm really sorry. That sounds so helpless, but I am. This is all no good.

BURTON DERRY

The War Is Everywhere

Houston flew to Paris to talk with rail car foundry executives about funding a metro car sale through the city, TA, and French government. The French cars were clearly superior to any American design and cheaper too, but it was just a junket. He knew a backstairs deal had been made for bigger, heavier, less dependable cars.

He had been talking with Beame's pixie sidekick, Cavanaugh, a Damon Runyon politician they called Abie's Irish Rose. He was *incredible*. Shabby. Ignorant. "We got a deal," he said. And "So they're expensive. We raise taxes." And "Banks raise interest; why can't we raise taxes?" The usual form of class resentment he'd seen in LBJ, too: Attack the banks.

Still, he was on the junket as a break because everyone had heard the tough news about little Sam. "Devastating!" he'd said. "Tragic!"—the clichés belying how truly stunned and anguished he was; but it had always been his reflex, even when pounded, to spring up and move on (run back to the huddle), so he gave those quick responses like running notes on a xylophone: *blink blank blonk!* Our family's done its bit! He had a lot of fun! Terrible luck!

Houston's sadness was overlaid with self-disgust at not having been able to get Sam out, too. Could they have finessed it with a little more effort? Fraker Chillingworth had mentioned Yale Divinity School—but of course he didn't know how young poor Sam was. The younger brothers and nephews of so many they knew were at Yale or some other seminary because they were lottery-proof.

*   *   *

"I just want it to stop," Ma said. Usually she had a bluff, cheerful manner, but she was ashen, too.

He had flown Pam Am (use American flag carriers on city business). He hated it. They lost his goddam luggage. *Où se trouve la change?* He wandered around Orly's long metal-and-glass concourses awhile, hoping Pan Am would find his luggage. His suit was wrinkled and gamy. His secretary hadn't known how to get him francs beforehand. City employee: goddam typical. Saw someone watching him behind the aluminum rail of a bar-café on the walkway. Beard, worn leather lapel jacket, black cloth cap. He didn't like to be looked at by someone dressed like that. He gave a dismissive glance.

"Houston Bridles!" His tone was crisp, unlike the way he looked.

Houston squinted. "Randolph. Mark." As he approached, he smelled foul Gitanes. The Rands already had much gray in his hair and beard. Houston was a bit unsettled by Mark's appearance but he gave a jovial squeeze and grin. "Am I glad to see you! Can't find the damn exchange. Can you change some dollars?"

"Don't want any. You need francs, though."

"Of course."

"Booth's over there. Opens in a few minutes. I'll buy you a beer." He asked for a *pression* in rapid French. "I live here now," he said, and when Houston asked why, said, "I got tired of seeing the same goddam things. War news. You can't get away from the war. People yowling. American cities are unlivable now."

"I wish I could get a situation like that," Houston said. Mark didn't rise to the bait. "Are you working?" he prompted.

"I'm working on a project. A couple of inventions. I had some luck in the market to give me leeway." Mark didn't ask Houston; he glanced at his wrinkled, expensive suit and, Houston felt, deduced enough.

Houston was about finished with his beer when Mark said, "I can't understand how everything got so royally screwed up. I was in Rome when the Cambodian invasion hit the news. Then the killings at Kent State. The Italian students rioted. Garbage strike at the same time. It was like opera—big mounds of garbage as a backdrop, the mob stepping this way, the riot police marching after them, the mob charging that way, low clouds of tear gas. At least their riot squads are professional. I don't think our government can find its ass with both hands. Kent State was one-eighty out from how troops should handle a riot."

"What do you mean?"

"You're supposed to have troops on line pushing and a couple of designated snipers in back. If someone shoots or throws rocks, only the snipers fire. The National Guard panicked. They're a mob of white draft dodgers."

"Perhaps that's a new technique."

"Older than us. Training film we used was shot in Italy in the occupation, in the Yankee-go-home riots. We know less now than we used to."

"You don't miss home."

"Don't have one. Don't miss the States, if that's what you mean. It's no good there now. I got so sick and tired of listening to . . . Americans. Europeans aren't perennially shocked and they don't have to *talk* so much. I think people imagine heroes who are the opposite of who they really are—you know, like the French have *galants* because they're so grasping themselves, and the Spanish have these deft bull-fighters 'cause so many of them are *shlemiels*. And in America we have these strong silent heroes like Gary Cooper or Clint Eastwood because we *talk* so goddam much. About silly— Anyway, I spend most of my time in Spain. I guess I'm a *shlemiel*, too. It's kind of interesting living in another nation that once owned half the world and pissed it away." He laughed his heehaw laugh.

Houston didn't think it was terribly funny.

"A lot of Americans are sinking into the earth over here, Houston. Not just hippies and heads—I mean clods like me who don't want to be noticed. Sayonara to the Land of the Big PX. It's like dial-an-age here, I can contemplate a street that once had knights' horses clatter-ing the stones and see women in black in a procession and a painted virgin going back to when she was a goddess, and I don't have to listen to—"

Houston mulled about this in the cab on the way to the George V, for which the cheapskate City of New York was not paying all the tariff. A man, after all, has his standards.

Mark had been one of those happy barflies who had never ques-tioned the standards; not just Yale values (God, Country, Yale; Manly Hearty Goodness), but also Deke values (being one of the guys, telling a raunchy joke when possible, flicking a pat of butter across a crowded dining room onto an oil portrait so some eighteenth-century dignitary had a yellow square on his nose, using a lacrosse stick to rifle a water balloon at some weenie down the block and splatter it all over him, arms flying, glasses and books falling.

Houston had seen him that May night after he'd met Phoebe, Mark and some chums rolling out of his battered car, giggling, carrying a little pig, tiptoeing, shushing, up the stairs in Davenport to slide it into Dean Roberts's quarters.

He was a meatball, all right, but such a high-hearted amusing meatball, the one you expected to show up with space in his car, with that happy blonde from Skidmore, sometimes with an extra girl, the one who'd carry the keg. But now to see him—smell him, too—as a musty, bearded, *caporal*-smoking *soi-disant* European in those dingy foreign clothes and talking, for God's sake, of American decline. Houston picked diffidently at this. Since his genius was to keep moving over the surface rather than dig his plow, as it were, into rocky soil, he quickly concluded, *Too bad!*

Nevertheless, seeing his classmate was important to Houston because it directed him to his next wife. It came to him in a flash: I want a *blonde*.

All the reasons, the justifying data, came after. The negative example of raven-haired Phoebe with her implacable bluestocking insistence on questioning, snapping, upsetting; her acidic sensibility, saying things like "I was never innocent"—even her showing up at Fence, singing, bringing chaos. Well, the breaks. No dark passion, no Merreleese.

Stupid Blinky Mawson was a blonde. Sexual, yes. Too depraved, though, really. She'd given someone a bead job at the Boston Cotillion with her heirloom pearls. That was a bit much. Good, happy, bouncy—someone like Marty Sanford! The reflections on her Ben Wa balls—yes! A blonde, of course. But this time from the right background—both of them could understand—a blonde to stand up with him at receptions, run the houses.

Write a job description. Find one who fills the bill!

The prospect of something to do, a person to win, following the ball, pepped him up immensely, and he had a nice time in Paris, hardly needing to leave those few blocks bounded by the Île de la Cité and the Place d'Étoile. Even there he was looking—the lovely women of a certain class, dressing like their American sisters in simple blouses and skirts, with brushed, shining hair. Find a blonde. A blonde is your future.

Phoebe had plenty of work to do and did not want to think about anything else. Inside she was empty and filling up; yin–yang, life in death. She got a call in the newsroom.

"Phoebe? It's Carole. I can't talk long. How are you?"

Phoebe heard street noises in the background. She had been preoccupied with a story about cops cleaning out the camera collection of a photographer who had died in his studio, and being upset and mad and unprofessional about it, and feeling stirrings inside and stretching pains, so it took a moment to place "Carole" and that tentative alto voice.

"Carole! How *are* you? *Where* are you?"

"I can't talk now. Can we meet?"

Two hours later she walked along Central Park South across from the St. Moritz. A yellow cab rolled by, stopped, the door opened, and a black-haired woman leaned out and took off her sunglasses. It was Carole.

"Hi. Get in."

They rode into Central Park, then got out and walked among the trees. Carole wore a long gray cape with hood that she said she'd got in Marrakech.

"Where have you *been*, Carole?"

"North Africa. And in . . . Europe, for a while."

"I know you liked Provence."

"Yeah, I was in northern Europe, though. Uh, Germany. For a while I thought I'd stay away. You know."

"I've been getting your cards but don't remember— You've been gone some time, and I wondered—"

"It was after Wisconsin," Carole said, lighting a cigarette and blowing smoke and steam into the cold air. All Phoebe could see of her face was her shades and the tip of her nose and the rough gray wool of her hood.

"Were you studying there?"

They were by the Alice in Wonderland bronze. Carole stopped. "Phoebe, why do you think I'm on the run?"

"I suppose it has something to do with Weather, but I'm not going to quiz you, Carole. You'll tell me if you want."

"I'm wanted for murder."

She turned her glasses toward Phoebe, her nose red from the cold, her head and body wrapped in that mysterious garment. She stood next to the Mad Hatter.

"We planted a device that killed some fucking cop who shouldn't have been there at the CIA office in Chicago."

"During the Days of Rage?"

"No." She shook her head.

"I didn't know, Carole. Usually the wire has information on who's wanted."

"That's just it! The conniving bastards! That's what Nixon's doing now to destroy the Movement! He's not giving publicity! They put out APB's without telling the press. They think the press will warn us or make celebrities out of us! Like when you showed Jane Fonda in Hanoi! He's destroying the First Amendment, and now people don't even know who's *wanted*, who's a suspect! It's like Arthur *Koestler!*" She threw away her cigarette. "Fuckin' West Coast pigs!"

They walked on.

"What have you been doing, Phoebe?"

"I'm pregnant by a dead man. Houston's nephew. He was drafted and killed the week after he got there."

"Oh, honey. How do you feel?"

"I don't know, Carole—I'm without connections. Schizzed out, it's all coming apart. I feel everything; I don't know what to do. I think anyone who wants an abortion should have one, those awful people out there who have children and beat them to death, but, Jesus, Carole, I saw it! With Houston! *And I want Sam! I want something of us!*"

People turned to look at her and looked away. Carole put her arm around her. "Come on, Phoebe." They went to Phoebe's place.

"I want to kill them all," Carole said. "If the XYY chromosome definitely means murder, the XY *probably* does. Men revel in it. I swear to God, Phoebe, I'll blow up my next Army depot as a dedication to you. I'll trash the center that drafted Sam if you like. I'm really very good. I learned a lot more about explosives in Algeria. Fuzes, chains, common substances that will trash a room. Pigs in the West think they know so much with their industrial shit! Fuck it! I can go to a grocery store and get enough for a bomb."

"You've lost a lot of weight, haven't you?"

"Yes." She was wearing Phoebe's robe. Between her breasts she had freckles from her last time in the sun, in the Mediterranean, and her skimpy blonde hair belied the dye on her head and eyebrows. She walked to the window and pushed between the plants to look down on the street, lit orange and blue. It was midnight. "I blew up four truckloads of Army ammunition in Wisconsin, Phoebe. The feds told the press it was an industrial accident. They don't want to admit how much we're doing."

"Is it doing any good?" Phoebe sat in the brown leather armchair with a blanket wrapped around her, chain-smoking. A cold coffee, her tenth cup, sat on the block table beside her.

"What is good?"

"For a good end?"

"I don't even care about the end anymore. The good is in the action, the process, not the progress. But yes, it does good."

"How?"

"It fucks up the enemy."

Phoebe shrugged.

"Don't be silly, Phoebe. I'd had enough of being a blonde dumb cunt. I was so *stupid*, Phoebe. I simply accepted this. Even after Peas destroyed me. I didn't know how any of that worked until later. I took it all in, like a clam in polluted water. It wasn't till after I saw some film, you know? On television? About a *woman* being shot in the war—then it clicked. That's their *game*—they'd just as soon kill us all. So when I focused my hate I didn't focus on Peas, I focused on where he came from. He's a Social Democrat with a bagful of concerned phrases and he hates women. He hates men, too, because he feared and resented people in authority and put all his poison into *me*. And he hates women for a different reason—he didn't want their love, didn't want mine. The more I gave, the worse he got. He wants what he can take. But he's the product of a diseased, twisted, perverted society. I know you've heard that."

"It's all right."

"I could have killed him, but that wouldn't have accomplished anything. I'm doing more good now."

"Carole, bombing won't solve anything."

"Bombing may not over there, but it does wonders here. Just think of it, honey. No one's smug here anymore."

"No, people aren't smug. Or they don't care. Look, I'm knocked up. I'm not horrified, but I don't know what to do."

"I wouldn't agonize over it, honey. Have your baby. Have it all by yourself. You're lucky. You liked him, didn't you?"

"It was crazy. Yes, I did. I miss him."

"Well, have the baby. You'll have the best of both worlds. You won't have a man to turn ugly on you later and you'll have a kid you can raise right. If you're lucky it'll be a girl. I mean, fuck, parthenogenesis is *it*, honey. If everyone'd ovulate during a cold snap and get pregnant *without men* and deliver females, we *couldn't* fuck up the world worse'n these assholes did."

"I wish I had a man now, Carole. I'm afraid."

"Your luck hasn't been much better than mine, Phoebe. No one's good enough for you."

"That's exactly it. It's my fault. It's not that I pick pick pick, really—it's all inside me. If the man does something *predictable* I feel like a tennis ball hitting the fence—*plop!* But if he's *too* different I think, Well, this isn't *possible*. You must have seen some interesting men."

"I was in love with a Wisconsin bomber," Carole said. "He was some heavy dude, Phoebe. We had a place in the woods and he rigged dynamite deals, ammonium nitrate—we took down a fuckin' *fertilizer shed* and the pigs couldn't snap on to *why*, and we used two tons of rose food to blow up a place—trashed that fucker ankle high. And he could fly, too. We stole a plane and dropped dynamite on a state pig office. I was ballin' him and this chick who was our cutout, and we're all on the run now. *She* was crazy. She was from Lake Forest. It was serendipity. I'm not queer—it's a bodily function, Phoebe. We get off together. We always had something bigger ahead of us. But, yeah, he was an interesting dude. He didn't fuck around. See a place, watch it, trash it. I knew he was strong. I didn't mind how crazy it was."

Carole had become so strong, vengeful, brave, a virago. "You reach out and I retreat," Phoebe told her.

"Why do you think? Have you talked about it in group?"

"No group," Phoebe said. "I don't want to tell a group."

"Tell me. It's hung you up."

Phoebe sighed. "You might as well know. It wasn't anything that *happened*—it was all implied, suppressed, unrealized tension, like Henry James. Daddy watching me in the tack room when I was twelve and thirteen, before I went away to school. He didn't *do* anything—he was always the soul of rectitude. I just felt—I knew—I was never innocent. It hasn't hurt my sex—it hurts the way I think. Whoever's a just-right WASP boy makes me tingle—wide eyes and a cotton shirt are like a tongue in my ear—but as time goes on and they head into substance and rectitude, I know too much. And then Houston finished it off. For someone to be, not consciously, viciously cruel, but *heartless*, to know someone just doesn't care about you beyond your function—well, for me they're either pricks or they don't wear well, don't last, don't survive."

"They want to use you," Carole said. "They only want to see what you've got, paw it, break it, get bored like white trash reject pioneers, and move on to new wilderness. The Indians should have had the H-Bomb. Name me one fucking man who was ever nice without trying to *get* something."

"Mark Randolph was for a while," Phoebe said. "After my miscarriage. We'd already slept together. I suppose there wasn't any curiosity, and he'd grown so much, he was used to thinking for others. Good soldiers *are* selfless, Carole, and I knew he cared—"

Carole was looking at her in profound flared-nostril lifted-lip disbelief. "Him! Oh, no!"

"Well, it's out of the question anyway—"

"Phoebe, *what* are you basing this on?"

"Oh, it doesn't matter. I always felt he felt something—well, personal. I don't—never mind."

"Phoebe, he is a collossal brain failure! He babbles, he's been in one disaster after another, and he *asks* for it! Listen—do you know what that asshole tried with me?"

"What?"

"It was in Morocco. I'd just come over the mountains from Algeria to Marrakech by the trucks they use as buses between villages and ran into Mark on the D'jma el F'naa, the big square where idle kids smoke hash and drink mint tea, wear jellabas and sheepskins, and watch the pigeon sellers and conjurors and black dudes from the south. Mark was there trying to dig it. He had on Spanish workers' clothes, canvas boots, so he didn't look like another head. He acted like a pig, aware of who was walking close to him, smoking a cigarette, looking this way and that.

"I needed a running mate to Casa—they'd raped a single woman on the Marrakech Express and I'd dropped off my escort on the way in—so I went up to him. 'What a coincidence!' I said."

"Did he recognize you?"

"Sure. I wasn't disguised. When I told him he went into this 'Okay, sugar, big man'll protect you' routine. We went to his pension and smoked some and talked. He said he'd left America forever; something wasn't right back home. 'No shit,' I said. 'Have you read Frantz Fanon?'

"No, he hadn't. 'I don't give a shit about revolution,' he said. 'I want to emigrate but actually to another century. Do you know anything about the Wobblies? People on the frontier were the only interesting ones,' he said.

"What he was saying made no sense. He was disaffected. 'Fuck everything' was his theory. We were stoned, and I asked if he didn't learn anything in Vietnam, and he blabbers on about how they'd move at night, and how he'd admire the skills of the enemy, and *no* revolutionary consciousness! None at all. I mean, *stooooopid!* Then he moved on me. We necked and he played with my boobs and was *panting*. He dropped his pants and said, 'I don't wear underwear anymore.' I mean, oh, wow, and I thought, What *is* this? He doesn't know *who I am!* He doesn't know my *role!*

"And I stood up and *told* him, '*You* can't exploit women, *you* can't exercise machismo anymore, *you* are what's wrong with America and the West! And you want to stick *your* dick into *me*? Ha! Ha! Ha!'

"He's standing with his pants down and his hard-on rapidly losing credibility and his jaw hanging open, not even understanding why I'm haranguing him. At the end, when I paused for breath, he said, 'Shit, it's too late to get another broad tonight,' and I was so pissed off I could have shot him! I wish now I'd had a piece. I just stomped out. I got a jellaba and a knife and rode to Casa alone, ready to stab any melon fucker who tried me."

Phoebe shook her head, laughing. "Mark *is* dumb. He walks into it."

"I gave it to him good," Carole said. "Don't like someone 'cause he's safe and stupid, Phoebe."

She left in midmorning, when she would not be noticed in the crowds, and said she was going west.

A well-bred person does not make scenes; sometimes, of course, things happen around one, and others lose control of themselves and become unattractive, but that is their problem.

Phoebe was walking down Madison in December, properly

dressed in a black jumper—she was showing—and her heavy tweed coat, when she saw Edith Hicks pushing Pa Bridles in a wheelchair out of the Carlyle. Tally ho! She felt like rising in the stirrups. Pinched apple face, black cloth under the cream and green and gilt canopy. Mrs. Bridles came out too. Where was Kelly and the car? How gay and bright the shop windows were. Phoebe walked close.

Edith looked haggard and hung over, fingers twisting beads at her neck. Mrs. Bridles fingered flowers on her coat. Her pleasant face did not light up at the sight of Phoebe.

"Halloo," Phoebe said. "I wish simply to tell you I am devastated by Sam's death. He was a wonderful young man. I loved him."

"Please," Edith said, looking at her mother, shaking her head, sawing her hand sideways.

"And I'm carrying his child."

"No!" Edith put her hand to her mouth.

"What do you want?" Mrs. Bridles said.

"I don't want anything. I want you to know."

"I'll be a grandmother!" Edith said. "I *can't* be a grandmother. Mummy!" She turned toward the shiny revolving door.

Phoebe looked at Mrs. Bridles. "Sam and I were lovers. We had a terrific time and loved each other very much. We were crazy about each other."

"You'd never have married."

"Whatever we might have done is moot."

"And you intend to use his name? What is it you want?" Mrs. Bridles said. "You cannot claim The Point. You have no claim!"

Pa Bridles said, "Miss Bishop."

"Yes, Mr. Bridles."

"Why didn't you go to Italy?"

"Houston," Mrs. Bridles said.

Pa Bridles looked benignly at Phoebe. A silver thread of drool dropped from the corner of his mouth to his tweed coat and hung there.

Edith screamed, *"You can't stand here!"* The doorman looked at her.

"You can't have a share," Mrs. Bridles said. "You must leave! Leave now, please."

"I want nothing," Phoebe said, "except that you acknowledge Sam's child."

"No! Oh, Mother!"

"Please go away."

Pa Bridles said something about takeoff.

"I can't—" Edith said, biting her lip. "You are just inexcusable!"

"He was better than the rest of you," Phoebe said.

She was pregnant. Do you know how it changes you? The stretching pain, nausea, rise in temperature, having to pee constantly? That she already knew. What surprised her this time was how calm she was—indeed, how sweet she became, how kind. She had something to look forward to, something that she knew in her bones would be good. Every day she felt this little mouse growing, she remembered Sam, felt love and kindness flowing through her, acceptance, patience. She was easily hurt and sometimes burst into tears for little reason.

It was this kindness more than physical discomfort that decided her to take a leave of absence from news work. She could not be incisive, suspicious, effective—so she took a leave of absence from the network for about two years. Her contract said she could return to specific duties when her leave ended. The age thirty distribution from the Duikermann side put her in good shape anyway. She still had AFTRA residuals and benefits, and intended in the meantime to assemble photographs and make a show.

Those were big years in the business.

President Nixon had managed to outrage every liberal interest by 1972, when his burglars were caught in the Democratic National Headquarters at the Watergate in Washington, a modern glass complex that looked somewhat like the Century Plaza in L.A., where LBJ's Presidency had begun to crash.

Both events showed a truth: that Presidents weren't magic, right, or even particularly bright. Why people would have to be reminded of this was another mystery, but Phoebe supposed it was an AC–DC function of her business, shooting pictures of pageantry and glorifying the institution and then trying to depict objectively these seedy, exhibitionist politicians who live in the glow. Watergate was an opportunity to put killing light on anything that stunk in government, anything they'd been told not to show—officials getting drunk, stealing, misusing cars, taping their visitors.

Nixon's staff leaked "news" about *other* Presidents' taping and bugging, trying to deflect attention from Nixon. "Congressmen are meeting with North Vietnamese!" Erlichman charged, which was true. Sandy Sanford and Liz Holtzman, among others, appeared at rallies where the crowd waved the blue, red, and yellow flag. But what Nixon didn't like was congressmen meeting with the press. All the leaks did was stir up more rage. It was a chance to use a flamethrower on dead limbs, to channel torrents of public rage against the caked dung of the institution.

Ash Loakes became one of the journalistic heroes of Watergate for his investigative series on the FBI. He discussed the mythology of the FBI, its part in radio shows like "Gangbusters" and "This Is Your FBI," and the Ford-sponsored TV show. The publicity shots of the bulldog-faced Hoover with a tommy gun—and the real Hoover, raising roses, living with another man, albeit an agent, and carrying slimy toilet photos of congressmen and appointees to Lyndon Johnson and Richard Nixon among others. The way Hoover padded the bureau's statistics with arrests of interstate car thieves and befuddled draft dodgers while doing nothing about organized crime, letting the Mob take over whole industries in cities like New York. The way Hoover demanded that local police muscle for big busts where shooting was expected, though the FBI television show always had agents in impeccable suits doing the shooting.

Phoebe saw Ash at Elaine's during this time and he was infuriated about the FBI, a crusader taking on authority. "I'm going to stick it in them and break it off!"

Chick De Vore, the short, smelly correspondent, also in New York now, told her—"Ya wanta know what *really* happened?"—that Ash got a lot of his material from Allard Lowenstein, who had been harassed by the FBI, and other bits from Lowenstein's benefactor, the CIA, which was having its own problems with the Bureau and the press. But that didn't matter. Ash won a Sigma Delta Chi award for connecting the Bureau with Ku Klux Klan kid killers and church bombers, with nuts who sniped at civil rights marches, and with spying on Martin Luther King. In the business, and in Western culture, truth has an intrinsic value, like gold, and it doesn't matter how you get it.

Chick De Vore told how he'd covered Nixon years earlier in California and how the man was always foxy and insinuating, a cynical master at telling voters what they wanted to hear. Many now bought the Checkers speech of 1952 and listened to it stoned, to pick out the tricks, the appeals to prejudice, stupidity, and sentiment. The way Nixon had handled the peace movement was the same—putting long-haired shill demonstrators out to stampede worried folk toward his programs, abolishing the draft so that young men had no personal reason to stay in the antiwar movement and it collapsed. Those who called themselves thinkers and articulators did not like to have Nixon prove that most people weren't high-minded or altruistic; they didn't like the mirror he held up. Many newspeople were pissed off at themselves, too, because Lyndon Johnson had been such a monster, and the news had covered up his lies and excesses for years until he had ruined too much.

Chick De Vore said when Nixon lost the 1962 California governor's race he was finished. He yelled at reporters. He knew he was dead. What brought him back to life was Johnson being so awful. So when Nixon tripped on Watergate, after invading Cambodia, after Kent State, newspeople had a chance to unload on him like Puff the Magic Dragon and have a catharsis of hatred at two dreadful Presidents.

The European press offered other reasons why Nixon got it with such vehemence, but there were always some stories American media couldn't run, even now.

Phoebe didn't have a chance to get the boot in, to use Jim Robinson's term. She was too sweet, loving, and self-absorbed that winter of 1971–72. The feelings came to her later.

She quit smoking and limited the amount she drank while she was pregnant, but she enjoyed going the few blocks to Elaine's to sit and talk. It was a parallel trip for her because some of the people who hung out there were *Paris Review* writers or former interns. Brian Beechwood often went there, now celebrated for his prize-winning book on Vietnam, *Burning Temples*. It explained the war by showing how the Vietnamese perceived themselves, their world, and us, and how American cultural weakness not only had made it impossible for us to address the political war there, but also, like the clumsiness of an attacker in martial arts, made us hurt ourselves more the harder we lunged.

Brian paid no attention to the old dove–hawk terms. He showed how the NLF could be cruel when it had to, but why it worked for them and not us. There was another angle concealed in the book but most readers didn't grasp it at the time.

Other former Apothekers and Musinskys from *The Paris Review* were there as well, and artists and writers of the previous generation. One game they played was called "Dynamite Museum," in which artists in one medium worked in another, as when Norman Mailer wrote poetry and read it at museum gatherings. Perhaps no great art came out of these left-handed soirées, but the term "dynamite" went into the arts and then into general use in the early seventies, so that at a party you could have dynamite wine, dynamite cheese, and a dynamite time.

Garde! Mark Randolph woke sweating and panicked, again uncertain where he was. The armoire. The chair. Not the BOQ—a *pensión*. Itching, sweating, the thick sourness of scratchy red wine on his tongue, half-evaporated brandy scraping inside his skull, lungs and mouth painted by cigarettes.

He hadn't got to the museum. A *chato*, a slender glassita of wine, *unas pocas copitas, hablamos, amigos,* shoot the shit, a few stories, watch the people. Watch the people who are living.

Jesus Christ, he was unhappy. Why had he wasted another day yesterday? Why hadn't he—? Why couldn't he—? Questions clawed around inside him like bugs on his flesh. He didn't know the lives of newspeople, though they'd defined part of his life, but he was scrabbling after their basic questions—who what when where why? Who was he? Why here? Why had he survived? In the dim shutter-striped light he saw pictures of horror like fragments of torn photographs—his mother and father squabbling and suffering—why? His men, cold, weary, wounded; the shooting. The blown-up shack. The Sidgee whose spine he'd snapped—a man whose family had been hostage to the VC, all those relationships, family and country, snapped like his spine. His ex-wife's angry face. The horror of his parents' deaths—a drink in the plane in mid-air, fire and earth, all the elements of a world of death. The face of Pike, ears bleeding, his men wounded, holding—and he, Randolph, was here. Why? No family, no wife, comrades tattering away in memory.

His resilience was shot. All through his youth and twenties he'd been able to slip and slide through God knows what and laugh about it and expect the next time to be easier. Now instead of saying, "Whew!" he asked, "Why?"—and expected the worst next time up. He didn't want to go on. He looked into the dark spiral of himself, like looking down a gun barrel, and saw black twisting tighter and tighter: Death.

But at least he knew how to move without a mind. Down the cold dusty tiles to the *baño* and clean up. Walk down worn blue-shadowed streets. Stones here forever. Find the quiet space, dark *iglesia*.

He sat on the dusty bench unnoticed, a thick-shouldered man in common worker's corduroy and a sagging sweater, his beard graying, gazing dully at the image of the Virgin in her layered garments of red, gold, black, white, blue. Her glass shining eyes. It was calm here. They made a religion of childbirth and death. The figure of the Virgin looked like La Dama de Elche, the ancient strong-jawed woman's stone head dug up on the coast, connected to some mysterious queendom before the Phoenicians and Romans, the strong jaw and high forehead like Phoebe's. The dark hair and shining eyes of the Virgin, dark and light, death and life. Christ, he had hurt women. Natasha. Tears came to his eyes. Judy. Carole. And he'd been flayed by them. He didn't know anything about women. Or life.

He was in a dark church with a few dim lights, a shadowy grove of cluster columns topped by intertwined animals, pagan art, stone curves touched by light. Surrounded by death, somehow alive. He didn't know why. It wasn't the current theology, it was this ancient arrangement: women, blood, wood, snakes, water, stone, bread. He wasn't so different from others who'd been baffled by life or had messed it up.

He sat until he became aware that his ass was sore on the old wood bench. God, he had a huge, skull-banging hangover. He left the church, sucked in cool air on the worn stone street shadowed by walls from the Moors and Goths. People in black, the smells of coffee and black tobacco. This place he loved where they'd seen it all before.

At first Phoebe didn't know any more about Carole's death than the rest of the public. She was at home on Lexington, not in a newsroom, so didn't hear any wire service bells go off when the terrific explosion pulverized a townhouse off Sheridan Square. Brian Beechwood had said, "The war is everywhere."

All channels ran pictures of the house that night. It looked like a 155-millimeter shell had hit it: the facade blown off, the rubble of brick, splintered timber, and dust over the sidewalk and filling the cellar, where the firemen found enough to say there had been three people and varieties of explosives. The police didn't say until two days later who the bodies belonged to.

Carole Tiddens, thirty-one, B.A., Vassar, history, fugitive, wanted on suspicion of murder, interstate flight, possession of explosives, possession of automatic weapons, assault, destruction of U.S. property, destruction of private property. The police released all the information Carole said the FBI had been holding out: her part in the Chicago Days of Rage, Wisconsin bombings, CIA office bombing, and other bits that weren't crime but fed the story; how she had visited communist countries to receive explosives training. After her visit with Phoebe, she had lived in a farmhouse in Pennsylvania used as a commune for radical athletes. She had not used the term "jock-fucker" on Phoebe during that last visit.

Among the effects found when the FBI, or local police, or both, raided the farmhouse was a letter to a friend in Wisconsin in which she described herself as a guerrilla and said, "My parents killed John Kennedy." She had put fifty thousand dollars in cash down on the townhouse a month earlier. It had come from her "floating fund."

Ash Loakes wrote a tender obit of her, with pictures, saying she had been "like so many concerned, affluent people of our generation" and reminiscing about her roots in Middle America, her interest in film as a statement of Now, her growing commitment to the Movement. He did it well, though as usual he was dishonest, for he had met her only once, that spring a decade earlier. But because he described her part in the Movement she became a heroine.

Adams Peabody called Phoebe and asked her what she knew. Phoebe gave a long and detailed account. He said nothing for the longest time—dead air. Finally he said, in a grim tone, "Thank you," and hung up.

Sammy was born at Lenox Hill. It was a normal birth. Phoebe was alone, crying and laughing when the doctor put him on her chest—this little, squinty cone-headed monkey with dark fuzz on his head and back and grasping tiny fingers and upper lip stuck out like an egg tooth, this tiny, helpless creature who needed her, for whom she could be everything, descended from angels, knowing nothing of the world.

The center of her life changed for those years. She nursed and changed him, bathed him, watched as his eyes registered, as his features rounded, as he gained weight and learned to move. She slept with him beside her, and then settled him in his crib, listened to his cries resolve into sounds; saw his motions turn into crawling, cruising, walking; watched him grow from instinct to awareness, watched him pick up things and turn them this way and that to examine them before he put them into his mouth.

By the time he was sitting up she was going through pounds of proof sheets to set up her show. Some of the Vassar shots were good and worth showing, but the best and most immediate were from Vietnam: the thin faces of the Cao Dai with their ammunition belts and religious discs, the shaved-head bonzes, a Catholic procession in a crowded market, and the combat shots—the weary, dusty faces of young soldiers, an officer talking into a telephone like an executive but with that extra dimension of fear and death stamped into the paper like a hologram. Vietnamese screaming and curled in bloody heaps by the restaurant.

Black-and-white war photos, our black side. War brought out the noblest and most disgusting traits. Men wreaked it and women suffered for it, losing husbands and children. It was a minotaur devouring the young, the monster in the shadows, but so immediate. Live or die now. Smoke a cigarette, have a drink, see a corpse, be a corpse. She understood Jim's fascination. It made her shudder coldly, the opposite of an orgasm.

She cried looking at the faces of the young men in uniform and the land that had blown up around them, the sandbags instead of pillows, the clattering helicopters instead of custom cars, the tracers in the night sky instead of drive-in movies. She didn't want Sammy to go through this. She held him to her body and vowed to protect him, the way she hadn't saved her men, hadn't stopped them somehow.

The faces of the young and soon-to-be-dead haunted her. Their deaths were criminal. This ugly, crooked government of slobs, egoists, narcissists, clever fools, liars, toilet spies, and thieves had sent young men off on stupid orders to get killed, caring no more about them than an ape jerking off in a zoo cares about flakes of dandruff falling from his head. Americans had used to revere public service and war as sacred duty, but the high priests of government had massacred their own innocents. She hated them all—men, government liars, bullshitting MACV officers—and she wanted to kill them.

She had already seen her body change from swollen, flushed lubricity with Sam before the mirror, in the bath, on the floor, in the cab, standing up—and swelling, smiling, feeling so gentle having

Sammy. Now she wanted sharp edges, battering, death to the killers. When Sammy was peacefully asleep in his crib, when she spread proof sheets and eight-by-tens over the floor to examine them and created a black field, she felt the black rage flood through her as she stood above the faces of the damaged young, and in her reflection in the window she saw black, black lines coursing down her face, black hair, black forces spinning around her, black arrows shot from her head; she had black claws. Men had done it, men had caused Sam's death, had ruined lives, had ruined this country full of promise when she had been in her twenties, and Phoebe had to destroy them.

You see living people as targets, Mark Randolph had said. You search the terrain systematically and find your enemy and point; the steel sight concentrates your vision. Targets. Figures in black. Death in life. The little bloody figure in Boston. The Dark Star.

No question about it. He'd killed. She wasn't a lawyer, didn't adjudicate, seek proportionality. She knew whom she must destroy.

She set to work the next day, using at the beginning Houston's *Who's Who* entry, the entries for his father and uncle, and then adulatory news copy about his White House and Lindsay administration years before it lost its charisma. The *Times* index led her to D-Section stories about Houston's ingenious financing. And she had her Xerox copy of Houston's journal that Sam had filched from Houston's office. Houston couldn't have noticed its absence—even before Sam was killed she'd copied the journal and right away had an apprentice drop it on the floor of Houston's office when a crew was shooting another magic funding story at City Hall.

But she hadn't delved into the journal pages until now. What she read made her hit the ceiling. That *prick!*

She called the Democratic National Committee, congressmen's offices, and finally located the person she needed.

"I think we should talk about something very important to both of us," Phoebe said. "Why don't we meet for lunch. At—at Schraft's? On Madison?"

She got there at one-thirty, when the room had begun clearing out.

"Miss Bishop? I'm Terry Menska."

She was tanned, fuller in the face than the day Phoebe had seen her at the White House, her smile brisk, officelike, nervous, her reddish-blonde hair longer. She wore a skirt, blouse, and green jacket a shade off.

"Would you like a drink?"

"Mmm—white wine?" Terry asked tentatively.

"I'm going to have a Manhattan," Phoebe said. "You may need one."

They had a long, for Schraft's, and busy lunch, and didn't waste time. Terry was working for the party in Manhattan. She had been on Bobby Kennedy's staff when he was a senator.

"I'm doing research on my ex-husband," Phoebe said.

"Any particular reason?"

"My contract calls for a number of features and interviews and I'm going back to work soon. I want to get him. To let the world know what part he had in all these disasters. I really want to kill him, but I'll settle for telling the truth and exposing his evil to destroy him."

"I'd love to help," she said.

Terry had her own scores to settle. She talked in her breathless way, ending sentences with a question. She told how big-idea people like Houston had ruined her home.

"I'm from Brooklyn? Do you know Gowanus—it's across from the Statue of Liberty? It's always been Democratic there—you'd go to committee picnics in the summer. My dad was a party regular? We have Polish butcher shops and our church. The Irish have the churches to the south, and they didn't want us, and the Italians in Carroll Gardens have theirs, and everything's been like that for generations. Nothing was wrong with the neighborhoods. The only thing that hurt a little was when the city tore out an el train line and put in an elevated car expressway along Third Avenue."

"Not the Third Avenue El?"

"No, in *Brooklyn?*" she said. "Right on the water, across from the Statue of Liberty? It ruined that street. You can have shops under an el but not under an expressway. But it still was all pleasant brownstones and houses. You didn't have anyone leaving to go to the suburbs. But then in nineteen sixty-four President Johnson tried to beautify the cities with what he called Urban Renewal and what the blacks called Urban Removal—lots of those projects were deals he'd cooked up to raze an area, drive out people who were just getting by, who'd put everything they had into their homes, get rid of them, and let developers come in and make money off it. And construction companies. All those companies paid him off."

"What did they do in your neighborhood?"

"They cut down all the trees and widened an avenue so people could drive through to the suburbs? The place looked like carpet bombing. People lost their houses. Old, charming houses and big, thick shade trees. The avenue's bare and ugly now. Houston expedited this, you know. 'It's the flow of power,' he said. 'Keynes is at work. Cities evolve. Some neighborhoods have to be pruned.' "

Phoebe turned over ways to show *that* on television, while Terry went on, talking about her family's butcher and what had happened to a little playground, but since it was gone, they couldn't show that, either. "What can you tell me about these decisions?" Phoebe asked, and read from her notes on Houston's journal telling about the key decisions to save Vietnam and our cities. Terry told Phoebe volumes.

It took weeks of going over the material and accusatory questions she would ask Houston to satisfy the network lawyers and a few days of jiggering to suit Houston's schedule. Phoebe appealed to his vanity, which had grown immensely.

"*Do* you have time? I know you're *so* busy—you're one of the few who can keep the city afloat—but millions want to hear about the city's finances and something about your experience at the top levels of government! You'd be terrific!" She put it breathlessly. She had formed it with the lawyers.

"Thanks, Phoebe—my secretary keeps my desk calendar."

Oh, ho, ho, ho, Phoebe thought. But not your journal. She *knew* how he left stuff around for his "batwomen" to pick up. "I'll hang on, dear. You can be hot news."

He was very busy then, because the city was heading into the fiscal crisis with workers striking and not being prosecuted, the TA paying twice as much for defective cars and buses, the schools losing millions and producing illiterates, and Houston was producing the notes and bonds that kept the government liquid. "We couldn't tape it?"

"No, we always go live," she said. He had to be shot live because she wanted all the glitches and confusions of live television to make it real.

Revenge from
the Air

They met in the corridor outside the armchair and coffee table studio used for "Issues." Phoebe wore an open-necked working blouse and skirt. They made small talk about sailing and sports. Houston said he'd been seeing "a nice girl named Virginia Hill who's just out of Finch—a great sailor! Enthusiastic! Young! Her family keeps a nice boat at Seventy-ninth Street."

"How nice for you," Phoebe murmured.

He had on a gray pinstripe, blue shirt, gold collar pin, and the round horn-rimmed glasses he had begun wearing. He complimented her on how nice she looked.

"Lovely. You've always been lovely, Phoebe. And your hair. No frizzy do yet? Isn't that what liberated women wear now? Frizzy hair?" His eyes twinkled.

"I know you like Afros," she said gaily. "No, they're not ready for it here. I'll see you inside."

The assistant producer checked around them and walked off. The red light came on.

"Tonight's guest is well known to government watchers," she began. "He has been inside many crucial decisions of our era, in the Johnson White House and in Mayor Lindsay's government. He's Houston Bridles—gentleman athlete, charmer, Presidential aide, financial wizard."

Camera Two's light went on and the man zoomed close on Houston, who grinned. "Thank you, Phoebe."

"What's on everyone's mind is the fiscal crisis. I know you've been asked this before, but for tonight, will we get out?"

"Yes."

"How?"

"By fine-tuning spending, watching costs, and tapping revenue the city hasn't touched before." He looked into the camera. "New York is a very rich city. The underlying fact is not that we're running out of money, but that formalities stand in the way of getting what's there."

"What is?"

"A cash flow. We're going to get full taxes where we haven't collected, charge for services like guarding UN diplomats. Also new short-term notes."

"So you'll get it through taxes and borrowing."

"More effective taxes and short-term borrowing."

"Who's losing money?"

"No one—other than the city right now."

"Who's making money?"

"I don't know what you mean."

"Who's profiting from the fiscal crisis?"

"Well, I don't know if it can be put quite that way."

"But you're talking about BANs, TANs, RANs, and so on—essentially banks are loan-sharking the city, aren't they?"

"I don't think it's quite accurate to use that term," he said without hesitating. He was far above it, much in command, and she had to bring him down.

"Loan-sharking? It *is* excessive interest, wouldn't you agree?"

"It's fair considering the city's— In order to go long term on this or buy lower, the city's got to improve its tax posture," he said. "We're building a better structure now."

"You wrote a terrific piece called 'Death and Taxes' for the *Times* Op-Ed." Houston inclined his head, smiling. "And one of your bravest acts, years ago, was, as you described it, to insist to President Johnson that he raise taxes to pay for the Vietnam War. That led to your break with the White House and New York's gain in getting you, didn't it?"

He smiled modestly. "Really, I wouldn't call it too much. Those were terribly mistaken policies, Phoebe. I felt the war had become a tragic enterprise."

"And you urged him to get out? Or to raise taxes?"

"My primary thrust, of course, was to attempt to manage programs efficiently, but beyond that I knew our power had its limits and could not, ah, be misused."

She turned toward the camera, made her most dazzling smile, and turned it like a lamp on him. "Really, Houston, that's nonsense. We were sleeping together then. You told me all about how Johnson could do anything he wanted. Remember?"

It didn't shake him. He made a knowing smile and moved his hand. "Fun, but we're getting a little off the—"

"But you *did* say that, Houston. Don't you remember saying that this President was a genius at amassing power? That by asking for consensus"— she consulted her notes—"I quote you from the night of May tenth, nineteen sixty-four: 'This President has an unparalleled ability to catch men and get them to do what he wants.' Do you deny that?"

Houston rubbed his jaw and looked at her coolly. She knew what he was thinking: How did this game work and how would he beat it? Did he suspect she knew from the journal? She didn't think so. The apprentice said the office had been crowded and no one saw him drop the journal behind a chair. Houston may have missed it, but he always had others pick up after him, so probably wasn't sure what had happened to it. He didn't seem apprehensive yet, just irritated.

"If you wish to lower yourself further by publicizing bed secrets, I'll answer, Phoebe, but I'm surprised you can single out what *I* said from the torrent of bed secrets you must have lain under after nights of drinking as much as you did. *Everyone* grasped that Johnson was accumulating great power then. The press *toadied* to him, that's all."

"I don't think the press was aware that some of his power came from blackmail of congressmen arranged by J. Edgar Hoover."

"I'm not aware of it, either," Houston said lightly, and faced the camera, his expression sober, concerned, and high-minded. "Unlike many of that era, I wasn't obsessed with gossip and don't trade in it."

"You don't?"

"No. Furthermore, I can assure you that long before the Vietnam War became a financial drain, I had grave doubts we'd be able to do well in it from a practical standpoint and, ah, felt it was morally flawed."

"Why did you doubt it on practical grounds? Didn't you think we were powerful enough?"

"I never thought our power was limitless, and I knew because Americans are fundamentally decent that many would not want to fight dirty in a nasty war."

"Yet the country wound up doing this. The President you assisted sent large numbers in."

"I don't think this is useful."

"But who said no to the President, Houston? With the publication of the Pentagon Papers, it's apparent it was stupid to go in there, and that once there the government went about fighting it in the most stupid way, using far too many aircraft, which is suspicious, considering Johnson's long ties to the aerospace industry."

"I don't think, Phoebe, you're qualified to comment on how a war is conducted. I saw how the decisions were made."

"I saw how they were carried out. I saw how lives and money were wasted. And innocent people killed—many by indiscriminate bombing."

"That was never the government's intention. We always felt we could control the air. And prevent needless harm, of course."

"You were concerned about that? And not just keeping your jobs?"

"We were concerned about doing right for America," Houston said. "You seem to forget right-wing extremists were yelling for the most aggressive outrages. We tempered our actions, gave our best counsel to the President, and challenged him when necessary. Certainly I did."

Phoebe smiled—unnecessarily, because Camera Two was on and locked on to Houston, whose face was unperturbed but whose hands gripped the armchair tightly.

She hoped the director in the control booth would hold on Houston's face while she signaled to Terry Menska in the wings. Yes—Two's light remained on, and Terry stepped out wearing her slightly wrong red office dress, blinking.

"Let me introduce Terry Menska, who also was at the White House in the Kennedy and Johnson years and saw some of these decisions being made."

Houston's face showed nothing but Phoebe could tell he had been dealt a blow by the way he breathed and moved his body. But he wasn't clutching.

"Miss Menska was a secretary," Houston said. "If you're trying to burke me off the stage in some game of guerrilla journalism, you'll fail and you'll also disqualify yourself morally. The American people still know that qualified men—and women, of course—make the decisions. Only they can see the facts."

Terry was smiling sweetly at Two; Phoebe got the light on One. "Terry Menska, what did you hear in the White House West Wing Basement in nineteen sixty-four?"

Terry took a deep breath. "Well, everyone talked about it quite a bit, the war? About the balloon going up, as they put it, and *when* the war would start? And what pretext President Johnson would use? Because they said it was inevitable. Everyone wanted some kind of military action because of what Mr. Bridles mentioned, not wanting to stir up people on the right? Then after President Johnson's landslide, they all said it was a good thing. We'd bomb them and teach them a lesson and it wouldn't cause a commotion at home."

Phoebe asked, "Who said this and where?"

"Oh." She colored. "Uh, Mr. Bridles said it often. In bed. To me."

Houston's teeth clenched. "Shit," he muttered.

"Good," the director said through her ear wire.

"What else did he say?"

"Oh, he said the advantage of doing it this way—bombing?—was that we could hammer them and yet keep it away from the press so they couldn't appeal to sentiment. But when the Marines landed, he said that was good too, because it showed them we meant business."

"The National Liberation Front?"

"Mmm. Yes. And Senator Dirksen."

"When did he say this?"

"Nineteen sixty-five. It was after you left but we still went to bed occasionally."

Houston shot a searing look at each of them. He was furious. His face flushed.

"He didn't object to the landings and buildup there?"

"Oh, no," Terry said. "He told me, 'Call me a hawk. This is the way history is going. This President is riding history. I'm not going to tell him we can't fight there.' "

"Let me break into your gossip," Houston said. "Government cannot function when its affairs are betrayed. Governments can't deal with each other if they betray obligations. We went in to honor a treaty. You, and this, ah, lower-level employee have betrayed trust and decency."

"Have you ever thought you might have betrayed the American people?" Phoebe asked sweetly.

"No, this is impossible," Houston said. "You're not conducting any kind of a proper interview. It's over." He stood, nodded to the camera, and walked off, Two following his back. From the side Phoebe could see his jaw muscles working like mice in a sack.

She kept a straight face long enough to say, "We'll break now for a message and come back for Terry Menska's reminiscences about the White House under two presidents and their aides. This is Phoebe Bishop in New York."

At the edge of the set Houston yelled, "You treacherous bitch!"

Dat Moi

It was December 17 and Phoebe and crew were finishing the story about Angel Acevedo, the small-time killer, and his important victim.

"That was quick," Pat Mulkin said. They had got past three shopping gridlocks in a merciful few minutes and were riding among the brick buildings of Loisaida to get Lydia Acevedo again, since she hadn't come off well the first time.

"I worked out a few more questions," Tom Hurley said. "We want to find out what happened at home to make Angel a criminal. Here."

When he handed the sheet to Phoebe, his fingertips brushed her hand and his eyes flashed. He wanted to try her, all right. His youth and slimness reminded her of Sam, too. And they were neighbors—she'd moved from Lex last year to Central Park West and he'd been on the Upper West Side since college. She felt a surge at the touch of his hot hand.

"She's in the same clothes?" Phoebe asked brusquely.

"*Ciertamente.*"

They climbed the piss-saddened steps. Lydia opened the door. At first Phoebe wasn't sure she was the same woman—she looked lively, her dark eyes dancing. "*Bienvenido!* Please come in!" Of course it was the same place, the worn couch and chrome-and-Formica table, the view of brick walls and vandalized park—but Lydia talked twice as fast as before about the weather, the kids outside, the traffic, complimenting Phoebe on her clothes. She had become a different person.

She explained why. *"Veo.* I see you." She touched her eye. "I see you on television. You are *really good*—I like to watch the way you talk. I know you now! But wait, I have coffee fix. Sit down, please!"

They sat in the kitchen, which was cleaner than before, pine scented, the worn floor waxed. A yellow bag of Bustelo stood by the stove. Lydia poured boiling water through a Caribbean cloth strainer and served steaming black coffee, the cameraman shooting her as she served, smiling. "You like to cook? Phoebe?"

"Mmm? No, I'm afraid I'm not very good at it."

"I *know!*" Lydia said. "I *thought* so! I was never cook either— never like. I thought you wasn'. I go next door and watch you, I can tell. I didn' bake. I bought cookies."

She served them from the package and told about Señor García and Angel the child.

"Before Angel was born, García and me drive a lot. He had a Chevy. He was so happy. I didn' know the cars then but he taught me how to know a Chevy. He was workin' at a kitchen and he come home with over a hundred twenty dollars a week."

Her voice followed street rhythms; she dropped her pitch when she ended phrases. "We go Staten *Island* on the new *bridge*, go White *Mountain*. It was real good. He was workin', we had place, I feel little baby grow in me, and I hol' García. I think I'm as happy as anyone in the world. I could die and never be happier—"

But the tale she told they could not get on tape. It went on and on, involved, composed of trivial scenes. García and she meeting on the street while the older people played dominoes. García hugging her, posing in his tight, rolled-up T-shirt. García taking his car apart and putting it together at the curb, *buen mecánico*. García showing off driving, waving to a pal from *la isla* and getting into a stupid rear-end collision.

"It wasn' his fault!" Lydia said.

And from the accident, García's tailspin of bad reactions. Trying to fix the car first, out of vanity. He wanted the car to look right. Being late for work. Losing his job. Not getting another because his English was lousy. Feeling lost and helpless. Blaming Lydia. "He got sad and quiet and wasn' nice to me. He never hit me! But he tell me I shouldn' got *embarazado*. He blame baby comin'."

Phoebe touched Lydia's hand. "That's when he went back? Before Angel was born?"

Lydia nodded. "He said he go back and make money—there's *campos* and a factory he work—he got money and come back."

"But it's more expensive here."

"No! It's *cheap*! A television there *twice* as much. An' his *car*—he couldn' *have* a car like that. Anyway, he sell the car and give me money and go back. I raise Angel myself."

"Did you ever hear from him?"

"Not *actually*—" She talked aimlessly about bits of news between *la isla* and *Nueva York, la Gran Manzana,* and Phoebe was aware of Tom making hot eyes at her. Then something Lydia said made her senses quicken. A flash of light like a tracer that connected the killer to the victim—the thing that told about how they lived in adjacent camps. "It was, see, the *campos* close down because factory there, an' then factory close, too, so they go out lookin' on *la isla* or come here—"

Her burst of energy had run out. She was getting low again. Phoebe said, "Lydia, when you feared Angel might get into trouble, you used spells to try to help him. Would you show us?"

"Yes!" She opened the red-marked package of herbs and held it up, then dumped them into an ashtray and lit them with strips of paper. "I say novena seven times seven, nine times nine, a hundred and one, and decorate this virgin." She gestured to a black-painted plaster Maria. "With the herbs I offer and pray."

"Did you think it worked?"

"I think maybe awhile, then Angel met those bad people. So many bad people in one place here, I can' do nothing about them."

They drove back on Houston Street, heading to the West Side Highway to avoid drivers gawking at stuffed windows.

Tom said, "I wonder if all that car stuff plays."

"Mmmm! We *need* it!" Pat said. "I mean, he loved her and was living a normal life and he went loco chasing some mass-produced shit he didn't need back on *la isla*."

"He wasn't on *la isla*," Tom said. "He tried to hide there."

"Well, he didn't have a *la isla* to go back to anyway," Pat said. "Our factories tore up the farms."

"Luddite," Tom said, making hot eyes at Phoebe. "That's sev-

enties dreamland. Less is more. Herbal tea. García and Lydia made
their own mistakes."

"Oh, sure," Pat said. "All she had to do was take her welfare
payments and invest in Chicago Bridge and Iron eighteen years ago.
García should have bought a nice sturdy Range Rover. You asshole."

They passed Lafayette. Mercer. West Broadway. Phoebe saw
the gallery where she'd had her first show of photos. The banners and
iron fronts of SoHo, which had become so hot in the seventies, with
its down-dressed urban style.

F. Scott Fitzgerald said there are no second acts in American
lives, but Phoebe thought he was as full of shit about that as he was
about luminous evenings. People she'd thought got flattened, destroyed, and zapped by truth in the upheavals came back just like
Nixon.

After Phoebe scourged Houston on the air, he dropped from
sight for a time. His appointment as deputy mayor was ending, he
didn't admire Beame as he had Lindsay, and he must have seen, on
videotape later, if he didn't under studio lights, that his inventory of
charms, noble excuses, and enlightened poses had become shopworn
and threadbare.

Infuriatingly, the beating she gave him did him a favor: It bap-
tized him as a public figure. He took the role of young elder statesman
essayist on the *Times* Op-Ed page and in *American Heritage, New York*,
and *Esquire*. He said the right things elegantly, shedding the kind of
sweet oil, not light and truth, that had got him so far.

When LBJ died on his ranch after ruining the nation and then
trying to occupy himself with Great Irrigation Problems, Houston
wrote a gentlemanly farewell, saying, "This flawed man meant well;
h. attempted greatness for all people, and it redeems him that he died
of a broken heart."

At Charley O's, where some television journalists hung out,
Phoebe heard a man from another channel say, "Bridles didn't believe
that. He told me, 'This man was a vulgarian on the order of Khrush-
chev. But I don't intend to let the ghost of what he really was ruin the
institution of our Presidency.' "

He sailed with Uncle Stu and stayed in Bermuda awhile. When
he came back he was seen at the Yacht Club with the woman he'd
mentioned to Phoebe, Virginia Hill, Finch, '70. Phoebe saw her. She

was tall, thin, with prominent clavicles, ruddy skin, big teeth, a compulsive smile, coarse, straight blonde hair, and a bouncy disposition. She was devoted to Houston. They always married younger, Phoebe noticed. Trotskyism to tchotchkeism.

Houston's most widely quoted essay was the 1977 piece revealing the astonishing news that America *did* have social classes, that people at the bottom are, sadly, helpless, and that the people at the top ("men *and* women," he noted gracefully) should run affairs and advise the president. "We need wise men, advisers, boards," he wrote, adding a fond recollection of Pa Bridles's work for the Agency. Part of his genius was like play-making to keep the game going: saying the pivotal thing at the right time, whether or not it was true and whether or not he believed it. He was a Confucian mandarin.

He had by then become known as a man of great negotiating skill and financial acumen. After Vietnam fell, he went to Ho Chi Minh City representing a New York bank. Several American banks resumed operating despite the bloodshed and mass arrests. The Soviets acknowledged giving Hanoi some $30-odd billion in aid. U.S. banks put in millions after the fall.

Brian Beechwood told Phoebe at Elaine's that he felt the attitude of upper-class Americans at the end of the Vietnam War was the same as that of the British aristocracy at the end of World War I: They didn't care who won as long as they kept their own relative position. Beechwood had emerged as the classiest and brainiest writer of her group. *Burning Temples*, his evocation of Vietnamese culture at war, continued to win prizes and to yield more treasures to careful readers. Years after it was published critics realized that, aside from delivering information about that war and culture, it functioned as a defense of the Eastern WASP establishment and CIA, however bumbling, against the brawling claims of the Sun Belt and weapons makers forming the forces that eventually took power. Brian had the gift of seeing what would last for years.

While Beechwood was the classiest of her set, Ash Loakes was easily the most visible vulgar journalist. No trick was too shaggy for him to use, and not just once. "I guess we're not innocent anymore," he quoted twenty-nine-year-old Emil Patzos as Watergate broke, and "I suppose we're not innocent anymore," he had thirty-five-year-old Martha Kahn saying when Saigon fell.

Loakes's specialty was the violin, the purple paragraph at the beginning of the newsmagazine that sets the tone and tells the dumb reader how to feel. He had one violin describing Dawn in America: "The copper sun touches Martha's Vineyard [where he had a place], New Haven, the Heartland—Cleveland [his birthplace]. . . ." He carried his self-importance like his fat and seemed as unaware of it. What made Phoebe *fume* was when print journalists ignored crap like Loakes's and attacked television news.

Ash Loakes edited *New Ideas*, a seventies soft, alternative-lifestyle magazine, with Sara Gelber. *New Ideas* did conventional pieces on drugs, sex, Gary Gilmore, and the CIA. It had a few good years and foundered. Ash moved to an achievement lifestyle magazine while Sara, tough and busy as ever, took over a Manhattan women's magazine. Phoebe photographed her stalking through the office, glasses swinging on her neck, dusting everything with cigarette ash and waving printouts at writers crouched by video display terminals.

Someone else Phoebe had run into in news did well with the printed word. The cop she'd bantered with after Century Plaza, Sergeant Eddie Donahue, wrote a funny and revealing novel about cops, made half a million dollars, wrote another, made more, and found a new life away from the gritty and ugly wars on the border.

Adams Peabody had a terrible time getting published. The best he could do in the mid-seventies was a letter to the editor of *Newsweek* defending low college standards. "Don't you understand," he wrote, "that a flunk was a sentence to Death in the Trenches?" Life had passed him by. He was depressed, gathering dust in California, his fifteen minutes of fame over. Kimberley called Phoebe to tell this, her voice catching.

Phoebe thought of them as the pastel seventies. No big stories, no surprises. They were like postcoital limbo—you could discuss anything without shocking anyone.

She and Sara talked over a drink about how the upheavals had opened up the business of telling truth or something like it. More women worked general assignment. Women's magazines like *Ms.* showed women as serious workers, not cute or glamorous. Sara said, "So we advanced. It was because men couldn't do their old things right, they blew up all their own macho fantasies. Generals, politicians—nebbishes, shlemiels. Male journalists *apologize* in the

lead. We've done better, but why? And look at all the counterfeits—
for every woman on camera like you, a real journalist, you've got a
couple of cutie pies with perfect teeth."

"Tchotchkeism," Phoebe said.

Despite the counterfeits in the market, Phoebe enjoyed what the
I Ching called "advancement." She signed contracts for six-figure
sums, had network features, showed photos on the side. Little Sammy
went to private school and was tended by an Irish illegal nanny who
took him to Central Park, the carousel, the Museum of Natural History, while Phoebe worked; Sammy had a bit of a lilt in the way he
talked now, too. Phoebe was doing what she wanted while all the men
she'd known had had parts shot out of the armor of their *amour-propre*.

But many of them turned it around, like Adams Peabody. She
saw him in New York, wearing German-frame glasses, a radical Eu-
robeard, and an expensive drape suit. He was quiet, intense. "I ran
into a stone wall out there, so I searched the *Chronicle* and took this
foundation job. We help Third World countries. It's our only chance
for sanity!"

They were eating canapés at a UN party in that big General
Assembly room overlooking the East River. "I revised my thinking, of
course," Peabody said. "Nostalgia about hair and music is fun, but we
failed in the sixties because we weren't disciplined. Look at the FLN.
Look at the NLF. Also we failed because the American left always
stumbles at Stalin. He was disciplined, rigorous, inexorable. But we
were buffaloed when people brought up his excesses. So what if he
purged millions? Read Dostoyevski! Read Gogol! Anyway, he won
his war. We purged Asian experts and got into an unjust war we lost.
At what cost in heartbreak to all sides? I'm going to make sure the
right parties are supported in our dealings." His employers, the
Belknap Foundation, had been set up by a New England missionary.

Peabody said that before he left California in the mid-seventies
he'd seen Mark Randolph, back from Europe, covered with long hair
and a beard, traveling by motorcycle up the coast. "He was going into
the woods," he said. "You should have seen this motorcycle. Big,
loud, mud spattered. He had stuff lashed on the back like an Afghan
mule skinner. He called once. Somewhere in British Columbia. He
and a girl named Mimi Lyons called from a motel. They'd met in a bar
there. I knew her from Boston—she went to Wellesley! Quite a few
people were going to the woods then."

"I went to Vermont a few times," Phoebe said. "Wood smoke bothers my eyes."

"It's great country," Peabody said. "*I* never had a chance to do it. I asked him, 'What are you doing for bread, man?' And brought up how ambitious he had been in the Marines. He told me to get fucked and I haven't heard from him since. He's somewhere out there in the trees shacked up with Mimi in a log cabin!"

She wondered if she'd been near Mark Randolph because late in the seventies Chet North had assigned her a feature on Vietnamese refugees, some of them in the northwest. She'd interviewed the two types—the generals, like Loan, Thieu, and Ky, who had come out well off, and the boat people, who'd come out a few years later with nothing.

One general said, "We had no supplies. We had no ammunition. You had stopped supplying us. I am a major general! I know how one does this! I am a major general!"

Another general, a staff man in Southern California, seemed more philosophical. He was thin with a sad smile. The NVA had killed or tortured anyone above colonel, so he'd been glad to escape with his family and glad he'd set money aside.

She asked him if the ARVN had indeed run out of supplies.

"Yes," he said.

"Was the *an cap* still going on? Were officers still siphoning money and supplies off at the end?"

He smiled and wiggled his fingers, dismissing the subject. "Those times are past."

One of the funny things about the last years of the war, he said, was the quality of assistance, which continued to improve surprisingly. "By the end, in the matters police, the Americans send Vietnamese speakers, but Americans—round eyes—they speak like me. Perhaps little accent. Excellent understanding. They listen to all the radios. Hanoi. Ours, too, perhaps." He laughed. "Americans learn. Not fast enough, but they learn." This one had a dry cleaners in Anaheim.

She talked with a colonel who said that in April 1975 as South Vietnam collapsed the Americans flew out high-ranking officers and their families and hired a ship to take others. He said the Koreans also had a ship, an LST, in the river. Shellfire fell on the city, which made driving difficult. Evacuees abandoned their cars, so the streets and parks were littered with cars. A VNAF friend of his drove all over Saigon with his family and two rifles in a new Peugeot, turning this way and that as shells fell and cadres closed off streets with machine gun fire. Finally he got on a ship, paying cash, and abandoned the car and rifles there.

Another refugee officer said a company of ARVN paratroopers took refuge in the cathedral, that severe French Jesuit-style building with high louvered steeple windows, and waited while NVA *bo doi* marched down the street cheering. The paras opened fire, cutting down many. The *bo doi* deployed and flanked immediately, pouring machine gun fire and RPG high explosive into the cathedral and assaulted it, killing all the paratroopers.

She flew to San Francisco and Seattle to interview boat people being processed through military facilities, debriefed, clothed, sent out to settlement committees. These wretched people had given up everything, risked their lives in hazardous vessels, drifted in the tropics, been prey to pirates, many dying on the way, the survivors reaching sanctuary half dead and in shock. A woman captured by Thai pirates had been held in their foul boat and raped for a month. Her family had been killed before her eyes.

The boat people bribed the NVA to get out. The NVA had machine-gun posts at every intersection and treated the southerners like tribesmen. They confiscated the property of ethnic Chinese and killed those they didn't like anyway.

Vietnamese community workers told Phoebe that war shock was one of the problems refugees faced. Once here and safe they grasped what they had been through and collapsed. She taped a kid wearing a field jacket and Levi's, yelling on the street, "*Ecouté moi*, fucking number ten, *nhac muoi!*"

Vietnamese settled quickly around Seattle. The harbor city already had a large Asian population and a tolerant white population. Other Vietnamese found the newcomers houses and jobs. They had a newspaper called *Dat Moi*, or New Land, to keep them informed. They built self-help groups. They had civic talents the Americans had not touched.

She talked with them in a community building on a hill above Puget Sound. A priest wore a chocolate-brown cassock, two bonzes wore saffron robes, but the laymen wore new American polyester suits and the women American store dresses. A businessman showed her his shining new Chevrolet.

She saw trees covering the Cascades to the east and the Olympics west across the Sound from her. She asked the Seattle crew if any of them had covered woods people and got snorts and laughs. "Don't go out there," one said. "If you don't have veterans, you got drunken Indians, crazy loggers, brush pickers, and dope farmers ready to shoot you." She left that angle alone. That was where Mark Randolph was living.

Back in New York she and Chet North went over what to do with the stories she had. Chet didn't want to run too much about North Vietnamese genocide because it might pull the stake from Nixon's heart. People would say he was right about other things.

She mentioned the purges to Brian Beechwood, who said, "The Vietnamese have conflicts we never can rationalize. They have a national neurosis. They're going to fight and suffer for another generation."

She told Peabody about the bloodletting at another public-interest cocktail party on the East Side and Peabody angrily denied it. "There are no power struggles! Socialists are capable of making sudden adjustments!" He had become by then an outspoken defender of Third World excesses and this put a curious twist on the story of the street killing.

"I know Adams Peabody is involved in killing my husband," Virginia Hill Bridles told Tom Hurley. "Houston found out in his trustee work that the Belknap Foundation sent around a hundred thousand dollars to Lima and that it wound up with those guerrillas, the shining whatever-they-call-themselves. He was checking on what was supposed to be a tractor purchase in Germany and saw it was weapons. He notified the FBI, and I think Adams Peabody had Houston killed. Or some of his agents. Weren't they Hispanic? He funds terrorists."

They had her on tape, her big teeth and sure, careless WASP way of speaking, but Phoebe wasn't inclined to use it, titillating as it might have been. Phoebe knew goddam well why that little killer's random violence had found Houston Bridles, and the random justice of it followed other causes entirely.

A Hamburger at
Fanelli's

It was Wednesday, December 18, and the "Anatomy of a Street Killer: An In-Depth Look" segment would air tomorrow night.

Barry Pendleton, the news vice president, had said he was dying to see a good hard look at crime. Barry had been a fierce muckraker during Watergate; he still thought he was a crusader, though he hadn't sent anyone to challenge any important public figure in years, like Mayor Koch or Cardinal O'Connor, or Reagan or Bush when they came to town. Phoebe couldn't recall Barry wanting in-depth stories on city officials indicted recently, or federal officials caught in the housing scandal. It was safer for Barry to demand a fearless story about street crime. Her profession was dominated by males still, and they were short-dick males.

She watched "Street Killer" with Tom Hurley and Pat Mulkin on the console. Pictures came up: Angel's mug shot; the crummy, sprung-suspension car in which Angel's spotter was killed; Lydia blinking dark eyes in her worn kitchen, telling about her hopes for Angel, the baby, and her feelings for García, the loser. Her voice and facial expressions came through fine—a three-quarter angle full-screen close-up catching Lydia's wrinkles and the ghost of her prettiness. "We go in his *car*, an' we look at the *country*. He say he miss the *campos*, the country. . . . He don' feel—he didn' wan' *see* me when he couldn' get *work*. . . ."

The Street Wolves president stood up in his chrome-studded

leather colors talking about the little girl who "shouldna been killed."
Back to Lydia talking about her lost marriage and lost son, to give the
viewers that special Christmas season poignancy. The segment came
out at 8:43.

"It seems okay," Pat said.

Tom said, "The talk is short enough. Woman's dumb, though."

"I can sympathize with her," Phoebe said. "I could be her."

"You're smarter," Tom said, giving her that hot look again. He
knew. The question was—when?

Phoebe wondered what happened on the street before Angel
killed Houston Bridles, whether Angel had said much to Houston
and whether Houston tried to talk his way out of it. Did Angel
know this man was the nephew, or son, of Stuart Bridles, who had
invested in Puerto Rico? García's family had left a farm to work in
a factory and had been thrown loose when the factory closed, so had
come to Nueva York, *la Gran Manzana*, a place García was unprepared for, just as he had been unprepared to be Angel's father. Did
Houston know this? Certainly not. In any case he had those benign,
well-bred manners and intentions that deflected blame. Did Angel
know who Houston was? Of course not. But to some, Angel would
be a hero.

The next morning Tom showed up looking like hell. He had a
black eye, his lips were swollen on one side, and his jaw had ugly
brown-purple scabs. He moved stiffly across the room into his work
space and sat with his back to them. Pat Mulkin came into Phoebe's
office.

"What happened?" Phoebe asked.

"He was jumped by two robbers. I saw it happen—I came out of
here a minute or so after him. He was walking toward Central Park
West under the trees and two guys knocked him down. I heard a
shout and some young men ran around me and jumped on the muggers. They hit them a couple of times and the muggers ran. They
didn't have weapons. Tom's lying there, moaning. The two who'd
helped him were Puerto Ricans."

Pat laughed. "They said, 'We're busboys at Oakferns, man!' One
said, 'Lots of robbers jumpin' people this late. They got our frien' last
night, all his tips.' And the other helped Tom up and said, 'Hey, man,

he hit you. You too thin, man, they pickin' on thin ones. You waiter at Miss Grimble's, no?' "

"A waiter at Miss Grimble's!" Phoebe laughed.

"No, and *listen*, Phoebe, Tom was so embarrassed and pissed off he *couldn't* say a *word*."

Tom stood in the door of his cubicle. He looked at Pat and went back to his desk and sat down facing the desktop.

They were due to air "Angel of Death" at 8:00 P.M. EST. At noon something sensational happened: Judge Lester Snyder threw out all murder charges against Angel Acevedo and released him. This was early enough so the *Post* got off a big headline: SLAY SUSPECT WALKS!

The story was that Judge Snyder had accepted defense pretrial motions for dropping homicide charges on the grounds that Angel had never been convicted of an adult crime and the DA could not establish the dead fat man hadn't fired the pistol Angel was holding, as no paraffin test had been taken on the corpse. The defense also argued that the dead fat man had been Angel's de facto guardian and that his death had disoriented Angel, thus flawing any statements he'd made to the anticrime cops.

Judge Snyder made an elegant short speech about the sanctity of the law and gave Angel an illegal weapons charge, which could get him up to a year in jail, and a possession-of-stolen-property charge, as Angel had Houston's gold money clip and the wallet of the other dead man when the cops opened fire. But he was out on the street until February 28. The DA's deputy insisted to the *Post* that these charges were proof that the defendant had not got off too lightly. Judge Snyder was in a hurry to get out for the holidays. He took off at two for Florida.

Angel's release was outrageous, but in news terms it was a *terrific* stroke of luck, because they had another peg to hang the in-depth mugger story on. They got fifteen seconds of him coming out of the house of detention and clasping his hands over his head, and ran teases in the P.M. news, so they got a 60 share for the show.

The next morning Pat Mulkin said, "Mark Randolph? Line three."

"Hello, Mark."

"I saw the show. That was a nice sketch. The reason I'm calling is I saw Houston just before he was killed—must have been that afternoon."

"Where?"

"World Trade Center."

"What were *you* doing there?" She was your usual New Yorker on the phone, abrupt and paranoid.

"Visiting a bank."

"Don't you live in the woods? Peabody said you were out west somewhere."

"Yeah, but I've been here for years." Pause. "We had a screwy conversation. You talk to him recently?"

"No." Dead air. What does he want? What was he doing?

"You're probably not interested in this anyway."

"Yes. What did you notice? I'm glad to hear your voice, by the way."

"Nice to hear yours, too. I don't watch television, so this was the first time I saw you. You have an engaging presence. It was about how he acted. I can't do it over the phone. Can I tell you about it? Lunch?"

"I don't have much time."

"Neither do I. Uptown? Downtown?"

"Where are you?"

"Downtown."

"I have to be at City Hall."

"Okay. You know Fanelli's in SoHo? We could have a burger."

"Yes. I'd like to."

Fanelli's is an old dark-wood bar now frequented by new people wearing the work shirts, dark canvas, and leather of the neighborhood. She arrived in shades and sent on her car. Mark stood at the door in a tweed jacket and flannels. They looked at each other. She looks good, he thought. He has a nice tan, she thought. So thin. Oh, God—AIDS? Nice jacket. Nice watch. Bally shoes. She measured as she always had. The winter sunlight was bright enough for him to see the little signs where she'd had her eyes and chin tucked in. He smiled at her warmly. Yeah, the face-lift didn't get everything, he thought; she's getting that old mouth that looks like the hole in a Bull Durham sack.

"It's so good to see you. You look terrific!"

"You too!"

They sat at a table in back. The girl asked for a drink order.

"Seltzer."

"For me too."

They looked at each other and laughed.

"We're a couple of live ones," Phoebe said. "I have to work."

"I'm off the sauce."

"Really?" They laughed.

"Okay, here's what happened. I'm in the WTC at the bank wearing a suit and Houston called to me across the room—"Rands!" he said. Came over and grabbed my shoulder and pumped my hand. I was bemused by all this because the last time I saw him I was in a different kind of clothes and he was pretty prickly. You see?"

She smiled playfully. "Was it a nice suit?"

"Not bad. Paul Stuart."

"Where was it you saw him before?"

"Orly. Over a dozen years ago." He waved his hand. "But see, he had all the grins and charm out this time when I'm in the right uniform, period. And he tells me about all the stuff he's doing for Yale—I think he was a candidate for a seat on the board, the corporation. And he told me he'd raised money for the Vietnam pillar there. They always do the war dead at Commons and this has the thirty-three Vietnam dead."

Mark laughed. "Houston said, 'Harvard only had thirteen killed!' And then he said, 'Yale thirty-three, Harvard thirteen!' "

"Oh, no!"

"And he repeated it, the way old people do. 'Yale thirty-three, Harvard thirteen!' "

Their burgers came.

"Good."

"A-one?"

Mark thought she was still pretty, attractive, he remembered all he'd felt for her at times, how he'd wanted her and how she'd pissed him off, but as far as fascinating him—well, she was a high WASP, so different, there was so much in between.

"It was—what? Peabody's second wedding?" she said. "Peas said you went to Europe and then to the woods. When did you move here? What are you doing?"

"Five years ago. I have a building in TriBeCa."

"Good for you! A big building?"

He rotated his hand this way and that as if unscrewing a faucet, meaning *mezzo mezzo.* "Five stories."

"Terrific! Well, what *happened?* Tell me!"

"Well, what? Out there I had a little land. You know how timber land is taxed?"

"No. My mother never told me." She made an arch face.

"Couple of lucky deals." He liked to shoot the shit but had that WASP diffidence about talking money with a woman. He'd always assumed he'd grab money somewhere. When he was sober in sales, he'd earned. And he was lucky. "You know how TriBeCa was a few years ago."

"Yes."

"We might buy another. My wife has a good eye for these things."

"How nice. This is Mimi from Mass?"

"Mimi?" He laughed. "What? Peabody said that? No, Mimi and I trucked around awhile exploring the woods."

"What were they like?"

"Pretty. Rough people."

"Who?"

"Indians and white trash—you know, WASPs, like us, but *abajo,* lots of violence. Anyway, we left."

"You and your wife. Who's she?"

"Yes. Her name's Teal. We've been together for years. Here. Pictures."

Teal? What kind of goddam name is Teal? Phoebe looked at the pictures. She was much younger and good-looking. Tchotchkeism. The children were cute. "So you've settled down?"

"Yes. Do you want dessert?"

"No. Coffee."

"Two coffees, please. Yes." He faced her. His face had the serenity and certainty she had admired in some men. "Yes. For the first time in my life I have a home. All I ever wanted was a home and family. I chased a lot of silly stuff—"

"You survived."

"Yeah, parts, anyway." He gazed at her, calmly, smiling.

She felt he was reading her in a way more personal than she was used to, and to move him along said, "What did you *do* in the woods?"

"First I tried subsistence farming. Kohlrabi. Corn. Goats. My dog killed the goats. Then I went back a notch to hunter-gathering."

They laughed. "It rains a lot out there. I could understand man in the pluvial, the way a deer looks red in summer in the mist and the way they painted him in red ocher."

He looked at her, wondering what he could tell her. It had been another world out there in the woods. Being away from people. Standing in a cluster of alders by silver water, the trees' limbs reaching up like people stretching arms and hands into the light. Alders lived about as long as people and then fell over and others stood in their places, like people in the city. And the animals trooping through—bears' voices crooning and whuffing, claws making wooden cracks as they split bark from dead trees to find grubs; the hoof strikes of deer, the screams of a couger. Surrounded by noises of other forms of life. The sense he got when light came through the branches, bird shadows moving among the leaves; the air was filled with scents of ferns, musk where deer had lain. Couger sign, such as super cat piss, rank, and straight claw marks in the earth.

He had understood by noting his living surroundings how much he was a part of the fabric of life. Whatever truths time brought, they were for the living, not the dead. And then going through that man-in-the-pluvial time, killing deer, eating venison by the fire, belching and aaahhing, his dog cracking and gnawing bones. This was the beginning of finding a home. And then, meeting his wife, Teal, a lovely, strong woman who laughed at what was screwy, including some of the things they'd taken so *seriously* years ago, because she was younger. Teal understood beauty and gave a sense of gentle calm.

Looking at Phoebe—dark-haired, pretty, classic-browed Phoebe —in the busy room, the clattering plates and bar noises behind her, he wondered what was really inside her. Maybe not a capability for repose. Something was turning over in her too quickly. No, no way could he tell her what he'd seen in the woods. That was another world. It was like trying to explain what you'd seen in a war. That was another world, too. Even people who'd been in the same place saw it from different angles. But he had to tell her again the truth about how he'd felt about her. Her lovely high forehead, like La Dama de Elche—but a different mystery lay in her. He said, "I should tell you, to be honest, so you know, how much I felt I loved you, and couldn't express it, Phoebe. But that's part of my good luck, isn't it? Since I wasn't important to you."

"I think you're marvelously interesting now." She opened her mouth, then drew back from complimenting him on what he'd escaped. Wreckage, murder charges, disasters.

"I had all my adventures years ago. You are very attractive." He put his hand on hers. A bit too aggressively stylish, he thought.

"I haven't had good luck with men."

"I know Houston—"

She waved her hand. I won't tell him about two lovers killed, these other mismatches.

"But you're doing terrifically well." Trouble, he thought. His night sense. "You look great and you're so quick. You've become a tough old news broad."

"You've always been kind, Mark."

He walked her out to Broadway to hail a cab.

"This was fun!" she said. "Watch me, won't you? I'm not bad. Are you in the book? I'd love to meet your wife and family."

"It's nice to see you."

She opened her mouth when she kissed him. He held her.

It probably was impossible, she thought in the cab.

Walking over on Prince, he thought about how nice she had looked, tasted, smelled, and felt. And that was all. She had been an illusion for so long. He was living his real life now.